A Mummy Omnibus: 1820s — 1920s (Abridged Edition)

A list of titles available from

A Bit O'Irish Press

Gothic Library Editions
#1: *Fitz-James O'Brien: Gothic Short Stories* (2017) – 3/e
#2: *William Austin: Gothic Short Stories* (2018)
#3: *Ambrose Bierce: Gothic Short Stories* (2018)
#4: *Edward Bellamy: Gothic Short Stories* (forthcoming)

Monster Omnibus Editions
#1: *A Mummy Omnibus: 1820s – 1920s* (2018) – 3/e
#2: *A Mummy Omnibus: 1820s – 1920s* Abridged Edition (2018)
#3: *A Werewolf Omnibus: 1820s – 1920s* (2018)
#4: *A Werewolf Omnibus: 1820s – 1920s* Abridged Edition (2018)
#5: *A Monster Omnibus: 1820s – 1920s* Abridged Edition (2018)

The Collected Writings of O'Brien
Volume I: Short Stories (1851 – 1855) (2017)
Volume II: Short Stories (1856 – 1864) (2017)
Volume III: Poetry & Music (2018)
Volume IV: Miscellaneous Writings (forthcoming)
Volume V: Biography & Letters (forthcoming)

Deism Library Editions
#1: *Elihu Palmer: Writings on Deism* (forthcoming)
#2: *Matthew Tindal: Writings on Deism* (forthcoming)

American Studies Library Editions

Monster Omnibus Editions

A MUMMY Omnibus: 1820s — 1920s

—— Abridged Edition ——

Edited, with introduction, selection and notes, by
JOHN P. IRISH

A Bit O'Irish Press

Bridgeport, Texas 76426
johnpirish@gmail.com

TABLE OF CONTENTS

vii   Note from the Editor
ix   Note on the Text
xi   Introduction

Mummy Stories: 1820s – 1920s

1	The Mummy's Foot (1840)	Gautier
11	Mr. Grubbe's Night with Memnon (1843)	Smith
19	Some Words with a Mummy (1845)	Poe
31	Lost in a Pyramid (1869)	Alcott
39	My New Year's Eve (1880)	Allen
51	The Ring of Thoth (1890)	Doyle
65	Lot No. 249 (1892)	Doyle
89	A Professor of Egyptology (1894)	Boothby
103	The Strange Discovery of Dr. Nosidy (1896)	Suffling
115	The Story of Baelbrow (1898)	Heron
125	The Awakening of Pharaoh (1898)	Hering
133	Two Professors and One Mummy (1901)	Hering
141	The Lost Elixir (1903)	Griffith
153	The Mummy of Thompson-Pratt (1904)	Hyne
161	The Nemesis of Fire (1908)	Blackwood
211	The Green God (1916)	Spencer
223	Death's Secret (1917)	Schoolcraft
263	The Whispering Mummy (1918)	Rohmer
275	The Wrath of Amen-Ra (1921)	Holloway
291	The Nameless City (1921)	Lovecraft
301	The Adventure of the Egyptian Tomb (1923)	Christie
313	The Outsider (1926)	Lovecraft
319	The Abominations of Yondo (1926)	Smith
325	Spider-Bite (1926)	Carr
345	Body and Soul (1928)	Quinn

365   Books for Further Reading

NOTE FROM THE EDITOR

Thanks to all my students who have been members of my Monster Book Club. Special thanks to lifetime member Candice Cramer. Also, thanks to all the students who have taken, and will take, my "Famous Monsters in Classic Literature" classes. They keep me going and keep me intellectually focused. The lack of proper resources, on this particular topic, caused me to begin thinking of the idea of an anthology of classic mummy stories.

Thanks to Prof. John M. Lewis, whose independent study course "Famous Monsters in Classic Literature" I took between my Masters and my Doctorate programs. This set me on a journey in searching out and reading the stories that keep us up at night and often serve as the source of many nightmares — some of which involve mummies! Also thanks to Prof. Gary Swaim, who also encouraged me and gave me some valuable advice about publishing.

Thanks to Brian J. Frost, whose book, *The Essential Guide to Mummy Literature*, was one of the main sources for deciding what stories to include in this anthology. In many ways, this anthology is a primer for that book. Many of the stories that ultimately found their way in this anthology were stories recommended by him. His other two surveys, on Werewolves and Vampires, are also great.

Thanks to my parents, Johnny and Sandra Irish, both of them inspired in me a love of learning and especially a love of working with individuals, leading me to pursue a career in teaching — one of which I could not imagine myself doing anything else. Also, thanks to Maurice Irish, who also provides much moral support. As well as my sister, Shannon Foster, who also encouraged me and allowed me to bounce ideas off her from time to time. As well as Emily Bowe, my mother-in-law, who has also shown a tremendous amount of support and encouragement to my wife and I for over ten years.

Most importantly, thanks to my wife, Elizabeth Irish and our kids (aka, our pets, Nellie, Annie, Teddy, Katy, Tom, and Lucy), who constantly allow me the opportunity to pursue various intellectual interests that I have, like the publication of this anthology.

To all these folks, I offer my most sincere gratitude!

John P. Irish
12/28/17
Bridgeport, Texas

Film poster for the 1932 movie, *The Mummy*

NOTE ON THE TEXT

There have been, over the years, some really good mummy anthologies, but they were limited in scope. The goal of this anthology is to provide a single source for what is considered to be all the classic stories, as well as supplementing the canon with minor and hard to find stories, in some cases, some of these stories have never been published in a modern edition.

I have, when possible, used the original stories as they appeared in the magazines in which most of these found their way to the public. In some instances, because of scarce manuscripts, I have consulted modern anthologies. In most cases, I have compared multiple versions of the stories.

The choice of stories to include in this anthology was extremely difficult. All the classics have been included, stories from Gautier, Alcott, Poe, Doyle, Rohmer, Blackwood, Smith, Quinn, and Lovecraft. But the goal of the anthology, as has been noted, is to broaden the canon by including minor or important works which have never been anthologized before, or even published since their original publication. Stories like, "Death's Secret," "Mr. Grubbe's Night with Memnon," and "The Wrath of Aman-Ra," for example, are rare gems. Some of the stories included in this anthology, it could be argued, whether they are mummy stories or not, but all of these include elements of mummies in some form or fashion. Many of these have personal connections to me. I have included Lovecraft's "The Outsider," for example, because it was the very first story I read from him and it immediately made me a fan. Also, I have interpreted mummy "story" in the widest possible meaning, to include short stories, novelettes, and novellas.

This anthology was put together solely by myself. I have done multiple readings of the original stories as well as the edited stories which appear in this anthology. Any errors in this manuscript are solely the responsibility of this editor.

Film poster for the 1955 movie, *Abbott and Costello Meet the Mummy*

INTRODUCTION

My first experience with the mummy as a monster was watching Boris Karloff playing the ancient Egyptian priest Imhotep in the 1932 Universal Studio Horror Film, *The Mummy*. The monster did not have quite the same fear factor that Dracula, the Wolfman, or the Creature from the Black Lagoon had, but he was a terror in his own way, pure and simple. One of my all-time favorite mummy movies was not even a horror film at all but instead a comedy, *Abbott and Costello Meet the Mummy*, made in 1955. That was to be the last film that the comedy duo would produce for Universal Studios. From there, things took a variety of different turns, as my experience with the mummy would evolve and grow.

My first significant literary experience with a mummy was reading Bram Stoker's *The Jewel of the Seven Stars*. I had a copy of the Penguin Classics edition, and that came with both endings — the disturbing original and the modified version which eventually became the official published version. I was also first introduced to H. P. Lovecraft, in a meaningful way, through his Mummy stories. I had tried reading "The Call of Cthulhu" — several times — but for some reason, I was never able to get past the first chapter. I kept having people tell me, "you have to read Lovecraft." So one day I was in a bookstore and came across a collection of his stories, I bought it and thought I would give him another chance. This time I began with "The Outsider," as that was the first story in the collection. That was all I needed to become a Lovecraft fan. I thought that was one of the best stories I had ever read and while technically it may not be a mummy story, there are elements in there and plenty of references to Egypt, so it found its way into this anthology. I have since gone back and reread, and of course, I now am a huge Cthulhu fan. I have included several of Lovecraft's "traditional" Mummy stories in this anthology.

I was a huge fan of the 1999 Universal Studio remake of *The Mummy*, with Brendan Fraser, as well as the new 2017 Universal Studio film of *The Mummy* with Tom Cruise. These, along with all the cinematic classics, were my first experiences with monsters and the mummy always held a place of importance and interest to me. Maybe it is the thought of immortality or perhaps my obsession with the past (my day job is a history teacher), regardless, I have enjoyed the mummy as a monster my whole life. But what has been the fascination with the mummy in the West?

Three important events helped popularize interest in Egypt in the West and consequently in the mummy as a monster. First, Napoleon Bonaparte's campaign into Ottoman Egypt from 1798 – 1801. The expedition led to the discovery of the Rosetta Stone and the creation of the field of Egyptology in Europe. This ultimately ended in the establishment of the Egyptian Institute and the publication of the *Description de l'Égypte* from 1809 – 1821. Second, the building of the Suez Canal, an artificial sea-level waterway in Egypt connecting the Mediterranean Sea to the Red Sea, constructed between 1859 and 1869.

And third, the discovery of the tomb of Tutankhamun (ruler of Egypt from 1332 – 1323 B.C.), by Howard Carter in 1922. It sparked a renewed public interest in ancient Egypt, for which Tutankhamun's mask, now in the Egyptian Museum, remains one of the most popular symbols.

These events brought Egypt to the West; they exposed Westerners to objects and ideas that they were unfamiliar with, which in turn, gave rise to an artistic expression which included many stories about Egypt and mummies. All the stories in this collection have been written by Westerners — all the stories selected were stories that were originally published from the 1820s to the 1920s. When the pulp magazines were at their height.

It is surprising to see how many "big name" writers wrote stories utilizing the mummy as a key figure. The newly discovered text from Louisa May Alcott, in 1995 (that's right, it's not a typo), "Lost in a Pyramid," was indeed a rare find and helped shed new light on a writer that was virtually all but type-cast. Of course, the creator of the popular detective Sherlock Holmes, Arthur Conan Doyle, also dabbled in many other venues, including writing two classic mummy stories, "The Ring of Thoth" and "Lot No. 249." All the famous pulp writers of the early twentieth-century engaged in storytelling that involved mummies as monsters: H. P. Lovecraft, Clark Ashton Smith, and fellow Texan Robert E. Howard round out the "Big Three." Unfortunately, the best weird fiction involving mummies, from Smith, was published in the 1930's, just missing the cut-off and scope of this anthology. But I was able to find one good story from him published in 1926, "The Abominations of Yando." It gives the reader a sense of what he is capable of as a master writer and storyteller. Several well know writers of the pulps, unfortunately, had to be left out. Writers like Ray Bradbury and Robert Bloch wrote a number of stories with the mummy as a main character, but these were published in the 1930s or 40s, hence, falling outside the scope of the anthology.

As in the movies and other forms of popular culture, mummy stories can also be satirical and humorous, or otherwise lighthearted. The two earliest versions of stories involved the mummy as the monster were satires. In fact, one of the first, if not the first, fictional and literary accounts of a mummy was also a satire. In 1827 Jane Webb, at the ripe old age of nineteen, wrote *The Mummy!: Or a Tale of the Twenty-Second Century.* This novel has been regarded as the first literary attempt to construct a story around the main character of a mummy. An interesting mix of science fiction, satire, horror, combined with humor led to the creation of a popular mummy story. Many have argued that she took her cue from probably the most famous female writer of horror, Mary Shelly and her publication of *Frankenstein.*

"Letter from a Revived Mummy," published anonymously in 1832 in New York and included in the complete *A Mummy Omnibus: 1820s – 1920s* (of which this current collection is an abridgement), is an interesting blend of social commentary and satire. Even the great gothic writer, Edgar Allan Poe, contributed to the mummy literature with his political satire, "Some Words with a Mummy" in 1845. Two stories, written at the end of the nineteenth and beginning of the twentieth-centuries, attempted to utilize humor, quite successfully. They were written by Henry A. Hering: "The Awakening of Pharaoh" and "Two Professors and One Mummy." This is the first time that either of these stories have been published outside their original publications in 1898 and 1901 respectfully.

Of course, the main focus of this series in general, and this anthology in particular, is to include some of the best mummy stories ever published and their intention is to evoke the emotions of fear and terror. A number of these stories find their way, for the first time, in a modern anthology. Brian J. Frost, in his survey of mummy literature, *The Essential Guide to Mummy Literature*, said of one of the stories included in this anthology, "A neglected novelette by an American author that deserves to be rescued from obscurity is J. L. Schoolcraft's 'Death's Secret' (1917), which is an unusual variation on the 'mummy's curse' theme. . . . *it would certainly be worthy of inclusion in an anthology of the best ever mummy stories.*" It is this story, along with William Holloway's "The Wrath of Amen-Ra" and Albert Smith's "Mr. Grubbe's Night with Memnon" that serve as highlights of this anthology. None of these stories have appeared in a modern edition. In fact, Smith's story has never been in the conversation of any survey of mummy literature — making this collection a unique and ground breaking anthology of mummy stories.

Mummies may never be as popular, romantic, or alluring as the other monsters, like the vampire, the werewolf, or the ghost, but the fact that so many writers have chosen to engage with and include this monster in their fictional work shows the enduring legacy that mummies will continue to have in our culture and on our imaginations.

*   *   *   *   *

This Abridged Edition contaiaes the "Top 25" mummy stories from the full version of *A Mummy Omnibus: 1820s – 1920s*. It is designed to be of use for students and teachers specifically looking for an anthology to use in courses on monster fiction.

The Mummy

From out the light of many a mightier day,
From Pharaonic splendour, Memphian gloom,
And from the night aeonian of the tomb
They brought him forth, to meet the modern ray, —
Upon his brow the unbroken seal of clay,
While gods have gone to a forgotten doom,
And desolation and the dust assume
Temple and cot immingling in decay.
From out the everlasting womb sublime
Of cyclopean death, within a land
Of tombs and cities rotting in the sun,
He is reborn to mock the might of time,
While kings have built against Oblivion
With walls and columns of the windy sand.

* "The Mummy" was written by Clark Ashton Smith and published in 1922.

The Mummy's Foot[*]

had entered, in an idle mood, the shop of one of those curiosity-vendors, who are called *marchands de bric-à-brac* in that Parisian *argot* which is so perfectly unintelligible elsewhere in France.

You have doubtless glanced occasionally through the windows of some of these shops, which have become so numerous now that it is fashionable to buy antiquated furniture, and that every petty stockbroker thinks he must have his *chambre au moyen âge*.

There is one thing there which clings alike to the shop of the dealer in old iron, the wareroom of the tapestry maker, the laboratory of the chemist, and the studio of the painter: — in all those gloomy dens where a furtive daylight filters in through the window-shutters the most manifestly ancient thing is dust; — the cobwebs are more authentic than the guimp laces; and the old pear-tree furniture on exhibition is actually younger than the mahogany which arrived but yesterday from America.

The warehouse of my bric-a-brac dealer was a veritable Capharnaum; all ages and all nations seemed to have made their rendezvous there; an Etruscan lamp of red clay stood upon a Boule cabinet, with ebony panels, brightly striped by lines of inlaid brass; a duchess of the court of Louis XV nonchalantly extended her fawn-like feet under a massive table of the time of Louis XIII, with heavy spiral supports of oak, and carven designs of chimeras and foliage intermingled.

Upon the denticulated shelves of several sideboards glittered immense Japanese dishes with red and blue designs relieved by gilded hatching; side by side with enameled works by Bernard Palissy, representing serpents, frogs, and lizards in relief.

From disemboweled cabinets escaped cascades of silver-lustrous Chinese silks and waves of tinsel, which an oblique sunbeam shot through with luminous beads; while portraits of every era, in frames more or less tarnished, smiled through their yellow varnish.

The striped breastplate of a damascened suit of Milanese armor glittered in one corner; Loves and Nymphs of porcelain; Chinese Grotesques, vases of *céladon* and crackle-ware; Saxon and old Sevres cups, encumbered the shelves and nooks of the apartment.

The dealer followed me closely through the tortuous way contrived between the piles of furniture; warding off with his hand the hazardous sweep of my coat-skirts; watching my elbows with the uneasy attention of an antiquarian and a usurer.

It was a singular face, that of the merchant: — an immense skull, polished like a knee, and surrounded by a thin aureole of white

---

[*] "The Mummy's Foot" was written by Théophile Gautier (1811 – 1872) and originally published in 1840. The text for this edition was taken from the short story collection *One of Cleopatra's Nights and Other Fantastic Romances* (1882), translated by Lafcadio Hearn (1850 – 1904).

hair, which brought out the clear salmon tint of his complexion all the more strikingly, lent him a false aspect of patriarchal *bonhomie*, counteracted, however, by the scintillation of two little yellow eyes which trembled in their orbits like two louis-d'or upon quicksilver. The curve of his nose presented an aquiline silhouette, which suggested the Oriental or Jewish type. His hands, — thin, slender, full of nerves which projected like strings upon the finger-board of a violin, and armed with claws like those on the terminations of bats' wings, — shook with senile trembling; but those convulsively agitated hands became firmer than steel pincers or lobsters' claws when they lifted any precious article, — an onyx cup, a Venetian glass, or a dish of Bohemian crystal. This strange old man had an aspect so thoroughly rabbinical and cabalistic that he would have been burnt on the mere testimony of his face three centuries ago.

"Will you not buy something from me to-day, sir? Here is a Malay kreese with a blade undulating like flame: look at those grooves contrived for the blood to run along, those teeth set backward so as to tear out the entrails in withdrawing the weapon, — it is a fine character of ferocious arm, and will look well in your collection: this two-handed sword is very beautiful, — it is the work of Josepe de la Hera; and this *colichemarde*, with its fenestrated guard, — what a superb specimen of handicraft!"

"No; I have quite enough weapons and instruments of carnage; — I want a small figure, something which will suit me as a paper-weight; for I cannot endure those trumpery bronzes which the stationers sell, and which may be found on everybody's desk."

The old gnome foraged among his ancient wares, and finally arranged before me some antique bronzes, — so-called, at least; fragments of malachite; little Hindoo or Chinese idols,— a kind of poussah-toys in jade-stone, representing the incarnations of Brahma or Vishnoo, and wonderfully appropriate to the very undivine office of holding papers and letters in place.

I was hesitating between a porcelain dragon, all constellated with warts, — its mouth formidable with bristling tusks and ranges of teeth, — and an abominable little Mexican fetish, representing the god Vitziliputzili *au naturel;* when I caught sight of a charming foot, which I at first took for a fragment of some antique Venus.

It had those beautiful ruddy and tawny tints that lend to Florentine bronze that warm living look so much preferable to the gray-green aspect of common bronzes, which might easily be mistaken for statues in a state of putrefaction: satiny gleams played over its rounded forms, doubtless polished by the amorous kisses of twenty centuries; for it seemed a Corinthian bronze, a work of the best era of art, — perhaps moulded by Lysippus himself.

"That foot will be my choice," I said to the merchant, who regarded me with an ironical and saturnine air, and held out the object desired that I might examine it more fully.

I was surprised at its lightness; it was not a foot of metal, but in sooth a foot of flesh, — an embalmed foot,— a mummy's foot: on examining it still more closely the very grain of the skin, and the almost imperceptible lines impressed upon it by the texture of the bandages, became perceptible. The toes were slender and delicate, and terminated by perfectly formed nails, pure and transparent as agates; the great toe slightly separated from the rest, afforded a happy contrast, in the antique style, to the position of the other toes, and lent it an aeriel lightness, — the grace of a bird's foot; — the sole, scarcely streaked by a few almost imperceptible cross lines, afforded evidence that it had never touched the bare ground, and had only come in contact with the finest matting of Nile rushes, and the softest carpets of panther skin.

"Ha, ha! — you want the foot of the Princess Hermonthis," — exclaimed the merchant, with a strange giggle, fixing his owlish eyes upon me — "ha, ha, ha! — for a paper-weight! — an original idea! — artistic idea! Old Pharaoh would certainly have been surprised had some one told him that the foot of his adored daughter would be used for a paper-weight after he had had a mountain of granite hollowed out as a receptacle for the triple coffin, painted and gilded, — covered with hieroglyphics and beautiful paintings of the Judgment of Souls," — continued the queer little merchant, half audibly, as though talking to himself!

"How much will you charge me for this mummy fragment?"

"Ah, the highest price I can get; for it is a superb piece: if I had the match of it you could not have it for less than five hundred francs; — the daughter of a Pharaoh! nothing is more rare."

"Assuredly that is not a common article; but, still, how much do you want? In the first place let me warn you that all my wealth consists of just five louis: I can buy anything that costs five louis, but nothing dearer; — you might search my vest pockets and most secret drawers without even finding one poor five-franc piece more."

"Five louis for the foot of the Princess Hermonthis! that is very little, very little indeed; 'tis an authentic foot," muttered the merchant, shaking his head, and imparting a peculiar rotary motion to his eyes. "Well, take it, and I will give you the bandages into the bargain," he added, wrapping the foot in an ancient damask rag — "very fine! real damask — Indian damask which has never been redyed; it is strong, and yet it is soft," he mumbled, stroking the frayed tissue with his fingers, through the trade-acquired habit which moved him to praise even an object of so little value that he himself deemed it only worth the giving away.

He poured the gold coins into a sort of mediaeval alms-purse hanging at his belt, repeating: —

"The foot of the Princess Hermonthis, to be used for a paper-weight!"

Then turning his phosphorescent eyes upon me, he exclaimed in a voice strident as the crying of a cat which has swallowed a fish-bone:

"Old Pharaoh will not be well pleased: he loved his daughter, — the dear man!"

"You speak as if you were a contemporary of his: you are old enough, goodness knows! but you do not date back to the Pyramids of Egypt," I answered, laughingly, from the threshold.

I went home, delighted with my acquisition.

With the idea of putting it to profitable use as soon as possible, I placed the foot of the divine Princess Hermonthis upon a heap of papers scribbled over with verses, in themselves an undecipherable mosaic work of erasures; articles freshly began; letters forgotten, and posted in the table drawer instead of the letter-box, — an error to which absent-minded people are peculiarly liable. The effect was charming, *bizarre* and romantic.

Well satisfied with this embellishment, I went out with the gravity and pride becoming one who feels that he has the ineffable advantage over all the passers-by whom he elbows, of possessing a piece of the Princess Hermonthis, daughter of Pharaoh.

I looked upon all who did not possess, like myself, a paper weight so authentically Egyptian, as very ridiculous people; and it seemed to me that the proper occupation of every sensible man should consist in the mere fact of having a mummy's foot upon his desk.

Happily I met some friends, whose presence distracted me in my infatuation with this new acquisition: I went to dinner with them; for I could not very well have dined with myself.

When I came back that evening, with my brain slightly confused by a few glasses of wine, a vague whiff of Oriental perfume delicately titillated my olfactory nerves: the heat of the room had warmed the natron, bitumen, and myrrh in which the *paraschistes,* who cut open the bodies of the dead, had bathed the corpse of the princess; — it was a perfume at once sweet and penetrating, — a perfume that four thousand years had not been able to dissipate.

The Dream of Egypt was Eternity: her odors have the solidity of granite, and endure as long.

I soon drank deeply from the black cup of sleep: for a few hours all remained opaque to me; Oblivion and Nothingness inundated me with their somber waves.

Yet light gradually dawned upon the darkness of my mind: dreams commenced to touch me softly in their silent flight.

The eyes of my soul were opened; and I beheld my chamber as it actually was: I might have believed myself awake, but for a vague consciousness which assured me that I slept, and that something fantastic was about to take place.

The odor of the myrrh had augmented in intensity: and I felt a slight headache, which I very naturally attributed to several glasses of champagne that we had drank to the unknown gods and our future fortunes.

I peered through my room with a feeling of expectation which I saw nothing to justify: every article of furniture was in its proper place; the lamp, softly shaded by its globe of ground crystal, burned upon its bracket; the water-color sketches shone under their Bohemian glass; the curtains hung down languidly; everything wore an aspect of tranquil slumber.

After a few moments, however, all this calm interior appeared to become disturbed; the woodwork cracked stealthily; the ash-covered log suddenly emitted a jet of blue flame; and the disks of the pateras seemed like great metallic eyes, watching, like myself, for the things which were about to happen.

My eyes accidentally fell upon the desk where I had placed the foot of the Princess Hermonthis.

Instead of remaining quiet — as behooved a foot which had been embalmed for four thousand years, — it commenced to act in a nervous manner; contracted itself, and leaped over the papers like a startled frog; — one would have imagined that it had suddenly been brought into contact with a galvanic battery: I could distinctly hear the dry sound made by its little heel, hard as the hoof of a gazelle.

I became rather discontented with my acquisition, inasmuch as I wished my paper-weights to be of a sedentary disposition, and thought it very unnatural that feet should walk about without legs; and I commenced to experience a feeling closely akin to fear.

Suddenly I saw the folds of my bed-curtain stir; and heard a bumping sound, like that caused by some person hopping on one foot across the floor. I must confess I became alternately hot and cold; that I felt a strange wind chill my back; and that my suddenly-rising hair caused my nightcap to execute a leap of several yards.

The bed-curtains opened and I beheld the strangest figure imaginable before me.

It was a young girl of a very deep coffee-brown complexion, like the bayadere Amani, and possessing the purest Egyptian type of perfect beauty: her eyes were almond-shaped and oblique, with eyebrows so black that they seemed blue; her nose was exquisitely chiseled, almost Greek in its delicacy of outline; and she might indeed have been taken for a Corinthian statue of bronze, but for the prominence of her cheek-bones and the slightly African fullness of her lips, which compelled one to recognize her as belonging beyond all doubt to the hieroglyphic race which dwelt upon the banks of the Nile.

Her arms, slender and spindle-shaped, like those of very young girls, were encircled by a peculiar kind of metal bands, and bracelets of glass beads; her hair was all twisted into little cords; and she wore upon her bosom a little idol-figure of green paste, bearing a whip with seven lashes, which proved it to be an image of Isis: her brow was adorned with a shining plate of gold; and a few traces of paint relieved the coppery tint of her cheeks.

As for her costume, it was very odd indeed.

Fancy a *pagne* or skirt all formed of little strips of material bedizened with red and black hieroglyphics, stiffened with bitumen, and apparently belonging to a freshly unbandaged mummy.

In one of those sudden flights of thought so common in dreams I heard the hoarse falsetto of the *bric-a-brac* dealer, repeating like a monotonous refrain, the phrase he had uttered in his shop with so enigmatical an intonation:

"Old Pharaoh will not be well pleased: he loved his daughter, the dear man!"

One strange circumstance, which was not at all calculated to restore my equanimity, was that the apparition had but one foot; the other was broken off at the ankle!

She approached the table where the foot was starting and fidgetting about more than ever; and there supported herself upon the edge of the desk. I saw her eyes fill with pearly-gleaming tears.

Although she had not as yet spoken, I fully comprehended the thoughts which agitated her: she looked at her foot — for it was indeed her own — with an exquisitely graceful expression of coquettish sadness; but the foot leaped and ran hither and thither, as though impelled on steel springs.

Twice or thrice she extended her hand to seize it, but could not succeed.

Then commenced between the Princess Hermonthis and her foot — which appeared to be endowed with a special life of its own — a very fantastic dialogue in a most ancient Coptic tongue, such as might have been spoken thirty centuries ago in the syrinxes of the land of Ser: luckily I understood Coptic perfectly well that night.

The Princess Hermonthis cried, in a voice sweet and vibrant as the tones of a crystal bell:

"Well, my dear little foot, you always flee from me; yet I always took good care of you. I bathed you with perfumed water in a bowl of alabaster; I smoothed your heel with pumice-stone mixed with palm oil; your nails were cut with golden scissors and polished with a hippopotamus tooth; I was careful to select *tatbebs* for you, painted and embroidered and turned up at the toes, which were the envy of all the young girls in Egypt: you wore on your great toe rings bearing the device of the sacred Scarabæus; and you supported one of the lightest bodies that a lazy foot could sustain."

The foot replied in a pouting and chagrined tone: —

"You know well that I do not belong to myself any longer: — I have been bought and paid for: the old merchant knew what he was about: he bore you a grudge for having refused to espouse him: — this is an ill turn which he has done you. The Arab who violated your royal coffin in the subterranean pits of the necropolis of Thebes was sent thither by him: he desired to prevent you from being present at the reunion of the shadowy nations in the cities below. Have you five pieces of gold for my ransom?"

"Alas, no!" — my jewels, my rings, my purses of gold and silver, were all stolen from me," answered the Princess Hermonthis, with a sob.

"Princess," I then exclaimed, "I never retained anybody's foot unjustly; — even though you have not got the five louis which it cost me, I present it to you gladly: I should feel unutterably wretched to think that I were the cause of so amiable a person as the Princess Hermonthis being lame."

I delivered this discourse in a royally gallant, troubadour tone which must have astonished the beautiful Egyptian girl.

She turned a look of deepest gratitude upon me; and her eyes shone with bluish gleams of light.

She took her foot, — which surrendered itself willingly this time, — like a woman about to put on her little shoe; and adjusted it to her leg with much skill.

This operation over, she took a few steps about the room; as though to assure herself that she was really no longer lame.

"Ah, how pleased my father will be! — he who was so unhappy because of my mutilation; and who from the moment of my birth, set a whole nation at work to hollow me out a tomb so deep that he might preserve me intact until that last day, when souls must be weighed in the balance of Amenthi! Come with me to my father; — he will receive you kindly; for you have given me back my foot."

I thought this proposition natural enough. I arrayed myself, in a dressing-gown of large-flowered pattern, which lent me a very Pharaonic aspect; hurriedly put on a pair of Turkish slippers; and informed the Princess Hermonthis that I was ready to follow her.

Before starting, Hermonthis took from her neck the little idol of green paste, and laid it on the scattered sheets of paper which covered the table.

"It is only fair," she observed, smilingly, "that I should replace your paper-weight."

She gave me her hand, which felt soft and cold, like the skin of a serpent; and we departed.

We passed for some time with the velocity of an arrow through a fluid and greyish expanse, in which half-formed silhouettes flitted swiftly by us, to right and left.

For an instant we saw only sky and sea.

A few moments later obelisks commenced to tower in the distance: pylons and vast flights of steps guarded by sphinxes became clearly outlined against the horizon.

We had reached our destination.

The princess conducted me to a mountain of rose-colored granite, in the face of which appeared an opening so narrow and low that it would have been difficult to distinguish it from the fissures in the rock, had not its location been marked by two stelæ wrought with sculptures.

Hermonthis kindled a torch, and led the way before me.

We traversed corridors hewn through the living rock: their walls, covered with hieroglyphics and paintings of allegorical processions, might well have occupied thousands of arms for thousands of years in their formation; — these corridors, of interminable length, opened into square chambers, in the midst of which pits had been contrived, through which we descended by cramp-irons or spiral stairways; — these pits again conducted us into other chambers, opening into other corridors, likewise decorated with painted sparrow-hawks, serpents coiled in circles, the symbols of the *tau* and *pedum*, — prodigious works of art which no living eye can ever examine, — interminable legends of granite which only the dead have time to read through all eternity.

At last we found ourselves in a hall so vast, so enormous, so immeasurable, that the eye could not reach its limits; files of monstrous columns stretched far out of sight on every side, between which twinkled livid stars of yellowish flame; — points of light which revealed further depths incalculable in the darkness beyond.

The Princess Hermonthis still held my hand, and graciously saluted the mummies of her acquaintance.

My eyes became accustomed to the dim twilight; and objects became discernible.

I beheld the kings of the subterranean races seated upon thrones, — grand old men, though dry, withered, wrinkled like parchment, and blackened with naphtha and bitumen, — all wearing *pshents* of gold, and breast-plates and gorgets glittering with precious stones; their eyes immovably fixed like the eyes of sphinxes, and their long beards whitened by the snow of centuries. Behind them stood their peoples, in the stiff and constrained posture enjoined by Egyptian art, all eternally preserving the attitude prescribed by the hieratic code. Behind these nations, the cats, ibixes, and crocodiles cotemporary with them, — rendered monstrous of aspect by their swathing bands, — mewed, flapped their wings, or extended their jaws in a saurian giggle.

All the Pharaohs were there — Cheops, Chephrenes, Psammetichus, Sesostris, Amenotaph — all the dark rulers of the pyramids and syrinxes: — on yet higher thrones sat Chronos and Xixouthros, — who was contemporary with the deluge; and Tubal Cain, who reigned before it.

The beard of King Xixouthros had grown seven times around the granite table, upon which he leaned, lost in deep reverie, — and buried in dreams.

Further back, through a dusty cloud, I beheld dimly the seventy-two Preadamite Kings, with their seventy-two peoples — forever passed away.

After permitting me to gaze upon this bewildering spectacle a few moments, the Princess Hermonthis presented me to her father Pharaoh, who favored me with a most gracious nod.

"I have found my foot again! — I have found my foot!" cried the princess, clapping her little hands together with every sign of frantic joy: "it was this gentleman who restored it to me."

The races of Kemi, the races of Nahasi, — all the black, bronzed, and copper-colored nations repeated in chorus:

"The Princess Hermonthis has found her foot again!"

Even Xixouthros himself was visibly affected.

He raised his heavy eyelids, stroked his moustache with his fingers, and turned upon me a glance weighty with centuries.

"By Oms, the dog of Hell, and Tmei, daughter of the Sun and of Truth! this is a brave and worthy lad!" exclaimed Pharaoh, pointing to me with his scepter which was terminated with a lotus-flower.

"What recompense do you desire?"

Filled with that daring inspired by dreams in which nothing seems impossible, I asked him for the hand of the Princess Hermonthis; — the hand seemed to me a very proper antithetic recompense for the foot.

Pharaoh opened wide his great eyes of glass in astonishment at my witty request.

"What country do you come from? and what is your age?"

"I am a Frenchman; and I am twenty-seven years old, venerable Pharaoh."

"——— Twenty-seven years old! and he wishes to espouse the Princess Hermonthis, who is thirty centuries old!" — cried out at once all the Thrones and all the Circles of Nations.

Only Hermonthis herself did not seem to think my request unreasonable.

"If you were even only two thousand years old," replied the ancient King, "I would willingly give you the Princess; but the disproportion is too great; and, besides, we must give our daughters husbands who will last well: you do not know how to preserve yourselves any longer; even those who died only fifteen centuries ago are already no more than a handful of dust; — behold! my flesh is solid as basalt; my bones are bars of steel!

"I will be present on the last day of the world, with the same body and the same features which I had during my life-time: my daughter Hermonthis will last longer than a statue of bronze.

"Then the last particles of your dust will have been scattered abroad by the winds; and even Isis herself, who was able to find the atoms of Osiris, would scarce be able to recompose your being.

"See how vigorous I yet remain, and how mighty is my grasp," he added, shaking my hand in the English fashion with a strength that buried my rings in the flesh of my fingers.

He squeezed me so hard that I awoke, and found my friend Alfred shaking me by the arm to make me get up.

"O you everlasting sleeper! — must I have you carried out into the middle of the street, and fireworks exploded in your ears? It is after noon; don't you recollect your promise to take me with you to see M. Aguado's Spanish pictures?"

"God! I forgot all, all about it," I answered, dressing myself hurriedly; "we will go there at once; I have the permit lying there on my desk."

I started to find it; — but fancy my astonishment when I beheld, instead of the mummy's foot I had purchased the evening before, the little green paste idol left in its place by the princess Hermonthis!

Mr. Grubbe's Night
With Memnon[*]

In the far west of London — preserving many traces of its original characteristics, amidst the wide expanse of architectural innovations which are continually springing up around it — there is a sober and antiquated, but withal respectable, locality, known to those travelers whose enterprise has led them thus far into the occidental suburbs, as Brompton. It is a district principally inhabited by theatricals, *literati,* and small annuitants; and is much esteemed on account of the salubrity of its climate, the mildness of its society, and the economy of its household arrangements. Its chief natural curiosities are teaparties and old ladies; and its overland journey to London is performed by omnibuses, unless the route by water is preferred. But this is somewhat circuitous — Cadogan pier, which is the nearest port, standing in the same relation to Brompton as Civita Vecchia does to Rome.

Mr. Withers Grubbe, who was an old inhabitant of this pleasant village, resided in a modest tenement, situate at the edge of the great Fulham road. His establishment comprised himself and his housekeeper — a staid woman, of matronly appearance — from which circumstance it may be fairly presumed that he was either a widower or a bachelor; but the uncertainty as to which of these two orders of single life he came under will be quite removed, when we state that he was an antiquary, an entomologist, and a general natural philosopher, somewhat resembling a cocoa-nut — being shriveled in external appearance, but possessing a good heart or kernel, and not entirely destitute of the milk of human kindness.

As his favorite pursuits had been, from time immemorial, at variance with matrimony, he had never taken unto himself a wife. Once, and once only, did his friends speak of his falling in love. It was in the Park, one bright frosty morning, when he saw a lady whose cloak somewhat resembled the delicate tintings of the privet moth; but this lepidopterous attachment was very transient, and the next chrysalis of the *Sphynx Atropos,* or number of the "Gentleman's Magazine," that came to hand, immediately banished it from his mind.

And he was an occasional correspondent to the afore-named humorous publication. He had sent them a drawing of the old key of his dust-bin, and a dissertation upon several worn-out brass button-tops he had from time to time picked up in his walks, believing them to be ancient coins; as well as a plan of the Roman encampment on the

[*] "Mr. Grubbe's Night with Memnon" was written by Albert Smith (1816 – 1860) and originally published in 1843, later published in *Putnam's Monthly Magazine,* Aug. 1857.

Birmingham railway, and other interesting articles, the majority of which were "declined with thanks," by the venerable and undying Mr. Urban.

He belonged also to most of the learned and scientific bodies, to all of whom he read the rejected contributions, so that his time was pretty well occupied, and more especially in the spring; for then his *larvæ* and *aureliæ* broke forth into a new life, and there was such a buzzing, and fluttering, and pinning, and labeling all over the house, with intrusive butterflies getting into the bed-rooms, and strange caterpillars walking up and down stairs, that people of ordinary nerves and uninterested in insect architecture were afraid to go into the house.

But he cherished all his living things with singular affection, even to the moths which had fattened upon his waistcoats, and the cockroaches which ran about his kitchen; although Mrs. Weston, the housekeeper, could never understand that the former insects only did any mischief in their first stage of existence, and that the latter were to be looked upon as sacred things, from the high veneration they were held in amongst the ancient Egyptians. The poor, ignorant woman, in the darkness of her intellect, classed them all as "warmint."

The great aim of Mr. Grubbe's labors was to get up some paper that should produce a striking sensation in the learned world, by the novel facts that it might disclose — a consummation which had never yet arrived, for his most interesting discoveries had always been forestalled. To this great end did he consume his midnight patent stearine; for this did he burn holes in all his carpets with the contents of his galvanic battery, and get phosphorus under his nails, or take all the color from his table-covers; in prosecuting this endeavor, by rubbing his buffer of black lead over cartridge-paper, laid upon engraved stones and brass tablets, to take the impression, was he three times apprehended for Swing, and once for sacrilege.

But hitherto he had never produced any extraordinary impression beyond that which his appearance created with the rustics; and although he was a walking catalogue of the British Museum — far more copious and elaborate than those hired by country visitors at contiguous fishmongers, and public-houses — he found every object therein had been so often and so minutely described, that nothing fresh was left to dilate upon. And this opinion for a time subdued his energy, until one evening he was present at the unrolling of a mummy. He listened with intense attention to the remarks of the lecturer, and envied him the proud position he was for a time placed in, as the descriptive link between the present and the long-past epochs.

But when the ceremony was finished, and Mr. Grubbe found, upon reviewing the lecture, that our acquaintance with the ancient Egyptians extended just far enough to show that we knew nothing at all about them, a fresh chain of research presented itself to his mind, and from that time every other pursuit was merged in the depths of the Great Pyramid, or perched upon the edge of Belzoni's sarcophagus. He made a mummy of his favorite cat; called his abode Sphynx-cottage; and allowed the kitchen to swarm with cockroaches — which he called *scarabæi*, and Mrs. Weston black beadles — more than ever.

Things stood thus, when, one sultry July morning, a learned friend called to beg his company in a visit to the Docks, to view some wonderful organic remains, not yet landed, which a ship had brought from a distant country. Mr. Grubbe immediately prepared for the excursion; and, after having drawn an odd pair of boots upon the wrong legs in his absence of mind, as well as omitted to take off his duffel dressing-gown, he gave himself up to the care of Mrs. Weston, who finally pronounced him fit to appear in the public streets. He accordingly started with his friend, taking the omnibus to the Bank, whence they proceeded to the Docks on foot, saving the other sixpence; and beguiling the journey with many curious arguments and opinions about *ichthyosauri* and the blue lias clay.

The inspection of the fossils was most satisfactory, and they were pronounced highly interesting, the more so because several of them were perfectly incomprehensible; and notwithstanding the confined and heated places in which they were stowed, Mr. Grubbe poked about amongst the packing cases, covered with dust and perspiration, and dragging his friend after him, until every available object had been investigated, and they emerged from the hold into the free air.

A fresh treat now awaited him. His friend was attached to everything old equally with himself, and old wine possessed no insignificant share of his affections. With praiseworthy foresight he had provided a tasting-order as a crowning finish to their excursion; and having raised Mr. Grubbe's curiosity by mysterious hints of pipes and casks that had long slumbered in cool excavations below the level of the Thames, and wine more generous, oily, and sparkling than ever came into the dealer's hands, they were not long in furnishing themselves with inches of candle in split laths, and following their guide — a priest of Bacchus in high lows and corduroys — into the bowels of the Docks.

How long they lingered therein we are ashamed to state; nor will we tell the world too ruthlessly how many casks were broached by the relentless gimlet; how the wine leaped bright and creaming from the wood; how the glasses held twice the ordinary quantity, and how they were even rinsed out with claret and madeira, which was thrown about amongst the sawdust like water. Neither will we betray the number of samples tasted by the visitors; nor do more than just hint at Mr. Grubbe's slapping the cellarman on the back for a good fellow, and endeavoring to strike up an ancient Bacchanalian melody, sung by Dignum in his young days.

We only know that this subterranean sojourn was protracted to a period we blush to chronicle, delayed, no doubt, by a learned disquisition, poured forth by Mr. Grubbe, upon the home-made wines of Thebes, which ended just as they got to the top of the staircase, and stood once more, blinking and confused, in the glaring sunshine of a July afternoon. And terrible was the effect of the hot atmosphere upon their temperaments before a few minutes had passed. Whiz-z-z-z-z went their eyes and brains together; the ships flew round and round like the revolving boats at Greenwich fair, and the warehouses heaved and rolled as the billows of the sea.

It was with the greatest difficulty, amidst this general *bouleversement* of surrounding objects, that the two men of science staggered to the gate, and deposited themselves in the first omnibus that passed. They had not particularly inquired in what direction it was going; and, in consequence, after much traveling, Mr. Grubbe was somewhat surprised to find the vehicle stop in Tottenham-court-read, when he expected to be at the White Horse Cellar. But he was in the humor for treating any mishap that might have occurred with exceeding levity; and finding that the locality suited his friend just as well, even better, than Piccadilly, he wished him good-by very affectionately, and took advantage of its proximity to pay a visit to his favorite British Museum, partly in the belief that its cool tranquillity would allay his cerebral excitement.

He left his inseparable gingham umbrella — which answered the double purpose of keeping off the rain when open and serving as a portmanteau of collected curiosities when shut — with the porter upon entering; and then turned his steps toward the Egyptian gallery, which was his usual lounge, still cherishing some vague notion that his skull had turned into a bag of hydrogen, so elastic and vivacious was his step.

There were, as usual, a great many people gaping about and asking foolish questions of the attendant; some mixing up the sphynx with the fossils they had seen, and asking if it ever was alive; others feeling rather afraid of going too near the mummies by themselves; and others lost in mental arguments as to whether the colossal fist of red granite was a thunderbolt or the hand of a petrified giant; together with a great many ill-conducted little boys, with no veneration for antiquities, who laughed at the different objects as they would have done at any of the wondrous creations in a pantomime.

Heedless of the visitors, Mr. Grubbe was soon lost in mighty speculations upon the mysterious productions by which he was surrounded; and so continued until the constant shuffling of feet and increasing influx of strangers, whose inane remarks grated upon his learned ears, drove him from the block upon which he was sitting, to some more remote corner of the gallery. Ensconcing himself in a recess behind one of the enormous heads, and screened by a sarcophagus, he fell into a fresh train of intense thought upon hieroglyphics in general, and those of mummies in particular. To this succeeded a confused picture of wine-vaults, pyramids, docks, claret-casks, and megatheria; and finally, overcome by the influence of heat, fatigue, and the tasting-order, he fell fast asleep.

How long he slumbered remains to this day a mystery, and probably ever will do so. But when he awoke all was still and quiet as the interior of the Theban tombs; the gallery was entirely deserted, and the moon was pouring a flood of light through the windows, which fell upon the statues and remains, rendering them still more cold and ghastly.

In an instant the truth broke upon the unhappy antiquary; he had been overlooked when the Museum was cleared at seven o'clock, and was locked in — bolted, barred, almost hermetically shut up in the gallery, in the most remote part of the building, with nothing but stony monsters and crumbling mortality for his associates! Chilled to the heart with terror, despair, and the reaction of his previous excitement, he started from his corner with the intention of trying the doors, when his movement was arrested by the chime of a clock. He knew the sound well; it was the bell of St. George's, Bloomsbury, and it proclaimed the hour of twelve. And he was there alone — alone, at midnight, in the Egyptian chamber of the British Museum!

In a frenzy of terror he rushed towards the large doors, in the hope of finding them open; but they were fast closed, and he rattled the handles until the whole building rang with the echoes. Hark! what was that sound? The echo had died away, and was now renewed, although he had desisted from his impotent attempts to gain some mode of egress. It sounded from above, and now came nearer and nearer, louder and louder, like the deadened and regular beat of muffled drums. There were footsteps too — he could plainly distinguish them, in audible progression, coming down stairs.

And now a fearful spectacle met his horrified gaze. The immense marble *scarabæus* on the floor of the gallery vibrated with incipient animation; then it stretched forth its huge feelers and opened its massy wings, like a newly born insect trying the properties of its novel limbs; and next, with the heavy cumbrous motion of a tortoise, it crept across the floor, throwing back the moonbeams from its polished surface, towards the principal entrance of the gallery. Tramp, tramp, tramp — onward came the noise as of a great assembly, the drums still keeping up their monotonous accompaniment, and at last they approached close to the door, which quivered immediately afterwards with three loud knocks upon its panels from without.

As the hapless Mr. Grubbe shrank still further into the recess, the large beetle scuffled nearer to the door, and then, raising one of its hideous feelers, it turned the handle. The gigantic granite first moved by itself towards the entrance, and repeated the signal on the panels; and, at the last blow, a sound like the low rumbling of thunder echoed through the edifice, and the doors flew open, admitting a glare of purple light, that for a few moments blinded the terrified intruder, whilst on either side the Memnon and the Sphynx retreated back against the wall, to allow room for the dismal *cortége* that approached.

The whole collection of mummy-cases in the rooms above had given up their inmates, who now glided down the staircase, one after another, to join their ancient compatriots of the gallery below, lifting up the covers of their painted tombs, and stretching forth their pitched and blackened arms to welcome them. And next, the curious monsters with the birds' heads, who, up to this moment, had remained patiently sitting against the side of the room with their hands upon their knees, rose courteously to salute their visitors.

The light which filled the apartment, although proceeding from no visible point, grew brighter and brighter until it assumed the brilliancy of oxyhydrogen, and when the last of the dusty and bandaged guests had arrived, the doors closed violently, and the orgies began. The figures in the pictures became animated and descended from the tablets, being by far the most attractive portion of the company, either male or female, as they were semblances of life, bearing *amphoræ* of the choicest wine from the vineyards of Memphis; strange birds in long striped tunics, and stranger creations, whose shapes inherited an attribute of every class of the animal kingdom, acted as attendants, and obsequiously waited upon the superior deities; whilst the greatest feature of the gallery, the mystic, awe inspiring Memnon, moved in stately progress to the end of the room, and commenced pouring forth that wondrous harmony with which at sunrise and twilight he welcomed his early worshipers.

Then commenced an unearthly *galopade* — a dreary carnival of the dead, to the music of their master, accompanied by the strange sounds of instruments brought by the mummies most inclined to conviviality, from the glass-cases up stairs. But the strangest sight in the whole spectacle was the curious way in which Mr. Grubbe, despite his fears, perceived that they mingled ancient with modern manners, when the dance came to an end.

Some of the animated Egyptians betook themselves to pipes and beer; others brought large aerolites from the different rooms and began to play at ninepins with the inferior household gods of blue glazed clay; one young Memphian even went so far as to thrust an enormous hook, as big as an anchor, through the body of a *scarabæus,* and then spin him at the end of a rope about the room; and, finally, they wheeled a sarcophagus into the centre of the gallery, and filled it with what Mr. Grubbe's nose told him was excellent mixed punch, which they tippled until the eyes of Memnon twinkled with conviviality, as he snuffed up the goodly aroma; and at length, forgetting his dignity altogether, volunteered to play the *Aurora* waltzes (in compliment of course to his mother) out of his head. The monumental punch-bowl was directly pushed on one side, and they began to dance again, Mr. Grubbe, getting gradually more and more excited by the music, until, unable to contain himself any longer, he rushed from his recess, and seizing a fair young daughter of the Nile round the waist, was in an instant whirling round in the throng of deities, mummies, hieroglyphics, ibises, and anomalous creations who composed the assembly.

The hours flew along like joyous minutes, and still the unearthly waltz was continued with persisting energy, until Mr. Grubbe's brain became giddy and bewildered. His strength also began to fail in spite of the attractions of his young *Memphienne,* whose soft downy cheeks, roguish kissable lips, and supernaturally-sparkling eyes, had for a time made him forget his age. He requested her to stop in their wild gyrations, but she heeded him not — breathless and exhausted, he was pulled round and round, whilst the Memnonian orchestra played itself louder and louder, until at length, losing all power, he fell down in the midst of the dancers.

Twenty others, who had been twirling onwards, not perceiving their prostrate companion, immediately lost their footing; and, finally, the whole assembly, like so many bent cards, giddy with wine and excitement, bundled one over the other, the unfortunate antiquary being the undermost of the party. In vain he struggled to be free — each moment the pressure of the superincumbent Egyptians increased; until, in a last extremity, unable to breathe, bruised by their legs and arms, and half suffocated with mummy-dust, he gave a few fruitless gasps for air, and then became insensible.

It was broad daylight when he once more opened his eyes; and the motes were dancing in the bright morning sunbeams that darted into the gallery. There were sounds of life and motion too, on every side (although no one had as yet entered the apartment), and the rumble of distant vehicles in the streets. It was some little time before Mr. Grubbe could collect his ideas for his brain was still slightly clouded — his lips, also, were parched, and his eyeballs smarting with the revelry of the night.

But there he still was, in the room, surrounded by his late company, though they had now resumed their usual situations: the Memnon and Sphynx were *vis-à-vis,* and the *scarabæus* in his customary place, as cold and inanimate as ever; whilst the gigantic fist had once more taken possession of its pedestal, and the gentlemen with the curious heads were sitting with their hands upon their knees in their wonted gravity. But, notwithstanding all this chill reality, the antiquary's mind was in a tumult of excitement. The dim undying magic of ancient Egypt was still in force, unconquered by time or distance. He had been admitted to the orgies of Memnon; he had watched the revelries and manners of the hitherto mysterious race; above all, he had gleaned information for a paper that would bring the Society of Antiquaries at his feet in wondrous veneration!

The doors were, ere long, thrown open, and Mr. Grubbe left the gallery unnoticed. On arriving at Brompton, he found Mrs. Weston in a state of extreme terror and exhaustion, having watched the whole night for her master's return, that worthy gentleman never having passed so long a period from home.

He retired immediately to his study, and labored until dusk with unceasing industry; and from that period Egypt alone occupied his thoughts. He thought of nothing else by day, and dreamed of that subject only by night. The subject grew beneath his hands and ideas, and what with the circumstances he imagined, and those he dreamed about — for in his labors he ever confounded them together — the work is still unfinished; and he will not give it to the world in an imperfect condition, although his most intimate friends already fear that his application is affecting his brain.

But, when his task is concluded, great will be his triumph: he will have furnished — at least such is his expectation — a key to all the mystic customs of the early Nile; the hidden lore of Memphis will be unraveled to the million; he will walk abroad a thing for men to gaze at and reverence; and his name will go down to posterity in company with Memnon and the Great Pyramid.

These are his own anticipations: his intimate friends have only one hope — that he will be spared from Bedlam sufficiently long to perfect his colossal undertaking; and that on no account will he be induced any more to venture, with a tasting-order, to the Docks.

Some Words with a Mummy[*]

The Symposium of the preceding evening had been a little too much for my nerves. I had a wretched headache, and was desperately drowsy. Instead of going out, therefore, to spend the evening, as I had proposed, it occurred to me that I could not do a wiser thing than just eat a mouthful of supper and go immediately to bed.

A *light* supper, of course. I am exceedingly fond of Welsh rabbit. More than a pound at once, however, may not at all times be advisable. Still, there can be no material objection to two. And really between two and three, there is merely a single unit of difference. I ventured, perhaps, upon four. My wife will have it five; but, clearly, she has confounded two very distinct affairs. The abstract number, five, I am willing to admit; but, concretely, it has reference to bottles of brown stout, without which, in the way of condiment, Welsh rabbit is to be eschewed.

Having thus concluded a frugal meal and donned my nightcap, with the serene hope of enjoying it till noon the next day, I placed my head upon the pillow, and through the aid of a capital conscience, fell into a profound slumber forthwith.

But when were the hopes of humanity fulfilled? I could not have completed my third snore when there came a furious ringing at the street-door bell, and then an impatient thumping at the knocker, which awakened me at once. In a minute afterward, and while I was still rubbing my eyes, my wife thrust in my face a note, from my old friend, Dr. Ponnonner. It ran thus:

> Come to me, by all means, my dear good friend, as soon as you receive this. Come and help us to rejoice. At last, by long persevering diplomacy, I have gained the assent of the directors of the City Museum, to my examination of the mummy - you know the one I mean. I have permission to unswathe it, and open it, if desirable. A few friends only will be present - you, of course. The mummy is now at my house, and we shall begin to unroll it at eleven tonight.
>
> Yours ever, Ponnonner

By the time I had reached the 'Ponnonner', it struck me that I was as wide awake as a man need be. I leaped out of bed in an ecstasy, overthrowing all in my way; dressed myself with a rapidity truly marvellous; and set off, at the top of my speed, for the doctor's.

There I found a very eager company assembled. They had been awaiting me with much impatience. The mummy was extended upon the

* "Some Words with a Mummy" was written by Edgar Allan Poe (1809 – 1849) and published in *American Review: A Whig Journal*, Apr. 1845.

dining-table; and the moment I entered, its examination was commenced.

It was one of a pair brought, several years previously, by Captain Arthur Sabretash, a cousin of Ponnonner's, from a tomb near Eleithias, in the Lybian Mountains, a considerable distance above Thebes on the Nile. The grottoes at this point, although less magnificent than the Theban sepulchres, are of higher interest, on account of affording more numerous illustrations of the private life of the Egyptians. The chamber from which our specimen was taken, was said to be very rich in such illustrations — the walls being completely covered with fresco-paintings and bas-reliefs, while statues, vases, and mosaic work of rich patterns, indicated the vast wealth of the deceased.

The treasure had been deposited in the museum precisely in the same condition in which Captain Sabretash had found it — that is to say, the coffin had not been disturbed. For eight years it had thus stood, subject only externally to public inspection. We had now, therefore, the complete mummy at our disposal; and to those who are aware how very rarely the unransacked antique reaches our shores, it will be evident, at once, that we had great reason to congratulate ourselves upon our good fortune.

Approaching the table, I saw on it a large box, or case, nearly seven feet long, and perhaps three feet wide, by two feet and a half deep. It was oblong — not coffin-shaped. The material was at first supposed to be the wood of the sycamore *(platanus),* but upon cutting into it, we found it to be pasteboard, or, more properly, papier mache, composed of papyrus. It was thickly ornamented with paintings, representing funeral scenes, and other mournful subjects — interspersed among which, in every variety of position, were certain series of hieroglyphical characters, intended, no doubt, for the name of the departed. By good luck, Mr. Gliddon formed one of our party; and he had no difficulty in translating the letters, which were simply phonetic, and represented the word, *Allamistakeo.*

We had some difficulty in getting this case open without injury; but, having at length accomplished the task, we came to a second, coffin-shaped, and very considerably less in size than the exterior one, but resembling it precisely in every other respect. The interval between the two was filled with resin, which had, in some degree, defaced the colours of the interior box.

Upon opening this latter (which we did quite easily) we arrived at a third case, also coffin-shaped, and varying from the second one in no particular, except in that of its material, which was cedar, and still emitted the peculiar and highly aromatic odour of that wood. Between the second and the third case there was no interval — the one fitting accurately within the other.

Removing the third case, we discovered and took out the body itself. We had expected to find it, as usual, enveloped in frequent rolls or bandages of linen; but, in place of these, we found a sort of sheath, made of papyrus, and coated with a layer of plaster, thickly gilt and painted. The paintings represented subjects connected with the various supposed duties of the soul, and its presentation to different divinities, with numerous identical human figures, intended, very probably, as portraits of the persons embalmed. Extending from head to foot, was a columnar, or perpendicular inscription, in phonetic hieroglyphics, giving again his name and titles, and the names and titles of his relations.

Around the neck thus ensheathed, was a collar of cylindrical glass beads, diverse in colour, and so arranged as to form images of deities, of the scarabaeus, etc., with the winged globe. Around the small of the waist was a similar collar or belt.

Stripping off the papyrus, we found the flesh in excellent preservation, with no perceptible odour. The colour was reddish. The skin was hard, smooth, and glossy. The teeth and hair were in good condition. The eyes (it seemed) had been removed, and glass ones substituted, which were very beautiful, and wonderfully lifelike, with the exception of somewhat too determined a stare. The fingers and the nails were brilliantly gilded.

Mr. Gliddon was of opinion, from the redness of the epidermis, that the embalmment had been effected altogether by asphaltum; but, on scraping the surface with a steel instrument, and throwing into the fire some of the powder thus obtained, the flavour of camphor and other sweet-scented gums became apparent.

We searched the corpse very carefully for the usual openings through which the entrails are extracted, but, to our surprise, we could discover none. No member of the party was at that period aware that entire or unopened mummies are not infrequently met. The brain it was customary to withdraw through the nose; the intestines through an incision in the side; the body was then shaved, washed, and salted; then laid aside for several weeks, when the operation of embalming, properly so called, began.

As no trace of an opening could be found, Dr. Ponnonner was preparing his instruments for dissection, when I observed that it was then past two o'clock. Hereupon it was agreed to postpone the internal examination until the next evening; and we were about to separate for the present, when someone suggested an experiment or two with the voltaic pile.

The application of electricity to a mummy three or four thousand years old at the least, was an idea, if not very sage, still sufficiently original, and we all caught it at once. About one-tenth in earnest and nine-tenths in jest, we arranged a battery in the doctor's study, and conveyed thither the Egyptian.

It was only after much trouble that we succeeded in laying bare some portions of the temporal muscle which appeared of less stony rigidity than other parts of the frame but which, as we had anticipated, of course, gave no indication of galvanic susceptibility when brought in contact with the wire. This, the first trial, indeed, seemed decisive, and, with a hearty laugh at our own absurdity, we were bidding each other good-night, when my eyes, happening to fall upon those of the mummy, were there immediately riveted in amazement. My brief glance, in fact, had sufficed to assure me that the orbs which we had all supposed to be glass, and which were originally noticeable for a certain wild stare, were now so far covered by the lids, that only a small portion of the *tunica albuginea* remained visible.

With a shout I called attention to the fact, and it became immediately obvious to all.

I cannot say that I was *alarmed* at the phenomenon, because 'alarmed' is, in my case, not exactly the word. It is possible, however, that, but for the brown stout, I might have been a little nervous. As for the rest of the company, they really made no attempt at concealing the downright fright which possessed them. Dr. Ponnonner was a man to be pitied. Mr. Gliddon, by some peculiar process, rendered himself invisible. Mr. Silk Buckingham, I fancy, will scarcely be so bold as to deny that he made his way, upon all fours, under the table.

After the first shock of astonishment, however, we resolved, as a matter of course, upon further experiment forthwith. Our operations were now directed against the great toe of the right foot. We made an incision over the outside of the exterior *os sesamoideum pollicis pedis,* and thus got at the root of the *abductor* muscle. Readjusting the battery, we now applied the fluid to the bisected nerves, when, with a movement of exceeding lifelikeness, the mummy first drew up its right knee so as to bring it nearly in contact with the abdomen, and then, straightening the limb with inconceivable force, bestowed a kick upon Dr. Ponnonner, which had the effect of discharging that gentleman, like an arrow from a catapult, through a window into the street below.

We rushed out *en masse* to bring in the mangled remains of the victim, but had the happiness to meet him upon the staircase, coming up in an unaccountable hurry, brimful of the most ardent philosophy, and more than ever impressed with the necessity of prosecuting our experiments with vigour and with zeal.

It was by his advice, accordingly, that we made, upon the spot, a profound incision into the tip of the subject's nose, while the doctor himself, laying violent hands upon it, pulled it into vehement contact with the wire.

Morally and physically — figuratively and literally — was the effect electric. In the first place, the corpse opened its eyes, and winked very rapidly for several minutes, as does Mr. Barnes in the pantomime; in the second place, it sneezed; in the third, it sat up on end; in the fourth, it shook its fist in Dr. Ponnonner's face; in the fifth, turning to Messieurs Gliddon and Buckingham, it addressed them, in very capital Egyptian, thus — 'I must say, gentlemen, that I am as much surprised as I am mortified, at your behaviour. Of Dr. Ponnonner nothing better was to be expected. He is a poor little fat fool who *knows* no better. I pity and forgive him. But you, Mr. Gliddon — and you, Silk — who have travelled and resided in Egypt until one might imagine you to the manner born — you, I say, who have been so much among us that you speak Egyptian fully as well, I think, as you write your mother tongue — you, whom I have always been led to regard as the firm friend of the mummies — I really did anticipate more gentlemanly conduct from *you.* What am I to think of your standing quietly by and seeing me thus unhandsomely used? What am I to suppose by your permitting Tom, Dick, and Harry to strip me of my coffins, and my clothes, in this wretchedly cold climate? In what light (to come to the point) am I to regard your aiding and abetting that miserable little villain, Dr. Ponnonner, in pulling me by the nose?'

It will be taken for granted, no doubt, that upon hearing this speech under the circumstances, we all either made for the door, or fell into violent hysterics, or went off in a general swoon. One of these three things, was, I say, to be expected. Indeed each and all of these lines of conduct might have been very plausibly pursued. And, upon my word, I am at a loss to know how or why it was that we pursued neither the one nor the other. But, perhaps, the true reason is to be sought in the spirit of the age, which proceeds by the rule of contraries altogether, and is now usually admitted as the solution of everything in the way of paradox and impossibility. Or perhaps, after all, it was only the mummy's exceedingly natural and matter-of-course air that divested his words of the terrible. However this may be, the facts are clear, and no member of our party betrayed any very particular trepidation, or seemed to consider that anything had gone very especially wrong.

For my part I was convinced it was all right, and merely stepped aside, out of the range of the Egyptian's fist. Dr. Ponnonner thrust his hands into his breeches pockets, looked hard at the mummy, and grew excessively red in the face. Mr. Gliddon stroked his whiskers and drew up the collar of his shirt. Mr. Buckingham hung down his head, and put his right thumb into the left corner of his mouth.

The Egyptian regarded him with a severe countenance for some minutes, and at length, with a sneer, said — 'Why don't you speak, Mr. Buckingham? Did you hear what I asked you, or not? *Do* take your thumb out of your mouth!'

Mr. Buckingham, hereupon, gave a slight start, took his right thumb out of the left corner of his mouth, and, by way of indemnification, inserted his left thumb in the right corner of the aperture above mentioned.

Not being able to get an answer from Mr. B., the figure turned peevishly to Mr. Gliddon, and, in a peremptory tone, demanded in general terms what we all meant.

Mr. Gliddon replied at great length, in phonetics; and but for the deficiency of American printing-offices in hieroglyphical type, it would afford me much pleasure to record here, in the original, the whole of his very excellent speech.

I may as well take this occasion to remark, that all the subsequent conversation in which the mummy took a part, was carried on in primitive Egyptian, through the medium (so far as concerned myself and other untravelled members of the company) — through the medium, I say, of Messieurs Gliddon and Buckingham, as interpreters. These gentlemen spoke the mother-tongue of the mummy with inimitable fluency and grace; but I could not help observing that (owing, no doubt, to the introduction of images entirely modern, and, of course, entirely novel to the stranger) the two travellers were reduced, occasionally, to the employment of sensible forms for the purpose of conveying a particular meaning. Mr. Gliddon, at one period, for example, could not make the Egyptian comprehend the term 'politics,' until he sketched upon the wall, with a bit of charcoal, a little carbuncle-nosed gentleman, out at elbows, standing upon a stump, with his left leg drawn back, his right arm thrown forward, with his fist shut, the eyes rolled up toward heaven, and the mouth open at an angle of ninety degrees. Just in the same way Mr. Buckingham failed to convey the absolutely modern idea, 'Whig,' until (at Dr. Ponnonner's suggestion) he grew very pale in the face, and consented to take off his own.

It will be readily understood that Mr. Gliddon's discourse turned chiefly upon the vast benefits accruing to science from the unrolling and disembowelling of mummies; apologising, upon this score, for any disturbance that might have been occasioned *him,* in particular, the individual mummy called Allamistakeo; and concluding with a mere hint (for it could scarcely be considered more) that, as these little matters were now explained, it might be as well to proceed with the investigation intended. Here Dr. Ponnonner made ready his instruments.

In regard to the latter suggestions of the orator, it appears that Allamistakeo had certain scruples of conscience, the nature of which I did not distinctly learn; but he expressed himself satisfied with the apologies tendered, and, getting down from the table, shook hands with the company all round.

When this ceremony was at an end, we immediately busied ourselves in repairing the damages which our subject had sustained from the scalpel. We sewed up the wound in his temple, bandaged his foot, and applied a square inch of black plaster to the tip of his nose.

It was now observed that the count (this was the title, it seems, of Allamistakeo) had a slight fit of shivering — no doubt from the cold. The doctor immediately repaired to his wardrobe, and soon returned with a black dress coat, made in Jennings' best manner, a pair of skyblue plaid pantaloons, with straps, a pink gingham *chemise,* a flapped vest of brocade, a white sack overcoat, a walking cane with a hook, a hat with no brim, patent-leather boots, straw-coloured kid gloves, an eyeglass, a pair of whiskers, and a waterfall cravat. Owing to the disparity of size between the count and the doctor (the proportion being as two to one), there was some little difficulty in adjusting these habiliments upon the person of the Egyptian; but when all was arranged, he might have been said to be dressed. Mr. Gliddon, therefore, gave him his arm, and led him to a comfortable chair by the fire, while the doctor rang the bell upon the spot and ordered a supply of cigars and wine.

The conversation soon grew animated. Much curiosity was, of course, expressed in regard to the somewhat remarkable fact of Allamistakeo's still remaining alive.

'I should have thought,' observed Mr. Buckingham, 'that it is high time you were dead.'

'Why,' replied the count, very much astonished, 'I am little more than seven hundred years old! My father lived a thousand, and was by no means in his dotage when he died.'

Here ensued a brisk series of questions and computations, by means of which it became evident that the antiquity of the mummy had been grossly misjudged. It had been five thousand and fifty years, and some months, since he had been consigned to the catacombs at Eleithias.

'But my remark,' resumed Mr. Buckingham, 'had no reference to your age at the period of interment (I am willing to grant, in fact, that you are still a young man); and my allusion was to the immensity of time during which, by your own showing, you must have been done up in asphaltum.'

'In what?' said the count.

'In asphaltum,' persisted Mr. B.

'Ah, yes; I have some faint notion of what you mean; it might be made to answer, no doubt — but in my time we employed scarcely anything else than the bichloride of mercury.'

'But what we are especially at a loss to understand,' said Dr. Ponnonner, 'is, how it happens that, having been dead and buried in Egypt five thousand years ago, you are here today all alive, and looking so delightfully well.'

'Had I been, as you say, *dead,*' replied the count, 'it is more than probable that dead I should still be; for I perceive you are yet in the infancy of galvanism, and cannot accomplish with it what was a common thing among us in the old days. But the fact is, I fell into catalepsy, and it was considered by my best friends that I was either dead or should be; they accordingly embalmed me at once — I presume you are aware of the chief principle of the embalming process?'

'Why, not altogether.'

'Ah, I perceive — a deplorable condition of ignorance! Well, I cannot enter into details just now; but it is necessary to explain that to embalm (properly speaking) in Egypt, was to arrest indefinitely *all* the animal functions subjected to the process. I use the word "animal" in its widest sense, as including the physical not more than the moral and *vital* being. I repeat that the leading principle of embalmment consisted, with us, in the immediately arresting, and holding in perpetual abeyance, *all* the animal functions subjected to the process. To be brief, in whatever condition the individual was, at the period of embalmment, in that condition he remained. Now, as it is my good fortune to be of the blood of the Scarabaeus, I was embalmed *alive,* as you see me at present.'

'The blood of the Scarabaeus!' exclaimed Dr. Ponnonner.

'Yes. The Scarabaeus was the *insignium,* or the "arms", of a very distinguished and very rare patrician family. To be "of the blood of the Scarabaeus", is merely to be one of that family of which the Scarabaeus is the *insignium.* I speak figuratively.'

'But what has this to do with your being alive?'

'Why, it is the general custom in Egypt, to deprive a corpse, before embalmment, of its bowels and brains; the race of the Scarabaei alone did not coincide with the custom. Had I not been a Scarabaeus, therefore, I should have been without bowels and brains; and without either it is inconvenient to live.'

'I perceive that,' said Mr. Buckingham; 'and I presume that all the *entire* mummies that come to hand are of the race of Scarabaei.'

'Beyond doubt.'

'I thought,' said Mr. Gliddon, very meekly, 'that the Scarabaeus was one of the Egyptian gods.'

'One of the Egyptian *what?*' exclaimed the mummy, starting to its feet.

'Gods!' repeated the traveller.

'Mr. Gliddon, I really am astonished to hear you talk in this style,' said the count, resuming his seat. 'No nation upon the face of the earth has ever acknowledged more than *one god*. The Scarabaeus, the Ibis, etc., were with us (as similar creatures have been with others) the symbols, or *media,* through which we offered worship to the creator too august to be more directly approached.'

There was here a pause. At length the colloquy was renewed by Dr. Ponnonner.

'It is not improbable, then, from what you have explained,' said he, 'that among the catacombs near the Nile, there may exist other mummies of the Scarabaeus tribe, in a condition of vitality.'

'There can be no question of it,' replied the count; 'all the Scarabaei embalmed accidentally while alive, are alive. Even some of those *purposely* so embalmed, may have been overlooked by their executors, and still remain in the tombs.'

'Will you be kind enough to explain,' I said, 'what you mean by "purposely so embalmed"?'

'With great pleasure,' answered the mummy, after surveying me leisurely through his eyeglass — for it was the first time I had ventured to address him a direct question.

'With great pleasure,' he said. 'The usual duration of man's life, in my time, was about eight hundred years. Few men died, unless by most extraordinary accident, before the age of six hundred; few lived longer than a decade of centuries; but eight were considered the natural term. After the discovery of the embalming principle, as I have already described it to you, it occurred to our philosophers that a laudable curiosity might be gratified, and, at the same time, the interests of science much advanced, by living this natural term in instalments. In the case of history, indeed, experience demonstrated that something of this kind was indispensable. An historian, for example, having attained the age of five hundred, would write a book with great labour and then get himself carefully embalmed; leaving instructions to his executors *pro tem,* that they should cause him to be revivified after the lapse of a certain period — say five or six hundred years. Resuming existence at the expiration of this time, he would invariably find his great work converted into a species of haphazard notebook — that is to say, into a kind of literary arena for the conflicting guesses, riddles, and personal squabbles of whole herds of exasperated commentators. These guesses, etc., which passed under the name of annotations, or emendations, were found so completely to have enveloped, distorted, and overwhelmed the text, that the author had to go about with a lantern to discover his own book. When discovered, it was never worth the trouble of the search. After rewriting it throughout, it was regarded as the bounden duty of the historian to set himself to work, immediately, in correcting, from his own private knowledge and experience, the traditions of the day concerning the epoch at which he had originally lived. Now this process of rescription and personal rectification, pursued by various individual sages, from time to time, had the effect of preventing our history from degenerating into absolute fable.'

'I beg your pardon,' said Dr. Ponnonner at this point, laying his hand gently upon the arm of the Egyptian — 'I beg your pardon, sir, but may I presume to interrupt you for one moment?'

'By all means, *sir,*' replied the count, drawing up.

'I merely wished to ask you a question,' said the doctor. 'You mentioned the historian's personal correction of *traditions* respecting his own epoch. Pray, sir, upon an average, what proportion of these Kabbala were usually found to be right?'

'The Kabbala, as you properly term them, sir, were generally discovered to be precisely on a par with the facts recorded in the un-rewritten histories themselves; that is to say, not one individual iota of either was ever known, under any circumstances, to be not totally and radically wrong.'

'But since it is quite clear,' resumed the doctor, 'that at least five thousand years have elapsed since your entombment, I take it for granted that your histories at that period, if not your traditions, were sufficiently explicit on that one topic of universal interest, the creation, which took place, as I presume you are aware, only about ten centuries before.'

'Sir!' said the Count Allamistakeo.

The doctor repeated his remarks, but it was only after much additional explanation that the foreigner could be made to comprehend them. The latter at length said, hesitatingly — 'The ideas you have suggested are to me, I confess, utterly novel. During my time I never knew anyone to entertain so singular a fancy as that the universe (or this world, if you will have it so) ever had a beginning at all. I remember once, and once only, hearing something remotely hinted by a man of many speculations concerning the origin *of the human race;* and by this individual the very word *Adam* (or red earth), which you make use of, was employed. He employed it, however, in a generical sense, with reference to the spontaneous germination from rank soil (just as a thousand of the lower *genera* of creatures are germinated) — the spontaneous germination, I say, of five vast hordes of men, simultaneously upspringing in five distinct and nearly equal divisions of the globe.'

Here, in general, the company shrugged their shoulders, and one or two of us touched our foreheads with a very significant air. Mr. Silk Buckingham, first glancing slightly at the occiput and then at the siniciput of Allamistakeo, spoke as follows — 'The long duration of human life in your time, together with the occasional practice of passing it, as you have explained, in instalments, must have had, indeed, a strong tendency to the general development and conglomeration of knowledge. I presume, therefore, that we are to attribute the marked inferiority of the old Egyptians in all particulars of science, when compared with the moderns, and more especially with the Yankees, altogether to the superior solidity of the Egyptian skull.' 'I confess again,' replied the count, with much suavity, 'that I am somewhat at a loss to comprehend you; pray, to what particulars of science do you allude?'

Here our whole party, joining voices, detailed, at great length, the assumptions of phrenology and the marvels of animal magnetism.

Having heard us to an end, the count proceeded to relate a few anecdotes, which rendered it evident that prototypes of Gall and Spurzheim had flourished and faded in Egypt so long ago as to have been nearly forgotten, and that the manoeuvres of Mesmer were really very contemptible tricks when put in collation with the positive miracles of the Theban *savans,* who created lice, and a great many other similar things.

I here asked the count if his people were able to calculate eclipses. He smiled rather contemptuously, and said they were.

This put me a little out; but I began to make other enquiries in regard to his astronomical knowledge, when a member of the company, who had never as yet opened his mouth, whispered in my ear, that for information on this head I had better consult Ptolemy (whoever Ptolemy is), as well as one Plutarch *de facic lunae.*

I then questioned the mummy about burning-glasses and lenses, and, in general, about the manufacture of glass; but I had not made an end of my queries before the silent member again touched me quietly on the elbow, and begged me, for God's sake, to take a peep at Diodorus Siculus. As for the count, he merely asked me, in the way of reply, if we moderns possessed any such microscopes as would enable us to cut cameos in the style of the Egyptians. While I was thinking how I should answer this question, little Dr. Ponnonner committed himself in a very extraordinary way.

'Look at our architecture!' he exclaimed, greatly to the indignation of both the travellers, who pinched him black and blue to no purpose.

'Look!' he cried, with enthusiasm, 'at the Bowling Green Fountain in New York! or, if this be too vast a contemplation, regard for a moment the Capitol at Washington, DC!' — and the good little medical man went on to detail, very minutely, the proportions of the fabric to which he referred. He explained that the portico alone was adorned with no less than four and twenty columns, five feet in diameter, and ten feet apart.

The count said that he regretted not being able to remember, just at that moment, the precise dimensions of any one of the principal buildings of the City of Aznac, whose foundations were laid in the night of Time, but the ruins of which were still standing, at the epoch of his entombment, in a vast plain of sand to the westward of Thebes. He recollected, however (talking of porticoes), that one affixed to an inferior palace in a kind of suburb called Carnac, consisted of a hundred and forty-four columns, thirty-seven feet each in circumference, and twenty-five feet apart. The approach of this portico, from the Nile, was through an avenue two miles long, composed of sphinxes, statues, and obelisks, twenty, sixty, and a hundred feet in height. The palace itself (as well as he could remember) was, in one direction, two miles long, and might have been, altogether, about seven in circuit. Its walls were richly painted all over, within and without, with hieroglyphics. He would not pretend to *assert* that even fifty or sixty of the doctor's Capitols might have been built within these walls, but he was by no means sure that two or three hundred of them might not have been squeezed in with some trouble. That palace at Carnac was an insignificant little building after all. He (the count), however, could not conscientiously refuse to admit the ingenuity, magnificence, and superiority of the fountain at the Bowling-green, as described by the doctor. Nothing like it, he was forced to allow, had ever been seen in Egypt or elsewhere.

I here asked the count what he had to say to our railroads.

'Nothing,' he replied, 'in particular.' They were rather slight, rather ill-conceived, and clumsily put together. They could not be compared, of course, with the vast, level, direct, iron-grooved causeways, upon which the Egyptians conveyed entire temples and solid obelisks of a hundred and fifty feet in altitude.

I spoke of our gigantic mechanical forces.

He agreed that we knew something in that way, but enquired how I should have gone to work in getting up the imposts on the lintels of even the little palace at Carnac.

This question I concluded not to hear, and demanded if he had any idea of Artesian wells; but he simply raised his eyebrows; while Mr. Gliddon winked at me very hard and said, in a low tone, that one had been recently discovered by the engineers employed to bore for water in the Great Oasis.

I then mentioned our steel; but the foreigner elevated his nose, and asked me if our steel could have executed the sharp carved work seen on the obelisks, and which was wrought altogether by edge-tools of copper.

This disconcerted us so greatly that we thought it advisable to vary the attack to metaphysics. We sent for a copy of a book called the *Dial,* and read out of it a chapter or two about something which is not very clear, but which the Bostonians call the Great Movement or progress.

The count merely said that Great Movements were awfully common things in his day, and as for progress, it was at one time quite a nuisance, but it never progressed.

We then spoke of the great beauty and importance of democracy, and were at much trouble in impressing the count with a due sense of the advantages we enjoyed in living where there was suffrage *ad libitum* and no king.

He listened with marked interest, and in fact seemed not a little amused. When we had done he said that, a great while ago, there had occurred something of a very similar sort. Thirteen Egyptian provinces determined all at once to be free, and so set a magnificent example to the rest of mankind. They assembled their wise men, and concocted the most ingenious constitution it is possible to conceive. For a while they managed remarkably well; only their habit of bragging was prodigious. The thing ended, however, in the consolidation of the thirteen states, with some fifteen or twenty others, in the most odious and insupportable despotism that ever was heard of upon the face of the earth.

I asked what was the name of the usurping tyrant.

As well as the count could recollect, it was *Mob.*

Not knowing what to say to this, I raised my voice, and deplored the Egyptian ignorance of steam.

The count looked at me with much astonishment, but made no answer. The silent gentleman, however, gave me a violent nudge in the ribs with his elbows — told me I had sufficiently exposed myself for once — and demanded if I was really such a fool as not to know that the modern steam-engine is derived from the invention of Hero, through Solomon de Caus.

We were now in imminent danger of being discomfited; but, as good luck would have it, Dr. Ponnonner, having rallied, returned to our rescue, and enquired if the people of Egypt would seriously pretend to rival the moderns in the all-important particular of dress.

The count, at this, glanced downwards to the straps of his pantaloons, and then taking hold of the end of one of his coat-tails, held it up close to his eyes for some minutes. Letting it fall, at last, his mouth extended itself very gradually from ear to ear; but I do not remember that he said anything in the way of reply.

Hereupon we recovered our spirits, and the doctor, approaching the mummy with great dignity, desired it to say candidly, upon its honour as a gentleman, if the Egyptians had comprehended at *any* period the manufacture of either Ponnonner's lozenges, or Brandreth's pills.

We looked, with profound anxiety, for an answer — but in vain. It was not forthcoming. The Egyptian blushed and hung down his head. Never was triumph more consummate; never was defeat borne with so ill a grace. Indeed, I could not endure the spectacle of the poor mummy's mortification. I reached my hat, bowed to him stiffly, and took leave.

Upon getting home I found it past four o'clock, and went immediately to bed. It is now ten a.m. I have been up since seven, penning these memoranda for the benefit of my family and of mankind. The former I shall behold no more. My wife is a shrew. The truth is, I am heartily sick of this life, and of the nineteenth century in general. I am convinced that everything is going wrong. Besides, I am anxious to know who will be president in 2045. As soon, therefore, as I shave and swallow a cup of coffee, I shall just step over to Ponnonner's and get embalmed for a couple of hundred years.

Lost in a Pyramid; or, the Mummy's Curse

I

nd what are these, Paul?" asked Evelyn, opening a tarnished gold box and examining its contents curiously.

"Seeds of some unknown Egyptian plant," replied Forsyth, with a sudden shadow on his dark face, as he looked down at the three scarlet grains lying in the white hand lifted to him.

"Where did you get them?" asked the girl.

"That is a weird story, which will only haunt you if I tell it," said Forsyth, with an absent expression that strongly excited the girl's curiosity.

"Please tell it, I like weird tales, and they never trouble me. Ah, do tell it; your stories are always so interesting," she cried, looking up with such a pretty blending of entreaty and command in her charming face, that refusal was impossible.

"You'll be sorry for it, and so shall I, perhaps; I warn you beforehand, that harm is foretold to the possessor of those mysterious seeds," said Forsyth, smiling, even while he knit his black brows, and regarded the blooming creature before him with a fond yet foreboding glance.

"Tell on, I'm not afraid of these pretty atoms," she answered, with an imperious nod.

"To hear is to obey. Let me read the facts, and then I will begin," returned Forsyth, pacing to and fro with the far-off look of one who turns the pages of the past.

Evelyn watched him a moment, and then returned to her work, or play, rather, for the task seemed well suited to the vivacious little creature, half-child, half-woman.

"While in Egypt," commenced Forsyth, slowly, "I went one day with my guide and Professor Niles, to explore the Cheops. Niles had a mania for antiquities of all sorts, and forgot time, danger and fatigue in the ardor of his pursuit. We rummaged up and down the narrow passages, half choked with dust and close air; reading inscriptions on the walls, stumbling over shattered mummy-cases, or coming face to face with some shriveled specimen perched like a hobgoblin on the little shelves where the dead used to be stowed away for ages. I was desperately tired after a few hours of it, and begged the professor to return. But he was bent on exploring certain places, and would not desist. We had but one guide, so I was forced to stay; but Jumal, my man, seeing how weary I was, proposed to us to rest in one of the larger passages,

* "Lost in a Pyramid; or, the Mummy's Curse" was written by Louisa May Alcott (1832 – 1888) and published in *The New World*, Vol. 1, No. 1, Jan. 16, 1869.

while he went to procure another guide for Niles. We consented, and assuring us that we were perfectly safe, if we did not quit the spot, Jumal left us, promising to return speedily. The professor sat down to take notes of his researches, and stretching my self on the soft sand, I fell asleep.

"I was roused by that indescribable thrill which instinctively warns us of danger, and springing up, I found myself alone. One torch burned faintly where Jumal had struck it, but Niles and the other light were gone. A dreadful sense of loneliness oppressed me for a moment; then I collected myself and looked well about me. A bit of paper was pinned to my hat, which lay near me, and on it, in the professor's writing were these words:

"'I've gone back a little to refresh my memory on certain points. Don't follow me till Jumal comes. I can find my way back to you, for I have a clue. Sleep well, and dream gloriously of the Pharaohs. N.N.'

"I laughed at first over the old enthusiast, then felt anxious then restless, and finally resolved to follow him, for I discovered a strong cord fastened to a fallen stone, and knew that this was the clue he spoke of. Leaving a line for Jumal, I took my torch and retraced my steps, following the cord along the winding ways. I often shouted, but received no reply, and pressed on, hoping at each turn to see the old man poring over some musty relic of antiquity. Suddenly the cord ended, and lowering my torch, I saw that the footsteps had gone on.

"'Rash fellow, he'll lose himself, to a certainty,' I thought, really alarmed now.

"As I paused, a faint call reached me, and I answered it, waited, shouted again, and a still fainter echo replied.

"Niles was evidently going on, misled by the reverberations of the low passages. No time was to be lost, and, forgetting myself, I stuck my torch in the deep sand to guide me back to the clue, and ran down the straight path before me, whooping like a madman as I went. I did not mean to lose sight of the light, but in my eagerness to find Niles I turned from the main passage, and, guided by his voice, hastened on. His torch soon gladdened my eyes, and the clutch of his trembling hands told me what agony he had suffered.

"'Let us get out of this horrible place at once,' he said, wiping the great drops off his forehead.

"'Come, we're not far from the clue. I can soon reach it, and then we are safe'; but as I spoke, a chill passed over me, for a perfect labyrinth of narrow paths lay before us.

"Trying to guide myself by such land-marks as I had observed in my hasty passage, I followed the tracks in the sand till I fancied we must be near my light. No glimmer appeared, however, and kneeling down to examine the footprints nearer, I discovered, to my dismay, that I had been following the wrong ones, for among those marked by a deep boor-heel, were prints of bare feet; we had had no guide there, and Jumal wore sandals.

"Rising, I confronted Niles, with the one despairing word, 'Lost!' as I pointed from the treacherous sand to the fast-waning light.

"I thought the old man would be overwhelmed but, to my surprise, he grew quite calm and steady, thought a moment, and then went on, saying, quietly:

"'Other men have passed here before us; let us follow their steps, for, if I do not greatly err, they lead toward great passages, where one's way is easily found.'

"On we went, bravely, till a misstep threw the professor violently to the ground with a broken leg, and nearly extinguished the torch. It was a horrible predicament, and I gave up all hope as I sat beside the poor fellow, who lay exhausted with fatigue, remorse and pain, for I would not leave him.

"'Paul,' he said suddenly, 'if you will not go on, there is one more effort we can make. I remember hearing that a party lost as we are, saved themselves by building a fire. The smoke penetrated further than sound or light, and the guide's quick wit understood the unusual mist; he followed it, and rescued the party. Make a fire and trust to Jumal.'

"'A fire without wood?' I began; but he pointed to a shelf behind me, which had escaped me in the gloom; and on it I saw a slender mummy-case. I understood him, for these dry cases, which lie about in hundreds, are freely used as firewood. Reaching up, I pulled it down, believing it to be empty, but as it fell, it burst open, and out rolled a mummy. Accustomed as I was to such sights, it startled me a little, for danger had unstrung my nerves. Laying the little brown chrysalis aside, I smashed the case, lit the pile with my torch, and soon a light cloud of smoke drifted down the three passages which diverged from the cell-like place where we had paused.

"While busied with the fire, Niles, forgetful of pain and peril, had dragged the mummy nearer, and was examining it with the interest of a man whose ruling passion was strong even in death.

"'Come and help me unroll this. I have always longed to be the first to see and secure the curious treasures put away among the folds of these uncanny winding-sheets. This is a woman, and we may find something rare and precious here,' he said, beginning to unfold the outer coverings, from which a strange aromatic odor came.

"Reluctantly I obeyed, for to me there was something sacred in the bones of this unknown woman. But to beguile the time and amuse the poor fellow, I lent a hand, wondering as I worked, if this dark, ugly thing had ever been a lovely, soft-eyed Egyptian girl.

"From the fibrous folds of the wrappings dropped precious gums and spices, which half intoxicated us with their potent breath, antique coins, and a curious jewel or two, which Niles eagerly examined.

"All the bandages but one were cut off at last, and a small head laid bare, round which still hung great plaits of what had once been luxuriant hair. The shriveled hands were folded on the breast, and clasped in them lay that gold box."

"Ah!" cried Evelyn, dropping it from her rosy palm with a shudder.

"Nay; don't reject the poor little mummy's treasure. I never have quite forgiven myself for stealing it, or for burning her," said

Forsyth, painting rapidly, as if the recollection of that experience lent energy to his hand.

"Burning her! Oh, Paul, what do you mean?" asked the girl, sitting up with a face full of excitement.

"I'll tell you. While busied with Madame la Momie, our fire had burned low, for the dry case went like tinder. A faint, far-off sound made our hearts leap, and Niles cried out: 'Pile on the wood; Jumal is tracking us; don't let the smoke fail now or we are lost!'

"'There is no more wood; the case was very small, and is all gone,' I answered, tearing off such of my garments as would burn readily, and piling them upon the embers.

"Niles did the same, but the light fabrics were quickly consumed, and made no smoke.

"'Burn that!' commanded the professor, pointing to the mummy.

"I hesitated a moment. Again came the faint echo of a horn. Life was dear to me. A few dry bones might save us, and I obeyed him in silence.

"A dull blaze sprung up, and a heavy smoke rose from the burning mummy, rolling in volumes through the low passages, and threatening to suffocate us with its fragrant mist. My brain grew dizzy, the light danced before my eyes, strange phantoms seemed to people the air, and, in the act of asking Niles why he gasped and looked so pale, I lost consciousness."

Evelyn drew a long breath, and put away the scented toys from her lap as if their odor oppressed her.

Forsyth's swarthy face was all aglow with the excitement of his story, and his black eyes glittered as he added, with a quick laugh:

"That's all; Jumal found and got us out, and we both forswore pyramids for the rest of our days."

"But the box: how came you to keep it?" asked Evelyn, eyeing it askance as it lay gleaming in a streak of sunshine.

"Oh, I brought it away as a souvenir, and Niles kept the other trinkets."

"But you said harm was foretold to the possessor of those scarlet seeds," persisted the girl, whose fancy was excited by the tale, and who fancied all was not told.

"Among his spoils, Niles found a bit of parchment, which he deciphered, and this inscription said that the mummy we had so ungallantly burned was that of a famous sorceress who bequeathed her curse to whoever should disturb her rest. Of course I don't believe that curse has anything to do with it, but it's a fact that Niles never prospered from that day. He says it's because he has never recovered from the fall and fright and I dare say it is so; but I sometimes wonder if I am to share the curse, for I've a vein of superstition in me, and that poor little mummy haunts my dreams still."

A long silence followed these words. Paul painted mechanically and Evelyn lay regarding him with a thoughtful face. But gloomy fancies were as foreign to her nature as shadows are to noonday, and presently she laughed a cheery laugh, saying as she took up the box again:

"Why don't you plant them, and see what wondrous flower they will bear?"

"I doubt if they would bear anything after lying in a mummy's hand for centuries," replied Forsyth, gravely.

"Let me plant them and try. You know wheat has sprouted and grown that was taken from a mummy's coffin; why should not these pretty seeds? I should so like to watch them grow; may I, Paul?"

"No, I'd rather leave that experiment untried. I have a queer feeling about the matter, and don't want to meddle myself or let anyone I love meddle with these seeds. They may be some horrible poison, or possess some evil power, for the sorceress evidently valued them, since she clutched them fast even in her tomb."

"Now, you are foolishly superstitious, and I laugh at you. Be generous; give me one seed, just to learn if it will grow. See I'll pay for it," and Evelyn, who now stood beside him, dropped a kiss on his forehead as she made her request, with the most engaging air.

But Forsyth would not yield. He smiled and returned the embrace with lover-like warmth, then flung the seeds into the fire, and gave her back the golden box, saying, tenderly:

"My darling, I'll fill it with diamonds or bonbons, if you please, but I will not let you play with that witch's spells. You've enough of your own, so forget the 'pretty seeds' and see what a Light of the Harem I've made of you."

Evelyn frowned, and smiled, and presently the lovers were out in the spring sunshine reveling in their own happy hopes, untroubled by one foreboding fear.

II

"I have a little surprise for you, love," said Forsyth, as he greeted his cousin three months later on the morning of his wedding day.

"And I have one for you," she answered, smiling faintly.

"How pale you are, and how thin you grow! All this bridal bustle is too much for you, Evelyn," he said, with fond anxiety, as he watched the strange pallor of her face, and pressed the wasted little hand in his.

"I am so tired," she said, and leaned her head wearily on her lover's breast. "Neither sleep, food, nor air gives me strength, and a curious mist seems to cloud my mind at times. Mamma says it is the heat, but I shiver even in the sun, while at night I burn with fever. Paul, dear, I'm glad you are going to take me away to lead a quiet, happy life with you, but I'm afraid it will be a very short one."

"My fanciful little wife! You are tired and nervous with all this worry, but a few weeks of rest in the country will give us back our blooming Eve again. Have you no curiosity to learn my surprise?" he asked, to change her thoughts.

The vacant look stealing over the girl's face gave place to one of interest, but as she listened it seemed to require an effort to fix her mind on her lover's words.

"You remember the day we rummaged in the old cabinet?"

"Yes," and a smile touched her lips for a moment.

"And how you wanted to plant those queer red seeds I stole from the mummy?"

"I remember," and her eyes kindled with sudden fire.

"Well, I tossed them into the fire, as I thought, and gave you the box. But when I went back to cover up my picture, and found one of those seeds on the rug, a sudden fancy to gratify your whim led me to send it to Niles and ask him to plant and report on its progress. Today I hear from him for the first time, and he reports that the seed has grown marvelously, has budded, and that he intends to take the first flower, if it blooms in time, to a meeting of famous scientific men, after which he will send me its true name and the plant itself. From his description, it must be very curious, and I'm impatient to see it."

"You need not wait; I can show you the flower in its bloom," and Evelyn beckoned with the *mechante* smile so long a stranger to her lips.

Much amazed, Forsyth followed her to her own little boudoir, and there, standing in the sunshine, was the unknown plant. Almost rank in their luxuriance were the vivid green leaves on the slender purple stems, and rising from the midst, one ghostly-white flower, shaped like the head of a hooded snake, with scarlet stamens like forked tongues, and on the petals glittered spots like dew.

"A strange, uncanny flower! Has it any odor?" asked Forsyth, bending to examine it, and forgetting, in his interest, to ask how it came there.

"None, and that disappoints me, I am so fond of perfumes," answered the girl, caressing the green leaves which trembled at her touch, while the purple stems deepened their tint.

"Now tell me about it," said Forsyth, after standing silent for several minutes.

"I had been before you, and secured one of the seeds, for two fell on the rug. I planted it under a glass in the richest soil I could find, watered it faithfully, and was amazed at the rapidity with which it grew when once it appeared above the earth. I told no-one, for I meant to surprise you with it; but this bud has been so long in blooming, I have had to wait. It is a good omen that it blossoms today, and as it is nearly white, I mean to wear it, for I've learned to love it, having been my pet for so long."

"I would not wear it, for, in spite of its innocent color, it is an evil-looking plant, with its adder's tongue and unnatural dew. Wait till Niles tells us what it is, then pet it if it is harmless. Perhaps my sorceress cherished it for some symbolic beauty — those old Egyptians were full of fancies.

It was very sly of you to turn the tables on me in this way. But I forgive you, since in a few hours, I shall chain this mysterious hand forever. How cold it is! Come out into the garden and get some warmth and color for tonight, my love."

But when night came, no-one could reproach the girl with her pallor, for she glowed like a pomegranate-flower, her eyes were full of fire, her lips scarlet, and all her old vivacity seemed to have returned. A more brilliant bride never blushed under a misty veil, and when her lover saw her, he was absolutely startled by the almost unearthly beauty which transformed the pale, languid creature of the morning into this radiant woman.

They were married, and if love, many blessings, and all good gifts lavishly showered upon them could make them happy, then this young pair were truly blest. But even in the rapture of the moment that made her his, Forsyth observed how icy cold was the little hand he held, how feverish the deep color on the soft cheek he kissed, and what a strange fire burned in the tender eyes that looked so wistfully at him.

Blithe and beautiful as a spirit, the smiling bride played her part in all the festivities of that long evening, and when at last light, life and color began to fade, the loving eyes that watched her thought it but the natural weariness of the hour. As the last guest departed, Forsyth was met by a servant, who gave him a letter marked "Haste." Tearing it open, he read these lines, from a friend of the professor's:

"DEAR SIR — Poor Niles died suddenly two days ago, while at the Scientific Club, and his last words were: 'Tell Paul Forsyth to beware of the Mummy's Curse, for this fatal flower has killed me.' The circumstances of his death were so peculiar, that I add them as a sequel to this message. For several months, as he told us, he had been watching an unknown plant, and that evening he brought us the flower to examine. Other matters of interest absorbed us till a late hour, and the plant was forgotten. The professor wore it in his buttonhole — a strange white, serpent-headed blossom, with pale glittering spots, which slowly changed to a glittering scarlet, till the leaves looked as if sprinkled with blood. It was observed that instead of the pallor and feebleness which had recently come over him, that the professor was unusually animated, and seemed in an almost unnatural state of high spirits. Near the close of the meeting, in the midst of a lively discussion, he suddenly dropped, as if smitten with apoplexy. He was conveyed home insensible, and after one lucid interval, in which he gave me the message I have recorded above, he died in great agony, raving of mummies, pyramids, serpents, and some fatal curse which had fallen upon him.

"After his death, livid scarlet spots, like those on the flower, appeared upon his skin, and he shriveled like a withered leaf. At my desire, the mysterious plant was examined, and pronounced by the best authority one of the most deadly poisons known to the Egyptian sorceresses. The plant slowly absorbs the vitality of whoever cultivates it, and the blossom, worn for two or three hours, produces either madness or death."

Down dropped the paper from Forsyth's hand; he read no further, but hurried back into the room where he had left his young wife. As if worn out with fatigue, she had thrown herself upon a couch, and lay there motionless, her face half-hidden by the light folds of the veil, which had blown over it.

"Evelyn, my dearest! Wake up and answer me. Did you wear that strange flower today?" whispered Forsyth, putting the misty screen away.

There was no need for her to answer, for there, gleaming spectrally on her bosom, was the evil blossom, its white petals spotted now with flecks of scarlet, vivid as drops of newly spilt blood.

But the unhappy bridegroom scarcely saw it, for the face above it appalled him by its utter vacancy. Drawn and pallid, as if with some wasting malady, the young face, so lovely an hour ago, lay before him aged and blighted by the baleful influence of the plant which had drunk up her life. No recognition in the eyes, no word upon the lips, no motion of the hand — only the faint breath, the fluttering pulse, and wide-opened eyes, betrayed that she was alive.

Alas for the young wife! The superstitious fear at which she had smiled had proved true: the curse that had bided its time for ages was fulfilled at last, and her own hand wrecked her happiness for ever. Death in life was her doom, and for years Forsyth secluded himself to tend with pathetic devotion the pale ghost, who never, by word or look, could thank him for the love that outlived even such a fate as this.

My New Year's Eve
Among the Mummies*

have been a wanderer and a vagabond on the face of the earth for a good many years now, and I have certainly had some odd adventures in my time; but I can assure you, I never spent twenty-four queerer hours than those which I passed some twelve months since in the great unopened Pyramid of Abu Villa.

The way I got there was itself a very strange one. I had come to Egypt for a winter tour with the Fitz-Simkinses, to whose daughter Editha I was at that precise moment engaged. You will probably remember that old Fitz-Simkins belonged originally to the wealthy firm of Simkinson and Stakoe, worshipful vintners; but when the senior partner retired from the business and got his knighthood, the College of Heralds opportunely discovered that his ancestors had changed their fine old Norman name for its English equivalent some time about the reign of King Richard I; and they immediately authorized the old gentleman to resume the patronymic and the armorial bearings of his distinguished forefathers. It's really quite astonishing how often these curious coincidences crop up at the College of Heralds.

Of course it was a great catch for a landless and briefless barrister like myself — dependent on a small fortune in South American securities, and my precarious earnings as a writer of burlesque — to secure such a valuable prospective property as Editha Fitz-Simkins. To be sure, the girl was undeniably plain; but I have known plainer girls than she was, whom forty thousand pounds converted into My Ladies: and if Editha hadn't really fallen over head and ears in love with me, I suppose old Fitz-Simkins would never have consented to such a match. As it was, however, we had flirted so openly and so desperately during the Scarborough season, that it would have been difficult for Sir Peter to break it off: and so I had come to Egypt on a tour of insurance to secure my prize, following in the wake of my future mother-in-law, whose lungs were supposed to require a genial climate — though in my private opinion they were really as creditable a pair of pulmonary appendages as ever drew breath.

Nevertheless, the course of true love did not run so smoothly as might have been expected. Editha found me less ardent than a devoted squire should be; and on the very last night of the old year she got up a regulation lovers' quarrel, because I had sneaked away from the boat that afternoon under the guidance of our dragoman, to witness the seductive performances of some fair Ghawázi, the dancing girls of a neighbouring town. How she found it out heaven only knows, for I gave that rascal

---

* "My New Year's Eve Among the Mummies" was written by Grant Allen (1848 – 1899) and published in *Belgravia Magazine*, 1880.

Dimitri five piastres to hold his tongue: but she did find it out somehow, and chose to regard it as an offence of the first magnitude: a mortal sin only to be expiated by three days of penance and humiliation.

I went to bed that night, in my hammock on deck, with feelings far from satisfactory. We were moored against the bank at Abu Villa, the most pestiferous hole between the cataracts and the Delta. The mosquitoes were worse than the ordinary mosquitoes of Egypt, and that is saying a great deal. The heat was oppressive even at night, and the malaria from the lotus beds rose like a palpable mist before my eyes. Above all, I was getting doubtful whether Editha Fitz-Simkins might not after all slip between my fingers. I felt wretched and feverish: and yet I had delightful interlusive recollections, in between, of that lovely little Gháziyah, who danced that exquisite, marvellous, entrancing, delicious, and awfully oriental dance that I saw in the afternoon.

By Jove, she *was* a beautiful creature. Eyes like two full moons; hair like Milton's Penseroso; movements like a poem of Swinburne's set to action. If Editha was only a faint picture of that girl now! Upon my word, I was falling in love with a Gháziyah!

Then the mosquitoes came again. Buzz — buzz — buzz. I make a lunge at the loudest and biggest, a sort of prima donna in their infernal opera. I kill the prima donna, but ten more shrill performers come in its place. The frogs croak dismally in the reedy shallows. The night grows hotter and hotter still. At last, I can stand it no longer. I rise up, dress myself lightly, and jump ashore to find some way of passing the time.

Yonder, across the flat, lies the great unopened Pyramid of Abu Villa. We are going to-morrow to climb to the top; but I will take a turn to reconnoitre in that direction now. I walk across the moonlit fields, my soul still divided between Editha and the Gháziyah, and approach the solemn mass of huge, antiquated granite blocks standing out so grimly against the pale horizon. I feel half awake, half asleep, and altogether feverish: but I poke about the base in an aimless sort of way, with a vague idea that I may perhaps discover by chance the secret of its sealed entrance, which has ere now baffled so many pertinacious explorers and learned Egyptologists.

As I walk along the base, I remember old Herodotus's story, like a page from the 'Arabian Nights', of how King Rhampsinitus built himself a treasury, wherein one stone turned on a pivot like a door; and how the builder availed himself of this his cunning device to steal gold from the king's storehouse. Suppose the entrance to the unopened Pyramid should be by such a door. It would be curious if I should chance to light upon the very spot.

I stood in the broad moonlight, near the north-east angle of the great pile, at the twelfth stone from the corner. A random fancy struck me, that I might turn this stone by pushing it inward on the left side. I leant against it with all my weight, and tried to move it on the imaginary pivot. Did it give way a fraction of an inch? No, it must have been mere fancy. Let me try again. Surely it is yielding! Gracious Osiris, it has moved an inch or more! My heart beats fast, either with fever or excitement, and I try a third time. The rust of centuries on the pivot wears slowly off, and the stone turned ponderously round, giving access to a low dark passage.

It must have been madness which led me to enter the forgotten corridor, alone, without torch or match, at that hour of the evening; but at any rate I entered. The passage was tall enough for a man to walk erect, and I could feel, as I groped slowly along, that the wall was composed of smooth polished granite, while the floor sloped away downward with a slight but regular descent. I walked with trembling heart and faltering feet for some forty or fifty yards down the mysterious vestibule: and then I felt myself brought suddenly to a standstill by a block of stone placed right across the pathway.

I had had nearly enough for one evening, and I was preparing to return to the boat, agog with my new discovery, when my attention was suddenly arrested by an incredible, a perfectly miraculous fact.

The block of stone which barred the passage was faintly visible as a square, by means of a struggling belt of light streaming through the seams. There must be a lamp or other flame burning within. What if this were a door like the outer one, leading into a chamber perhaps inhabited by some dangerous band of outcasts? The light was a sure evidence of human occupation: and yet the outer door swung rustily on its pivot as though it had never been opened for ages. I paused a moment in fear before I ventured to try the stone: and then, urged on once more by some insane impulse, I turned the massive block with all my might to the left. It gave way slowly like its neighbour, and finally opened into the central hall.

Never as long as I live shall I forget the ecstasy of terror, astonishment, and blank dismay which seized upon me when I stepped into that seemingly enchanted chamber. A blaze of light first burst upon my eyes, from jets of gas arranged in regular rows tier above tier, upon the columns and walls of the vast apartment. Huge pillars, richly painted with red, yellow, blue and green decorations, stretched in endless succession down the dazzling aisles. A floor of polished syenite reflected the splendour of the lamps, and afforded a base for red granite sphinxes and dark purple images in porphyry of the cat-faced goddess Pasht, whose form I knew so well at the Louvre and the British Museum. But I had no eyes for any of these lesser marvels, being wholly absorbed in the greatest marvel of all: for there, in royal state and with mitred head, a living Egyptian king, surrounded by his coiffured court, was banqueting in the flesh upon a real throne, before a table laden with Memphian delicacies!

I stood transfixed with awe and amazement, my tongue and my feet alike forgetting their office, and my brain whirling round and round, as I remember it used to whirl when my health broke down utterly at Cambridge after the Classical Tripos. I gazed fixedly at the strange picture before me, taking in all its details in a confused way, yet quite incapable of understanding or realizing any part of its true import. I saw the king in the centre of the hall, raised on a throne of granite inlaid with gold and ivory; his head crowned with the peaked cap of Rameses, and his curled hair flowing down his shoulders in a set and formal frizz. I saw priests and warriors on either side, dressed in the costumes which I had often carefully noted in our great collections; while bronze-skinned maids, with light garments round their waists, and limbs displayed in graceful picturesqueness, waited upon them, half nude, as in the wall paintings which we had lately examined at Karnak and Syene. I saw the ladies, clothed from head to foot in dyed linen garments, sitting apart in the background, banqueting by themselves at a separate table; while dancing girls, like older representatives of my yesternoon friends, the Ghawázi, tumbled before them in strange attitudes, to the music of four-stringed harps and long straight pipes. In short, I beheld as in a dream the whole drama of everyday Egyptian royal life, playing itself out anew under my eyes, in its real original properties and personages.

Gradually, as I looked, I became aware that my hosts were no less surprised at the appearance of their anachronistic guest than was the guest himself at the strange living panorama which met his eyes. In a moment music and dancing ceased; the banquet paused in its course, and the king and his nobles stood up in undisguised astonishment to survey the strange intruder.

Some minutes passed before any one moved forward on either side. At last a young girl of royal appearance, yet strangely resembling the Gháziyah of Abu Villa, and recalling in part the laughing maiden in the foreground of Mr. Long's great canvas at the previous Academy, stepped out before the throng.

'May I ask you,' she said in Ancient Egyptian, 'who you are, and why you come hither to disturb us?'

I was never aware before that I spoke or understood the language of the hieroglyphics: yet I found I had not the slightest difficulty in comprehending or answering her question. To say the truth, Ancient Egyptian, though an extremely tough tongue to decipher in its written form, becomes as easy as love-making when spoken by a pair of lips like that Pharaonic princess's. It is really very much the same as English, pronounced in a rapid and somewhat indefinite whisper, and with all the vowels left out.

'I beg ten thousand pardons for my intrusion,' I answered apologetically: 'but I did not know that this Pyramid was inhabited, or I should not have entered your residence so rudely. As for the points you wish to know, I am an English tourist, and you will find my name upon this card;' saying which I handed her one from the case which I had fortunately put into my pocket, with conciliatory politeness. The princess examined it closely, but evidently did not understand its import.

'In return,' I continued, 'may I ask you in what august presence I now find myself by accident?'

A court official stood forth from the throng, and answered in a set heraldic tone: 'In the presence of the illustrious monarch, Brother of the Sun, Thothmes the Twenty-seventh, king of the Eighteenth Dynasty.'

'Salute the Lord of the World,' put in another official in the same regulation drone.

I bowed low to his Majesty, and stepped out into the hall. Apparently my obeisance did not come up to Egyptian standards of courtesy, for a suppressed titter broke audibly from the ranks of bronze-skinned waiting-women. But the king graciously smiled at my attempt, and turning to the nearest nobleman, observed in a voice of great sweetness and self-contained majesty: 'This stranger, Ombos, is certainly a very curious person. His appearance does not at all resemble that of an Ethiopian or other savage, nor does he look like the pale-faced sailors who come to us from the Achaian land beyond the sea. His features, to be sure, are not very different from theirs; but his extraordinary and singularly inartistic dress shows him to belong to some other barbaric race.'

I glanced down at my waistcoat, and saw that I was wearing my tourist's check suit, of grey and mud colour, with which a Bond Street tairlor had supplied me just before leaving town, as the latest thing out in fancy tweeds. Evidently these Egyptians must have a very curious standard of taste not to admire our pretty and graceful style of male attire.

'If the dust beneath your Majesty's feet may venture upon a suggestion,' put in the officer whom the king had addressed, 'I would hint that this young man is probably a stray visitor from the utterly uncivilized lands of the North. The headgear which he carries in his hand obviously betrays an Arctic habitat.'

I had instinctively taken off my round felt hat in the first moment of surprise, when I found myself in the midst of this strange throng, and I was standing now in a somewhat embarrassed posture, holding it awkwardly before me like a shield to protect my chest.

'Let the stranger cover himself,' said the king.

'Barbarian intruder, cover yourself,' cried the herald. I noticed throughout that the king never directly addressed anybody save the higher officials around him.

I put on my hat as desired. 'A most uncomfortable and silly form of tiara indeed,' said the great Thothmes.

'Very unlike your noble and awe-spiring mitre, Lion of Egypt,' answered Ombos.

'Ask the stranger his name,' the king continued.

It was useless to offer another card, so I mentioned it in a clear voice.

'An uncouth and almost unpronounceable designation truly,' commented his Majesty to the Grand Chamberlain beside him. 'These savages speak strange languages, widely different from the flowing tongue of Memnon and Sesostris.'

The chamberlain bowed his assent with three low genuflexions. I began to feel a little abashed at these personal remarks, and I *almost* think (though I shouldn't like it to be mentioned in the Temple) that a blush rose to my cheek.

The beautiful princess, who had been standing near me meanwhile in an attitude of statuesque repose, now appeared anxious to change the current of the conversation. 'Dear father,' she said with a respectful inclination, 'surely the stranger, barbarian though he be, cannot relish such pointed allusions to his person and costume. We must let him feel the grace and delicacy of Egyptian refinement. Then he may perhaps carry back with him some faint echo of its cultured beauty to his northern wilds.'

'Nonsense, Hatasou,' replied Thothmes XXVII testily. 'Savages have no feelings, and they are as incapable of appreciating Egyptian sensibility as the chattering crow is incapable of attaining the dignified reserve of the sacred crocodile.'

'Your Majesty is mistaken,' I said, recovering my self-possession gradually and realizing my position as a freeborn Englishman before the court of a foreign despot — though I must allow that I felt rather less confident than usual, owing to the fact that we were not represented in the Pyramid by a British Consul — 'I am an English tourist, a visitor from a modern land whose civilization far surpasses the rude culture of early Egypt; and I am accustomed to respectful treatment from all other nationalities, as becomes a citizen of the First Naval Power in the World.'

My answer created a profound impression. 'He has spoken to the Brother of the Sun,' cried Ombos in evident perturbation. 'He must be of the Blood Royal in his own tribe, or he would never have dared to do so!'

'Otherwise,' added a person whose dress I recognized as that of a priest, 'he must be offered up in expiation to Amon-Ra immediately.'

As a rule I am a decent truthful person, but under these alarming circumstances I ventured to tell a slight fib with an air of nonchalant boldness. 'I am a younger brother of our reigning king,' I said without a moment's hesitation; for there was nobody present to gainsay me, and I tried to salve my conscience by reflecting that at any rate I was only claiming consanguinity with an imaginary personage.

'In that case,' said King Thothmes, with more geniality in his tone, 'there can be no impropriety in my addressing you personally. Will you take a place at our table next to myself, and we can converse together without interrupting a banquet which must be brief enough in any circumstances? Hatasou, my dear, you may seat yourself next to the barbarian prince.'

I felt a visible swelling to the proper dimensions of a Royal Highness as I sat down by the king's right hand. The nobles resumed their places, the bronze-skinned waitresses left off standing like soldiers in a row and staring straight at my humble self, the goblets went round once more, and a comely maid soon brought me meat, bread, fruits and date wine.

All this time I was naturally burning with curiosity to inquire who my strange host might be, and how they had preserved their existence for so many centuries in this undiscovered hall; but I was obliged to wait until I had satisfied his Majesty of my own nationality, the means by which I had entered the Pyramid, the general state of affairs throughout the world at the present moment, and fifty thousand other matters of a similar sort. Thothmes utterly refused to believe my reiterated assertion that our existing civilization was far superior to the Egyptian; 'because,' he said, 'I see from your dress that your nation is utterly devoid of taste or invention;' but he listened with great interest to my account of modern society, the steam-engine, the Permissive Prohibitory Bill, the telegraph, the House of Commons, Home Rule, and other blessings of our advanced era, as well as to a brief *résumé* of

European history from the rise of the Greek culture to the Russo-Turkish war. At last his questions were nearly exhausted, and I got a chance of making a few counter inquiries on my own account.

'And now,' I said, turning to the charming Hatasou, whom I thought a more pleasing informant than her august papa, 'I should like to know who *you* are.'

'What, don't you know?' she cried with unaffected surprise. 'Why, we're mummies.'

She made this astonishing statement with just the same quiet unconsciousness as if she had said, 'we're French,' or 'we're Americans.' I glanced round the walls, and observed behind the columns, what I had not noticed till then — a large number of empty mummy-cases, with their lids placed carelessly by their sides.

'But what are you doing here?' I asked in a bewildered way.

'Is it possible,' said Hatasou, 'that you don't really know the object of embalming? Though your manners show you to be an agreeable and well-bred young man, you must excuse my saying that you are shockingly ignorant. We are made into mummies in order to preserve our immortality. Once in every thousand years we wake up for twenty-four hours, recover our flesh and blood, and banquet once more upon the mummied dishes and other good things laid by for us in the Pyramid. To-day is the first day of a millennium, and so we have waked up for the sixth time since we were first embalmed.'

'The *sixth* time?' I inquired incredulously. 'Then you must have been dead six thousand years.'

'Exactly so.'

'But the world has not yet existed so long,' I cried, in a fervour of orthodox horror.

'Excuse me, barbarian prince. This is the first day of the three hundred and twenty-seven thousandth millennium.'

My orthodoxy received a severe shock. However, I had been accustomed to geological calculations, and was somewhat inclined to accept the antiquity of man; so I swallowed the statement without more ado. Besides, if such a charming girl as Hatasou had asked me at that moment to turn Mohammedan, or to worship Osiris, I believe I should incontinently have done so.

'You wake up only for a single day and night, then?' I said.

'Only for a single day and night. After that, we go to sleep for another millennium.'

'Unless you are meanwhile burned as fuel on the Cairo Railway,' I added mentally. 'But how,' I continued aloud, 'do you get these lights?'

'The Pyramid is built above a spring of inflammable gas. We have a reservoir in one of the side chambers in which it collects during the thousand years. As soon as we awake, we turn it on at once from the tap, and light it with a lucifer match.'

'Upon my word,' I interposed, 'I had no notion you Ancient Egyptians were acquainted with the use of matches.'

'Very likely not. "There are more things in heaven and earth, Cephrenes, than are dreamt of in your philosophy," as the bard of Philre puts it.'

Further inquiries brought out all the secrets of that strange tomb-house, and kept me fully interested till the close of the banquet. Then the chief priest solemnly rose, offered a small fragment of meat to a deified crocodile, who sat in a meditative manner by the side of his deserted mummy-case, and declared the feast concluded for the night. All rose from their places, wandered away into the long corridors or sideaisles, and formed little groups of talkers under the brilliant gas-lamps.

For my part, I strolled off with Hatasou down the least illuminated of the colonnades, and took my seat beside a marble fountain, where several fish (gods of great sanctity, Hatasou assured me) were disporting themselves in a porphyry basin. How long we sat there I cannot tell, but I know that we talked a good deal about fish, and gods, and Egyptian habits, and Egyptian philosophy, and, above all, Egyptian love-making. The last-named subject we found very interesting, and when once we got fully started upon it, no diversion afterwards occurred to break the even tenour of the conversation. Hatasou was a lovely figure, tall, queenly, with smooth dark arms and neck of polished bronze: her big black eyes full of tenderness, and her long hair bound up into a bright Egyptian headdress, that harmonized to a tone with her complexion and her robe. The more we talked, the more desperately did I fall in love, and the more utterly oblivious did I become of my duty to Editha Fitz-Simkins. The mere ugly daughter of a rich and vulgar brand-new knight, forsooth, to show off her airs before me, when here was a Princess of the Blood Royal of Egypt, obviously sensible to the attentions which I was paying her, and not unwilling to receive them with a coy and modest grace.

Well, I went on saying pretty things to Hatasou, and Hatasou went on deprecating them in a pretty little way, as who should say, 'I don't mean what I pretend to mean one bit;' until at last I may confess that we were both evidently as far gone in the disease of the heart called love as it is possible for two young people on first acquaintance to become. Therefore, when Hatasou pulled forth her watch — another piece of mechanism with which antiquaries used never to credit the Egyptian people — and declared that she had only three more hours to live, at least for the next thousand years, I fairly broke down, took out my handkerchief, and began to sob like a child of five years old.

Hatasou was deeply moved. Decorum forbade that she should console me with too much *empressement;* but she ventured to remove the handkerchief gently from my face, and suggested that there was yet one course open by which we might enjoy a little more of one another's society. 'Suppose,' she said quietly, 'you were to become a mummy. You would then wake up, as we do, every thousand years; and after you have tried it once, you will find it just as natural to sleep for a millennium as for eight hours. Of course,' she added with a slight blush, 'during the next three or four solar cycles there would be plenty of time to conclude any other arrangements you might possibly contemplate, before the occurrence of another glacial epoch.'

This mode of regarding time was certainly novel and somewhat bewildering to people who ordinarily reckon its lapse by weeks and months; and I had a vague consciousness that my relations with Editha imposed upon me a moral necessity of returning to the outer world, instead of becoming a millennial mummy. Besides, there was the awkward chance of being converted into fuel and dissipated into space before the arrival of the next waking day. But I took one look at Hatasou, whose eyes were filling in turn with sympathetic tears, and that look decided me. I flung Editha, life, and duty to the dogs, and resolved at once to become a mummy.

There was no time to be lost. Only three hours remained to us, and the process of embalming, even in the most hasty manner, would take up fully two. We rushed off to the chief priest, who had charge of the particular department in question. He at once acceded to my wishes, and briefly explained the mode in which they usually treated the corpse.

That word suddenly aroused me. 'The corpse!' I cried; 'but I am alive. You can't embalm me living,'

'We can,' replied the priest, 'under chloroform.'

'Chloroform!' I echoed, growing more and more astonished: 'I had no idea you Egyptians knew anything about it.'

'Ignorant barbarian!' he answered with a curl of the lip; 'you imagine yourself much wiser than the teachers of the world. If you were versed in all the wisdom of the Egyptians, you would know that chloroform is one of our simplest and commonest anæsthetics.'

I put myself at once under the hands of the priest. He brought out the chloroform, and placed it beneath my nostrils, as I lay on a soft couch under the central court. Hatasou held my hand in hers, and watched my breathing with an anxious eye. I saw the priest leaning over me, with a clouded phial in his hand, and I experienced a vague sensation of smelling myrrh and spikenard. Next, I lost myself for a few moments, and when I again recovered my senses in a temporary break, the priest was holding a small greenstone knife, dabbled with blood, and I felt that a gash had been made across my breast. Then they applied the chloroform once more; I felt Hatasou give my hand a gentle squeeze; the whole panorama faded finally from my view; and I went to sleep for a seemingly endless time.

When I awoke again, my first impression led me to believe that the thousand years were over, and that I had come to life once more to feast with Hatasou and Thothmes in the Pyramid of Abu Villa. But second thoughts, combined with closer observation of the surroundings, convinced me that I was really lying in a bedroom of Shepheard's Hotel at Cairo. An hospital nurse leant over me, instead of a chief priest; and I noticed no tokens of Editha Fitz-Simkins's presence. But when I endeavoured to make inquiries upon the subject of my whereabouts, I was peremptorily informed that I mustn't speak, as I was only just recovering from a severe fever, and might endanger my life by talking.

Some weeks later I learned the sequel of my night's adventure. The Fitz-Simkinses, missing me from the boat in the morning, at first imagined that I might have gone ashore for an early stroll. But after breakfast time, lunch time, and dinner time had gone past, they began to grow alarmed, and sent to look for me in all directions. One of their scouts, happening to pass the Pyramid, noticed that one of the stones near the north-east angle had been displaced, so as to give access to a dark passage, hitherto unknown. Calling several of his friends, for he was afraid to venture in alone, he passed down the corridor, and through a second gateway into the central hall. There the Fellahin found me, lying on the ground, bleeding profusely from a wound on the breast, and in an advanced stage of malarious fever. They brought me back to the boat, and the Fitz-Simkinses conveyed me at once to Cairo, for medical attendance and proper nursing.

Editha was at first convinced that I had attempted to commit suicide because I could not endure having caused her pain, and she accordingly resolved to tend me with the utmost care through my illness. But she found that my delirious remarks, besides bearing frequent reference to a princess, with whom I appeared to have been on unexpectedly intimate terms, also related very largely to our *casus belli* itself the dancing girls of Abu Villa. Even this trial she might have borne, setting down the moral degeneracy which led me to patronize so degrading an exhibition as a first symptom of my approaching malady: but certain unfortunate observations, containing pointed and by no means flattering allusions to her personal appearance — which I contrasted, much to her disadvantage, with that of the unknown princess — these, I say, were things which she could not forgive; and she left Cairo abruptly with her parents for the Riviera, leaving behind a stinging note, in which she denounced my perfidy and empty-heartedness with all the flowers of feminine eloquence. From that day to this I have never seen her.

When I returned to London and proposed to lay this account before the Society of Antiquaries, all my friends dissuaded me on the grounds of its apparent incredibility. They declare that I must have gone to the Pyramid already in a state of delirium, discovered the entrance by accident, and sunk exhausted when I reached the inner chamber. In answer, I would point out three facts. In the first place, I undoubtedly found my way unto the unknown passage — for which achievement I afterwards received the gold medal of the Société Khédiviale, and of which I retain a clear recollection, differing in no way from my recollection of the events. In the second place, I had in my pocket, when found, a ring of Hatasou's, which I drew from her finger just before I took the chloroform, and put into my pocket as a keepsake. And in the third place, I had on my breast the wound which I saw the priest inflict with a knife of greenstone, and the scar may be seen on the spot to the present day. The absurd hypothesis of my medical friends, that I was wounded by falling against a sharp edge of rock, I must at once reject as unworthy of a moment's consideration.

My own theory is either that the priest had not time to complete the operation, or else that the arrival of the Fitz-Simkins' scouts frightened back the mummies to their cases an hour or so too soon. At any rate, there they all were, ranged around the walls undisturbed, the moment the Fellahin entered.

Unfortunately, the truth of my account cannot be tested for another thousand years. But as a copy of this book will be preserved for the benefit of posterity in the British Museum, I hereby solemnly call upon Collective Humanity to try the veracity of this history by sending a deputation of archeologists to the Pyramid of Abu Villa, on the last day of December, Two thousand eight hundred and seventy-seven. If they do not then find Thothmes and Hatasou feasting in the central hall exactly as I have described, I shall willingly admit that the story of my New Year's Eve among the Mummies is a vain hallucination, unworthy of credence at the hands of the scientific world.

The Ring of Thoth*

Mr. John Vansittart Smith FRS of 147a Gower Street was a man whose energy of purpose and clearness of thought might have placed him in the very first rank of scientific observers. He was the victim, however, of a universal ambition which prompted him to aim at distinction in many subjects rather than pre-eminence in one. In his early days he had shown an aptitude for zoology and for botany which caused his friends to look upon him as a second Darwin, but when a professorship was almost within his reach he had suddenly discontinued his studies and turned his whole attention to chemistry. Here his researches upon the spectra of the metals had won him his fellowship in the Royal Society; but again he played the coquette with his subject, and after a year's absence from the laboratory, he joined the Oriental Society, and delivered a paper on the hieroglyphic and demotic inscriptions of El Kah, thus giving a crowning example both of the versatility and of the inconstancy of his talents.

The most fickle of wooers, however, is apt to be caught at last, and so it was with John Vansittart Smith. The more he burrowed his way into Egyptology, the more impressed he became by the vast field which it opened to the enquirer and by the extreme importance of a subject which promised to throw a light upon the first germs of human civilisation and the origin of the greater part of our arts and sciences. So struck was Mr. Smith that he straightway married an Egyptological young lady who had written upon the sixth dynasty, and having thus secured a sound base of operations he set himself to collect materials for a work which should unite the research of Lepsius and the ingenuity of Champollion. The preparation of this *magnum opus* entailed many hurried visits to the magnificent Egyptian collections of the Louvre, upon the last of which, no longer ago than the middle of last October, he became involved in a most strange and noteworthy adventure.

The trains had been slow and the Channel had been rough, so that the student arrived in Paris in a somewhat befogged and feverish condition. On reaching the Hôtel de France, in the Rue Laffitte, he had thrown himself upon a sofa for a couple of hours, but finding that he was unable to sleep, he determined, in spite of his fatigue, to make his way to the Louvre, settle the point which he had come to decide, and take the evening train back to Dieppe. Having come to his conclusion, he donned his greatcoat, for it was a raw rainy day, and made his way across the Boulevard des Italiens and down the Avenue de l'Opéra. Once in the Louvre he was on familiar ground, and he speedily made his way to the collection of papyri which it was his intention to consult.

* "The Ring of Thoth" was written by Arthur Conan Doyle (1859 – 1930) and published in *Cornhill Magazine*, Jan. 1890.

The warmest admirers of John Vansittart Smith could hardly claim for him that he was a handsome man. His high-beaked nose and prominent chin had something of the same acute and incisive character which distinguished his intellect. He held his head in a birdlike fashion, and birdlike, too, was the pecking motion with which, in conversation, he threw out his objections and retorts. As he stood, with the high collar of his greatcoat raised to his ears, he might have seen from the reflection in the glass case before him that his appearance was a singular one. Yet it came upon him as a sudden jar when an English voice behind him exclaimed in very audible tones, 'What a queer-looking mortal!'

The student had a large amount of petty vanity in his composition which manifested itself by an ostentatious and overdone disregard of all personal considerations. He straightened his lips and looked rigidly at the roll of papyrus, while his heart filled with bitterness against the whole race of travelling Britons.

'Yes,' said another voice, 'he really is an extraordinary fellow.'

'Do you know,' said the first speaker, 'one could almost believe that by the continual contemplation of mummies the chap has become half a mummy himself!'

'He has certainly an Egyptian cast of countenance,' said the other.

John Vansittart Smith spun round upon his heel with the intention of shaming his countrymen by a corrosive remark or two. To his surprise and relief, the two young fellows who had been conversing had their shoulders turned towards him and were gazing at one of the Louvre attendants who was polishing some brasswork at the other side of the room.

'Carter will be waiting for us at the Palais Royal,' said one tourist to the other, glancing at his watch, and they clattered away, leaving the student to his labours.

'I wonder what these chatterers call an Egyptian cast of countenance,' thought John Vansittart Smith, and he moved his position slightly in order to catch a glimpse of the man's face. He started as his eyes fell upon it. It was indeed the very face with which his studies had made him familiar. The regular statuesque features, broad brow, well-rounded chin and dusky complexion were the exact counterpart of the innumerable statues, mummy-cases and pictures which adorned the walls of the apartment. The thing was beyond all coincidence. The man must be an Egyptian. The national angularity of the shoulders and narrowness of the hips were alone sufficient to identify him.

John Vansittart Smith shuffled towards the attendant with some intention of addressing him. He was not light of touch in conversation, and found it difficult to strike the happy mean between the brusqueness of the superior and the geniality of the equal. As he came nearer, the man presented his side face to him, but kept his gaze still bent upon his work. Vansittart Smith, fixing his eyes upon the fellow's skin, was conscious of a sudden impression that there was something inhuman and preternatural about its appearance. Over the temple and cheek-bone it was as glazed and as shiny as varnished parchment. There was no suggestion of pores. One could not fancy a drop of moisture upon that arid surface. From brow to chin, however, it was cross-hatched by a million delicate wrinkles, which shot and interlaced as though nature in some Maori mood had tried how wild and intricate a pattern she could devise.

'Où est la collection de Memphis?' asked the student, with the awkward air of a man who is devising a question merely for the purpose of opening a conversation.

'C'est là,' replied the man brusquely, nodding his head at the other side of the room.

'Vous êtes un Egyptien, n'est-ce pas?' asked the Englishman.

The attendant looked up and turned his strange dark eyes upon his questioner. They were vitreous, with a misty dry shininess such as Vansittart Smith had never seen in a human head before. As he gazed into them he saw some strong emotion gather in their depths, which rose and deepened until it broke into a look of something akin both to horror and to hatred.

'Non, monsieur; je suis français.' The man turned abruptly and bent low over his polishing. The student gazed at him for a moment in astonishment, and then turning to a chair in a retired corner behind one of the doors he proceeded to make notes of his researches among the papyri. His thoughts, however, refused to return into their natural groove. They would run upon the enigmatical attendant with the sphinx-like face and the parchment skin.

'Where have I seen such eyes?' said Vansittart Smith to himself. 'There is something saurian about them, something reptilian. There's the *membrana nictitans* of the snakes,' he mused, bethinking himself of his zoological studies. 'It gives a shiny effect. But there was something more here. There was a sense of power, of wisdom — so I read them — and of weariness, utter weariness, and ineffable despair. It may be all imagination, but I never had so strong an impression. By Jove, I must have another look at them!' He rose and paced round the Egyptian rooms, but the man who had excited his curiosity had disappeared.

The student sat down again in his quiet corner, and continued to work at his notes. He had gained the information which he required from the papyri, and it only remained to write it down while it was still fresh in his memory. For a time his pencil travelled rapidly over the paper, but soon the lines became less level, the words more blurred and finally the pencil tinkled down upon the floor and the head of the student dropped heavily forward upon his chest. Tired out by his journey, he slept so soundly in his lonely post behind the door that neither the clanking civil guard, nor the footsteps of sightseers, nor even the loud hoarse bell which gives the signal for closing, were sufficient to arouse him.

Twilight deepened into darkness, the bustle from the Rue de Rivoli waxed and then waned, distant Notre Dame clanged out the hour of midnight, and still the dark and lonely figure sat silently in the shadow. It was not until close upon one in the morning that, with a sudden gasp and an intaking of the breath, Vansittart Smith returned to consciousness. For a moment it flashed upon him that he had dropped asleep in his study chair at home. The moon was shining fitfully though the unshuttered window, however, and as his eye ran along the lines of mummies and the endless array of polished cases, he remembered clearly where he was and how he came there. The student was not a nervous man. He possessed that love of a novel situation which is peculiar to his race. Stretching out his cramped limbs, he looked at his watch and burst into a chuckle as he observed the hour. The episode would make an admirable anecdote to be introduced into his next paper as a relief to the graver and heavier speculations. He was a little cold, but wide awake and much refreshed. It was no wonder that the guardians had overlooked him, for the door threw its heavy black shadow right across him.

The complete silence was impressive. Neither outside nor inside was there a creak or a murmur. He was alone with the dead men of a dead civilisation. What though the outer city reeked of the garish nineteenth century! In all this chamber there was scarce an article, from the shrivelled ear of wheat to the pigment-box of the painter, which had not held its own against four thousand years. Here was the flotsam and jetsam washed up by the great ocean of time from that far-off empire. From stately Thebes, from lordly Luxor, from the great temples of Heliopolis, from a hundred rifled tombs, these relics had been brought. The student glanced round at the long-silent figures who flickered vaguely up through the gloom, at the busy toilers who were now so restful, and he fell into a reverent and thoughtful mood. An unwonted sense of his own youth and insignificance came over him. Leaning back in his chair, he gazed dreamily down the long vista of rooms, all silvery with the moonshine, which extended through the whole wing of the widespread building. His eyes fell upon the yellow glare of a distant lamp.

John Vansittart Smith sat up on his chair with his nerves all on edge. The light was advancing slowly towards him, pausing from time to time, and then coming jerkily onwards. The bearer moved noiselessly. In the utter silence there was no suspicion of the pat of a footfall. An idea of robbers entered the Englishman's head. He snuggled up farther into the corner. The light was two rooms off. Now it was in the next chamber, and still there was no sound. With something approaching to a thrill of fear, the student observed a face, floating in the air as it were, behind the flare of the lamp. The figure was wrapped in shadow, but the light fell full upon the strange, eager face. There was no mistaking the metallic, glistening eyes and the cadaverous skin. It was the attendant with whom he had conversed.

Vansittart Smith's first impulse was to come forward and address him. A few words of explanation would set the matter clear, and lead doubtless to his being conducted to some side-door from which he might make his way to his hotel. As the man entered the chamber, however, there was something so stealthy in his movements, and so furtive in his expression, that the Englishman altered his intention. This was clearly no ordinary official walking the rounds. The fellow wore felt-soled slippers, stepped with a rising chest, and glanced quickly from left to right, while his hurried, gasping breathing thrilled the flame of his lamp. Vansittart Smith crouched silently back into the corner and watched him keenly, convinced that his errand was one of secret and probably sinister import.

There was no hesitation in the other's movements. He stepped lightly and swiftly across to one of the great cases, and drawing a key from his pocket, he unlocked it. From the upper shelf he pulled down a mummy, which he bore away with him, and laid it with much care and solicitude upon the ground. By it he placed his lamp, and then squatting down beside it in Eastern fashion he began with long, quivering fingers to undo the cerecloths and bandages which girt it round. As the crackling rolls of linen peeled off one after the other, a strong aromatic odour filled the chamber, and fragments of scented wood and of spices pattered down upon the marble floor.

It was clear to John Vansittart Smith that this mummy had never been unswathed before. The operation interested him keenly. He thrilled all over with curiosity, and his birdlike head protruded farther and farther from behind the door. When, however, the last roll had been removed from the four-thousand-year-old head, it was all that he could do to stifle an outcry of amazement. First, a cascade of long, black, glossy tresses poured over the workman's hands and arms. A second turn of the bandage revealed a low, white forehead, with a pair of delicately arched eyebrows. A third uncovered a pair of bright, deeply fringed eyes and a straight, well-cut nose, while a fourth and last showed a sweet, full, sensitive mouth and a beautifully curved chin. The whole face was one of extraordinary loveliness, save for the one blemish that in the centre of the forehead there was a single irregular, coffee-coloured splotch. It was a triumph of the embalmer's art. Vansittart Smith's eyes grew larger and larger as he gazed upon it, and he chirruped in his throat with satisfaction.

Its effect upon the Egyptologist was as nothing, however, compared with that which it produced upon the strange attendant. He threw his hands up into the air, burst into a harsh clatter of words, and then, hurling himself down upon the ground beside the mummy, he threw his arms round her and kissed her repeatedly upon the lips and brow. 'Ma petite!' he groaned in French. 'Ma pauvre petite!' His voice broke with emotion, and his innumerable wrinkles quivered and writhed, but the student observed in the lamplight that his shining eyes were still dry and tearless as two beads of steel. For some minutes he lay, with a twitching face, crooning and moaning over the beautiful head. Then he broke into a sudden smile, said some words in an unknown tongue, and sprang to his feet with the vigorous air of one who has braced himself for an effort.

In the centre of the room there was a large, circular case which contained, as the student had frequently remarked, a magnificent collection of early Egyptian rings and precious stones. To this the attendant strode, and unlocking it, threw it open. On the ledge at the side he placed his lamp, and beside it a small earthenware jar which he had drawn from his pocket. He then took a handful of rings from the case, and with a most serious and anxious face he proceeded to smear each in turn with some liquid substance from the earthen pot, holding them to the light as he did so. He was clearly disappointed with the first lot, for he threw them petulantly back into the case and drew out some more. One of these, a massive ring with a large crystal set in it, he seized and eagerly tested with the contents of the jar. Instantly he uttered a cry of joy, and threw out his arms in a wild gesture which upset the pot and set the liquid streaming across the floor to the very feet of the Englishman. The attendant drew a red handkerchief from his bosom, and mopping up the mess, he followed it into the corner, where in a moment he found himself face to face with his observer.

'Excuse me,' said John Vansittart Smith, with all imaginable politeness; 'I have been unfortunate enough to fall asleep behind this door.'

'And you have been watching me?' the other asked in English, with a most venomous look on his corpse-like face.

The student was a man of veracity. 'I confess,' said he, 'that I have noticed your movements, and that they have aroused my curiosity and interest in the highest degree.'

The man drew a long, flamboyantly bladed knife from his bosom. 'You have had a very narrow escape,' he said; 'had I seen you ten minutes ago, I should have driven this through your heart. As it is, if you touch me or interfere with me in any way you are a dead man.'

'I have no wish to interfere with you,' the student answered. 'My presence here is entirely accidental. All I ask is that you will have the extreme kindness to show me out through some side-door.' He spoke with great suavity, for the man was still pressing the tip of his dagger against the palm of his left hand, as though to assure himself of its sharpness, while his face preserved its malignant expression.

'If I thought — ' said he. 'But no, perhaps it is as well. What is your name?'

The Englishman gave it.

'Vansittart Smith,' the other repeated. 'Are you the same Vansittart Smith who gave a paper in London upon El Kab? I saw a report of it. Your knowledge of the subject is contemptible.'

'Sir!' cried the Egyptologist.

'Yet it is superior to that of many who make even greater pretensions. The whole keystone of our old life in Egypt was not the inscriptions or monuments of which you make so much, but was our hermetic philosophy and mystic knowledge of which you say little or nothing.'

'Our old life!' repeated the scholar, wide-eyed; and then suddenly, 'Good God, look at the mummy's face!'

The strange man turned and flashed his light upon the dead woman, uttering a long, doleful cry as he did so. The action of the air had already undone all the art of the embalmer. The skin had fallen away, the eyes had sunk inwards, the discoloured lips had writhed away from the yellow teeth, and the brown mark upon the forehead alone showed that it was indeed the same face which had shown such youth and beauty a few short minutes before.

The man flapped his hands together in grief and horror. Then mastering himself by a strong effort he turned his hard eyes once more upon the Englishman.

'It does not matter,' he said, in a shaking voice. 'It does not really matter. I came here tonight with the fixed determination to do something. It is now done. All else is as nothing. I have found my quest. The old curse is broken. I can rejoin her. What matter about her inanimate shell so long as her spirit is awaiting me at the other side of the veil!'

'These are wild words,' said Vansittart Smith. He was becoming more and more convinced that he had to do with a madman.

'Time presses, and I must go,' continued the other. 'The moment is at hand for which I have waited this weary time. But I must show you out first. Come with me.'

Taking up the lamp, he turned from the disordered chamber and led the student swiftly through the long series of the Egyptian, Assyrian and Persian apartments. At the end of the latter he pushed open a small door let into the wall and descended a winding, stone stair. The Englishman felt the cold, fresh air of the night upon his brow. There was a door opposite him which appeared to communicate with the street. To the right of this another door stood ajar, throwing a spurt of yellow light across the passage. 'Come in here!' said the attendant shortly.

Vansittart Smith hesitated. He had hoped that he had come to the end of his adventure. Yet his curiosity was strong within him. He could not leave the matter unsolved, so he followed his strange companion into the lighted chamber.

It was a small room, such as is devoted to a concierge. A wood fire sparkled in the grate. At one side stood a truckle bed, and at the other a coarse, wooden chair, with a round table in the centre, which bore the remains of a meal. As the visitor's eye glanced round he could not but remark with an ever-recurring thrill that all the small details of the room were of the most quaint design and antique workmanship. The candlesticks, the vases upon the chimneypiece, the fire-irons, the ornaments upon the walls were all such as he had been wont to associate with the remote past. The gnarled, heavy-eyed man sat himself down upon the edge of the bed, and motioned his guest into the chair.

'There may be design in this,' he said, still speaking excellent English. 'It may be decreed that I should leave some account behind as a warning to all rash mortals who would set their wits up against the workings of nature. I leave it with you. Make such use as you will of it. I speak to you now with my feet upon the threshold of the other world.

'I am, as you surmised, an Egyptian — not one of the downtrodden race of slaves who now inhabit the delta of the Nile, but a survivor of that fiercer and harder people who tamed the Hebrew, drove the Ethiopian back into the southern deserts, and built those mighty works which have been the envy and the wonder of all after generations. It was in the reign of Tuthmosis, sixteen hundred years before the birth of Christ, that I first saw the light. You shrink away from me. Wait, and you will see that I am more to be pitied than to be feared.

'My name was Sosra. My father had been the chief priest of Osiris in the great temple of Abaris, which stood in those days upon the Bubastic branch of the Nile. I was brought up in the temple and was trained in all those mystic arts which are spoken of in your own Bible. I was an apt pupil. Before I was sixteen I had learned all the wisest priest could teach me. From that time on I studied nature's secrets for myself, and shared my knowledge with no man.

'Of all the questions that attracted me there were none over which I laboured so long as over those which concern themselves with the nature of life. I probed deeply into the vital principle. The aim of medicine had been to drive away disease when it appeared. It seemed to me that a method might be devised which should so fortify the body as to prevent weakness or death from ever taking hold of it. It is useless that I should recount my researches. You would scarce comprehend them if I did. They were carried out partly upon animals, partly upon slaves and partly on myself. Suffice it that their result was to furnish me with a substance which, when injected into the blood, would endow the body with strength to resist the effects of time, of violence or of disease. It would not indeed confer immortality, but its potency would endure for many thousands of years. I used it upon a cat, and afterwards drugged the creature with the most deadly poisons. That cat is alive in Lower Egypt at the present moment. There was nothing of mystery or magic in the matter. It was simply a chemical discovery, which may well be made again.

'Love of life runs high in the young. It seemed to me that I had broken away from all human care now that I had abolished pain and driven death to such a distance. With a light heart I poured the accursed stuff into my veins. Then I looked round for someone whom I could benefit. There was a young priest of Thoth, Parmes by name, who had won my goodwill by his earnest nature and his devotion to his studies. To him I whispered my secret, and at his request I injected him with my elixir. I should now, I reflected, never be without a companion of the same age as myself.

'After this grand discovery I relaxed my studies to some extent, but Parmes continued his with redoubled energy. Every day I could see him working with his flasks and his distiller in the Temple of Thoth, but he said little to me as to the result of his labours. For my own part, I used to walk through the city and look around me with exultation as I reflected that all this was destined to pass away, and that only I should remain. The people would bow to me as they passed me, for the fame of my knowledge had gone abroad.

'There was war at this time, and the great king had sent down his soldiers to the eastern boundary to drive away the Hyksos. A governor, too, was sent to Abaris, that he might hold it for the king. I had heard much of the beauty of the daughter of this governor, but one day as I walked out with Parmes we met her, borne upon the shoulders of her slaves. I was struck with love as with lightning. My heart went out from me. I could have thrown myself beneath the feet of her bearers. This was my woman. Life without her was impossible. I swore by the head of Horus that she should be mine. I swore it to the priest of Thoth. He turned away from me with a brow which was as black as midnight.

'There is no need to tell you of our wooing. She came to love me even as I loved her. I learned that Parmes had seen her before I did, and had shown her that he, too, loved her, but I could smile at his passion, for I knew that her heart was mine. The white plague had come upon the city and many were stricken, but I laid my hands upon the sick and nursed them without fear or scathe. She marvelled at my daring. Then I told her my secret, and begged her that she would let me use my art upon her.

'"Your flower shall then be unwithered, Atma," I said. "Other things may pass away, but you and I, and our great love for each other, shall outlive the tomb of King Chefru."

'But she was full of timid, maidenly objections. Was it right? she asked, was it not a thwarting of "the will of the gods"? If the great Osiris had wished that our years should be so long, would he not himself have brought it about?

'With fond and loving words I overcame her doubts, and yet she hesitated. It was a great question, she said. She would think it over for this one night. In the morning I should know of her resolution. Surely one night was not too much to ask. She wished to pray to Isis for help in her decision.

'With a sinking heart and a sad foreboding of evil I left her with her tirewomen. In the morning, when the early sacrifice was over, I hurried to her house. A frightened slave met me upon the steps. Her mistress was ill, she said, very ill. In a frenzy I broke my way through the attendants, and rushed through hall and corridor to my Atma's chamber. She lay upon her couch, her head high upon the pillow, with a pallid face and a glazed eye. On her forehead there blazed a single angry, purple patch. I knew that hell-mark of old. It was the scar of the white plague, the sign-manual of death.

'Why should I speak of that terrible time? For months I was mad, fevered, delirious, and yet I could not die. Never did an Arab thirst after the sweet wells as I longed after death. Could poison or steel have shortened the thread of my existence, I should soon have rejoined my love in the land with the narrow portal. I tried, but it was of no avail. The accursed influence was too strong upon me. One night as I lay upon my couch, weak and weary, Parmes, the priest of Thoth, came to my chamber. He stood in the circle of the lamplight, and he looked down upon me with eyes which were bright with a mad joy.

'"Why did you let the maiden die?" he asked; "why did you not strengthen her as you strengthened me?"

'"I was too late," I answered. "But I had forgot. You also loved her. You are my fellow in misfortune. Is it not terrible to think of the centuries which must pass ere we look upon her again? Fools, fools, that we were to take death to be our enemy!"

'"You may say that," he cried with a wild laugh; "the words come well from your lips. For me they have no meaning."

'"What mean you?" I cried, raising myself upon my elbow. "Surely, friend, this grief has turned your brain." His face was aflame with joy, and he writhed and shook like one who hath a devil.

'"Do you know whither I go?" he asked.

'"Nay," I answered, "I cannot tell."

'"I go to her," said he. "She lies embalmed in the farther tomb by the double palm tree beyond the city wall."

'"Why do you go there?" I asked.

'"To die!" he shrieked, "to die! I am not bound by earthen fetters."

'"But the elixir is in your blood," I cried.

'"I can defy it," said he; "I have found a stronger principle which will destroy it. It is working in my veins at this moment, and in an hour I shall be a dead man. I shall join her, and you shall remain behind."

'As I looked upon him I could see that he spoke words of truth. The light in his eye told me that he was indeed beyond the power of the elixir.

'"You will teach me!" I cried.

'"Never!" he answered.

'"I implore you, by the wisdom of Thoth, by the majesty of Anubis!"

'"It is useless," he said coldly.

'"Then I will find it out," I cried.

'"You cannot," he answered; "it came to me by chance. There is one ingredient which you can never get. Save that which is in the ring of Thoth, none will ever more be made."

'"In the ring of Thoth!" I repeated, "where then is the ring of Thoth?"

'"That also you shall never know," he answered. "You won her love. Who has won in the end? I leave you to your sordid earth life. My chains are broken. I must go!" He turned upon his heel and fled from the chamber. In the morning came the news that the priest of Thoth was dead.

'My days after that were spent in study. I must find this subtle poison which was strong enough to undo the elixir. From early dawn to midnight I bent over the test-tube and the furnace. Above all, I collected the papyri and the chemical flasks of the priest of Thoth. Alas! they taught me little. Here and there some hint or stray expression would raise hope in my bosom, but no good ever came of it. Still, month after month, I struggled on. When my heart grew faint I would make my way to the tomb by the palm tree. There, standing by the dead casket from which the jewel had been rifled, I would feel her sweet presence, and would whisper to her that I would rejoin her if mortal wit could solve the riddle.

'Parmes had said that his discovery was connected with the ring of Thoth. I had some remembrance of the trinket. It was a large and weighty circlet, made not of gold but of a rarer and heavier metal brought from the mines of Mount Harbal. Platinum, you call it. The ring had, I remembered, a hollow crystal set in it, in which some few drops of liquid might be stored. Now, the secret of Parmes could not have to do with the metal alone, for there were many rings of that metal in the temple. Was it not more likely that he had stored his precious poison within the cavity of the crystal? I had scarce come to this conclusion before, in hunting through his papers, I came upon one which told me that it was indeed so, and that there was still some of the liquid unused.

'But how to find the ring? It was not upon him when he was stripped for the embalmer. Of that I made sure. Neither was it among his private effects. In vain I searched every room that he had entered, every box and vase and chattel that he had owned. I sifted the very sand of the desert in the places where he had been wont to walk; but, do what I would, I could come upon no traces of the ring of Thoth. Yet it may be that my labours would have overcome all obstacles had it not been for a new and unlooked-for misfortune.

'A great war had been waged against the Hyksos, and the captains of the great king had been cut off in the desert, with all their bowmen and horsemen. The shepherd tribes were upon us like the locusts in a dry year. From the wilderness of Shur to the great, bitter lake there was blood by day and fire by night. Abaris was the bulwark of Egypt, but we could not keep the savages back. The city fell. The governor and the soldiers were put to the sword, and I, with many more, was led away into captivity.

'For years and years I tended cattle in the great plains by the Euphrates. My master died, and his son grew old, but I was still as far from death as ever. At last I escaped upon a swift camel, and made my way back to Egypt. The Hyksos had settled in the land which they had conquered, and their own king ruled over the country. Abaris had been torn down, the city had been burned, and of the great temple there was nothing left save an unsightly mound. Everywhere the tombs had been rifled and the monuments destroyed. Of my Atma's grave no sign was left. It was buried in the sands of the desert, and the palm tree which marked the spot had long disappeared. The papers of Parmes and the remains of the temple of Thoth were either destroyed or scattered far and wide over the deserts of Syria. All search after them was vain.

'From that time I gave up all hope of ever finding the ring or discovering the subtle drug. I set myself to live as patiently as might be until the effect of the elixir should wear away. How can you understand how terrible a thing time is, you who have experience only of the narrow course which lies between the cradle and the grave! I know it to my cost, I who have floated down the whole stream of history. I was old when Ilium fell. I was very old when Herodotus came to Memphis. I was bowed down with years when the new gospel came upon earth. Yet you see me much as other men are with the cursed elixir still sweetening my blood, and guarding me against that which I would court. Now, at last, at last I have come to the end of it!

'I have travelled in all lands and I have dwelt with all nations. Every tongue is the same to me. I learned them all to help pass the weary time. I need not tell you how slowly they drifted by, the long dawn of modern civilisation, the dreary middle years, the dark times of barbarism. They are all behind me now. I have never looked with the eyes of love upon another woman. Atma knows that I have been constant to her.

'It was my custom to read all that the scholars had to say upon Ancient Egypt. I have been in many positions, sometimes affluent, sometimes poor, but I have always found enough to enable me to buy the journals which deal with such matters. Some nine months ago I was in San Francisco, and there I read an account of some discoveries made in the neighbourhood of Abaris. My heart leapt into my mouth as I read it. It said that the excavator had busied himself in exploring some tombs recently unearthed. In one there had been found an unopened mummy with an inscription upon the outer case setting forth that it contained the body of the daughter of the governor of the city in the days of Tuthmosis. It added that on removing the outer case there had been exposed a large platinum ring set with a crystal, which had been laid upon the breast of the embalmed woman. This, then, was where Parmes had hid the ring of Thoth. He might well say that it was safe, for no Egyptian would ever stain his soul by moving even the outer case of a buried friend.

'That very night I set off from San Francisco, and in a few weeks I found myself once more at Abaris, if a few sand-heaps and crumbling walls may retain the name of the great city. I hurried to the Frenchmen who were digging there and asked them for the ring. They replied that both the ring and the mummy had been sent to the Boulak Museum at Cairo. To Boulak I went, but only to be told that Mariette Bey had claimed them and had shipped them to the Louvre. I followed them, and there, at last, in the Egyptian chamber, I came, after close upon four thousand years, upon the remains of my Atma, and upon the ring for which I had sought so long.

'But how was I to lay hands upon them? How was I to have them for my very own? It chanced that the office of attendant was vacant. I went to the director. I convinced him that I knew much about Egypt. In my eagerness I said too much. He remarked that a professor's chair would suit me better than a seat in the conciergerie. I knew more, he said, than he did. It was only by blundering, and letting him think that he had overestimated my knowledge, that I prevailed upon him to let me move the few effects which I have retained into this chamber. It is my first and my last night here.

'Such is my story, Mr. Vansittart Smith. I need not say more to a man of your perception. By a strange chance you have this night looked upon the face of the woman whom I loved in those far-off days. There were many rings with crystals in the case, and I had to test for the platinum to be sure of the one I wanted. A glance at the crystal has shown me that the liquid is indeed within it, and that I shall at last be able to shake off that accursed health which has been worse to me than the foulest disease. I have nothing more to say to you. I have unburdened myself. You may tell my story or you may withhold it at your pleasure. The choice rests with you. I owe you some amends, for you have had a narrow escape of your life this night. I was a desperate man, and not to be baulked in my purpose. Had I seen you before the thing was done, I might have put it beyond your power to oppose me or to raise an alarm. This is the door. It leads into the Rue de Rivoli. Good-night.'

The Englishman glanced back. For a moment the lean figure of Sosra the Egyptian stood framed in the narrow doorway. The next the door had slammed, and the heavy rasping of a bolt broke on the silent night.

It was on the second day after his return to London that Mr. John Vansittart Smith saw the following concise narrative in the Paris correspondence of *The Times:*

> *Curious Occurrence in the Louvre* - Yesterday morning a
> strange discovery was made in the principal Eastern

chamber. The *ouvriers* who are employed to clean out the rooms in the morning found one of the attendants lying dead upon the floor with his arms round one of the mummies. So close was his embrace that it was only with the utmost difficulty that they were separated. One of the cases containing valuable rings had been opened and rifled. The authorities are of the opinion that the man was bearing away the mummy with some idea of selling it to a private collector, but that he was struck down in the very act by long-standing disease of the heart. It is said that he was a man of uncertain age and eccentric habits, without any living relations to mourn over his dramatic and untimely end.

Lot No. 249[*]

Of the dealings of Edward Bellingham with William Monkhouse Lee and of the cause of the great terror of Abercrombie Smith it may be that no absolute and final judgement will ever be delivered. It is true that we have the full and clear narrative of Smith himself and such corroboration as he could look for from Thomas Styles the servant, from the Reverend Plumptree Peterson, Fellow of Old's, and from such other people as chanced to gain some passing glance at this or that incident in a singular chain of events. Yet in the main, the story must rest upon Smith alone, and the most will think that it is more likely that one brain, however outwardly sane, has some subtle warp in its texture, some strange flaw in its workings, than that the path of nature has been overstepped in open day in so famed a centre of learning and light as the University of Oxford. Yet when we think how narrow and how devious this path of nature is, how dimly we can trace it, for all our lamps of science, and how from the darkness which girds it round great and terrible possibilities loom ever shadowly upwards, it is a bold and confident man who will put a limit to the strange bypaths into which the human spirit may wander.

In a certain wing of what we will call Old College in Oxford there is a corner turret of an exceeding great age. The heavy arch which spans the open door has bent downwards in the centre under the weight of its years, and the grey, lichen-blotched blocks of stone are bound and knitted together with withes and strands of ivy, as though the old mother had set herself to brace them up against wind and weather. From the door a stone stair curves upward spirally, passing two landings and terminating in a third one, its steps all shapeless and hollowed by the tread of so many generations of the seekers after knowledge. Life has flowed like water down this winding stair, and, waterlike, has left these smooth-worn grooves behind it. From the long-gowned, pedantic scholars of Plantagenet days down to the young bloods of a later age, how full and strong had been that tide of young, English life. And what was left now of all those hopes, those strivings, those fiery energies, save here and there in some old-world churchyard a few scratches upon a stone, and perchance a handful of dust in a mouldering coffin? Yet here were the silent stair and the grey, old wall, with bend and saltire and many another heraldic device still to be read upon its surface, like grotesque shadows thrown back from the days that had passed.

In the month of May, in the year 1884, three young men occupied the sets of rooms which opened on to the separate landings of the old stair. Each set consisted simply of a sitting-room and of a bedroom, while the two corresponding rooms upon the ground-floor were

[*] "Lot No. 249" was written by Arthur Conan Doyle (1859 – 1930) and published in *Harper's New Monthly Magazine*, Sep. 1892.

used, the one as a coal-cellar and the other as the living-room of the servant, or scout, Thomas Styles, whose duty it was to wait upon the three men above him. To right and to left was a line of lecture-rooms and of offices, so that the dwellers in the old turret enjoyed a certain seclusion, which made the chambers popular among the more studious undergraduates. Such were the three who occupied them now — Abercrombie Smith above, Edward Bellingham beneath him and William Monkhouse Lee upon the lowest storey.

It was ten o'clock on a bright, spring night, and Abercrombie Smith lay back in his armchair, his feet upon the fender and his briar-root pipe between his lips. In a similar chair, and equally at his ease, there lounged on the other side of the fireplace his old school friend Jephro Hastie. Both men were in flannels, for they had spent their evening upon the river, but apart from their dress no one could look at their hard-cut, alert faces without seeing that they were open-air men — men whose minds and tastes turned naturally to all that was manly and robust. Hastie, indeed, was stroke of his college boat, and Smith was an even better oar, but a coming examination had already cast its shadow over him and held him to his work, save for the few hours a week which health demanded. A litter of medical books upon the table, with scattered bones, models and anatomical plates, pointed to the extent as well as the nature of his studies, while a couple of single-sticks and a set of boxing-gloves above the mantelpiece hinted at the means by which, with Hastie's help, he might take his exercise in its most compressed and least-distant form. They knew each other very well — so well that they could sit now in that soothing silence which is the very highest development of companionship.

'Have some whisky,' said Abercrombie Smith at last between two cloudbursts. 'Scotch in the jug and Irish in the bottle.'

'No, thanks. I'm in for the sculls. I don't liquor when I'm training. How about you?'

'I'm reading hard. I think it best to leave it alone.'

Hastie nodded, and they relapsed into a contented silence. 'By the way, Smith,' asked Hastie, presently, 'have you made the acquaintance of either of the fellows on your stair yet?'

'Just a nod when we pass. Nothing more.'

'Hum! I should be inclined to let it stand at that. I know something of them both. Not much, but as much as I want. I don't think I should take them to my bosom if I were you. Not that there's much amiss with Monkhouse Lee.'

'Meaning the thin one?'

'Precisely. He is a gentlemanly little fellow. I don't think there is any vice in him. But then you can't know him without knowing Bellingham.'

'Meaning the fat one?'

'Yes, the fat one. And he's a man whom I, for one, would rather not know.'

Abercrombie Smith raised his eyebrows and glanced across at his companion. 'What's up, then?' he asked. 'Drink? Cards? Cad? You used not to be censorious.'

'Ah! you evidently don't know the man or you wouldn't ask. There's something damnable about him — something reptilian. My gorge always rises at him. I should put him down as a man with secret vices — an evil liver. He's no fool, though. They say that he is one of the best men in his line that they have ever had in the college.'

'Medicine or classics?'

'Eastern languages. He's a demon at them. Chillingworth met him somewhere above the second cataract last long, and he told me that he just prattled to the Arabs as if he had been born and nursed and weaned among them. He talked Coptic to the Copts, and Hebrew to the Jews, and Arabic to the Bedouins, and they were all ready to kiss the hem of his frock-coat. There are some old hermit Johnnies up in those parts who sit on rocks and scowl and spit at the casual stranger. Well, when they saw this chap Bellingham, before he had said five words they just lay down on their bellies and wriggled. Chillingworth said that he never saw anything like it. Bellingham seemed to take it as his right, too, and strutted about among them and talked down to them like a Dutch uncle. Pretty good for an undergrad of Old's, wasn't it?'

'Why do you say you can't know Lee without knowing Bellingham?'

'Because Bellingham is engaged to his sister Eveline. Such a bright little girl, Smith! I know the whole family well. It's disgusting to see that brute with her. A toad and a dove, that's what they always remind me of.'

Abercrombie Smith grinned and knocked his ashes out against the side of the grate.

'You show every card in your hand, old chap,' said he. 'What a prejudiced, green-eyed, evil-thinking old man it is! You have really nothing against the fellow except that.'

'Well, I've known her ever since she was as long as that cherry-wood pipe, and I don't like to see her taking risks. And it is a risk. He looks beastly. And he has a beastly temper, a venomous temper. You remember his row with Long Norton?'

'No; you always forget that I am a freshman.'

'Ah, it was last winter. Of course. Well, you know the towpath along by the river. There were several fellows going along it, Bellingham in front, when they came on an old market-woman coming the other way. It had been raining — you know what those fields are like when it has rained — and the path ran between the river and a great puddle that was nearly as broad. Well, what does this swine do but keep the path and push the old girl into the mud, where she and her marketings came to terrible grief. It was a blackguard thing to do, and Long Norton, who is as gentle a fellow as ever stepped, told him what he thought of it. One word led to another, and it ended in Norton laying his stick across the fellow's shoulders. There was the deuce of a fuss about it and it's a treat to see the way in which Bellingham looks at Norton when they meet now. By Jove, Smith, it's nearly eleven o'clock!'

'No hurry. Light your pipe again.'

'Not I. I'm supposed to be in training. Here I've been sitting gossiping when I ought to have been safely tucked up. I'll borrow your skull, if you can share it. Williams has had mine for a month. I'll take the little bones of your ear, too, if you are sure you won't need them. Thanks very much. Never mind a bag, I can carry them very well under my arm. Good-night, my son, and take my tip as to your neighbour.'

When Hastie, bearing his anatomical plunder, had clattered off down the winding stair, Abercrombie Smith hurled his pipe into the wastepaper basket, and drawing his chair nearer to the lamp, plunged into a formidable, green-covered volume, adorned with great, coloured maps of that strange, internal kingdom of which we are the hapless and helpless monarchs. Though a freshman at Oxford, the student was not so in medicine, for he had worked for four years at Glasgow and at Berlin, and this coming examination would place him finally as a member of his profession. With his firm mouth, broad forehead and clear-cut, somewhat hard-featured face, he was a man who, if he had no brilliant talent, was yet so dogged, so patient and so strong that he might in the end overtop a more showy genius. A man who can hold his own among Scotchmen and North Germans is not a man to be easily set back. Smith had left a name at Glasgow and at Berlin, and he was bent now upon doing as much at Oxford, if hard work and devotion could accomplish it.

He had sat reading for about an hour, and the hands of the noisy carriage clock upon the side-table were rapidly closing together upon the twelve, when a sudden sound fell upon the student's ear — a sharp, rather shrill sound, like the hissing intake of a man's breath who gasps under some strong emotion. Smith laid down his book and slanted his ear to listen. There was no one on either side or above him, so that the interruption came certainly from the neighbor beneath — the same neighbour of whom Hastie had given so unsavoury an account. Smith knew him only as a flabby, pale-faced man of silent and studious habits, a man whose lamp threw a golden bar from the old turret even after he had extinguished his own. This community in lateness had formed a certain silent bond between them. It was soothing to Smith when the hours stole on towards dawning to feel that there was another so close who set as small a value upon his sleep as he did. Even now, as his thoughts turned towards him, Smith's feelings were kindly. Hastie was a good fellow, but he was rough, strong-fibred, with no imagination or sympathy. He could not tolerate departures from what he looked upon as the model type of manliness. If a man could not be measured by a public-school standard, then he was beyond the pale with Hastie. Like so many who are themselves robust, he was apt to confuse the constitution with the character, to ascribe to want of principle what was really a want of circulation. Smith, with his stronger mind, knew his friend's habit, and made allowance for it now as his thoughts turned towards the man beneath him.

There was no return of the singular sound, and Smith was about to turn to his work once more, when suddenly there broke out in the silence of the night a hoarse cry, a positive scream — the call of a man who is moved and shaken beyond all control. Smith sprang out of his chair and dropped his book. He was a man of fairly firm fibre, but there was something in this sudden, uncontrollable shriek of horror which chilled his blood and prickled in his skin. Coming in such a place and at such an hour, it brought a thousand fantastic possibilities into his head. Should he rush down or was it better to wait? He had all the national hatred of making a scene, and he knew so little of his neighbour that he would not lightly intrude upon his affairs. For a moment he stood in doubt and even as he balanced the matter there was a quick rattle of footsteps upon the stairs, and young Monkhouse Lee, half-dressed and as white as ashes, burst into his room.

'Come down!' he gasped. 'Bellingham's ill.'

Abercrombie Smith followed him closely downstairs into the sitting-room which was beneath his own, and intent as he was upon the matter in hand, he could not but take an amazed glance around him as he crossed the threshold. It was such a chamber as he had never seen before — a museum rather than a study. Walls and ceiling were thickly covered with a thousand strange relics from Egypt and the East. Tall, angular figures bearing burdens or weapons stalked in an uncouth frieze round the apartments. Above were bull-headed, stork-headed, cat-headed, owl-headed statues, with viper-crowned, almond-eyed monarchs, and strange, beetle-like deities cut out of the blue Egyptian lapis lazuli. Horus and Isis and Osiris peeped down from every niche and shelf; while across the ceiling a true son of Old Nile, a great, hanging-jawed crocodile, was slung in a double noose.

In the centre of this singular chamber was a large, square table, littered with papers, bottles and the dried leaves of some graceful, palm-like plant. These varied objects had all been heaped together in order to make room for a mummy case, which had been conveyed from the wall, as was evident from the gap there, and laid across the front of the table. The mummy itself, a horrid, black, withered thing, like a charred head on a gnarled bush, was lying half out of the case, with its claw-like hand and bony forearm resting upon the table. Propped up against the sarcophagus was an old yellow scroll of papyrus and in front of it, in a wooden armchair, sat the owner of the room, his head thrown back, his widely opened eyes directed in a horrified stare to the crocodile above him and his blue, thick lips puffing loudly with every expiration.

'My God! he's dying!' cried Monkhouse Lee, distractedly.

He was a slim, handsome young fellow, olive-skinned and dark-eyed, of a Spanish rather than of an English type, with a Celtic intensity of manner which contrasted with the Saxon phlegm of Abercrombie Smith.

'Only a faint, I think,' said the medical student. 'Just give me a hand with him. You take his feet. Now on to the sofa. Can you kick all those little wooden devils off? What a litter it is! Now he will be all right if we undo his collar and give him some water. What has he been up to at all?'

'I don't know. I heard him cry out. I ran up. I know him pretty well, you know. It is very good of you to come down.'

'His heart is going like a pair of castanets,' said Smith, laying his hand on the breast of the unconscious man. 'He seems to me to be frightened all to pieces. Chuck the water over him! What a face he has got on him!'

It was indeed a strange and most repellent face, for colour and outline were equally unnatural. It was white, not with the ordinary pallor of fear, but with an absolutely bloodless white, like the under side of a sole. He was very fat, but gave the impression of having at sometime been considerably fatter, for his skin hung loosely in creases and folds, and was shot with a meshwork of wrinkles. Short, stubbly brown hair bristled up from his scalp, with a pair of thick, wrinkled ears protruding at the sides. His light-grey eyes were still open, the pupils dilated and the balls projecting in a fixed and horrid stare. It seemed to Smith as he looked down upon him that he had never seen nature's danger signals flying so plainly upon a man's countenance, and his thoughts turned more seriously to the warning which Hastie had given him an hour before.

'What the deuce can have frightened him so?' he asked. 'It's the mummy.' 'The mummy? How, then?'

'I don't know. It's beastly and morbid. I wish he would drop it. It's the second fright he has given me. It was the same last winter. I found him just like this, with that horrid thing in front of him.'

'What does he want with the mummy, then?'

'Oh, he's a crank, you know. It's his hobby. He knows more about these things than any man in England. But I wish he wouldn't! Ah, he's beginning to come to.'

A faint tinge of colour had begun to steal back into Bellingham's ghastly cheeks, and his eyelids shivered like a sail after a calm. He clasped and unclasped his hands, drew a long, thin breath between his teeth, and suddenly jerking up his head, threw a glance of recognition around him. As his eyes fell upon the mummy, he sprang off the sofa, seized the roll of papyrus, thrust it into a drawer, turned the key, and then staggered back on to the sofa.

'What's up?' he asked. 'What do you chaps want?'

'You've been shrieking out and making no end of a fuss,' said Monkhouse Lee. 'If our neighbour here from above hadn't come down, I'm sure I don't know what I should have done with you.'

'Ah, it's Abercrombie Smith,' said Bellingham, glancing up at him. 'How very good of you to come in! What a fool I am! Oh, my God, what a fool I am!'

He sank his head on to his hands, and burst into peal after peal of hysterical laughter.

'Look here! Drop it!' cried Smith, shaking him roughly by the shoulder. 'Your nerves are all in a jangle. You must drop these little midnight games with mummies or you'll be going off your chump. You're all on wires now.'

'I wonder,' said Bellingham, 'whether you would be as cool as I am if you had seen —'

'What then?'

'Oh, nothing. I meant that I wonder if you could sit up at night with a mummy without trying your nerves. I have no doubt that you are quite right. I dare say that I have been taking it out of myself too much lately. But I am all right now. Please don't go, though. Just wait for a few minutes until I am quite myself.'

'The room is very close,' remarked Lee, throwing open the window and letting in the cool night air.

'It's balsamic resin,' said Bellingham. He lifted up one of the dried palmate leaves from the table and frizzled it over the chimney of the lamp. It broke away into heavy smoke wreaths, and a pungent, biting odour filled the chamber. 'It's the sacred plant — the plant of the priests,' he remarked. 'Do you know anything of Eastern languages, Smith?'

'Nothing at all. Not a word.'

The answer seemed to lift a weight from the Egyptologist's mind.

'By the way,' he continued, 'how long was it from the time that you ran down, until I came to my senses?'

'Not long. Some four or five minutes.'

'I thought it could not be very long,' said he, drawing a long breath. 'But what a strange thing unconsciousness is! There is no measurement to it. I could not tell from my own sensations if it were seconds or weeks. Now that gentleman on the table was packed up in the days of the eleventh dynasty, some forty centuries ago, and yet if he could find his tongue, he would tell us that this lapse of time has been but a closing of the eyes and a reopening of them. He is a singularly fine mummy, Smith.'

Smith stepped over to the table and looked down with a professional eye at the black and twisted form in front of him. The features, though horribly discoloured, were perfect, and two little nut-like eyes still lurked in the depths of the black, hollow sockets. The blotched skin was drawn tightly from bone to bone, and a tangled wrap of black, coarse hair fell over the ears. Two thin teeth, like those of a rat, overlay the shrivelled lower lip. In its crouching position, with bent joints and craned head, there was a suggestion of energy about the horrid thing which made Smith's gorge rise. The gaunt ribs, with their parchment-like covering, were exposed, and the sunken, leaden-hued abdomen, with the long slit where the embalmer had left his mark; but the lower limbs were wrapped round with coarse, yellow bandages. A number of little clove-like pieces of myrrh and of cassia were sprinkled over the body and lay scattered on the inside of the case.

'I don't know his name,' said Bellingham, passing his hand over the shrivelled head. 'You see the outer sarcophagus with the inscriptions is missing. Lot 249 is all the title he has now. You see it printed on his case. That was his number in the auction at which I picked him up.'

'He has been a very pretty sort of fellow in his day,' remarked Abercrombie Smith.

'He has been a giant. His mummy is six feet seven in length, and that would be a giant over there, for they were never a very robust race. Feel these great, knotted bones, too. He would be a nasty fellow to tackle.'

'Perhaps these very hands helped to build the stones into the Pyramids,' suggested Monkhouse Lee, looking down with disgust in his eyes at the crooked, unclean talons.

'No fear. This fellow has been pickled in natron, and looked after in the most approved style. They did not serve hodsmen in that fashion. Salt or bitumen was enough for them. It has been calculated that this sort of thing cost about seven hundred and thirty pounds in our money. Our friend was a noble at the least. What do you make of that small inscription near his feet, Smith?'

'I told you that I know no Eastern tongue.'

'Ah, so you did. It is the name of the embalmer, I take it. A very conscientious worker he must have been. I wonder how many modern works will survive four thousand years?'

He kept on speaking lightly and rapidly, but it was evident to Abercrombie Smith that he was still palpitating with fear. His hands shook, his lower lip trembled and, look where he would, his eye always came sliding round to his gruesome companion. Through all his fear, however, there was a suspicion of triumph in his tone and manner. His eyes shone, and his footstep, as he paced the room, was brisk and jaunty. He gave the impression of a man who has gone through an ordeal, the marks of which he still bears upon him, but which has helped him to his end.

'You're not going yet?' he cried, as Smith rose from the sofa.

At the prospect of solitude, his fears seemed to crowd back upon him and he stretched out a hand to detain him.

'Yes, I must go. I have my work to do. You are all right now. I think that with your nervous system you should take up some less morbid study.'

'Oh, I am not nervous as a rule; and I have unwrapped mummies before.'

'You fainted last time,' observed Monkhouse Lee.

'Ah, yes, so I did. Well, I must have a nerve tonic or a course of electricity. You are not going, Lee?'

'I'll do whatever you wish, Ned.'

'Then I'll come down with you and have a shakedown on your sofa. Good-night, Smith. I am so sorry to have disturbed you with my foolishness.'

They shook hands, and as the medical student stumbled up the spiral and irregular stair he heard a key turn in a door and the steps of his two new acquaintances as they descended to the lower floor.

In this strange way began the acquaintance between Edward Bellingham and Abercrombie Smith, an acquaintance which the latter, at least, had no desire to push further. Bellingham, however, appeared to have taken a fancy to his rough-spoken neighbour, and made his advances in such a way that he could hardly be repulsed without absolute brutality. Twice he called to thank Smith for his assistance, and many times afterwards he looked in with books, papers and such other civilities as two bachelor neighbours can offer each other. He was, as Smith soon found, a man of wide reading, with catholic tastes and an extraordinary memory. His manner, too, was so pleasing and suave that one came, after a time, to overlook his repellent appearance. For a jaded and wearied man he was no unpleasant companion, and Smith found himself, after a time, looking forward to his visits, and even returning them.

Clever as he undoubtedly was, however, the medical student seemed to detect a dash of insanity in the man. He broke out at times into a high, inflated style of talk which was in contrast with the simplicity of his life.

'It is a wonderful thing,' he cried, 'to feel that one can command powers of good and of evil — a ministering angel or a demon of vengeance.' And again, of Monkhouse Lee, he said, 'Lee is a good fellow, an honest fellow, but he is without strength or ambition. He would not make a fit partner for a man with a great enterprise. He would not make a fit partner for me.'

At such hints and innuendoes stolid Smith, puffing solemnly at his pipe, would simply raise his eyebrows and shake his head, with little interjections of medical wisdom as to earlier hours and fresher air.

One habit Bellingham had developed of late which Smith knew to be a frequent herald of a weakening mind. He appeared to be forever talking to himself. At late hours of the night, when there could be no visitor with him, Smith could still hear his voice beneath him in a low, muffled monologue, sunk almost to a whisper, and yet very audible in the silence. This solitary babbling annoyed and distracted the student, so that he spoke more than once to his neighbour about it. Bellingham, however, flushed up at the charge, and denied curtly that he had uttered a sound; indeed, he showed more annoyance over the matter than the occasion seemed to demand.

Had Abercrombie Smith had any doubt as to his own ears he had not to go far to find corroboration. Tom Styles, the little wrinkled manservant who had attended to the wants of the lodgers in the turret for a longer time than any man's memory could carry him, was sorely put to it over the same matter.

'If you please, sir,' said he, as he tidied down the top chamber one morning, 'do you think Mr. Bellingham is all right, sir?'

'All right, Styles?'

'Yes, sir. Right in his head, sir.'

'Why should he not be, then?'

'Well, I don't know, sir. His habits has changed of late. He's not the same man he used to be, though I make free to say that he was never quite one of my gentlemen, like Mr. Hastie or yourself, sir. He's took to talkin' to himself something awful. I wonder it don't disturb you. I don't know what to make of him, sir.'

'I don't know what business it is of yours, Styles.'

'Well, I takes an interest, Mr. Smith. It may be forward of me, but I can't help it. I feel sometimes as if I was mother and father to my young gentlemen. It all falls on me when things go wrong and the relations come. But Mr. Bellingham, sir. I want to know what it is that walks about his room sometimes when he's out and when the door's locked on the outside.'

'Eh? you're talking nonsense, Styles.'

'Maybe so, sir; but I heard it mor'n once with my own ears.'

'Rubbish, Styles.'

'Very good, sir. You'll ring the bell if you want me.'

Abercrombie Smith gave little heed to the gossip of the old manservant, but a small incident occurred a few days later which left an unpleasant effect upon his mind, and brought the words of Styles forcibly to his memory.

Bellingham had come up to see him late one night, and was entertaining him with an interesting account of the rock tombs of Beni Hassan in Upper Egypt, when Smith, whose hearing was remarkably acute, distinctly heard the sound of a door opening on the landing below.

'There's some fellow gone in or out of your room,' he remarked.

Bellingham sprang up and stood helpless for a moment, with the expression of a man who is half-incredulous and half-afraid.

'I surely locked it. I am almost positive that I locked it,' he stammered. 'No one could have opened it.'

'Why, I hear someone coming up the steps now,' said Smith.

Bellingham rushed out through the door, slammed it loudly behind him, and hurried down the stairs. About halfway down Smith heard him stop and thought he caught the sound of whispering. A moment later the door beneath him shut, a key creaked in a lock, and Bellingham, with beads of moisture upon his pale face, ascended the stairs once more and re-entered the room.

'It's all right,' he said, throwing himself down in a chair. 'It was that fool of a dog. He had pushed the door open. I don't know how I came to forget to lock it.'

'I didn't know you kept a dog,' said Smith, looking very thoughtfully at the disturbed face of his companion.

'Yes, I haven't had him long. I must get rid of him. He's a great nuisance.'

'He must be, if you find it so hard to shut him up. I should have thought that shutting the door would have been enough, without locking it.'

'I want to prevent old Styles from letting him out. He's of some value, you know, and it would be awkward to lose him.'

'I am a bit of a dog-fancier myself,' said Smith, still gazing hard at his companion from the corner of his eyes. 'Perhaps you'll let me have a look at it.'

'Certainly. But I am afraid it cannot be tonight; I have an appointment. Is that clock right? Then I am a quarter of an hour late already. You'll excuse me, I am sure.'

He picked up his cap and hurried from the room. In spite of his appointment, Smith heard him re-enter his own chamber and lock his door upon the inside.

This interview left a disagreeable impression upon the medical student's mind. Bellingham had lied to him, and lied so clumsily that it looked as if he had desperate reasons for concealing the truth. Smith knew that his neighbour had no dog. He knew, also, that the step which he had heard upon the stairs was not the step of an animal. But if it were not, then what could it be? There was old Styles' statement about the something which used to pace the room at times when the owner was absent. Could it be a woman? Smith rather inclined to the view. If so, it would mean disgrace and expulsion to Bellingham if it were discovered by the authorities, so that his anxiety and falsehoods might be accounted for. And yet it was inconceivable that an undergraduate could keep a woman in his rooms without being instantly detected. Be the explanation what it might, there was something ugly about it, and Smith determined, as he turned to his books, to discourage all further attempts at intimacy on the part of his soft-spoken and ill-favoured neighbour.

But his work was destined to interruption that night. He had hardly caught up the broken threads when a firm, heavy footfall came three steps at a time from below, and Hastie, in blazer and flannels, burst into the room.

'Still at it!' said he, plumping down into his wonted armchair. 'What a chap you are to stew! I believe an earthquake might come and knock Oxford into a cocked hat, and you would sit perfectly placid with your books among the ruins. However, I won't bore you long. Three whiffs of baccy, and I am off.'

'What's the news, then?' asked Smith, cramming a plug of bird's-eye into his briar with his forefinger.

'Nothing very much. Wilson made seventy for the freshmen against the eleven. They say that they will play him instead of Buddicomb, for Buddicomb is clean off colour. He used to be able to bowl a little, but it's nothing but half-volleys and long hops now.'

'Medium right,' suggested Smith, with the intense gravity which comes upon a 'varsity man when he speaks of athletics.

'Inclining to fast, with a work from leg. Comes with the arm about three inches or so. He used to be nasty on a wet wicket. Oh, by the way, have you heard about Long Norton?'

'What's that?'

'He's been attacked.'

'Attacked?'

'Yes, just as he was turning out of the High Street, and within a hundred yards of the gate of Old's.'

'But who —'

'Ah, that's the rub! If you said 'what', you would be more grammatical. Norton swears that it was not human, and, indeed, from the scratches on his throat, I should be inclined to agree with him.'

'What, then? Have we come down to spooks?' Abercrombie Smith puffed his scientific contempt.

'Well, no; I don't think that is quite the idea, either. I am inclined to think that if any showman has lost a great ape lately, and the brute is in these parts, a jury would find a true bill against it. Norton passes that way every night, you know, about the same hour. There's a tree that hangs low over the path — the big elm from Rainy's garden. Norton thinks the thing dropped on him out of the tree. Anyhow, he was nearly strangled by two arms which, he says, were as strong and as thin as steel bands. He saw nothing; only those beastly arms that tightened and tightened on him. He yelled his head nearly off, and a couple of chaps came running, and the thing went over the wall like a cat. He never got a fair sight of it the whole time. It gave Norton a shake up, I can tell you. I tell him it has been as good as a change at the seaside for him.'

'A garrotter, most likely,' said Smith.

'Very possibly. Norton says not; but we don't mind what he says. The garrotter had long nails, and was pretty smart at swinging himself over walls. By the way, your beautiful neighbour would be pleased if he heard about it. He had a grudge against Norton, and he's not a man, from what I know of him, to forget his little debts. But hallo, old chap, what have you got in your noddle?'

'Nothing,' Smith answered curtly.

He had started in his chair, and the look had flashed over his face which comes upon a man who is struck suddenly by some unpleasant idea.

'You looked as if something I had said had taken you on the raw. By the way, you have made the acquaintance of Master B since I looked in last, have you not? Young Monkhouse Lee told me something to that effect.'

'Yes; I know him slightly. He has been up here once or twice.'

'Well, you're big enough and ugly enough to take care of yourself. He's not what I should call exactly a healthy sort of Johnny, though, no doubt, he's very clever, and all that. But you'll soon find out for yourself. Lee is all right; he's a very decent little fellow. Well, so long, old chap! I row Mullins for the vice-chancellor's pot on Wednesday week, so mind you come down, in case I don't see you before.'

Bovine Smith laid down his pipe and turned stolidly to his books once more. But with all the will in the world, he found it very hard to keep his mind upon his work. It would slip away to brood upon the man beneath him, and upon the little mystery which hung round his chambers. Then his thoughts turned to this singular attack of which Hastie had spoken, and to the grudge which Bellingham was said to owe the object of it. The two ideas would persist in rising together in his mind, as though there were some close and intimate connection between them. And yet the suspicion was so dim and vague that it could not be put down in words.

'Confound the chap!' cried Smith, as he shied his book on pathology across the room. 'He has spoiled my night's reading and that's reason enough, if there were no other, why I should steer clear of him in the future.'

For ten days the medical student confined himself so closely to his studies that he neither saw nor heard anything of either of the men beneath him. At the hours when Bellingham had been accustomed to visit him, he took care to sport his oak, and though he more than once heard a knocking at his outer door, he resolutely refused to answer it. One afternoon, however, he was descending the stairs when, just as he was passing it, Bellingham's door flew open, and young Monkhouse Lee came out with his eyes sparkling and a dark flush of anger upon his olive cheeks. Close at his heels followed Bellingham, his fat, unhealthy face all quivering with malignant passion.

'You fool!' he hissed. 'You'll be sorry.'

'Very likely,' cried the other. 'Mind what I say. It's off! I won't hear of it!'

'You've promised, anyhow.'

'Oh, I'll keep that! I won't speak. But I'd rather little Eva was in her grave. Once for all, it's off. She'll do what I say. We don't want to see you again.'

So much Smith could not avoid hearing, but he hurried on, for he had no wish to be involved in their dispute. There had been a serious breach between them, that was clear enough, and Lee was going to cause the engagement with his sister to be broken off. Smith thought of Hastie's comparison of the toad and the dove, and was glad to think that the matter was at an end. Bellingham's face when he was in a passion was not pleasant to look upon. He was not a man to whom an innocent girl could be trusted for life. As he walked, Smith wondered languidly what could have caused the quarrel, and what the promise might be which Bellingham had been so anxious that Monkhouse Lee should keep.

It was the day of the sculling match between Hastie and Mullins, and a stream of men were making their way down to the banks of the Isis. A May sun was shining brightly, and the yellow path was barred with the black shadows of the tall elm-trees. On either side the grey colleges lay back from the road, the hoary old mothers of minds looking out from their high, mullioned windows at the tide of young life which swept so merrily past them. Black-clad tutors, prim officials, pale, reading men, brown-faced, straw-hatted young athletes in white sweaters or many-coloured blazers, all were hurrying towards the blue, winding river which curves through the Oxford meadows.

Abercrombie Smith, with the intuition of an old oarsman, chose his position at the point where he knew that the struggle, if there were a struggle, would come. Far off he heard the hum which announced the start, the gathering roar of the approach, the thunder of running feet and the shouts of the men in the boats beneath him. A spray of half-clad, deep-breathing runners shot past him, and craning over their shoulders, he saw Hastie pulling a steady thirty-six, while his opponent, with a jerky forty, was a good boat's length behind him. Smith gave a cheer for his friend and, pulling out his watch, was starting off again for his chambers, when he felt a touch upon his shoulder and found that young Monkhouse Lee was beside him.

'I saw you there,' he said, in a timid, deprecating way. 'I wanted to speak to you, if you could spare me a half-hour. This cottage is mine. I share it with Harrington of King's. Come in and have a cup of tea.'

'I must be back presently,' said Smith. 'I am hard on the grind at present. But I'll come in for a few minutes with pleasure. I wouldn't have come out only Hastie is a friend of mine.'

'So he is of mine. Hasn't he a beautiful style? Mullins wasn't in it. But come into the cottage. It's a little den of a place, but it is pleasant to work in during the summer months.'

It was a small, square, white building, with green doors and shutters and a rustic trellis-work porch, standing back some fifty yards from the river's bank. Inside, the main room was roughly fitted up as a study — deal table, unpainted shelves with books and a few cheap oleographs upon the wall. A kettle sang upon a spirit-stove and there were tea things upon a tray on the table.

'Try that chair and have a cigarette,' said Lee. 'Let me pour you out a cup of tea. It's so good of you to come in, for I know that your time is a good deal taken up. I wanted to say to you that, if I were you, I should change my rooms at once.'

Smith sat staring with a lighted match in one hand and his unlit cigarette in the other.

'Yes; it must seem very extraordinary, and the worst of it is that I cannot give my reasons, for I am under a solemn promise — a very solemn promise. But I may go so far as to say that I don't think Bellingham is a very safe man to live near. I intend to camp out here as much as I can for a time.'

'Not safe! What do you mean?'

'Ah, that's what I mustn't say. But do take my advice and move your rooms. We had a grand row today. You must have heard us, for you came down the stairs.'

'I saw that you had fallen out.'

'He's a horrible chap, Smith. That is the only word for him. I have had doubts about him ever since that night when he fainted — you remember, when you came down. I taxed him today and he told me things that made my hair rise, and wanted me to stand in with him. I'm not strait-laced, but I am a clergyman's son, you know, and I think there are some things which are quite beyond the pale. I only thank God that I found him out before it was too late, for he was to have married into my family.'

'This is all very fine, Lee,' said Abercrombie Smith curtly. 'But either you are saying a great deal too much or a great deal too little.'

'I give you a warning.'

'If there is real reason for warning, no promise can bind you. If I see a rascal about to blow a place up with dynamite no pledge will stand in my way of preventing him.'

'Ah, but I cannot prevent him, and I can do nothing but warn you.'

'Without saying what you warn me against.'

'Against Bellingham.'

'But that is childish. Why should I fear him, or any man?'

'I can't tell you. I can only entreat you to change your rooms. You are in danger where you are. I don't even say that Bellingham would wish to injure you. But it might happen, for he is a dangerous neighbour just now.'

'Perhaps I know more than you think,' said Smith, looking keenly at the young man's boyish, earnest face. 'Suppose I tell you that someone else shares Bellingham's rooms.'

Monkhouse Lee sprang from his chair in uncontrollable excitement.

'You know, then?' he gasped.

'A woman.'

Lee dropped back again with a groan.

'My lips are sealed,' he said. 'I must not speak.'

'Well, anyhow,' said Smith, rising, 'it is not likely that I should allow myself to be frightened out of rooms which suit me very nicely. It would be a little too feeble for me to move out all my goods and chattels because you say that Bellingham might in some unexplained way do me an injury. I think that I'll just take my chance, and stay where I am, and as I see that it's nearly five o'clock, I must ask you to excuse me.'

He bade the young student adieu in a few curt words and made his way homeward through the sweet spring evening, feeling half-ruffled, half-amused, as any other strong, unimaginative man might who has been menaced by a vague and shadowy danger.

There was one little indulgence which Abercrombie Smith always allowed himself however closely his work might press upon him. Twice a week, on the Tuesday and the Friday, it was his invariable custom to walk over to Farlingford, the residence of Dr. Plumptree Peterson situated about a mile and a half out of Oxford. Peterson had been a close friend of Smith's elder brother, Francis, and as he was a bachelor, fairly well-to-do, with a good cellar and a better library, his house was a pleasant goal for a man who was in need of a brisk walk. Twice a week, then, the medical student would swing out there along the dark country roads and spend a pleasant hour in Peterson's comfortable study, discussing, over a glass of old port, the gossip of the varsity or the latest developments of medicine or of surgery.

On the day which followed his interview with Monkhouse Lee, Smith shut up his books at a quarter past eight, the hour when he usually started for his friend's house. As he was leaving his room, however, his eyes chanced to fall upon one of the books which Bellingham had lent him, and his conscience pricked him for not having returned it. However repellent the man might be, he should not be treated with discourtesy. Taking the book, he walked downstairs and knocked at his neighbour's door. There was no answer; but on turning the handle he found that it was unlocked. Pleased at the thought of avoiding an interview, he stepped inside and placed the book with his card upon the table.

The lamp was turned half down, but Smith could see the details of the room plainly enough. It was all much as he had seen it before — the frieze, the animal-headed gods, the hanging crocodile and the table littered over with papers and dried leaves. The mummy case stood upright against the wall, but the mummy itself was missing. There was no sign of any second occupant of the room, and he felt as he withdrew that he had probably done Bellingham an injustice. Had he a guilty secret to preserve, he would hardly leave his door open so that all the world might enter.

The spiral stair was as black as pitch, and Smith was slowly making his way down its irregular steps, when he was suddenly conscious that something had passed him in the darkness. There was a faint sound, a whiff of air, a light brushing past his elbow, but so slight that he could scarcely be certain of it. He stopped and listened, but the wind was rustling among the ivy outside and he could hear nothing else.

'Is that you, Styles?' he shouted.

There was no answer, and all was still behind him. It must have been a sudden gust of air, for there were crannies and cracks in the old turret. And yet he could almost have sworn that he heard a footfall by his very side. He had emerged into the quadrangle, still turning the matter over in his head, when a man came running swiftly across the smooth-cropped lawn.

'Is that you, Smith?'

'Hallo, Hastie!'

'For God's sake come at once! Young Lee is drowned! Here's Harrington of King's with the news. The doctor is out. You'll do, but come along at once. There may be life in him.'

'Have you brandy?'

'No.'

'I'll bring some. There's a flask on my table.'

Smith bounded up the stairs, taking three at a time, seized the flask and was rushing down with it, when, as he passed Bellingham's room, his eyes fell upon something which left him gasping and staring upon the landing.

The door, which he had closed behind him, was now open, and right in front of him, with the lamplight shining upon it, was the mummy case. Three minutes ago it had been empty. He could swear to that. Now it framed the lank body of its horrible occupant, who stood, grim and stark, with his black, shrivelled face towards the door. The form was lifeless and inert, but it seemed to Smith as he gazed that there still lingered a lurid spark of vitality, some faint sign of consciousness in the little eyes which lurked in the depths of the hollow sockets. So astounded and shaken was he that he had forgotten his errand and was still staring at the lean, sunken figure when the voice of his friend below recalled him to himself.

'Come on, Smith!' he shouted. 'It's life and death, you know. Hurry up! Now, then,' he added, as the medical student reappeared, 'let us do a sprint. It is well under a mile, and we should do it in five minutes. A human life is better worth running for than a pot.'

Neck and neck they dashed through the darkness, and did not pull up until, panting and spent, they had reached the little cottage by the river. Young Lee, limp and dripping like a broken water-plant, was stretched upon the sofa, the green scum of the river upon his black hair and a fringe of white foam upon his leaden-hued lips. Beside him knelt his fellow-student, Harrington, endeavouring to chafe some warmth back into his rigid limbs.

'I think there's life in him,' said Smith, with his hand to the lad's side. 'Put your watch glass to his lips. Yes, there's dimming on it. You take one arm, Hastie. Now work it as I do, and we'll soon pull him round.'

For ten minutes they worked in silence, inflating and depressing the chest of the unconscious man. At the end of that time a shiver ran through his body, his lips trembled and he opened his eyes. The three students burst out into an irrepressible cheer.

'Wake up, old chap. You've frightened us quite enough.'

'Have some brandy. Take a sip from the flask.'

'He's all right now,' said his companion Harrington. 'Heavens, what a fright I got! I was reading here, and he had gone out for a stroll as far as the river, when I heard a scream and a splash. Out I ran, and by the time I could find him and fish him out, all life seemed to have gone. Then

Simpson couldn't get a doctor, for he has a game-leg, and I had to run, and I don't know what I'd have done without you fellows. That's right, old chap. Sit up.'

Monkhouse Lee had raised himself on his hands, and looked wildly about him.

'What's up?' he asked. 'I've been in the water. Ah, yes; I remember.'

A look of fear came into his eyes, and he sank his face into his hands.

'How did you fall in?'

'I didn't fall in.'

'How then?'

'I was thrown in. I was standing by the bank and something from behind picked me up like a feather and hurled me in. I heard nothing and I saw nothing. But I know what it was, for all that.'

'And so do I,' whispered Smith.

Lee looked up with a quick glance of surprise.

'You've learned, then?' he said. 'You remember the advice I gave you?'

'Yes, and I begin to think that I shall take it.'

'I don't know what the deuce you fellows are talking about,' said Hastie, 'but I think, if I were you, Harrington, I should get Lee to bed at once. It will be time enough to discuss the why and the wherefore when he is a little stronger. I think, Smith, you and I can leave him alone now. I am walking back to college; if you are coming in that direction, we can have a chat.'

But it was little chat that they had upon their homeward path. Smith's mind was too full of the incidents of the evening, the absence of the mummy from his neighbour's rooms, the step that passed him on the stair, the reappearance — the extraordinary, inexplicable reappearance of the grisly thing — and then this attack upon Lee, corresponding so closely to the previous outrage upon another man against whom Bellingham bore a grudge. All this settled in his thoughts, together with the many little incidents which had previously turned him against his neighbour and the singular circumstances under which he was first called in to him. What had been a dim suspicion, a vague, fantastic conjecture, had suddenly taken form and stood out in his mind as a grim fact, a thing not to be denied. And yet, how monstrous it was! how unheard of! how entirely beyond all bounds of human experience. An impartial judge, or even the friend who walked by his side, would simply tell him that his eyes had deceived him, that the mummy had been there all the time, that young Lee had tumbled into the river as any other man tumbles into a river, and the blue pill was the best thing for a disordered liver. He felt that he would have said as much if the positions had been reversed. And yet he could swear that Bellingham was a murderer at heart and that he wielded a weapon such as no man had ever used in all the grim history of crime.

Hastie had branched off to his rooms with a few crisp and emphatic comments upon his friend's unsociability, and Abercrombie Smith crossed the quadrangle to his corner turret with a strong feeling of repulsion for his chambers and their associations. He would take Lee's advice and move his quarters as soon as possible, for how could a man study when his ear was ever straining for every murmur or footstep in the room below? He observed, as he crossed over the lawn, that the light was still shining in Bellingham's window, and as he passed up the staircase the door opened and the man himself looked out at him. With his fat, evil face he was like some bloated spider fresh from the weaving of his poisonous web.

'Good-evening,' said he. 'Won't you come in?'

'No,' cried Smith fiercely.

'No? You are as busy as ever? I wanted to ask you about Lee. I was sorry to hear that there was a rumour that something was amiss with him.' His features were grave, but there was the gleam of a hidden laugh in his eyes as he spoke. Smith saw it, and he could have knocked him down for it.

'You'll be sorrier still to hear that Monkhouse Lee is doing very well, and is out of all danger,' he answered. 'Your hellish tricks have not come off this time. Oh, you needn't try to brazen it out. I know all about it.' Bellingham took a step back from the angry student and half-closed the door as if to protect himself.

'You are mad,' he said. 'What do you mean? Do you assert that I had anything to do with Lee's accident?'

'Yes,' thundered Smith. 'You and that bag of bones behind you; you worked it between you. I tell you what it is, Master B, they have given up burning folk like you, but we still keep a hangman, and, by George! if any man in this college meets his death while you are here, I'll have you up, and if you don't swing for it, it won't be my fault. You'll find that your filthy Egyptian tricks won't answer in England.'

'You're a raving lunatic,' said Bellingham.

'All right. You just remember what I say, for you'll find that I'll be better than my word.'

The door slammed and Smith went fuming up to his chamber, where he locked the door upon the inside and spent half the night in smoking his old briar and brooding over the strange events of the evening.

Next morning Abercrombie Smith heard nothing of his neighbour, but Harrington called upon him in the afternoon to say that Lee was almost himself again. All day Smith stuck fast to his work, but in the evening he determined to pay the visit to his friend Dr. Peterson upon which he had started the night before. A good walk and a friendly chat would be welcome to his jangled nerves.

Bellingham's door was shut as he passed, but glancing back when he was some distance from the turret, he saw his neighbour's head at the window outlined against the lamplight, his face pressed apparently against the glass as he gazed out into the darkness. It was a blessing to be away from all contact with him, if but for a few hours, and Smith stepped out briskly and breathed the soft spring air into his lungs. The half-moon lay in the west between two Gothic pinnacles, and threw upon the silvered street a dark tracery from the stonework above. There was a brisk breeze and light, fleecy clouds drifted swiftly across the sky. Old's was on the very border of the town, and in five minutes Smith found himself beyond the houses and between the hedges of a May-scented, Oxfordshire lane.

It was a lonely and little-frequented road which led to his friend's house. Early as it was, Smith did not meet a single soul upon his way. He walked briskly along until he came to the avenue gate which opened into the long gravel drive leading up to Farlingford. In front of him he could see the cosy, red light of the windows glimmering through the foliage. He stood with his hand upon the iron latch of the swinging gate and he glanced back at the road along which he had come. Something was coming swiftly down it.

It moved in the shadow of the hedge, silently and furtively, a dark, crouching figure, dimly visible against the black background. Even as he gazed back at it, it had lessened its distance by twenty paces and was fast closing upon him. Out of the darkness he had a glimpse of a scraggy neck and of two eyes that will ever haunt him in his dreams. He turned and with a cry of terror he ran for his life up the avenue. There were the red lights, the signals of safety, almost within a stone's-throw of him. He was a famous runner, but never had he run as he ran that night.

The heavy gate had swung into place behind him but he heard it dash open again before his pursuer. As he rushed madly and wildly through the night, he could hear a swift, dry patter behind him, and could see, as he threw back a glance, that this horror was bounding like a tiger at his heels, with blazing eyes and one stringy arm out-thrown. Thank God, the door was ajar. He could see the thin bar of light which shot from the lamp in the hall. Nearer yet sounded the clatter from behind. He heard a hoarse gurgling at his very shoulder. With a shriek he flung himself against the door, slammed and bolted it behind him, and sank half-fainting on to the hall chair.

'My goodness, Smith, what's the matter?' asked Peterson, appearing at the door of his study.

'Give me some brandy.'

Peterson disappeared and came rushing out again with a glass and a decanter.

'You need it,' he said, as his visitor drank off what he poured out for him. 'Why, man, you are as white as a cheese.'

Smith laid down his glass, rose up, and took a deep breath. 'I am my own man again now,' said he. 'I was never so unmanned before. But, with your leave, Peterson, I will sleep here tonight, for I don't think I could face that road again except by daylight. It's weak, I know, but I can't help it.'

Peterson looked at his visitor with a very questioning eye.

'Of course you shall sleep here if you wish. I'll tell Mrs. Burney to make up the spare bed. Where are you off to now?'

'Come up with me to the window that overlooks the door. I want you to see what I have seen.'

They went up to the window of the upper hall whence they could look down upon the approach to the house. The drive and the fields on either side lay quiet and still, bathed in the peaceful moonlight.

'Well, really, Smith,' remarked Peterson, 'it is well that I know you to be an abstemious man. What in the world can have frightened you?'

'I'll tell you presently. But where can it have gone? Ah, now, look, look! See the curve of the road just beyond your gate.'

'Yes, I see; you needn't pinch my arm off. I saw someone pass. I should say a man, rather thin, apparently, and tall, very tall. But what of him? And what of yourself? You are still shaking like an aspen leaf.'

'I have been within hand-grip of the devil, that's all. But come down to your study, and I shall tell you the whole story.'

He did so. Under the cheery lamplight with a glass of wine on the table beside him and the portly form and florid face of his friend in front, he narrated, in their order, all the events, great and small, which had formed so singular a chain, from the night on which he had found Bellingham fainting in front of the mummy case until this horrid experience of an hour ago.

'There now,' he said as he concluded, 'that's the whole, black business. It is monstrous and incredible, but it is true.'

Dr. Plumptree Peterson sat for some time in silence with a very puzzled expression upon his face.

'I never heard of such a thing in my life, never!' he said at last. 'You have told me the facts. Now tell me your inferences.'

'You can draw your own.'

'But I should like to hear yours. You have thought over the matter, and I have not.'

'Well, it must be a little vague in detail, but the main points seem to me to be clear enough. This fellow Bellingham, in his Eastern studies, has got hold of some infernal secret by which a mummy — or possibly only this particular mummy — can be temporarily brought to life. He was trying this disgusting business on the night when he fainted. No doubt the sight of the creature moving had shaken his nerve, even though he had expected it. You remember that almost the first words he said were to call out upon himself as a fool. Well, he got more hardened afterwards, and carried the matter through without fainting. The vitality which he could put into it was evidently only a passing thing, for I have seen it continually in its case as dead as this table. He has some elaborate process, I fancy, by which he brings the thing to pass. Having done it, he naturally bethought him that he might use the creature as an agent. It has intelligence and it has strength. For some purpose he took Lee into his confidence; but Lee, like a decent Christian, would have nothing to do with such a business. Then they had a row, and Lee vowed that he would tell his sister of Bellingham's true character. Bellingham's game was to prevent him, and he nearly managed it by setting this creature of his on his track. He had already tried its powers upon another man — Norton — towards whom he had a grudge. It is the merest chance that he has not two murders upon his soul. Then, when I taxed him with the matter, he had the strongest reasons for wishing to get me out of the way before I could convey my knowledge to anyone else. He got his chance when I went out, for he knew my habits and where I was bound for. I have had a narrow shave, Peterson, and it is mere luck you didn't find me on your doorstep in the morning. I'm not a nervous man as a rule, and I never thought to have the fear of death put upon me as it was tonight.'

'My dear boy, you take the matter too seriously,' said his companion. 'Your nerves are out of order with your work, and you make too much of it. How could such a thing as this stride about the streets of Oxford, even at night, without being seen?'

'It has been seen. There is quite a scare in the town about an escaped ape, as they imagine the creature to be. It is the talk of the place.'

'Well, it's a striking chain of events. And yet, my dear fellow, you must allow that each incident in itself is capable of a more natural explanation.'

'What! even my adventure of tonight?'

'Certainly. You come out with your nerves all unstrung, and your head full of this theory of yours. Some gaunt, half-famished tramp steals after you, and seeing you run, is emboldened to pursue you. Your fears and imagination do the rest.'

'It won't do, Peterson; it won't do.'

'And again, in the instance of your finding the mummy case empty, and then a few moments later with an occupant, you know that it was lamplight, that the lamp was half turned down, and that you had no special reason to look hard at the case. It is quite possible that you may have overlooked the creature in the first instance.'

'No, no; it is out of the question.'

'And then Lee may have fallen into the river, and Norton been garrotted. It is certainly a formidable indictment that you have against Bellingham; but if you were to place it before a police magistrate, he would simply laugh in your face.'

'I know he would. That is why I mean to take the matter into my own hands.'

'Eh?'

'Yes; I feel that a public duty rests upon me, and, besides, I must do it for my own safety, unless I choose to allow myself to be hunted by this beast out of the college, and that would be a little too feeble. I have quite made up my mind what I shall do. And first of all, may I use your paper and pens for an hour?'

'Most certainly. You will find all that you want upon that side-table.'

Abercrombie Smith sat down before a sheet of foolscap, and for an hour and then for a second hour his pen travelled swiftly over it. Page after page was finished and tossed aside while his friend leaned back in his armchair, looking across at him with patient curiosity. At last, with an exclamation of satisfaction, Smith sprang to his feet, gathered his papers up into order, and laid the last one upon Peterson's desk.

'Kindly sign this as a witness,' he said.

'A witness? Of what?'

'Of my signature and of the date. The date is the most important. Why, Peterson, my life might hang upon it.'

'My dear Smith, you are talking wildly. Let me beg you to go to bed.'

'On the contrary, I never spoke so deliberately in my life. And I will promise to go to bed the moment you have signed it.'

'But what is it?'

'It is a statement of all that I have been telling you tonight. I wish you to witness it.'

'Certainly,' said Peterson, signing his name under that of his companion. 'There you are! But what is the idea?'

'You will kindly retain it, and produce it in case I am arrested.'

'Arrested? For what?'

'For murder. It is quite on the cards. I wish to be ready for every event. There is only one course open to me, and I am determined to take it.'

'For heaven's sake, don't do anything rash!'

'Believe me, it would be far more rash to adopt any other course. I hope that we won't need to bother you, but it will ease my mind to know that you have this statement of my motives. And now I am ready to take your advice and to go to roost, for I want to be at my best in the morning.'

Abercrombie Smith was not an entirely pleasant man to have as an enemy. Slow and easy-tempered, he was formidable when driven to action. He brought to every purpose in life the same deliberate resoluteness which had distinguished him as a scientific student. He had laid his studies aside for a day, but he intended that the day should not be wasted. Not a word did he say to his host as to his plans, but by nine o'clock he was well on his way to Oxford. In the High Street he stopped at Clifford's, the gun-maker's, and bought a heavy revolver with a box of central-fire cartridges. Six of them he slipped into the chambers, and half-cocking the weapon, placed it in the pocket of his coat. He then made his way to Hastie's rooms, where the big oarsman was lounging over his breakfast, with the *Sporting Times* propped up against the coffee-pot.

'Hallo! What's up?' he asked. 'Have some coffee?'

'No, thank you. I want you to come with me, Hastie, and do what I ask you.'

'Certainly, my boy.'

'And bring a heavy stick with you.'

'Hallo!' Hastie stared. 'Here's a hunting crop that would fell an ox.'

'One other thing. You have a box of amputating knives. Give me the longest of them.'

'There you are. You seem to be fairly on the war trail. Anything else?'

'No; that will do.' Smith placed the knife inside his coat, and led the way to the quadrangle. 'We are neither of us chickens, Hastie,' said he. 'I think I can do this job alone, but I take you as a precaution. I am going to have a little talk with Bellingham. If I have only him to deal with, I won't, of course, need you. If I shout, however, up you come, and lam out with your whip as hard as you can lick. Do you understand?'

'All right. I'll come if I hear you bellow.'

'Stay here, then. I may be a little time, but don't budge until I come down.'

'I'm a fixture.'

Smith ascended the stairs, opened Bellingham's door and stepped in. Bellingham was seated behind his table, writing. Beside him, among his litter of strange possessions, towered the mummy case, with its sale number 249 still stuck upon its front, and its hideous occupant stiff and stark within it. Smith looked very deliberately round him, closed the door, and then, stepping across to the fireplace, struck a match and set the fire alight. Bellingham sat staring, with amazement and rage upon his bloated face.

'Well, really now, you make yourself at home,' he gasped.

Smith sat himself deliberately down, placing his watch upon the table, drew out his pistol, cocked it, and laid it in his lap. Then he took the long amputating knife from his bosom, and threw it down in front of Bellingham.

'Now, then,' said he, 'just get to work and cut up that mummy.'

'Oh, is that it?' said Bellingham with a sneer.

'Yes, that is it. They tell me that the law can't touch you. But I have a law that will set matters straight. If in five minutes you have not set to work, I swear by the God who made me that I will put a bullet through your brain!'

'You would murder me?'

Bellingham had half-risen, and his face was the colour of putty.

'Yes.'

'And for what?'

'To stop your mischief. One minute has gone.'

'But what have I done?'

'I know and you know.'

'This is mere bullying.'

'Two minutes are gone.'

'But you must give reasons. You are a madman — a dangerous madman. Why should I destroy my own property? It is a valuable mummy.'

'You must cut it up, and you must burn it.'

'I will do no such thing.'

'Four minutes are gone.'

Smith took up the pistol and he looked towards Bellingham with an inexorable face. As the second-hand stole round, he raised his hand and the finger twitched upon the trigger.

'There! there! I'll do it!' screamed Bellingham.

In frantic haste he caught up the knife and hacked at the figure of the mummy, ever glancing round to see the eye and the weapon of his terrible visitor bent upon him. The creature crackled and snapped under every stab of the keen blade. A thick, yellow dust rose up from it. Spices and dried essences rained down upon the floor. Suddenly, with a rending crack, its backbone snapped asunder, and it fell, a brown heap of sprawling limbs, upon the floor.

'Now into the fire!' said Smith.

The flames leaped and roared as the dried and tinder-like debris was piled upon it. The little room was like the stokehole of a steamer and the sweat ran down the faces of the two men; but still the one stooped and worked, while the other sat watching him with a set face. A thick, fat smoke oozed out from the fire, and a heavy smell of burned resin and singed hair filled the air. In a quarter of an hour a few charred and brittle sticks were all that was left of Lot No. 249.

'Perhaps that will satisfy you,' snarled Bellingham, with hate and fear in his little grey eyes as he glanced back at his tormentor.

'No; I must make a clean sweep of all your materials. We must have no more devil's tricks. In with all these leaves! They may have something to do with it.'

'And what now?' asked Bellingham, when the leaves also had been added to the blaze.

'Now the roll of papyrus which you had on the table that night. It is in that drawer, I think.'

'No, no,' shouted Bellingham. 'Don't burn that! Why, man, you don't know what you do. It is unique; it contains wisdom which is nowhere else to be found.'

'Out with it!'

'But look here, Smith, you can't really mean it. I'll share the knowledge with you. I'll teach you all that is in it. Or, stay, let me only copy it before you burn it!'

Smith stepped forward and turned the key in the drawer. Taking out the yellow, curled roll of paper, he threw it into the fire, and pressed it down with his heel. Bellingham screamed, and grabbed at it; but Smith pushed him back and stood over it until it was reduced to a formless, grey ash.

'Now, Master B,' said he, 'I think I have pretty well drawn your teeth. You'll hear from me again if you return to your old tricks. And now good-morning, for I must go back to my studies.'

And such is the narrative of Abercrombie Smith as to the singular events which occurred in Old College, Oxford, in the spring of '84. As Bellingham left the university immediately afterwards, and was last heard of in the Sudan, there is no one who can contradict his statement. But the wisdom of men is small, and the ways of nature are strange, and who shall put a bound to the dark things which may be found by those who seek for them?

A Professor of Egyptology*

rom seven o'clock in the evening until half past, that is to say for the half-hour preceding dinner, the Grand Hall of the Hotel Occidental, throughout the season, is practically a lounge, and is crowded with the most fashionable folk wintering in Cairo. The evening I am anxiuos to describe was certainly no exception to the rule. At the foot of the fine marble staircase — the pride of its owner — a well-known member of the French Ministry was chatting with an English Duchess whose pretty, but somewhat delicate, daughter was flirting mildly with one of the Sirdar's Bimbashis, on leave from the Soudan. On the right-hand lounge of the Hall an Italian Countess, whose antecedents were as doubtful as her diamonds, was apparently listening to a story a handsome Greek *attaché* was telling her; in reality, however, she was endeavouring to catch scraps of a conversation being carried on, a few feet away, between a witty Russian and an equally clever daughter of the United States. Almost every nationality was represented there, but unfortunately for our prestige, the majority were English. The scene was a brilliant one, and the sprinkling of military and diplomatic uniforms (there was a Reception at the Khedivial Palace later) lent an additional touch of colour to the picture. Taken altogether, and regarded from a political point of view, the gathering had a significance of its own.

At the end of the Hall, near the large glass doors, a handsome, elderly lady, with grey hair, was conversing with one of the leading English doctors of the place — a grey-haired, clever-looking man, who possessed the happy faculty of being able to impress everyone with whom he talked with the idea that he infinitely preferred his or her society to that of any other member of the world's population. They were discussing the question of the most suitable clothing for a Nile voyage, and as the lady's daughter, who was seated next her, had been conversant with her mother's ideas on the subject ever since their first visit to Egypt (as indeed had been the Doctor), she preferred to lie back on the divan and watch the people about her. She had large, dark, contemplative eyes. Like her mother she took life seriously, but in a somewhat different fashion. One who has been bracketed third in the Mathematical Tripos can scarcely be expected to bestow very much thought on the comparative merits of Jæger, as opposed to dresses of the Common or Garden flannel. From this, however, it must not be inferred that she was in any way a blue stocking, that is, of course, in the vulgar acceptation of the word. She was thorough in all she undertook, and for the reason that mathematics interested her very much the same way that Wagner, chess, and, shall we say, croquet, interest other people, she made it her hobby, and it must be

---

* "A Professor of Egyptology" was written by Guy Boothby (1867 – 1905) and published in *The Graphic*, Dec. 10, 1894. The text for this edition was taken from short story collection *The Lady of the Island* (1904).

confessed she certainly succeeded in it. At other times she rode, drove, played tennis and hockey, and looked upon her world with calm, observant eyes that were more disposed to find good than evil in it. Contradictions that we are, even to ourselves, it was only those who knew her intimately, and they were few and far between, who realised that, under that apparently sober, matter-of-fact personality, there existed a strong leaning towards the mysterious, or, more properly speaking, the occult. Possibly she herself would have been the first to deny this — but that I am right in my surmise this story will surely be sufficient proof.

Mrs. Westmoreland and her daughter had left their comfortable Yorkshire home in September, and, after a little dawdling on the Continent, had reached Cairo in November the best month to arrive, in my opinion, for then the rush has not set in, the hotel servants have not had sufficient time to become weary of their duties, and what is better still, all the best rooms have not been bespoken. It was now the middle of December, and the fashionable caravanserai, upon which they had for many years bestowed their patronage, was crowded from roof to cellar. Every day people were being turned away, and the manager's continual lament was that he had not another hundred rooms wherein to place more guests. He was a Swiss, and for that reason regarded hotel-keeping in the light of a profession.

On this particular evening Mrs. Westmoreland and her daught Cecilia had arranged to dine with Dr. Forsyth — that is to say, they were to eat their meal at his table in order that they might meet a man of whom they had heard much, but whose acquaintance they had not as yet made. The individual in question was a certain Professor Constanides — reputed one of the most advanced Egyptologists, and the author of several well-known works. Mrs. Westmoreland was not of an exacting nature, and so long as she dined in agreeable company did not trouble herself very much whether it was with an English earl or a distinguished foreign *savant.*

'It really does not matter, my dear,' she was wont to observe to her daughter. 'So long as the cooking is good and the wine above reproach, there is absolutely nothing to choose between them. A Prime Minister and a country vicar are, after all, only men. Feed them well and they'll lie down and purr like tame cats. They don't want conversation.' From this it will be seen that Mrs. Westmoreland was well acquainted with her world. Whether Miss Cecilia shared her opinions is another matter. At any rate, she had been looking forward for nearly a fortnight to meeting Constanides, who was popularly supposed to possess an extraordinary intuitive knowledge — instinct, perhaps, it should be called — concerning the localities of tombs of the Pharaohs of the Eleventh, Twelfth and Thirteenth Dynasties.

'I am afraid Constanides is going to be late,' said the Doctor, who had consulted his watch more than once. 'I hope, in that case, as his friend and your host, you will permit me to offer you my apologies.'

The Doctor at no time objected to the sound of his own voice, and on this occasion he was even less inclined to do so. Mrs. Westmoreland was a widow with an ample income, and Cecilia, he felt sure, would marry ere long.

'He has still three minutes in which to put in an appearance,' observed that young lady, quietly. And then she added in the same tone, 'Perhaps we ought to be thankful if he comes at all.'

Both Mrs. Westmoreland and her friend the Doctor regarded her with mildly reproachful eyes. The former could not understand anyone refusing a dinner such as she felt sure the Doctor had arranged for them; while the latter found it impossible to imagine a man who would dare to disappoint the famous Dr. Forsyth, who, having failed in Harley Street, was nevertheless coining a fortune in the land of the Pharaohs.

'My good friend Constanides will not disappoint us, I feel sure,' he said, consulting his watch for the fourth time. 'Possibly I am a little fast, at any rate I have never known him to be unpunctual. A remarkable — a very remarkable man is Constanides. I cannot remember ever to have met another like him. And such a scholar!'

Having thus bestowed his approval upon him the worthy Doctor pulled down his cuffs, straightened his tie, adjusted his *pince-nez* in his best professional manner, and looked round the hall as if searching for someone bold enough to contradict the assertion he had just made.

'You have, of course, read his *Mythological Egypt,'* observed Miss Cecilia, demurely, speaking as if the matter were beyond doubt.

The Doctor looked a little confused.

'Ahem! Well, let me see,' he stammered, trying to find a way out of the difficulty. 'Well, to tell the truth, my dear young lady, I'm not quite sure that I have studied that particular work. As a matter of fact, you see, I have so little leisure at my disposal for any reading that is not intimately connected with my profession. That, of course, must necessarily come before everything else.'

Miss Cecilia's mouth twitched as if she were endeavouring to keep back a smile. At the same moment the glass doors of the vestibule opened and a man entered. So remarkable was he that everyone turned to look at him — a fact which did not appear to disconcert him in the least.

He was tall, well shaped, and carried himself with the air of one accustomed to command. His face was oval, his eyes large and set somewhat wide apart. It was only when they were directed fairly at one that one became aware of the power they possessed. The cheek bones were a trifle high, and the forehead possibly retreated towards the jet-black hair more than is customary in Greeks. He wore neither beard nor moustache, thus enabling one to see the wide, firm mouth, the compression of the lips which spoke for the determination of their possessor. Those who had an eye for such things noted the fact that he was faultlessly dressed, while Miss Cecila, who had the precious gift of observation largely developed, noted that, with the exception of a single ring and a magnificent pearl stud, the latter strangely set, he wore no jewellery of any sort.

He looked about him for Dr. Forsyth, and, when he had located him, hastened forward.

'My dear friend,' he said in English, which he spoke with scarcely a trace of foreign accent, 'I must crave your pardon a thousand times if I have kept you waiting.'

'On the contrary,' replied the Doctor, effusively, 'you are punctuality itself. Permit me to have the pleasure — the very great pleasure — of introducing you to my friends, Mrs. Westmoreland and her daughter, Miss Cecilia, of whom you have often heard me speak.'

Professor Constanides bowed and expressed the pleasure he experienced in making their acquaintance. Though she could not have told you why, Miss Cecilia found herself undergoing very much the same sensation as she had done when she had passed up the Throne Room at her presentation. A moment later the gong sounded, and, with much rustling of skirts and fluttering of fans, a general movement was made towards the dining-room.

As host, Dr. Forsyth gave his arm to Mrs. Westmoreland, Constanides following with Miss Cecilia. The latter was conscious of a vague feeling of irritation; she admired the man and his work, but she wished his name had been anything rather than what it was.

(It should be here remarked that the last Constanides she had encountered had swindled her abominably in the matter of a turquoise brooch, and in consequnce the name had been an offence to her ever since.)

Dr. Forsyth's table was situated at the further end, in the window, and from it a good view of the room could be obtained. The scene was an animated one, and one of the party, at least, I fancy, will never forget it — try how she may.

During the first two or three courses the conversation was practically limited to Cecilia and Constanides; the Doctor and Mrs. Westmoreland being too busy to waste time on idle chatter. Later, they became more amenable to the discipline of the table — or, in other words, they found time to pay attention to their neighbours.

Since then I have often wondered with what feelings Cecilia looks back upon that evening. In order, perhaps, to punish me for my curiosity, she has admitted to me since that she had never known, up to that time, what it was to converse with a really clever man. I submitted to the humiliation for the reason that we are, if not lovers, at least old friends, and, after all, Mrs. Westmoreland's cook is one in a thousand.

From that evening forward, scarcely a day passed in which Constanides did not enjoy some portion of Miss Westmoreland's society. They met at the polo ground, drove in the Gezîreh, shopped in the Muski, or listened to the band, over afternoon tea, on the balcony of Shepheard's Hotel. Constanides was always unobtrusive, always picturesque and invariably interesting. What was more to the point, he never failed to command attention whenever or wherever he might appear. In the Native Quarter he was apparently better known than in the European. Cecilia noticed that there he was treated with a deference such as one would only expect to be shown to a king. She marvelled, but said nothing. Personally, I can only wonder that her mother did not caution her before it was too late. Surely she must have seen how dangerous the intimacy was likely to become. It was old Colonel Bettenham who sounded the first note of warning. In some fashion or another he was connected with the Westmorelands, and therefore had more or less right to speak his mind.

'Who the man is, I am not in a position to say,' he remarked to the mother; 'but if I were in your place I should be very careful. Cairo at this time of year is full of adventurers.'

'But, my dear Colonel,' answered Mrs. Westmoreland, 'you surely do not mean to insinuate that the Professor is an adventurer. He was introduced to us by Dr. Forsyth, and he has written so many clever books.'

'Books, my dear madam, are not everything,' the other replied judicially, and with that fine impartiality which marks a man who does not read. 'As a matter of fact I am bound to confess that Phipps — one of my captains — wrote a novel some years ago, but only one. The mess pointed out to him that it wasn't good form, don't you know, so he never tried the experiment again. But as for this man, Constanides, as they call him, I should certainly be more than careful.'

I have been told since that this conversation worried poor Mrs. Westmoreland more than she cared to admit, even to herself. To a very large extent she, like her daughter, had fallen under the spell of the Professor's fascination. Had she been asked, point blank, she would doubtless have declared that she preferred the Greek to the Englishman — though, of course, it would have seemed flat heresy to say so. And yet — well, doubtless you can understand what I mean without my explaining further.

I am inclined to believe that I was the first to notice that there was serious trouble brewing. I could see a strained look in the girl's eyes for which I found it difficult to account. Then the truth dawned upon me, and I am ashamed to say that I began to watch her systematically. We have few secrets from each other, and she has told me a good deal of what happened during that extraordinary time — for extraordinary it certainly was. Perhaps none of us realised what a unique drama we were watching — one of the strangest, I am tempted to believe, that this world of ours has ever seen.

Christmas was just past and the New Year was fairly under way when the beginning of the end came. I think by that time even Mrs. Westmoreland had arrived at some sort of knowledge of the case. But it was then too late to interfere. I am as sure that Cecilia was not in love with Constanides as I am of anything. She was merely fascinated by him, and to a degree that, happily for the peace of the world, is as rare as the reason for it is perplexing.

To be precise, it was on Tuesday, January the 3rd, that the crisis came. On the evening of that day, accompanied by her daughter and escorted by Dr. Forsyth, Mrs. Westmoreland attended a reception at the palace of a certain Pasha, whose name I am obviously compelled to keep to myself. For the purposes of my story it is sufficient, however, that he is a man who prides himself on being up-to-date in most things, and for that and other reasons invitations to his receptions are eagerly sought after. In his drawing-room one may meet some of the most distinguished men in Europe, and on occasion it is even possible to obtain an insight into certain political intrigues that, to put it mildly, afford one an opportunity of reflecting on the instability of mundane affairs and of politics in particular.

The evening was well advanced before Constanides made his appearance. When he did, it was observed that he was more than usually quiet. Later, Cecilia permitted him to conduct her into the balcony, whence, since it was a perfect moonlight night, a fine view of the Nile could be obtained. Exactly what he said to her I have never been able to discover; I have, however, her mother's assurance that she was visibly agitated when she rejoined her. As a matter of fact, they returned to the hotel almost immediately, when Cecilia, pleading weariness, retired to her room.

And now this is the part of the story you will find as difficult to believe as I did. Yet I have indisputable evidence that it is true. It was nearly midnight and the large hotel was enjoying the only quiet it knows in the twenty-four hours. I have just said that Cecilia had retired, but in making that assertion I am not telling the exact truth, for though she had bade mother 'Goodnight' and had gone to her room, it was not to rest. Regardless of the cold night air she had thrown open the window, and was standing looking out into the moonlit street. Of what she was thinking I do not know, nor can she remember. For my own part, however, I incline to the belief that she was in a semi-hypnotic condition and that for the time being her mind was a blank.

From this point I will let Cecilia tell the story herself.

How long I stood at the window I cannot say; it may have been only five minutes, it might have been an hour. Then, suddenly, an extraordinary thing happened. I knew that it was imprudent, I was aware that it was even wrong, but an overwhelming craving to go out seized me. I felt as if the house were stifling me and that if I did not get out into the cool night air, and within a few minutes, I should die. Stranger still, I felt no desire to battle with the temptation. It was as if a will infinitely stronger than my own was dominating me and that I was powerless to resist. Scarcely conscious of what I was doing I changed my dress, and then, throwing on a cloak, switched off the electric light and stepped out into the corridor. The white-robed Arab servants were lying about on the floor as is their custom; they were all asleep. On the thick carpet of the great staircase my steps made no sound. The hall was in semi-darkness and the watchman must have been absent on his rounds, for there was no one there to spy upon me. Passing through the vestibule I turned the key of the front door. Still success attended me, for the lock shot back with scarcely a sound and I found myself in the street. Even then I had no thought of the folly of this escapade. I was merely conscious of the mysterious power that was dragging me on. Without hesitation I turned to the right and hastened along the pavement, faster I think than I had ever walked in my life. Under the trees it was comparatively dark, but out in the roadway it was well-nigh as bright as day. Once a carriage passed me and I could hear its occupants, who were French, conversing merrily — otherwise I seemed to have the city to myself. Later I heard a *muezzin* chanting his call to prayer from the minaret of some mosque in the neighbourhood, the cry being taken up and repeated from other mosques. Then at the corner of a street I stopped as if in obedience to a command. I can recall the fact that I was trembling, but for what reason I could not tell. I say this to show that while I was incapable of returning to the hotel, or of exercising my normal will power, I still possessed the faculty of observation.

I had scarcely reached the corner referred to, which, as a matter of fact, I believe I should recognise if I saw it again, when the door of a house opened and a man emerged. It was Professor Constanides, but his appearance at such a place and at such an hour, like everything else that happened that night, did not strike me as being in any way extraordinary.

'You have obeyed me,' he said by way of greeting. 'That is well. Now let us be going — the hour is late.'

As he said it there came the rattle of wheels and a carriage drove swiftly round the corner and pulled up before us. My companion helped me into it and took his place beside me. Even then, unheard-of as my action was, I had no thought of resisting.

'What does it mean?' I asked. 'Oh, tell me what it means? Why am I here?'

'You will soon know,' was his reply, and his voice took a tone I had never noticed in it before.

We had driven some considerable distance, in fact, I believe we had crossed the river, before either of us spoke again.

'Think,' said my companion, 'and tell me whether you can remember ever having driven with me before?'

'We have driven together many times lately,' I replied. 'Yesterday to the polo, and the day before to the Pyramids.'

'Think again,' he said, and as he did so he placed his hand on mine. It was as cold as ice. However, I only shook my head.

'I cannot remember,' I answered, and yet I seemed to be dimly conscious of something that was too intangible to be a recollection. He uttered a little sigh and once more we were silent. The horses must have been good ones for they whirled us along at a fast pace. I did not take much interest in the route we followed, but at last something attracted my attention and I knew that we were on the road to Gizeh. A few moments later the famous Museum, once the palace of the ex-Khedive Ismail, came into view. Almost immediately the carriage pulled up in the shadow of the *Lebbek* trees and my companion begged me to alight. I did so, whereupon he said something, in what I can only suppose was Arabic, to his coachman, who whipped up his horses and drove swiftly away.

'Come,' he said, in the same tone of command as before, and then led the way towards the gates of the old palace. Dominated as my will was by his I could still notice how beautiful the building looked in the moonlight. In the daytime it presents a faded and unsubstantial appearance, but now, with its Oriental tracery, it was almost fairylike. The Professor halted at the gates and unlocked them. How he had admitted us, I cannot say. It suffices that, almost before I was aware of it, we had passed through the garden and were ascending the steps to the main entrance. The doors behind us, we entered the first room. It is only another point in this extraordinary adventure when I declare that even now I was not afraid; and yet to find oneself in such a place and at such an hour at any other time would probably have driven me beside myself with terror. The moonlight streamed in upon us, revealing the ancient monuments and the other indescribable memorials of those long-dead ages. Once more my conductor uttered his command and we went on through the second room, passed the Skekh-El-Beled and the Seated Scribe. Room after room we traversed, and to do so it seemed to me that we ascended stairs innumerable. At last we came to one in which Constanides paused. It contained numerous mummy cases and was lighted by a skylight through which the rays of the moon streamed in. We were standing before one which I remembered to have remarked on the occasion of our last visit. I could distinguish the paintings upon it distinctly. Professor Constanides, with the deftness which showed his familiarity with the work, removed the lid and revealed to me the swathed-up figure within. The face was uncovered and was strangely well-preserved. I gazed down on it, and as I did so a sensation that I had never known before passed over me. My body seemed to be shrinking, my blood to be turning to ice. For the first time I endeavoured to exert myself, to tear myself from the bonds that were holding me. But it was in vain. I was sinking — sinking — sinking — into I knew not what. Then the voice of the man who had brought me to the place sounded in my ears as if he were speaking from a long way off. After that a great light burst upon me, and it was as if I were walking in a dream; yet I knew it was too real, too true to life to be a mere creation of my fancy.

It was night and the heavens were studded with stars. In the distance a great army was encamped and at intervals the calls of the sentries reached me. Somehow I seemed to feel no wonderment at my position. Even my dress caused me no surprise. To my left, as I looked towards the river, was a large tent, before which armed men paced continually. I looked about me as if I expected to see someone, but there was no one to greet me.

'It is for the last time,' I told myself. 'Come what may, it shall be the last time!'

Still I waited, and as I did so I could hear the night wind sighing through the rushes on the river's bank. From the tent near me — for Usirtasen, son of Amenemhait — was then fighting against the Libyans and was commanding his army in person — came the sound of revelry. The air blew cold from the desert and I shivered, for I was but thinly clad. Then I hid myself in the shadow of a great rock that was near at hand. Presently I caught the sound of a footstep, and there came into view a tall man, walking carefully, as though he had no desire that the sentries on guard before the Royal tent should become aware of his presence in the neighbourhood. As I saw him I moved from where I was standing to meet him. He was none other than Sinûhît — younger son of Amenemhait and brother of Usirtasen — who was at that moment conferring with his generals in the tent.

I can see him now as he came towards me, tall, handsome, and defiant in his bearing as a man should be. He walked with the assured step of one who has been a soldier and trained to warlike exercises from his youth up. For a moment I regretted the news I had to tell him — but only for a moment. I could hear the voice of Usirtasen in the tent, and after that I had no thought for anyone else.

'Is it thou, Nofrît?' he asked as soon as he saw me.

'It is I!' I replied. 'You are late, Sinûhît. You tarry too long over the wine cups.'

'You wrong me, Nofrît,' he answered, with all the fierceness for which he was celebrated. 'I have drunk no wine this night. Had I not been kept by the Captain of the Guard I should have been here sooner. Thou art not angry with me, Nofrît?'

'Nay, that were presumption on my part, my lord,' I answered. 'Art thou not the King's son, Sinûhît?'

'And by the Holy Ones I swear that it were better for me if I were not,' he replied. 'Usirtasen, my brother, takes all and I am but the jackal that gathers up the scraps wheresoever he may find them.' He paused for a moment. 'However, all goes well with our plot. Let me but have time and I will yet be ruler of this land and of all the Land of Khem beside.' He drew himself up to his full height and looked towards the sleeping camp. It was well known that between the brothers there was but little love, and still less trust.

'Peace, peace,' I whispered, fearing lest his words might be overheard. 'You must not talk so, my lord. Should you by chance be heard you know what the punishment would be!'

He laughed a short and bitter laugh. He was well aware that Usirtasen would show him no mercy. It was not the first time he had been suspected, and he was playing a desperate game. He came a step closer to me and took my hand in his. I would have withdrawn it — but he gave me no opportunity. Never was a man more in earnest than he was then.

'Nofrît,' he said, and I could feel his breath upon my cheek, 'what is my answer to be? The time for talking is past; now we must act. As thou knowest, I prefer deeds to words, and tomorrow my brother Usirtasen shall learn that I am as powerful as he.'

Knowing what I knew I could have laughed him to scorn for his boastful speech. The time, however, was not yet ripe, so I held my peace. He was plotting against his brother, whom I loved, and it was his desire that I should help him. That, however, I would not do.

'Listen,' he said, drawing even closer to me, and speaking in a voice that showed me plainly how much in earnest he was, 'thou knowest how much I love thee. Thou knowest that there is nought I would not do for thee or for thy sake. Be but faithful to me now and there is nothing thou shalt ask in vain of me hereafter. All is prepared, and ere the moon is gone I shall be Pharaoh and reign beside Amenemhait, my father.'

'Are you so sure that your plans will not miscarry?' I asked, with what was almost a sneer at his recklessness — for recklessness it surely was to think that he could induce an army that had been admittedly successful to swerve in its allegiance to the general who had won its battles for it, and to desert in the face of the enemy. Moreover, I knew that he was wrong in believing that his father cared more for him than for Usirtasen, who had done so much for the kingdom, and who was beloved by high and low alike. But it was not in Sinûhît's nature to look upon the dark side of things. He had complete confidence in himself and in his power to bring his conspiracy against his father and brother to a successful issue. He revealed to me his plans, and, bold though they were, I could see that it was impossible that they could succeed. And in the event of his failing, what mercy could he hope to receive? I knew Usirtasen too well to think that he would show any. With all the eloquence I could command I implored him to abandon the attempt, or at least to delay it for a time. He seized my wrist and pulled me to him, peering fiercely into my face.

'Art playing me false?' he asked. 'If it is so it were better that you should drown yourself in yonder river. Betray me and nothing shall save you — not even Pharaoh himself.'

That he meant what he said I felt convinced. The man was desperate; he was staking all he had in the world upon the issue of his venture. I can say with truth that it was not my fault that we had been drawn together, and yet on this night of all others it seemed as if there were nothing left for me but to side with him or to bring about his downfall.

'Nofrit,' he said, after a short pause, 'is it nothing, thinkest thou, to be the wife of a Pharaoh? Is it not worth striving for, particularly when it can be so easily accomplished?'

I knew, however, that he was deluding himself with false hopes. What he had in his mind could never come to pass. I was like dry grass between two fires. All that was required was one small spark to bring about a conflagration in which I should be consumed.

'Harken to me, Nofrit,' he continued. 'You have means of learning Usirtasen's plans. Send me word to-morrow as to what is in his mind and the rest will be easy. Your reward shall be greater than you dream of.'

Though I had no intention of doing what he asked, I knew that in his present humour it would be little short of madness to thwart him. I therefore temporised with him, and allowed him to suppose that I would do as he wished, and then, bidding him good-night, I sped away towards the hut where I was lodged. I had not been there many minutes when a messenger came to me from Usirtasen, summoning me to his presence. Though I could not understand what it meant I hastened to obey.

On arrival there I found him surrounded by the chief officers of his army. One glance at his face was sufficient to tell me that he was violently angry with someone, and I had the best of reasons for believing that that someone was myself. Alas! it was as I had expected. Sinûhît's plot had been discovered; he had been followed and watched, and my meeting with him that evening was known. I protested my innocence in vain. The evidence was too strong against me.

'Speak, girl, and tell what thou knowest,' said Usirtasen, in a voice I had never heard him use before. 'It is the only way by which thou canst save thyself. Look to it that thy story tallies with the tales of others!'

I trembled in every limb as I answered the questions he put to me. It was plain that he no longer trusted me, and that the favour I had once found in his eyes was gone, never to return.

'It is well,' he said when I had finished my story. 'And now we will see thy partner — the man who would have put me — the Pharaoh who is to be — to the sword had I not been warned in time.'

He made a sign to one of the officers who stood by, whereupon the latter left the tent, to return a few moments later with Sinûhît.

'Hail, brother!' said Usirtasen, mockingly, as he leaned back in his chair and looked at him through half-shut eyes. 'You tarried but a short time over the wine cup this night. I fear it pleased thee but little. Forgive me; on another occasion better shall be found for thee lest thou shouldst deem us lacking in our hospitality.'

'There were matters that needed my attention and I could not stay,' Sinûhît replied, looking his brother in the face. Thou wouldst not have me neglect my duties.'

'Nay! nay! Maybe they were matters that concerned our personal safety?' Usirtasen continued, still with the same gentleness. 'Maybe you heard that there were those in our army who were not well disposed towards us? Give me their names, my brother, that due punishment may be meted out to them.'

Before Sinûhît could reply, Usirtasen had sprung to his feet.

'Dog!' he cried, 'darest thou prate to me of matters of importance when thou knowest thou hast been plotting against me and my father's throne. I have doubted thee these many months and now all is made clear. By the Gods, the Holy Ones, I swear that thou shalt die for this ere cock-crow.'

It was at this moment that Sinûhît became aware of my presence. A little cry escaped him, and his face told me as plainly as any words could speak that he believed that I had betrayed him. He was about to speak, probably to denounce me, when the sound of voices reached us from outside. Usirtasen bade the guards to ascertain what it meant, and presently a messenger entered the tent. He was travel-stained and weary. Advancing towards where Usirtasen was seated, he knelt before him.

'Hail, Pharaoh,' he said. 'I come to three from the Palace of Titoui.'

An anxious expression came over Usirtasen's face as he heard this. I also detected beads of perspiration on the brow of Sinûhît. A moment latter it was known to us that Amenemhait was dead, and, therefore, Usirtasen reigned in his stead. The news was so sudden, and the consequences so vast, that it was impossible to realise quite what it meant. I looked across at Sinûhît and his eyes met mine. He seemed to be making up his mind about something. Then with lightning speed he sprang upon me; a dagger gleamed in the air; I felt as if a hot iron had been thrust into my breast, and after that I remember no more.

As I felt myself falling I seemed to wake from my dream — if dream it were — to find myself standing in the Museum by the mummy case, and with Professor Constanides by my side.

'You have seen,' he said. 'You have looked back across the centuries to that day when, as Nofrît, I believed you had betrayed me, and killed you. After that I escaped from the camp and fled into Kaduma. There I died; but it was decreed that my soul should never know peace till we had met again and you had forgiven me. I have waited all these years, and see — we meet at last.'

Strange to say, even then the situation did not strike me as being in any way improbable. Yet now, when I see it set down in black and white, I find myself wondering that I dare to ask anyone in their sober senses to believe it to be true. Was I in truth that same Nofrît who, four thousand years before, had been killed by Sinûhît, son of Amenemhait, because he believed that I had betrayed him? It seemed incredible, and yet, if it were a creation of my imagination, what did the dream mean? I fear it is a riddle of which I shall probably never know the answer.

My failure to reply to his question seemed to cause him pain.

'Nofrît,' he said, and his voice shook with emotion 'think' what your forgiveness means to me. Without it I am lost both here and hereafter.'

His voice was low and pleading and his face in the moonlight was like that of a man who knew the uttermost depths of despair.

'Forgive — forgive,' he cried again, holding out his hands to me. 'If you do not, I must go back to the sufferings which have been my portion since I did the deed which wrought my ruin.' I felt myself trembling like a leaf.

'If it is as you say, though I cannot believe it, I forgive you freely,' I answered, in a voice that I scarcely recognised as my own.

For some moments he was silent, then he knelt before me and took my hand, which he raised to his lips. After that, rising, he laid his head upon the breast of the mummy before which we were standing. Looking down at it he addressed it thus:

'Rest, Sinûhît, son of Amenemhait — for that which was foretold for thee is now accomplished, and the punishment which was decreed is at an end. Henceforth thou mayest sleep in peace.'

After that he replaced the lid of the coffin, and when this was done he turned to me.

'Let us be going,' he said, and we went together through the rooms by the way we had come.

Together we left the building and passsed through the gardens out into the road beyond. There we found the carriage waiting for us, and we took our places in it. Once more the horses sped along the silent road, carrying us swiftly back to Cairo. During the drive not a word was spoken by either of us. The only desire I had left was to get back to the hotel and lay my aching head upon my pillow. We crossed the bridge and entered the city. What the time was I had no idea, but I was conscious that the wind blew chill as if in anticipation of the dawn. At the same corner whence we had started, the coachman stopped his horses and I alighted, after which he drove away as if he had received his orders beforehand.

'Will you permit me to walk with you as far as your hotel?' said Constanides, with his customary politeness.

I tried to say something in reply, but my voice failed me. I would much rather have been alone, but as he would not allow this we set off together. At the corner of the street in which the hotel is situated we stopped.

'Here we must part,' he said. Then, after a pause, he added, 'And for ever. From this moment I shall never see your face again.'

'You are leaving Cairo?' was the only thing I could say.

'Yes, I am leaving Cairo,' he replied with peculiar emphasis. 'My errand here is accomplished. You need have no fear that I shall ever trouble you again.'

'I have no fear,' I answered, though I am afraid it was only a half truth.

He looked earnestly into my face.

'Nofrît,' he said, 'for, say what you will, you are the Nofrît I would have made my Queen and have loved beyond all other women, never again will it be permitted you to look into the past as you did to-night. Had things been ordained otherwise we might have done great things together, but the gods willed that it should not be. Let it rest therefore. And now — farewell! To-night I go to the rest for which I have so long been seeking.'

Without another word he turned and left me. Then I went on to the hotel. How it came about I cannot say, but the door was open and I passed quickly in. Once more, to my joy, I found the watchman was absent from the hall.

Trembling lest anyone might see me, I sped up the stairs and along the corridor, where the servants lay sleeping just as I had left them, and so to my room. Everything was exactly as I had left it, and there was nothing to show that my absence had been suspected. Again I went to the window, and, in a feeling of extraordinary agitation, looked out. Already there were signs of dawn in the sky. I sat down and tried to think over all that had happened to me that evening, endeavouring to convince myself, in the face of indisputable evidence, that it was not real and that I had only dreamt it. Yet it would not do! At last, worn out, I retired to rest. As a rule I sleep soundly; it is scarcely, however, a matter for wonderment that I did not do so on this occasion. Hour after hour I tumbled and tossed — thinking — thinking — thinking. When I rose and looked into the glass I scarcely recognised myself. Indeed, my mother commented on my fagged appearance when we met at the breakfast table.

'My dear child, you look as if you had been up all night,' she said, and little did she guess, as she nibbled her toast, that there was a considerable amount of truth in her remark.

Later she went shopping with a lady staying in the hotel, while I went to my room to lie down. When we met again at lunch it was easy to see that she had some news of importance to communicate.

'My dear Cecilia,' she said, 'I have just seen Dr. Forsyth, and he has given me a terrible shock. I don't want to frighten you, my girl, but have you heard that *Professor Constanides was found dead in bed this morning?* It is a most terrible affair! He must have died during the night!'

I am not going to pretend that I had any reply ready to offer her at that moment.

The Strange Discovery of Doctor Nosidy*

It is said proverbially, and I am quite aware of the fact, that a little knowledge is a dangerous thing, and that sharp tools should not be entrusted to the hands of unskilled persons; and it is because some may depreciate my knowledge, and class me among those to whom sharp tools are a danger, both to themselves and the community at large, that I have not placed my discovery before the scientific world.

I have no particular ambition to pose as a great genius or inventor; the things which I have discovered are so simple, that anybody else, following the same line of thought, would probably have stumbled upon the same truths. That my discoveries, placed in the hands of profane or frivolous persons, would be fraught with many and great evils I do not deny, and it is for this consideration that I refrain from giving my *exact* modus operandi in this narrative.

As will be seen from a perusal of this short recital, but little further thought and elaboration are required to place my experiments among the most astounding of this most marvellous age of discovery and invention.

It is a trite expression we make use of when we say that "Electricity is in its infancy." Of course it is; it is but in its swaddling clothes: but, by and by, it will grow such a powerful fellow as to claim by right the kingship of the whole mechanical and motive world.

Now to my mind the two greatest forces in the universe are brain power (or intellect) and electricity; and the time is rapidly approaching when these two subtle energies shall govern or control nearly everything under the sun. My friends infer that if I had a little more brain force I should not take such absurd views of these two great *Souls of Man and Motion,* as I am pleased to term intellect and electricity. That I am not so distraught as my friends are pleased to suppose, may be gathered from the outcome of those experiments which I am now about to explain, so far at least as that can be done without actually divulging the particular secrets which, for the present, I wish to withhold, even from the great *savants* of this scientific epoch. I am afraid, however, that some reader of these lines will, if he be of a keen, searching, inventive temperament, come in a short time very near the borders of that discovery which it has taken me a dozen years to experiment upon, and place in its present unfinished form.

Even when I was a lad I was a great reader and literary delver after things which were in any way obscure, unfinished, or apparently

* "The Strange Discovery of Doctor Nosidy" was written by Ernest R. Suffling (dates not known) and published in 1896. The text for this edition was taken from the short story collection *The Story Hunter or Tales of the Weird and Wild* (1896).

unfathomable; and among the many theories I formed upon subjects of which the world had written much, and talked more without advancing any nearer to their solution, was an idea regarding the soul of man!

I may say in a few words, without giving the precise chain of thought I employed, that my idea of man's soul was — that it was nothing more nor less than his *brain;* for is not that the very spirit, essence, conscience, reason, and vital principle of man?

Certainly: for in what degree can even a man's heart compare with his brain in the supremacy it asserts over his corporeal body? It is true that the heart is essential to him, and has a great work to perform, and can do it without help from his brain, even while the body and brain sleep; but, after all, it is a mere beautiful machine — a mechanical, monotonous slave, with nothing more to recommend it to notice than its faithfulness to its hidden duty.

Now let me affirm at once that the brain *is* the soul, and when you acquiesce in this, you will see more clearly how it is worked out as a substantial truth in my wonderful experiments, or rather, as their wonderful *result;* experiments, which after all were but my intellectual knowledge reduced to a reasonable system.

Very well. I commenced my experiments with this theory properly worked out in my own mind, but not substantiated with positive proof, *that the soul and the brain were synonymous.*

Now the soul never dies — consequently the brain never dies! It decays, and resolves itself into its constituent atoms, but it leaves behind it what I will term *brain-ether,* which is absolutely indestructible and immortal, and consequently lasts through all time.

Then came the thought — "If the brain-ether exists, where shall I find it?" I wanted *to* know this one thing; then I could work out the ideas I had in my mind, following them up with experiments to prove the correctness of my premises.

Just think for a few moments of the vast encyclopædia of knowledge stored in a human brain of ordinary calibre; think of the scenes, the faces, the technical knowledge, the music, the skill, and the secrets that human brain contains, and which, when the body decays, are turned into ethereal memories — memories *not lost,* but stored up in the brain-ether for ever.

Now it occurred to me, that if I could only ascertain what became of this brain-ether as the body decayed, that I might secure some of it, and with the help of modern scientific apparatus, so far capture its treasury of knowledge as to make that latent knowledge of incalculable service to mankind.

For many weeks I thought of places likely to be the earthly resting-place of what I considered to be the fugitive brain-ether, and, like every other mortal who has essayed the same intellectual feat, I failed because I had the words, "The soul has fled," ever present in my mind.

Naturally, when a human being dies, if one says, "His soul has fled," the person spoken to directly assumes that the soul has left the body, and gone no one knows whither. But, being scientifically artful, I took an opposite and antagonistic view of the usually accepted answer, and said to myself:

"Now suppose the soul has not fled, but is still present in the cranium in the form of brain-ether."

This startling hypothesis I took and worked upon. Forsaking the common theory, I resolved to see if I could not by some means discover the brain-ether, which I was morally certain existed *somewhere*, and which I quite believed was as likely, or more likely, to be found in its ordinary resting-place — the cranium — as elsewhere.

A recently deceased body or head was of no service to me to experimentalize upon, as the spirit or essential ether would not have become free till the disintegration of the pulpy matter of the brain was complete. What I wanted was a skeleton, or even a skull, which had neither been opened nor tampered with; and having no medical friends I was at a loss to know how I could supply my want, when a lucky accident gave me just what I required.

One day I was walking through Gower Street, London, when whom should I run against but my old friend Stairs. Stairs is an Egyptologist, great at reading hieroglyphics and cuneiform writing. Not having seen each other for two years, we naturally strolled into the Horseshoe Hotel to finish our chat in comfort, and to lubricate our throats, which have a wonderful knack of becoming dry when their owners meet old friends.

Stairs had been away for fifteen months in Egypt searching for any curious things having a commercial value in England. During his wanderings in the country of the Pharaohs, he had purchased a large number of curios, stones, amulets, rings, sarcophagi, and mummies, which he was now endeavouring to dispose of to the trustees of the British Museum.

After I had heard many of his adventures, it became his turn to inquire how I was employing myself, and this finally led to my explaining to Stairs all about my theory of the soul. Of course, being ignorant of the matter, he simply laughed, and suggested that I had better have one of his mummies to experiment upon!

Why not?

Just the very thing; what could be better than an ancient, unrolled mummy, some three thousand years old?

I was positively delighted; and in furtherance of my fancy he handed me his card, on the understanding that I was to proceed to his house, and make a selection of any mummy I thought would suit my purpose, take it home with me for a month to experiment upon, and at the end of that time return it to him.

That very evening I went to my friend's house in Gordon Square with a small covered van, and brought my precious Egyptian away, thankful to old Stairs for his kindly consideration. Stairs was off to Italy for a month, and I had his permission to do what I liked with the mummy, so long as I did not spoil its commercial value.

When the defunct Egyptian was safely deposited in my study I could have hugged him for very joy, but refrained from the embrace as he smelt a trifle musty.

I, Doctor Nosidy, scientist, mesmerist, thought-reader, and electrician, felt that evening that I stood upon the threshold of some brand discovery. The thought thrilled me as it did Columbus when he came in sight of the long-sought land, or Bernard Palissy when he discovered the true mode of firing his beautiful pottery-ware, or Galileo when he discovered the movement of the earth. I felt the sensations of these and other discoverers rolled into one; moreover, it was my conviction that I was about to find something by the side of which their discoveries would appear insignificant indeed.

Setting my apparatus in order, I commenced work by unrolling the head of the mummy; carefully stripping off the multitudinous layers of cerecloth, which were permeated quite through with a dark, brittle gum or resin of some kind. By and by I came to the leathery and gum-covered visage, wrinkled, emaciated, and black with the dry atmosphere of thirty centuries.

Dark curly hair still adhered to the skull, and was not so brittle but that, after bathing the compressed locks, I could lift them with the blade of a spatula quite away from the cranium without damage. The whole head was a very fine one — the nose prominent and hawk-like, the eyes cavernous, and the mouth excessively broad and grinning; the lips were so dried and compressed that they were flat with the face. The teeth were still white and glossy, and the entire absence of any signs of decay proclaimed the fact that the owner was young at his decease.

All these features I noticed as I worked away upon my subject, and having at length uncovered the whole head, I made a small hole through the apex of the cranium with a brad-awl. This done, I inserted, into the space once occupied by the brain, the ends of the wires connected with a certain electric instrument. Into the mouthpiece of the machine I spoke, asking,

"Do you hear me?"

I listened, but of course no reply came.

How could it?

I had been much too eager to commence my work, and of a certainty, this my first attempt could but end in one way — in absolute failure, and that from three causes.

1st. The brain of a deceased Egyptian was removed through the nostrils when the embalming took place.

2nd. Even if the brain-ether still tenanted the cranium the lips could form no answer to my query, as they were so dry and parched as to have no power of movement.

3rd. If the conditions of brain and lips were favourable, and I really obtained a sound, it would certainly be in the dead Egyptian tongue, which to me would be quite unintelligible. What should I do?

My defunct monarch, or whoever he might be, was suddenly transformed into a useless incumbrance, instead of a scientific help.

Instead of hugging him for joy I could now have beaten him as a scientific fraud.

There was nothing for it but to take a day or two and think the matter out in an intelligent and calm manner.

I did think it out; and on the third day had so far perfected my primal theory, that I resolved to give the mummy one more chance of communicating with a nineteenth-century scientist.

Starting with the assumption that the subject would have been dead from a few hours to a couple of days before the embalmers would commence their process, and that the brain being lifeless and cold, the spirit-ether might have escaped into its bony case and have remained in the skull after the actual brain-matter was abstracted by the cunning embalmer and his assistants, — I argued that it would be possible for me to communicate with this spirit-ether, which would still retain in an ethereal form the vast store of knowledge which the deceased had accumulated when on earth. In that spirit-ether would be indelibly written, as it were, a record of the whole life of the deceased, with all his cares and pleasures, knowledge of contemporary events, and the haunting memory of his sins.

Assuming, I say, that this record was present in an invisible, subtle form, how, even if I could communicate with the brain-ether, would it be possible to obtain a reply?

As I have said, I am a thought-reader, and my hope was that, if my query were understood by the soul (or brain-ether) of the mummy, I could, by the exercise of my peculiar function of reading thought, obtain a reply.

All seemed correct in theory, and to put it to the test, I, that very evening, opened communication with my ebony subject. One wire was inserted through the cranium and the other, instead of being attached to a sound receiver, I coiled several times around my own head!

Again I put the question "Do you hear me?"

Nothing at first transpired; but, on repeating the question several times, my brain became aware of the power of thought working in the dead skull, and this thought-voice gradually became coherent, until I could actually detect the vibration of certain words being formed, which were, however, not sufficiently distinct for me to understand.

My brain was quickly tired with the intense strain of sustained thought, and, lying down on the couch, I fell fast asleep, to dream of the land of the Pharaohs.

In my dream I seemed to hear people speaking to each other, and to see them going about their usual avocations. I appeared in my dream to be inside the shop of an Eastern hairdresser, where an Egyptian fop was having his hair curled and dressed for some evening function, possibly a ball or supper. The hair-dresser and his young patron appeared to be cracking jokes in their native tongue, of which I could not understand a word, but still I laughed at their jokes as heartily as if I fathomed every quip they uttered. At length I laughed so loudly in my sleep at one of the barber's witticisms, that I awoke to find tears of merriment streaming from my eyes.

My dream had solved part of the problem!

Of course the thought-words I had read, by means of the wire round my head, were in the *Egyptian* tongue, hence the reason for my not understanding them.

Here was a dilemma!

However, I did not give up my mummy; for, although I could neither ask intelligible questions nor receive answers that I could understand, I obtained Egyptian *thoughts* whenever I had a mind.

I kept the royal corpse for the allotted month, and then returned it in its deal case, with a letter of thanks to my friend in Gordon Square.

A dead subject was all very well, but a *dead language* was beyond me.

So far my success was very encouraging. I had learnt, among other things, that the soul, or brain-ether, still tenants the skull after the substance of the brain is entirely dissipated — provided it has not been removed from the cavity before decay set in.

With strong hopes of better success, I now resolved to obtain an English skull and try my skill upon it.

During my peregrinations in the South of England the following week, I found myself in the neighbourhood of X—— Cathedral, and strolling, almost unthinkingly, into its grand interior, admired its decorations and memorials. It was late in the day, and as in the gathering gloaming I wandered round the solemn building, I found myself gazing upon some curious painted coffins containing the remains of certain of our Saxon kings. Gazing upon them I became fascinated, for they suggested another step towards the realization of my grand scheme.

As I stood before these sepulchres of the long dead, I am sorry to say the longing came into my mind to possess a skull from one of the decorated coffins; and presently the longing became so intense, that, like some villainous body-snatcher, I hid myself behind a stack of chairs in the nave, remaining there seated comfortably on a hassock till the great bell tolled forth the noon of night, when, coming forth from my hiding-place, I effected my ghoulish purpose, and secreted under my cape the cranium of a Saxon monarch.

The weary hours of the night lagged in their monotonous round, for I dared not sleep, fearing I might not awaken before the opening of the south door for the eight o'clock service; but my vigil was ended at last by the arrival of a gaping old man, who came to ring the bell calling early worshippers to the holy fane. The entry of several persons to the building gave me an opportunity of walking quickly out without attracting attention, but I can scarcely describe my feelings of shame, nor is there perhaps any need of doing so. Necessity, the noble mother of invention, had made a very criminal of me; but whatever loathing I had for myself was condoned by the fact, that what I was doing was for the sake of mankind at large; and although I had purloined the principal part of a royal personage, I could not look upon it as a theft, but merely as a loan from one who had no further use for his ancient head.

A few hours brought me again to the mighty metropolis, and I quickly set to work with my elaborate apparatus, but, alas! only to be the victim of another disappointment.

Although I could obtain certain mental sounds (if I may so term them), and could, by the aid of my thought-reading power, understand that words were being thought by the brain-ether in the monarch's cranium, yet, unfortunately, to fathom their meaning was beyond me.

Pure Saxon was a language with which I was totally unacquainted!

Here was another stupid mistake of mine, of precisely the same nature as the one I made in my first experiment.

What could I do?

Very little.

I copied down, phonetically, a number of the words which the monarch was *thinking,* and showed them to a professor of Anglo-Saxon, but all he could do was to translate some of them into modern English, so giving a series of words without any sequence or connection whatever.

Angry with myself, and angry with the skull simply for being Saxon, and therefore not understandable, I took it in my hand, and, in my disappointment and rage, should doubtless have shattered it into fragments against the wall, but for the sudden ringing of my door bell, warning me of the arrival of a gentleman with whom I had an appointment.

When the interview was over my anger had ceased also, and that afternoon, with the skull in a bag, I took train for X——, and repaired to my stack of chairs in the cathedral. I hid myself again, like a felon, till the doors were closed, then restoring the skull uninjured to its resting-place, crept back to my hassock seat, and awaited the dawning.

I fell asleep, and I suppose snored, for, to my astonishment, I was awakened next morning by the verger, who, not believing my cock-and-bull story of having been shut in the cathedral while absorbed in the contemplation of the ancient structure and its interesting relics, haled me before a magistrate.

It was with difficulty I proved my identity, and doing so cost me all the loose cash I had about me in telegraphing to my friends, before the worthy magistrate would release me, although I had been twice searched to see if anything of value was secreted about my person.

Oh, science! what miseries thou hast for ages brought upon thy noblest sons! What sorrows; what disappointments; what troubles and trials, and alas, what terms of vile durance!, I being one of thy sons, have shared all these evils, though perhaps in a minor degree!

My failures, however, were not unmitigated: I had established the fact that brain-ether and brain-thought were present in skulls, whatever their nationality, and to whatever period they might belong; my failures were attributable principally to my lack of linguistic knowledge, a lack that might easily be remedied.

My business now became to seek a skull of a more modern period. I applied at a number of likely places, and at last was successful in obtaining a fine, large specimen, which had a clean and refined appearance. I paid but a small sum for it, and carried it home to my study in triumph. Surely at last I was on the road to the development of my pet project.

After dinner, all being quiet, I commenced experiments upon the skull, and having placed my apparatus in order, I asked my usual question:

"Who are you?"

"Sidney Smith," came the reply,

Good gracious, I thought, can this be the great wit?

"You do not mean to say," I asked," that you are the great Sidney Smith?"

"I reckon you have just hit the right nail on the head," was the immediate thought-reply.

What a piece of luck.

"Well, Mr. Smith, such men as you the world sees but too rarely; your name is still a household word among us, being constantly quoted as that of the brightest star of wit of your day."

"Whip you mean?" came from the skull.

"No; I said *wit;* a jocular person, you know."

"I ain't no wit nor jocular person," was the response, "not as I knows what 'jocular' is exactly, but if it is anything to do with a jockey it's nothing to do with me, for I stood six feet four, and weighed seventeen stone. If you calls me a 'whip' instead of a 'wit,' there you are right, for I drove the York and Manchester coach for over twenty years."

I found my subject very garrulous, very thick-headed, and very quarrelsome — a man of high stature but low breeding; one who knew nothing of any subjects but those of a horsey nature. One day our conversation became so warm, and such a string of bad language flooded the fellow's brain-ether, that I had to disconnect my battery. I left the cranium for some days, thinking that the man's temper would have cooled down, for I supposed that when I disconnected the electric wires the current of thought ceased; but when I applied the wires to my head, I found that the old store of abuse was still at work in the brain-ether of my giant subject, and the end of the matter was, that I smashed the beautiful skull into a thousand fragments against my study wall, thus dissipating the soul or brain-ether into space.

I did not regret the occurrence, for the fellow was most vituperative and impertinent whenever I wished to know anything of his family secrets or earthly career.

Still, when I think of it, I have a deal for which to thank that giant skull. It was during the fortnight that I possessed it that I, to a great extent, perfected my apparatus for Soul-Reading, Brain-Ether-Reviewing, Etherealized-Human-Record-Deciphering, or whatever men may term my discovery, for I have not yet invented a title for it myself.

I therefore thank that broken vase of humanity, though being broken, I cannot convey my thanks as I would wish, for there is no brain-ether left to convey it to.

Alas, poor giant!

Hundreds of skulls have come under my apparatus for examination during the past decade, and I possess facts that would make many great English families quake; facts asserted by ancestors' souls — *and souls cannot lie* — of how titles and estates have been wrongfully obtained, and rightful heirs darkly put aside to favour other candidates.

I know of facts, suppressed in history, which, were I to reveal their dark catalogue of murders, conspiracies and political intrigues, would put a fresh interpretation upon the records of our country. But of what avail would the disclosure be to our present generation? The heart of man in the nineteenth century is, what it has been in all ages, "desperately wicked."

On the other hand, it has been my good fortune to converse with kings and ambassadors, with men of learning, poets, statesmen, with artists and men of science, even with the great Isaac Newton himself, and am now in the position of being the best-informed man, upon past history and events, of any person in the world. Men say there is but a thin partition between a savant and a madman. I know better; I may be the former, but between me and madness a vast gap yawns, although my friends will have their little jibe at me. Great men ever had their traducers, and I, naturally, am no exception.

Of all those with whom I have chatted — and by my experiments I can converse with the spirit or soul of *any* person, provided I have the skull to which I can attach my apparatus — there has not been one equal in intellectual capacity to Sir Isaac Newton, a most steady, solid man of scientific sense.

Now Newton's idea of the brain and my own precisely coincide, and if I give *my* notion upon the subject I give his also. Here it is.

The brain is an elaborate storehouse of knowledge of every kind. It contains a record of *all* one has learned during one's lifetime; I say *all,* because if a person has learned a thing and forgotten it, it must not be supposed that that thing has vanished from the brain; not so; it is faithfully recorded in the brain substance, though the mental faculties may not be strong enough to *reproduce* the particular thing or theme when wanted.

Not only is everything once learnt retained by the brain, but it also contains a record of every *action* of one's life. All these actions and events are stored away in minute cells to the number of hundreds of thousands, and yet to the human eye they are not as visible as a pin's point; in fact, they have no dimensions whatever.

Now, supposing this theory to be correct, can we not see (and I say it with great reverence) how easy the task of the Recording Angel must be; can we not imagine the celestial one reading the record of a man's brain as easily as we poor mundane mortals can scan a book?

Are not many biblical texts elucidated by this theory; for instance, Ecclesiastes xii. 14; Matthew xii. 37; and Hebrews iv. 13?

But then the theory of the brain-ether, or the soul as some call it, goes further. I am of opinion that the soul is not *spirit* but *matter;* matter of such infinitely minute particles as to be perfectly invisible to even the most powerful microscope yet made.

Let me explain my meaning more fully.

Just as there are differences in the bulk and solidity of various materials, so is there a vast difference in the tangibility, if I may so term it, of various bodies and substances.

Take a cubic foot of steel — matter beyond all doubt — and of what closely-compacted solidity and enormous density! Then take a cubic foot of smoke, that again is matter, but what immeasurable difference in density, tangibility, and even visibility there is in the two substances!

Then go a step further, and imagine a cubic foot of gas: it is invisible, intangible, and possesses but little density, yet it is *matter,* it is not spirit.

Now, seeing the vast difference between various matters, can we not believe that the brain, instead of being soul or spirit, may still be matter of such a rare and subtle quality that there is even more difference between it and gas, than between gas and a solid lump of steel or granite?

If you can follow that suggestion you have my theory; but having spoken of my theory I go no farther. Of what my apparatus consists I have merely hinted, not mentioning one or two of its principal conditions. My secret is of such vast importance that it would go a great way to revolutionize science, history, and even religion, and I dare not divulge it to the world at large. The more I think over the matter, the more convinced I am that my experiments have so lifted the veil of death, that I have stepped within the bounds of things which should be unknown to man.

I have passed the Rubicon of the supernatural!

I tremble at my own temerity.

I have now but one Gordian knot to sever. Shall my secret die with me, and so save the civilized world much anxiety, or shall I divulge it to a small coterie of the world's greatest philosophers, and allow them to work upon and improve my ideas, so that they may benefit mankind, without revealing the secret power, which in profane hands would prove but a curse?

For the present the secret shall remain *mine alone,* but what I may decide to do with it in the future, who knows?

It is not every day that one has an opportunity of receiving a millionaire as a guest, and to have the privilege of hypnotizing one is a still rarer thing, yet both these experiences have been mine at one and the same time, and I will relate how it happened.

I was staying for a few days on the Cornish coast, and had drawn my van far on to the beach, by the side of a rivulet which, coming down from low neighbouring hills, murmured and tumbled along its rocky bed until it lost itself in the immeasurable sea.

My van was placed near some rocky cliffs, in such a position as to be snug and secluded, and yet so as to retain a view up the lovely valley through which the little river sparkled and foamed. I selected the spot because of its quietude and beauty; I do not care for the annoyance of children, or the obtrusive curiosity of their elders, when they can easily be avoided by a little forethought.

Once or twice I noticed a tall, middle-aged gentleman roaming quietly among the rocks and pools left by the low tide, and on one occasion passed the seal of day with him in a casual manner; but, as he seemed to be of a retiring disposition, I did not attempt to force my company upon him, and passed on.

One day I sat on a rock observing a wonderful storm-clouded sky; I watched the great, massive, vapour clouds rolling in from the west, growing blacker and denser each minute. I noticed the hush of the air and the subsidence of the wind, and so did the little birds, for they flew twittering overhead to hide themselves from the approaching storm. Then from the clouds burst the vivid zig-zags of lightning, and the accompanying roar of crashing thunder, gradually coming nearer and nearer, more frequent and louder. Presently, with a sudden blast, the wind came hurtling down with startling force and fury, licking up the sand and shingle as it drove along; and behind it came the rain, first a few sparse drops, then a full downpour, and finally a rushing torrent.

This drove me into the welcome shelter of my van; but although I securely closed the door it could not keep, from my startled ears, the thunder crashes, as they reverberated and rolled among the stupendous granite cliffs of the coast. My van shook, and my eyes were blinded by several intense flashes of the discharged electric element, which lighted up the wet rocks and the wind-swept pools with a luridly grand but awful effect.

The cliffs appeared as if they were being shattered and tumbled piecemeal to the shingle below, when an unmistakable tap, tap, tap rattled upon my door, and I fancied I heard a voice, but the crashing and roaring noises around me were so great that I paused before opening the door for a repetition of the sound. Indeed my nerves were strung up to such an intense pitch that, when the taps were repeated in a louder manner, I felt afraid to open, for fear of letting in some weird spirit of the storm.

Nervous, however, as I felt, I arose, and at the door, craving my van's humble shelter, was the silent gentleman I had spoken to a day or two previously. I welcomed him in, but he was already wet to the skin. That did not at all matter; I had plenty of dry clothes, which fitted him like his own — both his and my inches being more than those allotted to the average mortal.

In an hour the storm was over, the sun once more shone brilliantly over the heaving waters, while the larks rose warbling in the air, caroling their hymn of praise for the return of the welcome sunshine.

My guest accepted my invitation to stay and dine with me, and I found him a very pleasant companion. He helped me to prepare and cook the meal, and in the interval we played cribbage, smoked, and chatted.

He had come down to Cornwall, he informed me, to escape from his friends and mankind in general, for, having inherited some money, he was worried and pestered on all sides by impecunious persons and institutions; and to come to a place where he was unknown was his only means of obtaining a little peace, "far from the madding crowd."

Of course I brought hypnotism upon the *tapis* during dinner, and after the meal was discussed, he requested me to try my hand upon him, which of course I gladly did, with the result of obtaining from him the following story of "Two Ruined Towers."

I must here point out that, though while in a hypnotic trance I can cause my patient to tell me a story, yet when at its conclusion I awaken him, he does not remember a word of what he has divulged, and I do not on all occasions enlighten him; for, as I am at times the recipient of most remarkable family secrets, crimes, and misdeeds, I dare not commit to print a tithe of what is related to me.

The Story of Baelbrow*

It is a matter for regret that so many of Mr. Flaxman Low's reminiscences should deal with the darker episodes of his experiences. Yet this is almost unavoidable, as the more purely scientific and less strongly marked cases would not, perhaps, contain the same elements of interest for the general public, however valuable and instructive they might be to the expert student. It has also been considered better to choose the completer cases, those that ended in something like satisfactory proof, rather than the many instances where the thread broke off abruptly amongst surmisings, which it was never possible to subject to convincing tests.

North of a low-lying strip of country on the East Anglian coast, the promontory of Bael Ness thrusts out a blunt nose into the sea. On the Ness, backed by pinewoods, stands a square, comfortable stone mansion, known to the countryside as Baelbrow. It has faced the east winds for close upon three hundred years, and during the whole period has been the home of the Swaffam family, who were never in anywise put out of conceit of their ancestral dwelling by the fact that it had always been haunted. Indeed, the Swaffams were proud of the Baelbrow Ghost, which enjoyed a wide notoriety, and no one dreamt of complaining of its behaviour until Professor Van der Voort of Louvain laid information against it, and sent an urgent appeal for help to Mr. Flaxman Low.

The Professor, who was well acquainted with Mr. Low, detailed the circumstances of his tenancy of Baelbrow, and the unpleasant events that had followed thereupon.

It appeared that Mr. Swaffam, senior, who spent a large portion of his time abroad, had offered to lend his house to the Professor for the summer season. When the Van der Voorts arrived at Baelbrow, they were charmed with the place. The prospect, though not very varied, was at least extensive, and the air exhilarating. Also the Professor's daughter enjoyed frequent visits from her betrothed — Harold Swaffam — and the Professor was delightfully employed in overhauling the Swaffam library.

The Van der Voorts had been duly told of the ghost, which lent distinction to the old house, but never in any way interfered with the comfort of the inmates. For some time they found this description to be strictly true, but with the beginning of October came a change. Up to this time and as far back as the Swaffam annals reached, the ghost had been a shadow, a rustle, a passing sigh — nothing definite or troublesome. But early in October strange things began to occur, and the terror culminated when a housemaid was found dead in a corridor three weeks later. Upon this the Professor felt that it was time to send for Flaxman Low.

---

* "The Story of Baelbrow" was written by E. & H. Heron, pseud. of Kate and Hesketh Prichard (1876 – 1922), and published in *Pearson's Magazine*, Apr. 1898.

Mr. Low arrived upon a chilly evening when the house was already beginning to blur in the purple twilight, and the resinous scent of the pines came sweetly on the land breeze. Van der Voort welcomed him in the spacious, fire-lit hall. He was a stout man with a quantity of white hair, round eyes emphasised by spectacles, and a kindly, dreamy face. His life-study was philology, and his two relaxations chess and the smoking of a big bowled meerschaum.

'Now, Professor,' said Mr. Low when they had settled themselves in the smoking-room, 'how did it all begin?'

'I will tell you,' replied Van der Voort, thrusting out his chin, and tapping his broad chest, and speaking as if an unwarrantable liberty had been taken with him. 'First of all, it has shown itself to me!'

Mr. Flaxman Low smiled and assured him that nothing could be more satisfactory.

'But not at all satisfactory!' exclaimed the Professor. 'I was sitting here alone, it might have been midnight — when I hear something come creeping like a little dog with its nails, tick-tick, upon the oak flooring of the hall. I whistle, for I think it is the little "Rags" of my daughter, and afterwards opened the door, and I saw' — he hesitated and looked hard at Low through his spectacles, 'something that was just disappearing into the passage which connects the two wings of the house. It was a figure, not unlike the human figure, but narrow and straight. I fancied I saw a bunch of black hair, and a flutter of something detached, which may have been a handkerchief. I was overcome by a feeling of repulsion. I heard a few clicking steps, then it stopped, as I thought, at the museum door. Come, I will show you the spot.'

The Professor conducted Mr. Low into the hall. The main staircase, dark and massive, yawned above them, and directly behind it ran the passage referred to by the Professor. It was over twenty feet long, and about midway led past a deep arch containing a door reached by two steps. Van der Voort explained that this door formed the entrance to a large room called the Museum, in which Mr. Swaffam, senior, who was something of a dilettante, stored the various curios he picked up during his excursions abroad. The Professor went on to say that he immediately followed the figure, which he believed had gone into the museum, but he found nothing there except the cases containing Swaffam's treasures.

'I mentioned my experience to no one. I concluded that I had seen the ghost. But two days after, one of the female servants coming through the passage, in the dark, declared that a man leapt out at her from the embrasure of the Museum door, but she released herself and ran screaming into the servants' hall. We at once made a search but found nothing to substantiate her story.

'I took no notice of this, though it coincided pretty well with my own experience. The week after, my daughter Lena came down late one night for a book. As she was about to cross the hall, something leapt upon her from behind. Women are of little use in serious investigations — she fainted! Since then she has been ill and the doctor says "run down".' Here the Professor spread out his hands. 'So she leaves for a change tomorrow. Since then other members of the household have been attacked in much the same manner, with always the same result, they faint and are weak and useless when they recover.

'But, last Wednesday, the affair became a tragedy. By that time the servants had refused to come through the passage except in a crowd of three or four, — most of them preferring to go round by the terrace to reach this part of the house. But one maid, named Eliza Freeman, said she was not afraid of the Baelbrow Ghost, and undertook to put out the lights in the hall one night. When she had done so, and was returning through the passage past the Museum door, she appears to have been attacked, or at any rate frightened. In the grey of the morning they found her lying beside the steps dead. There was a little blood upon her sleeve but no mark upon her body except a small raised pustule under the ear. The doctor said the girl was extraordinarily anæmic, and that she probably died from fright, her heart being weak. I was surprised at this, for she had always seemed to be a particularly strong and active young woman.'

'Can I see Miss Van der Voort to-morrow before she goes?' asked Low, as the Professor signified he had nothing more to tell.

The Professor was rather unwilling that his daughter should be questioned, but he at last gave his permission, and next morning Low had a short talk with the girl before she left the house. He found her a very pretty girl, though listless and startlingly pale, and with a frightened stare in her light brown eyes. Mr. Low asked if she could describe her assailant.

'No,' she answered. 'I could not see him for he was behind me. I only saw a dark, bony hand, with shining nails, and a bandaged arm pass just under my eyes before I fainted.' 'Bandaged arm? I have heard nothing of this.'

'Tut-tut, mere fancy!' put in the Professor impatiently.

'I saw the bandages on the arm,' repeated the girl, turning her head wearily away, 'and I smelt the antiseptics it was dressed with.'

'You have hurt your neck,' remarked Mr. Low, who noticed a small circular patch of pink under her ear.

She flushed and paled, raising her hand to her neck with a nervous jerk, as she said in a low voice: 'It has almost killed me. Before he touched me, I knew he was there! I felt it!'

When they left her the Professor apologised for the unreliability of her evidence, and pointed out the discrepancy between her statement and his own.

'She says she sees nothing but an arm, yet I tell you it had no arms! Preposterous! Conceive a wounded man entering this house to frighten the young women! I do not know what to make of it! Is it a man, or is it the Baelbrow Ghost?'

During the afternoon when Mr. Low and the Professor returned from a stroll on the shore, they found a dark-browed young man with a bull neck, and strongly marked features, standing sullenly before the hall fire. The Professor presented him to Mr. Low as Harold Swaffam.

Swaffam seemed to be about thirty, but was already known as a far-seeing and successful member of the Stock Exchange.

'I am pleased to meet you, Mr. Low,' he began, with a keen glance, 'though you don't look sufficiently high-strung for one of your profession.'

Mr. Low merely bowed.

'Come, you don't defend your craft against my insinuations?' went on Swaffam. 'And so you have come to rout out our poor old ghost from Baelbrow? You forget that he is an heirloom, a family possession! What's this about his having turned rabid, eh, Professor?' he ended, wheeling round upon Van der Voort in his brusque way.

The Professor told the story over again. It was plain that he stood rather in awe of his prospective son-in-law.

'I heard much the same from Lena, whom I met at the station,' said Swaffam. 'It is my opinion that the women in this house are suffering from an epidemic of hysteria. You agree with me, Mr. Low?'

'Possibly. Though hysteria could hardly account for Freeman's death.'

'I can't say as to that until I have looked further into the particulars. I have not been idle since I arrived. I have examined the Museum. No one has entered it from the outside, and there is no other way of entrance except through the passage. The flooring is laid, I happen to know, on a thick layer of concrete. And there the case for the ghost stands at present.' After a few moments of dogged reflection, he swung round on Mr. Low, in a manner that seemed peculiar to him when about to address any person. 'What do you say to this plan, Mr. Low? I propose to drive the Professor over to Ferryvale, to stop there for a day or two at the hotel, and I will also dispose of the servants who still remain in the house for, say, forty-eight hours. Meanwhile you and I can try to go further into the secret of the ghost's new pranks?'

Flaxman Low replied that this scheme exactly met his views, but the Professor protested against being sent away. Harold Swaffam, however, was a man who liked to arrange things in his own fashion, and within forty-five minutes he and Van der Voort departed in the dogcart.

The evening was lowering, and Baelbrow, like all houses built in exposed situations, was extremely susceptible to the changes of the weather. Therefore, before many hours were over, the place was full of creaking noises as the screaming gale battered at the shuttered windows, and the tree-branches tapped and groaned against the walls.

Harold Swaffam on his way back was caught in the storm and drenched to the skin. It was, therefore, settled that after he had changed his clothes he should have a couple of hours' rest on the smoking-room sofa, while Mr. Low kept watch in the hall.

The early part of the night passed over uneventfully. A light burned faintly in the great wainscotted hall, but the passage was dark. There was nothing to be heard but the wild moan and whistle of the wind coming in from the sea, and the squalls of rain dashing against the windows. As the hours advanced, Mr. Low lit a lantern that lay at hand, and, carrying it along the passage tried the Museum door. It yeilded, and the wind came muttering through to meet him. He looked round at the shutters and behind the big cases which held Mr. Swaffam's treasures, to make sure that the room contained no living occupant but himself.

Suddenly he fancied he heard a scraping noise behind him, and turned round, but discovered nothing to account for it. Finally, he laid the lantern on a bench so that its light should fall through the door into the passage, and returned again to the hall, where he put out the lamp, and then once more took up his station by the closed door of the smoking-room. A long hour passed, during which the wind continued to roar down the wide hall chimney, and the old boards creaked as if furtive footsteps were gathering from every corner of the house. But Flaxman Low heeded none of these; he was awaiting for a certain sound.

After a while, he heard it — the cautious scraping of wood on wood. He leant forward to watch the Museum door. Click, click, came the curious dog-like tread upon the tiled floor of the Museum, till the thing, whatever it was, paused and listened behind the open door. The wind lulled at the moment, and Low listened also, but no further sound was to be heard, only slowly across the broad ray of light falling through the door grew a stealthy shadow.

Again the wind rose, and blew in heavy gusts about the house, till even the flame in the lantern flickered; but when it steadied once more, Flaxman Low saw that the silent form had passed through the door, and was now on the steps outside. He could just make out a dim shadow in the dark angle of the embrasure.

Presently, from the shapeless shadow came a sound Mr. Low was not prepared to hear. The thing sniffed the air with the strong, audible inspiration of a bear, or some large animal. At the same moment, carried on the draughts of the hall, a faint, unfamiliar odour reached his nostrils. Lena Van der Voort's words flashed back upon him — this, then, was the creature with the bandaged arm!

Again, as the storm shrieked and shook the windows, a darkness passed across the light. The thing had sprung out from the angle of the door, and Flaxman Low knew that it was making its way towards him through the illusive blackness of the hall. He hesitated for a second; then he opened the smoking-room door.

Harold Swaffam sat up on the sofa, dazed with sleep.

'What has happened? Has it come?'

Low told him what he had just seen. Swaffam listened half-smilingly.

'What do you make of it now?' he said.

'I must ask you to defer that question for a little,' replied Low.

'Then you mean me to suppose that you have a theory to fit all these incongruous items?'

'I have a theory, which may be modified by further knowledge,' said Low. 'Meantime, am I right in concluding from the name of this house that it was built on a barrow or burying-place?'

'You are right, though that has nothing to do with the latest freaks of our ghost,' returned Swaffam decidedly.

'I also gather that Mr. Swaffam has lately sent home one of the many cases now lying in the Museum?' went on Mr. Low.

'He sent one, certainly, last September.'

'And you have opened it,' asserted Low.

'Yes; though I flattered myself I had left no trace of my handiwork.'

'I have not examined the cases,' said Low. 'I inferred that you had done so from other facts.'

'Now, one thing more,' went on Swaffam, still smiling. Do you imagine there is any danger — I mean to men like ourselves? Hysterical women cannot be taken into serious account.'

'Certainly; the gravest danger to any person who moves about this part of the house alone after dark,' replied Low.

Harold Swaffam leant back and crossed his legs.

'To go back to the beginning of our conversation, Mr. Low, may I remind you of the various conflicting particulars you will have to reconcile before you can present any decent theory to the world?'

'I am quite aware of that.'

'First of all, our original ghost was a mere misty presence, rather guessed at from vague sounds and shadows — now we have a something that is tangible, and that can, as we have proof, kill with fright. Next Van der Voort declares the thing was a narrow, long and distinctly armless object, while Miss Van der Voort has not only seen the arm and hand of a human being, but saw them clearly enough to tell us that the nails were gleaming and the arm bandaged. She also felt its strength. Van der Voort, on the other hand, maintained that it clicked along like a dog — you bear out this description with the additional information that it sniffs like a wild beast. Now what can this thing be? It is capable of being seen, smelt, and felt, yet it hides itself, successfully in a room where there is no cavity or space sufficient to afford covert to a cat! You still tell me that you believe that you can explain?'

'Most certainly,' replied Flaxman Low with conviction.

'I have not the slightest intention or desire to be rude, but as a mere matter of common sense, I must express my opinion plainly. I believe the whole thing to be the result of excited imaginations, and I am about to prove it. Do you think there is any further danger to-night?'

'Very great danger to-night,' replied Low.

'Very well; as I said, I am going to prove it. I will ask you to allow me to lock you up in one of the distant rooms, where I can get no help from you, and I will pass the remainder of the night walking about the passage and hall in the dark. That should give proof one way or the other.'

'You can do so if you wish, but I must at least beg to be allowed to look on. I will leave the house and watch what goes on from the window in the passage, which I saw opposite the Museum door. You cannot, in any fairness, refuse to let me be a witness.'

'I cannot, of course,' returned Swaffam. 'Still, the night is too bad to turn a dog out into, and I warn you that I shall lock you out.'

'That will not matter. Lend me a macintosh, and leave the lantern lit in the Museum, where I placed it.'

Swaffam agreed to this. Mr. Low gives a graphic account of what followed. He left the house and was duly locked out, and, after groping his way round the house, found himself at length outside the window of the passage, which was almost opposite to the door of the

Museum. The door was still ajar and a thin band of light cut out into the gloom. Further down the hall gaped black and void. Low, sheltering himself as well as he could from the rain, waited for Swaffam's appearance. Was the terrible yellow watcher balancing itself upon its lean legs in the dim corner opposite, ready to spring out with its deadly strength upon the passer-by?

Presently Low heard a door bang inside the house, and the next moment Swaffam appeared with a candle in his hand, an isolated spread of weak rays against the vast darkness behind. He advanced steadily down the passage, his dark face grim and set, and as he came Mr. Low experienced that tingling sensation, which is so often the forerunner of some strange experience. Swaffam passed on towards the other end of the passage. There was a quick vibration of the Museum door as a lean shape with a shrunken head leapt out into the passage after him. Then all together came a hoarse shout, the noise of a fall and utter darkness.

In an instant, Mr. Low had broken the glass, opened the window, and swung himself into the passage. There he lit a match and as it flared he saw by its dim light a picture painted for a second upon the obscurity beyond.

Swaffam's big figure lay with outstretched arms, face downwards, and as Low looked a crouching shape extricated itself from the fallen man, raising a narrow vicious head from his shoulder.

The match spluttered feebly and went out, and Low heard a flying step click on the boards, before he could find the candle Swaffam had dropped. Lighting it, he stooped over Swaffam and turned him on his back. The man's strong colour had gone, and the wax-white face looked whiter still against the blackness of hair and brows, and upon his neck under the ear was a little raised pustule, from which a thin line of blood was streaked up to the angle of his cheekbone.

Some instinctive feeling prompted Low to glance up at this moment. Half extended from the Museum doorway were a face and bony neck — a high-nosed, dull-eyed, malignant face, the eye-sockets hollow, and the darkened teeth showing. Low plunged his hand into his pocket, and a shot rang out in the echoing passage-way and hall. The wind sighed through the broken panes, a ribbon of stuff fluttered along the polished flooring, and that was all, as Flaxman Low half dragged, half carried Swaffam into the smoking-room.

It was some time before Swaffam recovered consciousness. He listened to Low's story of how he had found him with a red angry gleam in his sombre eyes.

'The ghost has scored off me,' he said, with an odd, sullen laugh, 'but now I fancy it's my turn! But before we adjourn to the Museum to examine the place, I will ask you to let me hear your notion of things. You have been right in saying there was real danger. For myself I can only tell you that I felt something spring upon me, and I knew no more. Had this not happened I am afraid I should never have asked you a second time what your idea of the matter might be,' he added with a sort of sulky frankness.

'There are two main indications,' replied Low. 'This strip of yellow bandage, which I have just now picked up from the passage floor, and the mark on your neck.'

'What's that you say?' Swaffam rose quickly and examined his neck in a small glass beside the mantelshelf.

'Connect those two, and I think I can leave you to work it out for yourself,' said Low.

'Pray let us have your theory in full,' requested Swaffam shortly.

'Very well,' answered Low good-humouredly — he thought Swaffam's annoyance natural in the circumstances — 'The long, narrow figure which seemed to the Professor to be armless is developed on the next occasion. For Miss Van der Voort sees a bandaged arm and a dark hand with gleaming — which means, of course, gilded — nails. The clicking sound of the footsteps coincides with these particulars, for we know that sandals made of strips of leather are not uncommon in company with gilt nails and bandages. Old and dry leather would naturally click upon your polished floor.'

'Bravo, Mr. Low! So you mean to say that this house is haunted by a mummy!'

'That is my idea, and all I have seen confirms me in my opinion.'

'To do you justice, you held this theory before to-night — before, in fact, you had seen anything for yourself. You gathered that my father had sent home a mummy, and you went on to conclude that I had opened the case?'

'Yes. I imagine you took off most of, or rather all, the outer bandages, thus leaving the limbs free, wrapped only in the inner bandages which were swathed round each separate limb. I fancy this mummy was preserved on the Theban method with aromatic spices, which left the skin olive-coloured, dry and flexible, like tanned leather, the features remaining distinct, and the hair, teeth, and eyebrows perfect.'

'So far, good,' said Swaffam. 'But now, how about the intermittent vitality? The postule on the neck of those whom it attacks? And where is our old Baelbrow ghost to come in?'

Swaffam tried to speak in a rallying tone, but his excitement and lowering temper were visible enough, in spite of the attempts he made to suppress them.

'To begin at the beginning,' said Flaxman Low, 'everybody who, in a rational and honest manner, investigates the phenomena of spiritism will, sooner or later, meet in them some perplexing element, which is not to be explained by any of the ordinary theories. For reasons into which I need not now enter, this present case appears to me to be one of these. I am led to believe that the ghost which has for so many years given dim and vague manifestations of its existence in this house is a vampire.'

Swaffam threw back his head with an incredulous gesture.

'We no longer live in the middle ages, Mr. Low! And besides, how could a vampire come here?' he said scoffingly.

'It is held by some authorities on these subjects that under certain conditions a vampire may be self-created. You tell me that this house is built upon an ancient barrow, in fact, on a spot where we might naturally expect to find such an elemental psychic germ. In those dead human systems were contained all the seeds for good and evil. The power which causes these psychic seeds or germs to grow is thought, and from being long dwelt on and indulged, a thought might finally gain a mysterious vitality, which could go on increasing more and more by attracting to itself suitable and appropriate elements from its environment. For a long period this germ remained a helpless intelligence, awaiting the opportunity to assume some material form, by means of which to carry out its desires. The invisible is the real; the material only subserves its manifestation. The impalpable reality already existed, when you provided for it a physical medium for action by unwrapping the mummy's form. Now, we can only judge of the nature of the germ by its manifestation through matter. Here we have every indication of a vampire intelligence touching into life and energy the dead human frame. Hence the mark on the neck of its victims, and their bloodless and anæmic condition. For a vampire, as you know, sucks blood.'

Swaffam rose, and took up the lamp.

'Now, for proof,' he said bluntly. 'Wait a second, Mr. Low. You say you fired at this appearance?' And he took up the pistol which Low had laid down on the table.

'Yes, I aimed at a small portion of its foot which I saw on the step.'

Without more words, and with the pistol still in his hand, Swaffam led the way to the Museum.

The wind howled round the house, and the darkness, which precedes the dawn, lay upon the world, when the two men looked upon one of the strangest sights it has ever been given to men to shudder at.

Half in and half out of an oblong wooden box in a corner of the great room, lay a lean shape in its rotten yellow bandages, the scraggy neck surmounted by a mop of frizzled hair. The toe strap of a sandal and a portion of the right foot had been shot away.

Swaffam, with a working face, gazed down at it, then seizing it by its tearing bandages, he flung it into the box, where it fell into a life-like posture, its wide, moist-lipped mouth gaping up at them.

For a moment Swaffam stood over the thing; then with a curse he raised the revolver and shot into the grinning face again and again with a deliberate vindictiveness. Finally he rammed the thing down into the box, and, clubbing the weapon, smashed the head into fragments with a vicious energy that coloured the whole horrible scene with a suggestion of murder done.

Then, turning to Low, he said: 'Help me to fasten the cover on it.'

'Are you going to bury it?'

'No, we must rid the earth of it,' he answered savagely. 'I'll put it into the old canoe and burn it.'

The rain had ceased when in the daybreak they carried the old canoe down to the shore. In it they placed the mummy case with its ghastly occupant, and piled faggots about it. The sail was raised and the pile lighted, and Low and Swaffam watched it creep out on the ebb-tide, at first a twinkling spark, then a flare and waving fire, until far out to sea the history of that dead thing ended 3000 years after the priests of Armen had laid it to rest in its appointed pyramid.

The Awakening of Pharaoh[*]

I made his acquaintance at Tontine City Depôt while waiting for the Minneapolis express. He was sitting on a long packing case which was tightly bound with strong cord, and when the train at length drew up he was very anxious about this. He gave the baggage-master and the porters a good many instructions, which were carefully disregarded, and after he had seen it roughly hustled into the car he turned to me with a sigh.

"I guess, Colonel," said he, "there's some cons'lation in not bein' aval'able antiquity." With this profound reflection he got on board, and I followed him.

"You mentioned antiquities just now," I remarked, when we were comfortably settled. "No doubt that case of yours holds something of the sort?"

"Sir," he replied, "you've hit the bull dead in the eye. It does."

"Pottery?" I suggested.

A sneer curled round his lips and was lost in the surrounding furrows.'

"No," he said, "I don't pilot pots. At this pertic'ler moment I'm look in' after the remains of a king."

There was a republican emphasis on the last word which was nothing less than majestic.

"Indeed. Which king?"

"Pharaoh," he replied.

"There were several Pharaohs, if I remember rightly," I remarked.

"Only one that interests Amurricans," he answered. "Maybe you've heard of the Children of Israel? I guess there was only one Pharaoh fur them, an' he's in the baggagecar of thishyer express to-night."

"Why, he was lost in the Red Sea!" I exclaimed.

"Sir," he replied with a pitying look, "you air misinformed. His body was washed ashore an' embalmed, an' fur the last ten years it has been in the Municipal Museum of Tontine City, Dak., whar I'm curator. We air swoppin' spec'mins jest now to keep up our supply of new an' interestin' articles. I'm takin' Pharaoh to Minneapolis to-night, an' tomorrer I hope to return with three stuffed alligaters in exchange. We're dead nuts on Nat'ral Hist'ry in Tontine, Dak."

I saw he was disposed to be communicative, so went on:

"It's an interesting line of business, yours. You'll have had some curious articles to look after in your time."

* "The Awakening of Pharaoh" was written by Henry A. Hering (1874 – 1949) and published in *Cassell's Magazine*, May 1898.

"That's so, Colonel. I have," he replied; "but never one so cur'us as old Pharaoh. I could tell a yarn about him as 'ud astonish ye, if ye care to hear it."

"I should very much like to," I replied. "Have a smoke?"

"Thank you, sirree," said the old fellow. "I think thishyer will jest see me through it." He cut the end with great care, lighted it and puffed meditatively for an odd minute before he continued:

"When I got fixed up at Tontine I sorter thought it was fur life, an' I had no pertic'ler reason to think different till two years ago this fall. Then some mos' surprisin' things happened, an' at one time it looked uncommon as if I should have to yamoose.

"Ye see, Colonel, it's my duty to go roun' last thing an' see that all visitors have cleared, that the lights are down, an' that all is in order. I lock up the buildin' myself, an' am respons'ble fur its safety overnight. I live on the premises, an' when I come through my door nex' day I nat'rally expec' to find things pretty much as I left 'em. An' I wasn't disappointed till one fine mornin' I went into the Roman Secshun an' saw somethin' that fairly bristled my hair. Sir, sittin' on the top of the stove in the centre of the room was King Pharaoh! His swaddlin' ban's was loose, an' his lim's were free. He was restin' his dried-up old head on one stick of an arm, his legs were twisted like cross bones, an' he looked jest the biggest scarecrow ever seen this side of eternity.

"I was once a keeper at Keeley Cure Institute, so it takes a trifle to upset me, but I don't mind ownin' I was a bit skeered at the sight. However, I walked up to Pharaoh an' tetched him, an' he toppled over into my arms.

"I was feelin' pretty indignant jest then. Some derned cuss had been tryin' to get a rise outer me. I felt pretty certain he mus' be somewhar in the buildin', so I laid Pharaoh on the floor, an' had a brisk trot through the var'us secshuns. I didn't miss a single corner, but I found nobody, an' the windows were all snecked an' the doors locked, jest as I'd left 'em. In the Egyptian department — which at that pertic'ler moment consisted of Pharaoh an' an old she-mummy who hadn't a date or a dynasty to her label — I came across fresh tracks of the varmint's work. Pharaoh's glass case had the top an' one side smashed to bits.

"This riled me. No doubt it was derned funny to take a deceased king out of his skoffagus, where he'd lain fur a trifle of ten thousand years or more, an' put him in a ridic'l'us persition on the top of the stove in the Roman Secshun, but I'd be derned if I saw where the fun came in at smashin' plate glass at so many dollars a foot.

"I saw I should get all the derned blame for the fireworks, so I went down an' gathered Pharaoh together, bound him up tight ag'in an' stuck him in his skoffagus. Then I cleared the litter of glass away, an' only reported the breakage to the secretary when he came.

"He was mighty suspicious, was Calvert Hunt; said I'd broken it myself, an' wanted to blame someone else; told me I'd have to get Pharaoh glazed up at my own expense; an' orated like a senator about my future prospec's.

"Now, Colonel, it wasn't pertic'ler pleasant to be jawed at like that for somethin' I'd had no hand in, but I had to lay low an' say little, 'cause I had jest sent in an application for a rise in my remuneration, but on my way down to the glass fitter I sez to myself, 'If I catch you, my ole joker, y'u'll have a laugh on the wrong side of your face that'll reach down to Lower Egyp' an' back.'

"Now, Colonel, you bet I didn't rest much after that demonstration. I'd got an enemy, an' I reckoned he'd be showin' his hand ag'in afore long, an' I wanted to meet him a little more'n half-way. I watched that museum like a 'coon-dog. I took a chair, an' sat for hours at night in a corner or the Egyptian department hard by Pharaoh, and I'd get up at all times for a canter round, but never a surprise did I get for my pains.

"In about a month I slacked off an' began to keep my usual hours ag'in, an' then the derned trouble turned up once more. The joker had tackled the whole Egyptian Secshun that time, for I found both mummies on the floor over the hot air gratin' in the central hall. Pharaoh's ban's were loose as afore, but the she-mummy was bound up. She was lyin' on her back, an' her head was on Pharaoh's knees, an' he was contemplatin' her, sentimental-like, with a dried-up smile on his ugly face. I ran to their department. Two sides of plate glass smashed in both the cases!

"I tell ye, Colonel, I was jest mad at the sight. It wer'n't simply the glass bill-though that would be tough enough — but it showed I was never safe. I made sure that the humorist wasn't still in the show, an' then came the nat'ral question, How had he got out? An' fur the matter of that, how had he got in, an' why had he done it? Why had he fixed on that blamed foolish way of spitin' me; an' if it warn't me he was drivin' at, why should he want to get at Pharaoh? What had Pharaoh done to any Tontiner? There wasn't a Jew in the place, an' if there was, it was too late in the day to bear malice on account of old scores. If neither of these reasons held, what had anyone to gain by insultin' the deceased monarch?

I picked up the effigies an' carried 'em to their skoffagusses, an' when the secretary came I reported the whole matter to him.

"He wore an eye-glass, did Calvert Hunt, an' for all disbelievin' purposes an eye-glass does better'n any other mortal thing. If ever an eye-glass said you're a derned liar that one did. Then Calvert mentioned one or two things pertic'ler cuttin'. As how he'd give me one more chance, as how he didn't mind me breakin' plate glass at my own expense, but as how he distinctly objected to val'able antiquities bein' tampered with. If I liquored I'd better lock myself in my own house, an' break my own winders if I must smash glass, but if I tetched Pharaoh or the she-mummy or any other Museum article in my tantrums I'd have to git, even if it was only a pisin'd arrer I'd been suckin'. Then he cleared me out.

"I felt pretty sick of human nayter that mornin', an' more'n half resolved to chuck my billet straight off; but, as luck had it, I fell in with Morphine Tompkins, the coffin-man, on my way from the glass-fitter's. Morphine had the job at the Museum afore me, till the increasin' rate of mortality in Tontine City induced him to swop his vocation. He was a crusty, short-tempered 'coon, an' I never had much to do with him, but I guess he saw I was down on my luck, an' it cheered him up a bit, for he stopped fren'ly like:

"'Seem a bit off it this mornin', Pete,' sez he.

"'Like as not I am,' I growled, an' then I told him the whole blamed thing.

"We reached his lean-to while I was talkin', an' I finished my yarn there.

"'Now, Morphine,' sez I at last, 'can ye tell me what it all means?'

"Morphine is a busy man, an' he'd been sizin' a length of lumber with his pencil an' foot rule while I was jawin'.

"'Kin I?' sez he, lookin' up with more life in his ugly phiz than I'd ever seen thar afore. 'You bet I kin. If ye'd come to me at fust, I could have saved yer glass bill, I reckon. It don't require to be a Harvard etymoligist to know what's the matter."

"'Well, what is it?' I asked eagerly.

"'Have ye ever heard how them mummy seeds of corn kim to life ag'in after thousan's of years, an' sproutin'.'

"'Of course I have.'

"'Well,' sez he, 'Pharaoh's sproutin'.'

"'What!' I yelled.

"'Pharaoh's sproutin',' said he, smilin' grim-like. 'I don't say 'coz why, fur no one knows but Pharaoh, an' he aint in a persition ter tell, but somethin's agreed with him this fall an' he's got some life back.'

"'Morphine,' sez I, 'it'll be the biggest show we've had in Tontine when he sprouts altogether.'

"'Maybe it will,' sez Morphine, 'but jest yer wait till he does. It's an elephant to a flea he won't. I've had one or two busts like that in my time, an' the secretary afore this — Silas Cornu, yer know — took a big int'rest in 'em. One pertic'ler mummy broke his case ter bits every week fur a month afore we hitched onter the cause. Then we lay in wait fur him. One night we heard him fall on the floor, so we rushed in an' got some brandy down his throat, but that finished him straight off. He jest landed Silas Cornu one on the jaw an' then kerlaps'd. We got him back inter his bin, an' he never broke his glass ag'in. Two years after another of 'em started sproutin' — a female that time. We found her in a dead faint afore our mayor's prisitation statoo of himself, an' rememb'rin' how we'd fooled it before, we tried lemonade thishyer time. But it weren't no good. It brought on what Silas called ashfix'al spasims, an' all the sprout went out of her. Silas didn't give her up in a hurry, though. We applied 'lectricity to her, fixin' one wire to her big toe an' the other to her tongue. We started with two cells an' worked quietly up to eighteen of 'em. Twice she drewed her lim's as if we was a-ticklin' her, but that was all the sign she showed in four mortal hours, so we gave her up at last, an' she didn't cost anythin' more in glass.

"'Silas Cornu thought the matter over very careful, an' we'd many a jaw about it. Sez he, "It's the cirklashun wants restorin',

Morphine. They want their blood warmin', an' we've got to find out the best way fur to do it." An' Pharaoh's conduc' bears it out, Pete. He wanted warmth, an that's why he sot on the stove in the Roman Secshun, an' feelin' lonely he tried to revive his female fren' over the hot air gratin'. Yes, Silas thought all those p'ints out, an' he sez to me the very day he left, "Morphine," sez he, "if there's any more sproutin' try massij."

"'Massij, Morphine. What's that?' I asked.

"'It's the Harvard name fur rubbin', ' sez Morphine. 'You've got to restore the cirklashun,' said Silas, 'an' that's the best way fur to do it. 'Lectricity's all right fur Amurricans, or even Britishers, but these hyar 'Gyptians are so blamed modest that if they felt the current was a-doin' of 'em good they wouldn't own to it. You try massij nex' time,' an' that's my advice to you, Pete.'

"'Where shall I rub him, Morphine? His nose or his han's?'

"'That ain't massij rubbin',' sez Morphine, 'that's what they call chafin'. Massij is a derned scientific thing. I asked Silas where I could get a hint, an' he sez, "You have a Turkey bath nex' time y'u're at Minneapolis, an' they'll massij yer wi' soap in the shampooin' room." So I had a two-dollar wash nex' time I was thar, an' if yer want to have a tetch of hades, an' then be massijed as clean as an angel at a dime show, jest try the Minneapolis Turkey baths, an' they won't disappoint ye. Y'u'll know what massij is, anyway.'

"'Then as you know the dodge, will ye come an' massij Pharaoh?' I asked.

"'Don't mind if I do, Pete,' sez Morphine. 'I'm sorter growin' rusty in thishyer coffin bizness. Feel as I'd like ter bring somethin' ter life fur wunst. Jest yer git yer tackle ready ter-night, an' I'll kim roun' after closin' time.'

"'What tackle do yer want?' I asked.

"'Fur Turkey bath massij yer want some patent brushes fur fixin' on yer han's. Y'u'll git 'em at any gen'ral store, that's all yer need ter buy. Y'u'll want a power of hot an' cold water, an' plenty of soap fur lather, but I guess y'u'll have that at home.'

"I never had seen Morphine so talkative an' fren'ly afore. He was jest the surliest 'coon in Tontine as a rule, but that sproutin' bizness waked him up wonderful.

"I had some trouble to find those brushes, but I got 'em at last. I watched 'em fix Pharaoh's glass up with an easy mind. So long as I knew his movin' was constitootional I didn't trouble. It was the notion someone was gettin' at me as was rilin'.

"That night Morphine came.

"'Shall we take 'em up to Pharaoh?' sez I, p'intin' to my pails an' soap.

"'No,' sez he; 'it'll be a long job like as not, an' there'll be a sight of water wanted. We'll have to bring Pharaoh down ter yer wash kitchen. I guess that's the nearest approach to a Turkey bath we kin give him ter-night.'

"So we brought Pharaoh down, an' laid him on an ironin' board an' took off his ban's. He was a wisp of a thing, Colonel — a driedup, shrivelled gaspipe of a king as ever I saw. It didn't seem no credit to assist nayter in sproutin' sich an objec'.

"Morphine didn't stop to ruminate. He got a pail of warm water, put on his brushes, soaped 'em, an' then lathered the monarch. Seemed to me Morphine would have done well in that Turkey bizness from his gen'ral style. He polished that king all ends up fur two mortal hours with soap an' hot water, never restin', an' sisslin' all the time like a stable help. He turned him over an' over ag'in, an' when he tired of the brushes, he massijed him with his han's. Pharaoh never budged, but that didn't trouble Morphine.

"'Now we've got him in a dead heat,' sez he at last, 'we must give him the cold doosh. If the shock don't make him sprout it oughter.'

"We emptied half a dozen pails of cold spring water over Pharaoh. 'Now then,' Morphine sez, 'let's try towellin'.'

"We took two warm towels an' massijed him brisk with them, till he was in a warm glow all over. I was busy with his feet, when Morphine sings out, 'He's sproutin', Pete, he's sproutin';' an', sure enough, Pharaoh was movin'!

"Morphine fairly danced. 'If Silas Cornu was only here,' he sez. 'This beats his inventin' bizness holler. Now, Judge,' addressin' Pharaoh, 'take it easyful. Me an' Pete air only wantin' fur ter do yer good,' fur Pharaoh was strugglin' hard with the surroundin' atmosphere.

"'Raise him gently, Pete,' sez Morphine. 'There,' an' Pharaoh was a-sittin' on the end of the ironin' board.

"We wrapped a big warm dust-sheet round him, an' got him afore the fire. If ever a man tried hard to smile an' look pleased, that man was Pharaoh, but the crinckles an' ruts on his face was awful, an' he couldn't work through 'em.

"'Now, Colonel,' sez Morphine, 'kin yer hold up by yerself?'

"'Call him Gen'ral,' sez I. 'He was boss man at home–ran a Congress of his own like as not.'

"Pharaoh was limp, there was no getting over it. We stuck him back in an easy chair, an' there he sot, starin' at the fire, his face twitchin' contented like.

"'What about drinks, Morphine?' sez I. 'Seems to me he'd fancy one.'

"'Better wait till mornin',' sez Morphine. 'We overdid that afore. We'll have a physician's advice fust. He's done without liquor for some thousan's of years, so I reckon a few hours more won't signerfy. How's yer lordship feelin' now?' sez he, mighty perlite. He'd got the hang of that sentence through once showin' a Duke over the museum with a Congress-man.

"Pharaoh didn't answer. Once or twice it looked as if he wanted to open his mouth, but it seemed stuck.

"'Looks like lock-jaw,' said Morphine anxiously. 'P'r'aps you'd better go fur a docter now. Snakes! what's up with him?'

"He might well ask. Pharaoh's eyes were fixed on a print hangin' on the wall behind the stove. It was a coloured representation of Lake Michigan in a storm, the waves lashin' mount'ins high, an' the lightnin' flarin'. Pharaoh's eyes were froze on that print, an' a live red Injun couldn't have skeered him more. He jest shook with fear, an' then without a word of warnin', doubled up an' fell off his chair, knockin' his head agin the stove. His neck was dry an' parched, fur Morphine hadn't massijed it much. It snapped like a twig, an' his head rolled under the table.

"'Tarnation!' yelled Morphine, springin' up an' gettin' Pharaoh together. 'Where's his head? Quick, yer derned hayseed!'

"We stuck it on his shoulders agin, but it wouldn't fit, fur a big part of his neck had splintered off.

"'Well, of all the blamed do's,' sez Morphine, despairin' like, 'this tops the lot! Jest fancy thishyer happenin' when we'd got him nicely roun'. An' ter think that derned print of yours should have skeered him so. 'Tain't as if the waves were daubed in red, neither. What a mem'ry he had. He must have had a wettin' when he was drown'd. 'Tain't no good now, Pete. We've broken his varicus' vein. Let's cart him upstairs, an' bring yer glue-pot with ye.'

"We wrapped him up ag'in in his ban's an' things, an' put him in his skoffagus, an' then we glued his head on. Morphine made a good job of it; that's whar his coffin trainin' came in. He found the splinters of his neck an' stuck 'em in, an' smoothed 'em all round with sand-paper, an' it 'ud take an expert etymoligist to find it out.

"We never had any hope of Pharaoh after his head came off. Even sproutin' has its limits. So I didn't feel pertic'ler sorry when I heard they were goin' to swop him fur some stuffed alligators.

"The she-mummy is there yet, but her day hasn't come. Next time ye're in Tontine, sir, ye might look in at the Museum, an' maybe I shall have a yarn to spin about her."

Two Professors and One Mummy*

y dear Sir, or madam, medicine and treatment are of no avail in your particular case. What you require is a breath of your native air. That will do you more good than all the doctors' prescriptions in the world. Go to your birthplace to-morrow, and come and see me again in a month — cured."

The above airy advice has been addressed from time immemorial, alike by perplexed specialist and nonpulsed general practitioner, to the despairing patient, but there are no statistics available as to results. To those who have received this advice, and are hesitating whether to follow it, I give a remarkable instance of the beneficial results following the sojourn of a lady in her native air after the lapse of a considerable time, when all other attempts to restore her to her pristine vigor had signally failed.

The brothers Robinson are noted savants. The elder, Henry, resides in the Scilly Isles, and there pursues his remarkable investigations of fungi. The younger, Richard, is Professor of Egyptology at the University of Padua.

One day Professor Henry Robinson received the following letter, dated from the British Museum: —

> "My dear Sir, — we have just received from a correspondent in Samoa some funky of native growth, and seemingly most interesting character. As they are quite outside our province, I am forwarding them to you in the hope that they may be of use for your new work, which I trust will soon be through the press.
> "Yours faithfully,
> "James Munroe."

That week Professor Richard Robinson of Padua also received a note from the same source: —

> "Dear Robinson, — Padré has sent us a mummy of the XXV Dynasty. We are overstocked with this period, and as I remember your lament about the scarcity of specimens at your place, I am forwarding the case to you. You might report us if you find anything special about it.
> "We shall no doubt meet at Geneva next month.
> "With kindest regards to Mrs. Robinson,
> "Sincerely yours,
> "James Munroe."

---

* "Two Professors and One Mummy" was written by Henry A. Hering (1874 – 1949) and published in *Cassell's Magazine*, Oct. 1901.

These letters, though no doubt of importance to the gentleman to whom they were addressed, are of absolutely no interest to the outside world, and had the packages therein mentioned been duly forwarded to their respective destinations this story would not have been written; but owing to a clerical error this did not occur. The Egyptian mummy was addressed to the Scilly Isles, and Professor Richard Robinson received the case containing fungi.

There was hard swearing in Italy when the letter was opened, and for the moment, being early in April, it was thought that Mr. Munroe had been guilty of a practical joke, alike below the dignity of his office and unworthy of his high character.

Suddenly light flashed across the Egyptological brain of the Paduan Professor.

"I see how it is. Munroe has sent Richard my mummy, and I've got his fungi. There was a similar mistake made about ten years ago with some cuneiform and a prickly cactus. I will write at once."

So the learned gentleman sat down and penned a desultory effusion to his brother, winding up with —

"By the by, do you happen to have received a mummy? Munroe has advised me of one, and sent a box of fungi. I presume it is the old mistake. Anyway, I am sending you the fungi, and shall be glad to hear of my property."

A week later he received the following inconclusive reply: —

"Dear Richard, — Sinnot is an ass; the matter was settled by Duvine twenty years ago in his treaty on Tuberaceæ. Delighted to hear your boy is doing so well. Shall be glad to see him when he can spare time to run over.

"I hear you are going to Geneva. For Heaven's sake be careful. You are so rash in your conjectures. Lockett tells me that you are quite wrong in your conclusions about the orientation of the Temple of Pthah at Memphis.
"Your affectionate brother,
"Henry.
"P.S. — many thanks for the fungi you advise. Munroe ought to know my address by this time. "

"Confounded his impudence," said Professor Richard Robinson, when he read this letter. "I should like to know if my word isn't as good as Lockett's any day. 'Rash in my conjectures,' indeed! What about his own paper on potato disease? It was the laughing stock of Europe. And what about my mummy? He hasn't even the grace to mention it. I'll wire him."

So in considerable indignation the learned Professor sent off the following message —

"*Have you got my mummy?* — Richard," and in a few hours received the reply: "*There is no mummy in my house.* — Henry."

The Paduan Professor's language on receipt of this wire was loud and strong.

"Dick," he said to his son, "you can take your vacation now instead of next month. You must start for England to-morrow. Your uncle has sent me this wire in reply to mine. He's equivocating — that's the long and short of it. He's got my specimen and is detaining it for purposes best known to himself. You must get to the bottom of the matter; and my last instructions are — don't come home without the mummy."

On the following day Richard Robinson, junior, set off for the Scilly Isles inquest of the afore-mentioned antiquity.

Professor Richard Robinson was right in his surmise. His brother had received the mummy.

The size and form of the case excited his surprise and misgivings from the first, and deep was his disgust when its contents were finally reached.

"It's the old mistake over again," he plaintively murmured. "Munroe has sent my fungi to Richard. I hope you will have the sense to forward them to me. I'll repack this effigy to-morrow, and send it off to Padua at once."

Then the Professor resumed his interrupted work, and finished his celebrated chapter on the Hypodermiæ, thereby placing the name of Robinson among the Immortals.

The next day the Professor rose later than usual, for he was somewhat exhausted by the strain upon his brain of the previous evening. He had his breakfast, lit his pipe, read his letters and papers, and then entered his den to pack up the "effigy," as he contemptuously called it. On the threshold of the room he cast a glance at the package; then he stopped short and took a good look; then he rubbed his eyes and looked again.

"Re-markable!" he ejaculated, and with a certain amount of awe advanced towards the case.

"Re-markable!" he again ejaculated, and sank down on a chair before it.

The day before he had seen in the case the features of a mummy. They were not shriveled up and dried, as he had thought they always were, but they were wooden, lifeless and inert. Now he saw in their place the face of a girl. It was pale and heavy, and, it must be admitted, dirty; but it was the face of a living being, for the mummy was breathing!

For a few minutes the Professor gazed at her in absolute bewilderment, and the stupendous nature of his discovery only dawned upon him by degrees.

Here was a mummy, after the lapse of probably thousands of years, restored to life under his roof, seemingly without the action of any external agency whatever. It was simply marvelous. It was an incident unparalleled in the history of the human race. How Richard would envy him!

As these thoughts passed across his brain the eyes of the female slowly opened, and she looked dreamily around, then they closed, and then opened again. Her faculty seem to be slowly awakening, and in a confused manner she was taking in her surroundings. Then she saw the Professor. He was now standing with open eyes and mouth, and his hand grasped the hammer intended for nailing up the case. She evidently thought he was some monster intending to do her bodily harm, for no sooner did she see him than she gave a screech of terror, and fainted straight away.

Thereupon the Professor did a foolish thing, instead of summoning his housekeeper to the rescue, he ran for some water and dashed it in her face, and then noticing she was tightly strapped round, he hastily cut what wrappings he could, in order to give her relief. In a few minutes his exertions were rewarded by consciousness returning, and at length the eyes opened again.

"Pray, don't be afraid, madam," said the Professor in his most soothing tones. "I assure you I intend you no harm."

Her lips open, and she tried to speak; but long disuse had cloyed her tongue, and it refused to move. The ever alert Professor rushed off for more water, and poured the contents of a glass down her throat. Then her voice came; have first incoherent and spasmodic; finally fluent and melodious — but the words she uttered were incomprehensible to the Professor. He shook his head in response to her speech, and tried to make himself understood in what he remembered of Greek, as being the most likely language in his repertory, but without any satisfactory result. The lady was fast becoming distressed at her inability to make herself understood. At last she nodded to the cloths in which she was swaddled, then to the Professor, and then to the door.

"Oh! certainly, madame," he replied, quite forgetting his words would not be understood. "You will find some pins on my table. See, here they are. And when you are ready please call for me. My name is Robinson — Henry Robinson."

He said these words over and over again, pointing the while to himself. The lady guessed his meaning, and slowly repeated them after him — with a delicious in indescribable foreign accent.

The Professor withdrew from the room. In a quarter of an hour or so he heard the door open, and a silvery voice call out:

"Rob — in — son — 'En-ry — Rob — in — son."

From which it may be inferred that the lady had not been a custom to the use of the aspirate, or had forgotten it in the long years that had intervened since last she used it.

The Professor obeyed the call with alacrity. The late mummy had made the most of her time and opportunities. She was standing by the fire, and her clinging robe, held together by a multitude of pins, showed her lissom figure to great advantage. He now saw her features clearly for the first time, and he was surprised to find nothing Egyptian about them. Instead of the face being olive and oval, it was clear-colored and square-jawed. Her eyes were blue, and her hair fair. In fact, there was no trace of Eastern origin. She was slighter than he had thought, but exquisitely proportioned, and, notwithstanding the accumulated disadvantages of centuries, she looked like some dainty visitant from Fairy-land — or so thought the Professor, whose thoughts seldom ran on fairies.

Mr. Robinson hastened to express his gratification at her presence, but his polite phrases died away on his lips as she looked at him uncomprehendingly and almost tearfully.

"Poor thing! she must feel dreadfully lonely," he thought to himself. "I hope she isn't going to cry."

Then a brilliant idea struck him. He raised his hand to his mouth, and simulated, with a minimum of success, the operations of eating and drinking. The girl smiled and nodded. She understood.

The Professor left the room to see his housekeeper on the subject. He was so much impressed with his errand that he did not even think of any explanation being necessary to account for the presence of this interesting visitor.

"Mrs. Pridgett," said he, "will you please prepare some breakfast at once for a young lady."

"When do you expect her, sir?"

"She's here now."

"But I haven't unlocked the front door yet. When did she come, sir?"

"She came, Mrs. Pridgett — ah! yes, of course — she came overnight."

"Oh, indeed!" said Mrs. Pridgett in blank amazement.

"And I think you had better see about some clothing for her. She has very little on at present."

"Sir!" exclaimed Mrs. Pridgett in a most withering tone. But it passed the Professor unheeded.

"Don't be long with the breakfast, please. She has not broken her fast for some time."

Mrs. Pridgett bustled about indignantly, and in due course took in the meal. It was well she opened the door with empty hands, or the tray would most assuredly have fallen on the ground in her amazement, for the Professor was seated before the fire gently stroking the head of a thinly-clad lady. Who was seated on the hearthrug at his feet.

"There, my dear, don't be frightened. It's only Mrs. Pridgett," said the Professor reassuringly.

Indeed, some assurance of this nature was needed, for fierce indignation and undisguised contempt were written on the ladies features. She simply glared at the stranger as she flung down the tray upon the table. Then she bounced out of the room with her chin high in the air.

"Dear me!" said the Professor, who had surveyed this performance with some astonishment; "I have never seen Mrs. Pridgett taken like that before. I am afraid she must be unwell."

And Mrs. Pridgett seemed to be very unwell during the next few days.

That afternoon the Professor rang for her.

"Mrs. Pridgett, I wish you to be particularly kind and attentive to that young lady while she is here," said he.

Mrs. Pridgett sniffed.

"She naturally feels somewhat lonely, for she has no friend in the world but me."

"Ah!" gasped Mrs. Pridgett.

"See, here is some money for clothing. Just get her what you think best."

The housekeeper made no reply.

"I hope you quite understand me, Mrs. Pridgett."

"Perfectly, sir."

"That being so, perhaps you will go to — er, my ward at once."

"What did you say her name was, sir?"

"Well, really — I quite forgot to ask."

Mrs. Pridgett fled, banging the door behind her.

"She is really most unaccountable in her behavior to-day," said the savant, gazing at the door wonderingly.

The next day brought the letter from his brother, and in his reply the Professor prided himself upon having eluded the main question with considerable dexterity.

Some three days later he received a telegram from the same source, and he chuckled much as he rode out his diplomatic answer.

All the while he was educating and amusing his "ward."

A few days after the dispatch of his telegram, Professor Henry Robinson was seated on the floor playing "ring-taw" with his visitor. It was a game in which she had indulged with considerable zest on the banks of the Nile in earlier days. Whatever the Professor did he did thoroughly, and he was head and ears over in the intricacies of the game when there came a knock at the door.

"Come in," he shouted, without looking up. "Now, my dear, knuckle fair." Then, receiving no answer, he glanced towards his companion, whom he found gazing with unfeigned interest upon a young man who had just entered, and who returned her look tenfold.

"Well, when you've quite finished staring the lady out of countenance, perhaps you'll say how-do-you-do to me, said the Professor."

"I'm sure I beg your pardon, uncle, and the lady's also. I — er — did not expect to find a visitor here." And he looked inquiringly at her.

"Won't you introduce me, uncle?" he added.

"No; they did not introduce where she came from, but I'll explain who you are. Aïda is a foreigner, and I'm educating her. She is getting on famously with the language. Beautiful weather, my dear, isn't it?"

"Beautiful weather, my dear Robinson — 'Enry — Robinson," replied the girl, with much evident pride in her achievement.

"Bravo! bravo!" exclaimed her teacher. "This is my nephew Dick."

"My nephew Dick," she followed, with careful emphasis.

"He's a young scamp, my dear, a young scamp."

"A dear young scamp," she continued, to Dick's intense gratification.

Such was the manner of Dick Robinson's introduction to the lady his uncle had called Aïda, but who on earth she was, and where she came from, puzzled the young man's brain until after-dinner talk with the Professor.

"Oh, by the by, uncle," said he, when they were at last to themselves. "What about that mummy?"

"What about it?"

"Where is it?"

"I haven't a mummy in the house," said the Professor.

"So you wired; but the Museum people say they sent it to you."

"Do they?"

"So where is it?"

"Well, Dick, I'll tell you. Our fair friend Aïda is the very identical piece of goods you are inquiring after."

"What!" exclaimed Dick in a blank amazement.

"It's a fact — scarcely believable, but so it is. She came as a mummy, and now is what you see her."

For the moment Dick thought his uncle was mad.

"Yes, my boy, continued the Professor reflectively; it's really wonderful. Your father would have given a great deal for to have had this affair happen under his roof, but if the mummy had been sent to him it never could have happened, so it's nothing less than providential it was sent to me. I'll tell you all about it. But, first of all, tell me how old you think the young lady is."

"Twenty?"

"About two thousand five hundred and ninety-five! A few odd years one way or the other don't matter much, but that's her approximate age. She is rather ancient, eh? I have managed to extract enough information from her to form a very plausible theory to account for her restoration to life, and, like all great discoveries, it is an exceedingly simple one. But before I give it, I will ask for corroborative evidence. I found this role of papyrus in the case. The signs are unintelligible to me, but your father's son can, no doubt, decipher them."

For some time Dick puzzled over the time-faded and stained hieroglyphics. Then he turned to his uncle.

"I can't give you the exact translation as the guvn'r could have done, but, roughly speaking, this is the gist of it:

"'Aïda, the fair Lily from the lands of the setting sun, who fell asleep on the first of the festival of Osiris. Why she sleeps no man may say, and none may awaken her. Neither the cunning of the physicians nor the prayers and supplications of the high priest of the mighty mysteries have availed, and the great Sun-God Ra smiles upon her in vain. She is placed in the inner chamber of the sanctuary of the temple of Horus, and perchance the time may come when the soul of the sleeper will return, and tell of its wanderings in Amenti, unless without death it rest for ever in the fields of peace.'"

The Professor's face beamed with triumph while Dick was reading this.

"Splendid!" he ejaculated. "It makes my theory a dead certainty. Listen! About the year 700 B.C. our friend was born, if not in the Scilly Isles, at any rate on the coast hard by. Phoenician or other traders, calling for tin, carried her off with them and sold her into Egypt. How she past her years there I have not yet been able to find out, but at the age of twenty or twenty-one she fell ill, and there her memory ceases. Now my theory is, and it is remarkably confirmed by what you have just read, that she fell into a trance from which it was impossible to rouse her. She was eventually put aside as dead, but on account of her comatose condition and possible revocation she was not embalmed. As time passed on her history was forgotten, and she was eventually enclosed in a sarcophagus.

"Now mark the marvelous sequence of events. After the lapse of two thousand and so many hundred years she attracted the attention of those who sent her to London. Munroe intended her for your father, but by a wonderfully lucky mistake she was forwarded to me — at her birthplace. Observe the result. Within a few hours of her arrival here her native air acted as a reviving agent, and set in motion those springs of life which had lain inactive for so long. Just as grains of corn taken from mummy cases and planted after long centuries in congenial soil come to life again, so has Aïda. Earth is to seed what air is to humanity, so there is nothing so very wonderful about it after all; or rather, the one wonder is so common that we think nothing about it, while the other is marvelously simple on account of its rarity. I was first led to this train of thought by her appearance, which is distinctly Celtic, and notably different from that of an Egyptian. Hers is an absolutely English face. Then as to the action of the air. You know that the doctors often order their patients to breathe their native air, and that it frequently has most beneficial effects. In this case the results have been more than beneficial. They have been startling."

Dick listened to this explanation in open eyed amazement. It was altogether too wonderful a history to grasp in a moment. It was incredible. Yet here was the girl restored to life; and there in writing, her history. It must be so. His uncle's tale was true. He fell asleep that night thinking of the wonderful history of the mummy, but it was the face of the living girl that haunted his dreams, and the next day it was Richard Robinson, junior, who played ring-taw with Aïda, the fair lily from the lands of the setting sun.

*   *   *   *   *

Professor Richard Robinson of Padua anxiously awaited news of the mummy from his son, but the information he received was enigmatical and unsatisfactory, so much so that at lasts he threatened to run over to the Scilly Isles and see for himself what had happened. Then Dick sent word he was returning, for he had made good use of his time, and further delay was unnecessary.

One evening the Paduan Professor was seated in his study. He kept anxiously looking at the clock, for his boy and the coveted specimen were due.

At length the door opened.

Dick entered, and with him a lady.

The Professor rose, and looked at his son inquiringly.

Dick took hold of his companions hand and advanced.

"Father," he said, "I have brought home the mummy."

The Lost Elixir[*]

A week after I had passed my examination before the committee of the Narrative Club, which, as you may know, is an assembly into which none are admitted save those who have many wanderings to their account and are able to tell tales about them, I received a notice from the Secretary to the effect that he was in a position to accept my cheque in payment of my entrance fee, and, further, that he would be happy to introduce me to my fellow-wanderers at the usual monthly supper on the following Sunday, at 9pm.

"You are rather in luck as regards your introduction to-night," he said, when we met in his rooms. "According to the strict rules you would have been called upon to justify your calling and election by telling us a story; but it so happens that this evening will be the only one for nearly a year that we can get hold of a man who is, perhaps, our most distinguished member. You know him by name, and you may have run across him in some of your travels — Professor Hessetine."

Of course the world-famed name was familiar to me as it is to everybody who has read anything outside novels and newspapers; but as I had had the great privilege of sitting at the same table with him a couple of years before on a West Coast boat from Panama to Lima — whither he was going to write a monograph on the prehistoric tombs of the ancient seaboard towns — the freemasonry of travel entitled me to claim acquaintance with him.

"Then that's all right," said the Secretary, himself a noted climber of hills and slayer of retiring beasts which affect the most neck-breaking localities to be found above the snow-line, when I had mentioned this: "he'll be delighted to see you again and have a chat about Inca-land with you. Personally, I am expecting quite a treat, apart from any story he may have to tell us; for he promised me, in his letter accepting the invitation to be the narrator of the evening, that we should be the first to hear of what he has done at Susa. Even before the scientific papers get it, I mean."

"If he does that I don't much care whether he tells us a story or not," I said. "I can hardly imagine any ordinary travel yarn that would be anything like as interesting as Hessetine on Susa."

"That, my dear fellow," he replied, with a smile, "is probably because you have only just become a member of the Tale Club, as some of our irresponsible globe-trotters have christened it. Oh, and, by the way, that reminds me," he went on, turning towards me, "there's just one hint I ought to give you. You'll have to expect some pretty tough-laid yarns at our distinguished symposia, but we have a tacit understanding as to the

---

[*] "The Lost Elixir" was written by George Griffith, working name of George Chetwynd Griffith-Jones (1857 – 1906), and published in *Pall Mall Magazine*, Oct. 1903.

acceptance of the aphorism that truth is often stranger than fiction, and so we often give truth — and the narrator — the benefit of the doubt."

"That's nothing," I laughed: "I know some myself, perfectly true, which no British jury would believe if I told them on oath in the witness-box."

Now this was a true saying, but — well, if anyone else than a man of European reputation had told Professor Hessetine's story and staked that reputation on its truth I should still have had my doubts as to the complete purity of his facts.

It so happened that during supper — by the way, a supper at the Narrative Club is quite the most delightfully free-and-easy meal in the confines of civilisation — the conversation, led off by a young doctor who had just been making a long study of the so-called miracle-healing prectised by the priest-physicians of Corea, turned upon the many well-authenticated traditions which exist among nearly all peoples belonging to the older civilisations as to the possibility of prolonging human life, and even youth, indefinitely by the regular eating of certain combinations of herbs, or the direct mingling of certain animal and vegetable essences with the blood.

I noticed that, although the Professor listened most attentively to the conversation, he only assisted it by an odd remark, always very much to the point, thrown in here and there, and every now and then an approving nod or a dissenting head-shake. When the table was cleared, and the chairman, according to custom, gave up the post of honour to the Narrator of the evening, it was not very long before we discovered that he had a reason for his reticence, for the first words that he spoke after the glasses had been filled and the pipes loaded were:

"Fellow-wanderers by sea and land," — that is the usual form of address — "I daresay you will have noticed that I have been exceedingly interested in the conversation which took place during supper. It is, of course, a most absorbing topic for all students of human things who are able to approach the most impossible-seeming subjects with that perfectly open mind which, as most of us believe, only long study and intensive travel can give. But whether it be what is commonly called a coincidence or not, I may as well preface the story I am going to tell you by saying that it bears with exceeding closeness upon that very subject."

While the Narrator was saying this he seemed to some of us, certainly to myself, to have grown — I was almost saying — centuries younger. That, however, was not quite what I mean. He might himself have been of any age, clime or nationality, and his features and expression had suddenly undergone a subtle change which seemed a reversion to some former state of being. In other words, he appeared to transfer his personality from the present into that remote epoch of which he was going to tell us, an epoch of which he certainly knows more than any man alive — that is, as far as we know, now alive.

"You must not think," he went on, perhaps having noticed a certain involuntary lifting of eyebrows round the table, "that I am going to tell you that since our last meeting I have had the privilege of making the acquaintance of the Flying Dutchman or the Wandering Jew, although I fear I shall have to make an almost equal demand upon your credulity — for, gentlemen, I am going to ask you not to disbelieve me when I tell you that I, who am speaking to you to-night with the lips of flesh, only a few weeks ago spoke, also in the flesh, with one who, as I have every reason to believe, lived and toiled, loved and thought in the long-buried city of Susa in the far-off days when Rameses the Great was king."

In any other assembly such a tremendous announcement, coming in all seriousness from the lips of such a man, would have been received with what the reporters are accustomed to describe parenthetically as "sensation"; but among the Wanderers by Sea and Land not an eye winked. Only a deeper silence fell upon us as we waited for the Professor to continue.

"I may presume," he went on after a little pause, "that you all know I have just returned after some months' work in connexion with the excavations at Susa, one of the buried cities of Upper Egypt, which appears to have been a sort of pleasure resort on the shores of a now vanished lake, to which the aristocracy of Thebes were accustomed to go as Londoners and Parisians now go to Homburg or Aix. Indeed, as a matter of fact, I am now quite certain that this was so, for I have in my possession an almost unique treasure in the shape of a complete plan of it, illustrated with drawings of its principal buildings, from the hand of one who saw it in all its pride and beauty.

"This is, however, a slight anticipation. I have the plan with me, and you shall see it afterwards. I was engaging my staff of skilled diggers and excavators — quite a different class from the common fellah labourers — at Memphis, as the best men are nearly always to be found there; and one day, when I had almost completed my staff and was thinking of making a start northward, I was taking my usual evening stroll among the ruins to the north of the modern city, when I was considerably startled by hearing a man's voice speaking in strangely musical tones and in a tongue totally foreign to me. It came from the other side of the fallen statue of Rameses, at the back of which I was leaning, smoking a contemplative pipe.

"I say that I was startled, because I think I may affirm without boasting that I am familiar, not only with all the dialects spoken in the Nile Valley, but with most of the languages of the far and the near East. Yet I searched my memory in vain for the recollection of a single syllable or inflection, until I heard him say quite distinctly, and yet with an accent and intonation utterly strange to me, the words, or rather the exclamation, 'O Rameses, Rameses!'

"No one could have pronounced the name with such exquisite purity and such profound depth of feeling — I had almost said sorrow. Gentlemen, I am not ashamed to admit that in that moment a keen thrill of awe passed through my soul, for the accents seemed to awaken some long-stilled echo of a memory belonging to a life that had been lived in other ages, and with it came the thought, I know not whence, that I was listening to a speech that human lips had not uttered for nearly thirty centuries.

"I put out my pipe and went round the base of the statue, and there I found myself face to face with such a man as I had never set eyes on before. He might have stood as model to the sculptor who designed the statue beside which we were standing. There was the broad, square, low forehead, and under it looked out at me the large, level-set eyes that might have belonged to the Great King himself. The straight, massive nose, the full, delicately-curved, sensuous lips, and the firm, commanding chin — I recognised them all, and the whole countenance wore that almost indescribable expression of contemptuous repose which is so inevitably characteristic of the royal race of Old Egypt.

"He did not show the slightest sign of surprise at my appearance. His eyes looked too weary with seeing for that. He returned my salute with a grave dignity that was, even there, in strange contrast to the scanty rags and the frayed and faded cotton shawl which hung from his shoulders. I addressed him in Arabic — for somehow the pure and ancient speech of the desert suggested itself as the most fitting medium at my command — and asked him if he would do me the favour of telling what language he had been speaking when I had unintentionally overheard him a few moments before. He replied in Arabic which was far more fluent and idiomatic than my own:

"'That, Effendi, was the speech in which my brother Rameses, by whose time-worn effigy we stand, wooed our cousin Nephert-Anat, the star-eyed Lily of the Upper Nile, in the days when the desert that has buried our glories laughed and sang with the joy of its fruitfulness, and Egypt was Queen of the Earth.'

"Now, you are very well aware, gentlemen, that insanity, in its milder and more inoffensive forms, is not regarded in the East as it is here. It is treated with tolerance and by most people with respect as a sign of the special protection of the Deity. You will, I am sure, understand me when I say that my new acquaintance's first utterance inclined me to the belief that he was a scholar whom over-study and underfeeding had made mad. But there was no sign of madness in the calm, luminous eyes which looked so steadily into mine while he was making this extraordinary speech. There was none of the restlessness of the feet and hands, or the sideways movements of the head, which are the almost certain accompaniments of insanity. On the contrary, his attitude was easy and yet full of dignity, and his manner was rather that of a man who is uttering a commonplace which has become wearisome to him.

"I, of course, realised at once that no good end could possibly be served by any show of incredulity, and so I replied just as seriously as he had spoken: 'Truly, then, O brother of the Great King, since thy days have been prolonged on earth so far beyond the common span of mortal life, great must be the blessing or grievous the curse that the High Gods have laid upon thee. Is it permitted that a stranger from a far-off land should ask thee of why the shade of thy mighty brother hath waited so many cycles for thee in the Halls of Amenti?'

"'Ah,' he exclaimed, bending down towards me — for, as I have said, he was a man of splendid stature, fully a head taller than I am — and bringing his eyes to a level with mine, 'dost thou believe me, then? or is it only thy charity which thus listens with a show of credulity to what thou, like the others, takest for the idle tale of a madman? Speak truly, Effendi, as thy soul liveth, for on thy faith hangs the fate of one who, in the days that are forgotten, by his own rash and presumptious act, brought upon his soul the anger of the High Gods, and cut himself off from the common lot of man.'

"I confess that I was strangely and deeply moved; and I replied, as though some inner impulse had been prompting me: 'O Egyptian, who am I, the child of yesterday, that I should say what is and is not possible to the might of the Gods? Shall the sand-grain by the seashore say to its fellow, "With thee and me the limits of Ocean end"? I would make no trespass on thy confidence, yet if thou hast the will to tell me, thy story will not fall on idle ears, and when the proof is given belief shall not be wanting.'

"'It is just,' he said, his lips making the faintest movement of a smile. 'Yet it is well said that trust is twofold. Will the Effendi trust me in a small matter if I will trust him in a great one?'

"It may seem to you like a piece of arrant foolishness in an old traveller, but I positively could not distrust the man, and so I answered: 'So far as it is lawful and fair dealing between man and man, Egyptian, I will trust thee to the half of my goods.'

"'I have no need of thy goods, Effendi,' he replied, with a sigh which was the saddest I have ever heard from a human breast: 'I who have feasted with kings and conquerors and scattered gold and jewels to the four winds of heaven till wealth became as dross in my hands and I had sickened of all that earth could sell — what is thy poor little fortune to me? Yet it is because I am what men call poor in money that I would ask for thy faith and thy help. The matter is in this wise. Thou art going to Susa, the city of my youth and happiness, and the scene of the crime against the High Gods which made the one unfading and destroyed the other for ever. At Susa thou wilt seek to clear the dust of ages from the house in which I and mine dwelt, the temples in which we worshipped and the tombs where the mummies of my dear ones are resting: while I, self-doomed, count on the countless suns of endless days. Now, what I ask is this: that thou shouldst make me one of thy company, the meanest of them if thou wilt and take me to Susa, and there I will show thy workmen where to dig that they may find that which thou seekest. I will draw thee pictures of the temples and the theatres and the tombs, and mark out the streets and the squares, until all Susa in its ruins shall be as plain to thee as it was in its glory to me.'

"I don't suppose that any archaeologist had ever had such an astoundingly tempting offer made to him, and I candidly admit that I was not only tempted — I fell. But there was still the undeniable fact that, under all known human conditions, such a thing was absolutely impossible. Certain doubts, too, which I will come to shortly, had occured to me while he was making his proposition. Still all said and done, I stood to risk nothing but his railway fare and keep — I was already risking them and absurdly high wages too for men not half as likely-looking as my strange friend — even if I was only able to use that commanding air of his by making him an overseer, so I held out my hand, and said:

"'It is agreed, Egyptian. To-morrow we start by the train that leaves at sun-down. Come to me after the early coffee and I will tell the dragoman and the overseer that I have engaged thee. After the paper is signed I will advance money to buy what thou hast need of. Then in thine own time thou shalt make plain those things which are now dark to my eyes.

"'Our hands met. As I believe now, it was a grip which drew two living men together across a gulf of thirty centuries. That strikes you, no doubt, as a somewhat fantastic and farfetched notion, but I am not without hope that your opinion will change when you have heard my reason for believing as I do."

The Professor, who had so far told his extraordinary story in the most commonplace conversational tone, paused and took a draught from a great tankard of lager before him. The silence was so strained that no one seemed to care to break it, even to get a drink. When he put his tankard down and faced us again, some of us began to find a sort of likeness in those symmetrically-cut features of his to others that we had seen on the wall-paintings at Luxor and Karnac and other familiar places on the now, if possible, vulgarised Nile, as well as on the mighty carved monoliths which even now raise their giant bulk above the sands of time, changeless in the midst of change, silently contemptuous of the roar of the noisy centuries and the chatter of their yester-born children.

"'During the journey to Thebes," he went on, just as quietly as before, my friend the Egyptian took his place among the other men in my employment, and scarcely exchanged a score of words with me. This was, of course, perfectly natural. In the East master is master and servant is servant, and there are no board schools. But as soon as we had left the train at Thebes and began to prepare for crossing the fifty-odd miles of desert to the site of what once was the pleasure-city of Susa, a sudden change came over him. Those of you who have seen a man breathing his native air after years of exile will understand what I mean. He began to exert a sort of unofficial authority which not even the dragoman or the overseer tried to resist after the first few hours, during which they somehow learnt that he was at home and they were not.

"We reached the semicircle of granite hills under which the long-dead citizens of Susa once found protection from the worst of the desert winds, during the second march of the third day. We chose our camping-ground and pitched our tents. After supper I took my pipe and went for a stroll round the encampment, to see that everything was shipshape. There was such a moon in the sky as one only sees from the desert; and when my inspection was over I wandered towards the edge of the bay of smooth sand, broken by outcrops of stone which were for vanished Susa what the Monument and Nelson's Column may some day be for London — if they last as long.

"I had not gone far from the camp when I heard close by me the grave, gentle voice of my Egyptian saying, still in the classic Arabic of the Koran:

"'Effendi, thou has kept thy part of that which was agreed between us. This is Susa, and my eyes already see the flood of ages rolled back, the sands swept away, and the likeness of the temples and the palaces once more reflected in the blue mirror of the lake which washed their everlasting walls. Diana, as I have heard the old Greeks say, is smiling full-eyed on us tonight. Hast thou the leisure and the will to learn why Pent-ar, priest of the Royal Blood in the House of Amen-ra and Writer of the Sacred Records, sought thy help and charity to return to the place of his birth?'

"I confess that I started a little at the mention of that name, so famous to all Egyptian scholars, by the lips of a man who claimed it as his own, but I managed to tell him in my usual tone that if he was prepared to give me his confidence I was quite ready to receive it; and so I sat down on a huge slab of granite, and he, declining with a graceful gesture my request that he too would be seated, stood before me, a strangely eloquent figure in the bright moonlight, and told me his story with a simple dignity of diction and expression which, translating from his exquisite Arabic as I am, I cannot hope to emulate.

"'My history, Effendi.' he began, after a long look over the wilderness of ruins, 'shall be brief, since no man could tell even in many hours the narrative of the changing ages. And first I will explain what may have seemed strange to thee — that I, who, as I told thee at Memphis, have squandered uncounted treasures, should be too poor to pay my way here and do the work for myself which I am to do for thee. It comes about in this wise. Not many months ago I learned from such a seeker as thou art for the hidden glories of my people that a certain papyrus had been found at Thebes which was of the time of the Great King and a little after, and signed by one Panit-Ahmes, priest of Sekhet and scribe of the College of Physicians at Thebes. Further, I was told that this papyrus, which is now in your great Museum of London, contained certain passages which, though plain to decipher, had no outward meaning, and contained, moreover, characters which the most learned of those skilled in the writing of the old Egyptians could not make words or phrases of.

"'Now in the days of the Great King this Panit-Ahmes shared with me the fame which in those days was greater than that which men could win with bow and spear, the fame of learning and of the knowledge of hidden things. This of itself, though it might have made us rivals for the favour of the High Gods, would not by necessity have made us enemies; but there was that between us which hath set man's hand against his brother since first the world began — the love of a fair woman. I divined instantly that the passages which your scholars could not read were written in the Hermetic character which was known only to the initiates of the Sacred Mysteries, and that, since this lore has been lost for many ages, there was no other on earth who could read them save myself.

"'That day I sold a few curious jewels, the last of a once great store, to the explorer, bought myself some clothes of the European fashion, and took passage to London. As I can speak your language, as I can all others which I have seen come into being since my nurse taught me the ancient tongue of Khem, I went to the chief keeper of manuscripts in your Museum and offered to translate this papyrus for him, though in doing so I was breaking the oath of my initiation, so strong upon me was the desire to learn what Panit-Ahmes had hidden in the Hermetic passages.

"'He looked on me at first in wonder, as thou didst, Effendi, when we stood that evening by the statue of Rameses; but there was unbelief as well as wonder in his eyes and his speech, so I went to a case in which some papyri of the time of the Second Amen-ho-tep, who took the great city of Ninevah, rested, and these I read off into English as quickly as you, Effendi, would translate from an Arabic writing. Then he believed, but his wonder grew greater; and in the end, after much talk and writing to many people, as is the fashion of the English, the permission I craved was given to me, and in a day I made the translation and a copy of the Hermetic passages for myself. The scholars of the Museum were greatly amazed, and offered me a high stipend to remain and work for them; but how could I, Pent-ar the Initiate, take money for the revealing of the Holy Mysteries to unbelievers? Also, I had deceived them, for the meaning I wrote down of the mystic sentences was not the true one. Had I written them they would have laughed at me, and I should have broken my oath for nothing.

"'Now the meaning of the passages was this — and by it thou shalt learn, ere that many days have passed, whether Pent-ar the Scribe hath told thee the truth or a lie:

"'*O thou who in the days to come shalt be weary of the burden of years: Behold, my hate shall be buried in my tomb, that I may greet thee as friend in the Halls of the Assessor.*

"'*When the High Gods, whose holiness thine impiety hath outraged, shall judge thy cup of penance to be full, it may be that thine eyes shall see this writing, which thou alone of men wilt in those days be able to read with understanding.*

"'*Then shalt thou learn that the flame lit in thy veins by the Elixir of Long-Drawn Days may be quenched only by the dew which thou shalt find even then moist on the waiting lips of Love. It was given to me to learn the secret of the poison which was the antidote to the venom of endless days. Thy mistaken love bound her soul in the flesh — fetters which through ages of weariness thou shalt learn to curse. My love gave her rest.*

"'*From her lips, in the good time of the High Gods, it may be given to thee to drink the Elixir of the Lesser Death. On the green shores of Amenti we wait and pray for thee.*

"'Effendi, thou hast already heard the story of Pent-ar, for beyond the recital of the Passages of Panit-Ahmes — once my rival and enemy, and now my friend and only hope — there is little to tell that thou hast not already guessed.

"'In many climes and ages I have seen men seeking the essence which they in their ignorance called the Elixir of Life. I could have given it to them, as I could give it to thee if I wished to repay thy friendship with a curse; for it was I who, guided by the malice of the Infernal Gods, discovered the reality of which they were seeking the shadow and the manner of finding it was this:

"'When the Great King was building the Hall of Seti at Luxor, many structures were cleared away to make room, and great excavations were necessary for its foundations. In one of these I, when, as Keeper of the Records, examining the ground that no hidden sacred place might be violated by the workmen, found a very ancient temple, so old that it was buried in those days even as Susa is buried in these. By virtue of my office I passed into it alone; — would that my feet had rotted to the ankles before I had crossed that fatal threshold! In the inmost sanctuary, in the place of hiding behind the chief altar, I found a golden casket of scrolls, which, as was my right, I took home with me, that I might if possible discover new secrets amongst their contents. That which I sought I found, and more.

"'Fastened by a blood — red seal to the smallest of the scrolls was a great emerald wrapped in many folds of leaf of gold. The scroll, deciphered after much labour, told me that it was hollow, and that its cavity was filled with the Elixir of Long — Drawn Days. "O thou," ran the scroll, "whose learning shall teach thee the meaning of these words: know that the Elixir of the Emerald is the last of the secrets of the Infernal Gods vouchsafed to man. If thou hast courage, and wouldst outlive the changing ages, thyself unchanged amidst them; if thou wouldst see the generations of men pass away like shadows from the bright morning of thine eternal youth, mingle but a drop of this ichor — which is the tears of Isis — with thy blood, and never shall it be chilled with frosts of age, nor its flow arrested by the hand of Death. Dost thou love? Then shall one drop more in the veins of thy beloved give thee and her the delights of quenchless love and deathless passion as long as the ages last. Immortal — the Infernal Gods greet thee!"

"'Alas! Effendi, I loved, and through my love I was lost. I would fain spare myself and thee, Son of the Younger Days, the story of that which was the same then as it is now and as it shall be when the last son and daughter of man pledge their troth on the brink of the common grave. Let it therefore suffice to say that Amaris was in my eyes even fairer and more desirable than her sister the lovely Nefert-Anat herself, who was honoured by the love of the Great King. Endless days of fadeless youth with her — what more could the Gods themselves give me? I took the elixir in my satchel one evening when I was to walk with her through our favourite paradise among the palms. I read the scroll to her and showed her the emerald. Then I tempted her as I had been tempted, and because she loved me I won my way with her.

"'Soon afterwards we were married, for I was of the Royal Blood and Panit-Ahmes was not. Moreover Rameses and Nefert were my friends and pleaded my cause well. My rival cloaked his wrath and his hate under a guise of resignation, but the fires burnt still in his breast and well-nigh consumed him.

"'On our marriage night I instilled the elixir into my veins and hers, and we went to rest dreaming that, as long as the sands of time should run, for us all nights would be like this, all mornings like the morrow. The next day, in the boasting pride of my happiness and triumph, I told Panit-Ahmes of what I had done, and then, telling him that I and my Amaris, alone of the sons and daughters of men, should live and love for ever, I flung the emerald and what was left in it of the tears of Isis far out among the brown waves of the Nile.

"'What hidden lore Panit-Ahmes may have known then or discovered later I know not, but he laughed when he saw me throw away what kings would have given their dominions for, and told me that since I had kept part of the curse of the Infernal Gods for myself I was welcome to do what I would with the rest. "As for Amaris thy wife," he said, as he turned away from me, "I have loved her, and I will save her from the doom that thou shalt some day pray the High Gods in vain to take away from thee."

"'For a year, Effendi, I was happy — happy, perchance, as no other wedded lover has been since then, for that year was to me only the first of the countless years which should all be as bright as it was. Then Panit came to me, and told me that he had found in a dream, which was a revelation from the High Gods, the secret of the antidote to the tears of Isis. I laughed him to scorn, so marvellously had the elixir renewed my already fading youth within the short space of a year. I boasted that I would drink a measure of it as I would a draught of the red wine of Cos, but he flung my laugh back at me, saying that since I loved the life of the flesh so well, I should live it. It was not for me but for Amaris that she might lay down the burden of living when the Gods pleased or she was weary of carrying it.

"'Then said I, in my pride, "O Panit-Ahmes, Amaris will be singing the songs of youth in the days when thy mummy is dust. Let her drink if she will. She is my most precious gift from the Gods; thou canst not take her from me."

"'Never was vainglorious boast more bitterly requited, never was boaster made more humble than I was. Amaris, full of faith and vivid life as I was, took the hazard of the draught laughingly, and seemingly was none the worse for it. Yet another year had not gone by before she sickened of a fever that followed a low Nile, and died. Mad with grief, I took the fever too, and for many days lay in delirium. When I returned to health and reason, the mummy of Amaris already lay in its place in the City of the Dead, over yonder behind the northern spur of the hills, and Panit-Ahmes too was dead and had taken his secret with him over the River of Darkness into the Land of Shadows.

"'Effendi, my tale is told, nor will I weary thee further by telling thee the awful story of the years that have passed between then and now. I have seen the races of men come and go, and their empires wax and wane. I have seen altars rise and fall, faiths born and die, like shadows drifting over the eternal sea. I have learnt the vanity of human things — the shame of glory and the poverty of wealth and the dream of dominion — and here I stand before thee, poor and lonely, without a friend or a lover among all the myriads of men, weary of living, and asking only of the High Gods and thee to find the tomb of Amaris, that I may lay my lips on hers, and from them receive the sweet summons to join her waiting shade on the green shores of Amenti.'

"Such, gentlemen," continued the Professor, laying down a few slips of paper which he had used every now and then to help his memory, such was the extraordinary story which I heard under such singular circumstances amidst the ruins of Susa. I will tell you the sequel to it in as few words as possible, for I must confess that my theme has somewhat run away from me. Marvellous as it may seem to you, I must ask you to accept it as I saw it and as I tell it to you. There are some things which do not admit of discussion or explanation, and I think you will agree with me that this is one of them.

"Pent-ar was as good as his word, so far as his knowledge of the locality went. The precision with which he indicated the course of the streets and the positions of the hidden buildings was little short of miraculous. For upwards of a month he possessed his world-weary soul in patience, until he had completed the plan of which I spoke some time ago. When he brought it to me, soon after sunrise one morning, he said, with that strange, joyless smile of his:

"'Effendi, have I kept faith with thee? Have I promised aught that I have not performed? If thou art content with me give me now my freedom, that I may go and seek the tomb of Amaris.'

"My answer was an order to my overseer to move the camp at once under his direction to the City of the Dead. Once there, his whole manner changed. His eyes burned with the fire of an eager anticipation, and he worked with pick and shovel harder than the best of the labourers. At the end of a week we had laid bare a small pyramid, the apex of which, only showing a couple of feet or so above the sand, he had found with unerring instinct or memory after an hour's survey of the wilderness of ruins amidst which it stood. Just before sunset on the last day he came to me with two lamps in one hand and a powerful crowbar in the other.

"'My friend,' he said, using the term for the first time, 'Pent-ar has come to bid thee farewell. The tomb is found, and Amaris waits for me within. I go to open the way to her. If thou wouldst see with thine own eyes the proof of the things which I have told thee, come with me now to the Gate of Death. But bring all thy courage with thee, for it may be thou wilt need it.'

"'I will come, Pent-ar,' I said. It did not seem a time for more words, so I took one of the lamps and followed him to the tomb in silence. It would have taken my workmen hours to remove the great stone slab which closed the entrance; but he, evidently knowing all the secrets of the lost art, laid the passage open in less than an hour. Still silent, we went in, he leading. After I had counted twenty paces the passage ended in a chamber about twelve feet square and fifteen high. In the middle of it, on a huge cube of polished black marble, lay two splendidly adorned sarcophagi. One was open and empty, the other closed.

"'The resting place of him who died not,' Pent-ar whispered, holding his lamp over it. Then he gave the lamp to me, and set to work with a chisel and mallet, which he had picked up outside the pyramid, on the lid of the other sarcophagus. When he had loosened it I helped him to raise it. A mummy case lay inside, and this with reverent hands we lifted out and laid across the end of the stone. For a moment Pent-ar stood beside it, with hands raised above his head, and murmured in the ancient tongue what was doubtless a prayer for forgiveness and the favour of his outraged Gods. This finished, he took his knife from his belt and with a few deft silent movements detached and removed the cover of the case.

"'Amaris! Amaris!' he murmured again, falling on his knees beside the case, and saying some more words in his own speech.

"I looked over his shoulders, and to my amazement I saw, not the mummy I had expected to find, but the unswathed, white-robed figure of an exquisitely beautiful girl, who, instead of having lain there hidden from the sight of men for thirty centuries, might have fallen asleep only an hour before.

"'It is time,' said Pent-ar, rising and taking my hands. 'Is she not beautiful, my love, my bride? See, are not her sweet lips moist still with the dew of love, as Panit said? Now farewell, Son of the Younger Days and last of my friends on earth. In a few moments Pent-ar will be walking in the groves of Amenti hand in hand with Amaris. Farewell, and let not thy courage fail thee in the presence of Death the Releaser."

"As I pressed his hands and bade him farewell, a flood of memories swept over my soul, I know not whence. Was it possible that I, with other eyes, had once looked with love on that fair face? Who knows? But before I could frame the question I would have asked Pent-ar, he had stretched himself lengthways over the case and pressed his lips to those of his dead love.

"Gentlemen, I hope I may never see such another sight as that which I beheld in the next few moments. No sooner had their lips met than the fair flesh of the mummy grew dark and shrivelled into a thousand wrinkles. The eyes sank back into the sockets, the gloss faded from the gold-brown hair, and the rounded form shrank together under the garments. But even this was as nothing to the awful change which the magic of the Death-kiss had wrought on Pent-ar. He who a moment before had stood with me, a living breathing man, holding my hands and speaking to me in his now familiar voice, became, as it were in an instant, not a corpse, but a skeleton covered with a dry brown skin, through which the grey bones broke their way as they dropped with a gentle rustling sound into the case in which the ashes of the long-parted lovers at length were permitted to mingle.

"In my wonder and horror I dropped the lamps I was holding, and when I had groped my way into the outer air I found it full of flying grains of sand. I fought my way, half choked, back into camp. That night the worst sandstorm I have ever seen raged until morning, and when I was able to go back to the City of the Dead I found nothing but a wide, level plain of driven sand where our excavations had been made. It was the winding-sheet of Pent-ar and Amaris, and beneath it their ashes shall, I trust, rest in peace until the dawn of the day whose sun will never set."

The Mummy of
Thompson-Pratt[*]

argrave was a Fellow of Clare with rooms in College, who lectured twice a week on Constructive Egyptology, as a rule to empty benches. He was one of the most profound Egyptologists of the day, and had a clever knack of keeping all interesting items to himself, and discoursing the dry bran of theory only. At the beginning of each October term he had quite a crowd to hear him. The undergraduate who thought he ought to do something up at Cambridge on which to report progress to parent or guardian, would run his eye down the list, and pitch upon Constructive Egyptology as a subject likely to be of the light fiction order, and one which would probably offer him pleasant entertainment. But one hearing of Gargrave soon knocked this notion on the head, and that undergraduate in future wasted no more time drawing caricatures on lecture-room foolscap with spluttering lecture-room quills, whilst Gargrave prosed about the true significance of an accidental scratch on a scarabeus, but spent his mornings in bed, or on the river, or merely playing poker, as Nature had originally intended. And the lecture-room benches remained vacant till the next batch of green freshmen arrived in the succeeding October.

This result was pointed out clearly to Gargrave by candid friends. But this made no difference in the discourses. He held to the solid Cambridge theory that 'Varsity lectures were not intended to amuse, or teach anything that was useful; but merely to educate; which was a very different matter. "D'ye think I'm a music hall?" Gargrave would say, "Or is it a damned board-school you take me for?" The rest of the Clare fellows wished Gargrave would take orders, and then they could give him a college living and get rid of him. But Gargrave refused to do this thing, on the plea of religious scruples; and rumour got about in Cambridge that his creed was that of the ancient gods or Egypt.

Of the same college, and the bye-term senior to Gargrave, was Thompson-Pratt, Demonstrator in Chemistry at the Cavendish laboratories. He was not a Fellow of Clare, or even likely to be made one. Why he had ever got a first class in the National Science tripos was an abstruse mystery. He was not a man of brilliant intellect, nor did he, in his undergraduate days, ever resort to excessive reading. When he graduated at the end of his third year, he tried school-mastering for a twelve-month, disliked it, and stumbled into this demonstratorship in chemistry which was then vacant. Envious people said he got it by sheer favouritism. He himself suggested that it was a just reward for his powers of blarney.

---

[*] "The Mummy of Thompson-Pratt" was written by C. J. Cutcliffe Hyne (1866 – 1944) and published in *Atoms of Empire* (1904).

Thompson-Pratt always had matches and strong tobacco ready in his pocket for any one who needed them, and in the waiting spaces during a lingering experiment he could re-spin a yarn from back numbers of the *Pink 'Un* as deftly as one could wish to hear it. He was a distinctly popular man in a small way, and got asked out more than was good for his health.

Gargrave dined daily at the high table in hall, drank two glasses of port and ate four walnuts in the Combination Room afterwards, and then returned to his own rooms on the Don's staircase and worked till 2 A.M. Thompson-Pratt kept in Green Street, dined at the Hoop, and spent his evenings at threepenny-rise poker with four other Bachelors who entertained one another in turn and sat up till daylight. He knew Gargrave and disliked him candidly, and Gargrave despised Thompson-Pratt. So here are the men, and these are the relations between them.

Gargrave brought home the mummy himself by long sea from Alexandria in a P. & O. boat, and as I happened to be on board, and was a man of his own year and college, he looked upon me as his especial prey and bored me accordingly. I told him at the outset that except as fuel I was not interested in mummies in any degree whatever. But that did not choke him off in the least; and he poured conversational mummy-dust into my ears all down the Mediterranean, and through the Straits, and across the Bay, and down Channel till we fetched up in Southampton. I gave him the slip there in the Custom-House, and hoped he'd get run over by a cab in the street.

Two years later I went up to Cambridge to take my M.A. degree. I was paying my fees in the butteries, when in came Gargrave and passed the time of day. "Look here," he said, "I wish you'd come round to my rooms after you've finished your business in the Senate House. I've got an experiment I want you to be in at."

"What sort of experiment?" I asked. "Not mummies?"

"It has to do with a mummy. The one you saw me bring home from Egypt."

"No, thanks, old man," I said. "I hate the whole breed of them. Besides, I've another engagement."

He pawed my coat sleeve. "I know you hate them. That's just the very reason I want you. You'll be an unprejudiced witness. Now do stay. You needn't put up at the Bull. I've got a spare bed, and I'll tell my gyp to make it up for you. I believe I've got hold of the finest thing that was ever hit upon since Egyptology started, and I want you to be there to confirm my notes."

"But I should be no good at taking down notes. I'm merely a novelist. I haven't climbed as far as being a reporter yet. Shorthand is clean beyond me."

"I've got a phonograph to take it all down," he said. "Writing would be no use even though you knew the language, which you don't. The accent we use now is probably quite wrong. You wouldn't be able to catch hold of one word in ten."

"I wish you wouldn't talk hieroglyphics."

"I can't explain it more to you here," he said. "You must come and see for yourself, and I can promise you the entertainment will be exciting enough and suit even your lively tastes. If you stay away, you'll regret it all the rest of your life."

"Why?"

He was getting exasperated. "You'll see why, you fool, when my book comes out in a year's time."

It was really cheering to see Gargrave human enough to lose his temper. "All right," I said, "I'll come after I've been through the mill in the Senate House and can smoke in Cambridge streets at night without danger of being proctorised and fined the gentle six-and-eight. So long," I said, and turned into the butteries to talk over past undergraduate high-jinks with my old gyp.

Now if anything better had turned up, it is more than possible that I should have forgotten my engagement with Gargrave and gone elsewhere. I had had a very excellent three years in Cambridge some time before, as an irresponsible undergraduate, and was by no means averse to having a short retaste of the old lively scenes. But I could find no one that I knew who seemed at all interesting; the current undergraduates, looked at from the light of after years, seemed mere schoolboys; and in fact the larger part of my acquaintance seemed to consist of gyps, bedmakers, or tradesmen's assistants; and so *faute de mieux,* after I had been raised to the sublime degree of Magister Artiurn, I restored my borrowed hood, cap, gown, and bands to the tailor's, and strolled across to Gargrave's staircase.

I went in without knocking, *more Cantab.* He was fitting a new wax cylinder to a phonograph, and as he leaned over the machine and I saw the curves of his head, I thought of what a thousand pities it was that a man with such a magnificent brain should fritter it on such a useless life-work. The mummy case stood open against one of the walls, the mummy in it stripped of its swathings. The air was full of the sickly flavour of spices. I pulled out a cigar and lit it.

"Don't smoke," said Gargrave. "I must have the air here quite clear."

"Then open the window," I said. "The place stinks."

"You'll be used to the atmosphere directly. There's the mummy. What do you think of him?"

"Toughish *biltong.* Newer meat for me. He's well tattooed about the chest and arms, though."

"Those are not tattoo marks. Look closer. They are a pattern in the grain of the epidermis."

"So they are. Mr. Menen-Ra — isn't that his name? — is a curious beast."

"Curious! He's unique. Or at least he and his descendants are."

"Oh, those markings would not pass on to his son."

"So you say. But it appears they did."

"Have you got another mummy here, then?"

"I've got more than that. I've got one of his living descendants, he's due in this room almost directly."

"Humbug."

"You shall judge for yourself. You know the very man. He's Thompson-Pratt, of the bye-term above us."

"What, the demonstrator in the labs?"

"That same man. He's the lineal descendant of this mummy, as I've been at infinite pains to find out."

"And has he got the strawberry mark, or whatever you call it?"

"He has, line for line, pustule for pustule."

"Did he see your mummy and come up and claim it as a cousin?"

"He did not. I discovered his markings for myself long before I saw the mummy. It was the term after you had gone down. He'd been on this staircase here to see the Dean, who was out. He slipped in coming down, and took a header, and got all the sense knocked out of him. I heard the noise. I was the only man in. So I went and picked him up, and brought him in here. He lay so still I thought he was dead, so I ripped open his shirt to see if I could feel his heart beating; and it was then that incidentally I came across the markings. I got him back to his senses again soon afterwards, and whilst he was lying on my sofa getting his nerves straight again, I told him what I had seen and asked him how they came there.

"He was furiously angry and said I'd taken a great liberty.

"'My good man,' I said, 'I didn't look for the things. I merely stumbled across them by accident.'

"'They are the curse of my life,' said he. 'I love swimming, and yet I daren't bathe in public. People hoot at me if I do. Look,' he said, and pulled back his shirt and showed me his chest and the tops of his arms. 'I'm marked like the spotted man at the fair. I'm a blooming spectacle. My father's the same way, and so's the grand gov'nor, and so was his father before him. I suppose it's a sort of family curse, or some such rot as that, only we're too ashamed of the whole thing to have any yarn about it.' And then he pinned me not to tell about him and then he went. I didn't worry my head more about the matter. Biology's outside my line, and Thompson-Pratt was not a man I had any special interest in at that period.

"Well, then, of course I went on with my work, and in time went to Egypt and got this mummy of Menen-Ra. I brought it home in its swathings, and didn't open it out till I got here. I'd procured it, as you know, for a certain purpose connected with one of my theories. But when I'd had the first glance at those markings on its skin, I let my original ideas go to the winds for the time being. So far as I could remember, they were the exact repetition of those carried by Thompson-Pratt.

"Here was a strange thing! I sat and thought of it hour after hour, and day after day. I tell you theories fairly bubbled out of me. At last I made up my mind what was to be done. But before I went further, I had got to know if the markings were exactly the same as Thompson-Pratt's. He made a big difficulty about it, and for a man who pretends to be scientific, I must say he was absurdly prejudiced. But he gave in at last, and let me take a photograph. I tell you it was simply marvellous: line for line, pustule for pustule, his markings were the same as the mummy's.

"Well, that was strong evidence, you'll say, but I wanted to go deeper. I've put an enormous amount of work into it; I've had scores of genealogy experts working for me; and I've had amazing luck. I've worked out the chain of descent in Egypt, Italy, France, England, Scotland, and England again without a break; and I've learned for an absolute certainty that Thompson-Pratt is the direct descendant of the Egyptian Menen-Ra, whose mummy you see against the wall yonder.

"And now," he went on, "I'll explain to you what I intend to do." But he did not explain to me then. The door opened and Thompson-Pratt came into the room. He nodded curtly enough to Gargrave, but he greeted me kindly. "Hullo, old man. How's the world using you? Heard you were up taking out your M.A. Staying up long?"

"Going down to-morrow. I've just come in here because Gargrave wanted to show me some tricks with his mummy."

"Damnation," said Thompson-Pratt to the owner of the rooms, "you haven't been talking about — er — secrets, have you'!"

"No secrets will be given away unless you do it yourself," said Gargrave, oracularly. "I've just asked him in to be an independent witness."

"Oh, I see," said Thompson-Pratt, getting into a chair. "But look here, you know. I don't half like this experiment of yours."

"It's in the cause of science."

"Science be sugared." He stared thoughtfully into the fire and then turned round and faced Gargrave squarely. "Look here, sir, if you are going to make use of me, I'm going to share some of the profits. You say that wrinkled, smelly person in the coffin yonder is my ancestor, and you are going to make me to talk his thoughts. Well, you may do it, or you mayn't. But if it does come off, it's just on the cards the old boy may let slip something in the natural science line which is strange to us to-day. I've a notion those old Egyptians were a lot ahead of us in some branches of chemistry, and if I could get hold of the way of making some new dye, for instance, to use with alizerene ——"

"You shall have a copy of every word that's said," Gargrave promised.

"From the phonograph? Yes, I see. But it'll be in what-d'you-call-em language — hieroglyphics, isn't it? Ancient Egyptian, I mean."

"You shall overlook my translation as I make it. Man, I mean to do fairly by you."

"Oh, all right," said Thompson-Pratt. "Don't get shirty. Only, a man must look after his own interests, y' know, that's all; and besides, it's a hundred to one the whole thing's a fizzle."

Gargrave set his teeth. "Have you any more to say?" he inquired.

"No," said Thompson-Pratt, with a bored yawn. "Wire in."

Now from where I sat on the table, I was watching the proceedings pretty carefully; and it struck me that Gargrave merely got a hypnotic influence over Thompson-Pratt in the usual way. He has told me since that he did something more, and perhaps this may be so; but anyway the patient seemed to go to sleep and to wake up again, and be entirely under the control of Gargrave's will. He made him lie down on the hearthrug in front of the fire, and then he took the mummy out of its case and laid that down on the hearthrug also, side by side with its living descendant. Then he told me to go out of the room.

"Whatever for?" I asked. "I thought you invited me here to see an experiment?"

"So I did. And you shall see it when the time comes. But I have one or two more preparations to make first, which I don't choose to be overlooked. You must go into my inner room."

"I have a rare big mind to go out of the place altogether."

"You can do it if you like, of course, but you are a fool if you do."

Well, perhaps it was undignified, but I shrugged my shoulders, and swallowed my pride, and marched off to the inner room. I will own I was getting curious as to what was coming next.

Gargrave came after me, and had the impertinence to lock the door on my heels. So there I was anyway, and as he seemed to have a dislike for smoking, I lit a pipe and filled the room with heavy reek.

I will give him credit for one thing, though. He did not keep me waiting long. He opened the door in a minute or so and said: "Sorry, old man, but I must keep my processes secret at any cost. Come in."

I went in. Thompson-Pratt and the man who had predeceased him some 3000 years were lying side by side on the hearthrug, to all appearance exactly as I had left them.

Evening was come on, the lamps had not been lit, and only the dancing, uncanny firelight illuminated the faces; and as I gazed a little closer, a curious thrill went through me. It was Thompson-Pratt's which seemed to be the dead face now. Behind the shrivelled mask of the mummy there was surely some flicker of life. Gargrave was bending down, arranging the mouthpiece of the phonograph over the mummy's lips, and as he moved aside I could have sworn I saw the long-dead limbs twitch. I took out a handkerchief and wiped my forehead. Gargrave saw me do it.

"Now don't be an idiot," he said. "There's nothing to be scared of. Just keep cool, and take accurate mental notes of all you see and hear." He tried to talk calmly, but I saw he was quivering with excitement for all that. He turned to the mummy and said something in a tongue I could not understand, enunciating each syllable most distinctly. I distinguished the word "Menen-Ra," but could make out nothing else.

Neither the mummy nor Thompson-Pratt gave any sign of having heard.

He repeated the sentence again, varying the pronunciation of the words, and this time got a reply.

"You must speak English if you wish me to understand," came the answer in a stifled, dusty voice directly from the mummy's lips.

Gargrave started, and I think he swore. "Why?" he asked savagely.

"Because I have forgotten the other — the old tongue."

"If I am being played with," said Gargrave, "there is one man here who will carry out of this room my marks on him for life."

There was no answer. He went on: "Do you know your name?"

"Menen-Ra."

"Where buried?"

"Thebes."

"You were not."

"I was buried at Thebes; but I should be taken afterwards to our family vault on the estate by Koorkoor, according to our custom."

"It was in the desert by the oasis of Koorkoor I found you. In what manner of grave?"

"Rock-hewn, with my titles carved above me."

"Alone?"

"No, my four uncles, killed in war, would be with me."

"Were they all sound men?"

"No, my uncle Nepo, the last buried and so the next to me, had his right arm lopped off at the elbow: an old wound."

Gargrave broke off his questioning and hit the table excitedly. "That settles it," he cried. "No living soul knows what the grave was like except myself, and no one could have guessed it. And it's all absolutely exact. It's a miracle, but I've done it. The soul of Thompson-Pratt has gone back to its old abiding-place, and now I shall be told the history of 3000 years ago exactly as it happened, and I can give that history to the modern world. When he spoke English I thought there was fraud; but there isn't; it's just part of the natural lapse." He rubbed his hands. "Lord! how simple it is, and I'm the only man that's got the key." He turned again to the mummy. "Menen-Ra, I command you that you lift up your voice now in history, and tell us of the Government of Egypt, and of Pharaoh, and of Pharaoh's inner life, and the daily life you lived yourself, and the daily life of the people."

And the mummy in its dusty tones began to speak. There was no doubt about the genuineness of it all, that I can vouch for. The phraseology was certainly that of Thompson-Pratt, reader of the *Pink 'Un,* and Demonstrator in Chemistry at the Cavendish Labs. But the sentiments were those of ancient Egypt, spoken as no other men now living (except Gargrave and myself) ever heard them, but startlingly fresh and real. Not even the most imaginative student, redolent in the lore of that long-dead land, could have invented them. They were marvelous in their vivid truth. They were nothing short of a revelation.

But Gargrave cursed as he listened. He had looked for a dissertation on history, and he was getting *chroniques scandaleuses*; he had expected talk about Kings' policies, and he was hearing the tales of flirtations with their housemaids. He wanted descriptions of Council Chambers, and he got the dimensions of wine-shops. He had fallen into the error of thinking that all the men of bygone Egypt were as thoughtful and ponderous as the hoary few whose scribings have remained; and when he found that the ancient land contained devil-may-care pleasure-eaters like those that live in this land of ours to-day, he could have beaten himself in the fury of his disappointment.

For myself, as I listened whilst Menen-Ra prattled on, I laughed till the tears came, and my only regret — a professional one — was that I could not use up that unmatchable subject-matter hereafter. I was listening to the talk of a man-about-town, who lived in Thebes 3000 years ago and learning in detail exactly how he wasted his days and how he enjoyed his nights. He told us of his bets, his bouts, his light loves, and his serious entanglements. Every third sentence referred to a long-dead

Chloe, evidently the Thais of her day in that far-forgotten Thebes. Even allowing for Menen-Ra's obvious partiality, Chloe must have been a lady of wonderful powers, albeit she was a mere dancer by recognized profession. It was a gorgeous piece of description. But as it was given to us it would not publish; no, not even inside a yellow cover. And though I did note down a few items to make into future copy, I think I shall give them as my own. They are quite new, and no one will accuse me of lifting them; and, besides, it is merely foolishness to offer unasked-for explanations which no one will believe.

But I cannot say I heard as much as I wished. It was evident that Menen-Ra, after his silence of 3000 years, was equal to going on till midnight. But his was a mouth which could only speak on its own topic. Again and again Gargrave tried to lead this wanderer from a long-forgotten past on to the more weighty matters of state, and time after time he got back to talk about cockfights, and dicing bouts, and ape-racing on the dry Nile banks; or else he would speak to us of Chloe and his other loves with a freedom which is quite obsolete to-day. He brimmed with these reminiscences. But he had no others of a graver sort. This Menen-Ra had lived for nothing but his own personal pleasure, and beyond the limits of that he knew no more than we moderns did about the larger affairs of his country.

Gargrave tried him on every topic. He asked about the army. Menen-Ra started off loud in the praises of his favourite gladiator, and gave us the latest betting on his approaching fight. Gargrave asked for some song of the priests of Osiris, and this faded roysterer promptly trolled forth a drinking chant that nearly split his dusky throat.

And at last, seeing the futility of getting what he wanted, Gargrave savagely put an end to the inquisition. He clapped a large sponge over the still white face of Thompson-Pratt, and took a green powder from the mantelpiece and threw it on the sponge. There was a *paff* of streaky flame, and Thompson-Pratt sprang up choking and spluttering.

"I say, good Lord, Gargrave, what devil's game have you been up to now? What have you been putting me to bed on the hearthrug with that old image for? Here! I say, have you got a whisky-and-soda? Get me some whisky, for heaven's sake. I'm nearly parched to death."

I mixed a drink, and handed it to him. He gulped half of it thirstily. Then he bethought him of a toast. He nodded towards the mummy on the floor. "Here's to you, old cock," said he, and emptied his tumbler to the dregs. "I wonder what the equivalent of whisky was in your benighted day? I bet you had your share of it, if you are ancestor of mine."

"You're a Goth," I said.

"I know," said Thompson-Pratt, "and I had a far better time of it than — say — a Constructive Egyptologist has. Come along to the Hoop and have some dinner. We'll leave Gargrave to go on thumbing at my unpleasant forefather."

The Nemesis of Fire[*]

By some means which I never could fathom, John Silence always contrived to keep the compartment to himself, and as the train had a clear run of two hours before the first stop, there was ample time to go over the preliminary facts of the case. He had telephoned to me that very morning, and even through the disguise of the miles of wire the thrill of incalculable adventure had sounded in his voice.

"As if it were an ordinary country visit," he called, in reply to my question; "and don't forget to bring your gun."

"With blank cartridges, I suppose?" for I knew his rigid principles with regard to the taking of life, and guessed that the guns were merely for some obvious purpose of disguise.

Then he thanked me for coming, mentioned the train, snapped down the receiver, and left me, vibrating with the excitement of anticipation, to do my packing. For the honour of accompanying Dr. John Silence on one of his big cases was what many would have considered an empty honour — and risky. Certainly the adventure held all manner of possibilities, and I arrived at Waterloo with the feelings of a man who is about to embark on some dangerous and peculiar mission in which the dangers he expects to run will not be the ordinary dangers to life and limb, but of some secret character difficult to name and still more difficult to cope with.

"The Manor House has a high sound," he told me, as we sat with our feet up and talked, "but I believe it is little more than an overgrown farmhouse in the desolate heather country beyond D —, and its owner, Colonel Wragge, a retired soldier with a taste for books, lives there practically alone, I understand, with an elderly invalid sister. So you need not look forward to a lively visit, unless the case provides some excitement of its own."

"Which is likely?"

By way of reply he handed me a letter marked "Private." It was dated a week ago, and signed "Yours faithfully, Horace Wragge."

"He heard of me, you see, through Captain Anderson," the doctor explained modestly, as though his fame were not almost world-wide; "you remember that Indian obsession case —" I read the letter. Why it should have been marked private was difficult to understand. It was very brief, direct, and to the point. It referred by way of introduction to Captain Anderson, and then stated quite simply that the writer needed help of a peculiar kind and asked for a personal interview — a morning interview, since it was impossible for him to be absent from the house at night. The letter was dignified even to the point of abruptness, and it is difficult to explain how it managed to convey to me the impression of a

---

* "The Nemesis of Fire" was written by Algernon Blackwood (1869 – 1951) and published in *John Silence, Physician Extraordinary* (1908).

strong man, shaken and perplexed. Perhaps the restraint of the wording, and the mystery of the affair had something to do with it; and the reference to the Anderson case, the horror of which lay still vivid in my memory, may have touched the sense of something rather ominous and alarming. But, whatever the cause, there was no doubt that an impression of serious peril rose somehow out of that white paper with the few lines of firm writing, and the spirit of a deep uneasiness ran between the words and reached the mind without any visible form of expression.

"And when you saw him —?" I asked, returning the letter as the train rushed clattering noisily through Clapham Junction.

"I have not seen him," was the reply. "The man's mind was charged to the brim when he wrote that; full of vivid mental pictures. Notice the restraint of it. For the main character of his case psychometry could be depended upon, and the scrap of paper his hand has touched is sufficient to give to another mind — a sensitive and sympathetic mind — clear mental pictures of what is going on. I think I have a very sound general idea of his problem."

"So there may be excitement, after all?"

John Silence waited a moment before he replied.

"Something very serious is amiss there," he said gravely, at length. "Some one — not himself, I gather, — has been meddling with a rather dangerous kind of gunpowder. So — yes, there may be excitement, as you put it."

"And my duties?" I asked, with a decidedly growing interest. "Remember, I am your 'assistant'."

"Behave like an intelligent confidential secretary. Observe everything, without seeming to. Say nothing — nothing that means anything. Be present at all interviews. I may ask a good deal of you, for if my impressions are correct this is —"

He broke off suddenly.

"But I won't tell you my impressions yet," he resumed after a moment's thought. "Just watch and listen as the case proceeds. Form your own impressions and cultivate your intuitions. We come as ordinary visitors, of course," he added, a twinkle showing for an instant in his eye; "hence, the guns."

Though disappointed not to hear more, I recognised the wisdom of his words and knew how valueless my impressions would be once the powerful suggestion of having heard his own lay behind them. I likewise reflected that intuition joined to a sense of humour was of more use to a man than double the quantity of mere "brains," as such.

Before putting the letter away, however, he handed it back, telling me to place it against my forehead for a few moments and then describe any pictures that came spontaneously into my mind.

"Don't deliberately look for anything. Just imagine you see the inside of the eyelid, and wait for pictures that rise against its dark screen."

I followed his instructions, making my mind as nearly blank as possible. But no visions came. I saw nothing but the lines of light that pass to and fro like the changes of a kaleidoscope across the blackness. A momentary sensation of warmth came and went curiously.

"You see — what?" he asked presently.

"Nothing," I was obliged to admit disappointedly; "nothing but the usual flashes of light one always sees. Only, perhaps, they are more vivid than usual."

He said nothing by way of comment or reply.

"And they group themselves now and then," I continued, with painful candour, for I longed to see the pictures he had spoken of, "group themselves into globes and round balls of fire, and the lines that flash about sometimes look like triangles and crosses — almost like geometrical figures. Nothing more."

I opened my eyes again, and gave him back the letter.

"It makes my head hot," I said, feeling somehow unworthy for not seeing anything of interest. But the look in his eyes arrested my attention at once.

"That sensation of heat is important," he said significantly.

"It was certainly real, and rather uncomfortable," I replied, hoping he would expand and explain. "There was a distinct feeling of warmth — internal warmth somewhere — oppressive in a sense."

"That is interesting," he remarked, putting the letter back in his pocket, and settling himself in the corner with newspapers and books. He vouchsafed nothing more, and I knew the uselessness of trying to make him talk. Following his example I settled likewise with magazines into my corner. But when I closed my eyes again to look for the flashing lights and the sensation of heat, I found nothing but the usual phantasmagoria of the day's events — faces, scenes, memories, — and in due course I fell asleep and then saw nothing at all of any kind.

When we left the train, after six hours' travelling, at a little wayside station standing without trees in a world of sand and heather, the late October shadows had already dropped their sombre veil upon the landscape, and the sun dipped almost out of sight behind the moorland hills. In a high dogcart, behind a fast horse, we were soon rattling across the undulating stretches of an open and bleak country, the keen air stinging our cheeks and the scents of pine and bracken strong about us. Bare hills were faintly visible against the horizon, and the coachman pointed to a bank of distant shadows on our left where he told us the sea lay. Occasional stone farmhouses, standing back from the road among straggling fir trees, and large black barns that seemed to shift past us with a movement of their own in the gloom, were the only signs of humanity and civilisation that we saw, until at the end of a bracing five miles the lights of the lodge gates flared before us and we plunged into a thick grove of pine trees that concealed the Manor House up to the moment of actual arrival.

Colonel Wragge himself met us in the hall. He was the typical army officer who had seen service, real service, and found himself in the process. He was tall and well built, broad in the shoulders, but lean as a greyhound, with grave eyes, rather stern, and a moustache turning grey. I judged him to be about sixty years of age, but his movements showed a suppleness of strength and agility that contradicted the years. The face was full of character and resolution, the face of a man to be depended upon, and the straight grey eyes, it seemed to me, wore a veil of perplexed anxiety that he made no attempt to disguise. The whole appearance of the man at once clothed the adventure with gravity and importance. A matter that gave such a man cause for serious alarm, I felt, must be something real and of genuine moment.

His speech and manner, as he welcomed us, were like his letter, simple and sincere. He had a nature as direct and undeviating as a bullet. Thus, he showed plainly his surprise that Dr. Silence had not come alone.

"My confidential secretary, Mr. Hubbard," the doctor said, introducing me, and the steady gaze and powerful shake of the hand I then received were well calculated, I remember thinking, to drive home the impression that here was a man who was not to be trifled with, and whose perplexity must spring from some very real and tangible cause. And, quite obviously, he was relieved that we had come. His welcome was unmistakably genuine.

He led us at once into a room, half library, half smoking-room, that opened out of the low-ceilinged hall. The Manor House gave the impression of a rambling and glorified farmhouse, solid, ancient, comfortable, and wholly unpretentious. And so it was. Only the heat of the place struck me as unnatural. This room with the blazing fire may have seemed uncomfortably warm after the long drive through the night air; yet it seemed to me that the hall itself, and the whole atmosphere of the house, breathed a warmth that hardly belonged to well-filled grates or the pipes of hot air and water. It was not the heat of the greenhouse; it was an oppressive heat that somehow got into the head and mind. It stirred a curious sense of uneasiness in me, and I caught myself thinking of the sensation of warmth that had emanated from the letter in the train.

I heard him thanking Dr. Silence for having come; there was no preamble, and the exchange of civilities was of the briefest description. Evidently here was a man who, like my companion, loved action rather than talk. His manner was straightforward and direct. I saw him in a flash: puzzled, worried, harassed into a state of alarm by something he could not comprehend; forced to deal with things he would have preferred to despise, yet facing it all with dogged seriousness and making no attempt to conceal that he felt secretly ashamed of his incompetence.

"So I cannot offer you much entertainment beyond that of my own company, and the queer business that has been going on here, and is still going on," he said, with a slight inclination of the head towards me by way of including me in his confidence.

"I think, Colonel Wragge," replied John Silence impressively, "that we shall none of us find the time hang heavy. I gather we shall have our hands full."

The two men looked at one another for the space of some seconds, and there was an indefinable quality in their silence which for the first time made me admit a swift question into my mind; and I wondered a little at my rashness in coming with so little reflection into a big case of this incalculable doctor. But no answer suggested itself, and to withdraw was, of course, inconceivable. The gates had closed behind me now, and the spirit of the adventure was already besieging my mind with its advance guard of a thousand little hopes and fears.

Explaining that he would wait till after dinner to discuss anything serious, as no reference was ever made before his sister, he led the way upstairs and showed us personally to our rooms; and it was just as I was finishing dressing that a knock came at my door and Dr. Silence entered.

He was always what is called a serious man, so that even in moments of comedy you felt he never lost sight of the profound gravity of life, but as he came across the room to me I caught the expression of his face and understood in a flash that he was now in his most grave and earnest mood. He looked almost troubled. I stopped fumbling with my black tie and stared.

"It is serious," he said, speaking in a low voice, "more so even than I imagined. Colonel Wragge's control over his thoughts concealed a great deal in my psychometrising of the letter. I looked in to warn you to keep yourself well in hand — generally speaking."

"Haunted house?" I asked, conscious of a distinct shiver down my back.

But he smiled gravely at the question.

"Haunted House of Life more likely," he replied, and a look came into his eyes which I had only seen there when a human soul was in the toils and he was thick in the fight of rescue. He was stirred in the deeps.

"Colonel Wragge — or the sister?" I asked hurriedly, for the gong was sounding.

"Neither directly," he said from the door. "Something far older, something very, very remote indeed. This thing has to do with the ages, unless I am mistaken greatly, the ages on which the mists of memory have long lain undisturbed."

He came across the floor very quickly with a finger on his lips, looking at me with a peculiar searchingness of gaze.

"Are you aware yet of anything — odd here?" he asked in a whisper. "Anything you cannot quite define, for instance. Tell me, Hubbard, for I want to know all your impressions. They may help me."

I shook my head, avoiding his gaze, for there was something in the eyes that scared me a little. But he was so in earnest that I set my mind keenly searching.

"Nothing yet," I replied truthfully, wishing I could confess to a real emotion; "nothing but the strange heat of the place."

He gave a little jump forward in my direction.

"The heat again, that's it!" he exclaimed, as though glad of my corroboration. "And how would you describe it, perhaps?" he asked quickly, with a hand on the door knob.

"It doesn't seem like ordinary physical heat," I said, casting about in my thoughts for a definition.

"More a mental heat," he interrupted, "a glowing of thought and desire, a sort of feverish warmth of the spirit. Isn't that it?"

I admitted that he had exactly described my sensations.

"Good!" he said, as he opened the door, and with an indescribable gesture that combined a warning to be ready with a sign of praise for my correct intuition, he was gone.

I hurried after him, and found the two men waiting for me in front of the fire.

"I ought to warn you," our host was saying as I came in, "that my sister, whom you will meet at dinner, is not aware of the real object of your visit. She is under the impression that we are interested in the same line of study — folklore — and that your researches have led to my seeking acquaintance. She comes to dinner in her chair, you know. It will be a great pleasure to her to meet you both. We have few visitors."

So that on entering the dining-room we were prepared to find Miss Wragge already at her place, seated in a sort of bath-chair. She was a vivacious and charming old lady, with smiling expression and bright eyes, and she chatted all through dinner with unfailing spontaneity. She had that face, unlined and fresh, that some people carry through life from the cradle to the grave; her smooth plump cheeks were all pink and white, and her hair, still dark, was divided into two glossy and sleek halves on either side of a careful parting. She wore gold-rimmed glasses, and at her throat was a large scarab of green jasper that made a very handsome brooch.

Her brother and Dr. Silence talked little, so that most of the conversation was carried on between herself and me, and she told me a great deal about the history of the old house, most of which I fear I listened to with but half an ear.

"And when Cromwell stayed here," she babbled on, "he occupied the very rooms upstairs that used to be mine. But my brother thinks it safer for me to sleep on the ground floor now in case of fire."

And this sentence has stayed in my memory only because of the sudden way her brother interrupted her and instantly led the conversation on to another topic. The passing reference to fire seemed to have disturbed him, and thenceforward he directed the talk himself.

It was difficult to believe that this lively and animated old lady, sitting beside me and taking so eager an interest in the affairs of life, was practically, we understood, without the use of her lower limbs, and that her whole existence for years had been passed between the sofa, the bed, and the bath-chair in which she chatted so naturally at the dinner-table. She made no allusion to her affliction until the dessert was reached, and then, touching a bell, she made us a witty little speech about leaving us "like time, on noiseless feet," and was wheeled out of the room by the butler and carried off to her apartments at the other end of the house.

And the rest of us were not long in following suit, for Dr. Silence and myself were quite as eager to learn the nature of our errand as our host was to impart it to us. He led us down a long flagged passage to a room at the very end of the house, a room provided with double doors, and windows, I saw, heavily shuttered. Books lined the walls on every side, and a large desk in the bow window was piled up with volumes, some open, some shut, some showing scraps of paper stuck between the leaves, and all smothered in a general cataract of untidy foolscap and loose-half sheets.

"My study and workroom," explained Colonel Wragge, with a delightful touch of innocent pride, as though he were a very serious scholar. He placed arm-chairs for us round the fire. "Here," he added significantly, "we shall be safe from interruption and can talk securely."

During dinner the manner of the doctor had been all that was natural and spontaneous, though it was impossible for me, knowing him as I did, not to be aware that he was subconsciously very keenly alert and already receiving upon the ultra-sensitive surface of his mind various and vivid impressions; and there was now something in the gravity of his face, as well as in the significant tone of Colonel Wragge's speech, and something, too, in the fact that we three were shut away in this private chamber about to listen to things probably strange, and certainly mysterious — something in all this that touched my imagination sharply and sent an undeniable thrill along my nerves. Taking the chair indicated by my host, I lit my cigar and waited for the opening of the attack, fully conscious that we were now too far gone in the adventure to admit of withdrawal, and wondering a little anxiously where it was going to lead.

What I expected precisely, it is hard to say. Nothing definite, perhaps. Only the sudden change was dramatic. A few hours before the prosaic atmosphere of Piccadilly was about me, and now I was sitting in a secret chamber of this remote old building waiting to hear an account of things that held possibly the genuine heart of terror. I thought of the dreary moors and hills outside, and the dark pine copses soughing in the wind of night; I remembered my companion's singular words up in my bedroom before dinner; and then I turned and noted carefully the stern countenance of the Colonel as he faced us and lit his big black cigar before speaking.

The threshold of an adventure, I reflected as I waited for the first words, is always the most thrilling moment — until the climax comes.

But Colonel Wragge hesitated — mentally — a long time before he began. He talked briefly of our journey, the weather, the country, and other comparatively trivial topics, while he sought about in his mind for an appropriate entry into the subject that was uppermost in the thoughts of all of us. The fact was he found it a difficult matter to speak of at all, and it was Dr. Silence who finally showed him the way over the hedge.

"Mr. Hubbard will take a few notes when you are ready — you won't object," he suggested; "I can give my undivided attention in this way."

"By all means," turning to reach some of the loose sheets on the writing table, and glancing at me. He still hesitated a little, I thought. "The fact is," he said apologetically, "I wondered if it was quite fair to trouble you so soon. The daylight might suit you better to hear what I have to tell. Your sleep, I mean, might be less disturbed, perhaps."

"I appreciate your thoughtfulness," John Silence replied with his gentle smile, taking command as it were from that moment, "but really we are both quite immune. There is nothing, I think, that could prevent either of us sleeping, except — an outbreak of fire, or some such very physical disturbance."

Colonel Wragge raised his eyes and looked fixedly at him. This reference to an outbreak of fire I felt sure was made with a purpose. It certainly had the desired effect of removing from our host's manner the last signs of hesitancy.

"Forgive me," he said. "Of course, I know nothing of your methods in matters of this kind — so, perhaps, you would like me to begin at once and give you an outline of the situation?"

Dr. Silence bowed his agreement. "I can then take my precautions accordingly," he added calmly.

The soldier looked up for a moment as though he did not quite gather the meaning of these words; but he made no further comment and turned at once to tackle a subject on which he evidently talked with diffidence and unwillingness.

"It's all so utterly out of my line of things," he began, puffing out clouds of cigar smoke between his words, "and there's so little to tell with any real evidence behind it, that it's almost impossible to make a consecutive story for you. It's the total cumulative effect that is so — so disquieting." He chose his words with care, as though determined not to travel one hair's breadth beyond the truth.

"I came into this place twenty years ago when my elder brother died," he continued, "but could not afford to live here then. My sister, whom you met at dinner, kept house for him till the end, and during all these years, while I was seeing service abroad, she had an eye to the place — for we never got a satisfactory tenant — and saw that it was not allowed to go to ruin. I myself took possession, however, only a year ago.

"My brother," he went on, after a perceptible pause, "spent much of his time away, too. He was a great traveller, and filled the house with stuff he brought home from all over the world. The laundry — a small detached building beyond the servants' quarters — he turned into a regular little museum. The curios and things I have cleared away — they collected dust and were always getting broken — but the laundry — house you shall see tomorrow."

Colonel Wragge spoke with such deliberation and with so many pauses that this beginning took him a long time. But at this point he came to a full stop altogether. Evidently there was something he wished to say that cost him considerable effort. At length he looked up steadily into my companion's face.

"May I ask you — that is, if you won't think it strange," he said, and a sort of hush came over his voice and manner, "whether you have noticed anything at all unusual — anything queer, since you came into the house?"

Dr. Silence answered without a moments hesitation.

"I have" he said. "There is a curious sensation of heat in the place."

"Ah!" exclaimed the other, with a slight start. "You have noticed it. This unaccountable heat —"

"But its cause, I gather, is not in the house itself — but outside," I was astonished to hear the doctor add.

Colonel Wragge rose from his chair and turned to unhook a framed map that hung upon the wall. I got the impression that the movement was made with the deliberate purpose of concealing his face.

"Your diagnosis, I believe, is amazingly accurate," he said after a moment, turning round with the map in his hands. "Though, of course, I can have no idea how you should guess —"

John Silence shrugged his shoulders expressively. "Merely my impression," he said. "If you pay attention to impressions, and do not allow them to be confused by deductions of the intellect, you will often find them surprisingly, uncannily, accurate."

Colonel Wragge resumed his seat and laid the map upon his knees. His face was very thoughtful as he plunged abruptly again into his story.

"On coming into possession," he said, looking us alternately in the face, "I found a crop of stories of the most extraordinary and impossible kind I had ever heard — stories which at first I treated with amused indifference, but later was forced to regard seriously, if only to keep my servants. These stories I thought I traced to the fact of my brothers death — and, in a way, I think so still."

He leant forward and handed the map to Dr. Silence.

"It's an old plan of the estate," he explained, "but accurate enough for our purpose, and I wish you would note the position of the plantations marked upon it, especially those near the house. That one," indicating the spot with his finger, "is called the Twelve Acre Plantation. It was just there, on the side nearest the house, that my brother and the head keeper met their deaths."

He spoke as a man forced to recognise facts that he deplored, and would have preferred to leave untouched — things he personally would rather have treated with ridicule if possible. It made his words peculiarly dignified and impressive, and I listened with an increasing uneasiness as to the sort of help the doctor would look to me for later. It seemed as though I were a spectator of some drama of mystery in which any moment I might be summoned to play a part.

"It was twenty years ago," continued the Colonel, "but there was much talk about it at the time, unfortunately, and you may, perhaps, have heard of the affair. Stride, the keeper, was a passionate, hot-tempered man but I regret to say, so was my brother, and quarrels between them seem to have been frequent."

"I do not recall the affair," said the doctor. "May I ask what was the cause of death?" Something in his voice made me prick up my ears for the reply.

"The keeper, it was said, from suffocation. And at the inquest the doctors averred that both men had been dead the same length of time when found."

"And your brother?" asked John Silence, noticing the omission, and listening intently.

"Equally mysterious," said our host, speaking in a low voice with effort.

"But there was one distressing feature I think I ought to mention. For those who saw the face — I did not see it myself — and though Stride carried a gun its chambers were undischarged —" He stammered and hesitated with confusion. Again that sense of terror moved between his words. He stuck.

"Yes," said the chief listener sympathetically.

"My brother's face, they said, looked as though it had been scorched. It had been swept, as it were, by something that burned — blasted. It was, I am told, quite dreadful. The bodies were found lying side by side, faces downwards, both pointing away from the wood, as though they had been in the act of running, and not more than a dozen yards from its edge."

Dr. Silence made no comment. He appeared to be studying the map attentively.

"I did not see the face myself," repeated the other, his manner somehow expressing the sense of awe he contrived to keep out of his voice, "but my sister unfortunately did, and her present state I believe to be entirely due to the shock it gave to her nerves. She never can be brought to refer to it, naturally, and I am even inclined to think that the memory has mercifully been permitted to vanish from her mind. But she spoke of it at the time as a face swept by flame — blasted."

John Silence looked up from his contemplation of the map, but with the air of one who wished to listen, not to speak, and presently Colonel Wragge went on with his account. He stood on the mat, his broad shoulders hiding most of the mantelpiece.

"They all centred about this particular plantation, these stories. That was to be expected, for the people here are as superstitious as Irish peasantry, and though I made one or two examples among them to stop the foolish talk, it had no effect, and new versions came to my ears every week. You may imagine how little good dismissals did, when I tell you that the servants dismissed themselves. It was not the house servants, but the men who worked on the estate outside. The keepers gave notice one after another, none of them with any reason I could accept; the foresters refused to enter the wood, and the beaters to beat in it. Word flew all over the countryside that Twelve Acre Plantation was a place to be avoided, day or night.

"There came a point," the Colonel went on, now well in his swing, "when I felt compelled to make investigations on my own account. I could not kill the thing by ignoring it; so I collected and analysed the stories at first hand. For this Twelve Acre Wood, you will see by the map, comes rather near home. Its lower end, if you will look, almost touches the end of the back lawn, as I will show you tomorrow, and its dense growth of pines forms the chief protection the house enjoys from the east winds that blow up from the sea. And in olden days, before my brother interfered with it and frightened all the game away, it was one of the best pheasant coverts on the whole estate."

"And what form, if I may ask, did this interference take?" asked Dr. Silence.

"In detail, I cannot tell you, for I do not know — except that I understand it was the subject of his frequent differences with the head keeper; but during the last two years of his life, when he gave up travelling and settled down here, he took a special interest in this wood, and for some unaccountable reason began to build a low stone wall around it. This wall was never finished, but you shall see the ruins tomorrow in the daylight."

"And the result of your investigations — these stories, I mean?" the doctor broke in, anxious to keep him to the main issues.

"Yes, I'm coming to that," he said slowly, "but the wood first, for this wood out of which they grew like mushrooms has nothing in any way peculiar about it. It is very thickly grown, and rises to a clearer part in the centre, a sort of mound where there is a circle of large boulders — old Druid stones, I'm told. At another place there's a small pond. There's nothing distinctive about it that I could mention — just an ordinary pine-wood, a very ordinary pine-wood — only the trees are a bit twisted in the trunks, some of 'em, and very dense. Nothing more.

"And the stories? Well, none of them had anything to do with my poor brother, or the keeper, as you might have expected; and they were all odd — such odd things, I mean, to invent or imagine. I never could make out how these people got such notions into their heads."

He paused a moment to relight his cigar.

"There's no regular path through it," he resumed, puffing vigorously, "but the fields round it are constantly used, and one of the gardeners whose cottage lies over that way declared he often saw moving lights in it at night, and luminous shapes like globes of fire over the tops of the trees, skimming and floating, and making a soft hissing sound — most of 'em said that, in fact — and another man saw shapes flitting in and out among the trees, things that were neither men nor animals, and all faintly luminous. No one ever pretended to see human forms — always queer, huge things they could not properly describe. Sometimes the whole wood was lit up, and one fellow — he's still here and you shall see him — has a most circumstantial yarn about having seen great stars lying on the ground round the edge of the wood at regular intervals —"

"What kind of stars?" put in John Silence sharply, in a sudden way that made me start.

"Oh, I don't know quite; ordinary stars, I think he said, only very large, and apparently blazing as though the ground was alight. He was too terrified to go close and examine, and he has never seen them since."

He stooped and stirred the fire into a welcome blaze — welcome for its blaze of light rather than for its heat. In the room there was already a strange pervading sensation of warmth that was oppressive in its effect and far from comforting.

"Of course," he went on, straightening up again on the mat, "this was all commonplace enough — this seeing lights and figures at night. Most of these fellows drink, and imagination and terror between them may account for almost anything. But others saw things in broad daylight. One of the woodmen, a sober, respectable man, took the shortcut home to his midday meal, and swore that he was followed the whole length of the wood by something that never showed itself, but dodged from tree to tree, always keeping out of sight, yet solid enough to make the branches sway and the twigs snap on the ground. And it made a noise, he declared — but really" — the speaker stopped and gave a short laugh — "it's too absurd —"

"Please!" insisted the doctor; "for it is these small details that give me the best clues always."

"— it made a crackling noise, he said, like a bonfire. Those were his very words: like the crackling of a bonfire," finished the soldier, with a repetition of his short laugh.

"Most interesting," Dr. Silence observed gravely. "Please omit nothing."

"Yes," he went on, "and it was soon after that the fires began — the fires in the wood. They started mysteriously burning in the patches of coarse white grass that cover the more open parts of the plantation. No one ever actually saw them start, but many, myself among the number, have seen them burning and smouldering. They are always small and circular in shape, and for all the world like a picnic fire. The head keeper has a dozen explanations, from sparks flying out of the house chimneys to the sunlight focusing through a dewdrop, but none of them, I must admit, convince me as being in the least likely or probable. They are most singular, I consider, most singular, these mysterious fires, and I am glad to say that they come only at rather long intervals and never seem to spread.

"But the keeper had other queer stories as well, and about things that are verifiable. He declared that no life ever willingly entered the plantation; more, that no life existed in it at all. No birds nested in the trees, or flew into their shade. He set countless traps, but never caught so much as a rabbit or a weasel. Animals avoided it, and more than once he had picked up dead creatures round the edges that bore no obvious signs of how they had met their death.

"Moreover, he told me one extraordinary tale about his retriever chasing some invisible creature across the field one day when he was out with his gun. The dog suddenly pointed at something in the field at his feet, and then gave chase, yelping like a mad thing. It followed its imaginary quarry to the borders of the wood, and then went in — a thing he had never known it to do before. The moment it crossed the edge — it is darkish in there even in daylight — it began fighting in the most frenzied and terrific fashion. It made him afraid to interfere, he said. And at last, when the dog came out, hanging its tail down and panting, he found something like white hair stuck to its jaws, and brought it to show me. I tell you these details because —"

"They are important, believe me," the doctor stopped him. "And you have it still, this hair?" he asked.

"It disappeared in the oddest way," the Colonel explained. "It was curious looking stuff, something like asbestos, and I sent it to be analysed by the local chemist. But either the man got wind of its origin, or else he didn't like the look of it for some reason, because he returned it to me and said it was neither animal, vegetable, nor mineral, so far as he could make out, and he didn't wish to have anything to do with it. I put it away in paper, but a week later, on opening the package — it was gone! Oh, the stories are simply endless. I could tell you hundreds all on the same lines."

"And personal experiences of your own, Colonel Wragge?" asked John Silence earnestly, his manner showing the greatest possible interest and sympathy.

The soldier gave an almost imperceptible start. He looked distinctly uncomfortable.

"Nothing, I think," he said slowly, "nothing — er — I should like to rely on. I mean nothing I have the right to speak of, perhaps — yet."

His mouth closed with a snap. Dr. Silence, after waiting a little to see if he would add to his reply, did not seek to press him on the point.

"Well," he resumed presently, and as though he would speak contemptuously, yet dared not, "this sort of thing has gone on at intervals ever since. It spreads like wildfire, of course, mysterious chatter of this kind, and people began trespassing all over the estate, coming to see the wood, and making themselves a general nuisance. Notices of man-traps and spring-guns only seemed to increase their persistence; and — think of it," he snorted, "some local Research Society actually wrote and asked permission for one of their members to spend a night in the wood! Bolder fools, who didn't write for leave, came and took away bits of bark from the trees and gave them to clairvoyants, who invented in their turn a further batch of tales. There was simply no end to it all."

"Most distressing and annoying, I can well believe," interposed the doctor.

"Then suddenly, the phenomena ceased as mysteriously as they had begun, and the interest flagged. The tales stopped. People got interested in something else. It all seemed to die out. This was last July. I can tell you exactly, for I've kept a diary more or less of what happened."

"Ah!"

"But now, quite recently, within the past three weeks, it has all revived again with a rush — with a kind of furious attack, so to speak. It has really become unbearable. You may imagine what it means, and the general state of affairs, when I say that the possibility of leaving has occurred to me."

"Incendiarism?" suggested Dr. Silence, half under his breath, but not so low that Colonel Wragge did not hear him.

"By Jove, sir, you take the very words out of my mouth!" exclaimed the astonished man, glancing from the doctor to me and from me to the doctor, and rattling the money in his pocket as though some explanation of my friend's divining powers were to be found that way.

"It's only that you are thinking very vividly," the doctor said quietly, "and your thoughts form pictures in my mind before you utter them. It's merely a little elementary thought-reading."

His intention, I saw, was not to perplex the good man, but to impress him with his powers so as to ensure obedience later.

"Good Lord! I had no idea —" He did not finish the sentence, and dived again abruptly into his narrative.

"I did not see anything myself, I must admit, but the stories of independent eye-witnesses were to the effect that lines of light, like streams of thin fire, moved through the wood and sometimes were seen to shoot out precisely as flames might shoot out — in the direction of this house. There," he explained, in a louder voice that made me jump, pointing with a thick finger to the map, "where the westerly fringe of the plantation comes up to the end of the lower lawn at the back of the house

— where it links on to those dark patches, which are laurel shrubberies, running right up to the back premises — that's where these lights were seen. They passed from the wood to the shrubberies, and in this way reached the house itself. Like silent rockets, one man described them, rapid as lightning and exceedingly bright."

"And this evidence you spoke of?"

"They actually reached the sides of the house. They've left a mark of scorching on the walls — the walls of the laundry building at the other end. You shall see 'em tomorrow." He pointed to the map to indicate the spot, and then straightened himself and glared about the room as though he had said something no one could believe and expected contradiction.

"Scorched — just as the faces were," the doctor murmured, looking significantly at me.

"Scorched — yes," repeated the Colonel, failing to catch the rest of the sentence in his excitement.

There was a prolonged silence in the room, in which I heard the gurgling of the oil in the lamp and the click of the coals and the heavy breathing of our host. The most unwelcome sensations were creeping about my spine, and I wondered whether my companion would scorn me utterly if I asked to sleep on the sofa in his room. It was eleven o'clock, I saw by the clock on the mantelpiece. We had crossed the dividing line and were now well in the movement of the adventure. The fight between my interest and my dread became acute. But, even if turning back had been possible, I think the interest would have easily gained the day.

"I have enemies, of course," I heard the Colonel's rough voice break into the pause presently, "and have discharged a number of servants —"

"It's not that," put in John Silence briefly.

"You think not? In a sense I am glad, and yet — there are some things that can be met and dealt with —"

He left the sentence unfinished, and looked down at the floor with an expression of grim severity that betrayed a momentary glimpse of character. This fighting man loathed and abhorred the thought of an enemy he could not see and come to grips with. Presently he moved over and sat down in the chair between us. Something like a sigh escaped him. Dr. Silence said nothing.

"My sister, of course, is kept in ignorance, as far as possible, of all this," he said disconnectedly, and as if talking to himself. "But even if she knew, she would find matter-of-fact explanations. I only wish I could. I'm sure they exist."

There came then an interval in the conversation that was very significant. It did not seem a real pause, or the silence real silence, for both men continued to think so rapidly and strongly that one almost imagined their thoughts clothed themselves in words in the air of the room. I was more than a little keyed up with the strange excitement of all I had heard, but what stimulated my nerves more than anything else was the obvious fact that the doctor was clearly upon the trail of discovery. In his mind at that moment, I believe, he had already solved the nature of this perplexing psychical problem. His face was like a mask, and he employed the absolute minimum of gesture and words. All his energies were directed inwards, and by those incalculable methods and processes he had mastered with such infinite patience and study, I felt sure he was already in touch with the forces behind these singular phenomena and laying his deep plans for bringing them into the open, and then effectively dealing with them.

Colonel Wragge meanwhile grew more and more fidgety. From time to time he turned towards my companion, as though about to speak, yet always changing his mind at the last moment. Once he went over and opened the door suddenly, apparently to see if any one were listening at the keyhole, for he disappeared a moment between the two doors, and I then heard him open the outer one. He stood there for some seconds and made a noise as though he were sniffing the air like a dog. Then he closed both doors cautiously and came back to the fireplace. A strange excitement seemed growing upon him. Evidently he was trying to make up his mind to say something that he found it difficult to say. And John Silence, as I rightly judged, was waiting patiently for him to choose his own opportunity and his own way of saying it. At last he turned and faced us, squaring his great shoulders, and stiffening perceptibly.

Dr. Silence looked up sympathetically.

"Your own experiences help me most," he observed quietly.

"The fact is," the Colonel said, speaking very low, "this past week there have been outbreaks of fire in the house itself. Three separate outbreaks — and all — in my sister's room."

"Yes," the doctor said, as if this was just what he had expected to hear.

"Utterly unaccountable — all of them," added the other, and then sat down. I began to understand something of the reason of his excitement. He was realising at last that the "natural" explanation he had held to all along was becoming impossible, and he hated it. It made him angry.

"Fortunately," he went on, "she was out each time and does not know. But I have made her sleep now in a room on the ground floor."

"A wise precaution," the doctor said simply. He asked one or two questions. The fires had started in the curtains — once by the window and once by the bed. The third time smoke had been discovered by the maid coming from the cupboard, and it was found that Miss Wragge's clothes hanging on the hooks were smouldering. The doctor listened attentively, but made no comment.

"And now can you tell me," he said presently, "what your own feeling about it is — your general impression?"

"It sounds foolish to say so," replied the soldier, after a moment's hesitation, "but I feel exactly as I have often felt on active service in my Indian campaigns: just as if the house and all in it were in a state of siege; as though a concealed enemy were encamped about us — in ambush somewhere." He uttered a soft nervous laugh. "As if the next sign of smoke would precipitate a panic — a dreadful panic."

The picture came before me of the night shadowing the house, and the twisted pine trees he had described crowding about it, concealing some powerful enemy; and, glancing at the resolute face and figure of the old soldier, forced at length to his confession, I understood something of all he had been through before he sought the assistance of John Silence.

"And tomorrow, unless I am mistaken, is full moon," said the doctor suddenly, watching the other's face for the effect of his apparently careless words.

Colonel Wragge gave an uncontrollable start, and his face for the first time showed unmistakable pallor.

"What in the world —?" he began, his lip quivering.

"Only that I am beginning to see light in this extraordinary affair," returned the other calmly, "and, if my theory is correct, each month when the moon is at the full should witness an increase in the activity of the phenomena."

"I don't see the connection," Colonel Wragge answered almost savagely, "but I am bound to say my diary bears you out." He wore the most puzzled expression I have ever seen upon an honest face, but he abhorred this additional corroboration of an explanation that perplexed him.

"I confess," he repeated, "I cannot see the connection."

"Why should you?" said the doctor, with his first laugh that evening. He got up and hung the map upon the wall again. "But I do — because these things are my special study — and let me add that I have yet to come across a problem that is not natural, and has not a natural explanation. It's merely a question of how much one knows and admits."

Colonel Wragge eyed him with a new and curious respect in his face. But his feelings were soothed. Moreover, the doctor's laugh and change of manner came as a relief to all, and broke the spell of grave suspense that had held us so long. We all rose and stretched our limbs, and took little walks about the room.

"I am glad, Dr. Silence, if you will allow me to say so, that you are here," he said simply, "very glad indeed. And now I fear I have kept you both up very late," with a glance to include me, "for you must be tired, and ready for your beds. I have told you all there is to tell," he added, "and tomorrow you must feel perfectly free to take any steps you think necessary."

The end was abrupt, yet natural, for there was nothing more to say, and neither of these men talked for mere talking's sake.

Out in the cold and chilly hall he lit our candles and took us upstairs. The house was at rest and still, every one asleep. We moved softly. Through the windows on the stairs we saw the moonlight falling across the lawn, throwing deep shadows. The nearer pine trees were just visible in the distance, a wall of impenetrable blackness.

Our host came for a moment to our rooms to see that we had everything. He pointed to a coil of strong rope lying beside the window, fastened to the wall by means of an iron ring. Evidently it had been recently put in.

"I don't think we shall need it," Dr. Silence said, with a smile.

"I trust not," replied our host gravely. "I sleep quite close to you across the landing," he whispered, pointing to his door, "and if you — if you want anything in the night you will know where to find me."

He wished us pleasant dreams and disappeared down the passage into his room, shading the candle with his big muscular hand from the draughts.

John Silence stopped me a moment before I went.

"You know what it is?" I asked, with an excitement that even overcame my weariness.

"Yes," he said, "I'm almost sure. And you?"

"Not the smallest notion."

He looked disappointed, but not half as disappointed as I felt.

"Egypt," he whispered, "Egypt!"

Nothing happened to disturb me in the night — nothing, that is, except a nightmare in which Colonel Wragge chased me amid thin streaks of fire, and his sister always prevented my escape by suddenly rising up out of the ground in her chair — dead. The deep baying of dogs woke me once, just before the dawn, it must have been, for I saw the window frame against the sky; there was a flash of lightning, too, I thought, as I turned over in bed. And it was warm, for October oppressively warm.

It was after eleven o'clock when our host suggested going out with the guns, these, we understood, being a somewhat thin disguise for our true purpose. Personally, I was glad to be in the open air, for the atmosphere of the house was heavy with presentiment. The sense of impending disaster hung over all. Fear stalked the passages, and lurked in the corners of every room. It was a house haunted, but really haunted; not by some vague shadow of the dead, but by a definite though incalculable influence that was actively alive, and dangerous. At the least smell of smoke the entire household quivered. An odour of burning, I was convinced, would paralyse all the inmates. For the servants, though professedly ignorant by the master's unspoken orders, yet shared the common dread; and the hideous uncertainty, joined with this display of so spiteful and calculated a spirit of malignity, provided a kind of black doom that draped not only the walls, but also the minds of the people living within them.

Only the bright and cheerful vision of old Miss Wragge being pushed about the house in her noiseless chair, chatting and nodding briskly to every one she met, prevented us from giving way entirely to the depression which governed the majority. The sight of her was like a gleam of sunshine through the depths of some ill-omened wood, and just as we went out I saw her being wheeled along by her attendant into the sunshine of the back lawn, and caught her cheery smile as she turned her head and wished us good sport.

The morning was October at its best. Sunshine glistened on the dew-drenched grass and on leaves turned golden-red. The dainty messengers of coming hoar-frost were already in the air, a search for permanent winter quarters. From the wide moors that everywhere swept up against the sky, like a purple sea splashed by the occasional grey of rocky clefts, there stole down the cool and perfumed wind of the west. And the keen taste of the sea ran through all like a master-flavour, borne over the spaces perhaps by the seagulls that cried and circled high in the air.

But our host took little interest in this sparkling beauty, and had no thought of showing off the scenery of his property. His mind was otherwise intent, and, for that matter, so were our own.

"Those bleak moors and hills stretch unbroken for hours," he said, with a sweep of the hand; "and over there, some four miles," pointing in another direction, "lies S — Bay, a long, swampy inlet of the sea, haunted by myriads of seabirds. On the other side of the house are the plantations and pine-woods. I thought we would get the dogs and go first to the Twelve Acre Wood I told you about last night. It's quite near."

We found the dogs in the stable, and I recalled the deep baying of the night when a fine bloodhound and two great Danes leaped out to greet us. Singular companions for guns, I thought to myself, as we struck out across the fields and the great creatures bounded and ran beside us, nose to ground.

The conversation was scanty. John Silence's grave face did not encourage talk. He wore the expression I knew well — that look of earnest solicitude which meant that his whole being was deeply absorbed and preoccupied. Frightened, I had never seen him, but anxious often — it always moved me to witness it — and he was anxious now.

"On the way back you shall see the laundry building," Colonel Wragge observed shortly, for he, too, found little to say. "We shall attract less attention then."

Yet not all the crisp beauty of the morning seemed able to dispel the feelings of uneasy dread that gathered increasingly about our minds as we went.

In a very few minutes a clump of pine trees concealed the house from view, and we found ourselves on the outskirts of a densely grown plantation of conifers. Colonel Wragge stopped abruptly, and, producing a map from his pocket, explained once more very briefly its position with regard to the house. He showed how it ran up almost to the walls of the laundry building — though at the moment beyond our actual view — and pointed to the windows of his sister's bedroom where the fires had been. The room, now empty, looked straight on to the wood. Then, glancing nervously about him, and calling the dogs to heel, he proposed that we should enter the plantation and make as thorough examination of it as we thought worth while. The dogs, he added, might perhaps be persuaded to accompany us a little way — and he pointed to where they cowered at his feet — but he doubted it. "Neither voice nor whip will get them very far, I'm afraid," he said. "I know by experience."

"If you have no objection," replied Dr. Silence, with decision, and speaking almost for the first time, "we will make our examination alone — Mr. Hubbard and myself. It will be best so."

His tone was absolutely final, and the Colonel acquiesced so politely that even a less intuitive man than myself must have seen that he was genuinely relieved.

"You doubtless have good reason," he said.

"Merely that I wish to obtain my impressions uncoloured. This delicate clue I am working on might be so easily blurred by the thought-currents of another mind with strongly preconceived ideas."

"Perfectly. I understand," rejoined the soldier, though with an expression of countenance that plainly contradicted his words. "Then I will wait here with the dogs; and we'll have a look at the laundry on our way home."

I turned once to look back as we clambered over the low stone wall built by the late owner, and saw his straight, soldierly figure standing in the sunlit field watching us with a curiously intent look on his face. There was something to me incongruous, yet distinctly pathetic, in the man's efforts to meet all far-fetched explanations of the mystery with contempt, and at the same time in his stolid, unswerving investigation of it all. He nodded at me and made a gesture of farewell with his hand. That picture of him, standing in the sunshine with his big dogs, steadily watching us, remains with me to this day.

Dr. Silence led the way in among the twisted trunks, planted closely together in serried ranks, and I followed sharp at his heels. The moment we were out of sight he turned and put down his gun against the roots of a big tree, and I did likewise.

"We shall hardly want these cumbersome weapons of murder," he observed, with a passing smile.

"You are sure of your clue, then?" I asked at once, bursting with curiosity, yet fearing to betray it lest he should think me unworthy. His own methods were so absolutely simple and untheatrical.

"I am sure of my clue," he answered gravely. "And I think we have come just in time. You shall know in due course. For the present — be content to follow and observe. And think, steadily. The support of your mind will help me."

His voice had that quiet mastery in it which leads men to face death with a sort of happiness and pride. I would have followed him anywhere at that moment. At the same time his words conveyed a sense of dread seriousness. I caught the thrill of his confidence; but also, in this broad light of day, I felt the measure of alarm that lay behind.

"You still have no strong impressions?" he asked. "Nothing happened in the night, for instance? No vivid dreamings?"

He looked closely for my answer, I was aware.

"I slept almost an unbroken sleep. I was tremendously tired, you know, and, but for the oppressive heat —"

"Good! You still notice the heat, then," he said to himself, rather than expecting an answer. "And the lightning?" he added, "that lightning out of a clear sky — that flashing — did you notice that?"

I answered truly that I thought I had seen a flash during a moment of wakefulness, and he then drew my attention to certain facts before moving on.

"You remember the sensation of warmth when you put the letter to your forehead in the train; the heat generally in the house last evening, and, as you now mention, in the night. You heard, too, the Colonel's stories about the appearances of fire in this wood and in the house itself, and the way his brother and the gamekeeper came to their deaths twenty years ago."

I nodded, wondering what in the world it all meant.

"And you get no clue from these facts?" he asked, a trifle surprised.

I searched every corner of my mind and imagination for some inkling of his meaning, but was obliged to admit that I understood nothing so far.

"Never mind, you will later. And now," he added, "we will go over the wood and see what we can find."

His words explained to me something of his method. We were to keep our minds alert and report to each other the least fancy that crossed the picture-gallery of our thoughts. Then, just as we started, he turned again to me with a final warning.

"And for your safety," he said earnestly, "imagine now — and for that matter, imagine always until we leave this place — imagine with the utmost keenness, that you are surrounded by a shell that protects you. Picture yourself inside a protective envelope, and build it up with the most intense imagination you can evoke. Pour the whole force of your thought and will into it. Believe vividly all through this adventure that such a shell, constructed of your thought, will and imagination, surrounds you completely, and that nothing can pierce it to attack."

He spoke with dramatic conviction, gazing hard at me as though to enforce his meaning, and then moved forward and began to pick his way over the rough, tussocky ground into the wood. And meanwhile, knowing the efficacy of his prescription, I adopted it to the best of my ability.

The trees at once closed about us like the night. Their branches met overhead in a continuous tangle, their stems crept closer and closer, the brambly undergrowth thickened and multiplied. We tore our trousers, scratched our hands, and our eyes filled with fine dust that made it most difficult to avoid the clinging, prickly network of branches and creepers. Coarse white grass that caught our feet like string grew here and there in patches. It crowned the lumps of peaty growth that stuck up like human heads, fantastically dressed, thrusting up at us out of the ground with crests of dead hair. We stumbled and floundered among them. It was hard going, and I could well conceive it impossible to find a way at all in the night-time. We jumped, when possible, from tussock to tussock, and it seemed as though we were springing among heads on a battlefield, and that this dead white grass concealed eyes that turned to stare as we passed.

Here and there the sunlight shot in with vivid spots of white light, dazzling the sight, but only making the surrounding gloom deeper by contrast. And on two occasions we passed dark circular places in the grass where fires had eaten their mark and left a ring of ashes. Dr. Silence pointed to them, but without comment and without pausing, and the sight of them woke in me a singular realisation of the dread that lay so far only just out of sight in this adventure.

It was exhausting work, and heavy going. We kept close together. The warmth, too, was extraordinary. Yet it did not seem the warmth of the body due to violent exertion, but rather an inner heat of the mind that laid glowing hands of fire upon the heart and set the brain in a kind of steady blaze. When my companion found himself too far in advance, he waited for me to come up. The place had evidently been untouched by hand of man, keeper, forester or sportsman, for many a year; and my thoughts, as we advanced painfully, were not unlike the state of the wood itself — dark, confused, full of a haunting wonder and the shadow of fear.

By this time all signs of the open field behind us were hid. No single gleam penetrated. We might have been groping in the heart of some primeval forest. Then, suddenly, the brambles and tussocks and string-like grass came to an end; the trees opened out; and the ground began to slope upwards towards a large central mound. We had reached the middle of the plantation, and before us stood the broken Druid stones our host had mentioned. We walked easily up the little hill, between the sparser stems, and, resting upon one of the ivy-covered boulders, looked round upon a comparatively open space, as large, perhaps, as a small London Square.

Thinking of the ceremonies and sacrifices this rough circle of prehistoric monoliths might have witnessed, I looked up into my companion's face with an unspoken question. But he read my thought and shook his head.

"Our mystery has nothing to do with these dead symbols," he said, "but with something perhaps even more ancient, and of another country altogether."

"Egypt?" I said half under my breath, hopelessly puzzled, but recalling his words in my bedroom.

He nodded. Mentally I still floundered, but he seemed intensely preoccupied and it was no time for asking questions; so while his words circled unintelligibly in my mind I looked round at the scene before me, glad of the opportunity to recover breath and some measure of composure. But hardly had I time to notice the twisted and contorted shapes of many of the pine trees close at hand when Dr. Silence leaned over and touched me on the shoulder. He pointed down the slope. And the look I saw in his eyes keyed up every nerve in my body to its utmost pitch.

A thin, almost imperceptible column of blue smoke was rising among the trees some twenty yards away at the foot of the mound. It curled up and up, and disappeared from sight among the tangled branches overhead. It was scarcely thicker than the smoke from a small brand of burning wood.

"Protect yourself! Imagine your shell strongly," whispered the doctor sharply, "and follow me closely."

He rose at once and moved swiftly down the slope towards the smoke, and I followed, afraid to remain alone. I heard the soft crunching of our steps on the pine needles. Over his shoulder I watched the thin blue spiral, without once taking my eyes off it. I hardly know how to describe the peculiar sense of vague horror inspired in me by the sight of that streak of smoke pencilling its way upwards among the dark trees.

And the sensation of increasing heat as we approached was phenomenal. It was like walking towards a glowing yet invisible fire.

As we drew nearer his pace slackened. Then he stopped and pointed, and I saw a small circle of burnt grass upon the ground. The tussocks were blackened and smouldering, and from the centre rose this line of smoke, pale, blue, steady. Then I noticed a movement of the atmosphere beside us, as if the warm air were rising and the cooler air rushing in to take its place: a little centre of wind in the stillness. Overhead the boughs stirred and trembled where the smoke disappeared. Otherwise, not a tree sighed, not a sound made itself heard. The wood was still as a graveyard. A horrible idea came to me that the course of nature was about to change without warning, had changed a little already, that the sky would drop, or the surface of the earth crash inwards like a broken bubble. Something, certainly, reached up to the citadel of my reason, causing its throne to shake.

John Silence moved forward again. I could not see his face, but his attitude was plainly one of resolution, of muscles and mind ready for vigorous action. We were within ten feet of the blackened circle when the smoke of a sudden ceased to rise, and vanished. The tail of the column disappeared in the air above, and at the same instant it seemed to me that the sensation of heat passed from my face, and the motion of the wind was gone. The calm spirit of the fresh October day resumed command.

Side by side we advanced and examined the place. The grass was smouldering, the ground still hot. The circle of burned earth was a foot to a foot and a half in diameter. It looked like an ordinary picnic fireplace. I bent down cautiously to look, but in a second I sprang back with an involuntary cry of alarm, for, as the doctor stamped on the ashes to prevent them spreading, a sound of hissing rose from the spot as though he had kicked a living creature. This hissing was faintly audible in the air. It moved past us, away towards the thicker portion of the wood in the direction of our field, and in a second Dr. Silence had left the fire and started in pursuit.

And then began the most extraordinary hunt of invisibility I can ever conceive.

He went fast even at the beginning, and, of course, it was perfectly obvious that he was following something. To judge by the poise of his head he kept his eyes steadily at a certain level — just above the height of a man — and the consequence was he stumbled a good deal over the roughness of the ground. The hissing sound had stopped. There was no sound of any kind, and what he saw to follow was utterly beyond me. I only know, that in mortal dread of being left behind, and with a biting curiosity to see whatever there was to be seen, I followed as quickly as I could, and even then barely succeeded in keeping up with him.

And, as we went, the whole mad jumble of the Colonel's stories ran through my brain, touching a sense of frightened laughter that was only held in check by the sight of this earnest, hurrying figure before me. For John Silence at work inspired me with a kind of awe. He looked so diminutive among these giant twisted trees, while yet I knew that his purpose and his knowledge were so great, and even in hurry he was dignified. The fancy that we were playing some queer, exaggerated game together met the fact that we were two men dancing upon the brink of some possible tragedy, and the mingling of the two emotions in my mind was both grotesque and terrifying.

He never turned in his mad chase, but pushed rapidly on, while I panted after him like a figure in some unreasoning nightmare. And, as I ran, it came upon me that he had been aware all the time, in his quiet, internal way, of many things that he had kept for his own secret consideration; he had been watching, waiting, planning from the very moment we entered the shade of the wood. By some inner, concentrated process of mind, dynamic if not actually magical, he had been in direct contact with the source of the whole adventure, the very essence of the real mystery. And now the forces were moving to a climax. Something was about to happen, something important, something possibly dreadful. Every nerve, every sense, every significant gesture of the plunging figure before me proclaimed the fact just as surely as the skies, the winds, and the face of the earth tell the birds the time to migrate and warn the animals that danger lurks and they must move.

In a few moments we reached the foot of the mound and entered the tangled undergrowth that lay between us and the sunlight of the field. Here the difficulties of fast travelling increased a hundredfold. There were brambles to dodge, low boughs to dive under, and countless tree trunks closing up to make a direct path impossible. Yet Dr. Silence never seemed to falter or hesitate. He went, diving, jumping, dodging, ducking, but ever in the same main direction, following a clean trail. Twice I tripped and fell, and both times, when I picked myself up again, I saw him ahead of me, still forcing a way like a dog after its quarry. And sometimes, like a dog, he stopped and pointed — human pointing it was, psychic pointing — and each time he stopped to point I heard that faint high hissing in the air beyond us. The instinct of an infallible dowser possessed him, and he made no mistakes.

At length, abruptly, I caught up with him, and found that we stood at the edge of the shallow pond Colonel Wragge had mentioned in his account the night before. It was long and narrow, filled with dark brown water, in which the trees were dimly reflected. Not a ripple stirred its surface.

"Watch!" he cried out, as I came up. "It's going to cross. It's bound to betray itself. The water is its natural enemy, and we shall see the direction."

And, even as he spoke, a thin line like the track of a water-spider, shot swiftly across the shiny surface; there was a ghost of steam in the air above; and immediately I became aware of an odour of burning.

Dr. Silence turned and shot a glance at me that made me think of lightning. I began to shake all over.

"Quick!" he cried with excitement, "to the trail again! We must run around. It's going to the house!"

The alarm in his voice quite terrified me. Without a false step I dashed round the slippery banks and dived again at his heels into the sea of bushes and tree trunks. We were now in the thick of the very dense belt that ran around the outer edge of the plantation, and the field was near; yet so dark was the tangle that it was some time before the first shafts of white sunlight became visible. The doctor now ran in zigzags. He was following something that dodged and doubled quite wonderfully, yet had begun, I fancied, to move more slowly than before.

"Quick!" he cried. "In the light we shall lose it!"

I still saw nothing, heard nothing, caught no suggestion of a trail; yet this man, guided by some interior divining that seemed infallible, made no false turns, though how he failed to crash headlong into the trees has remained a mystery to me ever since. And then, with a sudden rush, we found ourselves on the skirts of the wood with the open field lying in bright sunshine before our eyes.

"Too late!" I heard him cry, a note of anguish in his voice. "It's out and, by God, it's making for the house!"

I saw the Colonel standing in the field with his dogs where we had left him. He was bending double, peering into the wood where he heard us running, and he straightened up like a bent whip released. John Silence dashed passed, calling him to follow.

"We shall lose the trail in the light," I heard him cry as he ran. "But quick! We may get there in time!"

That wild rush across the open field, with the dogs at our heels, leaping and barking, and the elderly Colonel behind us running as though for his life, shall I ever forget? Though I had only vague ideas of the meaning of it all, I put my best foot forward, and, being the youngest of the three, I reached the house an easy first. I drew up, panting, and turned to wait for the others. But, as I turned, something moving a little distance away caught my eye, and in that moment I swear I experienced the most overwhelming and singular shock of surprise and terror I have ever known, or can conceive as possible.

For the front door was open, and the waist of the house being narrow, I could see through the hall into the dining-room beyond, and so out on to the back lawn, and there I saw no less a sight than the figure of Miss Wragge — running. Even at that distance it was plain that she had seen me, and was coming fast towards me, running with the frantic gait of a terror-stricken woman. She had recovered the use of her legs.

Her face was a livid grey, as of death itself, but the general expression was one of laughter, for her mouth was gaping, and her eyes, always bright, shone with the light of a wild merriment that seemed the merriment of a child, yet she was singularly ghastly. And that very second, as she fled past me into her brother's arms behind, I smelt again most unmistakably the odour of burning, and to this day the smell of smoke and fire can come very near to turning me sick with the memory of what I had seen.

Fast on her heels, too, came the terrified attendant, more mistress of herself, and able to speak — which the old lady could not do — but with a face almost, if not quite, as fearful.

"We were down by the bushes in the sun," — she gasped and screamed in reply to Colonel Wragge's distracted questionings, — "I was wheeling the chair as usual when she shrieked and leaped — I don't know exactly — I was too frightened to see — Oh, my God! she jumped clean out of the chair — and ran! There was a blast of hot air from the wood, and she hid her face and jumped. She didn't make a sound — she didn't cry out, or make a sound. She just ran."

But the nightmare horror of it all reached the breaking point a few minutes later, and while I was still standing in the hall temporarily bereft of speech and movement; for while the doctor, the Colonel and the attendant were half-way up the staircase, helping the fainting woman to the privacy of her room, and all in a confused group of dark figures, there sounded a voice behind me, and I turned to see the butler, his face dripping with perspiration, his eyes starting out of his head.

"The laundry's on fire!" he cried; "the laundry building's a-caught!"

I remember his odd expression "a-caught," and wanting to laugh, but finding my face rigid and inflexible.

"The devil's about again, s'help me Gawd!" he cried, in a voice thin with terror, running about in circles.

And then the group on the stairs scattered as at the sound of a shot, and the Colonel and Dr. Silence came down three steps at a time, leaving the afflicted Miss Wragge to the care of her single attendant.

We were out across the front lawn in a moment and round the corner of the house, the Colonel leading, Silence and I at his heels, and the portly butler puffing some distance in the rear, getting more and more mixed in his addresses to God and the devil; and the moment we passed the stables and came into view of the laundry building, we saw a wicked-looking volume of smoke pouring out of the narrow windows, and the frightened women-servants and grooms running hither and thither, calling aloud as they ran.

The arrival of the master restored order instantly, and this retired soldier, poor thinker perhaps, but capable man of action, had the matter in hand from the start. He issued orders like a martinet, and, almost before I could realise it, there were streaming buckets on the scene and a line of men and women formed between the building and the stable pump.

"Inside," I heard John Silence cry, and the Colonel followed him through the door, while I was just quick enough at their heels to hear him add, "the smoke's the worst part of it. There's no fire yet, I think."

And true enough, there was no fire. The interior was thick with smoke, but it speedily cleared and not a single bucket was used upon the floor or walls. The air was stifling, the heat fearful.

"There's precious little to burn in here; it's all stone," the Colonel exclaimed, coughing. But the doctor was pointing to the wooden covers of the great cauldron in which the clothes were washed, and we saw that these were smouldering and charred. And when we sprinkled half a bucket of water on them the surrounding bricks hissed and fizzed and sent up clouds of steam. Through the open door and windows this passed out with the rest of the smoke, and we three stood there on the brick floor staring at the spot and wondering, each in our own fashion, how in the name of natural law the place could have caught fire or smoked at all. And each was silent — myself from sheer incapacity and befuddlement, the Colonel from the quiet pluck that faces all things yet speaks little, and John Silence from the intense mental grappling with this latest manifestation of a profound problem that called for concentration of thought rather than for any words.

There was really nothing to say. The facts were indisputable. Colonel Wragge was the first to utter.

"My sister," he said briefly, and moved off. In the yard I heard him sending the frightened servants about their business in an excellently matter-of-fact voice, scolding some one roundly for making such a big fire and letting the flues get over-heated, and paying no heed to the stammering reply that no fire had been lit there for several days. Then he dispatched a groom on horseback for the local doctor.

Then Dr. Silence turned and looked at me. The absolute control he possessed, not only over the outward expression of emotion by gesture, change of colour, light in the eyes, and so forth, but also, as I well knew, over its very birth in his heart, the masklike face of the dead he could assume at will, made it extremely difficult to know at any given moment what was at work in his inner consciousness. But now, when he turned and looked at me, there was no sphinx-expression there, but rather the keen triumphant face of a man who had solved a dangerous and complicated problem, and saw his way to a clean victory.

"Now do you guess?" he asked quietly, as though it were the simplest matter in the world, and ignorance were impossible.

I could only stare stupidly and remain silent. He glanced down at the charred cauldron-lids, and traced a figure in the air with his finger. But I was too excited, or too mortified, or still too dazed, perhaps, to see what it was he outlined, or what it was he meant to convey. I could only go on staring and shaking my puzzled head.

"A fire-elemental," he cried, "a fire-elemental of the most powerful and malignant kind —"

"A what?" thundered the voice of Colonel Wragge behind us, having returned suddenly and overheard.

"It's a fire-elemental," repeated Dr. Silence more calmly, but with a note of triumph in his voice he could not keep out, "and a fire-elemental enraged."

The light began to dawn in my mind at last. But the Colonel — who had never heard the term before, and was besides feeling considerably worked up for a plain man with all this mystery he knew not how to grapple with — the Colonel stood, with the most dumfounded look ever seen on a human countenance, and continued to roar, and stammer, and stare.

"And why," he began, savage with the desire to find something visible he could fight — "why, in the name of all the blazes —?" and then stopped as John Silence moved up and took his arm.

"There, my dear Colonel Wragge," he said gently, "you touch the heart of the whole thing. You ask 'Why.' That is precisely our problem." He held the soldier's eyes firmly with his own. "And that, too, I think, we shall soon know. Come and let us talk over a plan of action — that room with the double doors, perhaps."

The word "action" calmed him a little, and he led the way, without further speech, back into the house, and down the long stone passage to the room where we had heard his stories on the night of our arrival. I understood from the doctor's glance that my presence would not make the interview easier for our host, and I went upstairs to my own room — shaking.

But in the solitude of my room the vivid memories of the last hour revived so mercilessly that I began to feel I should never in my whole life lose the dreadful picture of Miss Wragge running — that dreadful climax after all the non-human mystery in the wood — and I was not sorry when a servant knocked at my door and said that Colonel Wragge would be glad if I would join them in the little smoking-room.

"I think it is better you should be present," was all Colonel Wragge said as I entered the room. I took the chair with my back to the window. There was still an hour before lunch, though I imagine that the usual divisions of the day hardly found a place in the thoughts of any one of us.

The atmosphere of the room was what I might call electric. The Colonel was positively bristling; he stood with his back to the fire, fingering an unlit black cigar, his face flushed, his being obviously roused and ready for action. He hated this mystery. It was poisonous to his nature, and he longed to meet something face to face — something he could gauge and fight. Dr. Silence, I noticed at once, was sitting before the map of the estate which was spread upon a table. I knew by his expression the state of his mind. He was in the thick of it all, knew it, delighted in it, and was working at high pressure. He recognised my presence with a lifted eyelid, and the flash of the eye, contrasted with his stillness and composure, told me volumes.

"I was about to explain to our host briefly what seems to me afoot in all this business," he said without looking up, "when he asked that you should join us so that we can all work together." And, while signifying my assent, I caught myself wondering what quality it was in the calm speech of this undemonstrative man that was so full of power, so charged with the strange, virile personality behind it and that seemed to inspire us with his own confidence as by a process of radiation.

"Mr. Hubbard," he went on gravely, turning to the soldier, "knows something of my methods, and in more than one — er — interesting situation has proved of assistance. What we want now" — and here he suddenly got up and took his place on the mat beside the Colonel, and looked hard at him — "is men who have self-control, who are sure of themselves, whose minds at the critical moment will emit positive forces, instead of the wavering and uncertain currents due to negative feelings — due, for instance, to fear."

He looked at us each in turn. Colonel Wragge moved his feet farther apart, and squared his shoulders; and I felt guilty but said nothing, conscious that my latent store of courage was being deliberately hauled to the front. He was winding me up like a clock.

"So that, in what is yet to come," continued our leader, "each of us will contribute his share of power, and ensure success for my plan."

"I'm not afraid of anything I can see," said the Colonel bluntly.

"I'm ready," I heard myself say, as it were automatically, "for anything," and then added, feeling the declaration was lamely insufficient, "and everything."

Dr. Silence left the mat and began walking to and fro about the room, both hands plunged deep into the pockets of his shooting-jacket. Tremendous vitality streamed from him. I never took my eyes off the small, moving figure; small, yes — and yet somehow making me think of a giant plotting the destruction of worlds. And his manner was gentle, as always, soothing almost, and his words uttered quietly without emphasis or emotion. Most of what he said was addressed, though not too obviously, to the Colonel.

"The violence of this sudden attack," he said softly, pacing to and fro beneath the bookcase at the end of the room, "is clue, of course, partly to the fact that tonight the moon is at the full" — here he glanced at me for a moment — "and partly to the fact that we have all been so deliberately concentrating upon the matter. Our thinking, our investigation, has stirred it into unusual activity. I mean that the intelligent force behind these manifestations has realised that some one is busied about its destruction. And it is now on the defensive: more, it is aggressive."

"But 'it' — what is 'it'?" began the soldier, fuming. "What, in the name of all that's dreadful, is a fire-elemental?"

"I cannot give you at this moment," replied Dr. Silence, turning to him, but undisturbed by the interruption, "a lecture on the nature and history of magic, but can only say that an Elemental is the active force behind the elements, — whether earth, air, water, or fire — it is impersonal in its essential nature, but can be focused, personified, ensouled, so to say, by those who know how — by magicians, if you will — for certain purposes of their own, much in the same way that steam and electricity can be harnessed by the practical man of this century.

"Alone, these blind elemental energies can accomplish little, but governed and directed by the trained will of a powerful manipulator they may become potent activities for good or evil. They are the basis of all magic, and it is the motive behind them that constitutes the magic 'black' or 'white'; they can be the vehicles of curses or of blessings, for a curse is nothing more than the thought of a violent will perpetuated. And in such cases — cases like this — the conscious, directing will of the mind that is using the elemental stands always behind the phenomena —"

"You think that my brother —!" broke in the Colonel, aghast.

"Has nothing whatever to do with it — directly. The fire-elemental that has here been tormenting you and your household was sent upon its mission long before you, or your family, or your ancestors, or even the nation you belong to — unless I am much mistaken — was even in existence. We will come to that a little later; after the experiment I propose to make we shall be more positive. At present I can only say we have to deal now, not only with the phenomenon of Attacking Fire merely, but with the vindictive and enraged intelligence that is directing it from behind the scenes — vindictive and enraged," — he repeated the words.

"That explains —" began Colonel Wragge, seeking furiously for words he could not find quickly enough.

"Much," said John Silence, with a gesture to restrain him.

He stopped for a moment in the middle of his walk, and a deep silence came down over the little room. Through the windows the sunlight seemed less bright, the long line of dark hills less friendly, making me think of a vast wave towering to heaven and about to break and overwhelm us. Something formidable had crept into the world about us. For, undoubtedly, there was a disquieting thought, holding terror as well as awe, in the picture his words conjured up: the conception of a human will reaching its deathless hand, spiteful and destructive, down through the ages, to strike the living and afflict the innocent.

"But what is its object?" burst out the soldier, unable to restrain himself longer in the silence. "Why does it come from that plantation? And why should it attack us, or any one in particular?" Questions began to pour from him in a stream.

"All in good time," the doctor answered quietly, having let him run on for several minutes. "But I must first discover positively what, or who, it is that directs this particular fire-elemental. And, to do that, we must first" — he spoke with slow deliberation —"seek to capture — to confine by visibility — to limit its sphere in a concrete form."

"Good heavens almighty!" exclaimed the soldier, mixing his words in his unfeigned surprise.

"Quite so," pursued the other calmly; "for in so doing I think we can release it from the purpose that binds it, restore it to its normal condition of latent fire, and also" — he lowered his voice perceptibly — "also discover the face and form of the Being that ensouls it."

"The man behind the gun!" cried the Colonel, beginning to understand something, and leaning forward so as not to miss a single syllable.

"I mean that in the last resort, before it returns to the womb of potential fire, it will probably assume the face and figure of its Director, of the man, of magical knowledge who originally bound it with his incantations and sent it forth upon its mission of centuries."

The soldier sat down and gasped openly in his face, breathing hard; but it was a very subdued voice that framed the question.

"And how do you propose to make it visible? How capture and confine it? What d'ye mean, Dr. John Silence?"

"By furnishing it with the materials for a form. By the process of materialisation simply. Once limited by dimensions, it will become slow, heavy, visible. We can then dissipate it. Invisible fire, you see, is dangerous and incalculable; locked up in a form we can perhaps manage it. We must betray it — to its death."

"And this material?" we asked in the same breath, although I think I had already guessed.

"Not pleasant, but effective," came the quiet reply; "the exhalations of freshly-spilled blood."

"Not human blood!" cried Colonel Wragge, starting up from his chair with a voice like an explosion. I thought his eyes would start from their sockets.

The face of Dr. Silence relaxed in spite of himself, and his spontaneous little laugh brought a welcome though momentary relief.

"The days of human sacrifice, I hope, will never come again," he explained. "Animal blood will answer the purpose, and we can make the experiment as pleasant as possible. Only, the blood must be freshly spilled and strong with the vital emanations that attract this peculiar class of elemental creature. Perhaps — perhaps if some pig on the estate is ready for the market —"

He turned to hide a smile; but the passing touch of comedy found no echo in the mind of our host, who did not understand how to change quickly from one emotion to another. Clearly he was debating many things laboriously in his honest brain. But, in the end, the earnestness and scientific disinterestedness of the doctor, whose influence over him was already very great, won the day, and he presently looked up more calmly, and observed shortly that he thought perhaps the matter could be arranged.

"There are other and pleasanter methods," Dr. Silence went on to explain, "but they require time and preparation, and things have gone much too far, in my opinion, to admit of delay. And the process need cause you no distress: we sit round the bowl and await results. Nothing more. The emanations of blood — which, as Levi says, is the first incarnation of the universal fluid — furnish the materials out of which the creatures of discarnate life, spirits if you prefer, can fashion themselves a temporary appearance. The process is old, and lies at the root of all blood sacrifice. It was known to the priests of Baal, and it is known to the modern ecstasy dancers who cut themselves to produce objective phantoms who dance with them. And the least gifted clairvoyant could tell you that the forms to be seen in the vicinity of slaughter-houses, or hovering above the deserted battlefields, are — well, simply beyond all description. I do not mean," he added, noticing the uneasy fidgeting of his host, "that anything in our laundry-experiment need appear to terrify us, for this case seems a comparatively simple one, and it is only the vindictive character of the intelligence directing this fire-elemental that causes anxiety and makes for personal danger."

"It is curious," said the Colonel, with a sudden rush of words, drawing a deep breath, and as though speaking of things distasteful to him, "that during my years among the Hill Tribes of Northern India I came across — personally came across — instances of the sacrifices of blood to certain deities being stopped suddenly, and all manner of disasters happening until they were resumed. Fires broke out in the huts, and even on the clothes, of the natives — and — and I admit I have read, in the course of my studies," — he made a gesture toward his books and heavily laden table, —"of the Yezidis of Syria evoking phantoms by means of cutting their bodies with knives during their whirling dances — enormous globes of fire which turned into monstrous and terrible forms — and I remember an account somewhere, too, how the emaciated forms and pallid countenances of the spectres, that appeared to the Emperor Julian, claimed to be the true Immortals, and told him to renew the sacrifices of blood 'for the fumes of which, since the establishment of Christianity, they had been pining' — that these were in reality the phantoms evoked by the rites of blood."

Both Dr. Silence and myself listened in amazement, for this sudden speech was so unexpected, and betrayed so much more knowledge than we had either of us suspected in the old soldier.

"Then perhaps you have read, too," said the doctor, "how the Cosmic Deities of savage races, elemental in their nature, have been kept alive through many ages by these blood rites?"

"No," he answered; "that is new to me."

"In any case," Dr. Silence added, "I am glad you are not wholly unfamiliar with the subject, for you will now bring more sympathy, and therefore more help, to our experiment. For, of course, in this case, we only want the blood to tempt the creature from its lair and enclose it in a form —"

"I quite understand. And I only hesitated just now," he went on, his words coming much more slowly, as though he felt he had already said too much, "because I wished to be quite sure it was no mere curiosity, but an actual sense of necessity that dictated this horrible experiment."

"It is your safety, and that of your household, and of your sister, that is at stake," replied the doctor. "Once I have seen, I hope to discover whence this elemental comes, and what its real purpose is."

Colonel Wragge signified his assent with a bow.

"And the moon will help us," the other said, "for it will be full in the early hours of the morning, and this kind of elemental-being is always most active at the period of full moon. Hence, you see, the clue furnished by your diary."

So it was finally settled. Colonel Wragge would provide the materials for the experiment, and we were to meet at midnight. How he would contrive at that hour — but that was his business. I only know we both realised that he would keep his word, and whether a pig died at midnight, or at noon, was after all perhaps only a question of the sleep and personal comfort of the executioner.

"Tonight, then, in the laundry," said Dr. Silence finally, to clinch the plan; "we three alone — and at midnight, when the household is asleep and we shall be free from disturbance."

He exchanged significant glances with our host, who, at that moment, was called away by the announcement that the family doctor had arrived, and was ready to see him in his sister's room.

For the remainder of the afternoon John Silence disappeared. I had my suspicions that he made a secret visit to the plantation and also to the laundry building; but, in any case, we saw nothing of him, and he kept strictly to himself. He was preparing for the night, I felt sure, but the nature of his preparations I could only guess. There was movement in his room, I heard, and an odour like incense hung about the door, and knowing that he regarded rites as the vehicles of energies, my guesses were probably not far wrong.

Colonel Wragge, too, remained absent the greater part of the afternoon, and, deeply afflicted, had scarcely left his sister's bedside, but in response to my inquiry when we met for a moment at tea-time, he told me that although she had moments of attempted speech, her talk was quite incoherent and hysterical, and she was still quite unable to explain the nature of what she had seen. The doctor, he said, feared she had recovered the use of her limbs, only to lose that of her memory, and perhaps even of her mind.

"Then the recovery of her legs, I trust, may be permanent, at any rate," I ventured, finding it difficult to know what sympathy to offer. And he replied with a curious short laugh, "Oh yes; about that there can be no doubt whatever."

And it was due merely to the chance of my overhearing a fragment of conversation — unwillingly, of course — that a little further light was thrown upon the state in which the old lady actually lay. For, as I came out of my room, it happened that Colonel Wragge and the doctor were going downstairs together, and their words floated up to my ears before I could make my presence known by so much as a cough.

"Then you must find a way," the doctor was saying with decision; "for I cannot insist too strongly upon that — and at all costs she must be kept quiet. These attempts to go out must be prevented — if necessary, by force. This desire to visit some wood or other she keeps talking about is, of course, hysterical in nature. It cannot be permitted for a moment."

"It shall not be permitted," I heard the soldier reply, as they reached the hall below.

"It has impressed her mind for some reason —" the doctor went on, by way evidently of soothing explanation, and then the distance made it impossible for me to hear more.

At dinner Dr. Silence was still absent, on the public plea of a headache, and though food was sent to his room, I am inclined to believe he did not touch it, but spent the entire time fasting.

We retired early, desiring that the household should do likewise, and I must confess that at ten o'clock when I bid my host a temporary goodnight, and sought my room to make what mental preparation I could, I realised in no very pleasant fashion that it was a singular and formidable assignation, this midnight meeting in the laundry building, and that there were moments in every adventure of life when a wise man, and one who knew his own limitations, owed it to his dignity to withdraw discreetly. And, but for the character of our leader, I probably should have then and there offered the best excuse I could think of, and have allowed myself quietly to fall asleep and wait for an exciting story in the morning of what had happened. But with a man like John Silence, such a lapse was out of the question, and I sat before my fire counting the minutes and doing everything I could think of to fortify my resolution and fasten my will at the point where I could be reasonably sure that my self — control would hold against all attacks of men, devils, or elementals.

At a quarter before midnight, clad in a heavy ulster, and with slippered feet, I crept cautiously from my room and stole down the passage to the top of the stairs. Outside the doctor's door I waited a moment to listen. All was still; the house in utter darkness; no gleam of light beneath any door; only, down the length of the corridor, from the direction of the sick-room, came faint sounds of laughter and incoherent talk that were not things to reassure a mind already half a-tremble, and I made haste to reach the hall and let myself out through the front door into the night.

The air was keen and frosty, perfumed with night smells, and exquisitely fresh; all the million candles of the sky were alight, and a faint breeze rose and fell with far-away sighings in the tops of the pine trees. My blood leaped for a moment in the spaciousness of the night, for the splendid stars brought courage; but the next instant, as I turned the corner of the house, moving stealthily down the gravel drive, my spirits sank again ominously. For, yonder, over the funereal plumes of the Twelve Acre Plantation, I saw the huge and yellow face of the full moon just rising in the east, staring down like some vast Being come to watch upon the progress of our doom. Seen through the distorting vapours of the earth's atmosphere, her face looked weirdly unfamiliar, her usual expression of benignant vacancy somehow a-twist. I slipped along by the shadows of the wall, keeping my eyes upon the ground.

The laundry-house, as already described, stood detached from the other offices, with laurel shrubberies crowding thickly behind it, and the kitchen-garden so close on the other side that the strong smells of soil and growing things came across almost heavily. The shadows of the haunted plantation, hugely lengthened by the rising moon behind them, reached to the very walls and covered the stone tiles of the roof with a dark pall. So keenly were my senses alert at this moment that I believe I could fill a chapter with the endless small details of the impression I received — shadows, odour, shapes, sounds — in the space of the few seconds I stood and waited before the closed wooden door.

Then I became aware of some one moving towards me through the moonlight, and the figure of John Silence, without overcoat and bareheaded, came quickly and without noise to join me. His eyes, I saw at once, were wonderfully bright, and so marked was the shining pallor of his face that I could hardly tell when he passed from the moonlight into the shade.

He passed without a word, beckoning me to follow, and then pushed the door open, and went in.

The chill air of the place met us like that of an underground vault; and the brick floor and whitewashed walls, streaked with damp and smoke, threw back the cold in our faces. Directly opposite gaped the black throat of the huge open fireplace, the ashes of wood fires still piled and scattered about the hearth, and on either side of the projecting chimney-column were the deep recesses holding the big twin cauldrons for boiling clothes. Upon the lids of these cauldrons stood the two little oil lamps, shaded red, which gave all the light there was, and immediately in front of the fireplace there was a small circular table with three chairs set about it. Overhead, the narrow slit windows, high up the walls, pointed to a dim network of wooden rafters half lost among the shadows, and then came the dark vault of the roof. Cheerless and unalluring, for all the red light, it certainly was, reminding me of some unused conventicle, bare of pews or pulpit, ugly and severe, and I was forcibly struck by the contrast between the normal uses to which the place was ordinarily put, and the strange and mediæval purpose which had brought us under its roof tonight.

Possibly an involuntary shudder ran over me, for my companion turned with a confident look to reassure me, and he was so completely master of himself that I at once absorbed from his abundance, and felt the chinks of my failing courage beginning to close up. To meet his eye in the presence of danger was like finding a mental railing that guided and supported thought along the giddy edges of alarm.

"I am quite ready," I whispered, turning to listen for approaching footsteps.

He nodded, still keeping his eyes on mine. Our whispers sounded hollow as they echoed overhead among the rafters.

"I'm glad you are here," he said. "Not all would have the courage. Keep your thoughts controlled, and imagine the protective shell round you — round your inner being."

"I am all right," I repeated, cursing my chattering teeth.

He took my hand and shook it, and the contact seemed to shake into me something of his supreme confidence. The eyes and hands of a strong man can touch the soul. I think he guessed my thought, for a passing smile flashed about the corners of his mouth.

"You will feel more comfortable," he said, in a low tone, "when the chain is complete. The Colonel we can count on, of course. Remember, though," he added warningly, "he may perhaps become controlled — possessed — when the thing comes, because he won't know how to resist. And to explain the business to such a man —!" He shrugged his shoulders expressively. "But it will only be temporary, and I will see that no harm comes to him."

He glanced round at the arrangements with approval.

"Red light," he said, indicating the shaded lamps, "has the lowest rate of vibration. Materialisations are dissipated by strong light — won't form, or hold together — in rapid vibrations."

I was not sure that I approved altogether of this dim light, for in complete darkness there is something protective — the knowledge that one cannot be seen, probably — which a half-light destroys, but I remembered the warning to keep my thoughts steady, and forbore to give them expression.

There was a step outside, and the figure of Colonel Wragge stood in the doorway. Though entering on tiptoe, he made considerable noise and clatter, for his free movements were impeded by the burden he carried, and we saw a large yellowish bowl held out at arms' length from his body, the mouth covered with a white cloth. His face, I noted, was rigidly composed. He, too, was master of himself. And, as I thought of this old soldier moving through the long series of alarms, worn with watching and wearied with assault, unenlightened yet undismayed, even down to the dreadful shock of his sister's terror, and still showing the dogged pluck that persists in the face of defeat, I understood what Dr. Silence meant when he described him as a man "to be counted on."

I think there was nothing beyond this rigidity of his stern features, and a certain greyness of the complexion, to betray the turmoil of the emotions that was doubtless going on within; and the quality of these two men, each in his own way, so keyed me up that, by the time the door was shut and we had exchanged silent greetings, all the latent courage I possessed was well to the fore, and I felt as sure of myself as I knew I ever could feel.

Colonel Wragge set the bowl carefully in the centre of the table.

"Midnight," he said shortly, glancing at his watch, and we all three moved to our chairs.

There, in the middle of that cold and silent place, we sat, with the vile bowl before us, and a thin, hardly perceptible steam rising through the clamp air from the surface of the white cloth and disappearing upwards the moment it passed beyond the zone of red light and entered the deep shadows thrown forward by the projecting wall of chimney.

The doctor had indicated our respective places, and I found myself seated with my back to the door and opposite the black hearth. The Colonel was on my left, and Dr. Silence on my right, both half facing me, the latter more in shadow than the former. We thus divided the little table into even sections, and sitting back in our chairs we awaited events in silence.

For something like an hour I do not think there was even the faintest sound within those four walls and under the canopy of that vaulted roof. Our slippers made no scratching on the gritty floor, and our breathing was suppressed almost to nothing; even the rustle of our clothes as we shifted from time to time upon our seats was inaudible. Silence smothered us absolutely — the silence of night, of listening, the silence of a haunted expectancy. The very gurgling of the lamps was too soft to be heard, and if light itself had sound, I do not think we should have noticed the silvery tread of the moonlight as it entered the high narrow windows and threw upon the floor the slender traces of its pallid footsteps.

Colonel Wragge and the doctor, and myself too for that matter, sat thus like figures of stone, without speech and without gesture. My eyes passed in ceaseless journeys from the bowl to their faces, and from there faces to the bowl. They might have been masks, however, for all the signs of life they gave; and the light steaming from the horrid contents beneath the while cloth had long ceased to be visible.

Then presently, as the moon rose higher, the wind rose with it. It sighed, like the lightest of passing wings, over the roof; it crept most softly round the walls; it made the brick floor like ice beneath our feet. With it I saw mentally the desolate moorland flowing like a sea about the old house, the treeless expanse of lonely hills, the nearer copses, somber and mysterious in the night. The plantation, too, in particular I saw, and imagined I heard the mournful whisperings that must now be a-stirring among its tree-tops as the breeze played down between the twisted stems. In the depth of the room behind us the shafts of moon-light met and crossed in a growing network.

It was after an hour of this wearing and unbroken attention, and I should judge about one o'clock in the morning, when the baying of the dogs in the stableyard first began, and I saw John Silence move suddenly in his chair and sit up in an attitude of attention. Every force in my being instantly leaped into the keenest vigilance. Colonel Wragge moved too, though slowly, and without raising his eyes from the table before him.

The doctor stretched his arm out and took the white cloth from the bowl.

It was perhaps imagination that persuaded me the red glare of the lamps grew fainter and the air over the table before us thickened. I had been expecting something for so long that the movement of my companions, and the lifting of the cloth, may easily have caused the momentary delusion that something hovered in the air before my face, touching the skin of my cheeks with a silken run. But it was certainly not a delusion that the Colonel looked up at the same moment and glanced over his shoulder, as though his eyes followed the movements of something to and fro about the room, and that he then buttoned his overcoat more tightly about him and his eyes sought my own face first, and then the doctor's. And it was no delusion that his face seemed somehow to have turned dark, become spread as it were with a shadowy blackness. I saw his lips tighten and his expression grow hard and stern, and it came to me then with a rush that, of course, this man had told us but a part of the experiences he had been through in the house, and that there was much more he had never been able to bring himself to reveal at all. I felt sure of it. The way he turned and stared about him betrayed a familiarity with other things than those he had described to us. It was not merely a sight of fire he looked for; it was a sight of something alive, intelligent, something able to evade his searching; it was a person. It was the watch for the ancient Being who sought to obsess him.

And the way in which Dr. Silence answered his look — though it was only by a glance of subtlest sympathy — confirmed my impression.

"We may be ready now," I heard him say in a whisper, and I understood that his words were intended as a steadying warning, and braced myself mentally to the utmost of my power.

Yet long before Colonel Wragge had turned to stare about the room, and long before the doctor had confirmed my impression that things were at last beginning to stir, I had become aware in most singular fashion that the place held more than our three selves. With the rising of the wind this increase to our numbers had first taken place. The baying of the hounds almost seemed to have signalled it. I cannot say how it may be possible to realise that an empty place has suddenly become — not empty, when the new arrival is nothing that appeals to any one of the senses; for this recognition of an "invisible," as of the change in the balance of personal forces in a human group, is indefinable and beyond proof. Yet it is unmistakable. And I knew perfectly well at what given moment the atmosphere within these four walls became charged with the presence of other living beings besides ourselves. And, on reflection, I am convinced that both my companions knew it too.

"Watch the light," said the doctor under his breath, and then I knew too that it was no fancy of my own that had turned the air darker, and the way he turned to examine the face of our host sent an electric thrill of wonder and expectancy shivering along every nerve in my body.

Yet it was no kind of terror that I experienced, but rather a sort of mental dizziness, and a sensation as of being suspended in some remote and dreadful altitude where things might happen, indeed were about to happen, that had never before happened within the ken of man.

Horror may have formed an ingredient, but it was not chiefly horror, and in no sense ghostly horror.

Uncommon thoughts kept beating on my brain like tiny hammers, soft yet persistent, seeking admission; their unbidden tide began to wash along the far fringes of my mind, the currents of unwonted sensations to rise over the remote frontiers of my consciousness. I was aware of thoughts, and the fantasies of thoughts, that I never knew before existed. Portions of my being stirred that had never stirred before, and things ancient and inexplicable rose to the surface and beckoned me to follow. I felt as though I were about to fly off, at some immense tangent, into an outer space hitherto unknown even in dreams. And so singular was the result produced upon me that I was uncommonly glad to anchor my mind, as well as my eyes, upon the masterful personality of the doctor at my side, for there, I realised, I could draw always upon the forces of sanity and safety.

With a vigorous effort of will I returned to the scene before me, and tried to focus my attention, with steadier thoughts, upon the table, and upon the silent figures seated round it. And then I saw that certain changes had come about in the place where we sat.

The patches of moonlight on the floor, I noted, had become curiously shaded; the faces of my companions opposite were not so clearly visible as before; and the forehead and cheeks of Colonel Wragge were glistening with perspiration. I realised further, that an extraordinary change had come about in the temperature of the atmosphere. The increased warmth had a painful effect, not alone on Colonel Wragge, but upon all of us. It was oppressive and unnatural. We gasped figuratively as well as actually.

"You are the first to feel it," said Dr. Silence in low tones, looking across at him. "You are in more intimate touch, of course —"

The Colonel was trembling, and appeared to be in considerable distress. His knees shook, so that the shuffling of his slippered feet became audible. He inclined his head to show that he had heard, but made no other reply. I think, even then, he was sore put to it to keep himself in hand. I knew what he was struggling against. As Dr. Silence had warned me, he was about to be obsessed, and was savagely, though vainly, resisting.

But, meanwhile, a curious and whirling sense of exhilaration began to come over me. The increasing heat was delightful, bringing a sensation of intense activity, of thoughts pouring through the mind at high speed, of vivid pictures in the brain, of fierce desires and lightning energies alive in every part of the body. I was conscious of no physical distress, such as the Colonel felt, but only of a vague feeling that it might all grow suddenly too intense — that I might be consumed — that my personality as well as my body, might become resolved into the flame of pure spirit. I began to live at a speed too intense to last. It was as if a thousand ecstasies besieged me —

"Steady!" whispered the voice of John Silence in my ear, and I looked up with a start to see that the Colonel had risen from his chair. The doctor rose too. I followed suit, and for the first time saw down into the bowl. To my amazement and horror I saw that the contents were troubled. The blood was astir with movement.

The rest of the experiment was witnessed by us standing. It came, too, with a curious suddenness. There was no more dreaming, for me at any rate.

I shall never forget the figure of Colonel Wragge standing there beside me, upright and unshaken, squarely planted on his feet, looking about him, puzzled beyond belief, yet full of a fighting anger. Framed by the white walls, the red glow of the lamps upon his streaming cheeks, his eyes glowing against the deathly pallor of his skin, breathing hard and making convulsive efforts of hands and body to keep himself under control, his whole being roused to the point of savage fighting, yet with nothing visible to get at anywhere — he stood there, immovable against odds. And the strange contrast of the pale skin and the burning face I had never seen before, or wish to see again.

But what has left an even sharper impression on my memory was the blackness that then began crawling over his face, obliterating the features, concealing their human outline, and hiding him inch by inch from view. This was my first realisation that the process of materialisation was at work. His visage became shrouded. I moved from one side to the other to keep him in view, and it was only then I understood that, properly speaking, the blackness was not upon the countenance of Colonel Wragge, but that something had inserted itself between me and him, thus screening his face with the effect of a dark veil. Something that apparently rose through the floor was passing slowly into the air above the table and above the bowl. The blood in the bowl, moreover, was considerably less than before.

And, with this change in the air before us, there came at the same time a further change, I thought, in the face of the soldier. One-half was turned towards the red lamps, while the other caught the pale illumination of the moonlight falling aslant from the high windows, so that it was difficult to estimate this change with accuracy of detail. But it seemed to me that, while the features — eyes, nose, mouth — remained the same, the life informing them had undergone some profound transformation. The signature of a new power had crept into the face and left its traces there — an expression dark, and in some unexplained way, terrible.

Then suddenly he opened his mouth and spoke, and the sound of this changed voice, deep and musical though it was, made me cold and set my heart beating with uncomfortable rapidity. The Being, as he had dreaded, was already in control of his brain, using his mouth.

"I see a blackness like the blackness of Egypt before my face," said the tones of this unknown voice that seemed half his own and half another's. "And out of this darkness they come, they come."

I gave a dreadful start. The doctor turned to look at me for an instant, and then turned to centre his attention upon the figure of our host, and I understood in some intuitive fashion that he was there to watch over the strangest contest man ever saw — to watch over and, if necessary, to protect.

"He is being controlled — possessed," he whispered to me through the shadows. His face wore a wonderful expression, half triumph, half admiration.

Even as Colonel Wragge spoke, it seemed to me that this visible darkness began to increase, pouring up thickly out of the ground by the hearth, rising up in sheets and veils, shrouding our eyes and faces. It stole up from below — an awful blackness that seemed to drink in all the radiations of light in the building, leaving nothing but the ghost of a radiance in their place. Then, out of this rising sea of shadows, issued a pale and spectral light that gradually spread itself about us, and from the heart of this light I saw the shapes of fire crowd and gather. And these were not human shapes, or the shapes of anything I recognised as alive in the world, but outlines of fire that traced globes, triangles, crosses, and the luminous bodies of various geometrical figures. They grew bright, faded, and then grew bright again with an effect almost of pulsation. They passed swiftly to and fro through the air, rising and falling, and particularly in the immediate neighbourhood of the Colonel, often gathering about his head and shoulders, and even appearing to settle upon him like giant insects of flame. They were accompanied, moreover, by a faint sound of hissing — the same sound we had heard that afternoon in the plantation.

"The fire-elementals that precede their master," the doctor said in an undertone. "Be ready."

And while this weird display of the shapes of fire alternately flashed and faded, and the hissing echoed faintly among the dim rafters overhead, we heard the awful voice issue at intervals from the lips of the afflicted soldier. It was a voice of power, splendid in some way I cannot describe, and with a certain sense of majesty in its cadences, and, as I listened to it with quickly beating heart, I could fancy it was some ancient voice of Time itself, echoing down immense corridors of stone, from the depths of vast temples, from the very heart of mountain tombs.

"I have seen my divine Father, Osiris," thundered the great tones. "I have scattered the gloom of the night. I have burst through the earth, and am one with the starry Deities!"

Something grand came into the soldier's face. He was staring fixedly before him, as though seeing nothing.

"Watch," whispered Dr. Silence in my ear, and his whisper seemed to come from very far away.

Again the mouth opened and the awesome voice issued forth.

"Thoth," it boomed, "has loosened the bandages of Set which fettered my mouth. I have taken my place in the great winds of heaven."

I heard the little wind of night, with its mournful voice of ages, sighing round the walls and over the roof.

"Listen!" came from the doctor at my side, and the thunder of the voice continued —

"I have hidden myself with you, O ye stars that never diminish. I remember my name — in — the — House — of — Fire!"

The voice ceased and the sound died away. Something about the face and figure of Colonel Wragge relaxed, I thought. The terrible look passed from his face. The Being that obsessed him was gone.

"The great Ritual," said Dr. Silence aside to me, very low, "the Book of the Dead. Now it's leaving him. Soon the blood will fashion it a body."

Colonel Wragge, who had stood absolutely motionless all this time, suddenly swayed, so that I thought he was going to fall, — and, but for the quick support of the doctor's arm, he probably would have fallen, for he staggered as in the beginning of collapse.

"I am drunk with the wine of Osiris," he cried, — and it was half with his own voice this time — "but Horus, the Eternal Watcher, is about my path — for — safety." The voice dwindled and failed, dying away into something almost like a cry of distress.

"Now, watch closely," said Dr. Silence, speaking loud, "for after the cry will come the Fire!"

I began to tremble involuntarily; an awful change had come without warning into the air; my legs grew weak as paper beneath my weight and I had to support myself by leaning on the table. Colonel Wragge, I saw, was also leaning forward with a kind of droop. The shapes of fire had vanished all, but his face was lit by the red lamps and the pale, shifting moonlight rose behind him like mist.

We were both gazing at the bowl, now almost empty; the Colonel stooped so low I feared every minute he would lose his balance and drop into it; and the shadow, that had so long been in process of forming, now at length began to assume material outline in the air before us.

Then John Silence moved forward quickly. He took his place between us and the shadow. Erect, formidable, absolute master of the situation, I saw him stand there, his face calm and almost smiling, and fire in his eyes. His protective influence was astounding and incalculable. Even the abhorrent dread I felt at the sight of the creature growing into life and substance before us, lessened in some way so that I was able to keep my eyes fixed on the air above the bowl without too vivid a terror.

But as it took shape, rising out of nothing as it were, and growing momentarily more defined in outline, a period of utter and wonderful silence settled down upon the building and all it contained. A hush of ages, like the sudden centre of peace at the heart of the travelling cyclone, descended through the night, and out of this hush, as out of the emanations of the steaming blood, issued the form of the ancient being who had first sent the elemental of fire upon its mission. It grew and darkened and solidified before our eyes. It rose from just beyond the table so that the lower portions remained invisible, but I saw the outline limn itself upon the air, as though slowly revealed by the rising of a curtain. It apparently had not then quite concentrated to the normal proportions, but was spread out on all sides into space, huge, though rapidly condensing, for I saw the colossal shoulders, the neck, the lower portion of the dark jaws, the terrible mouth, and then the teeth and lips — and, as the veil seemed to lift further upon the tremendous face — I saw the nose and cheek bones. In another moment I should have looked straight into the eyes —

But what Dr. Silence did at that moment was so unexpected, and took me so by surprise, that I have never yet properly understood its nature, and he has never yet seen fit to explain in detail to me. He uttered some sound that had a note of command in it — and, in so doing, stepped forward and intervened between me and the face. The figure, just nearing completeness, he therefore hid from my sight — and I have always thought purposely hid from my sight.

"The fire!" he cried out. "The fire! Beware!"

There was a sudden roar as of flame from the very mouth of the pit, and for the space of a single second all grew light as day. A blinding flash passed across my face, and there was heat for an instant that seemed to shrivel skin, and flesh, and bone. Then came steps, and I heard Colonel Wragge utter a great cry, wilder than any human cry I have ever known. The heat sucked all the breath out of my lungs with a rush, and the blaze of light, as it vanished, swept my vision with it into enveloping darkness.

When I recovered the use of my senses a few moments later I saw that Colonel Wragge with a face of death, its whiteness strangely stained, had moved closer to me. Dr. Silence stood beside him, an expression of triumph and success in his eyes. The next minute the soldier tried to clutch me with his hand. Then he reeled, staggered, and, unable to save himself, fell with a great crash upon the brick floor.

After the sheet of flame, a wind raged round the building as though it would lift the roof off, but then passed as suddenly as it came. And in the intense calm that followed I saw that the form had vanished, and the doctor was stooping over Colonel Wragge upon the floor, trying to lift him to a sitting position.

"Light," he said quietly, "more light. Take the shades off."

Colonel Wragge sat up and the glare of the unshaded lamps fell upon his face. It was grey and drawn, still running heat, and there was a look in the eyes and about the corners of the mouth that seemed in this short space of time to have added years to its age. At the same time, the expression of effort and anxiety had left it. It showed relief.

"Gone!" he said, looking up at the doctor in a dazed fashion, and struggling to his feet. "Thank God! it's gone at last." He stared round the laundry as though to find out where he was. "Did it control me — take possession of me? Did I talk nonsense?" he asked bluntly. "After the heat came, I remember nothing —"

"You'll feel yourself again in a few minutes," the doctor said. To my infinite horror I saw that he was surreptitiously wiping sundry dark stains from the face. "Our experiment has been a success and —"

He gave me a swift glance to hide the bowl, standing between me and our host while I hurriedly stuffed it down under the lid of the nearest cauldron.

"— and none of us the worse for it," he finished.

"And fires?" he asked, still dazed, "there'll be no more fires?"

"It is dissipated — partly, at any rate," replied Dr. Silence cautiously.

"And the man behind the gun," he went on, only half realising what he was saying, I think; "have you discovered that?"

"A form materialised," said the doctor briefly. "I know for certain now what the directing intelligence was behind it all."

Colonel Wragge pulled himself together and got upon his feet. The words conveyed no clear meaning to him yet. But his memory was returning gradually, and he was trying to piece together the fragments into a connected whole. He shivered a little, for the place had grown suddenly chilly. The air was empty again, lifeless.

"You feel all right again now," Dr. Silence said, in the tone of a man stating a fact rather than asking a question.

"Thanks to you — both, yes." He drew a deep breath, and mopped his face, and even attempted a smile. He made me think of a man coming from the battlefield with the stains of fighting still upon him, but scornful of his wounds. Then he turned gravely towards the doctor with a question in his eyes. Memory had returned and he was himself again.

"Precisely what I expected," the doctor said calmly; "a fire-elemental sent upon its mission in the days of Thebes, centuries before Christ, and tonight, for the first time all these thousands of years, released from the spell that originally bound it."

We stared at him in amazement, Colonel Wragge opening his lips for words that refused to shape themselves.

"And, if we dig," he continued significantly, pointing to the floor where the blackness had poured up, "we shall find some underground connection — a tunnel most likely — leading to the Twelve Acre Wood. It was made by — your predecessor."

"A tunnel made by my brother!" gasped the soldier. "Then my sister should know — she lived here with him —" He stopped suddenly.

John Silence inclined his head slowly. "I think so," he said quietly. "Your brother, no doubt, was as much tormented as you have been," he continued after a pause in which Colonel Wragge seemed deeply preoccupied with his thoughts, "and tried to find peace by burying it in the wood, and surrounding the wood then, like a large magic circle, with the enchantments of the old formulæ. So the stars the man saw blazing —"

"But burying what?" asked the soldier faintly, stepping backwards towards the support of the wall.

Dr. Silence regarded us both intently for a moment before he replied. I think he weighed in his mind whether to tell us now, or when the investigation was absolutely complete.

"The mummy," he said softly, after a moment; "the mummy that your brother took from its resting place of centuries, and brought home — here."

Colonel Wragge dropped down upon the nearest chair, hanging breathlessly on every word. He was far too amazed for speech.

"The mummy of some important person — a priest most likely — protected from disturbance and desecration by the ceremonial magic of the time. For they understood how to attach to the mummy, to lock up with it in the tomb, an elemental force that would direct itself even after ages upon any one who dared to molest it. In this case it was an elemental of fire."

Dr. Silence crossed the floor and turned out the lamps one by one. He had nothing more to say for the moment. Following his example,

I folded the table together and took up the chairs, and our host, still dazed and silent, mechanically obeyed him and moved to the door.

We removed all traces of the experiment, taking the empty bowl back to the house concealed beneath an ulster.

The air was cool and fragrant as we walked to the house, the stars beginning to fade overhead and a fresh wind of early morning blowing up out of the east where the sky was already hinting of the coming day. It was after five o'clock.

Stealthily we entered the front hall and locked the door, and as we went on tiptoe upstairs to our rooms, the Colonel, peering at us over his candle as he nodded good-night, whispered that if we were ready the digging should be begun that very day.

Then I saw him steal along to his sister's room and disappear.

But not even the mysterious references to the mummy, or the prospect of a revelation by digging, were able to hinder the reaction that followed the intense excitement of the past twelve hours, and I slept the sleep of the dead, dreamless and undisturbed. A touch on the shoulder woke me, and I saw Dr. Silence standing beside the bed, dressed to go out.

"Come," he said, "it's tea-time. You've slept the best part of a dozen hours."

I sprang up and made a hurried toilet, while my companion sat and talked. He looked fresh and rested, and his manner was even quieter than usual.

"Colonel Wragge has provided spades and pickaxes. We're going out to unearth this mummy at once," he said; "and there's no reason we should not get away by the morning train."

"I'm ready to go tonight, if you are," I said honestly.

But Dr. Silence shook his head.

"I must see this through to the end," he said gravely, and in a tone that made me think he still anticipated serious things, perhaps. He went on talking while I dressed.

"This case is really typical of all stories of mummy-haunting, and none of them are cases to trifle with," he explained, "for the mummies of important people — kings, priests, magicians — were laid away with profoundly significant ceremonial, and were very effectively protected, as you have seen, against desecration, and especially against destruction.

"The general belief," he went on, anticipating my questions, "held, of course, that the perpetuity of the mummy guaranteed that of its Ka, — the owner's spirit — but it is not improbable that the magical embalming was also used to retard reincarnation, the preservation of the body preventing the return of the spirit to the toil and discipline of earth-life; and, in any case, they knew how to attach powerful guardian-forces to keep off trespassers. And any one who dared to remove the mummy, or especially to unwind it — well," he added, with meaning, "you have seen — and you will see."

I caught his face in the mirror while I struggled with my collar. It was deeply serious. There could be no question that he spoke of what he believed and knew.

"The traveller-brother who brought it here must have been haunted too," he continued, "for he tried to banish it by burial in the wood, making a magic circle to enclose it. Something of genuine ceremonial he must have known, for the stars the man saw were of course the remains of the still flaming pentagrams he traced at intervals in the circle. Only he did not know enough, or possibly was ignorant that the mummy's guardian was a fire-force. Fire cannot be enclosed by fire, though, as you saw, it can be released by it."

"Then that awful figure in the laundry?" I asked, thrilled to find him so communicative.

"Undoubtedly the actual Ka of the mummy operating always behind its agent, the elemental, and most likely thousands of years old."

"And Miss Wragge —?" I ventured once more.

"Ah, Miss Wragge," he repeated with increased gravity, "Miss Wragge."

A knock at the door brought a servant with word that tea was ready, and the Colonel had sent to ask if we were coming down. The thread was broken. Dr. Silence moved to the door and signed to me to follow. But his manner told me that in any case no real answer would have been forthcoming to my question.

"And the place to dig in," I asked, unable to restrain my curiosity, "will you find it by some process of divination or —?"

He paused at the door and looked back at me, and with that he left me to finish my dressing.

It was growing dark when the three of us silently made our way to the Twelve Acre Plantation; the sky was overcast, and a black wind came out of the east. Gloom hung about the old house and the air seemed full of sighings. We found the tools ready laid at the edge of the wood, and each shouldering his piece, we followed our leader at once in among the trees. He went straight forward at some twenty yards and then stopped. At his feet lay the blackened circle of one of the burned places. It was just discernible against the surrounding white grass.

"There are three of these," he said, "and they all lie in a line with one another. Any one of them will tap the tunnel that connects the laundry — the former Museum — with the chamber where the mummy now lies buried."

He at once cleared the burnt grass and began to dig; we all began to dig. While I used the pick, the others shovelled vigorously. No one spoke. Colonel Wragge worked the hardest of the three. The soil was light and sandy, and there were only a few snake-like roots and occasional loose stones to delay us. The pick made short work of these. And meanwhile the darkness settled about us and the biting wind swept roaring through the trees overhead.

Then, quite suddenly, with a cry, Colonel Wragge disappeared up to his neck.

"The tunnel!" cried the doctor, helping to drag him out, red, breathless, and covered with sand and perspiration. "Now, let me lead the way." And he slipped down nimbly into the hole, so that a moment later we heard his voice, muffled by sand and distance, rising up to us.

"Hubbard, you come next, and then Colonel Wragge — if he wishes," we heard.

"I'll follow you, of course," he said, looking at me as I scrambled in.

The hole was bigger now, and I got down on all-fours in a channel not much bigger than a large sewer — pipe and found myself in total darkness. A minute later a heavy thud, followed by a cataract of loose sand, announced the arrival of the Colonel.

"Catch hold of my heel," called Dr. Silence, "and Colonel Wragge can take yours."

In this slow, laborious fashion we wormed our way along a tunnel that had been roughly dug out of the shifting sand, and was shored up clumsily by means of wooden pillars and posts. Any moment, it seemed to me, we might be buried alive. We could not see an inch before our eyes, but had to grope our way feeling the pillars and the walls. It was difficult to breathe, and the Colonel behind me made but slow progress, for the cramped position of our bodies was very severe.

We had travelled in this way for ten minutes, and gone perhaps as much as ten yards, when I lost my grasp of the doctor's heel.

"Ah!" I heard his voice, sounding above me somewhere. He was standing up in a clear space, and the next moment I was standing beside him. Colonel Wragge came heavily after, and he too rose up and stood. Then Dr. Silence produced his candles and we heard preparations for striking matches.

Yet even before there was light, an indefinable sensation of awe came over us all. In this hole in the sand, some three feet under ground, we stood side by side, cramped and huddled, struck suddenly with an over whelming apprehension of something ancient, something formidable, something incalculably wonderful, that touched in each one of us a sense of the sublime and the terrible even before we could see an inch before our faces. I know not how to express in language this singular emotion that caught us here in utter darkness, touching no sense directly, it seemed, yet with the recognition that before us in the blackness of this underground night there lay something that was mighty with the mightiness of long past ages.

I felt Colonel Wragge press in closely to my side, and I understood the pressure and welcomed it. No human touch, to me at least, has ever been more eloquent.

Then the match flared, a thousand shadows fled on black wings, I saw John Silence fumbling with the candle, his face lit up grotesquely by the flickering light below it.

I had dreaded this light, yet when it came there was apparently nothing to explain the profound sensations of dread that preceded it. We stood in a small vaulted chamber in the sand, the sides and roof shored with bars of wood, and the ground laid roughly with what seemed to be tiles. It was six feet high, so that we could all stand comfortably, and may have been ten feet long by eight feet wide. Upon the wooden pillars at the side I saw that Egyptian hieroglyphics had been rudely traced by burning.

Dr. Silence lit three candles and handed one to each of us. He placed a fourth in the sand against the wall on his right, and another to mark the entrance to the tunnel. We stood and stared about us, instinctively holding our breath.

"Empty, by God!" exclaimed Colonel Wragge. His voice trembled with excitement. And then, as his eyes rested on the ground, he added, "And footsteps — look — footsteps in the sand!"

Dr. Silence said nothing. He stooped down and began to make a search of the chamber, and as he moved, my eyes followed his crouching figure and noted the queer distorted shadows that poured over the walls and ceiling after him. Here and there thin trickles of loose sand ran fizzing down the sides. The atmosphere, heavily charged with faint yet pungent odours, lay utterly still, and the flames of the candles might have been painted on the air for all the movement they betrayed.

And, as I watched, it was almost necessary to persuade myself forcibly that I was only standing upright with difficulty in this little sand-hole of a modern garden in the south of England, for it seemed to me that I stood, as in vision, at the entrance of some vast rock-hewn Temple far, far down the river of Time. The illusion was powerful, and persisted. Granite columns, that rose to heaven, piled themselves about me, majestically uprearing, and a roof like the sky itself spread above a line of colossal figures that moved in shadowy procession along endless and stupendous aisles. This huge and splendid fantasy, borne I knew not whence, possessed me so vividly that I was actually obliged to concentrate my attention upon the small stooping figure of the doctor, as he groped about the walls, in order to keep the eye of imagination on the scene before me.

But the limited space rendered a long search out of the question, and his footsteps, instead of shuffling through loose sand, presently struck something of a different quality that gave forth a hollow and resounding echo. He stooped to examine more closely.

He was standing exactly in the centre of the little chamber when this happened, and he at once began scraping away the sand with his feet. In less than a minute a smooth surface became visible — the surface of a wooden covering. The next thing I saw was that he had raised it and was peering down into a space below. Instantly, a strong odour of nitre and bitumen, mingled with the strange perfume of unknown and powdered aromatics, rose up from the uncovered space and filled the vault, stinging the throat and making the eyes water and smart.

"The mummy!" whispered Dr. Silence, looking up into our faces over his candle; and as he said the word I felt the soldier lurch against me, and heard his breathing in my very ear.

"The mummy!" he repeated under his breath, as we pressed forward to look.

It is difficult to say exactly why the sight should have stirred in me so prodigious an emotion of wonder and veneration, for I have had not a little to do with mummies, have unwound scores of them, and even experimented magically with not a few. But there was something in the sight of that grey and silent figure, lying in its modern box of lead and wood at the bottom of this sandy grave, swathed in the bandages of centuries and wrapped in the perfumed linen that the priests of Egypt had prayed over with their mighty enchantments thousands of years before — something in the sight of it lying there and breathing its own spice-laden atmosphere even in the darkness of its exile in this remote land, something that pierced to the very core of my being and touched that root of awe which slumbers in every man near the birth of tears and the passion of true worship.

I remember turning quickly from the Colonel, lest he should see my emotion, yet fail to understand its cause, turn and clutch John Silence by the arm, and then fall trembling to see that he, too, had lowered his head and was hiding his face in his hands.

A kind of whirling storm came over me, rising out of I know not what utter deeps of memory, and in a whiteness of vision I heard the magical old chauntings from the Book of the Dead, and saw the Gods pass by in dim procession, the mighty, immemorial Beings who were yet themselves only the personified attributes of the true Gods, the God with the Eyes of Fire, the God with the Face of Smoke. I saw again Anubis, the dog-faced deity, and the children of Horus, eternal watcher of the ages, as they swathed Osiris, the first mummy of the world, in the scented and mystic bands, and I tasted again something of the ecstasy of the justified soul as it embarked in the golden Boat of Ra, and journeyed onwards to rest in the fields of the blessed.

And then, as Dr. Silence, with infinite reverence, stooped and touched the still face, so dreadfully staring with its painted eyes, there rose again to our nostrils wave upon wave of this perfume of thousands of years, and time fled backwards like a thing of naught, showing me in haunted panorama the most wonderful dream of the whole world.

A gentle hissing became audible in the air, and the doctor moved quickly backwards. It came close to our faces and then seemed to play about the walls and ceiling.

"The last of the Fire — still waiting for its full accomplishment," he muttered; but I heard both words and hissing as things far away, for I was still busy with the journey of the soul through the Seven Halls of Death, listening for echoes of the grandest ritual ever known to men.

The earthen plates covered with hieroglyphics still lay beside the mummy, and round it, carefully arranged at the points of the compass, stood the four jars with the heads of the hawk, the jackal, the cynocephalus, and man, the jars in which were placed the hair, the nail parings, the heart, and other special portions of the body. Even the amulets, the mirror, the blue clay statues of the Ka, and the lamp with seven wicks were there. Only the sacred scarabæus was missing.

"Not only has it been torn from its ancient resting-place," I heard Dr. Silence saying in a solemn voice as he looked at Colonel Wragge with fixed gaze, "but it has been partially unwound," — he pointed to the wrappings of the breast — "and — the scarabreus has been removed from the throat."

The hissing, that was like the hissing of an invisible flame, had ceased; only from time to time we heard it as though it passed backwards and forwards in the tunnel; and we stood looking into each other's faces without speaking.

Presently Colonel Wragge made a great effort and braced himself. I heard the sound catch in his throat before the words actually became audible.

"My sister," he said, very low. And then there followed a long pause, broken at length by John Silence.

"It must be replaced," he said significantly.

"I knew nothing," the soldier said, forcing himself to speak the words he hated saying. "Absolutely nothing."

"It must be returned," repeated the other, "if it is not now too late. For I fear — I fear —"

Colonel Wragge made a movement of assent with his head.

"It shall be," he said.

The place was still as the grave.

I do not know what it was then that made us all three turn round with so sudden a start, for there was no sound audible to my ears, at least.

The doctor was on the point of replacing the lid over the mummy, when he straightened up as if he had been shot.

"There's something coming," said Colonel Wragge under his breath, and the doctor's eyes, peering down the small opening of the tunnel, showed me the true direction.

A distant shuffling noise became distinctly audible coming from a point about half-way down the tunnel we had so laboriously penetrated.

"It's the sand falling in," I said, though I knew it was foolish.

"No," said the Colonel calmly, in a voice that seemed to have the ring of iron, "I've heard it for some time past. It is something alive and it is coming nearer."

He stared about him with a look of resolution that made his face almost noble. The horror in his heart was overmastering, yet he stood there prepared for anything that might come.

"There's no other way out," John Silence said.

He leaned the lid against the sand, and waited. I knew by the masklike expression of his face, the pallor, and the steadiness of the eyes, that he anticipated something that might be very terrible — appalling.

The Colonel and myself stood on either side of the opening. I still held my candle and was ashamed of the way it shook, dripping the grease all over me; but the soldier had set his into the sand just behind his feet.

Thoughts of being buried alive, of being smothered like rats in a trap, of being caught and done to death by some invisible and merciless force we could not grapple with, rushed into my mind. Then I thought of fire — of suffocation — of being roasted alive. The perspiration began to pour from my face.

"Steady!" came the voice of Dr. Silence to me through the vault.

For five minutes, that seemed fifty, we stood waiting, looking from each other's faces to the mummy, and from the mummy to the hole, and all the time the shuffling sound, soft and stealthy, came gradually nearer. The tension, for me at least, was very near the breaking point when at last the cause of the disturbance reached the edge. It was hidden for a moment just behind the broken rim of soil. A jet of sand, shaken by the close vibration, trickled down on to the ground; I have never in my life seen anything fall with such laborious leisure. The next second, uttering a cry of curious quality, it came into view.

And it was far more distressingly horrible than anything I had anticipated.

For the sight of some Egyptian monster, some god of the tombs, or even of some demon of fire, I think I was already half prepared; but when, instead, I saw the white visage of Miss Wragge framed in that round opening of sand, followed by her body crawling on all-fours, her eyes bulging and reflecting the yellow glare of the candles, my first instinct was to turn and run like a frantic animal seeking a way of escape.

But Dr. Silence, who seemed no whit surprised, caught my arm and steadied me, and we both saw the Colonel then drop upon his knees and come thus to a level with his sister. For more than a whole minute, as though struck in stone, the two faces gazed silently at each other: hers, for all the dreadful emotion in it, more like a gargoyle than anything human; and his, white and blank with an expression that was beyond either astonishment or alarm. She looked up; he looked down. It was a picture in a nightmare, and the candle, stuck in the sand close to the hole, threw upon it the glare of impromptu footlights.

Then John Silence moved forward and spoke in a voice that was very low, yet perfectly calm and natural.

"I am glad you have come," he said. "You are the one person whose presence at this moment is most required. And I hope that you may yet be in time to appease the anger of the Fire, and to bring peace again to your household, and," he added lower still so that no one heard it but myself, "safety to yourself."

And while her brother stumbled backwards, crushing a candle into the sand in his awkwardness, the old lady crawled farther into the vaulted chamber and slowly rose upon her feet.

At the sight of the wrapped figure of the mummy I was fully prepared to see her scream and faint, but on the contrary, to my complete amazement, she merely bowed her head and dropped quietly upon her knees. Then, after a pause of more than a minute, she raised her eyes to the roof and her lips began to mutter as in prayer. Her right hand, meanwhile, which had been fumbling for some time at her throat suddenly came away, and before the gaze of all of us she held it out, palm upwards, over the grey and ancient figure outstretched below. And in it we beheld glistening the green jasper of the stolen scarabæus.

Her brother, leaning heavily against the wall behind, uttered a sound that was half cry, half exclamation, but John Silence, standing directly in front of her, merely fixed his eyes on her and pointed downwards to the staring face below.

"Replace it," he said sternly, "where it belongs."

Miss Wragge was kneeling at the feet of the mummy when this happened. We three men all had our eyes riveted on what followed. Only the reader who by some remote chance may have witnessed a line of mummies, freshly laid from their tombs upon the sand, slowly stir and bend as the heat of the Egyptian sun warms their ancient bodies into the semblance of life, can form any conception of the ultimate horror we experienced when the silent figure before us moved in its grave of lead and sand. Slowly, before our eyes, it writhed, and, with a faint rustling of the immemorial cerements, rose up, and through sightless and bandaged eyes, stared across the yellow candle-light at the woman who had violated it.

I tried to move — her brother tried to move — but the sand seemed to hold our feet. I tried to cry — her brother tried to cry — but the sand seemed to fill our lungs and throat. We could only stare — and, even so, the sand seemed to rise like a desert storm and cloud our vision. . . .

And when I managed at length to open my eyes again, the mummy was lying once more upon its back, motionless, the shrunken and painted face upturned towards the ceiling, and the old lady had tumbled forward and was lying in the semblance of death with her head and arms upon its crumbling body.

But upon the wrappings of the throat I saw the green jasper of the sacred scarabæus shining again like a living eye.

Colonel Wragge and the doctor recovered themselves long before I did, and I found myself helping them clumsily and unintelligently to raise the frail body of the old lady, while John Silence carefully replaced the covering over the grave and scraped back the sand with his foot, while he issued brief directions.

I heard his voice as in a dream; but the journey back along that cramped tunnel, weighted by a dead woman, blinded with sand, suffocated with heat, was in no sense a dream. It took us the best part of half an hour to reach the open air. And, even then, we had to wait a considerable time for the appearance of Dr. Silence. We carried her undiscovered into the house and up to her own room.

"The mummy will cause no further disturbance," I heard Dr. Silence say to our host later that evening as we prepared to drive for the night train, "provided always," he added significantly, "that you, and yours, cause it no disturbance."

It was in a dream, too, that we left.

"You did not see her face, I know," he said to me as we wrapped our rugs about us in the empty compartment. And when I shook my head, quite unable to explain the instinct that had come to me not to look, he turned toward me, his face pale, and genuinely sad.

"Scorched and blasted," he whispered.

The Green God*

They were following the last of the storm, climbing soggily the great rollers, nursing the boat carefully through the white-caps, making consistently for the island with the dead tree spire.

Rill, with head sagging on his narrow chest, scraped rhythmically with the bailing-pail, along the bottom, over the side, scrape and over, scrape and over, never ceasing, rarely looking up, his thin face lined with fatigue.

The other man swung forlornly on a pair of great oars. His head was thrown back, exposing the neck-column that sat on the thick torso, beautiful as the neck of a Greek vase. The two rarely spoke, unless concerning the course.

They had not changed posture since the day before, when, after the delirium of the Bertha's foundering, they had found themselves as they were now, the one rowing, the other, of lesser physique, bailing. The storm had driven the packet boat that plied north from Skagway out of her course. They were somewhere in the Aleutian Islands. That was all they knew, that, and a hunger that lost itself somewhere in thirst.

The danger of capsizing hourly had grown less, seeming queerly enough to lessen with the weakening of the men's resistance; or possibly it was the other way round. Late in the afternoon, with the sun beginning to shine palely, they came to the island. The surf crashed upon the rocky line in steady thunder. Sea-birds swooped and beat above it, their cawing inaudible.

"Guess it's all up," the big man at the oars said. "If we go round to make shore on the lee side, the current'll carry us past like a shot. If we get in the surf, them rocks'll chop us up — for the gulls."

They both stared at the spuming shoreline that momentarily became plainer. The oarsman had the better eyes.

"There's a cove," he said presently. "Sometimes that means a stretch of sand. If the breakers catch you right, you kin carry through, sometimes. Try it?"

The slim man peered through the lank black hair that fell over his red-lidded eyes, noting his informant as he had the shore.

"I don't know you yet," he said. "You a sailor? Got good judgment? Can we do anything else?"

"Name's Pug Norton, sir — cook on the Bertha, sailed regular before the mast in the old days up here. Ain't much I don't know about landin' a boat. I'd rather get it over quick, there in the pound, than take days to it. I've helped pick up fellows that croaked from the thirst — I swore when my turn came I'd go a quick way. You feel the same?"

* "The Green God" was written by William Call Spencer (fl. 1910s) and published in *All-Story Weekly*, Vol. 64, No. 1, Oct. 28, 1916.

Rill nodded his head, and went to baling again, head drooped forward, shoulders bent. The sailor, Pug, gazed more frequently over his shoulder and sent the boat along a bit faster. Perhaps he intended to try the wild ride before dusk put a false light on things. They had no more speech, for they had said quite all that was necessary to say with thickening tongues.

The moment came when the boat was opposite the little cove, and the sailor simply, without hesitation, headed in for the breakers. They were big, as they usually are in Alaska, and always after a storm. Pug had a parting fragment of advice to give:

"If this here boat founders way out, just hang on tight. If she busts on shore, keep away from her. I've seen a Malay get his nut cracked between the boat and the sand. An' I guess you know enough not to fight — if we ain't carried in, we don't get it, that's all."

Rill dropped the bucket and hung on to the gunwales as the other, choosing his time, strained at the oars. They shot in, lifted by a swell, dropped, were carried again, and again dropped just before the wave foamed and curled. The sailor had timed it well. He had the boat further in by the next break, so that at any rate the tremendous fall of water did not bash them. Instead they met the crazy blanket of foam. Rill perceived vaguely the other flashing the oars frantically, then the boat sank from under him, and he went down, clinging like a barnacle to the gunwale. He remembered coming to the top again, and swirling madly, giddily over and under the boat. Finally he let go. He felt his arm seized, and then his consciousness went.

When it came back he was lying with his face in the sand a foot or so beyond high-water line. He coughed weakly and opened his eyes to see the sailor, Pug, reeling toward him through the dusk, carrying something in his cap. Rill wondered pettishly how the sailor had kept that cap.

"Pool of rain-water back there," Pug said. "Scummy-like, but good enough to rinse the salt water out of your mouth. Here."

He lay down on the sand above Rill, and before the latter was through with the water he was sleeping. Rill had time to note the brine still dripping from him into the sand and to observe the same phenomenon occurring in his own case before he too fell back with a relaxing sigh into deep slumber. That was the end of their first day.

The second held other problems, chiefly those of food and water and shelter. They spread their clothes to dry on the sand, and occupied that time in collecting sections of the boat that had come ashore. Tangled and caught with sea-weed they found the long painter-rope. Norton patiently worked it free and coiled it to dry. But most pressing was the question of food. Later they could unravel a bit of the rope and form a fish-line, but the need was immediate. They put on their shoes and scoured among the rocks, catching little crabs and minnows, of which six might make a mouthful. They ate these raw for an hour or so, with the help of Norton's jack-knife.

"I got a tin of matches in my pants for next time," the latter explained. "But they eat good this way, huh?"

The sailor was the provident man, forehanded, capable. The thin-faced one with the wide forehead and loose lip would not have seen the practical wisdom of carrying matches in a water-tight receptacle.

In the afternoon they circuited the island and partially explored the interior, which indicates its size. Of man they found no trace, except, on the highest point, charred wood from some signal-fire. They were concerned chiefly at their failure to discover running water, for what pools they found in the rocks were brackish and filled with life, both animal and vegetable.

"If we had a kettle we could cook it," Pug observed. "But we ain't."

The dead tree they had seen the day before was a pine, and they collected the brown needles for a bed. The day passed very quickly with the multitude of tasks. At night they slept close together for the warmth. The sailor got up once to see to the fire, but the other slept through without a wink of the eyelid.

They fashioned a low shelter, roofing it with needles and with green from the profuse underbrush. They made a fireplace that would endure the heavy rains. In all these things the sailor advised and directed, and Rill, unaccustomed to that, had to conceal his irritation. He did as the other advised, however, because invariably that was the best method. He had to admit that to himself, and the sailor took it as a matter of course. The latter would not have comprehended passing a mistake for the sake of the other's self-satisfaction.

For instance, the cook had made a bird-snare and caught a gull. After their meal from it Rill threw carelessly the bones into the fire and leaned back. Pug swore and forked them out.

"You got to be more careful," he admonished the other. "Them bones is valuable."

Rill considered Pug, sucking his loose under lip.

"You got the bulge on me out here," he answered. "If we were in town I might appear in other light — what an you doing?"

Pug had cleaned the clavicles or furcula, which in a chicken is the wishbone, and was carving it.

"Fish-hook," he replied, and opened up the other phase. "I knew you was a city guy. I piped you stringing along with the other passengers on the Bertha. You was mostly at the tables in the smoking-room, wasn't you? But I ain't placed you — sometimes I think you're educated, and next minute you're spielin' as if you was raised on the water-front."

Rill did not avail himself of the request for an autobiography. He got to his feet and scanned lazily the empty sea.

"Yep, Pug, I've been arbiter elegantia, so to speak, among the esthetes and the patricians, and again I've mooched a plate of beans from a Cholo tamale man. While you're fishing this afternoon, I'll go over the island again."

Pug watched him put his hands in his pockets and stroll easily around the curve in the shore.

"He'd bag a gink for a dime, if he thought he could get away with it," he murmured to himself, and went on with the hook-making.

He was cleaning a meager catch of fish when the one who had gone exploring came back and sat down beside him.

"You got to be expert to bring 'em in with this here hook," Pug announced, and considered that he had done his duty in the matter of small talk. But the other appeared engrossed.

"You can't read Egyptian hieroglyphics or Chinese ideographs, can you?" he asked presently.

That was a good joke. Pug chuckled loudly and laughed again at the straight face the other kept.

"Sure, an' deaf an' dumb languige, too. You need that?"

"Remember that big regular-shaped rock we saw on the other side of the island? That's a monolith."

"A which?"

"The big one near the shore, that stuck up like a pillar, flat on top — now you remember?"

"What about it?"

"I thought it looked queer, and I peeled off some of the moss. The thing is all carved with some ancient writing, related, I think, both to Egyptian and Chinese, maybe Mexican. And another thing, the stone is granite. You won't find another piece on the island."

"Whew!" Pug waited for a moment, studying these bits of information in the light of the other's facial expression. But a solution not immediately presenting itself, he turned again to the fish.

"And that wasn't all," Rill went on. "It looked as if there might have been a road into the island there, and I followed it up. About fifty yards from the monolith there's a big hole, some twenty feet across. I dropped in a rock or two and judged they fell maybe a hundred feet, and then rolled down a slanting shaft. To-morrow we'll go look it over. There's copper indications near there."

There was new excitement in the sailor that had not appeared even in the fight with the surf. After the meal the explanation came:

"I ran across a poor bum," Pug said, "down in Sitka a couple of years ago. We had a drink, and he spieled a lot of queer bunk. They said he'd gone nuts. Anyhow, he sez he was with a party of Indians in these here islands, prospecting for ore. There was a small island with a big pine in the middle of it what the Indians called 'The Island of the Lost God.' They wouldn't land him till he pulled his gun and threatened to shoot them — said a green devil lived there in a deep cave; a bad one."

"This guy laughs at 'em an' makes 'em lower him into this here cave on a rope — he sez it looks to him like an old copper-mine shaft. The boys up top get scared as soon as he hits the bottom and light out for keeps. He doesn't know it, though, and goes on in. It's great, the story he tells about that, about how he meets this green devil coming, grinning at him. He takes a pot-shot at him and shinnies the rope like he was a cat. By an' by somebody picks him up — crazy with the thirst and the fright and all. But he ain't never forgot that green thing. Say, I wish we could get picked up right now —"

Rill allowed himself an ironical smile.

"Why, you believe in the story?" he asked.

"No, I don't say that — but still, my mother was Irish, and she saw the banshee once, an' she knew the runes of the fairies — we'd best go 'round the hole.'"

"No devil'll scare me away from a lost copper, mine. If there's anything there you can buy out fifty devils."

"Make fun if you want — I'll keep clear." Rill made for the inscriptured rock the next day and the sailor followed, somewhat curious. The characters were large and deeply cut, excellently preserved by the six-inch skin of moss that covers everything in that region. Rill scraped merely enough to determine that the entire monolith was carved.

They dug also below the surface, and still finding the strange characters, determined that what they saw was merely the summit or upper half, possibly, of an obelisk. The writing ran in regular lines, sometimes horizontally and sometimes vertically. Rill discovered one line larger and more freely written than the rest, with simpler glyphs. He studied long over this, so long that the sailor tired of it and began to saunter off.

"Wait," Rill said. "I've got part of it. I happen to have a smattering of this science — and when I go down the shaft I want to know as much as this will tell us."

He began to elucidate, pointing to the row that ran around the stone:

"This line was written in a hurry; it's more elemental. It's the original stuff. See the serpent in the second group? — that stands for wisdom. The Pharaohs used the asp, symbol of their wisdom. The serpent tempted Adam and Eve, that is, the beginnings of wisdom or thought brought them self-knowledge. The dragon is the Chinese development of that idea; Hermes's caduceus has the serpents of wisdom intertwined; there's a Hindu god that holds out in one hand a big snake — all the same idea.

"Now, that first mark is the anthropomorphic sign and can stand for God. Right under it is a mouth, sign of talk. See the zigzag sign in the second group? — that's water. Then comes the moon or month and the setting sun; the one like a dead bush is a hand, sign of force or power. The zigzag on a line means mountains sometimes, and in the next group is forest. The triangle thing's got me guessing, but I can get the epic out of it, anyway."

"You mean you can read the stuff?" Pug was somewhat incredulous, this feat appearing miraculous.

"It starts like this — the god speaks, evidently in warning, because the wise ones take to their boats and go off on the water, six to the boat rowing, I think. Then elapses the time from the new moon to the old moon and two days besides. Again the god warns in some way, and again a period of time. Finally the god acts or uses his power (you see the hand), and some terrible catastrophe occurs.

"The writer tells us of the chaos by putting the sun upside down, as if to say they never saw the sun or the days. But still the men number as the trees of a forest. They had no understanding, and put to sea. You can read the next sign — a big storm, all perish. And finally the god speaks once more, saying that man's day is over. Some story, Pug?"

"It must have been the green god that did the talking and all. We'd best let the shaft alone. There's always somebody scouting around these islands: we'll get took off before long."

They did wait. The sailor fished and performed the practical duties. The other was absorbed in the efforts to perfect the message, blocked by the meaning of the triangle signs. Together they struggled with the water supply. The pools were slowly drying, and becoming more brackish and filled with life. That was the big problem, the daily mounting worry — water.

The shaft held the only hope. Yet Pug preferred on the whole to struggle with the known phenomena of the surface, and Rill could not bring himself to the point of contending with the physical difficulties, the trusting himself to the rope, the dangers. There was also their mutual suspicion, natural and inevitable, that precluded, short of imminent necessity a combining of forces wherein one must trust the other.

A morning came when Rill, of weaker constitution, vomited after a swallow of the green water. That was enough; he determined immediately to explore the hole. They got the rope, and Pug came presently with a couple of pine-knots and burning brands from the fire to light them.

The edge of the shaft was clean-cut in the soft rock, so that they could peer over and down. Kneeling there, Rill whispered and the sibilance rushed back and forth ended finally in a subdued, venomous hissing at the bottom.

They dropped a stone, and the crash of its impacts mounted in a hollow roar now loudly, now softly, multitudinously. They could distinguish various upper strata, but the lower portion was shrouded in impenetrable black. The sailor glanced at Rill, and saw a sheen of damp on his forehead.

"What's up?" he asked, thinking himself of the green thing of the legend.

"Suppose the rope isn't long enough, or should cut on the rock — sure you can pull me up — and will?"

They did not talk much while the sailor knotted a loop in the rope for Rill's foot, and tied the other end to a stake driven in a deft of the rock. Perhaps Rill did feel a qualm, but if so it was not again apparent to the other.

As his end of the rope eventually came into Pug's hands a frown of worry lowered his eyebrows. He was certain that it was not long enough, when the tension laxed. He peered down. Far away the smoky yellow of the torch wavered upon the roughness of the rock. The man holding it called up, but long before the words came to the sailor they had been mingled and churned into a confused rumble.

Then the torch moved slowly into the wall until the blaze itself was hidden, though he could still see the moving light playing from the tunnel upon the wall of the vertical shaft. With the minutes that grew fainter. There came up a sharp cry of fright, and immediately the yellow glow vanished. The still menacing darkness of the centuries swooped once more, like the drop of a hawk, over the caverns.

With his back to the sun, the sailor listened intently at the edge, waiting for some explanation of that sudden shout and the succeeding silence. He called once or twice, but the sound echoed back to him raucously, mockingly. Presently apprehensions of the green thing, that had lain dormant for a time, swept over him.

His imagination pictured Rill in the grasp of some awful being, some green-tentacled, green-eyed chimera. That heavy darkness might hide any terror. Then he had a moment wherein common sense dictated that Rill had met with some natural accident; had fallen down a hole or dislodged a fall of rock.

It was good to look up at the placid sea and the two or three islands hazy in the distance, the lazy smoke of their signal-fire, the white birds floating and careering along the shore. The sense of freedom, the absence of the strain of always watching the other man, gave him a sort of pleasure.

He was almost glad that he was alone, and sauntered toward camp. But that act did not seem right; somehow he felt guilty; he felt that he had a duty, difficult and abhorrent, but nevertheless necessary. He went over to the rope and tested the firmness of the peg.

Rill had thrown down the extra torch. The sailor filled a pocket with dry leaves and twigs, enough to light it at the bottom. To slip over the side and descend hand under hand was not difficult. He had had a lifetime of that. But as he went down through the dusk-lit strata to the depths, his fear of that unknown enlarged.

The noise of his descent came back to him from the walls, almost maliciously, he imagined. From the bottom he looked up. He had never seen a sky of so intense a blue, clotted with winking stars. Though he had heard of this, nevertheless he wished that he had not looked up. It lent too much of an air of unreality to the whole undertaking. He sighed relievedly when he found the torch and got it flaring. The stale air smelt of the passage of Rill's torch. Sweat came out on his forehead, perhaps caused as much by mental as by physical discomfort. He shouted and waited, but no answer came. The passage curved evidently, for he could not see far. Where it passed through soft strata the sides had been shored up with stone work, with great rocks patiently fitted into each other, narrowing toward the top.

He took a step forward and halted. If he could have found the smallest excuse he would have dropped the torch and the whole business. This adventure was trying him in his weakest part. He felt that his scalp was moving, there was a giddy nausea at the pit of his stomach. The crux of his hesitation lay in his doubt as to whether there existed a green thing in there or whether Rill had met with a natural accident. Some low instinct of superstitious belief insisted on the former, and years of common sense scoffed.

He nerved himself to go forward somewhat as a swimmer brings himself to the point of the first plunge into water that he fears is cold. With sweat pouring from him he edged into the passage, holding aloft the blazing pine-knot, ready to dash back. After the first slight curve the tunnel straightened to such length that his light did not carry to the end. As he advanced he grew more confident; the action involved in keeping his feet occupied him.

The air grew heavier, his lungs worked as if caught in the stricture of a great snake.

The torch burned lower and redly. Once more he called. This time he was startled by an answer, a dull moan that issued a few feet beyond, from between two great boulders. He stooped over Rill, but could find no signs of harm or violence.

"What's the matter?" he asked.

Rill rolled his head weakly and muttered. He tried it again, muttering the second time plainly enough for the other to hear:

"Be careful — knocked me out —"

Pug's torch was nearly gone. He stood up and searched for the one that Rill must have dropped. His eyes wandered up the passage, and abruptly held, dilating. He stood woodenly, nerveless with terror.

His pale light glimmered vaguely upon the green thing that half-sat, half-reclined in a heap of earth a few feet from them. In the quivering light the twisted limbs appeared to move and contort. The green skin upon the skull, drawn back until the cruel mouth grinned insanely, the hollowed cheeks, the deep eye-sockets that stared at him, the taut, glistening parchment upon the forehead — these fascinated the sailor so that he could not look away. He expected it to stand over him to point its skinny, withered arm at him or to open its jaws, in a shattering laugh.

He heard a coughing choke behind him, and jumped backward, ramming against the wall of the passage. But it was merely Rill.

"Water," he was trying to articulate, "Some water."

Swept from his immobility, Pug acted feverishly. He backed over to Rill. In such case, as this prayer might be efficacious. He remembered one his mother had taught him that invoked God against devils. He recited it quickly and ran his arm around Rills shoulders. Nothing happened; obviously the magic had done its work!

He spelled it out again and backed off, dragging the limp body with one arm while the other held the light upon the green thing, until the returning gloom blotted it out. Then he turned about and, with Rill on his shoulder, strode heavily and hurriedly back. The torch went out and he stumbled along, caroming from side to side, slipping, gasping harshly in the close fetid air.

When he got to the vertical shaft he was forced to lay Rill down and to rest for several moments. The blood-vessels in his neck and head throbbed from the pressure in the lungs. Rill began to talk:

"I was following along the vein in the roof," he said. "Climbed up on the rock. I saw the green thing. I think the rock wobbled with me, and I fell. I'll be all right with a drink of water."

The sailor moved Rill over to the rope and succeeded in knotting it around his shoulders. That was fairly difficult as it was necessary to lift him into the air while he tied. But still, that was easy compared with his next move. He began to climb the rope hand over hand. With Rill weighting the end he mounted painfully inch by inch the long stretch. If he could have rested midway it would have helped, but that was impossible. The skin began to tear from his hands, a numbness entered the arm muscles, so terribly three times he wrapped his legs in the rope and in a way eased the strain, but his strength appeared to evaporate with these rests.

He had been fatigued before he undertook the climb, from the violent work in the vitiated air. The last ten feet drew from him as much energy and pain as the first half of the feat. He became dizzy, black spots moved before his eyes, the rope in his hands appeared as tenuous as a fine thread, and as difficult to grasp. He had climbed to where the rope went over the edge. He would have to spring his body up two feet and catch the rope beyond the edge before he fell back. How easy to coil about the rope and slide again to the bottom!

He considered that for a long time, but he knew that if he fell he would not be able again to get that far. He summoned all his reserve, worked up till one hand was wedged tightly between the rope and the rock, and made the supreme effort. The hand that reached over for the new hold slipped, he began to fall back, the knuckles scraping along the rock. They passed over a ledge, a fissure. He let go the rope and held to that with the ends of his fingers, got the other arm up, and slowly worked his body over.

He lay there on his back, his feet hanging over the shaft, for another period of time. Pain began to enter his skinned hands, a sign of recuperation. There remained the task of pulling up the weak man. The signal fire was nearly out, they had no food on hand, they had found no water.

Dusk was settling before the sailor stood up and essayed to haul on the rope. He brought up a few feet, but the torture in his hands was excruciating. It was common sense, he decided, to wait until he could surely finish the job. Rill, below, was too far gone to protest. Pug mentally could see him hanging there, swaying loosely in the rope, head hanging to his flat chest.

The sailor shuffled over to their dead campfire. There had been scraps on the fish-bones they had thrown away at their midday meal. He needed those. As he worked along he looked out to sea, as the habit had grown, upon them to do.

In the gray light he could not see far. He was looking away when he got an impression of some life upon the great expanse, of something moving between the shore and the horizon. He stopped and stared, his heart palpitating with fear lest there had been a chance of rescue that they had missed. He became certain that it was a small craft of some sort. He shouted crazily; the call carried as far as the sound of a falling leaf in a breeze.

Then he remembered their signal-fire and clambered hurriedly the little summit. He piled on the scanty provision of fuel recklessly, and blew it into a blaze. He could no longer distinguish any movement in the soft darkness, but between the fire and the sea he stood and waved his arms. The glow spread about him, his shadow, gigantic, monstrous, filling half the world.

Twice he replenished the fire, always returning to his position with his back to it. His hope had vanished, he was satisfied he had been mistaken, when cries came from the water edge. While he was climbing down he heard a boat being beached on the sand.

It proved to be a dugout load of Huyda Indians on a cruise. It was for them a simple, smiling matter to draw up the man still swinging on the rope. They became loquacious between each other in their guttural way, marveling at the white men's capacity for dried meat and meal. Rill was weak, still suffering from the shock and his wound and his long lack of water. The Indians, however, refused to remain overnight on the island, fearful perhaps of the green devil, and put to sea with the two white men lying at length on the canoe bottom.

The full moon came up in the clear night, illuming the far islands. The atmosphere was unusually clear, and miles away they made out a tall peak ringed by a mushroom-shaped cloud. It had never previously been visible.

"Him Grewink," the nearest Indian explained in answer to their questioning gaze. "Him smoke all time." He laughed heartily at his own little joke, and asked:

"Mebbe you like smoke, too?"

Rill contemplated the distant peak and presently turned to the sailor beside him:

"Remember the triangle in the inscription that I couldn't make out? I've got it now. That stands for old Grewink or a fellow just like him. See what happened? The volcano began to stir up, and the wise ones left in a hurry. Then they had a big time here, and what with the volcano spouting and earthquakes, they thought the world was ending. Of course it was their god that did it for vengeance, they'd say, and put to sea. A tidal wave or a big storm finished that batch, and the survivors wrote it up on their altar stone. That's some story, Pug."

"But the green thing — that was what drove them out. I don't see how we got away ourselves. I wouldn't go down that shaft again if it was lined with gold —"

Rill, sucking his under lip, gazed up at the spangled cloth of the heavens. The Indians paddled steadily, talking among themselves, guiding the canoe over the lazy, dark swells. Rill appeared to have reached a decision.

"You're a good scout, Pug," he said "You've always been there in the pinch. I was counting on your scare of the green fellow to keep you out of it; I was going to claim the mine and get capital to work it, with you out of the way. But you've been square with me, and I'll play the game square for once. The green devil you saw was just a mummy. He's one of the miners that got caught in the earthquake — mighty bad to look at but perfectly harmless, Pug."

"A mummy? You're kidding!"

"No. You see, he was buried in the copper ore, and instead of decaying, he absorbed certain minerals that petrified him, preserved him. Next time you're in New York go to the museum and look at one of them that they found in a copper mine in Chile. In the case of this fellow, somebody must have begun digging, probably the Indian that started the legend, and uncovered him. We'll work up the mine proposition together."

Death's Secret*

et me see," said Talcott, "you have everything, have you?" He stepped to the laden pony and ran his hands over the multitude of things strapped to his sides. "You have your spade, your bar, your tackle. Better take another water-bottle; you never can tell about water by what the natives say, and you want enough to bring you back as well as take you out there. You have forage for this beast. And one, two, three tins of food for yourself. And picket rope. It is a bit unpleasant to be out in the desert and have your horses run away."

He stepped back a pace, looked the equipment over with a keen professional glance, nodded his satisfaction, and then turned to the young man who stood at his side.

"Now stand up here and let me inspect you. Tumble your things out here on this box and let me make sure that you have everything here that you ought to have."

Williamson smiled and took from his many pockets his watch, his compass, his medical kit, his map. Talcott looked at them keenly, nodded, and the younger man put them all back.

"And now let's look at your horse. Lift up, here!" He went around the four feet of the horse, inspecting each hoof carefully, peered at his eyes and into his mouth.

"Everything all right. You must forgive me if I seem to be a bit of an old maid about these things, but you remember that it was for want of a nail that the battle was lost."

"That's all right, sir," said the younger man; "just what I want."

"Now for the final instructions," said Talcott; "it ought to be just about eight miles out to this oasis that the natives told us about. You may find something there, and you may not. Sketch anything that interests you, and remember that it is always better to err on the side of fullness than the other way. If there is anything there to be brought back which you cannot bring yourself, heliograph me, and I will come. There is a lot of interesting stuff in Samarkund, but I think that it is all here in the city. There would be no sense in putting anything away off there in the desert."

Williamson mounted and Talcott took his hand in his own strong grasp.

"You have my leave to depart," he said, smiling.

As the other dug his heels into the sides of his mount, he called out, "Williamson! Perhaps you had better take this. There is only one

* "Death's Secret" was written by J.L. Schoolcraft, pseud. of Frederick Faust (1892 – 1944) and originally published in 1917 (source unknown). The text for this edition came from *Fantastic Novels*, Jul. 1950.

chance in a thousand that you will have any use for it, but scientists should be prepared for just that thousandth chance."

He came alongside the other and pressed an automatic pistol into his hand.

"Here is ammunition."

"Nothing out there but a scorpion and a wild date or two," laughed the younger man, "but I suppose I had best take it."

With that he slapped the pony across the flank and started up what had once been the main thoroughfare of the ancient city of Samarkund. Now there was nothing to mark it but a pair of jagged stone stumps of what had been the posts to the gate. They were twice as thick as a man's body, and near one lay a capital of red stone, richly and curiously carved with the palm leaves as motif. Away on either side of the street stretched jagged lines of wall that had been uncovered. About them lay all the equipment of the expedition — shovels, small for the puny laborers that they had, and a narrow track with a car running out to a sand dump.

Williamson passed this and circled the laborers' camp. Tiny fires glowed like cigarette-butts in the dusk; goat-bells tinkled suddenly and were still. He turned his back to the camp and struck off through the desert.

The light in the heavens died with startling quickness, and stars, still strange to his northern eyes, burned in the velvet arc above him. Ahead of him rolled a ghostly procession of small hills. This was the desert of Panarshot — "The road to hell."

"And well named, too," said Williamson to himself. Like most men who are much alone, he had the habit of thinking aloud. "Sand and sand, and the only harvest those red knobs of rock!"

For two hours he rode, halting at half-hour intervals to breathe his horse. About the feet of the little beast the sand sucked in a silken whisper. It was hard going.

At the sixth halt a moon the color of ripe grain pushed up over the horizon with theatrical quickness. The whole country was bathed in a mellow, strong light, so clear that each wave in the sand threw a shadow black as ink. Where the moon struck, the sand glistened, making a path of light for all the world like that which it was casting somewhere else on a smooth water.

"Like a summer sea," said Williamson, "like a frozen summer sea."

He stood for a moment, lost in the vast beauty of the scene, then mounted, and struck off to the south. Soon he saw a delicate black filigree of palm trees — three of them — sprung from one base and drooping apart with languid grace.

"That must be Anarshan," he said.

The filigree slid slowly across the great; bright circle. When it had been quite gone for a half-hour, his horse raised his head, whinnied, and struck into a shuffling trot which carried him shortly to the edge of the oasis.

It was hardly more than twenty feet across. A carpet of coarse grass which gave up a pungent smell when crushed under the pony's hoofs spread about a spring that gushed up at the foot of the three palms. The water flowed, flaked with great patches of liquid silver where the moon struck it, then seeped off into the sand.

Williamson dismounted, eased the girths of the saddle, washed out the pony's mouth, and allowed him a few gulps of water.

From somewhere out on the desert came a queer, quavering cry. It began as a low wail and sharpened to a high scream of seeming anguish. The pony threw up his head and stood with nervously pointing ears.

"Steady!" said his master, and slipped back into the shadow of the trees, and threw a clip of cartridges into his pistol. He looked in the direction from which the pony was snuffing wind. He saw nothing but a rolling flat of country, silver with black patches where the red rock broke through the sand.

The pony was stock-still, trembling slightly.

For five minutes he stood tense, listening. Then his mount dropped his head to his forage and went on munching contentedly.

"Probably a jackal," said Williamson.

"Odd, though. Never heard one that sounded at all like that. Somewhere between animal and human. But the pony seems contented."

Still watchful, he opened a food tin and supped on army biscuit, chocolate, and raisins, washing them down with water from the spring. When he was finished, and had completed unsaddling his horse, the moon had ridden half across the heavens. He pressed the spring of his repeater, and the strokes beat upon the air like tiny silver hammers — three for the quarters, twelve for the hour.

"Quarter to one," he said. "Must be at work at four. Remember to whinny, Bucephalus, if anything comes around."

He leaned against a tree-trunk, started to light a cigarette, then thought of the strange cry, did not, put his automatic close at hand, and fell asleep. When he awoke, the world was white with dawn. He stretched, walked up and down to get the stiffness out of his back and legs, washed, and started on a tour of inspection.

"Jove!" he exclaimed, as he rounded the tree-trunks. "Here is something!"

He was standing in front of a low, oblong structure about as long as a tall man, and a yard and a half wide. It was almost covered with sand; the door, however, was clear of it. From ground to roof he estimated it as being about five feet, although the sand made it impossible to know exactly.

Excitement leaped up in his eyes, and he started for the spade which stuck up out of his pile of equipment. But he checked himself and laughed.

"Food first!" he said. "Anyone would think that this was the first time you ever had seen an ancient tomb. It is almost the first."

He boiled some chocolate over a spirit lamp, made some soup from the concentrated powder he carried with him, breakfasted, fed the horse, and turned to examine his find.

As he looked, admiration grew. It was a beautiful piece of workmanship, built of the red porous rock in which the country abounded. He knew how difficult it was to work the soft material, but here the slabs had been so carefully made that in no joint could be thrust a leaf of the thinnest paper. The dryness of the country had prevented erosion; the joints stood out in thin, straight lines. For this reason and because there was no decoration, he could not even estimate the age of the structure.

There was a door, a single slab, with a crack running from top to bottom. To push it in might crush some relic of priceless value. A plan of campaign opened out in his mind; he would enlarge that crevice, draw out each half of the door. He took hammer and chisel from his equipment and set to work.

At noon he threw them aside impatiently. The heat was insufferable; to go on might mean that he would never return to camp. He sat down in the shade of the palms, made a sketch of the tomb as it stood, and waited for the sun to pass the meridian.

The sun was low in the west when he cut through for the first time. He paused long enough to eat, and feed his horse. The stars came out with the suddenness of city lights, and he was at it again. The rock lay about him in broad flakes.

At last the crack down the middle was broadened to a gap three inches in breadth. He inserted his iron bar, pried gently, and one side of the broken door fell outward. Using his bar as a lever, he worked it outward, and propped it against the side of the tomb. The other slab followed and the broad doorway yawned blackly before him. A breath of hot air came out of it laden with an odor of spicy sweetness.

Williamson flashed his torchlight into the darkness. The light came back to him from a dozen colors of great richness.

Exultant, he put his head and shoulders inside the door, but withdrew quickly. It was stifling; the rock held the heat of a day, and the odor, while indescribably sweet, was almost overpowering.

Patiently he sat, fanning with his helmet in an endeavor to get new air into the black, tunnel-like structure before him. The sky yellowed; it was almost time for the moon to be up.

The odor that flowed out, heavily sweet, seemed to be compounded of that given off by some fragrant wood, a strong cinnamon-like smell and delicate lily-like scent. After he had fanned a quarter of an hour, he put his head within the doorway again. The air was comparatively fresh. He wriggled his body in and flashed his torch about him.

As the circle of brilliant white light struck the walls, an exclamation of joy escaped him.

The whole interior was a mass of brilliant decoration. The soft stone had been polished with the greatest care; even so, it did not take on the mirror-like finish that a harder stone would have; instead, the decoration lay on a background of satiny red.

"It's Egyptian!" he exclaimed as the patch of light struck upon a frieze of alternate lotus and Anubis figures. This frieze ran about the four sides, close under the roof. The roof itself was a maze of running arabesques filled with gold. The pattern was repeated in the floor without the filling of gold. The walls were paneled broadly, and within each panel were stripes of raw red and blue.

At his side he felt the smooth roundness of a mummy case. He threw his light on it.

Outside, on the still air came the queer, blood-curdling cry. His heart caught. As best he could in his cramped position, he whirled about. His horse was whickering and plunging. One of the slabs which had made half of the door slid slowly from its position and fell across the opening. He jerked in his feet and saved them by the fraction of an inch. He fired once through the open door.

The acrid smell of powder curled about him. Outside was the sand glistening in the serene light of the moon. His horse's hoofs clattered against the stone as he raced up and down at the end of his tether.

For five minutes he lay, scarcely breathing. Then he put his helmet on his foot and protruded it through the opening. It remained, black against the light outside, undisturbed. There was still room for his body in the door; he squirmed out as best he could and sprang to his feet, clutching the comforting butt of his automatic.

The desert slept, mile upon mile, gentle wave after gentle wave of impassive, dreaming sand. The shadows of the palms fell inky black and deadly still. The spring whispered and snickered at his feet.

"Where is it, old fellow," he said to the horse, which stood snuffing and trembling, "and what is it?"

His mount turned his head this way and that, rolled his eyes, then dropped his head to his forage again.

"It may be that I did not prop up that slab squarely enough," he said slowly, "and it may be that I did. At any rate, I stay outside tonight."

Weary from his labor of the day before, he slept through until long after dawn. When he awoke he circled the camp, but there were no prints either in the sand or on the rock. But the desert sand is almost a living thing, endowed with a motion of its own; even if the wind did not blow, he knew that it moved and covered things with what seemed to be of its own will.

As soon as the sun was up he mounted a little hillock and began flashing a message to Talcott. For a quarter of an hour his call shot across the desert. Then an answering flash of light winked out, and he signaled:

"Come at once. Bring a draft animal."

"Am starting at once," came the answer.

With that he turned to breakfast, feeding his horse and making his little camp clean for the keen eyes of his chief.

Then he stood looking at his find.

"Too bad we have not a tractor," he said regretfully; "the whole thing ought to be in the British Museum."

His resolution to stay outside until someone was there to watch weakened under the spell of the fascinating mystery before him. He entered the tomb, this time to look at the mummy case.

The floor was a solid slab, and, part of it, two trestles rose to the height of about six inches. They supported a case of what had been yellow wood, superbly lacquered. But age had turned the bright yellow to a golden brown. It was a short case, almost that of a child. He thought that it must be that of a child until he looked at the face of the occupant which was painted on the outside.

Instead of the conventionalized face common to most of the cases he had seen, this one was done with consummate art. It was a portrait — the portrait of a girl just coming to womanhood. The eyes were opened, deep with mystery. The lips were full and still bright in color. Eyebrows, small and fine, and the hair, almost concealing the low, broad forehead, were inky black. The smooth roundness of the case told him, too, that this was all that was left of some girl grown into womanhood with the sudden bloom of the tropics.

The rest of the cover held only conventionalized patterns; yet he found, there, the wavy line which stands for the Nile and the dog-headed figure of Anubis.

The wood of the case had shrunk; a long crack showed where the cover had been joined, and the pegs could be seen like uncovered tendons. It was only necessary to grip with the fingers and pull strongly in order to lift the cover quite off. This Williamson did, revealing a figure, wrapped with the finest of cloth, which still retained the roundness of youth.

There were no jewels or gold. In one end of the case was a small porphyry case filled with some substances which still gave off a poignantly sweet, lily-like odor. The treasure lay in the profusion of decoration and in the infinite care with which it was executed.

In the foot of the case was a small bamboo box, sealed at either end with a tarlike substance. It was becoming unbearably warm in the tomb; he took the bamboo case out with him into the open, chipped off the ends, and drew out a tightly rolled manuscript made on papyrus of wafer thinness, still soft.

He laid it across his knees. The writing was Egyptian, the black and red still bright. Sitting in the shade of palms, he set to deciphering it.

This is the story of Nalinthia, daughter of Notki, priest of Anubis.

"All right, my dear," he said; "but how did you get up here?"

I tell this my story in order that vengeance may be taken for me and in order that my body may be buried after the fashion of my kind, and not be burned as is the custom among these beasts living here.

For my body must be whole against the time when the spirit will come again. I shudder to think of my soul wandering through eternity looking for a body. And the flames curling about me!

Williamson laughed gently at this naïve touch. But his amusement deepened to intense interest as he read into the story. Abruptly the tone changed to that of passionate appeal.

Oh, my beloved one! Thou who wouldst have been my husband had I not been torn from thee by those I loathe to name. A child I was, for since my birth fourteen summers had flooded the Nile when I was taken by these who were guests in my father's house.

But for the memory of thee I had died long since. For I knew that some time thou wouldst find me and we could be happy again. But now my body has become a loathing to me, and even thy love, great as the Nile, could not accept me.

I have taken my life, which is against the express command of Anubis, but I have been told by a sign that for me it is fit. And I shall rest easy in the halls of the dead, knowing that for each of my wrongs thou wilt take a life. And some time when the rolling years have come to a new time we shall be together again, for I know that my soul will find these as long as I am I.

Read, then, the story of my wrongs.

For upward of an hour Williamson toiled with the hieroglyphics.

When he had finished he sat motionless for a long time. The sun was at its height; the desert was a mass of leaping, vaporous heat-waves through which the patches of rock nodded and leaped.

At last he rose to his feet.

"Poor little kid!" he murmured. "Poor little kid!"

He passed his hand over his brow, trying to dispel the sense of reality that the story inspired in him. It was a tale of cruelty and refined wickedness that made his clean Anglo-Saxon blood run cold.

He turned again to the manuscript. There was a sentence at the bottom which he had overlooked. There was the conventional figure of the story-teller — a man squatting before another. Then there was the sun and an arc indicating the passage of twenty-four hours. Then there was the figure of the boatman which stood for death.

"Whoever tells this story will die within twenty-four hours," he translated; *"it is not good that such things be in the minds of men. I have had a sign that this shall be so."*

"You may trust me," he said earnestly; "you may trust me! I hope that revenge was taken, and fully." He turned to the tomb. "So that was how this came to be built. Done by her sweetheart. A labor of love!"

It was with a feeling of reverence that he entered the structure again and set about sketching the decoration. As he worked away, this new contact with reality led him to say, "Of course I do not believe that the curse holds."

Nevertheless, when the distorted figures of Talcott's caravan hove in sight, he resolved for the time being to say nothing about his find. He slipped it into his sketching-case. The figures came sliding across the long slope, leaping to gigantic proportions one minute and dwindling to absurdity the next. The sun had declined, and the faint breeze was talking hoarsely in the palms, but heat-waves still bounded from the sand, and each nubbin of red rock was a center of fanning irradiation.

"What ho!" sang out Talcott as his figure drew down to normal. His browned, strong face was shiny with sweat. With him was Purdy, the engineer of the expedition, a short, blond man with a continual worried pucker between his eyes. His first words were:

"Well, let's get things started. Lord only knows what those natives are doing while we are gone."

"What did you find?" asked Talcott.

"A tomb done in pure Egyptian, a mummy, a sick jackal yowling, are all that I have to report."

"Anything in the mummy case?"

"No, sir."

Talcott wedged his broad shoulders into the opening, and the others could hear him muttering to himself, "Extraordinary! The whole thing ought to be in the British Museum! Beautiful work! Purest Egyptian. Cannot get it out with our present equipment. Marvelous perfume. Still sweet after twenty-five centuries. Lotus, I should say."

At last he backed out.

"It's a find, all right!" he said, wiping the sweat from his forehead. "There was nothing in the case to explain how this Egyptian work came into existence three hundred leagues from the Nile?"

"No, sir; nothing there but the body and the porphyry box."

"Well, it will give us all some beautiful chances for theory, and there is nothing that a scientist loves more than a hypothesis. We can sling the mummy and case on one of the camels. It is a shame that we have not the wheeled equipment to take the whole thing right with us. It is a remarkable find, all right. You deserve the credit. Young man," he said, looking down at his subordinate, while a kindly smile played around his earnest eyes, "it will make you famous, for the whole story of this part of the expedition will be done by you in a separate monograph."

Williamson laughed like a boy.

"Thank you, sir," he said. "This is certainly kind of you."

The mummy case was brought out with infinite care, wrapped in many yards of burlap and dried moss, put in a box that Purdy knocked together out of some lumber which had ridden on the back of a camel, and the whole was hoisted to the back of the grunting beast.

By starlight they set out, and the palms faded behind them into the limitless darkness of the desert night. The sand flowed about the feet of the animals in a silken whisper; the natives chattered in high, feminine voices; the pony bridles clinked, and the camels grunted heavily.

The men pushed up over the hills; each wrinkle in the sand lay clear, silver and jet; back of them the palm fronds were touched into a fine tracery of the same colors.

Williamson turned in his saddle to say good-by to this place where so much had come to him. It was to make him, a comparatively young and unknown man, into one whose name would be heard with respect by the scientific world.

Was that a cry that he heard — a sound that began in the low register and climbed to a scream almost feminine in shrillness? It was ghostly thin. His horse pricked up its ears and turned its head, paused, blew through its nostrils, then put his head down and plodded on.

Williamson pushed ahead where the chunky figure of Talcott loomed up at the head of the procession.

"Did you hear that jackal, sir?"

"No." said the other: "riding close to these grunting beasts, one could not hear the trump of doom."

Back in the camp, Williamson turned to working up the report which would make his name famous in the world of Oriental science. An Egyptian tomb found in the desert of Puntarshot, a thousand miles from the Nile, had just the touch of the unusual necessary to stimulate interest in his work. He knew how the strangeness of such a thing would tantalize the curiosity of his colleagues.

What to do with the story of the girl, he did not know. He had fibbed instinctively to Talcott. The story had touched him deeply, and at the time when Talcott had put his question he was still under the spell of it. He had the same hesitation at repeating the story as he would have had about retelling a bit of gossip about some of his own women friends in England.

But how to make the report complete without telling the story he did not know. He was certain that sooner or later, unless he did tell the thing, some one of his colleagues would hint that young explorer's imagination had run away with him, and that this Egyptian tomb was not all that was claimed for it.

As he went deeper and deeper into the work and saw what a treasure he had come across, the feeling of reluctance faded, and the passion of the scientist to tell the truth grew.

At length he decided to put the matter up to Talcott, a man of great experience, whose high scientific ideals were tempered by a kindly spirit.

He found Talcott sitting in front of his tent on a camp-stool that bent perilously under his weight. Before him, he had some fragments of pottery which had been unearthed that day. He was inspecting them by the light of an acetylene lamp at his side.

"Nothing new," he said, in response to the greeting of his subaltern. Nevertheless, he wrapped them carefully, marked them, and put them away in his tent.

"Sit down, my boy," he said. "You will find a box in the tent."

When Williamson was seated and drawing on his pipe, Talcott said, "How is the report coming? Have you any theory as to how this tomb came to be here, so far from home?"

"No, sir," said Williamson quietly. "I know."

"Indeed! How?"

"I found a manuscript in the mummy case, which I told no one about. I am not sure I ought to tell any one about it now. It is partly a matter of sentiment and partly a matter of honor."

For a moment the older man pulled away at his pipe.

"I do not see why I should not leave it to you," he said, with kindly seriousness. "Of course we have a duty to the men who sent us out here and another duty to the truth. As a matter of fact, that is the only allegiance that men of our sort have — an allegiance to the truth."

"Quite right, sir. But suppose this is of no value to science?"

Talcott sat upright in his chair.

"Anything that is true is of value," he said earnestly; "anything that is true! We may not see the bearing of it at once; some day some one may come along and build on the humble foundations we have laid. I knew a man at Oxford who spent his time counting the words in the world's great books. He numbered them in the Bible, the Koran, Shakespeare, Cervantes, and so on. We used to laugh at him; but one day he went into a court, testified in a lawsuit between printer and editor, and saved a grave injustice. You have heard of Burnside, who spent most of his life in Australia classifying the insects there. He died, but in the next generation some one built on his work and saved the commonwealth millions of dollars by using Burnside's notes in his work of exterminating insect pests.

"The chain may not be clear to you in this case, but remember that we live in a present which has its roots in the past. The slightest knowledge we have of that past may mean a great deal to us in the present.

"It is the great glory of science that it has but one allegiance — the truth!"

"I forgot to say, sir, that there is a threat at the end of the manuscript, which says that any one who tells this story will die within twenty-four hours. Of course, I have no fear of this threat. A fifteen-year old girl, dying twenty-five centuries ago, more or less, could have no effect on men today."

"Undoubtedly not," said his chief.

"Sir, I will put it to you. The manuscript in the mummy case told the story of a girl, written by herself, who was abducted and subjected to such torture, mental and physical, as I had not dreamed possible. She told the story in order that her sweetheart might avenge her, and I hope to God that he did! At the end she says that it is not good that such things be in the minds of men, and adds the threat which I have spoken of — that any one who tells the story will be dead within twenty-four hours. You know that I am not afraid, but I felt, somehow or other, that the girl was putting me on my honor."

"M-m," said the chief. "In love with a mummy?"

"Not at all."

For a long time Talcott was silent.

"I see no reason why I should not leave it to you," he said finally. "I put this thing into your hands. I see your point, and it does you credit to feel as you do.

"Of course there is nothing to be afraid of. We are Europeans living in an age which worships test tubes, not Egyptians living in an age which worshipped cats."

"Very well, sir," said Williamson. "I shall tell you the whole thing, and you can give me some advice as to how best to present the story. It ought to be a sensation in the scientific world."

There was the rasp of hobnails on the ground, and Purdy drifted in out of the darkness.

The worried pucker was deeper.

"Sorry to bother you," he said, "but the beggars seem to be a bit restless tonight. Think there is anything wrong?"

Talcott bent his head and listened to the hum that came from the jumbled mass of shadows and tiny points of light that stood for the laborers' camp.

"Any liquor?"

"Not that I know of."

"Any speeches?"

"No."

Talcott listened for a moment more.

"Sounds normal," he said. "Look out for speeches and liquor. You do a great deal of unnecessary worrying, Purdy. Sit down. Williamson has something interesting to impart."

"This is the story of Nalinthia, daughter of Notki, priest of Anubis," began Williamson.

For fifteen minutes his voice sounded in the quiet night. Talcott's pipe went out. Purdy sat with his head bent, staring at the ground. The hum of busy life in the native camp softened as the brown men dropped off to sleep.

When the voice had ceased, they were all silent for a moment.

Then Purdy leaped to his feet.

"My God!" he cried. "Isn't there some thing that can be done to make up for that? What incredible beasts! I hope to God there is a future life, and I hope that the little girl's curse against them holds, and that somewhere those hyenas are stewing in boiling oil."

"You forget," said Talcott in his strong, even voice, "that if the curse against them holds good, so does the curse against the man who repeats the yarn. That man happens to be our young friend who is here."

"You're right!" said Purdy. "Good Lord! I would not tell that story for all the money in the world!"

"You are a rank sentimentalist!" said Talcott. "The girl has been at peace now for several thousands of years. So have those who are responsible for her death. We might hang them in effigy or send up prayers that their souls be tortured; I see no other way for us to do anything against them."

"But aren't you afraid?" said Purdy to Williamson.

"Of course he is not!" interposed the chief crisply. "Of course not! This is the twentieth century."

"Twentieth century or not," said Purdy in retort, "I have seen just enough to know that the Orient is closer to the twentieth century before Christ than it is to the twentieth century after Christ.

"Eleven o'clock," said Talcott. "Time we all turned in."

The next day Williamson ran into a snag in making his report. There was one point in his sketch of the frieze of the tomb which was not quite clear. It had been dark in the place when he made his drawings, and he had put in but one section of the frieze, since all the sections were the same. But whether the dog-headed figure faced to the right or the left, he was not sure. The sketch seemed to show that it faced to the left, but this was in defiance of all Egyptian tradition. He must make sure. There was nothing for it but to make a trip to the tomb and settle the matter.

"I can go tonight," he calculated. "Make sure in about five minutes, and be back before noon tomorrow."

He went to where Purdy and Talcott were directing the excavation of a temple site.

"Can you spare me? I must go back to the tomb to make sure about a detail in the decoration."

"Certainly," said Talcott.

"Good Lord!" said Purdy, "if I were you I would put myself in a safety deposit vault until the twenty-four hours which you are given after telling that yarn have expired."

"Rot!" said Williamson, and the chief joined him in his laugh at Purdy's fear.

Talcott gave him his customary inspection before he started. Williamson found that his watch had run down, set it to accord with the dial on Talcott's wrist, and started out for his journey to the oasis of Anarshan.

For one who professed such contempt for the threat of the dead princess, Talcott was rather attentive to the time of his subaltern's return. Noontime came and with it no Williamson.

"What time did he say he would be back?" asked Purdy.

"According to his estimate, he should be back now," replied the other, "but his work may have taken him more time than he thought."

They sat down to a lunch of tinned beef, army soup, jam, and tea.

"You know, chief," said Purdy, "if I were you I would not have let that boy out of my sight for those twenty-four hours. I may be a fool."

"You are," was the prompt response. "The boy is much safer here than he would be in his own home in London. Safest place in the world. No trains to push you down, no buses to run over you, no disease germs."

"Yes," replied the engineer, "nothing here but a lot of grinning hyenas who would knife you for a copper cent. They have been milling around a bit tonight."

"Purdy, you are an efficient man all right, but you would be much more efficient if you did not worry so much."

Supper time came but Williamson did not. Talcott undressed and lay on his cot. It was only after he had lain there for a moment that he realized that mechanically he had put his revolver close to his side and that his hand was clutching the butt of it, and that he was gaining a great deal of subconscious comfort thereby.

He laughed shortly, put the pistol out of bed, and resolutely fell asleep.

He was awakened by Purdy's scratching on his tent wall.

"Yes," he said, instantly awake and collected, "anything wrong?"

"Oh, nothing special," was the reply, "I just could not sleep and wondered if you had some bromide."

"Bromide nothing! What are you worrying about now?"

"Nothing. On my word, chief!"

"What time is it?" asked Talcott.

"One o'clock."

"He ought to be back," said Talcott.

"I was thinking that, too," said the other.

"Let's see," said Talcott, "it is eight miles out there. He started at evening — at six. I remember that he set his watch. He would be there by ten at least, unless he lost his way and this is highly improbable. His sketching may have taken him five minutes and it may have taken him five hours. If it took him five minutes, he should have been back yesterday at noon; if it took him five hours, he should have been back last evening."

He stood with his head bent, calm, self-possessed, every faculty of a trained mind, a strong body, and a calm spirit bent on the problem before him. Purdy was comforted in the presence of the strength before him. He never ceased to wonder at his chief — a man who never made a joke, and yet who was never lacking in kindness and thoughtfulness, a man who was never so much himself as in the presence of a difficult problem.

"We will wait here one hour," said Talcott crisply. "If, at the end of that time, he has not come back, you go out with two of the best natives. I will stay here. I can handle anything that might arise here and can keep the work going."

Silently they walked to Purdy's tent, which stood on the edge of the native camp. They piled saddle, bridle, water bottles, forage in front of it and stood waiting. From somewhere out on the desert came a faint, rhythmic sound. It ceased. Talcott stood with his head bent, impassive, ears strained to this new note in the heavy silence.

Somewhere near them a native started to his feet and ran, his hands over his head, eyes closed, moaning in a dream. Talcott's heavy boot caught him in the shins, he tumbled and lay prone, silent.

The sounds came again.

"Thank God!" said Purdy. "Here he comes!"

"Hush!" said Talcott.

The sound strengthened to a drumbeat of horse's hoofs.

"That horse is running with an empty saddle," said Talcott calmly. "No man would ride like that. Hear him stumble."

There was a slithering clatter on the rock and for a moment the beat of hoofs stopped, only to be taken up again with increased sound. About them, in the dark, shrill voices arose and they could see the dark glimmer of naked bodies as the sleepers sprang up in a wild scramble.

Williamson's horse careened through the camp, stirrups flying.

Talcott caught him by the rein and threw the whole weight of his body against the already exhausted beast. He came to a stop and stood with his head scarce six inches from the ground. The sand flew up in puffs to his labored breathing; he stood with his legs apart and his belly sucked up in an agony of exhaustion.

Talcott was at the saddle in an instant, throwing the white light of an electric torch over its surface. From that he went to the other equipment, examining it all with the greatest care and trying to apply logic to the evidence at hand.

"First, we must know whether or not the accident took place before he reached the tomb, or after," he said, more to himself than to Purdy, who was standing with the lines in his brow deepened to helplessness.

"The water bottles are full, but he might have filled them at the spring. We might tell by the taste of the water except that the canteen flavors everything. The forage is gone; therefore the probability is that he used it all up and was starting back. But this is weakened by the fact that the pony has been galloping and may have thrown it off. The same with his sketches. There are no marks on the saddle. Some of the food tins are gone, but they may also have been thrown. There are no marks on the saddle or on the pony's back.

"Purdy, take two of the best men from the camp and go out. Take your rifle. Scour the country on each side of the trail. You will find no prints in the sand worth anything because of its shifting. Watch for marks on the rock."

He led the staggering pony away and then put the expedition in motion.

During the day and the night in which Purdy was gone, Talcott had never been more exact or more exacting. The records for work done on those days surpassed any others. His finds were scrupulously labeled and filed away; any native loafing behind a foundation wall was sure to hear the deep voice booming at him.

In the early morning Purdy came riding in, white, the pucker between his eyes deeper than ever. Talcott met him, talked calmly in the presence of the natives and followed Purdy to his tent, helped him off with his boots, and mixed him a bromide.

"No signs at all," said Purdy helplessly. "Tomb sealed up as we left it. I opened it, but there was nothing there. There are no signs on the road. I sent men out on each side, but they found nothing."

Talcott nodded, and left his subordinate to sleep.

For two days they worked with nothing to indicate that anything was wrong. They were hard put for records — Williamson had been the only man who could sketch — the heat had made photographic plates useless.

On the third day there was trouble in the native camp. When the dawn came, a half dozen of them did not arise, but lay snoring stertorously.

In some way native liquor had been smuggled into the camp — villainous stuff made of young palm shoots, crushed and fermented.

Another half dozen of the natives reeled under the lashes of the headmen. One of them, a short, undernourished thing, staggered past Talcott, stumbled and fell. From his breech clout rolled something that glistened in the new light, trundled over the sand in a long, eccentric curve, and came to rest at Talcott's feet.

It was Williamson's watch.

He stooped, picked it up.

"Bring that man to my tent," he said to the headman, "he needs punishment."

He turned to where Purdy was scolding helplessly, trying to get the gangs into some sort of organization. With a few words of brisk command, Talcott had them under control, fed, and at work.

For an hour he watched them. "Come to my tent soon. Make it casual," he said to Purdy.

In his tent he found the native lying doubled, the whites of his eyes showing through parted lids. The white man straightened him, gagged him with a tightly rolled bandage from his medicine kit, sprinkled water on his head, and put a bottle of aromatic spirits under his nose.

The man groaned, rolled his head from side to side, and opened his eyes.

Purdy strolled in, stopped still at the sight.

Talcott held up a warning hand.

"This rolled out of his breech clout just now," he said and held out the watch.

"Murder," gasped Purdy, "with robbery as motive!"

The blank, rolling eyes of the native looked about, with intelligence dawning in them, and after intelligence, fear.

"What do you know about this?" Talcott demanded.

The eyes closed, and the face took on the impassivity of a sphinx.

Talcott jerked the man to a sitting posture.

"Tell me!" he said in a low voice. "You are the man who has bad dreams. I saw you running in your sleep, pursued by a dream. Tell, or I swear that for the rest of your days you will be haunted by visions of drowned men and women who have died by violence."

The face remained impassive.

"I speak the truth," Talcott went on, "and I give you this for a sign."

He tore a piece of fine paper into a dozen pieces, rolled them into a ball, breathed upon it, unrolled them. The paper came out untorn.

The tobacco brown eyes of the native widened in terror at this. He drew himself to Talcott's feet, touched them twice with his forehead.

He looked up like a frightened spaniel and nodded his head.

"And remember that this is to be spoken of by no one. If you tell aught that has passed here, the curse will hold."

The native nodded again, and his inquisitor took the gag from his mouth.

"Where did you get this?"

He held up the watch.

"From the body of the sketching effendi."

"What does he say? What does he say?" asked Purdy, whose mastery of the native tongue had never been too complete.

"And where does the body lie?"

"Two leagues from this camp on the road to Anarshan."

"You killed the sketching effendi to get his watch and his money," said Talcott. "Tell me the truth or I swear that you will suffer so that each day of your life will be as a year."

The thin body twitched and trembled, and he broke into a flood of protest.

"No, effendi, I swear by the soul of my mother! The effendi's body lay by the side of the road. I did not tell master for fear he would stop the work and then we all should starve. I had of him his watch. Others had of him his pistol and other things. I swear by my hope of Nirvana that he was not struck by me or by any other man of this camp. We know not how he came to his death. His head was split so" — he drew his finger in a curved line from crown to brow — "and his face was not the face we knew."

"He lies!" said Purdy, who had gathered the drift of what was being said. "His body is not by the roadside. I looked, and two others marched on each side of the road to see. There is no body there."

"The engineer effendi says that you lie. He looked through his glass which sees all things, and no body lies by the road."

"It did," said the native humbly. "We moved it — two others and myself, for the jackals were about and we feared that if it were found the work would cease and we should all starve. I will fetch the other things which we had of him."

"What beasts," groaned Purdy. "Typical native logic. As though we would not find him sooner or later."

"Go!" said Talcott to the native. "Bring the other things that were the sketching effendi's property. Speak no word of this!"

The native slid out of the tent, and Purdy wiped his brow.

"I did not know you were a juggler," he said to Talcott.

His chief made no answer, but stood with his brows knitted.

Within five minutes there was a scratching at the tent wall, and a brown arm laid Williamson's pistol, his belt, his pen, and his purse on the ground.

"Wait," said Talcott. "Be ready to go with us in a moment."

"My God! My God!" said Purdy. "What a fine lad he was!"

"Was!" said Talcott sharply. "Is! How do we know the beggar is not lying? You make me weary with your imaginings!"

As they swung into saddle, he said, "I beg your pardon for speaking bruskly. Of course you are right. There is not one chance in a thousand."

They found Williamson lying in a crevice about a hundred yards off the road. The head was crushed. In addition it was swollen almost beyond recognition. There were deep scratches in the flesh, perhaps made by being dragged over the rock by a maddened horse.

Purdy wept as they straightened the clean young body, and folded the hands across the breast. Talcott stood at the head and repeated as best he could the prayer of the English church for those fallen far from home.

"Dust to dust — ashes to ashes. Amen."

They filled in the grave with loose stones, marked it as best they could, noted its location carefully on a map, and turned toward camp.

Two nights later, Purdy scratched at his chief's tent flap.

"Come in," said the latter in a low voice. "I was not sleeping, either."

"See here!" Purdy burst out." This thing is getting on my nerves. What I want to know is: did the boy die within twenty-four hours after telling that damned story!"

"I do not know," said Talcott.

"Isn't there some way of finding out?" groaned Purdy. "I am not such an inhuman machine as you are. It's getting on my nerves!"

"I do not blame you," said his chief patiently; "it is a gruesome thing."

"If he died on the way out," said Purdy, "he died before those twenty-four hours were up. He was found about six miles out. It would take him about three hours to get there. He started at six, which means that he died at about nine. That is, if he were thrown on the way to Anarshan. And if he was thrown on the way out, that damned story did him in! If he was killed on the way back, it did not. The point is, when did it happen, when he was going out or coming back?"

"As far as I can see, it makes no difference," said Talcott calmly; "the boy is dead and that is the end of it."

But he added, a moment later, throwing up his head, "It does make a difference. I persuaded the boy to tell his story. It is a good thing to know. We are all working in the cause of science, and it is my duty as a scientist to know all that can be known!"

"Yes, but how?" said Purdy helplessly. "How?"

"I have his watch. The crystal is broken, the case is dented, and the hands are bent. But I have ascertained that the works are all right and that the man who found it did not know enough to wind it."

He brought out the watch and pressed the spring of the repeating mechanism. The strokes rang out on the still night — nine for the hour and no more.

"It stopped at nine o'clock," he said.

"Just as I said," exclaimed Purdy. "He was killed at nine o'clock; just as I said!"

"It may have been nine in the morning," replied his chief calmly. With his strong fingers which could be so gentle with some fragile treasure which he had unearthed, he bent the hands until one stood at nine and the other at twelve.

"I saw the boy wind this watch tightly at six just as he started. It is a Swiss movement and will run accurately just twenty-eight hours. At the end of that time it stops. This watch has run from six until nine. If it stopped at nine in the morning, it will run for twenty-eight less fifteen, making thirteen hours. If it stopped at nine o'clock in the evening it will run twenty-five hours. The only thing to do is to start the thing off and see if it goes beyond thirteen hours."

He looked at the luminous dial strapped to his own wrist.

"It is now one o'clock. If this watch runs past two tomorrow, we shall know."

He shook the watch gently and held it to his ear to make sure that it was going.

"Go to bed, Purdy," he said. "I shall put it under my pillow to keep it safe."

"My God!" breathed Purdy. "I could no more sleep with that under my pillow than an insomniac with a trip hammer under his window."

The next morning Talcott called Purdy into conference.

"We have done as much as we can," he said, "with our present equipment. We had best lay our plans to leave within the week. Put up as many sand fences as you can. They will keep the stuff partly uncovered, and perhaps we shall all be back here in a year with a tractor or two. With Williamson gone there is not much we can do with the sketching. Fortunately the best things are light enough to be carried."

"I suppose that means the mummy."

"It certainly does!"

Talcott called in the three headmen from the village.

"Within seven days we go," he said.

All morning he worked, packing away the smaller articles in square, gray boxes, marked with the O.E.S. of the Oriental Exploration Society.

Purdy drifted in and stood like a restless schoolboy.

"Is it running?" he asked.

"What?" said Talcott. "Your tongue?"

"You know what I mean. The watch."

"Yes," was the reply, "and going strong."

As the morning wore on, Purdy grew more and more restless. A native dropped a shovel behind him; he jumped and swore. He ordered his lunch served in Talcott's tent. The watch lay on the top of a cracker box, its beating abnormally loud because of the sounding board beneath it.

"We have found some good things," rumbled the chief, "and established a new theory about trade routes. The Germans think that the main line of travel lay north of here, but the walls of the great caravansary which we have uncovered will prove that the route lay much farther south than any so far projected."

"Farther south than what?" asked Purdy vaguely.

"Purdy, you old woman! I suppose I shall have to sit here and watch you fidget until that timepiece stops at two o'clock."

In spite of his coolness, both real and assumed, Talcott grew a bit silent as his own watch drew toward two o'clock and the hands of the repeater moved toward ten. At five minutes before the hour the engineer arose and stood over the timepiece. The twisted hands moved with infinite slowness; but eventually the long hand stood at twelve and the short one at ten.

"Gosh!" breathed Purdy, "it's stopping, isn't it?"

His chief said nothing. The long hand moved to one minute past twelve, two minutes, three minutes. When it stood at five minutes past, Purdy said, "That settles it, doesn't it? It is still going."

"Wait," said Talcott. "Make sure."

Five minutes more they watched. The ticking still went on. Talcott took the watch and gently tested the spring. It was still taut.

"That settles it," he said. "The chances are ninety-nine out of a hundred that he died at nine in the evening on his way out. But see here, Purdy, you do not think for a moment that his telling the story had anything to do with it?"

"I do not know," said the engineer helplessly. "I suppose not. All the same I would not tell the yarn!"

At a quarter of two o'clock the next morning Talcott arose from his cot and stood over the watch.

At two it was clicking briskly; as the hands drew past ten the clicking halted; there were one or two spasmodic ticks and then silence.

In the early dawn of a week later, Talcott stood alone in what had been the main thoroughfare of the ancient city of Samarkund. About him lay the great, crude rectangles of what had been the market, a temple, a caravansary, a palace. They were partly concealed by sand fences, queer shutter-like structures that deflected the drifting sand.

And yet he knew that the desert would soon take to itself what he had forced her to yield up. The sand was a living, slow, malignant thing with consciousness. It would climb above the puny instruments set to keep it out; soon there would be no sign of Samarkund except perhaps the lonely capital lying on a ledge of rock.

Beyond him he saw the long line of black figures that made up his caravan, dwindling to nodding absurdity in the distance. A man does nothing for the last time without regret. Here he had put the whole strength of his nature for over a year. For the last time he walked about the ancient streets. He turned and looked out toward Anarshan. Beyond was the desert, impassive, dreaming in the white dawn.

"Good-by, my boy," he said. "Good-by!"

He turned to his pony and set one foot in the stirrup.

Was that a cry he heard out in the limitless void about him, a low wail climbing to a sharp scream — something between animal and human? It came a phantom voice — thin as the light which lay over everything.

For five minutes he stood, immobile, head bent.

Then he swung himself into his saddle and made off after his caravan. The sound had not been repeated.

Once on shipboard and bound for home the worried pucker smoothed itself out of Purdy's brow. He became, in the words of Mrs. Vandeventer, who occupied the one luxurious cabin aboard, the "life of the ship." He started a movement for a concert to be given in the saloon with himself as announcer of the program. It was he who organized the shuffleboard tournament. It was he who took the first cabin passengers to the steerage and lectured to them on the different races represented in the chattering mob of Orientals.

Most of all it was Purdy who sat by the hour in the smoking-room looking into the bottom of tall glasses which were apparently self-emptying.

He came to Talcott's cabin one day where the latter spent all of his time putting his notes in order.

"Chief," he said, slapping Talcott on the back, a familiarity he had never quite dared before, "I promised Mrs. Vandeventer that you would give a talk in the saloon to-night on some of your explorations in the Orient. Something informal and chatty, you know. Little anecdotes about the use of hairpins among the ancient Samarkundians or the habits of the wild gazelle fish. Anything! If you don't want to tell the truth, make up something, and if you do not want to make up something, give me the word and I will compose something for you." He giggled and hiccupped and stood swaying just a little more than the smooth motion of the ship warranted.

"Nonsense!" said Talcott stiffly. "You have been drinking."

"No, 'm not," said Purdy earnestly. "No 'm not. Had nothing to-day but something to ward off seasickness with a couple lifelong friends I met on the boat."

"Lifelong friends you never saw before!" said Talcott. He shrugged his shoulders. "However, you are your own master. But I wish you would shave and put on clean linen and keep yourself a credit to your profession in looks at least."

Purdy, a bit sobered by his chief's icy manner, rubbed his hand over his chin.

"Sure thing, chief," he mumbled apologetically. "I'll attend to all that."

He went out, swaying perilously, forgetting all about the speech by Dr. Talcott, which he had promised Mrs. Vandeventer.

Outside, he ran into that charming lady; accompanied by another old friend of his, a fat man who traveled extensively in the service of an American harvesting machinery corporation.

"Oh, you interesting man!" cried the lady. "Do come and tell me what Dr. Talcott said."

"I bear his apologies to you," said Purdy. "He is ill and cannot appear tonight."

"Oh, how screamingly unfortunate," exclaimed Mrs. Vandeventer. "He is so fascinating! Don't you love a mysterious man!"

"Huh!" grunted the harvester salesman.

They made their way to the cafe, a small screened-off part of the stuffy smoking-room.

Mrs. Vandeventer ordered a drink compounded of ginger ale and lemon juice; the men ordered whisky and soda.

"You must run into perfectly fascinating mysterious things away off in the desert," gushed the lady. "I had so hoped that Dr. Talcott would tell us some of them to-night."

"I'm sorry," said Purdy, "very ill!"

"Now I knew a charming man — a Frenchman —" said Mrs. Vandeventer. "He lived in Martinique, and he knew the most delightfully gruesome stories about the Witchcraft there, what do they call it? Oh, yes, hoodoo!"

"Voodoo, you mean," said the harvester salesman.

"Oh, yes, voodoo! Well, it appears that if one person hates another person, all that he needs to do is to go to one of these witch doctors and he makes a small image of wax and puts it up in front of the fire and it melts and when the last bit is melted the person dies! Honestly! He gave me his word that he had seen it done!"

"Nonsense!" said the fat man. "Like as not the witch doctor sent around word that he was operating on the party and his imagination just got the better of him. Probably killed himself; paid to do so by the witch doctor."

"I could tell a tale," said Purdy, wagging his head mysteriously — so mysteriously that he almost forgot to cease wagging.

"Oh, do let us hear it!" screamed Mrs. Vandeventer. "Is it horrible and mysterious and everything!"

"It is," said Purdy, "all of that."

"Let's have it," said the fat man, "come on, trot it out!"

"Me!" almost shrieked Purdy. "Me tell it! Why, man! The person who tells this story is bound to die in twenty-four hours, absolutely bound to die within twenty-four hours. One of our men told it —"

"Well, did he die?" asked the fat man.

"He did," said Purdy.

"Coincidence," said the other. "I don't believe that stuff and neither do you. You are a scientist; I am a business man. Now take business. If things don't sell, there is a good reason, that's all."

"Grapenuts!" giggled Purdy and almost fell out of his chair. "Of course," he went on, "cause and effect. I am a scientist; expect to be elected to the Royal Geographic Society on the strength of what I have done in Samarkund."

"Samarkund," exclaimed Mrs. Vandeventer —" what a perfectly beautiful, delightful, mysterious name! Can't you imagine camels and antelopes and wild horses and horrible witchy things happening in a place like that!"

"Come on," said the fat man; "let's have the story."

"Not I," said Purdy.

"Afraid?"

"Sir," said Purdy, "you are insulting! I afraid! A man who has been through what I have been through! I am not afraid of anything on this earth, above it, or below it!"

"Prove it," said the fat man.

"Well, it was this way. We had a young fellow who found a tomb away off in the desert. Funny, it was Egyptian, and a thousand miles away from the Nile. He opened it, found a mummy-case and the story of the occupant. This is the story."

At the end of three minutes Mrs. Vandeventer screamed, put her hands to her ears, and ran away.

Purdy went on doggedly for fifteen minutes, interrupted only by changing glasses. At the end of that time he stopped, looked around triumphantly, and said thickly:

"Afraid! I? Afraid! Where's Mrs. What-do-you-call-'em?"

"Whew!" said the harvester man. "What rotten people they were in those days."

"What?" said Purdy sleepily.

The huge figure of Talcott loomed in the door. He stood for a moment looking uncertainly about, and then strode over and laid his hand on Purdy's shoulder.

"Purdy!" he said.

Purdy made no answer. His head was sinking lower and lower.

"He's been having a round or two with old King Al," said the harvester man. "Will you have a sniff yourself, doc?"

"No, thank you," said Talcott stiffly. "Purdy, you fool!"

"Ouch!" said Purdy. "Leggo."

Talcott dragged him to his feet and half carried him out to the deck. A heavy fog had settled, and above them sounded the melancholy, measured hoot of the foghorn.

For half an hour Talcott marched his engineer briskly up and down the slippery deck.

At the end of that time the glassy look began to wear out of his eyes.

"Listen, Purdy," said Talcott, "I have had an important wireless which you ought to know about it. It is from Barbour, president of the society. He has been on the continent, and he says that there is some sort of trouble between Austria and Serbia, and that there is a chance of our being drawn in. Aren't you in the territorials?"

"Yes," said Purdy, passing his hand over his forehead. The worried look was coming back. "I'm captain in an engineer regiment."

"I thought you should know."

"Do you think England will be drawn in?"

"No," said Talcott, after a long pause. "The time is past for brutalities of that sort. Even if she is, reason will soon get the upper hand. It will amount to nothing."

He marched Purdy to the latter's stateroom.

"Good night," he said. "I think you had better stay here until morning."

"Good night," said Purdy, sitting on the edge of his bunk. The pucker between his brows deepened.

He arose.

"Talcott! Good God!"

"Well?"

"For God's sake, don't leave me!"

"Why not?"

"I've gone and told that damned story!"

"About the princess?"

"Yes."

"And you are afraid?"

"My God, yes!"

"Purdy, when we go to London, I am going to recommend that you sever your connection with the Oriental Society. Are you sure, in the first place, that you told it?"

"Did I?" said Purdy, trying painfully hard to collect his thoughts. "Maybe I did not."

That night the ship ran onto a derelict. Talcott was awake in an instant, collected, deducing from the orders above and the drumming of feet on deck just what the danger was.

He ran to Purdy's stateroom and opened the door. It was not locked. Purdy was not there.

He made a circuit of the deck, but could not find him. The steerage passengers were swarming up the stairs to the boat-deck. An officer with a drawn pistol stood at the head of the stairs, keeping them back.

Talcott ran back to his stateroom and threw together the things which were most important. When he came back on deck, the boats had been lowered and lay about the ship in a pale ring of upturned faces. The fog lifted and lay above them in a white woolly sheet. The ship listed slightly to port, but did not settle.

Within an hour the passengers were back on the boat, and she was proceeding toward Liverpool, only six hours away, at half speed.

The only life lost was that of Purdy. He could not be found on the ship. Talcott waited a week in Liverpool, but gained no news of him. He gave him up for lost, went to London, submitted a preliminary report to the society, and journeyed on to his cottage near the east coast.

Wexham lay within a league of the sea — a small village of less than a hundred souls. About it rolled the treeless downs, crossed by one white road. A mile from the village stood Talcott's cottage, a low structure of wood and stone, surrounded by a stone wall as high as a man, banked with flourishing shrubs. At the back was a small garden, empty now, for Talcott had been gone a year, and a stable. A walk made of crushed shells ran from the road to the gate in the wall, and the other walks which crossed the garden were made of the same material.

Here he set to work on the report. It was already almost finished, for his care in taking notes had been so great that it was only a question of putting them in some sort of sequence. He worked undisturbed, for he had few callers — the doctor, the rector, and Edmunds, the constable, who had been in charge of the place during his absence.

The inevitable question arose as to whether or not he should print the story of the princess. His first impulse was to tell it; but, after all, there might be something in the thing. It had certainly worked twice. If he turned the thing loose on the world and there was a power for evil in it, he would be eternally responsible.

Characteristically, he gave a day to the consideration of the problem, with the firm resolve to make up his mind at the end of that day. He spent it on the downs walking across them to the sea, and along the sands that were cold and wet in the shadow of the white cliffs that towered above them. All day he tramped, lunching at an inn. But when he turned homeward, the customary decision was lacking in his walk. He dawdled along, switching at the gorse with a heavy walking stick. He had come to no decision. At his gate he paused, reminded of his promise to settle the question.

"I will do it," he said aloud; "it is my duty. And who can believe that these things were anything but coincidence!"

In the house he found a message from London telling him to come at once. The name — Vandeventer — meant nothing to him at first. Then he remembered the foolish, simpering creature on the boat.

The message said it was a matter of life and death, and he went up to London, depressed, irritated at this new invasion on the serenity of life.

He found Mrs. Vandeventer in a house full of sisters and aunts and other women, all in tears. One worried-looking doctor was in charge. Talcott answered very bruskly the storm of talk that came upon him from the women and shut himself up with the doctor.

"Why was I sent for?" he demanded.

"Well, sir, it is a most peculiar case. Do you know anything about a princess named Nalinthia?"

"Yes," said Talcott calmly, "I do."

"The lady came home here with some cock-and-bull story which she said she heard on the boat from some one in your party. I believe there was a penalty for repeating it, wasn't there?"

"Yes," was the calm reply; "death within twenty-four hours."

"Well, from what I gathered from the ladies here, she knew a part of it. She kept it to herself as long as she could, but the strain became too great and she babbled it all out one evening by the fire here. The next morning she felt this sickness coming on, and thought it was the penalty. She went quite out of her head and has been more or less crazy ever since."

"Any other symptoms?" asked Talcott after a silence of a few minutes.

The doctor shrugged his black-clad shoulders.

"Well, yes. Some fever. Increased blood pressure, of course. Delirium; but I give you my word, I do not know whether it is or is not insanity."

"Insanity as a penalty for telling part of the story?" murmured Talcott. "Impossible!"

"May I see the lady?" he asked abruptly.

"Yes, certainly."

They went through the weeping throng at the door, up the broad stairs and into a dark bedroom.

Mrs. Vandeventer lay with an ice-pack at her head. The physician lifted the shade and Talcott bent over restless figure.

The pretty, foolish face was flushed and a constant babble of talk escaped her. Her eyes, light blue and very bright, were wide open, gazing this way and that, but seeing nothing.

The doctor shook his head.

"I think that all is being done that can be done. I called you in the hope that you might know something more about this than is apparent to the eyes. As for the permanency of this condition, that we must wait for time to show."

Talcott escaped through the ring of questioning women at the door and walked away from the house, head bent, brows knitted. Here was a new twist to the situation. Death for telling the story! Insanity for telling half of it!

His depression deepened. He walked the streets until eight o'clock, dined, walked again, undecided as to what he should do. London irritated him; this continual darkening of the streets against an improbable air raid made it so difficult to get about.

He remembered a note that he carried in his pocket about a matter concerning Egyptian decoration that he wished to look up. The note gave the name of an author famous for his explorations in Egypt and the title of a book known to the world as the authoritative work on Egyptian decoration.

He stopped short and struck his hands together.

"Stupid! Why did I not think of this before."

He stopped under a dimly burning gas light and ran through the names in his address book.

"Brandon, that's the name," he said with satisfaction, noted the address, and set off at top speed to find his man.

Brandon lived in a gloomy house which faced a dingy park. A dim gas light burned in the hall; Talcott pulled the bell and heard a harsh jingle somewhere in the depths of the building. Brandon himself answered the door, a slight man with shining, bald brow, and a slim, white hand that was lost in Talcott's hearty grip.

"And whom have I the honor of seeing?" murmured Brandon, a bit suspicious.

His suspicion thawed out as Talcott named himself and spoke of a meeting some years ago at a scientific congress in Copenhagen. He led the way into a dark, paneled library, lined with books on spiritualism and all the other isms which have to do with the survival of a life after death.

"I came to you on a matter of business," said Talcott abruptly, refusing the chair which the other drew up for him. "I have had a matter on my mind for some time. It has caused me considerable worry, for I have not known just how much to believe. As I was walking the streets tonight, I remembered a notation that I made while in the country, relative to looking up a detail of Egyptian decoration in Rheinhardt's great work on that subject. Suddenly I asked myself why I went to Rheinhardt. And the answer is, of course, that he is the one who knows more about these things than any one. Persons wishing to know about Samarkund will come to me, and persons like myself who wish to know anything about psychical matters, come to you."

"Of course there is a distinction," said Brandon, who had been watching his visitor with keen, but veiled interest. "You remember that Kant said the three problems which human beings can never settle are God, immortality, and freedom of the will."

"Exactly," said Talcott, "but you more than any other man are able to say whether or not there is anything in a curse made some twenty-five centuries ago which can operate to-day."

"Well," said Brandon slowly, "that is a hard question. Undoubtedly there have been cases in which it seemed as though things of that sort continued to be powerful. But in those cases science has not had a chance to apply her rules to the game. I know of few cases in things of that sort which, when put to the test of science, have not turned out to be fakes of one sort and another. I have here an interesting collection of such." He waved his hand toward the darker half of the room and Talcott saw glass cases filled with spirit trumpets, wooden toes for knocking, phosphoric masks and other apparatus for the séance.

"Are there any cases in which science has not been able to get at the bottom of the matter?" demanded Talcott.

"Yes, there have been some in which cause and effect as we know them have not seemed to apply. Notice that I say as we know them, for science is always taking to itself false science and legitimatizing it. Time was when Mesmerism was such a false science, and mesmeric demonstrations might well have been called witchcraft. But in time it became a valuable and true science."

He waited for his visitor to answer, but Talcott was silent, his heavy brows knitted in thought.

"Of course," Brandon went on, "as to the matter of the curse, there are all sorts of cults now which believe that thought is an active, living thing, independent of the thinking person. Their whole effort is to put themselves in contact with healthy, happy, prosperous currents of thought. They would undoubtedly say that a curse might live as a part of an evil current of thought and whoever put himself in contact with that evil current, consciously or unconsciously, would feel the effects of the curse. Perhaps," he finished delicately, "a concrete instance might help me to a decision."

"Do you remember Williamson," his caller asked abruptly, "a young man who was with me at the Copenhagen congress in nineteen-twelve?"

"Quite well," said Brandon. "A splendid chap."

"He found a tomb in the desert at Anarshan, a little oasis about eight miles from Samarkund. He opened it, found a superb mummy-case there. In it was the body of a girl who had been carried away from her home by the Nile. She suffered untold cruelties. She killed herself and left a record of her story in order that she might be avenged by her sweetheart, who was to come from Egypt to take that revenge. At the foot of the manuscript was an injunction against repeating this story, for such things should not be in the minds of men. And as a threat, she said that a sign had been given her by the god Anubis that whoever told the story would die within twenty-four hours.

"Williamson said nothing about this parchment for several days. Then he came to me and asked me whether or not he should tell the story, because his report would be incomplete without it. He was not afraid of the curse, understand, but he felt that the girl had put him on his honor. I did not directly persuade him to tell the story, but I am sure that

I am more or less responsible for his doing so. He told it to Purdy and me. Within twenty-four hours, twenty-three to be exact, he was dead, probably from a fall from his horse.

"Coming across on the boat Purdy got himself drunk and blabbed the story out to a woman and a man. I do not know who the man was, but the woman was Mrs. Vandeventer, whose name you have undoubtedly heard."

"Yes," nodded Brandon, "a rather pretty, giggling sort of person."

"Exactly. The ship ran onto a derelict within six hours from the English coast; all hands were put off in boats, floated around for a time in a calm sea, and then came back on board. That is, all except Purdy. Somewhere in the shuffle he was lost, and I have no doubt that he was killed. I have heard nothing of him."

"Extraordinary!"

"And that is not all. This Mrs. Vandeventer heard only part of the story. You will understand that no woman would care to listen to it in the presence of men. She hurried away before it was finished. However, she knew the prohibition attached, kept it to herself as long as she possibly could, and then babbled the thing out to her sisters. She is now more or less a maniac, with doubtful chances of recovery."

"Extraordinary!" murmured Brandon again. He was silent for a time, looking at the tall, strong figure in front of him.

"You are not afraid for yourself, of course," he said finally. "The problem is whether or not you ought to turn such a thing loose on the world. If it were not for the command at the end, you might do it, but just as soon as people were told that they must not repeat the yarn, they would all be doing so."

"My report will be incomplete without it," said Talcott. "My impulse is of course, to disregard the command and tell the story. My whole nature rebels against accepting any such restriction. But if there is power for evil in this curse, it is obviously my duty not to let it go farther than it has gone already."

"I can come to no decision on it," said Brandon. But he added, looking obliquely at his caller, "There is one way of settling it and that is the only way that I can see."

Talcott raised his head and met the eyes of his host squarely.

"I have thought of that," he said.

"Of course," ruminated Brandon, his eyes alight with the excitement of the thing, "you would be a great loss to the scientific world. Practically, it is absurd to think of telling the story just to see whether or not it works; scientifically, it is an experiment of inestimable value.

"You have nerve and physique. Where are you living?"

"I have a cottage near Wexham on the east coast."

"Ideal! If you were in London you might be run over by a bus or fall down a manhole, or be shot by some of these amateur soldiers. At Wexham every possible outside influence would be eliminated."

"When could we go down?"

"In the morning."

"Is there any one else we could get? Three observers are better than two. Two are better than one, I should say, for you yourself can scarcely be classed as an observer."

Talcott meditated for a moment.

"Yes," he said, "there is Edmunds, who has been watching my place while I have been gone. He is an old soldier; at present constable."

"Ideal!" exclaimed Brandon. "Was there ever such an experiment?"

A moment later he added, "What children men can be when they are interested in a thing! It is nonsense to think of your taking any risk, Let us drop the thing!"

"I shall go through with it," replied the other calmly.

Brandon looked at the deep-set blue eyes, the short, determined nose, the strong lines of jaw beneath the short beard.

"I can see that you are not one to be persuaded," he said, "and I will admit that I am not interested in persuading you to give this up."

"I have a duty," said Talcott calmly, "a twofold duty — partly to those who have gone before me and partly to science."

Talcott had telegraphed Edmunds to meet them at the station with a conveyance and he was there, touching his hat respectfully as they dismounted from the train. They drove across the mile of white road that separated Talcott's cottage from the village. Away to their left they could see the blue sparkle of the sea and over the fragrant downs came a strong breeze, with a tang of salt in it.

Ahead of them Talcott's cottage and stable nestled in a low mass, scarcely distinguishable from the country about it. Brandon took in the sun, the strong breeze, and the treeless country.

"Not much of a place for ghosts, is it? I would be out of a job down here."

"Very interesting subject," said Edmunds, touching his cap. "I have read Mr. Brandon's name in connection with the reports of the psychical society."

"Indeed!" said Brandon. "Interested in that sort of thing, Edmunds?"

"Not exactly hinterested, sir, but I 'ave seen some strange things in India."

"You are just our man," replied the other. "I suppose Talcott has told you that there is to be an experiment along that line to-day."

"Something of that sort was 'inted at in his telegram," replied the constable.

They drew up in front of the cottage and Edmunds took out their bags. Brandon exclaimed over the cheery interior, light walls, many windows now open to the warm breeze, bare brown floor, fireplace, books.

He was in favor of starting the ball rolling by having Talcott reel off the story at once. But Edmunds, once he understood the situation, interposed meekly, "Begging your pardon, sir, but I must get the horse back to the village and tend to some little legal matters. Also, I suggest that the story be told at midnight. It will be a strain, sirs, although you may laugh now. If it is told at midnight, it will give us a greater variety of night and day — a short spell of night, then a long spell of day and another short spell of night. And night will be the 'ard time, I take it."

The advantage of such an arrangement was quickly seen and Edmunds drove away, to return at a quarter before twelve that night.

As the clock rang the three chimes for that hour there was the rasp of hobnails outside and Edmund's knock at the door. He came in wrapped in a oilskin.

"A bit thick outside, gentlemen, a bit thick. A fine night for deviltry of any sort. We shall need to keep a close watch."

He took off his slicker and helmet, displaying an army pistol reposing in a holster, rich brown from wear, but polished with all the care which an old trooper of the queen could lavish on his equipment.

"Will you have something to drink, Edmunds?" asked Brandon.

"No, thank you, sir," said the constable respectfully. "You can't tell what may turn up here, and we ought to be ready for anything. Cool 'eads and steady 'ands, that's the ticket, sir, on a night like this."

"By George, you are right," said Brandon, and put back the decanter, which he had taken from a triangular cupboard that stood in the corner.

The clock hands drew toward twelve. There was a whirr of wheels and the chimes rang out — four peals for the quarter and then twelve slow strokes for the hour.

Edmunds and Brandon sat in chairs drawn up front of the fire. Talcott rose and stood in front of them. As the last heavy note died away, his rich, strong voice began.

"This is the story of Nalinthia, daughter of Notki, priest of Anubis."

For fifteen minutes the room resounded to his voice.

Then he stopped; the clock rang a peal for the quarter.

The story was told.

Edmunds cleared his throat.

"My word, sir, living in Hengland 'as its blessings, 'asn't it, sir? Things like that could not 'appen 'ere and now. Law and order, gentlemen, that's the ticket, law and order."

"Curious tale," said Brandon. "Now to see what's the result. I hate to think of staying awake all night without any stimulus whatever."

"Beg pardon, gentlemen," said Edmunds respectfully, "but my advice is that we stand watch turn and about, as it were. If we get no sleep at all, to-morrow night at this time we will be seeing all sorts of things that ain't there at all. I will go on from now until four in the morning, Mr. Brandon can stand watch from four until eight, Mr. Talcott from eight till twelve, and then we can start all over again. Those who are not on watch can sleep."

"Edmunds," exclaimed Brandon, "you are the prince of constables!"

"Thank you, sir. You gentlemen can go to sleep here. I will be going in and out at about 'alf hour intervals, so do not be disturbed if you 'ear me. Sort of patrol as it were."

Talcott pulled out the cot from his sleeping alcove; Brandon lay on it fully dressed. His host spread a blanket on the floor. The lights were put out; Edmunds took his position by the fireplace in a straight-backed chair. The red light of the fire touched the forms of the two reclining men and the keen, lined face of the old trooper. In the corner the face of the clock took on a rosy tint from the fire, and its ticking with the intermittent cracking of the coal in the fireplace were the only sounds.

When the two peals on the chimes rang for the half-hour, Edmunds slipped outside and made the circuit of the place. He was back again within five minutes, for the grounds were so small as to be easily encompassed in that time. The mist was still heavy outside; he came in dripping.

At the end of the first half-hour, Talcott's deep breathing told that he was asleep. Brandon's eyes were shut, but a telltale flutter now and then and his constant turning indicated that he had not found it so easy to forget the threat that hung over Talcott.

Each peal of the chimes he heard, and each time Edmunds went out he opened his eyes drowsily and watched him go. Four times the constable had gone, and the clock was striking half after two. Edmunds arose, slipped on his rainproof and tiptoed softly out of the door.

In a moment there came a shout, a pistol shot and the sound of a falling body.

Brandon reared up in bed, calling helplessly, "Talcott! Talcott!"

The latter rose from the floor, instantly awake, cool, self-possessed.

"There was a shot outside," cried Brandon, "and somebody fell!"

His host seized the heavy poker that stood by the fire, went to the shutter in his sleeping alcove, opened it, and slipped out into the night.

In a moment he came back through the door, half carrying the constable. The latter's face was terribly cut up; he was blinded by blood that poured into his eyes from a half dozen savage cuts in his forehead. Otherwise he was uninjured and his cool voice was saying:

"Didn't see which way it went, sir, whatever it was. Don't be alarmed, sir, my eyes are all right. Just can't see where I am going. Don't forget to bolt the door; there is some deviltry in the wind."

Brandon stared helplessly while Talcott tended the wounds on his side. He washed them carefully, examined them by the fierce light of an electric torch. All the time the cool voice of the wounded man was running on.

"I had just come out of the door, gentlemen, and my eyes were still a bit puckered up by the change from light to dark. I stood just under the eaves around the corner from the door, when something struck me. It may have been from above or from below or from in front. It may have been a man or a beast. It was inky dark and it occurred so quickly that I knew nothing except that my face was being chewed up. Whatever it was, it was gone in the flash of an eye."

"I am sorry, gentlemen, not to have seen more clearly."

"What do you think?" asked Brandon of Talcott.

"It must have been done by a man armed with some fiendish weapon," said Talcott slowly. "We have no animals in Wexham that could make such marks."

It was still dark outside; their routine of standing watch was broken up. Brandon should have gone on, but one look at his concerned face told Talcott that he was not the man to patrol the place in the dark hours of a misty morning.

He took upon himself the labor of watching until dawn.

When he returned from his second round he found Brandon watching the constable with a puzzled look. The old man was sitting bolt upright in his chair.

"Right wheel!" he said sharply. "Load with ball!"

"What is it, Edmunds?" asked Talcott.

The other paid no attention, but broke into a babble of meaningless talk.

"Orders for the day are to let no one pass this white post," he said rapidly. "Corporal of the guard! Relief, number three! Steady my man, take it easy. A deep breath and a light touch at the trigger. You got him!"

Edmunds jumped up from his chair, but Talcott caught him by the shoulders and pushed him back. He forced his head back. The bandages covered most of his face; what was visible was angry red, and the eyes were pulled almost shut.

"Get me warm water and my medical kit from the corner cupboard."

He unwrapped the bandages, which were pulled tightly by the swelling of Edmunds' wounds. Each scratch was turning black on its edges, the wounded man's head was grotesquely puffed.

Talcott made a tourniquet and bound it lightly about his patient's head. Then he compressed each wound, washed it time and time again. Edmunds ceased his babble and slumped down in his chair.

"What is it?" asked Brandon, who had been doing nothing but wet fresh cloths, for each one that had been used was thrown upon the fire.

Talcott looked at him vaguely.

He had almost forgotten the existence of Brandon.

"Poison of some sort. He was cut with a poisoned knife of some sort."

He lifted the chunky figure of the wounded man in his arms and laid him out on the cot.

"Brandon," he said rapidly, "you will have to go to the village. Wake up the men at the inn first, get some sort of conveyance and bring the doctor back with you. Edmunds must have good care, and we cannot give it to him here."

When Brandon opened the door to go out, the dawn was already showing whitely through the mist.

Alone with his charge, Talcott worked feverishly to keep up the failing pulse. At quarter-hour intervals, he loosened the tourniquet for a few moments. The bathing and compressing of the wounds he did not cease. The constable lay in a coma, silent, inert, scarcely breathing. His face was turned almost entirely black.

Suddenly Talcott paused, straightened himself up.

Somewhere in the back of his mind an answering chord responded faintly to the sight of the dark and swollen face before him. Once he had seen such a sight — cheeks black, eyes puffed shut, head crushed from crown to brow.

It was Williamson, as he had lain in the crevice of rock near the road to Anarshan!

His mind leaped upon this slender bit of evidence, while his body went mechanically through the process of wrapping his patient in blankets, forcing brandy between his lips, and then putting hot bricks at his feet.

Was there a connection there? Could he be sure that Williamson had suffered something of this sort, or had he been dragged by his horse?

The matter was still milling around in his mind when Brandon returned with the doctor and a carriage.

The constable was breathing more deeply, the blue color had gone from his lips; if he suffered no reaction, the doctor decided, he would live.

When it was decided that he could be moved, it was well on into the morning. Edmunds spoke rationally.

"My 'ead is very 'eavy," he said. "My word, sir, I think I owe my life to you."

"You had a very narrow escape," said the doctor. "If it had not been for the prompt cleansing of the wounds and tourniquet, which kept the poison out of your heart, you would have been a gone man. Extraordinary," he said. "Is this England or is this the Orient?"

Talcott answered his question very shortly, telling him nothing of the experiment that was under way. He left Brandon in charge of the house and rode off to the village with Edmunds. He wanted to get a gun of some sort, for one thing; a pistol is accurate up to twenty feet; but whatever there was roaming the moors might need to be downed at longer range than that.

He started back across the downs at noon. Everywhere the mist lay, thick, dripping fog. Over the rolling land came the boom of fog-horns along the coast, and he heard the piping cry of unseen birds wheeling above him. Ahead of him the road slid into sight scarce a dozen feet away; on either side the downs faded into gray mist.

A breeze fanned the fog gently. It brought to his nostrils the pungent odor of smoke. He quickened his pace and as he drew near his own property the smoke odor thickened. He saw a red glow through the mist, and broke into a run. His cottage was burning!

His first thought was for Brandon and he dashed open the door. The room was full of swirling smoke. Brandon was lying fully dressed on the cot, sleeping heavily.

Talcott picked him up bodily and carried him out into the garden. He propped him up against the wall and turned to fighting the fire. One corner of the building which contained his sleeping quarters was in flames; evidently it had started close to the ground.

He seized an ax and tore the burning timbers from the house and tossed them into the dripping bushes where they blazed harmlessly. A pump stood in the garden and a tub. From this he threw water on to the small blaze that was left. The roof was too wet to burn. Steam curled up from it, but the flames that licked up there soon died out.

Three quarters of the cottage was intact; one corner gaped with a great black hole, showing the comfortable interior, sleeping alcove, and beyond, chairs drawn up in front of the fire, blue dishes on a table, a small jar of gorse in the corner.

He turned to Brandon who was sitting up, passing his hand over his brow.

"What is it?" he said weakly. "A fire?"

"No," said his host somewhat impatiently, "a picnic."

"I must have fallen asleep," said Brandon, "the first I knew I came to out here. Everything was all right before. I was tired and lay down for a moment.

He struggled to his feet.

"Ouch!" he said, and burst into a fit of coughing. "I must have breathed some of that smoke into my lungs. They are very painful."

"I hope you feel all right otherwise," said Talcott. "I hope there is no such thing as poisoned smoke."

"You don't think there is!" cried Brandon.

"Of course not," was the reply. "Had there been, you would be dead now. But I think that from the looks you had better go to the village and go to bed with your windows wide open."

"And leave you here alone?" protested Brandon feebly.

"Yes," said Talcott, "this is my problem, and I ought to see it through alone. There is no reason why any one else should take any risk. When I consented to your coming, I did not think that things would turn out as they have."

Brandon took his traveling bag, shook hands with his host, and walked away.

The daylight ended early; at six it was murky and dark as night. Talcott dined, washed his dishes, put his bed back into the alcove, and swept the place free from bits of blackened timber. He stirred up the fire and sat down in front of it. Near his hand leaned a fowling piece; he had not been able to get a rifle in the village.

As he sat gazing into the coals, the whole affair of the tomb at Anarshan passed before him, in pictures formed by the shifting colors in the fire. He saw young Williamson standing at the edge of the oasis, waving his sun helmet, and shouting, "Come on, sir, a big find!" And then the night in front of his tent, the boy sitting just at the edge of the white light thrown from his acetylene lamp, saying, "Not that I am afraid of the threat, but I rather felt that she was putting me on my honor."

Then Purdy had drifted in and the boy had reeled off, the story and Purdy had blurted out his ridiculous fear.

Ridiculous? Could he call Purdy's fear ridiculous when the scene reproduced itself before him: the boy lying in a crevice just off the road, his head crushed and blackened?

Then came Purdy's obstinate drunkenness on the ship, the collision and the white ring of boats lying about the heeling vessel, Purdy's empty stateroom, his hunt for him about the ship, and the days of waiting in Liverpool.

In his mind's eye he saw the simpering face of Mrs. Vandeventer under the white edge of the ice-pack and heard her high voice babbling on.

Outside he heard a low roar coming from the sea. A wind was up, scouring across the treeless downs. It struck his house and the sturdy little structure trembled beneath the blow. The dripping of the fog from the roof ceased, and as he went to the window to secure a banging shutter, he saw the fog running before the wind in long, gray streaks.

He went back to his place by the fire and the low, steady roar of the wind outside brought back to him the sound of his own voice as he stood there at the last midnight, telling the story of Nalinthia. Twenty of his allotted hours had already gone; the clock had just ceased booming the hour of eight.

What if the dead hand of this girl could reach across twenty-seven centuries and touch him! What if somewhere or somehow Nalinthia was still Nalinthia; her command a living thing, jealously kept by some power beyond the physical, yet working through it. For the death of Williamson had been accomplished by physical means, so probably had the death of Purdy. About Mrs. Vandeventer he could not be sure; she might have thought herself into a state of approaching insanity. What if somewhere the feud went on between Nalinthia and her persecutors!

And then almost on the heels of his telling the story had come the wounding of Edmunds, ghastly cuts that swelled and blackened almost within the hour. And after that the fire and the narrow escape of Brandon from death by smoke strangulation.

The wind strengthened; the curtain that hung between the living room and his sleeping-alcove stood straight out, struck a small jar of gorse that stood on his bookshelves, and sent it rolling and crashing across the floor. He arose and turned toward the black opening of his sleeping-room. A strong blast of air swept through the opening made by the fire of the afternoon.

And in that opening, which yawned blackly into the outer night, flashed a pair of sinister green eyes.

Talcott stood while the eyes drew near through the darkness, disembodied, for he could see nothing but them, changing from green to red and back. He leaped back, seized the fowling-piece, and fired once from the hip. He jumped back into the shadow.

A cry rang out above the roar of the wind — a cry that he had heard before — a sound that began as a low wail and sharpened to a scream of animal anguish. A yellow body came hurtling through the air toward him and he fired again. There was the thump of a heavy body falling.

Talcott leaped to the door, bolted it, bolted the windows, fastened the curtain down by laying the heavy poker across the lower edge, and turned to his find.

On the floor lay something between a house-cat and leopard as to size; in color it was an even, dirty yellow. Its back was broken, and its legs lay in a curious, sprawled, impotent attitude. The ragged ears lay flat against the sinister, snakelike head, and the eyes, slowly glazing, looked up at him through slanting lids with incredible ferocity.

He stood watching until the twitching of the yellow body ceased. Exultation was in his eyes; he broke into a laugh of triumph. For here was the starting-point on which he could build up a structure of reasoning. He had heard that cry before — as he was mounting his horse to leave the waste sands of Samarkund. There was the point on which he could begin. He quoted the axiom of Archimedes, rolling out the sonorous Greek periods, "Give me but a place to rest my lever, and I will unhinge the universe!"

The body was quite lifeless by now; he lifted it and placed it on the table under the lamp. It was emaciated; the ribs protruded through the thick, matted fur, but even so it was a heavy weight. The head was small, with strong, vicious jaws, the legs were long and strongly muscled. He gazed at it, searching in his memories of natural history for some clue to its identity. It was too large for a common house-cat, although he knew that in the Orient, where such animals are bred with care, they reach proportions unknown to the housewives of England. It was too small to be a leopard, and the smooth color of the coat precluded any possibility of its being such. There were no tufts to the ears, therefore it could not be any sort of a lynx.

He turned to his books and ran through a number which had to do with the Orient. In one he came across a picture, showing a group of animals such as this one. It was an artist's sketch; not that of a scientist, and showed these animals standing by a riverbank with a heron under the paw of one.

"Desert cat," read the title under the picture, "common to Egypt. These creatures are supposed to be descendants of the ancient temple cats. They live in bands and hunt so. Surly, ferocious, have been known to attack men. The natives sometimes train them for hunting birds but on account of the sullen disposition, this is rarely successful."

He turned and looked at the yellow splotch under the light.

"Egypt in Samarkund again," he mused.

There was a knock at his door; because of the increasing violence of the wind outside, he had heard no footsteps on the walk.

He put the animal out of sight, and opened the door. A blast of air swept in, and with it a boy from the village. Talcott had to throw his whole weight against the door to close it again; he could hear the tumbling of the surf coming on the wind.

The boy had a message from Edmunds saying that he was doing well and was sorry not to be with Talcott, another from Brandon expressing the same regret and adding that if the wind went down he would drive out later, provided the doctor would come with him.

There was also a letter from London written by Mrs. Vandeventer's physician saying that a famous specialist had identified the lady's trouble as an obscure Oriental fever evidently contracted on her way to England. Her mind was impaired; there were doubts as to her ever being sane again, but such was the natural course of the malady under which she suffered.

"Terrible night, sir," said the boy. "The steeple is down at the church and the rectory orchard is all up by the roots."

"Too bad," murmured Talcott absently and tipped the boy. He slipped out into the howling night and the scientist returned to the problem before him.

Another step which would prove that everything that had to do with the telling of the story was coincidence! Mrs. Vandeventer had not been made insane because she told the story, but because she had contracted a definite form of sickness.

He put the cat upon the table again, raised one foot and pressed upon the pad of the foot gently. Claws, long and keen pushed out in a sinister half-circle. Without the aid of his reading-glass he could see that they had been smeared with some yellowish black venom.

"Some one brought you to England!" he exclaimed, his voice deep with exultation.

The wind moaned hoarsely as it raced overhead. The curtain broke loose from its mooring and stood straight out in the room. Talcott left it so, unbolted the windows, unlocked the door and sat down in front of the fire. The fire glowed and flickered in the strong draft. Outside the wind raced over the downs and dashed against the walls of his house, bringing with it bits of stone that pattered like hailstones. The far-off sound of the surf, which on quiet days was no more than a murmur, had deepened to a thunderous roar.

The clock struck half-after nine.

He pictured to himself the death of young Williamson; this animal springing upon him, and then the mad plunging of his horse and the boy catapulted over the beast's head.

The clock ticked around to ten, to half-past, and still the storm strengthened outside until the wind flew past with a melancholy scream. The firelight played over the motionless figure of the man and shone upon the glazed, sinister slits which stood for the eyes of the beast upon the table.

Suddenly Talcott jumped to his feet, whirled about, and struck once with the heavy poker that lay close at hand. Once more he bolted the door and the shutters and moored the curtain to the floor; this time with a heavy chair. Then he turned back into the room with exultation gleaming in his eyes.

Back of his chair lay a slim, brown man, thin, looking emaciated in the cast-off European clothes which he wore. At his side lay a curved knife. Talcott picked it up gracefully. Its keen edge was dark with the same cruel venom that had been smeared on the claws of the cat. He threw the knife into the fire, plunging the blade deep into the glowing coals.

His captive's hat had fallen off, showing a smooth long head, a straight nose finely formed, a small full lipped mouth and a round chin. He was not of the brown color which was characteristic of the natives about Samarkund; there was a coppery tint to the skin.

Talcott's brows knitted.

"Egyptian features," he said, "if I know anything about the inhabitants of that land. That slim head and straight nose are certainly not characteristic of any other Oriental race."

He bound the feet and hands of the unconscious man with fine strong cord, passing the bonds about the hands just below the roots of the fingers. There was a welt on the smooth head, but he had not struck out to kill. A touch on the thin chest told him that his captive still lived.

He looked in triumph from the cat to the man and back. The first had almost got him; the second he had deliberately played for, leaving all avenues of entrance open and trusting the mirror-like surface of the chimney-piece to tell him when anything came up behind him.

The slim, brown body twitched, moved; almond eyes opened and looked up at him blankly. Then hate blazed up in them; the native whipped himself over and snapped at his captor's leg.

Talcott sidestepped and then threw the body of the dead cat beside the other. The face writhed into an expression of animal grief at sight of the lifeless body.

"What has happened to this foul thing will happen to you!" said the scientist, speaking in the tongue which was used about Samarkund. "I must know of the young effendi and the engineer effendi!"

There was no answer and he could not be sure that he had been understood. He took the fowling-piece, slipped a cartridge into it, and placed the muzzle against the head of his prisoner.

"I must know!" he said.

The eyes closed and the face became as calm as a graven image. The lips moved as if in prayer. Talcott bent close, and although the sound of the wind outside made the voice almost inaudible, heard that he was praying, and in the tongue of the Samarkund region.

"That is all I wanted to know," he said, putting the fowling piece back by the fire-place; "whether or not you understood me."

"I must know!" he went on. "By you men have lost their lives and there must be an accounting. You do not fear death; you fear pain. I swear that you will suffer the pangs of those in hell if you do not tell."

Still there was no answer.

He slipped the cleaning-rod of his pistol through the fine cord that went about the thin knuckles of his captive. He gave the rod a turn, and the cord cut deep into the hands, and the slender bones of the hand crunched. The body writhed in pain.

"Tell me."

Still there was silence. For a quarter of an hour he kept the pressure unrelaxed; as the clock was striking eleven, the native burst into a flood of cursing and wailing.

The sweat was pouring from Talcott's forehead as he arose. This sort of thing sickened him, but it must be done, and he had seen it through with all the thoroughness at his command.

"Tell me!" he said and pointed to the cat.

"It is mine," wailed the brown man, "mine. I brought it with me across the sea. Two of you have felt its claws."

"And who are those two?"

"The foolish young effendi who opened the tomb and the one who has gone back to the village to die."

"He will not die," said Talcott; "he will live and will see that you are punished. He is of the law. Why did you kill the young effendi?"

"He broke into the sacred tomb." The native laughed shrilly, a laugh that mingled with the hideous chorus of the wind.

"He broke into the sacred tomb. He was near to death when first he entered it, for if the slab had fallen more quickly, his feet would have been crushed."

Talcott looked down with loathing into the maniacal face with its rolling eyes, and lips drawn back over brown teeth.

"Did you kill the young effendi?"

"I did not strike him! I swear it! He felt the claws of this one and then his horse plunged and he fell."

"Beast!" cried Talcott. "You set this thing to hunt him. You will suffer!"

"I am not afraid to die."

"But you shall suffer. What became of the engineer effendi?"

"He was a fool! I struck him once when the ship was shaking, and he fell into the water."

"And what of the laughing lady on the ship?"

"Of her I know nothing!"

"Tell me," said Talcott in a terrible voice. He placed the heel of his boot on the slender hand. The face of the native turned ashen and his tobacco brown eyes rolled in apprehension.

"Of her I know nothing! She came among us with the engineer effendi and laughed at us. One of us was sick. He touched her."

Here was how Mrs. Vandeventer had contracted the obscure Oriental fever. Talcott turned away for a moment. Another link in the chain of evidence, and another fact to disprove the theory that to tell the story entailed a penalty.

"And what other things have you done?"

The native lay exhausted. Strange lands and strange food had weakened him. When he spoke again, Talcott could scarcely hear him above the hideous chorus which the wind made outside.

"It was I who brought liquor to the camp at Samarkund. I paid two of those pigs to kill you. And the fire in this house I started."

There was still the question of why this Egyptian looking face should be near Samarkund.

"Of what race are you?"

"I am not of the pigs who were at Samarkund. My ancestors were river gods and sacred cats."

The river god, Talcott thought, could be nothing but the Nile; the cat was sacred only in ancient Egypt. His mind harked back to the lover of Nalinthia who was to take vengeance on her persecutors.

"And did one of them do a great deed of blood in the country of Samarkund, after leaving his own land?"

"That he did, and took a wife of the people of his own land. His sons have guarded the sacred tomb at Anarshan ever since. There is always one, and when he dies another takes the duty upon him."

"And what of him who tells the tale of her that was in the tomb?" demanded Talcott.

The blank stare came back at him.

"Of that I know nothing, nor of her that was in the tomb. It is sacred."

"Why did you come for me?"

"You were one of those who broke open the sacred place, and it is our duty to take vengeance for that."

"Where is your city?"

"That I will never tell, nor where our dead lie buried, not burned, as is the custom of the pigs about Samarkund!"

Triumphantly the scientist looked at the clock. It was a quarter before twelve and the three peals on the chimes sounded faintly in the din that went on outside. The wind had been steadily mounting; the shutters shivered, and the latch of the door clacked as gusts of wind swept against the heavy panels.

Within fifteen minutes his time would be up!

He mused on the strangeness of the thing, and felt joy that Nalinthia's wrongs had been avenged. Her sweetheart had done a great deed of blood in Samarkund — undoubtedly the murder of the human jackals who had abducted her. Then for twenty-seven centuries his people had guarded her tomb. There must be a city of them — hidden away in the rocky hills somewhere. He thought of the houses built in the Egyptian fashion, dotting some valley surrounded by hills of the galleries of mummied figures there must be there, awaiting the return of the soul.

He looked at the clock again. Ten more minutes and his time would be up!

He had settled the threat forever — laid its ghost — so that he could publish the story of Nalinthia and people could tell it again and again without fear. Cause and effect — cause and effect had been responsible for all the strange things which had puzzled him — cause and effect working in material channels.

Outside the wind arose in a long melancholy shriek. The house tottered under the blow; the heavy chair that held down the curtain in his sleeping-alcove overturned with a crash and the cloth was snapped from its fastenings. Talcott was almost blown flat by the rushing current of wind that stormed into the room. With it came bits of stone, of timber, of up-torn gorse from the downs. The roof creaked under the in-blowing blast and seemed to rise a fraction of an inch.

The blast sank. The running roar of the sea seemed to be at his very door. He turned to straighten the chair, and there was a roar as another blast came running over the downs. This time the latch of the door gave way and the panel swung round with a crash, breaking into two long splinters as it struck against the stone doorpost. The shutters sprang outward and were borne off on the wings of the wind. A long crack appeared in the ceiling with a splitting roar. The windows fell in with a jingle of breaking glass, and the house groaned almost humanly as the roof moved.

The native struggled to his knees.

"God Anubis!" he screamed. "I pray thee, strike thou this defiler of the sacred tomb. Thou movest in many ways, but all to the one end that he who defiles what is sacred feels the smart. Punish this one with death!"

He bowed twice, touching his forehead to the floor, and fixed his malignant eyes on Talcott, who stood, calm, opposing his body to the blast that swept through the house wildly.

The wind slackened and there was a grinding creak as the house settled together again. Then came another long running roar as a fresh blast swept in from the sea.

"God Anubis!" screamed the native. "Strike!"

There was a crash in the garden as a portion of the stone wall went down under the wind. The roof rose slowly, broke and whirled down into the room. A heavy beam struck Talcott squarely in the head, and he fell at the feet of the wild-eyed native, dead.

"God Anubis! I thank thee!"

A frenzied laugh mingled with the scream of the wind that swept through the shattered cottage.

The wind slackened to a deadly stillness. On the coast a surf poured thunderously, shaking the downs.

In the corner of the wrecked building there was a whir of wheels, a click, and the clock struck — four peals on the chimes for the quarters, and then twelve booming strokes.

The Whispering Mummy*

I

elix Bréton and I were the only occupants of the raised platform at the end of the hall; and the inartistic performance of the bulky dancer who occupied the stage promised to be interminable. From motives of sheer boredom I studied the details of her dress — a white dress, fitting like a vest from shoulder to hip, and having short, full sleeves under which was a sort of blue gauze. Her hair, wrists, and ankles glittered with barbaric jewelery and strings of little coins.

A deafening orchestra consisting of tambourines, shrieking Arab viols, and the inevitable *daràbukeh,* surrounded the performer in a half-circle; and three other large-sized *ghawâzi* mingled their shrill voices with the barbaric discords of the musicians. I yawned.

"As a quest of local color, Bréton," I said, "this evening's expedition can only be voted a dismal failure."

Felix Bréton turned to me, with a smile, resting his elbows upon the dirty little marble-topped table. He looked sufficiently like an artist to have been merely a painter; yet his gruesome picture "Le Roi S'Amuse" had proved the salvation of the previous Salon.

"Have patience," he said; "it is Shejeret ed-Durr (Tree of Pearls) that we have come to see, and she has not yet appeared."

"Unless she appears shortly," I replied, stifling another yawn, "I shall disappear."

But even as I spoke, there arose a hum of excitement throughout the crowded room; the fat dancer, breathless from her unpleasing exertions, resumed her seat; and all the performers turned their heads towards a door at the side of the stage. A veiled figure entered, with slow, lithe step; and her appearance was acclaimed excitely. Coming to the centre of the stage, she threw off her veil with a swift movement, and confronted the audience, a slim, barbaric figure. I glanced at Felix Bréton. His eyes were glittering with excitement. Here at last was the *ghazîyeh* of romance, the *ghazîyeh* of the Egyptian monuments; a true daughter of that mysterious tribe who, in the remote past of the Nile-land, wove spells of subtle moon-magic before the golden Pharaoh.

A monstrous crash from the musicians opened the music of the dance — the famous Gazelle dance — which commenced to a measure of long, monotonous cadences. Shejeret ed-Durr began slowly to move her arms and body in that indescribable manner which, like the stirring of palm fronds, speaks the veritable language of the voluptuous Orient. The

* "The Whispering Mummy" was written by Sax Rohmer, pseud. of Arthur Sarsfield Ward (1883 – 1959), and published in *The Premier Magazine*, No. 47, Mar. 1918. The source for this edition came from the short story collection *Tales of Secret Egypt* (1918).

attendant dancers clashing their miniature cymbals, the measure quickened, and swift passion informed the languorous body, which magically became transformed into that of a leaping nymph, a bacchante, a living illustration of Keats' wonder-words:

> "Like to a moving vintage, down they came,
> Crown'd with green leaves, and faces all aflame;
> All madly dancing through the pleasant valley,
> To scare thee, Melancholy!"

At the conclusion of her dance, Shejeret ed-Durr, resuming her veil, descended to the floor of the hall and passed from table to table, exchanging light badinage with those patrons known to her.

"Do you think you could induce her to come up here, Kernaby?" said Bréton excitedly; "she is simply the ideal model for my 'Danse Funebre.'"

"Any inducement other than our presence in this select part of the establishment," I replied, offering him a cigarette, "is unnecessary. She will present herself with all reasonable despatch."

Indeed, I had seen the dark eyes glance many times towards us, as we sat there in distinguished isolation; and, even as I spoke, the girl was ascending the steps, from whence she approached our table, smiling in friendly fashion. Bréton's surprise was rather amusing when she confidently seated herself, giving an order to the cross-eyed waiter in close attendance. It would be our privilege, of course, to pay the bill. Of its being a privilege, no one could doubt who had observed the envious glances cast in our direction by less favored patrons.

As Bréton spoke no Arabic, the task of interpreter devolved upon me; and I was carrying on quite mechanically when my attention was drawn to a peculiarly sinister-looking person seated alone at a table close beside the corner of the stage. I remembered having observed him address some remark to Shejeret ed-Durr, and having noted that she seemed to avoid him. Now, he was directing upon us a glare so electrically baleful that when I first detected it I was conscious of a sort of shock. The man was rather oddly dressed, wearing a black turban and a sort of loose robe not unlike the *burnûs* of the desert Arabs. I concluded that he belonged to some religious order, and that his bosom was inflamed with a hatred of a most murderous character towards myself, Felix Bréton, and the dancer.

I endeavored, without attracting the girl's notice to indicate to Bréton the presence of the Man of the Glare; but the artist was so engrossed in contemplation of Shejeret ed-Durr and kept me so busy interpreting, that I abandoned the attempt in despair. Having made his wishes evident to her, the girl readily consented to pose for him; and when next I glanced at the table near the stage, the Man of the Glare had disappeared.

What induced me to look towards the rear of the platform upon which we were seated I know not, unless I did so in obedience to a species of hypnotic suggestion; but something prompted me to glance over my shoulder. And, for the second time that night, I encountered the gaze of mysterious eyes. From a little square window these compelling eyes regarded me fixedly, and presently I distinguished the outline of a head surmounted by a white turban.

The second watcher was Abû Tabâh!

What business could have brought the mysterious *imám* to such a place was a problem beyond my powers of conjecture, but that he was silently directing me to depart with all speed I presently made out. Having signified, by a gesture, that I had grasped the purport of his message, I turned again to Bréton, who was struggling to carry on a conversation with Shejeret ed-Durr in his native French.

I experienced some difficulty in inducing him to leave, but my arguments finally prevailed, and we passed out into the dimly lighted street. About us in the darkness pipes wailed, and there was the dim throbbing of the eternal *darábukeh.* We were in that part of El-Wasr adjoining the notorious Square of the Fountain. Discordant woman voices filled the night, and strange figures flitted from the shadows into the light streaming from the open doorways. It was the centre of secret Cairo, the midnight city; and three paces from the door of the dance hall, a slim, black-robed figure suddenly appeared at my elbow, and the musical voice of Abû Tabâh spoke close to my ear:

"Be on the terrace of Shepheard's in half an hour."

The mysterious figure melted again into the shadows about us.

II

On the deserted hotel balcony, Abû Tabâh awaited me.

"It was indeed fortunate, Kernaby Pasha," he said, "that I observed you this evening."

"I am greatly obliged to you," I replied, "for watching over me with such paternal solicitude. May I inquire what danger I have incurred?"

I was angrily conscious of feeling like a schoolboy suffering reproof.

"A very great danger," Abû Tabâh assured me, his gentle, musical voice expressing real concern. "Ahmad es-Kebîr is the lover of the dancer called Shejeret ed-Durr, although she who is of the *ghawâzi* of Keneh does not return his affections."

"Ahmad es-Kebîr? — do you refer to a malignant looking person in a black turban?" I inquired.

Abû Tabâh gravely inclined his head.

"He is one of the *Rifa'íyeh,* the Black *Darwîshes.* They practise strange rites and are by some accredited with supernatural powers. For you the danger is not so great as for your friend, who seemed to be speaking words of love to the *ghazîyeh.*"

I laughed shortly.

"You are mistaken, Abû Tabâh," I replied; "his interest was not of the character which you suppose. He is an artist and merely desired the girl to pose for him."

Abû Tabâh shrugged his shoulders.

"She is an unveiled woman," he said contemptuously, "but love in the heart of such a one as Ahmad is a terrible passion, consuming the vitals and rendering whom it afflicts either a partaker of Paradise or as one of the evil *ginn*."

"In the particular case under consideration," I said, "it would seem distinctly to have produced the latter and less agreeable symptoms."

"Let your friend step warily," advised Abû Tabâh; "for some who have aroused the enmity of the Black *Darwîshes* have met with strange ends, nor has it been possible to fix responsibility upon any member of the order."

"You think my poor friend, Felix Bréton, may be discovered some morning in an unpleasantly messy condition?"

"The Black *Darwîshes* do not employ the knife," answered Abû Tabâh; "they employ strange and more subtle weapons."

I stared hard at him in the darkness. I thought I knew my Cairo, but this sounded unpleasantly mysterious. However —

"I am indebted to you, Abû Tabâh," I said, "for your timely warning. As you know, I always personally avoid any possibility of misunderstanding in regard to my relations with Egyptian womenfolk."

"With some rare exceptions," agreed Abû Tabâh, "particulars of which escape my memory at the moment, you have always been a model of discretion, Kernaby Pasha."

"I will warn my friend," I said hastily, "of the view of his conduct mistakenly taken by the gentleman in the black turban."

"It is well," replied Abû Tabâh; "we shall meet again ere long."

With that and the customary dignified salutations he departed, leaving me wondering what hidden significance lay in his words, "we shall meet again ere long."

Experience had taught me that Abû Tabâh's warnings were not to be lightly dismissed, and I knew enough of the fanaticism of those strange Eastern sects whereof the *Rifâ'îyeh*, or Black *Darwîshes*, was one, to realize that it would prove an unhealthy amusement to interfere with their domestic affairs. Felix Bréton, who possessed the rare gift of capturing and transferring to canvas the atmosphere of the East with the opulent colorings and vivid contrasts which constitute its charm, had nevertheless but little practical experience of the manners and customs of the golden Orient. He had leased a large studio situated on the roof of a fine old Cairene palace hidden away behind the Street of the Booksellers and almost in the shadow of the Mosque of el-Azhar. His romantic spirit had prompted him after a time to give up his rooms at the Continental and to take up his abode in the apartment adjoining the studio; that is to say, completely to cut himself off from European life and to become an inhabitant of the Oriental city. With his imperfect knowledge of the practical side of native life in the East, I did not envy him; but I was fully alive to his danger, isolated as he was from the European community, indeed from modernity; for out of the boulevards of modern Cairo into the streets of the *Arabian Nights* is but a step, yet a step that bridges the gulf of centuries.

As I entered his studio on the following morning, I discovered him at work upon the extraordinary picture "Danse Funébre." Shejeret ed-Durr was posing in the dress of an ancient priestess of Isis. Bréton briefly greeted me, waving his hand towards a cushioned *dîwan* before which stood a little coffee-table bearing decanters, siphons, cigarettes, and other companionable paraphernalia. Making myself comfortable, I studied the picture and the model.

"Danse Funébr" was an extraordinary conception, representing an elaborately furnished modern room, apparently that of an antiquary or Egyptologist; for a multitude of queer relics decorated the walls, cabinets, and the large table at which a man was seated. Boldly represented immediately to the left of his chair stood a mummy in an ornate sarcophagus, and forth from the swathed figure into the light cast downwards from an antique lamp, floated a beautiful spirit shape — that of an Egyptian priestess. Upon her face was an expression of intense anger, as, her fingers crooked in sinister fashion, she bent over the man at the table.

The mummy and sarcophagus depicted on the canvas stood before me against the wall of the studio, the lid resting beside the case. It was moulded, as is sometimes seen, to represent the face and figure of the occupant and was as fine an example of the kind as I had met with. The mummy was that of a priestess and dancer of the Great Temple at Philæ, and it had been lent by the museum authorities for the purpose of Bréton's picture.

His enthusiasm at first seeing Shejeret ed-Durr was explainable by the really uncanny resemblance which the girl bore to the modeled figure. Studying her, from my seat on the *dîwan,* as she posed in that gauzy raiment depicted upon the lid of the sarcophagus, it seemed indeed that the ancient priestess was reborn in the form of Shejeret ed-Durr the *ghazîyeh.* Bréton had evidently tabooed make-up, with the exception of the characteristic black bordering to the eyes (which appeared in the presentment of the servant of Isis); and seen now in its natural coloring the face of the dancing-girl had undoubted beauty.

Presently, whilst the model rested, I informed Bréton of my conversation with Abû Tabâh; but, as I had anticipated, he was sceptical to the point of derision.

"My dear Kernaby," he said, "is it likely that I am going to interrupt my work now that I have found such an inspiring model, because some ridiculous *darwîsh* disapproves?"

"It is highly unlikely," I admitted; "but do not make the mistake of treating the matter lightly. You are right off the map here, and Cairo is not Paris."

"It is a great deal safer!" he cried in his boisterous fashion, "and infinitely more interesting."

But my mind was far from easy; for in the dark eyes of the model, when their glance rested upon Felix Bréton, there was that to have aroused poisonous sentiments in the bosom of the Man of the Glare.

III

During the course of the following month I saw Felix Bréton two or three times, and he was enthusiastic about the progress of his picture and the beauty of his model. The first hint that I received of the strange idea which was to lead to stranger happenings came one afternoon when he had called upon me at Shepheard's.

"Do you believe in reincarnation, Kernaby?" he asked suddenly.

I stared at him in surprise.

"Regardless of my personal views on the matter," I replied, "in what way does the subject interest you?"

Momentarily he hesitated; then —

"The resemblance between Yâsmîn" (this was the real name of Shejeret ed-Durr) "and the priestess of Isis," he said, "appears to me too marked to be explainable by mere coincidence. If the mummy were my personal property I should unwrap it —"

"Do you seriously desire me to believe that you regard Yâsmîna as a reincarnation of the elder lady?"

"That or a lineal descendant," he answered. "The tribe of the *Ghawâzi* is of unknown antiquity and may very well be descended from those temple dancers of the days of the Pharaohs. If you have studied the ancient wall paintings, you cannot have failed to observe that the dancing girls represented have entirely different forms from those of any other women depicted and from those of the ordinary Egyptian women of to-day."

His enthusiasm was tremendous; he was one of those uncomfortable fanatics who will ride a theory to the death.

"I cannot say that I have noticed it," I replied. "Your knowledge of the female form divine is doubtless more extensive than mine."

"My dear Kernaby," he cried excitedly, "to the trained eye the difference is extraordinary. Until I saw Yâsmîna I had believed the peculiar form to which I refer to be extinct like the blue enamel and the sacred lotus. If it is not reincarnation it is heredity."

I could not help thinking that it more closely resembled insanity than either; but since Bréton had made no reference to the wearer of the black turban, I experienced less anxiety respecting his physical than his mental welfare.

Three days later there was a dramatic development. Drifting idly into Bréton's studio one morning I found him pacing the place in despair and glaring at his unfinished canvas like a man distraught.

"Where is Shejeret ed-Durr?" I inquired.

"Gone!" he replied. "She disappeared yesterday and I can find no trace of her."

"Surely the excellent Suleyman, proprietor of the dancing establishment, can assist you?"

"I tell you," cried Bréton savagely, "that she has disappeared. No one knows what has become of her."

I looked at him in dismay. He presented a mournful spectacle. He was unshaven and his dark hair was wildly disordered. His despair was more acute than I should have supposed possible in the circumstances; and I concluded that his interest in Yâsmîna was deeper than I had assumed or that I was incapable of comprehending the artistic temperament. I suppose the Gallic blood in him had something to do with it, but I was unspeakably distressed to observe that the man was on the verge of tears.

Consolation was impossible, and I left him pacing his empty studio distractedly. That night at an unearthly hour, long after I had retired to my own apartments, he came to Shepheard's. Being shown into my room, and the servant having departed —

"Yâsmîna is dead!" he burst out, standing there, a disheveled figure, just within the doorway.

"What!" I exclaimed, standing up from the table at which I had been writing and confronting him. "Dead? Do you mean —"

"He has murdered her!" said Bréton, in a dull monotonous voice — "that fiend of whom you warned me."

I was appalled; for I had been utterly unprepared for such a tragedy.

"Who discovered her?"

"No one discovered her; she will never be discovered! He has buried her body in some secret spot in the desert."

My amazement grew with every word that he uttered, and presently —

"Then how in Heaven's name did you learn of her murder?" I asked.

Felix Bréton, who had begun to pace up and down the room, a truly pitiable figure, paused and looked at me wildly.

"You will think that I am mad, Kernaby," he said; "but I must tell you — I must tell someone. I could see that you were incredulous when I spoke to you of reincarnation, but I was right, Kernaby, I was right! Either that or my reason is deserting me."

My opinion inclined distinctly in the direction of the latter theory, but I remained silent, watching Bréton's haggard face.

"To-night," he continued, "as I sat looking at my unfinished picture and trying to imagine what could have become of Yâsmîna, the mummy — the mummy of the priestess — *spoke to me!*"

I slowly sank back into my chair. I was now assured that Felix Bréton had formed a sudden and intense infatuation for Yâsmîna and that her mysterious disappearance had deranged his sensitive mind. Words failed me; I could think of nothing to say; and bending towards me his haggard face —

"It whispered to me," he said, "in *her* voice — in my own language, French, as I have taught it to her; just a few imperfect words, but sufficient to convey to me the story of the tragedy. Kernaby, what does it mean? Is it possible that her spirit, released from the body of Yâsmîna, has returned to that which I firmly believe it formerly inhabited? . . ."

I had had the misfortune to be a party to some distressing scenes, but few had affected me so unpleasantly as this. That poor Felix Bréton was raving I could not doubt, but having persuaded him to spend the night at Shepheard's and having seen him safely to bed, I returned to my own room to endeavor to work out the problem of what steps I should take regarding him on the morrow.

In the morning, however, he seemed more composed, having shaved and generally rendered himself more presentable; but the wild look still lingered in his eyes and I could see that the strange obsession had secured a firm hold upon him. He discussed the matter quite calmly during breakfast, and invited met to visit the scene of this supernatural happening. I assented, and hailing *arabîyeh* we drove together to the studio.

There was nothing abnormal in the appearance of the place, but I examined the mummy and the mummy case with a new curiosity; for if Felix Bréton was not mad (and this was a point upon which I recognized my incompetence to decide) the phantom voice was clearly the product of some trick. However, I was unable to discover anything to account for it. The sarcophagus stood against the outer wall of the studio and near to a large lattice window before which was draped a heavy tapestry curtain for the purpose of excluding undesirable light upon that side of the model's throne. There was no balcony outside the window, which was fully, thirty feet from the street below; therefore unless someone had been hiding in the window recess beside the sarcophagus, trickery appeared to be out of the question. Turning to Bréton, who was watching me haggardly —

"You searched the recess last night?" I said.

"I did — immediately. There was no one there. There was no one anywhere in the studio; and when I looked out of the open window, the street below, was deserted from end to end."

Naturally, I took it for granted that he would avoid the place, at any rate by night; and I said as much, as we passed along the Mûski together. I can never forget the wildness in his eyes as he turned to me.

"I *must* go back, Kernaby," he said. "It seems like desertion, base and cowardly."

IV

Bréton did not join me at dinner that evening as we had arranged that he should do, and towards the hour of ten o'clock, growing more and more uneasy on his behalf, I set out for the studio, half hoping that I should meet him. I saw nothing of him, however, as I crossed the Ezbekîyeh Gardens and the Atabet el-Khadrâ into the Mûski. From thence onward to the Eondpoint the dark and narrow streets were almost deserted, and from the corner of the Shâria el-Khordâgîya to the Street of the Bookbinders I met with no living thing save a lean and furtive cat.

My footsteps echoed hollowly from wall to wall of the overhanging buildings, as I approached the door giving access to the courtyard from which a stair communicated with the studio above. The moonlight, slanting down into the ancient place, left more than half of it in densest shadow, but just touched the railing of the balcony and the lower part of the *mushrabîyeh* screen masking what once had been the *harêm* apartments from the view of one entering the courtyard. Far above me, through an open lattice, a dim light shone out, though vaguely. This part of the house was bathed in the radiance of the moon, which dimmed that of the studio lamp; for the open window was the window of Bréton's studio.

The door at the foot of the stairs was partly open, and I ascended slowly, since the place was quite dark and I was forced to feel my way around the eccentric turnings introduced by an Arab architect to whom simplicity had evidently been an abomination.

A modern door had been fitted to the studio; and although this door was also unfastened, I rapped loudly, but, receiving no answer, entered the studio. It was empty. The lamp was lighted, as I had observed from below, and a faint aroma of Turkish tobacco smoke hung in the air. Clearly, Bréton had left but a few moments earlier; and I judged it probable that he would be returning very shortly, for had he set out for Shepheard's he would not have left his door unlocked, and in any event I should have met him on the way. Therefore, having glanced into the inner room, which, latterly, Bréton had been using as a bedroom, I sat down on the *dîwân* and prepared to await his return.

The lamp whose light I had seen shining through the window was that which hung before the model's throne, and the curtain which usually draped the window recess had been partially pulled aside, so that from where I sat I could see part of the centre lattice, which was open. My mind at this time was entirely occupied with uneasy speculations regarding Bréton, and although I had glanced more than once at the large unfinished picture on the easel, from which the face of Shejeret ed-Durr peered out across the shoulder of the seated man, and several times had looked at the mummy set upright in its painted sarcophagus, no sense of the uncanny had touched me or in any way prepared me for the amazing manifestation which I was about to witness.

How long I had sat there I cannot say exactly; possibly for ten minutes or a quarter of an hour: when, suddenly, an eerie whisper crept through the stillness of the big room!

Since I had more than once been temporarily tricked into belief in the supernatural, by means of certain ingenious devices, I did not readily fall a victim to the mysterious nature of the present occurrence. Yet I must confess that my heart gave a great leap and I was forced to exert all my will to control my nerves. I sat quite still, listening intently for a repetition of that evil whisper. Then, in the stillness, it came again.

"Felix," it breathed, "because of you I lie dead in a grave in the desert. . . . I died for you, Felix, and now I am so lonely. . . ."

The whispering voice offered no clue to the age or the sex of the speaker; for a true whisper is toneless. But the words, as Bréton had declared, were uttered in broken French and spoken with a curious accent.

It ceased, that ghostly whispering; and I realized that my nerves could stand no more of it; for that it came or seemed to come from the mummy of the priestess was a fact as undeniable as it was horrible.

Resorting to action, I sprang up and leaped across the room, grasping first at the curtain draped in the window on the right of the sarcophagus. I jerked it fully aside. The recess was empty. All three lattices were open, on the right, left, and in the centre of the window; but, craning out from the latter, I saw the street below to be vacant from end to end.

Stepping back into the room, and metaphorically clutching my courage with both hands, I approached the sarcophagus, peered behind it, all around it, and, finally, into the swathed face of the mummy itself. Nothing rewarded my search. But the studio of Felix Bréton seemed to have become icily cold; at any rate I found myself to be shivering; and walking deliberately, although it cost me a monstrous effort to do so, I descended the dark winding stairway into the courtyard, and, on regaining the street, discovered to my intense annoyance that my brow was wet with cold perspiration.

I had taken no more than ten paces in the direction of the Sûk es-Sûdan when I heard the sound of approaching footsteps, and for some reason (I can only suppose as a result of my highly strung condition) I stepped into the shelter of a narrow gateway, where I could see without being seen, and there awaited the appearance of the one who approached.

It was Felix Bréton, his face showing ghastly in the moonlight as he turned the corner. I could not be certain if a mere echo had deceived me, but I thought I could detect faintly the softer footfalls of someone who was following him. From my cover I had an uninterrupted view of the entrance to the house which I had just left; and without showing myself I watched Bréton approach the door. At its threshold he seemed to hesitate; and in that brief hesitancy were illustrated the conflicting emotions driving the man. I recalled the words he had spoken to me that morning. "I must go back, Kernaby; it seems like desertion, base and cowardly." He opened the door and disappeared.

As he did so, a second figure crossed from the shadows on the opposite side of the street — that is, the side upon which I was concealed; and in turn advanced towards the door. As he passed my hiding-place I acted. Without an instant's hesitation I hurled myself upon him.

How he avoided that furious attack — if he did avoid it — or whether in the darkness I miscalculated my spring, I do not know to this day: I only know that I missed my objective, stumbled, recovered myself . . . and turned with clenched fists to find *Abû Tabâh* confronting me!

"Kernaby Pasha!" he cried.

"Abû Tabâh!" said I dazedly.

"I perceive that I am not alone in my anxiety for the welfare of M. Felix Bréton."

"But why were you following him? I narrowly missed assaulting you."

"Very narrowly," he agreed in his gentle manner; "but you ask me why I was following M. Bréton. I was following him because I have seen so many of those who have crossed the path of the Black *Darwîshes* meet with violent and inexplicable deaths."

"Murder?" I whispered.

"Not murder — suicide. Therefore, observing, as I had anticipated, a strangeness in your friend's behavior, I have watched him."

"The strangeness of his behavior is easily accounted for," I said. And excitedly, for the horror of the episode in the studio was still strongly upon me, I told him of the whispering mummy.

"These are very dreadful things of which you speak, Kernaby Pasha," he admitted, "but I warned you that it was ill to incur the enmity of the Black *Darwîshes*. That there is a scheme afoot to compass the self-destruction or insanity of your friend is now evident to me; and he has brought this calamity upon himself; for the words which he believed to be spoken by the spirit of the girl Yâsmîna would not have affected him so unpleasantly if his attitude towards her had been marked by proper restraint and the affair confined within suitable limitations."

"Quite so. But although the Black *Darwîshes* may be both malignant and clever, that uncanny whispering is beyond the control of natural forces."

"Such is not my opinion," replied Abû Tabâh. "A spirit does not mistake one person for another; and the whispering voice addressed itself to 'Felix' when Felix was not present. I believe, Kernaby Pasha, that you are the possessor of a pair of excellent opera-glasses? May I suggest that you return to Shepheard's and procure them."

V

The platform of the minaret seemed very cold to the touch of my stockinged feet; for I had left my shoes at the entrance to the mosque below in accordance with custom; and now, from the wooden balcony, I overlooked the neighboring roofs of Cairo, and Abû Tabâh, beside me, pointed to where a vague patch of light broke the darkness beneath us to the left.

"The window of M. Felix Bréton's studio," he said.

Raising the glasses to his eyes, he gazed in that direction, whilst I also peered thither and succeeded in making out the well of the courtyard and the roofs of the buildings to right and left of it. It was not evident to me for what Abû Tabâh was looking, and when presently he lowered the glasses and turned to me I expressed my doubts in words.

"It is surely evident," I said, speaking, as I now almost invariably did to the *imam*, in English, of which he had a perfect mastery, "that we have little chance of discovering anything from here, since nothing was visible from the studio window. Furthermore, who save Yâsmîna could have spoken in the manner which I have related and in broken French?"

"An eavesdropper," he replied, "might have profited by the lessons which Yâsmîna received from M. Bréton; and all vocal characteristics are lost in a whisper. In the second place, Yâsmîna is not dead."

"What!" I cried.

Although, when Bréton had informed me of her death, I myself had doubted him, for some reason the ghostly whisper had convinced me as it had convinced him.

"She has been kept a prisoner during the past week in a house belonging to one of the Black *Darwîshes*," continued Abû Tabâh; "but my agents succeeded in tracing her this morning. By my orders, however, she has not been allowed to return to her home."

"And what was the object of those orders?"

"That I might learn for what purpose she had been made to disappear," replied Abû Tabâh; "and I have learned it to-night."

"Then you think that the whispering mummy —"

He suddenly clutched my arm.

"Quick! raise your glasses!" he said softly. "On the roof of the house to the left of the light. There is the whispering mummy!"

Strung up to a high pitch of excitement, I gazed through the glasses in the direction indicated by my companion. Without difficulty I discerned him? — a man wearing a black turban — who crept like some ungainly cat along the flat roof, carrying in his hand what looked like one of those sugar canes which pass for a delicacy among the natives, but which to European eyes appear more suitable for curtain-poles than sweetmeats. Springing perilously across a yawning gulf, the wearer of the black turban gained the roof of the studio, crept along for some little distance further, and then, lying prone, began slowly to lower the bamboo rod in the direction of the lighted window.

I found that unconsciously I had suspended my respiration, and now, breathlessly, as the truth came home to me —

"It is a speaking-tube!" I cried, "I cannot see the end of it, but no doubt it is curved so as to protrude through the side of the lattice window. Do you look, Abû Tabâh: I propose to act."

Thrusting the glasses into the *imám's* hand, I took my Colt repeater from my pocket, and, having peered for some seconds steadily in the direction of the dimly visible *Darwîsh,* I opened fire! I had fired five shots in the heat of my anger at that sinister crouching figure, ere Abû Tabâh seized my wrist.

"Stop!" he cried; "do you forget where you stand?"

Truly I had forgotten in my indignation, or I should not have outraged his feelings by firing from the minaret of a mosque. But sufficient of my wrath remained to occasion me a thrill of satisfaction, when, peering through the dusk, I saw the *Darwîsh* throw up his arms and disappear from view.

*　　*　　*　　*　　*　　*

"There is blood in the courtyard," said Abû Tabâh; "but Ahmad es-Kebîr has fled. Therefore he still lives, and his anger will be not the less but the greater. Depart from Cairo, M. Bréton: it is my counsel to you."

"But," cried Felix Bréton, glaring wildly at the big canvas on the easel, "I must finish my picture. As Yâsmîna is alive, she must return, and I must finish my picture!"

"Yâsmîna cannot return," replied Abû Tabâh, fixing his weird eyes upon the speaker. "I have caused her to be banished from Cairo." He raised his hand, checking Bréton's hot words ere they were uttered. "Recriminations are unavailing. Her presence disturbs the peace of the city, and the peace of the city it is my duty to maintain."

The Wrath of Amen-Ra*

hroughout the strange chain of events that uncoiled itself beneath the blazing Egyptian sky, Jimmy Stayner remained a skeptic. For one thing, Egypt bored him inexpressibly. The colossal temples were too colossal, the mighty statues entirely too mighty, while the tombs, carved with hieroglyphics, gave him that nightmare feeling of the morning after.

To be perfectly honest, an X-ray of Jimmy Stayner's mind would have shown a profound conviction that the cigarette and not the pyramids has made Egypt famous. What wonder then that he attributed the odd things he saw merely to coincidence?

There was, of course, no question about his meeting with Professor Upton. That was chance, entirely chance — if there is such a thing in this marvelously balanced universe. And had the encounter taken place in America, Jimmy would have passed on his way without a word. But in the desert, miles from human habitation, the sight of a human being in distress calls for different treatment; wherefore he gave the two quick whistles which ordered Hassan, his Bedouin guide, to bring the tiny caravan to a halt.

The camel Jimmy was riding was a peculiarly sad-faced, musty, misbegotten specimen of an overadvertized race. After two days of suffering Jimmy had become so accustomed to him that he was beginning to think that in a year or two he might care to take some solid food. Now as the brute began to sink to its knees with that peculiar motion that is compounded of the movements of a bucking bronco mingled with the uplift produced by the discharge of a depth bomb, Jimmy shut his eyes and decided that the year or two should be lengthened. Next instant the churning ceased and he set foot upon the sandy floor of the desert.

The sun being high in the heavens the sand was unpleasantly hot, wherefore Jimmy, like King Agag, walked "delicately." Dangling from his fingers was the old police-whistle — gift of a friend — which had once halted crowds in far-off Pittsburgh, and which, a minute before, had brought the caravan to a standstill. And, seated on, a camp-stool, beneath the shelter of a large white umbrella, was the gray old man whose sudden appearance in the midst of the desert had so surprised him.

"I am Stayner — Jimmy Stayner," he announced; "thought you might be in trouble, so I stopped." He glanced about the deserted encampment, where overturned equipment and scattered supplies told of hasty, apparently unpremeditated flight. "All alone?"

* "The Wrath of Amen-Ra" was written by William Holloway (dates unknown) and was originally published in 1921 (source unknown). The text for this edition came from *Fantastic Novels*, Jan. 1949.

"My name is Upton," answered the old man with a quick lift of cold gray eyes which Stayner, least fanciful of men, found oddly disturbing. "James Upton, professor of the Egyptian and Coptic languages and of Egyptian archaeology in —" He gazed expectantly at Stayner as he paused, but that individual giving no signs of having heard the name before, the old man shrugged his shoulders and went on. "In a western university, making a trip to a buried temple. Ali, my dragoman and his rascals deserted me this morning."

"That's odd!" commented Stayner. He gazed past Professor Upton at Hassan, who was making frantic gestures behind the old man's back, in a vain endeavor to arrest his employer's attention. What the man meant by his ridiculous antics Stayner had no means of knowing; nor did he greatly care. "What was the trouble with them?"

"Superstition!" was the curt reply. "You know what the natives are like. Well, then —"

Hassan's gestures were growing more emphatic. What did he mean? Probably something was the matter with the caravan — something of no importance to any one but Hassan. Jimmy Stayner looked about him at the kneeling camels, at the desert shimmering peacefully in the sunshine, and a vague feeling of annoyance crept over him that any man should disturb that stately calm.

Besides, when you save an Arab's life in a native brawl in Wady Halfa and in addition hire him as guide through the Libyan Desert, you scarcely expect to find him waving windmill arms behind the first white man you encounter.

Consequently, Jimmy, shaking his head at Hassan, proceeded to explain his own presence in the desert.

He was an engineer, he said briefly, killing time while British experts at Cairo went over the details of an important engineering project he had brought from Pittsburgh. Part of his boyhood had been spent in Arizona, which accounted for the call of the desert. He was on his way, for no particular reason, to a small oasis of which his guide had spoken. And if Professor Upton would care to join him.

The old man inclined his snowy head politely as he expressed his thanks; and Jimmy Stayner, hail fellow, well met with half the world, went forward to give instructions to Hassan regarding the new member of the caravan. He was doing a good turn to an entire stranger, but it never occurred to him that this was at all eccentric. Hassan promptly undeceived him.

"The mad American!" he whispered hoarsely.

"The one you were telling me of last night?" Jimmy was frankly incredulous. The story of the night before had been a strange one. It had possessed a certain sinister attraction, told in the moonlight, with the desert full of strange shadows, but here in open day, and applied to Professor Upton, the thing seemed too ridiculous for words. "That man is just as mad as you or I."

Hassan, who had traversed the desert many times from Biskra to Sinai and who had picked up a surprising command of English from a long line of tourists, exhausted his knowledge in a long explanation. The mad American had been coming to Egypt for many years. He came for the reason Hassan had mentioned the night before. Else why should Ali have deserted him, a dragoman above reproach and a true believer of the tribe Ouled Nail?

"Ah, shucks!" cried Jimmy Stayner. "That old man isn't mad at all. And why shouldn't he come to Egypt every year if he wants to? Forget it!"

"There are ancient devils in this land — devils such as no man dreams of," said Hassan firmly. "He comes to talk to them."

Stayner stared blankly as the son of the desert went on with his explanation. Before the coming of the true faith of Islam there had been other gods in Egypt, gods of majesty and power. These false gods fled before the caliphs, the servants of Allah. Some went to other lands; others remained in Egypt and took refuge in lonely mountain passes or in hidden tombs.

They were not gods, of course. There is but one god — here Hassan eyed his employer proudly — he who begets not nor is begotten. These were devils. And it was these the mad American came each year to seek. No! He was not like the wise men, who study the great pylons at Karnak. Hassan had been dragoman for many of these. This old man was different.

Jimmy Stayner drew a deep breath of satisfaction. Then he smiled. "I never thought I'd catch up with the Arabian Nights," he remarked. "But I've done it all right."

Hassan's face relaxed in turn at mention of the great classic of his race. "The Thousand Nights and One!" he exclaimed. "There it tells of Suliman the Magnificent — the one of the unbelievers call Solomon — who imprisoned the jinn in bottles of brass and sealed them with a holy seal. But that was not in Egypt. In Egypt the jinn were left free."

"Holy mackerel!" exclaimed Jimmy Stayner. He stood looking at the Arab an instant in comical amazement; then, the combined influence of Pittsburgh and the engineering profession asserted itself.

"We make our midday camp right here, Hassan," he said quietly. "The old gentleman goes with us, but don't talk to the men about him. See?"

Hassan, who belonged to the oldest and most well-bred race in the world, bowed gravely. He had given warning of the danger. If his employer disregarded the danger, death would probably tap him on the shoulder. That would be a pity. But it was Kismet. And, mindful of a certain evening in Wady Halfa, when the young man had saved his life at the risk of his own, Hassan knew that he would follow him to the end. Which, also, was Kismet.

The next few hours Stayner spent in the seclusion of his tent, in a restless doze. The sun was reaching his full power now and the surface of the desert shimmered with waves of heat that rose from the blistering sand. Above, the sun blazed in a cloudless sky, its rays striking down with the force of bullets.

No wonder, thought Stayner dreamily, that the superstitious Egyptians had made Amen-Ra, the god of the sun, the chief deity of their religion; for if ever there was a country where the sun deserved to be a god Egypt is that very country. He grew more and more sure of it as the day wore on and his tent thermometer mounted to unbelievable heights.

That evening Professor Upton made a curious proposal. Seated like Abraham before their tent "in the cool of the evening," he turned suddenly to the younger man.

"Know anything about Amen-Ra?"

"The old-timer, who was the big noise around Egypt?" asked Jimmy. "The Sun-God?"

"Exactly!" was the quiet answer. "Amen-Ra!"

"The father of the gods and the most powerful," remarked Stayner slowly. "That's the limit of my knowledge."

"The most powerful? That is the common opinion, which I do not share. But that is of no importance just now. What matters is that I was on my way to an ancient shrine of Amen-Ra's, when Ali deserted; a ruined temple hidden in an almost inaccessible mountain gorge. And I have been wondering this afternoon if you would care to go there with me."

"I'll try anything once," answered Jimmy Stayner flippantly, and the next instant regretted his decision. There would be another row with Hassan, of course, and, anyway, hunting up old temples is not the liveliest sport in the world. So that presently he fell silent and sat watching the moon rise over the desert.

Now to Jimmy Stayner what men term the mystery of Egypt was absolutely non-existent. When he spoke of Egypt he referred to modern Egypt only and not to the ancient land, which lies hidden beneath the sand of the desert. But this evening, with the Etesian wind blowing waves of grateful coolness in his face, the fathomless sky throbbing with stars, the moonlight beginning to cast strange shadows, everything seemed different.

Of course, he assured himself, it was all very foolish, all a reflex of his conversation with the old man; yet the fact remained that for the first time he was seeing the land as others saw it. The weight and oppression of long-dead centuries seemed upon the dreaming sand ocean. Other deserts — the Mojave for example — give a feeling of loneliness and death; this seemed clamorous with thoughts of a mysterious alien life, the roots of which were ages deep in the past.

He mentioned the thought to Professor Upton, who stooped down and caught up a handful of sand, which he allowed to trickle slowly through his fingers. "I doubt if there is a single grain of sand in the Nile Valley that has not once formed part of some human organism," he said quietly. "Think of the narrow land, the enormous population and the almost endless centuries!"

They broke camp next morning when dawn was visible only in a faint glow upon the horizon. Hassan, hearing from his employer of the change in his plans, made no protest, much to the other's surprise. It is true that for a moment his dark face wore a look of horror, but this passed quickly.

"Better not tell the men," he suggested. "They will find out soon enough."

"You think they will desert when they know?" asked Stayner with some curiosity.

Hassan nodded gravely. It was only a question of time, he explained.

"And you?" was Stayner's blunt question.

The Bedouin did not reply directly. For a moment his black eyes were full upon Stayner's face, and Jimmy, watching, saw a gleam appear and then disappear in their soundless depths. Thinking back, it always reminded him of a flash of lightning reflected in a quiet mountain pool. Then Hassan said quietly, "Wady Halfa." And it was as though everything had been spoken that could be spoken.

The little caravan moved westward through the tremulous glories of the dawn. Dew lay upon scattered thorn bushes and upon stray patches of half a grass in faintest tracery. Camel bells tinkled with an immemorial sound, swarthy Bedouins strode across the sand as their ancestors had done for countless centuries, and Jimmy Stayner, gazing about him, felt himself for the first time part of the pageant of history.

That evening two of the camel drivers deserted. There was nothing underhanded nor evasive in their procedure. They merely unloaded the beasts of burden which they had hired to Hassan, and announced their intention of turning back. There followed a long discussion in which Hassan — so Stayner judged by his gestures — tried to persuade the two men to continue. A waving of hands followed, mingled with gestures toward Professor Upton's tent. Then the voice died away and the two departed, leaving the remainder of Hassan's men visibly uneasy.

A change had come over the spirit of the expedition. That night the men made a larger fire than usual, utilizing thorn bushes recklessly. Yet Stayner noticed that there was none of the usual camp-fire gaiety in the air. Perhaps gaiety is too strong an impression for the quiet Oriental. At all events there was none of the telling of ancient stories that is the customary amusement of the desert camp-fire. It grew strangely chill as the sunlight faded and the Arabs gathered closely about the blaze. But it was a silent group and not once did a voice raise itself above the others.

Next day the appearance of the country began to change. Mountains loomed in sight; not in picturesque peaks, but in long, flat ranges of barren rock, scarred by sandstorms with a sort of dry erosion until they represented the ultimate extent of barren, reddish-yellow desolation. Among the crags and the sand-dunes the little expedition wound its way, Hassan speaking gently to his men in an evident endeavor, as Stayner interpreted it, to coax them to continue as long as possible. But they were plainly uneasy as their questioning glances showed. Once, when turning a corner of rock, a small hare ran quickly across the track and more than one man started at the sight.

Professor Upton had curiously little to say. Perched on top of a camel, he passed the day in a kind of feverish doze, raising his head at intervals to gave about him and then closing his eyes. At night he was almost as uncommunicative, though once or twice he began to speak, only to break off abruptly and resume his silent brooding.

There was something on the old man's mind. Of that Jimmy Stayner was positive; what it might be, of course he could not tell, but it was a fair conjecture that it related in some way to the subject of his quest. Jimmy was curious, but questions did not seem in order; so he talked to Hassan and waited patiently for the situation to develop.

An odd change had taken place in Jimmy Stayner's view of the expedition. He was much like a man who unwillingly sits down at the card-table and contemplates his first hand with a feeling of complete boredom, only to draw a card that changes his whole outlook on the game. He had agreed to go upon Professor Upton's search in a mood of careless good fellowship. Now he was vitally interested in the expedition. Hassan's attitude and that of his people had helped to change him. And the actions of the old Egyptologist had completed the turn about.

There was something odd about the old man; there was no question of that. When a man welcomes the dawn with the ritual of an ancient religion, he is, to put it mildly, peculiar. And it was Professor Upton's fad or folly to stand with arms up-raised, chanting an invocation in the stately tongue of dead Egypt.

The second morning Jimmy Stayner yawned profoundly.

"I always used a 'pony' when I studied foreign languages, professor," he said frankly. "Can you run that stuff off in English?"

"It is a prayer written over three thousand years ago by the Pharaoh Amenhotep IV to the god, Aton, the greatest god of Egypt. He is represented by the sun."

"I thought old Amen-Ra was the sun god and the big noise generally," interrupted the other.

The old man's face grew black.

"Fools thought so in ancient Egypt," he said shortly, "but Amenhotep IV destroyed the worship of Amen-Ra and set up that of Aton in its place. This prayer begins —"

He lifted up his hands, closed his eyes and spoke in a curious, singsong voice:

"Thy dawning is beautiful in the horizon of heaven, O thou, Aton, initiator of life.

"When thou risest in the east, thou fillest the earth with thy beauty; thou art beautiful, sublime and exalted above the earth. Thy beams envelop the lands and all that thou hast made."

"Oh, all right," interrupted Jimmy hastily. "I get you. Some little prayer!"

What had caused a man as entirely unromantic as Jimmy Stayner to call a halt was a very simple thing. Trained in the rough-and-tumble school of life it was one of his boasts that he could tell whether or not a man believed what he was saying. Now a shiver ran through him as he realized that the little ceremony he had witnessed was not a mere intellectual amusement, such as, for example, the reciting of the Rubáiyát, but an act of religious devotion.

The old man really believed what he was saying. Jimmy would have sworn to that. Yet that meant that from Jimmy's standpoint he was crazy. And if there are advantages in exploring ancient tombs in company with a madman they had hitherto escaped Jimmy's attention.

On the fourth day of this strange expedition the children of the desert succumbed to their fears and refused to go further, despite Hassan's entreaties and verbal scourgings. Rocks hemmed them in on all sides now; the scenery had become indescribably grim and awe-inspiring; they seemed entering upon untrodden ways that might lead who knows where. Stayner could scarcely blame them as he saw them hastily beginning the march back to civilization, though he was well aware that their departure meant a doubling and trebling of the difficulties of the expedition.

It throws a sharp side light upon Jimmy Stayner's character to report that it never once entered his head that Professor Upton should in the slightest degree change his plans. He had drawn cards in a curious game; he was going to stay in it to the end.

The caravan now consisted of only three camels. Professor Upton, with some of his baggage, accounted for one. The other two, piled with traveling equipment and supplies, padded softly on their way behind Hassan and his employer. It was the first time Jimmy had taken charge of one of the creatures on foot, and for some moments he had a vague impression that the brute behind him was only waiting occasion to pasture on his ears.

The road grew momentarily more difficult. They were now working their way through a narrow gorge, cloven in the rock ages since, the frowning sides of which threw somber shadows across their path.

Here and there were huge boulders, set in little mounds of eroded rock, which the wind at intervals set dancing in clouds of gritty, brownish-yellow dust that irritated the lungs almost to the point of suffocation.

After several hours travel the gorge ended abruptly in an overhanging rock, and the caravan came to a sudden halt. The younger man glanced doubtfully at Professor Upton, whose face wore a smile of satisfaction.

"Once before I came this far and had to turn back," he explained. "Short of water!"

"I don't see any gate," remarked Stayner, glancing at the rocky barrier. "I suppose there is a way up."

"We leave the animals here," said the old man. "There is a footpath behind the rock, leading to the plateau above. On that plateau, sunken in the sand I expect to find a temple of Amen-Ra's. It is unique because I think it about the only one of its kind that was left untouched when Amenhotep IV destroyed the worship of Amen-Ra and set up in its place that of Aton. All the temples of Amen-Ra were forcibly entered, the sanctuaries violated, the name of Amen-Ra chiseled from the stone inscriptions, the priesthood — the most powerful in the world — driven into exile. But this temple hidden in the desert, escaped the fate of the others. It was in charge of a very famous high priest, whose mummy I feel sure we shall be able to discover."

"And then," asked Stayner, "what are you going to do?"

"You will see," was the enigmatic answer.

Hassan attended to the matter-of-fact camels and the upward climb began, Professor Upton, who showed surprising agility, leading the way. They had ascended perhaps fifty feet when Stayner, who was second in line, was startled to observe the old man stumble over a projecting spur of rock and fall forward on his face, a distance of several feet, his cork helmet ricocheting down the trail like a spent bullet.

To leap to his side was the work of only an instant. He was not injured, Stayner could see at a glance, although somewhat shaken. But his forehead, damp with perspiration, had evidently been in contact with the earth for, marked upon it, evidently by pressure, was a curious oval containing within it a distinct impression of some kind of figures, the exact nature of which Stayner could not determine in the first quick glance allowed him.

Professor Upton rose slowly to his feet and smiled reassuringly. No! He was not hurt in the least. He had been careless. He hoped he had given no alarm to his companions — all of which was spoken in a firm, even voice that testified to the strength of his nerves. He was about to add something else when his gaze fell upon a fragment of sculpture lying in the sand.

"Excellent! Excellent!" he cried with unconcealed delight. "A cartouch of Amen-Ra!" He pointed at a strange mark, not unlike a picture of the sun. "See! The sign of Amen-Ra! We are on the right track."

Stayner made no reply. With wide eyes he was staring at the old man's forehead, across which lay an oval mark, having within it the sign of Amen-Ra. There was, of course, no mystery about it. Professor Upton had merely chanced to stumble in such a manner that his forehead, damp with perspiration, had come into close contact with the cartouch of Amen-Ra. There was absolutely nothing to it, yet Jimmy Stayner could not help but smile as he thought of the absurdity of the old Egyptologist being even momentarily marked with the sign of the god whose temple they were about to invade. Poetic justice? That was about what they would call it, Jimmy decided.

"You fell on it," he explained, "and it left a mark on your forehead. The sign of Amen-Ra!"

For a moment he expected that the old man's anger would surely strangle him, so furious was it. With passionate swiftness he swept his handkerchief across his forehead in an endeavor to remove all traces of the mark of Amen-Ra. In this he was partly successful, though the sign of the great god still remained in blurred red upon the skin. Then, Hassan having retrieved the missing cork helmet, the march upward was resumed.

Sometimes the slightest incident will change the current of a man's thoughts. The thing now happened to Jimmy Stayner. Hitherto the expedition had bored him inexpressibly; he had only continued in it because it was one way of killing time and because he had foolishly given a promise. But now he began to see that there might be a comic side to the affair. This little incident of the cartouch of Amen-Ra being marked across the forehead of a man who despised the god's power struck him as decidedly amusing. When they reached the temple of the ancient god there was a good prospect of more fun. Wherefore, Jimmy smiled to himself and possessed his soul in patience.

He had not long to wait. They mounted the crest of rock and stood looking down upon an amphitheater perhaps a couple of miles in width, sunken in the far recesses of the Libyan desert. What in primeval times had apparently been a series of terraces lifted in slow undulations to the opposite wall of rock, from which projected the facade of a great temple. A lane of sphinxes of huge size led to the massive pylon, or entrance gate, a vast structure in two parts, between which was the gateway to the outer court of the temple. So much was plain at the first glance.

A second and more careful inspection showed a second terrace some yards above the first and in the distance beyond it yet another. On the second terrace was another court, surrounded by a double row of pillars, and adorned with two small temples, one on either side. What there might be on the third terrace, which melted into the background of the eternal rocks, Stayner could not determine. Coming from the dimness of the gully into the glare of the noonday sun, his eyes were dazzled by the rays that beat upon the shining white wall opposite. But he saw enough to understand that the temple of Amen-Ra, facing him, was no mean huddle of buildings, but a structure or structures of the highest class.

He turned to Professor Upton. There was a curious glint in the old man's eyes that might have meant a number of things. Stayner did not pause to analyze it. Now that the end of the journey was in sight he was anxious to have the matter over and done with. Their position in the recesses of the Libyan desert had unpleasant features about it. He for one, and no doubt Hassan for two, wished he were on the homeward trail. Wherefore, despite the fact that the noonday heat made rest imperative, he suggested an exploration of the temple.

Professor Upton agreed with suspicious alacrity.

"It will only take a couple of hours," the old man said hastily. "Then my errand will be finished and we can make camp."

Jimmy Stayner was very thoughtful as they descended to the sandy amphitheater beneath. All inclination to laugh was gone. When a man undergoes trouble and privation in order to reach a given point and then announces that his errand will take only a couple of hours it is obvious that he knows exactly the object of his search and where it is to be found. Now what but treasure of some sort, the hiding-place of which he had in some manner discovered, could have brought the old man to this desolate mass of ruins? And that there are immense possibilities for "finds" in such situations is merest commonplace: So that, from this point on, Jimmy Stayner began to take the expedition very seriously.

The other member of the trio, Hassan, took the matter even more seriously. This was evidenced a moment later, when he flatly refused to proceed. He knew the place now. It was accursed, haunted by a mighty jinn. This was the reason why the Arabs of the desert gave it a wide berth. He would remain where he was until they returned.

Stayner nodded as he heard Hassan give his decision. Professor Upton was fumbling with a heavy knapsack which he wore, and Stayner was anxious to see the reason. A minute later the old man produced a hammer and chisel. Evidently, Jimmy Stayner told himself, they were about to burglarize the temple in the distance. Whether this were so or not, Professor Upton had other and more immediate uses for the hammer, for presently he paused before a narrow slab of limestone, upon which were cut various names of Amen-Ra, and, hastily, almost savagely, began defacing the hieroglyphics with quick strokes of the hammer. Stayner, whose ideas of hieroglyphics were somewhat vague, although he fancied he did recognize one of the emblems of the Sun God, asked pointblank for an explanation. When one did come it was peculiar.

"I think I told you that Amenhotep IV, after forbidding the worship of Amen-Ra, ordered all Amen-Ra's emblems to be chiseled from the stone of the temples and monuments. It was done all over Egypt except here. This particular temple was probably saved because of its distance from the rest of the world. At any rate, there took refuge here the man you might call the high priest of Amen-Ra. It was he who afterward restored the worship of Amen-Ra and destroyed the pure worship of Aton. The symbols I am destroying are those of Amen-Ra."

"Yes," remarked Jimmy Stayner politely. "Rather a nice temple." The old man was, of course, queer, but there is always something to be learned from a study of the engineering problems of ancient structures; and the terracing of this series of rock temples afforded interesting comparisons with other work of the sort Stayner had studied in America. So the ill-assorted pair went on their way, Hassan perched like a dejected fly on the hillside behind them.

The lane of sphinxes, leading to the pylon gate, was of extraordinary interest; but neither paid it much attention. Then came the first court, after which the ground rose about fifty feet to the terrace which formed the second court. The stone work here was exquisitely finished as Stayner noticed, the wall of white limestone in the rear being a gem of construction. On either side of the white limestone wall were temples. The old man pointed to each in turn. "Hathor!" he said curtly. "Anubis!" And Stayner knew he was looking upon shrines that Egyptologists would probably rave over.

What puzzled him was the fact that Professor Upton paid no attention to the two temples. With face set and eyes gleaming he mounted the central incline to still another and higher terrace that lay beyond. Here, passing through a granite portico, they entered a vestibule rectangular in shape and considerably smaller than either of the two outer courts, though nevertheless of considerable size. This vestibule was built against the mountainside, a doorway leading through the rock into the innermost temple, the Holy of Holies, within the mountain.

They paused momentarily before the doorway, Stayner to look about him, the older man to wipe the perspiration from his damp forehead. It was very warm where they stood in the full rays of the Egyptian sun, yet a faint cooling current made itself felt from the opening in the mountainside and suggested unbelievable depths of coolness within. But Jimmy Stayner was not concerned with the temperature. For the first time he was seeing a bit of ancient Egypt without being annoyed by tourists, guide-book in hand, in search of souvenirs; and for the first time Egypt had begun to bind him with her spell.

The sky was clear, yet he could fancy it dark with the wings of the mighty gods who had here accepted worship at their shrines. A vague sense of unknown presences, ancient beyond all telling, seemed to hover about them. It was all fancy, he told himself an instant later as he flung the thought from him; but while it lasted it certainly gave a man a jolt.

He turned to look at Professor Upton, who was now replacing his cork helmet. The old man's face was crimson; his eyes sparkled with excitement; he appeared worn and tired and old, as though wearied with the very violence of his emotions. As Stayner surveyed him, he saw him strike angrily with his hammer at a hieroglyphic inscription of Amen-Ra which adorned the wall near the doorway.

The blow was a glancing one and a slender spear of stone, flashing upward under the stroke, struck into the soft flesh of his neck. There was a tiny smear of blood as the old man brushed the splinter aside, but Stayner was quite grave. A trifle to one side and there might have been serious trouble with one of the larger blood-vessels. As it was the thing was of no importance whatever, unless a man was superstitious — and Stayner was surely not that.

The coolness of the temple within the mountain was peculiarly refreshing. In a moment it seemed to Stayner that he was revivified and strengthened. Leaving to Professor Upton the task of penetrating to the interior of the shrine, Jimmy Stayner perched himself upon a mass of diorite and waited. A stray bat blew out of the dark recesses within and brushed his ears as it passed, without attracting his attention.

He was debating several little problems of interest as he sat there. When the Englishmen gave him the contract — for of course, they would do that — he would leave this God-forsaken country on the jump. Imagine a country dependent on the whims of a single river! Suppose the river got balky? He smiled at the idea as he lit his pipe. Of course, too, he was going to get that contract. He could hear Professor Upton hammering within the Holy of Holies now. The old boy was certainly active for such a hot day.

The pipe had been smoked and so had its successor before the old man appeared from the dim recesses of the temple and put an end to the desultory current of his thoughts. Professor Upton's face was flushed with triumph as he dragged behind him the shrouded figure of a mummy.

"The easiest mummy-case I ever opened," he said cheerfully, lowering the mummy to the floor. "Generally a man of his importance has a heavier case than usual; but this brute" — he touched the shrouded and recumbent figure contemptuously with his foot — "somehow didn't."

There was something decidely unpleasant in the old man's voice and manner. After all, as Stayner told himself, this prostrate form had once been instinct with the mystery of human life, had once played a great part in the affairs of a vanished people. To treat it with disrespect seemed a childish bit of impertinence. Yet, Professor Upton was acting in just that way. And Stayner admitted to himself that he was puzzled.

"But what is the whole thing about?" he asked. "Why did you come here? And what are you going to do with the mummy?"

Professor Upton now unbent.

"I suppose you think me crazy," he said with a smile. "Well, I am not; though I own to being a bit of a crank on some phases of Egyptian history. For one thing I have always been interested in Amenhotep IV and his attempts to do away with the worship of Amen-Ra. The fact of his failure does not alter the other fact that he was the greatest religious reformer the world has ever known. The only trouble is that he died before he had entirely uprooted the influence of Amen-Ra. This was chiefly due to the high priest of Amen-Ra, whose mummy lies yonder. He it was who led the forces of the old god to triumph. The temples of the new god, Aton, were destroyed and the reformed worship overthrown.

"Now, many years ago I heard of this lonely temple in the desert and I determined" — the old man smiled reminiscently as a man might smile at the follies of his youth — "that if I ever found the temple my first step would be to unwind the mummy of the high priest and throw it out upon the sands of the desert to decay."

"But what's the big idea?" protested Stayner. "I don't quite get you."

"If I do that," the older man explained, "I practically destroyed the man body and soul, according to Egyptian philosophy. I suppose it's a small thing to do, but I've had it in my mind for thirty years, and I intend to do it now."

There was a curious ring of triumph in Professor Upton's voice, and Jimmy Stayner, glancing at him, saw that he was smiling to himself as though highly pleased. "You see," he continued, "the Egyptians embalmed the body because they thought the soul would one day return to earth, when the man would need his body again. Should the soul come back and find the body destroyed, it meant practical annihilation. That is what is going to happen to the high priest of Amen-Ra."

Stayner thought rapidly. The destruction of one mummy or a thousand meant absolutely nothing to him. What did matter was the conviction that the old man was undeniably crazy. The very fact of his chanting hymns to an Egyptian god was proof enough of that. Men, Stayner knew, have studied insanity for years only to become insane themselves; in a similar manner Professor Upton had studied the religion of Amenhotep IV until he actually, incredible as it seemed, believed it. And not only was he crazy, but his insanity, judging from his excited eyes and reddened face, had reached a climax.

It might have been the sudden termination of his long search that had finally upset him. It was more likely, Stayner told himself, the sudden change from the coolness of the rock temple to the blazing sun of noonday. At all events, when Stayner glanced at him again, he was dancing about the rocky floor in triumph, pausing at intervals to kick the prostrate mummy as he passed, his face working convulsively. The sight was so unpleasant that the younger man acted promptly.

"Suppose we go back to the camels?" he suggested. "You are ill." Professor Upton looked at Stayner with an air of profound attention. Then, without saying a word, he began unwinding from around his waist several yards of heavy cord, such as tent-dwellers use in bracing tent-poles. Still in complete silence he went to one of the pillars which guarded the entrance to the rock-cavern, and fastened securely around it one end of his cord, after which he turned briskly about again. "If you will come over here I'll be obliged," he said quietly.

"I don't get you," began Jimmy Stayner; "that is, I —" The words seemed to choke him for, staring him full in the face, was a little round circle of steel, which he dimly knew to be the muzzle of a revolver.

"Hurry up!" came the sharp command. "I have no time to waste."

There was such a note of inflexible determination in the old man's voice that Jimmy Stayner did exactly as ordered. It was only when he knew himself to be bound securely to the pillar that he uttered a protest.

"Say! What the devil are you trying to do?" he asked hotly.

Professor Upton, kneeling beside the mummy, was beginning to unfasten its bandages of fine linen. As he did so a strong aromatic odor that spoke of tropical spices, floated out upon the air. "I told you I was going to unwrap the mummy of the high priest of Amen-Ra, and let it decay in the sun. Maybe I'll set fire to it. That's all; but I have been planning to do that very thing for thirty years, so do you think it likely I would tolerate any interference? Afterward, I'll untie you and we'll go back to the camels. My life work will then be finished."

As he spoke the crazy old man was busy with the linen bandages that swatched the mummy; bandages that ages before had been wrapped about it by the priests of ancient Egypt and sealed with mighty enchantments to protect it from harm. As Stayner watched the unrolling of the yards of aromatic linen a sense of the futility of it all came over him. There were charms upon that soft, stained linen that should, by all rights, have blasted Professor Upton where he stood. Yet, nothing occurred. The old Egyptologist went on with his gruesome work as calmly as though it were the most usual thing in the world, while, above, the Egyptian sun blazed down remorselessly.

Presently the task was ended and the ancient figure of the high priest of Amen-Ra lay bare and dishonored upon the blistering pavement of the temple court. From the yards upon yards of discarded wrappings a heavy smell of spices floated up in the warm air. And the gods of Egypt, deified in the person of the high priest, gave no sign. By all rights, Jimmy Stayner told himself, there should have been the rustling of vast wings, a quivering in the atmosphere as the monstrous procession of the ancient gods, headed by Amen-Ra, came to avenge the violator of their hoary faith. But there was absolutely nothing but a great peace.

Yes! There was something. And it came, strangely enough, from the old man. His face darkened with anger as he pointed toward a small, insignificant snake, with markings curiously like a sprawling cross upon its brown and yellow back. He stamped his feet while he spoke.

"It came out of the rock temple. I suppose I disturbed it," he explained. "It interrupted my prayer to Aton."

"Dangerous?" asked Stayner indifferently. "Better kill it, hadn't you?"

The little reptile crawled slowly across the pavement toward the pile of aromatic linen wrappings, doubtless attracted by their strong perfume. Both men watched it an instant; then Jimmy Stayner turned his attention to the mummy of the high priest.

For the sun, the emblem of Amen-Ra, was beginning to work upon the shrunken limbs of the dead man. He saw the brownish-yellow limbs writhe and twist with a sickening simulation of real life, saw the body of the high priest move upon his shoulders, lift partly from the ground, and falling back, struggle once more to move.

It was, of course, only a coincidence that the action of the sunlight should have made it seemingly endeavor to move toward Professor Upton. It merely chanced, as Stayner assured himself, that the sun drew more strongly in that direction. But the effect was as though the dumb, dead thing, centuries old, that lay upon the pavement, were vainly striving to reach the man who had violated its solemn repose.

Professor Upton apparently noticed it also, for his face wore a startled look and he drew back. Then, once more he stepped forward, close to the mummy, watching its stirrings with gloating eyes. The tiny snake, which had been crawling toward the linen wrappings on the other side of the mummy, reached them, circle about them and twined up the high priest's arm where it partly uncoiled to raise a menacing head, after which it ran down to the upturned right palm.

What followed came so quickly that Jimmy Stayner had no time to cry out. The body, which had not ceased to stir with an odious semblance to life, was suddenly violently contorted as Professor Upton bent forward to watch. The right hand straightened and lifted from the ground as the body twisted, until it fell across the shrunken breast, while the snake, poised upon the palm, was tossed lightly in Professor Upton's face. There was a sharp cry from the old Egyptologist, one hand flung the reptile far across the pavement while the other clutched fast to his throat.

"It got me!" he cried thickly.

To Stayner, bound helplessly to the stone pillar, the happenings of the next half-hour seemed to fill years. He could see the sightless gaze of the mummy fixed upon his enemy as the suffering man sank upon the pavement with an expression of abiding malice. Then, the sun having done its work, its limbs gradually grew quiet again. It seemed to settle down upon the pavement much as it had done at first, and much as Professor Upton was doing now.

For the latter, bitten in the throat, there was never the remotest chance in the world. Even had he been able to unloosen Stayner's bonds, the latter would have been able to do nothing more than watch his passing. The end came speedily. An hour later Jimmy Stayner was watching the black and horribly swollen face of a dead man, when Hassan stole furtively into view. He had grown uneasy, he said, as he untied the rope, and though he mentioned no names, Jimmy Stayner knew he was reaping the reward of a good evening at Wady Halfa.

For a moment the two stared at the two bodies that lay near. "Surely there are devils in these old places," said Hassan.

"Devils your grandmother!" cried Jimmy Stayner. "That's all bunk. It was just the sun's heat moving the mummy. But it was odd. It gave me the creeps. But, shucks! There was nothing to it." He looked about him. "If you hand me that stick, Hassan, I'll kill that useless snake and then we can see about the body."

He paused a minute. "The cartouch was a little queer, but there was nothing to it but chance."

And the silent mummy of the high priest of Amen-Ra lay with calm face upturned to the sun the symbol of his god.

The Nameless City[*]

When I drew nigh the nameless city, I knew it was accursed. I was travelling in a parched and terrible valley under the moon, and afar I saw it protruding uncannily above the sands as parts of a corpse may protrude from an ill-made grave. Fear spoke from the age-worn stones of this hoary survivor of the deluge, this great-grandfather of the eldest pyramid; and a viewless aura repelled me and bade me retreat from antique and sinister secrets that no man should see, and no man else had dared to see.

Remote in the desert of Araby lies the nameless city, crumbling and inarticulate, its low walls nearly hidden by the sands of uncounted ages. It must have been thus before the first stones of Memphis were laid, and while the bricks of Babylon were yet unbaked. There is no legend so old as to give it a name, or to recall that it was ever alive; but it is told of in whispers around campfires and muttered about by grandams in the tents of sheiks so that all the tribes shun it without wholly knowing why. It was this place that Abdul Alhazred the mad poet dreamed of the night before he sang his unexplained couplet:

That is not dead which can eternal lie,
And with strange aeons death may die.

I should have known that the Arabs had good reason for shunning the nameless city, the city told of in strange tales but seen by no living man, yet I defied them and went into the untrodden waste with my camel. I alone have seen it, and that is why no other face bears such hideous lines of fear as mine; why no other man shivers so horribly when the night wind rattles the windows. When I came upon it in the ghastly stillness of unending sleep it looked at me, chilly from the rays of a cold moon amidst the desert's heat. And as I returned its look I forgot my triumph at finding it, and stopped still with my camel to wait for the dawn.

For hours I waited, till the east grew grey and the stars faded, and the grey turned to roseate light edged with gold. I heard a moaning and saw a storm of sand stirring among the antique stones though the sky was clear and the vast reaches of desert still. Then suddenly above the desert's far rim came the blazing edge of the sun, seen through the tiny sandstorm which was passing away, and in my fevered state I fancied that from some remote depth there came a crash of musical metal to hail the fiery disc as Memnon hails it from the banks of the Nile. My ears rang and my imagination seethed as I led my camel slowly across the sand to that unvocal place, that place which I alone of living men had seen.

---

[*] "The Nameless City" was written by H. P. Lovecraft (1890 – 1937) and published in *The Wolverine*, Nov. 1921.

In and out amongst the shapeless foundations of houses and places I wandered, finding never a carving or inscription to tell of these men, if men they were, who built this city and dwelt therein so long ago. The antiquity of the spot was unwholesome, and I longed to encounter some sign or device to prove that the city was indeed fashioned by mankind. There were certain *proportions* and *dimensions* in the ruins which I did not like. I had with me many tools, and dug much within the walls of the obliterated edifices; but progress was slow, and nothing significant was revealed. When night and the moon returned I felt a chill wind, which brought new fear, so that I did not dare to remain in the city. And as I went outside the antique walls to sleep, a small sighing sandstorm gathered behind me, blowing over the grey stones though the moon was bright and most of the desert still.

I awakened just at dawn from a pageant of horrible dreams, my ears ringing as from some metallic peal. I saw the sun peering redly through the last gusts of a little sandstorm that hovered over the nameless city, and marked the quietness of the rest of the landscape. Once more I ventured within those brooding ruins that swelled beneath the sand like an ogre under a coverlet, and again dug vainly for relics of the forgotten race. At noon I rested, and in the afternoon I spent much time tracing the walls and bygone streets, and the outlines of the nearly vanished buildings. I saw that the city had been mighty indeed, and wondered at the sources of its greatness. To myself I pictured all the splendours of an age so distant that Chaldaea could not recall it, and thought of Sarnath the Doomed, that stood in the land of Mnar when mankind was young, and of Ib, that was carven of grey stone before mankind existed.

All at once I came upon a place where the bedrock rose stark through the sand and formed a low cliff; and here I saw with joy what seemed to promise further traces of the antediluvian people. Hewn rudely on the face of the cliff were the unmistakable façades of several small, squat rock-houses or temples, whose interiors might preserve many secrets of ages too remote for calculation, though sandstorms had long effaced any carvings which may have been outside.

Very low and sand-choked were all the dark apertures near me, but I cleared one with my spade and crawled through it, carrying a torch to reveal whatever mysteries it might hold. When I was inside I saw that the cavern was indeed a temple, and beheld plain signs of the race that had lived and worshipped before the desert was a desert. Primitive altars, pillars, and niches, all curiously low, were not absent; and though I saw no sculptures or frescoes, there were many singular stones clearly shaped into symbols by artificial means. The lowness of the chiselled chamber was very strange, for I could hardly kneel upright; but the area was so great that my torch showed only part of it at a time. I shuddered oddly in some of the far corners; for certain altars and stones suggested forgotten rites of terrible, revolting and inexplicable nature and made me wonder what manner of men could have made and frequented such a temple. When I had seen all that the place contained, I crawled out again, avid to find what the temples might yield.

Night had now approached, yet the tangible things I had seen made curiosity stronger than fear, so that I did not flee from the long moon-cast shadows that had daunted me when first I saw the nameless city. In the twilight I cleared another aperture and with a new torch crawled into it, finding more vague stones and symbols, though nothing more definite than the other temple had contained. The room was just as low, but much less broad, ending in a very narrow passage crowded with obscure and cryptical shrines. About these shrines I was prying when the noise of a wind and my camel outside broke through the stillness and drew me forth to see what could have frightened the beast.

The moon was gleaming vividly over the primitive ruins, lighting a dense cloud of sand that seemed blown by a strong but decreasing wind from some point along the cliff ahead of me. I knew it was this chilly, sandy wind which had disturbed the camel and was about to lead him to a place of better shelter when I chanced to glance up and saw that there was no wind atop the cliff. This astonished me and made me fearful again, but I immediately recalled the sudden local winds that I had seen and heard before at sunrise and sunset, and judged it was a normal thing. I decided it came from some rock fissure leading to a cave, and watched the troubled sand to trace it to its source, soon perceiving that it came from the black orifice of a temple a long distance south of me, almost out of sight. Against the choking sand-cloud I plodded toward this temple, which as I neared it loomed larger than the rest, and shewed a doorway far less clogged with caked sand. I would have entered had not the terrific force of the icy wind almost quenched my torch. It poured madly out of the dark door, sighing uncannily as it ruffled the sand and spread among the weird ruins. Soon it grew fainter and the sand grew more and more still, till finally all was at rest again; but a presence seemed stalking among the spectral stones of the city, and when I glanced at the moon it seemed to quiver as though mirrored in unquiet waters. I was more afraid than I could explain, but not enough to dull my thirst for wonder; so as soon as the wind was quite gone, I crossed into the dark chamber from which it had come.

This temple, as I had fancied from the outside, was larger than either of those I had visited before; and was presumably a natural cavern since it bore winds from some region beyond. Here I could stand quite upright, but saw that the stones and altars were as low as those in the other temples. On the walls and roof I beheld for the first time some traces of the pictorial art of the ancient race, curious curling streaks of paint that had almost faded or crumbled away; and on two of the altars I saw with rising excitement a maze of well-fashioned curvilinear carvings. As I held my torch aloft it seemed to me that the shape of the roof was too regular to be natural, and I wondered what the prehistoric cutters of stone had first worked upon. Their engineering skill must have been vast.

Then a brighter flare of the fantastic flame showed that form which I had been seeking, the opening to those remoter abysses whence the sudden wind had blown; and I grew faint when I saw that it was a small and plainly artificial door chiselled in the solid rock. I thrust my torch within, beholding a black tunnel with the roof arching low over a rough flight of very small, numerous and steeply descending steps. I shall always see those steps in my dreams, for I came to learn what they meant. At the time I hardly knew whether to call them steps or mere footholds in a precipitous descent. My mind was whirling with mad thoughts, and the words and warning of Arab prophets seemed to float across the desert from the land that men know to the nameless city that men dare not know. Yet I hesitated only for a moment before advancing through the portal and commencing to climb cautiously down the steep passage, feet first, as though on a ladder.

It is only in the terrible phantasms of drugs or delirium that any other man can have such a descent as mine. The narrow passage led infinitely down like some hideous haunted well, and the torch I held above my head could not light the unknown depths toward which I was crawling. I lost track of the hours and forgot to consult my watch, though I was frightened when I thought of the distance I must be traversing. There were changes of direction and of steepness; and once I came to a long, low, level passage where I had to wriggle my feet first along the rocky floor, holding my torch at arm's length beyond my head. The place was not high enough for kneeling. After that were more of the steep steps, and I was still scrambling down interminably when my failing torch died out. I do not think I noticed it at the time, for when I did notice it I was still holding it above me as if it were ablaze. I was quite unbalanced with that instinct for the strange and the unknown which had made me a wanderer upon earth and a haunter of far, ancient and forbidden places.

In the darkness there flashed before my mind fragments of my cherished treasury of daemonic lore; sentences from Alhazred the mad Arab, paragraphs from the apocryphal nightmares of Damascius and infamous lines from the delirious *Image du Monde* of Gauthier de Metz. I repeated queer extracts, and muttered of Afrasiab and the daemons that floated with him down the Oxus, later chanting over and over again a phrase from one of Lord Dunsany's tales — 'The unreverberate blackness of the abyss'. Once when the descent grew amazingly steep I recited something in sing-song from Thomas Moore until I feared to recite more:

> *A reservoir of darkness, black*
> *As witches' cauldrons are, when fill'd*
> *With moon-drugs in th' eclipse distill'd.*
> *Leaning to look if foot might pass*
> *Down thro' that chasm, I saw, beneath,*
> *As far as vision could explore,*
> *The jetty sides as smooth as glass,*
> *Looking as if just varnish'd o'er*
> *With that dark pitch the Seat of Death*
> *Throws out upon its slimy shore.*

Time had quite ceased to exist when my feet again felt a level floor, and I found myself in a place slightly higher than the rooms in the two smaller temples now so incalculably far above my head. I could not quite stand, but could kneel upright, and in the dark I shuffled and crept hither and thither at random. I soon knew that I was in a narrow passage whose walls were lined with cases of wood having glass fronts. As in that Palaeozoic and abysmal place I felt of such things as polished wood and glass I shuddered at the possible implications. The cases were apparently ranged along each side of the passage at regular intervals, and were oblong and horizontal, hideously like coffins in shape and size. When I tried to move two or three for further examination, I found that they were firmly fastened.

I saw that the passage was a long one, so floundered ahead rapidly in a creeping run that would have seemed horrible had any eye watched me in the blackness; crossing from side to side occasionally to feel of my surroundings and be sure the walls and rows of cases still stretched on. Man is so used to thinking visually that I almost forgot the darkness and pictured the endless corridor of wood and glass in its low-studded monotony as though I saw it. And then, in a moment of indescribable emotion, I did see it.

Just when my fancy merged into real sight I cannot tell; but there came a gradual glow ahead, and all at once I knew that I saw the dim outlines of a corridor and the cases, revealed by some unknown subterranean phosphorescence. For a little while all was exactly as I had imagined it, since the glow was very faint; but as I mechanically kept stumbling ahead into the stronger light I realised that my fancy had been but feeble. This hall was no relic of crudity like the temples in the city above, but a monument of the most magnificent and exotic art. Rich, vivid and daringly fantastic designs and pictures formed a continuous scheme of mural paintings whose lines and colours were beyond description. The cases were of a strange golden wood, with fronts of exquisite glass, and containing the mummified forms of creatures outreaching in grotesqueness the most chaotic dreams of man.

To convey any idea of these monstrosities is impossible. They were of the reptile kind, with body lines suggesting sometimes the crocodile, sometimes the seal, but more often nothing of which either the naturalist or the palaeontologist ever heard. In size they approximated a small man, and their fore-legs bore delicate and evident feet curiously like human hands and fingers. But strangest of all were their heads, which presented a contour violating all known biological principles. To nothing can such things be well compared — in one flash I thought of comparisons as varied as the cat, the bullfrog, the mythic Satyr and the human being. Not Jove himself had had so colossal and protuberant a forehead, yet the horns and the noselessness and the alligator-like jaw placed the things outside all established categories. I debated for a time on the reality of the mummies, half suspecting they were artificial idols; but soon decided they were indeed some Palaeogene species, which had lived when the nameless city was alive. To crown their grotesqueness, most of them were gorgeously enrobed in the costliest of fabrics, and lavishly laden with ornaments of gold, jewels and unknown shining metals.

The importance of these crawling creatures must have been vast, for they held first place among the wild designs on the frescoed walls and ceiling. With matchless skill had the artist drawn them in a world of their own, wherein they had cities and gardens fashioned to suit their dimensions; and I could not help but think that their pictured history was allegorical, perhaps shewing the progress of the race that worshipped them. These creatures, I said to myself, were to men of the nameless city what the she-wolf was to Rome, or some totem-beast is to a tribe of Indians.

Holding this view, I could trace roughly a wonderful epic of the nameless city; the tale of a mighty seacoast metropolis that ruled the world before Africa rose out of the waves, and of its struggles as the sea shrank away, and the desert crept into the fertile valley that held it. I saw its wars and triumphs, its troubles and defeats, and afterwards its terrible fight against the desert when thousands of its people — here represented in allegory by the grotesque reptiles — were driven to chisel their way down though the rocks in some marvellous manner to another world whereof their prophets had told them. It was all vividly weird and realistic, and its connection with the awesome descent I had made was unmistakable. I even recognised the passages.

As I crept along the corridor toward the brighter light I saw later stages of the painted epic — the leave-taking of the race that had dwelt in the nameless city and the valley around for ten million years; the race whose souls shrank from quitting scenes their bodies had known so long where they had settled as nomads in the earth's youth, hewing in the virgin rock those primal shrines at which they had never ceased to worship. Now that the light was better I studied the pictures more closely and, remembering that the strange reptiles must represent the unknown men, pondered upon the customs of the nameless city. Many things were peculiar and inexplicable. The civilisation, which included a written alphabet, had seemingly risen to a higher order than those immeasurably later civilisations of Egypt and Chaldaea, yet there were curious omissions. I could, for example, find no pictures to represent deaths or funeral customs, save such as were related to wars, violence and plagues; and I wondered at the reticence shown concerning natural death. It was as though an ideal of immortality had been fostered as a cheering illusion.

Still nearer the end of the passage were painted scenes of the utmost picturesqueness and extravagance: contrasted views of the nameless city in its desertion and growing ruin, and of the strange new realm of paradise to which the race had hewed its way through the stone. In these views the city and the desert valley were shewn always by moonlight, golden nimbus hovering over the fallen walls, and half-revealing the splendid perfection of former times, shown spectrally and elusively by the artist. The paradisal scenes were almost too extravagant to be believed, portraying a hidden world of eternal day filled with glorious cities and ethereal hills and valleys. At the very last I thought I saw signs of an artistic anticlimax. The paintings were less skilful, and much more bizarre than even the wildest of the earlier scenes. They seemed to record a slow decadence of the ancient stock, coupled with a growing ferocity toward the outside world from which it was driven by the desert. The forms of the people — always represented by the sacred reptiles — appeared to be gradually wasting away, though their spirit as shewn hovering above the ruins by moonlight gained in proportion. Emaciated priests, displayed as reptiles in ornate robes, cursed the upper air and all who breathed it; and one terrible final scene shewed a primitive-looking man, perhaps a pioneer of ancient Irem, the City of

Pillars, torn to pieces by members of the elder race. I remembered how the Arabs fear the nameless city, and was glad that beyond this place the grey walls and ceiling were bare.

As I viewed the pageant of mural history I had approached very closely to the end of the low-ceiled hall, and was aware of a gate through which came all of the illuminating phosphorescence. Creeping up to it, I cried aloud in transcendent amazement at what lay beyond; for instead of other and brighter chambers there was only an illimitable void of uniform radiance, such as one might fancy when gazing down from the peak of Mount Everest upon a sea of sunlit mist. Behind me was a passage so cramped that I could not stand upright in it; before me was an infinity of subterranean effulgence.

Reaching down from the passage into the abyss was the head of a steep flight of steps — small numerous steps like those of black passages I had traversed — but after a few feet the glowing vapours concealed everything. Swung back open against the left-hand wall of the passage was a massive door of brass, incredibly thick and decorated with fantastic bas-reliefs, which could if closed shut the whole inner world of light away from the vaults and passages of rock. I looked at the steps, and for the nonce dared not try them. I touched the open brass door, and could not move it. Then I sank prone to the stone floor, my mind aflame with prodigious reflections, which not even a death-like exhaustion could banish.

As I lay still with closed eyes, free to ponder, many things I had lightly noted in the frescoes came back to me with new and terrible significance — scenes representing the nameless city in its heyday — the vegetations of the valley around it, and the distant lands with which its merchants traded. The allegory of the crawling creatures puzzled me by its universal prominence, and I wondered that it would be so closely followed in a pictured history of such importance. In the frescoes the nameless city had been shewn in proportions fitted to the reptiles. I wondered what its real proportions and magnificence had been, and reflected a moment on certain oddities I had noticed in the ruins. I thought curiously of the lowness of the primal temples and of the underground corridor, which were doubtless hewn thus out of deference to the reptile deities there honoured; though it perforce reduced the worshippers to crawling. Perhaps the very rites here involved crawling in imitation of the creatures. No religious theory, however, could easily explain why the level passages in that awesome descent should be as low as the temples — or lower, since one could not even kneel in it. As I thought of the crawling creatures, whose hideous mummified forms were so close to me, I felt a new throb of fear. Mental associations are curious, and I shrank from the idea that except for the poor primitive man torn to pieces in the last painting, mine was the only human form amidst the many relics and symbols of the primordial life.

But as always in my strange and roving existence, wonder soon drove out fear; for the luminous abyss and what it might contain presented a problem worthy of the greatest explorer. That a weird world of mystery lay far down that flight of peculiarly small steps I could not doubt, and I hoped to find there those human memorials which the painted corridor had failed to give. The frescoes had pictured unbelievable cities, and valleys in this lower realm, and my fancy dwelt on the rich and colossal ruins that awaited me.

My fears, indeed, concerned the past rather than the future. Not even the physical horror of my position in that cramped corridor of dead reptiles and antediluvian frescoes, miles below the world I knew and faced by another world of eerie light and mist, could match the lethal dread I felt at the abysmal antiquity of the scene and its soul. An ancientness so vast that measurement is feeble seemed to leer down from the primal stones and rock-hewn temples of the nameless city, while the very latest of the astounding maps in the frescoes shewed oceans and continents that man has forgotten, with only here and there some vaguely familiar outlines. Of what could have happened in the geological ages since the paintings ceased and the death-hating race resentfully succumbed to decay, no man might say. Life had once teemed in these caverns and in the luminous realm beyond; now I was alone with vivid relics, and I trembled to think of the countless ages through which these relics had kept a silent deserted vigil.

Suddenly there came another burst of that acute fear which had intermittently seized me ever since I first saw the terrible valley and the nameless city under a cold moon, and despite my exhaustion I found myself starting frantically to a sitting posture and gazing back along the black corridor toward the tunnels that rose to the outer world. My sensations were like those which had made me shun the nameless city at night, and were as inexplicable as they were poignant. In another moment, however, I received a still greater shock in the form of a definite sound — the first which had broken the utter silence of these tomb-like depths. It was a deep, low moaning, as of a distant throng of condemned spirits, and came from the direction in which I was staring. Its volume rapidly grew, till it soon reverberated frightfully through the low passage, and at the same time I became conscious of an increasing draught of cold air, likewise flowing from the tunnels and the city above. The touch of this air seemed to restore my balance, for I instantly recalled the sudden gusts which had risen around the mouth of the abyss each sunset and sunrise, one of which had indeed revealed the hidden tunnels to me. I looked at my watch and saw that sunrise was near, so braced myself to resist the gale that was sweeping down to its cavern home as it had swept forth at evening. My fear again waned low, since a natural phenomenon tends to dispel broodings over the unknown.

More and more madly poured the shrieking, moaning night wind into the gulf of the inner earth. I dropped prone again and clutched vainly at the floor for fear of being swept bodily through the open gate into the phosphorescent abyss. Such fury I had not expected, and as I grew aware of an actual slipping of my form toward the abyss I was beset by a thousand new terrors of apprehension and imagination. The malignancy of the blast awakened incredible fancies; once more I compared myself shudderingly to the only human image in that frightful corridor, the man who was torn to pieces by the nameless race, for in the fiendish clawing of the swirling currents there seemed to abide a vindictive rage all the stronger because it was largely impotent. I think I screamed frantically near the last — I was almost mad — but if I did so my cries were lost in the hell-born babel of the howling wind-wraiths. I tried to crawl against the murderous invisible torrent, but I could not even hold my own as I was pushed slowly and inexorably toward the unknown world. Finally reason must have wholly snapped, for I fell to babbling over and over that unexplainable couplet of the mad Arab Alhazred, who dreamed of the nameless city:

> *That is not dead which can eternal lie,*
> *And with strange aeons even death may die.*

Only the grim brooding desert gods know what really took place — what indescribable struggles and scrambles in the dark I endured or what Abaddon guided me back to life, where I must always remember and shiver in the night wind till oblivion — or worse — claims me. Monstrous, unnatural, colossal, was the thing — too far beyond all the ideas of man to be believed except in the silent damnable small hours of the morning when one cannot sleep.

I have said that the fury of the rushing blast was infernal — cacodaemoniacal — and that its voices were hideous with the pent-up viciousness of desolate eternities. Presently these voices, while still chaotic before me, seemed to my beating brain to take articulate form behind me; and down there in the grave of unnumbered aeondead antiquities, leagues below the dawn-lit world of men, I heard the ghastly cursing and snarling of strange-tongued fiends. Turning, I saw outlined against the luminous aether of the abyss what could not be seen against the dusk of the corridor — a nightmare horde of rushing devils; hate-distorted, grotesquely panoplied, half transparent devils of a race no man might mistake — the crawling reptiles of the nameless city.

And as the wind died away, I was plunged into the ghoul-pooled darkness of earth's bowels; for behind the last of the creatures the great brazen door clanged shut with a deafening peal of metallic music whose reverberations swelled out to the distant world to hail the rising sun as Memnon hails it from the banks of the Nile.

The Adventure of the Egyptian Tomb[*]

I have always considered that one of the most thrilling and dramatic of the many adventures I have shared with Poirot was that of our investigation into the strange series of deaths which followed upon the discovery and opening of the Tomb of King Men-her-Ra.

Hard upon the discovery of the Tomb of Tutankh-Amen by Lord Carnarvon, Sir John Willard and Mr. Bleibner of New York, pursuing their excavations not far from Cairo, in the vicinity of the Pyramids of Giza, came unexpectedly on a series of funeral chambers. The greatest interest was aroused by their discovery. The Tomb appeared to be that of King Men-her-Ra, one of those shadowy kings of the Eighth Dynasty, when the Old Kingdom was falling to decay. Little was known about this period, and the discoveries were fully reported in the newspapers.

An event soon occurred which took a profound hold on the public mind. Sir John Willard died quite suddenly of heart failure.

The more sensational newspapers immediately took the opportunity of reviving all the old superstitious stories connected with the ill luck of certain Egyptian treasures. The unlucky Mummy at the British Museum, that hoary old chestnut, was dragged out with fresh zest, was quietly denied by the Museum, but nevertheless enjoyed all its usual vogue.

A fortnight later Mr. Bleibner died of acute blood poisoning, and a few days afterwards a nephew of his shot himself in New York. The "Curse of Men-her-Ra" was the talk of the day, and the magic power of dead and gone Egypt was exalted to a fetish point.

It was then that Poirot received a brief note from Lady Willard, widow of the dead archaeologist, asking him to go and see her at her house in Kensington Square. I accompanied him.

Lady Willard was a tall, thin woman, dressed in deep mourning. Her haggard face bore eloquent testimony to her recent grief.

"It is kind of you to have come so promptly, Monsieur Poirot."

"I am at your service, Lady Willard. You wished to consult me?"

"You are, I am aware, a detective, but it is not only as a detective that I wish to consult you. You are a man of original views, I know, you have imagination, experience of the world — tell me, Monsieur Poirot, what are your views on the supernatural?"

---

[*] "The Adventure of the Egyptian Tomb" was written by Agatha Christie (1890 – 1976) and published in *The Sketch*, Sep. 26 1923. The text for this edition was taken from the short story collection *Poirot Investigates* (1924).

Poirot hesitated for a moment before he replied. He seemed to be considering.

Finally he said:

"Let us not misunderstand each other, Lady Willard. It is not a general question that you are asking me there. It has a personal application, has it not? You are referring obliquely to the death of your late husband?"

"That is so," she admitted.

"You want me to investigate the circumstances of his death?"

"I want you to ascertain for me exactly how much is newspaper chatter, and how much may be said to be founded on fact. Three deaths, Monsieur Poirot — each one explicable taken by itself, but taken together surely an almost unbelievable coincidence, and all within a month of the opening of the tomb! It may be mere superstition, it may be some potent curse from the past that operates in ways undreamed of by modern science. The fact remains — three deaths! And I am afraid, Monsieur Poirot, horribly afraid. It may not yet be the end."

"For whom do you fear?"

"For my son. When the news of my husband's death came I was ill. My son, who has just come down from Oxford, went out there. He brought the — the body home, but now he has gone out again, in spite of my prayers and entreaties. He is so fascinated by the work that he intends to take his father's place and carry on the system of excavations. You may think me a foolish, credulous woman, but, Monsieur Poirot, I am afraid. Supposing that the spirit of the dead king is not yet appeased? Perhaps to you I seem to be talking nonsense —"

"No, indeed, Lady Willard," said Poirot quickly. "I, too, believe in the force of superstition, one of the greatest forces the world has ever known."

I looked at him in surprise. I should never have credited Poirot with being superstitious. But the little man was obviously in earnest.

"What you really demand is that I shall protect your son? I will do my utmost to keep him from harm."

"Yes, in the ordinary way, but against an occult influence?"

"In volumes of the Middle Ages, Lady Willard, you will find many ways of counteracting black magic. Perhaps they knew more than we moderns with all our boasted science. Now let us come to facts, that I may have guidance. Your husband had always been a devoted Egyptologist, hadn't he?"

"Yes, from his youth upwards. He was one of the greatest living authorities upon the subject."

"But Mr. Bleibner, I understand, was more or less of an amateur?"

"Oh, quite. He was a very wealthy man who dabbled freely in any subject that happened to take his fancy. My husband managed to interest him in Egyptology, and it was his money that was so useful in financing the expedition."

"And the nephew? What do you know of his tastes? Was he with the party at all?"

"I do not think so. In fact I never knew of his existence till I read of his death in the paper. I do not think he and Mr. Bleibner can have been at all intimate. He never spoke of having any relations."

"Who are the other members of the party?"

"Well, there is Dr. Tosswill, minor official connected with the British Museum; Mr. Schneider of the Metropolitan Museum in New York; a young American secretary; Dr. Ames, who accompanies the expedition in his professional capacity; and Hassan, my husband's devoted native servant."

"Do you remember the name of the American secretary?"

"Harper, I think, but I cannot be sure. He had not been with Mr. Bleibner very long, I know. He was a very pleasant young fellow."

"Thank you, Lady Willard."

"If there is anything else —?"

"For the moment, nothing. Leave it now in my hands, and be assured that I will do all that is humanly possible to protect your son."

They were not exactly reassuring words, and I observed Lady Willard wince as he uttered them. Yet, at the same time, the fact that he had not pooh-poohed her fears seemed in itself to be a relief to her.

For my part I had never before suspected that Poirot had so deep a vein of superstition in his nature. I tackled him on the subject as we went homewards. His manner was grave and earnest.

"But yes, Hastings. I believe in these things. You must not underrate the force of superstition."

"What are we going to do about it?"

"*Toujours pratique,* the good Hastings! *Eh bien,* to begin with we are going to cable to New York for fuller details of young Mr. Bleibner's death."

He duly sent off his cable. The reply was full and precise. Young Rupert Bleibner had been in low water for several years. He had been a beachcomber and a remittance man in several South Sea islands, but had returned to New York two years ago, where he had rapidly sunk lower and lower. The most significant thing, to my mind, was that he had recently managed to borrow enough money to take him to Egypt. "I've a good friend there I can borrow from," he had declared. Here, however, his plans had gone awry. He had returned to New York cursing his skinflint of an uncle who cared more for the bones of dead and gone kings than his own flesh and blood. It was during his sojourn in Egypt that the death of Sir John Willard occurred. Rupert had plunged once more into his life of dissipation in New York, and then, without warning, he had committed suicide, leaving behind him a letter which contained some curious phrases. It seemed written in a sudden fit of remorse. He referred to himself as a leper and an outcast, and the letter ended by declaring that such as he were better dead.

A shadowy theory leapt into my brain. I had never really believed in the vengeance of a long dead Egyptian king. I saw here a more modern crime. Supposing this young man had decided to do away with his uncle — preferably by poison. By mistake, Sir John Willard receives the fatal dose. The young man returns to New York, haunted by his crime. The news of his uncle's death reaches him. He realizes how unnecessary his crime has been, and stricken with remorse takes his own life.

I outlined my solutions to Poirot. He was interested.

"It is ingenious what you have thought of there — decidedly it is ingenious. It may even be true. But you leave out of count the fatal influence of the Tomb."

I shrugged my shoulders.

"You still think that has something to do with it?"

"So much so, *mon ami,* that we start for Egypt tomorrow."

"What?" I cried, astonished.

"I have said it." An expression of conscious heroism spread over Poirot's face. Then he groaned. "But, oh," he lamented, "the sea! The hateful sea!"

It was a week later. Beneath our feet was the golden sand of the desert. The hot sun poured down overhead. Poirot, the picture of misery, wilted by my side. The little man was not a good traveler. Our four days' voyage from Marseilles had been one long agony to him. He had landed at Alexandria the wraith of his former self, even his usual nearness had deserted him. We had arrived in Cairo and had driven out at once to the Mena House Hotel, right in the shadow of the Pyramids.

The charm of Egypt had laid hold of me. Not so Poirot. Dressed precisely the same as in London, he carried a small clothes-brush in his pocket and waged an unceasing war on the dust which accumulated on his dark apparel.

"And my boots," he wailed. "Regard them, Hastings. My boots, of the neat patent leather, usually so smart and shining. See, the sand is inside them, which is painful, and outside them, which outrages the eyesight. Also the heat, it causes my mustaches to become limp — but limp!"

"Look at the Sphinx," I urged. "Even I can feel the mystery and the charm it exhales."

Poirot looked at it discontentedly.

"It has not the air happy," he declared. "How could it, half-buried in sand in that untidy fashion. Ah, this cursed sand!"

"Come, now, there's a lot of sand in Belgium," I reminded him, mindful of a holiday spent at Knocke-sur-mer in the midst of *"les dunes impeccables"* as the guide-book had phrased it.

"Not in Brussels," declared Poirot. He gazed at the Pyramids thoughtfully. "It is true that they, at least, are of a shape solid and geometrical, but their surface is of an unevenness most unpleasing. And the palm trees I like them not. Not even do they plant them in rows!"

I cut short his lamentations, by suggesting that we should start for the camp. We were to ride there on camels, and the beasts were patiently kneeling, waiting for us to mount, in charge of several picturesque boys headed by a voluble dragoman.

I pass over the spectacle of Poirot on a camel. He started by groans and lamentations and ended by shrieks, gesticulations and invocations to the Virgin Mary and every saint in the calendar. In the end, he descended ignominiously and finished the journey on a diminutive donkey. I must admit that a trotting camel is no joke for the amateur. I was stiff for several days.

At last we neared the scene of the excavations. A sunburnt man with a gray beard, in white clothes and wearing a helmet, came to meet us.

"Monsieur Poirot and Captain Hastings? We received your cable. I'm sorry that there was no one to meet you in Cairo. An unforeseen event occurred which completely disorganized our plans."

Poirot paled. His hand, which had stolen to his clothes-brush, stayed its course.

"Not another death?" he breathed.

"Yes."

"Sir Guy Willard?" I cried.

"No, Captain Hastings. My American colleague, Mr. Schneider."

"And the cause?" demanded Poirot.

"Tetanus."

I blanched. All around me I seemed to feel an atmosphere of evil, subtle and menacing. A horrible thought flashed across me. Supposing I were the next?

"Mon Dieu," said Poirot, in a very low voice, "I do not understand this. It is horrible. Tell me, monsieur, there is no doubt that it was tetanus?"

"I believe not. But Dr. Ames will tell you more than I can do."

"Ah, of course, you are not the doctor."

"My name is Tosswill."

This, then, was the British expert described by Lady Willard as being a minor official at the British Museum. There was something at once grave and steadfast about him that took my fancy.

"If you will come with me," continued Dr. Tosswill, "I will take you to Sir Guy Willard. He was most anxious to be informed as soon as you should arrive."

We were taken across the camp to a large tent. Dr. Tosswill lifted up the flap and we entered. Three men were sitting inside.

"Monsieur Poirot and Captain Hastings have arrived, Sir Guy," said Tosswill.

The youngest of the three men jumped up and came forward to greet us. There was a certain impulsiveness in his manner which reminded me of his mother. He was not nearly so sunburnt as the others, and that fact, coupled with a certain haggardness round the eyes, made him look older than his twenty-two years. He was clearly endeavoring to bear up under a severe mental strain.

He introduced his two companions, Dr. Ames, a capable-looking man of thirty odd, with a touch of graying hair at the temples, and Mr. Harper, the secretary, a pleasant lean young man wearing the national insignia of horn-rimmed spectacles.

After a few minutes' desultory conversation the latter went out, and Dr. Tosswill followed him. We were left alone with Sir Guy and Dr. Ames.

"Please ask any questions you want to ask, Monsieur Poirot," said Willard. "We are utterly dumfounded at this strange series of disasters, but it isn't — it can't be, anything but coincidence."

There was a nervousness about his manner which rather belied the words. I saw that Poirot was studying him keenly.

"Your heart is really in this work, Sir Guy?"

"Rather. No matter what happens, or what comes of it, the work is going on. Make up your mind to that."

Poirot wheeled round on the other.

"What have you to say to that, *monsieur le docteur?*"

"Well," drawled the doctor, I'm not for quitting myself."

Poirot made one of those expressive grimaces of his.

"Then, *évidemment,* we must find out just how we stand. When did Mr. Schneider's death take place?"

"Three days ago."

"You are sure it was tetanus?"

"Dead sure."

"It couldn't have been a case of strychnine poisoning, for instance?"

"No, Monsieur Poirot. I see what you're getting at. But it was a clear case of tetanus."

"Did you not inject anti-serum?"

"Certainly we did," said the doctor dryly. "Every conceivable thing that could be done was tried."

"Had you the anti-serum with you?"

"No. We procured it from Cairo."

"Have there been any other cases of tetanus in the camp?"

"No, not one."

"Are you certain that the death of Mr. Bleibner was not due to tetanus?"

"Absolutely plumb certain. He had a scratch upon his thumb which became poisoned, and septicemia set in. It sounds pretty much the same to a layman, I dare say, but the two things are entirely different."

"Then we have four deaths — all totally dissimilar, one heart failure, one blood poisoning, one suicide and one tetanus."

"Exactly, Monsieur Poirot."

"Are you certain that there is nothing which might link the four together?"

"I don't quite understand you."

"I will put it plainly. Was any act committed by those four men which might seem to denote disrespect to the spirit of Men-her-Ra?"

The doctor gazed at Poirot in astonishment.

"You're talking through your hat, Monsieur Poirot. Surely you've not been guyed into believing all that fool talk?"

"Absolute nonsense," muttered Willard angrily.

Poirot remained placidly immovable, blinking a little out of his green cat's eyes.

"So you do not believe it, *monsieur le docteur?*"

"No, sir, I do not," declared the doctor emphatically. "I am a scientific man, and I believe only what science teaches."

"Was there no science then in Ancient Egypt?" asked Poirot softly. He did not wait for a reply, and indeed Dr. Ames seemed rather at a loss for the moment. "No, no, do not answer me; but tell me this. What do the native workmen think?"

"I guess," said Dr. Ames, "that, where white folk lose their heads, natives aren't going to be far behind. I'll admit that they're getting what you might call scared — but they've no cause to be."

"I wonder," said Poirot noncommittally.

Sir Guy leant forward.

"Surely," he cried incredulously, "you cannot believe in — oh, but the thing's absurd! You can know nothing of Ancient Egypt if you think that."

For answer Poirot produced a little book from his pocket — an ancient tattered volume. As he held it out I saw its title, *The Magic of the Egyptians and Chaldeans.* Then, wheeling round, he strode out of the tent. The doctor stared at me.

"What is his little idea?"

The phrase, so familiar on Poirot's lips, made me smile as it came from another.

"I don't know exactly," I confessed. "He's got some plan of exorcising the evil spirits, I believe."

I went in search of Poirot, and found him talking to the lean-faced young man who had been the late Mr. Bleibner's secretary.

"No," Mr. Harper was saying, "I've only been six months with the expedition. Yes, I knew Mr. Bleibner's affairs pretty well."

"Can you recount to me anything concerning his nephew?"

"He turned up here one day, not a bad-looking fellow. I'd never met him before, but some of the others had — Ames, I think, and Schneider. The old man wasn't at all pleased to see him. They were at it in no time, hammer and tongs. 'Not a cent,' the old man shouted. 'Not one cent now or when I'm dead. I intend to leave my money to the furtherance of my life's work. I've been talking it over with Mr. Schneider today.' And a bit more of the same. Young Bleibner lit out for Cairo right away."

"Was he in perfectly good health at the time?"

"The old man?"

"No, the young one."

"I believe he did mention there was something wrong with him. But it couldn't have been anything serious, or I should have remembered."

"One thing more, has Mr. Bleibner left a will?"

"So far as we know, he has not."

"Are you remaining with the expedition, Mr. Harper?"

"No, sir, I am not. I'm for New York as soon as I can square up things here. You may laugh if you like, but I'm not going to be this blasted old Men-her-Ra's next victim. He'll get me if I stop here."

The young man wiped the perspiration from his brow.

Poirot turned away. Over his shoulder he said with a peculiar smile: "Remember, he got one of his victims in New York."

"Oh, hell!" said Mr. Harper forcibly.

"That young man is nervous," said Poirot thoughtfully. "He is on the edge, but absolutely on the edge."

I glanced at Poirot curiously, but his enigmatical smile told me nothing. In company with Sir Guy Willard and Dr. Tosswill we were taken round the excavations. The principal finds had been removed to Cairo, but some of the tomb furniture was extremely interesting. The enthusiasm of the young baronet was obvious, but I fancied that I detected a shade of nervousness in his manner as though he could not quite escape from the feeling of menace in the air. As we entered the tent which had been assigned to us, for a wash before joining the evening meal, a tall dark figure in white robes stood aside to let us pass with a graceful gesture and a murmured greeting in Arabic. Poirot stopped.

"You are Hassan, the late Sir John Willard's servant?"

"I served my Lord Sir John, now I serve his son." He took a step nearer to us and lowered his voice. "You are a wise one, they say, learned in dealing with evil spirits. Let the young master depart from here. There is evil in the air around us."

And with an abrupt gesture, not waiting for a reply, he strode away.

"Evil in the air," muttered Poirot. "Yes, I feel it."

Our meal was hardly a cheerful one. The floor was left to Dr. Tosswill, who discoursed at length upon Egyptian antiquities. Just as we were preparing to retire to rest, Sir Guy caught Poirot by the arm and pointed. A shadowy figure was moving amidst the tents. It was no human one: I recognized distinctly the dog-headed figure I had seen carved on the walls of the tomb.

My blood literally froze at the sight.

"Mon Dieu!" murmured Poirot, crossing himself vigorously. "Anubis, the jackal-headed, the god of departing souls."

"Some one is hoaxing us," cried Dr. Tosswill, rising indignantly to his feet.

"It went into your tent, Harper," muttered Sir Guy, his face dreadfully pale.

"No," said Poirot, shaking his head, "into that of the Dr. Ames."

The doctor stared at him incredulously; then, repeating Dr. Tosswill's words, he cried:

"Some one is hoaxing us. Come, we'll soon catch the fellow."

He dashed energetically in pursuit of the shadowy apparition. I followed him, but, search as we would, we could find no trace of any living thing having passed that way. We returned, somewhat disturbed in mind, to find Poirot taking energetic measures, in his own way, to ensure his personal safety. He was busily surrounding our tent with various diagrams and inscriptions which he was drawing in the sand. I recognized the five-pointed star or Pentagon many times repeated. As was his wont, Poirot was at the same time delivering an impromptu lecture on witchcraft and magic in general, White Magic as opposed to Black, with various references to the Ka and the Book of the Dead thrown in.

It appeared to excite the liveliest contempt in Dr. Tosswill, who drew me aside, literally snorting with rage.

"Balderdash, sir," he exclaimed angrily. "Pure balderdash. The man's an impostor. He doesn't know the difference between the superstitions of the Middle Ages and the beliefs of Ancient Egypt. Never have I heard such a hotch-potch of ignorance and credulity."

I calmed the excited expert, and joined Poirot in the tent. My little friend was beaming cheerfully.

"We can now sleep in peace," he declared happily. "And I can do with some sleep. My head, it aches abominably. Ah, for a good *tisane!*"

As though in answer to prayer, the flap of the tent was lifted and Hassan appeared, bearing a steaming cup which he offered to Poirot. It proved to be chamomile tea, a beverage of which he is inordinately fond. Having thanked Hassan and refused his offer of another cup for myself, we were left alone once more. I stood at the door of the tent some time after undressing, looking out over the desert.

"A wonderful place," I said aloud, "and a wonderful work. I can feel the fascination. This desert life, this probing into the heart of a vanished civilization. Surely, Poirot, you, too, must feel the charm?"

I got no answer, and I turned, a little annoyed. My annoyance was quickly changed to concern. Poirot was lying back across the rude couch, his face horribly convulsed. Beside him was the empty cup. I rushed to his side, then dashed out and across the camp to Dr. Ames's tent.

"Dr. Ames!" I cried. "Come at once."

"What's the matter?" said the doctor, appearing in pajamas.

"My friend. He's ill. Dying. The chamomile tea. Don't let Hassan leave the camp."

Like a flash the doctor ran to our tent. Poirot was lying as I left him.

"Extraordinary," cried Ames. "Looks like a seizure — or — what did you say about something he drank?" He picked up the empty cup.

"Only I did not drink it!" said a placid voice.

We turned in amazement. Poirot was sitting up on the bed. He was smiling.

"No," he said gently. "I did not drink it. While my good friend Hastings was apostrophizing the night, I took the opportunity of pouring it, not down my throat, but into a little bottle. That little bottle will go to the analytical chemist. No" — as the doctor made a sudden movement — "as a sensible man, you will understand that violence will be of no avail. During Hastings brief absence to fetch you, I have had time to put the bottle in safe keeping. Ah, quick, Hastings, hold him!"

I misunderstood Poirot's anxiety. Eager to save my friend, I flung myself in front of him. But the doctor's swift movement had another meaning. His hand went to his mouth, a smell of bitter almonds filled the air, and he swayed forward and fell.

"Another victim," said Poirot gravely, "but the last. Perhaps it is the best way. He has three deaths on his head."

"Dr. Ames?" I cried, stupefied. "But I thought you believed in some occult influence?"

"You misunderstood me, Hastings. What I meant was that I believe in the terrific force of superstition. Once get it firmly established that a series of deaths are supernatural, and you might almost stab a man in broad daylight, and it would still be put down to the curse, so strongly is the instinct of the supernatural implanted in the human race. I suspected from the first that a man was taking advantage of that instinct. The idea came to him, I imagine, with the death of Sir John Willard. A fury of superstition arose at once. As far as I could see, nobody could derive any particular profit from Sir John's death. Mr. Bleibner was a different case. He was a man of great wealth. The information I received from New York contained several suggestive points. To begin with, young Bleibner was reported to have said he had a good friend in Egypt from whom he could borrow. It was tacitly understood that he meant his uncle, but it seemed to me that in that case he would have said so outright. The words suggest some boon companion of his own. Another thing, he scraped up enough money to take him to Egypt, his uncle refused outright to advance him a penny, yet he was able to pay the return passage to New York. Some one must have lent him the money."

"All that was very thin," I objected.

"But there was more. Hastings, there occur often enough words spoken metaphorically which are taken literally. The opposite can happen too. In this case, words which were meant literally were taken metaphorically. Young Bleibner wrote plainly enough: 'I am a leper,' but nobody realized that he shot himself because he believed that he had contracted the dread disease of leprosy."

"What?" I ejaculated.

"It was the clever invention of a diabolical mind. Young Bleibner was suffering from some minor skin trouble, he had lived in the South Sea Islands, where the disease is common enough. Ames was a former friend of his, and a well-known medical man, he would never have dreamed of doubting his word. When I arrived here, my suspicions were divided between Harper and Dr. Ames, but I soon realized that only the doctor could have perpetrated and concealed the crimes, and I learnt from Harper that he was previously acquainted with young Bleibner. Doubtless the latter at some time or another had made a will or had insured his life in favor of the doctor. The latter saw his chance of acquiring wealth. It was easy for him to inoculate Mr. Bleibner with the deadly germs. Then the nephew, overcome with despair at the dread news his friend had conveyed to him, shot himself. Mr. Bleibner, whatever his intentions, had made no will. His fortune would pass to his nephew and from him to the doctor."

"And Mr. Schneider?"

"We cannot be sure. He knew young Bleibner too, remember, and may have suspected something, or, again, the doctor may have thought that a further death motiveless and purposeless would strengthen the coils of superstition. Furthermore, I will tell you an interesting psychological fact, Hastings. A murderer has always a strong desire to repeat his successful crime, the performance of it grows upon him. Hence my fears for young Willard. The figure of Anubis you saw tonight was Hassan, dressed up by my orders. I wanted to see if I could frighten the doctor. But it would take more than the supernatural to frighten him. I could see that he was not entirely taken in by my pretenses of belief in the occult. The little comedy I played for him did not deceive him. I suspected that he would endeavor to make me the next victim. Ah, but in spite of *la mer maudite,* the heat abominable, and the annoyances of the sand, the little gray cells still functioned!"

Poirot proved to be perfectly right in his premises. Young Bleibner, some years ago, in a fit of drunken merriment, had made a jocular will, leaving "my cigarette case you admire so much and everything else of which I die possessed which will be principally debts to my good friend Robert Ames who once saved my life from drowning."

The case was hushed up as far as possible, and, to this day, people talk of the remarkable series of deaths in connection with the Tomb of Men-her-Ra as a triumphal proof of the vengeance of a bygone king upon the desecrators of his tomb — a belief which, as Poirot pointed out to me, is contrary to all Egyptian belief and thought.

The Outsider[*]

That night the Baron dreamt of many a woe;
And all his warrior-guests, with shade and form
Of witch, and demon, and large coffin-worm,
Were long be-nightmared.

— Keats

Unhappy is he to whom the memories of childhood bring only fear and sadness. Wretched is he who looks back upon lone hours in vast and dismal chambers with brown hangings and maddening rows of antique books, or upon awed watches in twilight groves of grotesque, gigantic, and vine-encumbered trees that silently wave twisted branches far aloft. Such a lot the gods gave to me — to me, the dazed, the disappointed; the barren, the broken. And yet I am strangely content and cling desperately to those sere memories, when my mind momentarily threatens to reach beyond to *the other.*

I know not where I was born, save that the castle was infinitely old and infinitely horrible, full of dark passages and having high ceilings where the eye could find only cobwebs and shadows. The stones in the crumbling corridors seemed always hideously damp, and there was an accursed smell everywhere, as of the piled-up corpses of dead generations. It was never light, so that I used sometimes to light candles and gaze steadily at them for relief, nor was there any sun outdoors, since the terrible trees grew high above the topmost accessible tower. There was one black tower which reached above the trees into the unknown outer sky, but that was partly ruined and could not be ascended save by a well-nigh impossible climb up the sheer wall, stone by stone.

I must have lived years in this place, but I cannot measure the time. Beings must have cared for my needs, yet I cannot recall any person except myself, or anything alive but the noiseless rats and bats and spiders. I think that whoever nursed me must have been shockingly aged, since my first conception of a living person was that of somebody mockingly like myself, yet distorted, shrivelled, and decaying like the castle. To me there was nothing grotesque in the bones and skeletons that strewed some of the stone crypts deep down among the foundations. I fantastically associated these things with everyday events, and thought them more natural than the coloured pictures of living beings which I found in many of the mouldy books. From such books I learned all that I know. No teacher urged or guided me, and I do not recall hearing any human voice in all those years — not even my own; for although I had read of speech, I had never thought to try to speak aloud. My aspect was a matter equally unthought of, for there were no mirrors in the castle, and I merely regarded myself by instinct as akin to the youthful figures I saw

* "The Outsider" was written by H. P. Lovecraft (1890 – 1937) and published in *Weird Tales*, Apr. 1926.

drawn and painted in the books. I felt conscious of youth because I remembered so little.

Outside, across the putrid moat and under the dark mute trees, I would often lie and dream for hours about what I read in the books; and would longingly picture myself amidst gay crowds in the sunny world beyond the endless forests. Once I tried to escape from the forest, but as I went farther from the castle the shade grew denser and the air more filled with brooding fear; so that I ran frantically back lest I lose my way in a labyrinth of nighted silence.

So through endless twilights I dreamed and waited, though I knew not what I waited for. Then in the shadowy solitude my longing for light grew so frantic that I could rest no more, and I lifted entreating hands to the single black ruined tower that reached above the forest into the unknown outer sky. And at last I resolved to scale that tower, fall though I might; since it were better to glimpse the sky and perish, than to live without ever beholding day.

In the dank twilight I climbed the worn and aged stone stairs till I reached the level where they ceased, and thereafter clung perilously to small footholds leading upward. Ghastly and terrible was that dead, stairless cylinder of rock; black, ruined, and deserted, and sinister with startled bats whose wings made no noise. But more ghastly and terrible still was the slowness of my progress; for climb as I might, the darkness overhead grew no thinner, and a new chill as of haunted and venerable mould assailed me. I shivered as I wondered why I did not reach the light, and would have looked down had I dared. I fancied that night had come suddenly upon me, and vainly groped with one free hand for a window embrasure, that I might peer out and above, and try to judge the height I had attained.

All at once, after an infinity of awesome, sightless, crawling up that concave and desperate precipice, I felt my head touch a solid thing, and I knew I must have gained the roof, or at least some kind of floor. In the darkness I raised my free hand and tested the barrier, finding it stone and immovable. Then came a deadly circuit of the tower, clinging to whatever holds the slimy wall could give; till finally my testing hand found the barrier yielding, and I turned upward again, pushing the slab or door with my head as I used both hands in my fearful ascent. There was no light revealed above, and as my hands went higher I knew that my climb was for the nonce ended, since the slab was the trapdoor of an aperture leading to a level stone surface of greater circumference than the lower tower, no doubt the floor of some lofty and capacious observation chamber. I crawled through carefully, and tried to prevent the heavy slab from falling back into place, but failed in the latter attempt. As I lay exhausted on the stone floor I heard the eerie echoes of its fall, but hoped when necessary to pry it up again.

Believing I was now at prodigious height, far above the accursed branches of the wood, I dragged myself up from the floor and fumbled about for windows, that I might look for the first time upon the sky, and the moon and stars of which I had read. But on every hand I was disappointed, since all that I found were vast shelves of marble, bearing odious oblong boxes of disturbing size. More and more I reflected, and wondered what hoary secrets might abide in this high apartment so many aeons cut off from the castle below. Then unexpectedly my hands came upon a doorway, where hung a portal of stone, rough with strange chiselling. Trying it, I found it locked; but with a supreme burst of strength I overcame all obstacles and dragged it open inward. As I did so there came to me the purest ecstasy I have ever known; for shining tranquilly through an ornate grating of iron, and down a short stone passageway of steps that ascended from the newly found doorway, was the radiant full moon, which I had never before seen save in dreams and in vague visions I dared not call memories.

Fancying now that I had attained the very pinnacle of the castle, I commenced to rush up the few steps beyond the door; but the sudden veiling of the moon by a cloud caused me to stumble, and I felt my way more slowly in the dark. It was still very dark when I reached the grating — which I tried carefully and found unlocked, but which I did not open for fear of falling from the amazing height to which I had climbed. Then the moon came out.

Most demoniacal of all shocks is that of the abysmally unexpected and grotesquely unbelievable. Nothing I had before undergone could compare in terror with what I now saw; with the bizarre marvels that sight implied. The sight itself was as simple as it was stupefying, for it was merely this: instead of a dizzying prospect of treetops seen from a lofty eminence, there stretched around me on the level through the grating nothing less than *the solid ground,* decked and diversified by marble slabs and columns, and overshadowed by an ancient stone church, whose ruined spire gleamed spectrally in the moonlight.

Half unconscious, I opened the grating and staggered out upon the white gravel path that stretched away in two directions. My mind, stunned and chaotic as it was, still held the frantic craving for light; and not even the fantastic wonder which had happened could stay my course. I neither knew nor cared whether my experience was insanity, dreaming, or magic; but was determined to gaze on brilliance and gaiety at any cost. I knew not who I was or what I was, or what my surroundings might be; though as I continued to stumble along I became conscious of a kind of fearsome latent memory that made my progress not wholly fortuitous. I passed under an arch out of that region of slabs and columns, and wandered through the open country; sometimes following the visible road, but sometimes leaving it curiously to tread across meadows where only occasional ruins bespoke the ancient presence of a forgotten road. Once I swam across a swift river where crumbling, mossy masonry told of a bridge long vanished.

Over two hours must have passed before I reached what seemed to be my goal, a venerable ivied castle in a thickly wooded park, maddeningly familiar, yet full of perplexing strangeness to me. I saw that the moat was filled in, and that some of the well-known towers were demolished, whilst new wings existed to confuse the beholder. But what I observed with chief interest and delight were the open windows — gorgeously ablaze with light and sending forth sound of the gayest revelry. Advancing to one of these I looked in and saw an oddly dressed company indeed; making merry, and speaking brightly to one another. I had never, seemingly, heard human speech before and could guess only vaguely what was said. Some of the faces seemed to hold expressions that brought up incredibly remote recollections, others were utterly alien.

I now stepped through the low window into the brilliantly lighted room, stepping as I did so from my single bright moment of hope to my blackest convulsion of despair and realization. The nightmare was quick to come, for as I entered, there occurred immediately one of the most terrifying demonstrations I had ever conceived. Scarcely had I crossed the sill when there descended upon the whole company a sudden and unheralded fear of hideous intensity, distorting every face and evoking the most horrible screams from nearly every throat. Flight was universal, and in the clamour and panic several fell in a swoon and were dragged away by their madly fleeing companions. Many covered their eyes with their hands, and plunged blindly and awkwardly in their race to escape, overturning furniture and stumbling against the walls before they managed to reach one of the many doors.

The cries were shocking; and as I stood in the brilliant apartment alone and dazed, listening to their vanishing echoes, I trembled at the thought of what might be lurking near me unseen. At a casual inspection the room seemed deserted, but when I moved towards one of the alcoves I thought I detected a presence there — a hint of motion beyond the golden-arched doorway leading to another and somewhat similar room. As I approached the arch I began to perceive the presence more clearly; and then, with the first and last sound I ever uttered — a ghastly ululation that revolted me almost as poignantly as its noxious cause — I beheld in full, frightful vividness the inconceivable, indescribable, and unmentionable monstrosity which had by its simple appearance changed a merry company to a herd of delirious fugitives.

I cannot even hint what it was like, for it was a compound of all that is unclean, uncanny, unwelcome, abnormal, and detestable. It was the ghoulish shade of decay, antiquity, and dissolution; the putrid, dripping eidolon of unwholesome revelation, the awful baring of that which the merciful earth should always hide. God knows it was not of this world — or no longer of this world — yet to my horror I saw in its eaten-away and bone-revealing outlines a leering, abhorrent travesty on the human shape; and in its mouldy, disintegrating apparel an unspeakable quality that chilled me even more.

I was almost paralysed, but not too much so to make a feeble effort towards flight; a backward stumble which failed to break the spell in which the nameless, voiceless monster held me. My eyes, bewitched by the glassy orbs which stared loathsomely into them, refused to close, though they were mercifully blurred, and showed the terrible object but indistinctly after the first shock. I tried to raise my hand to shut out the sight, yet so stunned were my nerves that my arm could not fully obey my will. The attempt, however, was enough to disturb my balance; so that I had to stagger forward several steps to avoid falling. As I did so I became suddenly and agonizingly aware of the *nearness* of the carrion thing, whose hideous hollow breathing I half fancied I could hear. Nearly mad, I found myself yet able to throw out a hand to ward off the foetid apparition which pressed so close; when in one cataclysmic second of cosmic nightmarishness and hellish accident *my fingers touched the rotting outstretched paw of the monster beneath the golden arch.*

I did not shriek, but all the fiendish ghouls that ride the night wind shrieked for me as in that same second there crashed down upon my mind a single fleeting avalanche of soul-annihilating memory. I knew in that second all that had been; I remembered beyond the frightful castle and the trees, and recognized the altered edifice in which I now stood; I recognized, most terrible of all, the unholy abomination that stood leering before me as I withdrew my sullied fingers from its own.

But in the cosmos there is balm as well as bitterness, and that balm is nepenthe. In the supreme horror of that second I forgot what had horrified me, and the burst of black memory vanished in a chaos of echoing images. In a dream I fled from that haunted and accursed pile, and ran swiftly and silently in the moonlight. When I returned to the churchyard place of marble and went down the steps I found the stone trap-door immovable; but I was not sorry, for I had hated the antique castle and the trees. Now I ride with the mocking and friendly ghouls on the night-wind, and play by day amongst the catacombs of Nephren-Ka in the sealed and unknown valley of Hadoth by the Nile. I know that light is not for me, save that of the moon over the rock tombs of Neb, nor any gaiety save the unnamed feasts of Nitokris beneath the Great Pyramid; yet in my new wildness and freedom I almost welcome the bitterness of alienage.

For although nepenthe has calmed me, I know always that I am an outsider; a stranger in this century and among those who are still men. This I have known ever since I stretched out my fingers to the abomination within that great gilded frame; stretched out my fingers and touched *a cold and unyielding surface of polished glass.*

The Abominations of Yondo*

he sand of the desert of Yondo is not as the sand of other deserts; for Yondo lies nearest of all to the world's rim; and strange winds, blowing from a gulf no astronomer may hope to fathom, have sown its ruinous fields with the gray dust of corroding planets, the black ashes of extinguished suns. The dark, orb-like mountains which rise from its wrinkled and pitted plain are not all its own, for some are fallen asteroids half-buried in that abysmal sand. Things have crept in from nether space, whose incursion is forbid by the gods of all proper and well-ordered lands; but there are no such gods in Yondo, where live the hoary genii of stars abolished, and decrepit demons left homeless by the destruction of antiquated hells.

It was noon of a vernal day when I came forth from that interminable cactus-forest in which the Inquisitors of Ong had left me, and saw at my feet the gray beginnings of Yondo. I repeat, it was noon of a vernal day; but in that fantastic wood I had found no token or memory of spring; and the swollen, fulvous, dying and half-rotten growths through which I had pushed my way, were like no other cacti, but bore shapes of abomination scarcely to be described. The very air was heavy with stagnant odours of decay; and leprous lichens mottled the black soil and russet vegetation with increasing frequency. Palegreen vipers lifted their heads from prostrate cactus-boles and watched me with eyes of bright ochre that had no lids or pupils. These things had disquieted me for hours past; and I did not like the monstrous fungi, with hueless stems and nodding heads of poisonous mauve, which grew from the sodden lips of fetid tarns; and the sinister ripples spreading and fading on the yellow water at my approach, were not reassuring to one whose nerves were still taut from unmentionable tortures. Then, when even the blotched and sickly cacti became more sparse and stunted, and rills of ashen sand crept in among them, I began to suspect how great was the hatred my heresy had aroused in the priests of Ong; and to guess the ultimate malignancy of their vengeance.

I will not detail the indiscretions which had led me, a careless stranger from far-off lands, into the power of those dreadful magicians and mysteri-archs who serve the lion-headed Ong. These indiscretions, and the particulars of my arrest, are painful to remember; and least of all do I like to remember the racks of dragon-gut strewn with powdered adamant, on which men are stretched naked; or that unlit room with six-inch windows near the sill, where bloated corpse worms crawled in by hundreds from a neighboring catacomb. Sufficient to say that, after expanding the resources of their frightful fantasy, my inquisitors had borne me blindfolded on camel-back for incomputable hours, to leave me

---

* "The Abominations of Yondo" was written by Clark Ashton Smith (1893 – 1961) and published in *The Overland Monthly*, Vol. 4, No. 84, Apr. 1926.

at morning twilight in that sinister forest. I was free, they told me, to go whither I would; and in token of the clemency of Ong, they gave me a loaf of coarse bread and a leathern bottle of rank water by way of provision. It was at noon of the same day that I came to the desert of Yondo.

So far, I had not thought of turning back, for all the horror of those rotting cacti, or the evil things that dwelt among them. Now, I paused, knowing the abominable legend of the land to which I had come; for Yondo is a place where few have ventured wittingly and of their own accord. Fewer still have returned — babbling of unknown horrors and strange treasure; and the lifelong palsy which shakes their withered limbs, together with the mad gleam in their staring eyes beneath whitened brows and lashes, is not an incentive for others to follow. So it was that I hesitated on the verge of those ashen sands, and felt the tremor of a new fear in my wrenched vitals. It was dreadful to go on, and dreadful to go back, for I felt sure that the priests had made provision against the latter contingency. So after a little I went forward, sinking at each step in loathly softness, and followed by certain long-legged insects that I had met among the cacti. These insects were the color of a week-old corpse and were as large as tarantulas; but when I turned and trod upon the foremost, a mephitic stench arose that was more nauseous even than their color. So, for the nonce, I ignored them as much as possible.

Indeed, such things were minor horrors in my predicament. Before me, under a huge sun of sickly scarlet, Yondo reached interminable as the land of a hashish-dream against the black heavens. Far-off, on the utmost rim, were those orb-like mountains of which I have told; but in between were awful blanks of gray desolation, and low, treeless hills like the backs of half-buried monsters. Struggling on, I saw great pits where meteors had sunk from sight; and divers-colored jewels that I could not name glared or glistened from the dust. There were fallen cypresses that rotted by crumbling mausoleums, on whose lichen-blotted marble fat chameleons crept with royal pearls in their mouths. Hidden by the low ridges, were cities of which no stela remained unbroken — immense and immemorial cities lapsing shard by shard, atom by atom, to feed infinities of desolation. I dragged my torture-weakened limbs over vast rubbish-heaps that had once been mighty temples; and fallen gods frowned in rotting psammite or leered in riven porphyry at my feet. Over all was an evil silence, broken only by — the satanic laughter of hyenas, and the rustling of adders in thickets of dead thorn or antique gardens given to the perishing nettle and fumitory.

Topping one of the many mound-like ridges, I saw the waters of a weird lake, unfathomably dark and green as malachite, and set with bars of profulgent salt. These waters lay far beneath me in a cup-like hollow; but almost at my feet on the wave-worn slopes were heaps of that ancient salt; and I knew that the lake was only the bitter and ebbing dregs of some former sea. Climbing down, I came to the dark waters, and began to lave my hands; but there was a sharp and corrosive sting in that immemorial brine, and I desisted quickly, preferring the desert dust that had wrapped me about like a slow shroud.

Here I decided to rest for a little; and hunger forced me to consume part of the meagre and mocking fare with which I had been provided by the priests. It was my intention to push on if my strength would allow and reach the lands that lie to the north of Yondo. These lands are desolate, indeed, but their desolation is of a more usual order than that of Yondo; and certain tribes of nomads have been known to visit them occasionally. If fortune favored me, I might fall in with one of these tribes.

The scant fare revived me, and, for the first time in weeks of which I had lost all reckoning, I heard the whisper of a faint hope. The corpse-colored insects had long since ceased to follow me; and so far despite the eeriness of the sepulchral silence and the mounded dust of timeless ruin, I had met nothing half so horrible as those insects. I began to think that the terrors of Yondo were somewhat exaggerated.

It was then that I heard a diabolic chuckle on the hillside above me. The sound began with a sharp abruptness that startled me beyond all reason, and continued endlessly, never varying its single note, like the mirth of an idiotic demon. I turned, and saw the mouth of a dark cave fanged with green stalactites, which I had not perceived before. The sound appeared to come from within this cave.

With a fearful intentness I stared at the black opening. The chuckle grew louder, but for awhile I could see nothing. At last I caught a whitish glimmer in the darkness; then, with all the rapidity of nightmare, a monstrous Thing emerged. It had a pale, hairless, egg-shaped body, large as that of a gravid she-goat; and this body was mounted on nine long, wavering legs with many flanges, like the legs of some enormous spider. The creature ran past me to the water's edge; and I saw that there were no eyes in its oddly sloping face; but two knife-like ears rose high above its head, and a thin, wrinkled snout hung down across its mouth, whose flabby lips, parted in that eternal chuckle, revealed rows of bats' teeth.

It drank avidly of the bitter lake; then, with thirst satisfied, it turned and seemed to sense my presence, for the wrinkled snout rose and pointed toward me, sniffing audibly. Whether the creature would have fled, or whether it meant to attack me, I do not know; for I could bear the sight no longer but ran with trembling limbs amid the massive boulders and great bars of salt along the lakeshore.

Utterly breathless, I stopped at last, and saw that I was not pursued. I sat down, still trembling, in the shadow of a boulder. But I was to find little respite, for now began the second of those bizarre adventures which forced me to believe all the mad legends I had heard.

More startling even than that diabolic chuckle was the scream that rose at my elbow, from the salt-compounded sand — the scream of a woman possessed by some atrocious agony, or helpless in the grip of devils. Turning, I beheld a veritable Venus, naked in a white perfection that could fear no scrutiny, but immersed to her navel in the sand. Her terror-widened eyes implored me and her lotus hands reached out with beseeching gesture. I sprang to her side — and touched a marble statue, whose carven lids were drooped in some enigmatic dream of dead cycles, and whose hands were buried with the lost loveliness of hips and thighs.

Again I fled, shaken with a new fear; and again I heard the scream of a woman's agony. But this time I did not turn to see the imploring eyes and hands.

Up the long slope to the north of that accursed lake, stumbling over boulders of basanite and ledges that were sharp with verdigris-covered metals; floundering in pits of salt, on terraces wrought by the receding tide in ancient aeons. I fled as a man flies from dream to baleful dream of some cacodemoniacal night. At whiles there was a cold whisper in my ear, which did not come from the wind of my flight; and looking back as I reached one of the upper terraces, I perceived a singular shadow that ran pace by pace with my own. This shadow was not the shadow of man nor ape nor any known beast; the head was too grotesquely elongated, the squat body too gibbous; and I was unable to determine whether the shadow possessed five legs, or whether what appeared to be the fifth was merely a tail.

Terror lent me new strength, and I had reached the hilltop when I dared to look back again. But still the fantastic shadow kept pace by pace with mine; and now I caught a curious and utterly sickening odour, foul as the odour of bats who have hung in a charnel-house amid the mould of corruption. I ran for leagues, while the red sun slanted above the asteroidal mountains to the west; and the weird shadow lengthened with mine but kept always at the same distance behind me.

An hour before sunset I came to a circle of small pillars that rose miraculously unbroken amid ruins that were like a vast pile of potsherds. As I passed among these pillars I heard a whimper, like the whimper of some fierce animal, between rage and fear, and saw that the shadow had not followed me within the circle. I stopped and waited, conjecturing at once that I had found a sanctuary my unwelcome familiar would not dare to enter; and in this the action of the shadow confirmed me, for the Thing hesitated, then ran about the circle of columns, pausing often between them; and, whimpering all the while, at last went away and disappeared in the desert toward the setting sun.

For a full half hour I did not dare to move; then, the imminence of night, with all its probabilities of fresh terror, urged me to push on as far as I could to the north. For I was now in the very heart of Yondo, where demons or phantoms might dwell who would not respect the sanctuary of the unbroken columns.

Now, as I toiled on, the sunlight altered strangely; for the red orb, nearing the mounded horizon, sank and smouldered in a belt of miasmal haze, where floating dust from all the shattered fanes and necropoli of Yondo was mixed with evil vapors coiling skyward from black enormous gulfs lying beyond the utmost rim of the world. In that light, the entire waste, the rounded mountains, the serpentine hills, the lost cities, were drenched with phantasmal and darkening scarlet.

Then, out of the north, where shadows mustered, there came a curious figure — a tall man fully caparisoned in chainmail — or, rather, what I assumed to be a man. As the figure approached me, clanking dismally at each step on the sharded ground, I saw that its armour was of brass mottled with verdigris; and a casque of the same metal, furnished with coiling horns and a serrate comb, rose high above its head. I say its head, for the sunset was darkening, and I could not see clearly at any distance; but when the apparition came abreast, I perceived that there was no face beneath the brows of the bizarre helmet, whose empty edges were outlined for a moment against the smoldering light. Then the figure passed on, still clanking dismally, and vanished.

But on its heels, ere the sunset faded, there came a second apparition, striding with incredible strides and halting when it loomed almost upon me in the red twilight — the monstrous mummy of some ancient king, still crowned with untarnished gold, but turning to my gaze a visage that more than time or the worm had wasted. Broken swathings flapped about the skeleton legs, and above the crown that was set with sapphires and orange rubies, a black Something swayed and nodded horribly; but, for an instant, I did not dream what it was. Then, in its middle, two oblique and scarlet eyes opened and glowed like hellish coals, and two ophidian fangs glittered in an ape-like mouth. A squat, furless, shapeless head on a neck of disproportionate extent leaned unspeakably down and whispered in the mummy's ear. Then, with one stride, the titanic lich took half the distance between us, and from out the folds of the tattered sere-cloth a gaunt arm arose, and fleshless, taloned fingers, laden with glowering gems, reached out and fumbled for my throat . . .

Back, back through aeons of madness and dread, in a prone, precipitate flight, I ran from those fumbling fingers that hung always on the dusk behind me; back, back forever, unthinking, unhesitating, to all the abominations I had left; back in the thickening twilight toward the nameless and sharded ruins, the haunted lake, the forest of evil cacti, and the cruel and cynical inquisitors of Ong who waited my return.

Spider-Bite[*]

"By the tomb of Ner-Taul, in the chamber of the pool, lies Za, the scribe. By the sting of the box and the juice of the jar he shall arise. Keeper is he to the jewels of Ahma-Ka."

I

rofessor Ashbrooke frowned as Phil finished translating. "It does sound a little odd," he admitted, "but it's hardly worth getting so excited over, do you think? Still, those old Egyptians generally had something to say when they wrote on the stone tablets."

"Perhaps the tomb of Ner-Taul never was thoroughly examined," suggested Phil; "let's investigate this 'chamber of the pool' business. That inscription sounds as though the earlier excavators might have overlooked something valuable."

Ashbrooke smiled. "You do like to organize wild goose chases, don't you? That riddle you just ran across probably doesn't mean anything at all."

"But there's the chance of discovering a new tomb — and it mentioned the jewels of Ahma-Ka." Phil's face was pleading and boyish.

The professor laughed shortly. "Egyptology is no hobby for a modern young romanticist — you get excited too easily." He turned and stared out of the window across the rock-strewn little valley that lay baking in the Egyptian sun.

"I think we're passing up an interesting clue," persisted Phil.

Ashbrooke suddenly relented. "All right," he said, "we'll go, but the chances are ninety-nine out of a hundred that we shan't find a thing."

II

"Was I right?"

Professor Ashbrooke swept the bare, dusty tomb-chamber with a half-contemptuous fling of his arm. Phil was silent.

"But then," continued the professor patronizingly, "there wasn't any digging to do, so there's nothing wasted but our time."

Phil bit his lip. "We knew before we came here that there was nothing here in *this* tomb," he exclaimed a trifle indignantly; "it has already been opened. What I want to do is see if we can get some clue to the meaning of that riddle about 'the sting of the box and the juice of the jar.' Look here." He took from his pocket a paper bearing the English translation of the puzzling inscription. "This says *'by* the tomb of Ner-

---

[*] "Spider-Bite" was written by Robert S. Carr (1909 – 1994) and published in *Weird Tales*, Jun. 1926.

Taul,' not *in* it. It plainly states that the tomb of Za, the scribe, is near here somewhere. All we have to do is find it."

"Exactly." Ashbrooke was mildly sarcastic. "And how do you intend to go about it?"

"Well, first I'm going to have a good look at every inch of this place." Phil strode over to a far corner of the tomb and began to tap along the wall with a small geologist's hammer. Suddenly he stepped back in alarm.

"What's the matter?" snapped the professor quickly.

Phil smiled a bit shamefacedly. "Just a loose stone in the floor. Kind of gave me a start." He turned around and resumed his tapping.

Ashbrooke pursed his lips in silence a moment, then exclaimed: "There couldn't be a loose stone in here — this whole room is carved out of solid rock!"

Phil's eyebrows lifted. He stepped back and rejoined his companion. "That may be," he said slowly, "but nevertheless the floor moved under my feet right over there." He pointed to where his boot-tracks showed in the heavy dust.

The professor darted forward, knelt, and began to dust the stone floor with his handkerchief. A moment later Phil was following his example.

"Here's a straight crack," he announced presently. "Seems to be the edge of a block. Yes, it is — here's the corner!" Soon they had uncovered what seemed to be a separate section of stone, roughly four feet long and three feet wide.

"You say it moved?"

For answer Phil placed one hand on the stone and shoved vigorously downward. With a low grating sound that end of the block sank into the floor while the other raised itself slightly.

"A stone slab mounted on an axle through the center," analyzed the professor quickly. "Push down again and harder, Phil."

Phil complied. When the under edge of the end of the block appeared, Ashbrooke hooked his strong fingers over it, and their combined efforts succeeded in raising it to an almost perpendicular position. Phil gave one more tug. As it swung perfectly upright, both men heard a metallic click.

"Wonder if it will stay that way now?"

"It seems to be pretty solid." Phil pushed against the stone to see if it would roll on its axle. To his surprise it was firm. He pushed harder, but he might as well have tried to move the rocky walls on either side, for the revolving slab was now securely locked in its upright position. He shrugged, then stepped back from the opening as a strong current of air arose; icy with the clammy coldness that comes to dead air long imprisoned underground. Like the breath of a phantom the young man felt it on his cheek. He shuddered at its faint but ghastly odor — an aromatic mustiness that hinted of grim-visaged mummies peering into the eternal blackness of their underground tombs. . . .

He involuntarily moved closer to the professor. "Queer odor, isn't it?" he said slowly. "Makes one think of spooks and open graves and things like that."

Ashbrooke silenced him with an irritated gesture. "Rot!" he exclaimed brusquely. "Phil, your imagination is your greatest fault. . . . But it certainly is strange how *wet* that air is!"

"'The chamber of the pool'," quoted Phil. Try as he would, he could not keep a certain hollow ring out of his voice. The professor turned and frowned.

"What's the matter with you? You're beginning to get on my nerves. Go outside and get some fresh air if you feel nervous — don't stand around in here and croak like Poe's raven." He consulted his watch. "Time for lunch anyhow; let's both go."

Phil felt immensely and inexplicably relieved as he stepped out into the bright glare of the Egyptian sun and was immediately ashamed of himself for it. He wouldn't let his imagination run wild again, he promised himself. When they re-entered the tomb a half-hour later, his step was almost jaunty.

Accompanying them were Beeba, their native foreman, and another native, carrying small picks, shovels and electric lanterns. The slab still held its perpendicular position and seemed as firm as before. Phil turned his flash light's strong beam down into the hole, revealing smooth sides and a level stone floor some seven or eight feet below. He lay down and projected the light around the interior of the pit.

"There's a tunnel, leading off to the left," he announced.

"Let me see," exclaimed the professor. He lay down by Phil's side and craned his neck. "It's carved out of the solid rock, so there's no danger of a cave-in. I wonder how the air is down there." He sat up, tore a leaf from his notebook, lighted it and tossed it down a few feet back in the tunnel. It burned brightly.

"It's all right," he said, satisfied as to the safety.

Phil leaped down into the stone-walled pit, holding his flashlight before him. In a moment the professor and the two natives had joined him. In single file they started through the tunnel, their elbows brushing the walls.

They walked a moment in silence. Suddenly Ashbrooke halted, so abruptly that Phil, in second place, collided with him.

"What is it?" he whispered. The professor moved aside so that Phil could look ahead. Immediately before them the ceiling of the tunnel sloped sharply to the floor, barring further progress. The angle where the ceiling met the floor was filled with an accumulation of dust and debris. Phil dropped to his hands and knees and poked in the litter.

"Give me a shovel," he said presently, turning to one of the natives.

In a few minutes he revealed that the slope of the ceiling was not complete, but ceased as abruptly as it had begun at a point about ten inches from the floor, leaving an aperture the full width of the tunnel at the bottom. A gust of air, colder and wetter than before, swept past them like a ghost escaping from a sepulcher. Phil was busy with his flash light.

"I think the tunnel continues," he said after a brief inspection. "I'll crawl through and see what's on the other side. If there's anything we want, we can break down this part of the wall and get it."

"I'm going with you," said the professor. He stopped and surveyed the ten-inch crack dubiously, then regarded his rather rotund waistline. "I don't think I can make it," he added; "let's see."

He experimented, then stood up and brushed the dust off his clothes. "Impossible," he laughed. "One's enough, though; there's no danger." He spoke the last sentence in a slightly louder tone. An instant later an eery voice echoed out of the blackness behind them. Faintly it came, a single word — "Danger!"

Both natives started, the whites of their eyes plainly visible. Ashbrooke coughed. "Peculiar echo," he remarked evenly. Phil licked his dry lips. To him the echo had had an entirely different inflection from that the professor had given it. . . . Why hadn't the other words come echoing back too?

Then he shook himself, dropped flat and, flashlight in hand, crawled slowly into the forbidding hole before him. Ashbrooke had an uneasy feeling, a premonition almost, as he watched the tips of Phil's boots disappear.

"See anything?" he called, to dispel his nervousness.

"Not yet." The voice came as if from the bowels of the earth. When it ceased the silence was so intense that to Ashbrooke the ticking of his watch in his trousers pocket was as loud as the rapid, rhythmic dropping of coins into a metal bowl close at hand. He was relieved when the sepulchral voice resumed its reporting.

"It's high enough to stand up, I guess. Wider —" There was an instant of scuffling, the smacking thud of a body falling violently upon unyielding rock, a groan — then silence.

For an instant Ashbrooke was petrified. Then he quickly prostrated himself before the opening, cupped his hands and called.

"Phil! Oh, Phil! Answer me! Are you hurt?" He listened intently for a reply. None came. He could hear a liquid dripping somewhere beyond in the blackness. . . . Again he called. A steady drip, drip, drip, now quite audible, was his only answer.

He wheeled on the terrified natives. "Break through that rock!" he commanded. Although numb with fright, they moved forward to obey, only to stop short as a new horror presented itself.

Ashbrooke followed their wide-eyed stare and his lips curled back in revulsion, for there, crawling slowly up the wall before them, was a huge white spider, a creature occasionally encountered in very old tombs.

The frightful thing was fully as large as the fingers and palm of a grown man's hand, with a bloated body and unusually thick legs — legs that looked as though possessed of a strength far out of proportion to the size of the body. Covered as it was with matted white hair, it stood out against the dark rock like a bleached skull mounted on black velvet. It crawled slowly, deliberately, as if gorged to repletion on some hideous meal, the probable nature of which caused Ashbrooke an involuntary shudder.

The two natives were absolutely paralyzed with fear. Their eyes bulged in their sockets and on their foreheads a cold sweat stood out in great beads, for not only is the Egyptian tomb-spider a fearsome and horrible thing to behold, but the legends and superstitions which surround it are of such a nature as would cause the most harmless and mild-appearing creature to be regarded with mortal terror.

Ashbrooke regained control of himself with an effort. He drew his revolver, took careful aim, and fired. The soft-nosed bullet spattered the huge spider into a sticky clot that drooled slowly down the rocks. With the roar of the revolver the natives bolted screaming into the darkness dropping the tools and lanterns in their mad flight.

The thin pencil of illumination from the flashlight his only guide, the professor hurriedly made his way back along the tunnel. He broke into a run when he heard the natives' screams double in volume. At the end of the tunnel he found them, pointing upward. He took a startled glance, then stepped back aghast.

The trap-door was closed!

For an instant he felt a hysterical impulse to scream with them, but the very panic of the others steeled his own nerves against giving way. He grasped Beeba roughly by the arm and shook him.

"Brace up!" he barked; "we've got to get the door open! Down on your hands and knees — quick!"

They obeyed his command, and in a moment were braced together in a corner of the wall, with their bare knees padded against the coming pressure with Ashbrooke's jacket. Still holding his flashlight, he stepped lightly upon them one foot on each of the bare, brown backs. He settled himself, snapped out his light and pocketed it, placed both hands against the cold stone of the door overhead, took a deep breath and — pushed.

For a moment he was assailed by the horrible suspicion that someone had placed a heavy weight over the trap-door, for it seemed immovable. Then to his great relief it gave, slowly and ponderously, but enough to assure him that it was moving on its axle.

Inch by inch the great stone slab swung upward. The effort was tremendous. Though the atmosphere in the tunnel beneath the old tomb was chilly, hot perspiration streaked down Ashbrooke's face. The natives winced and cried out softly as the steel hobnails of his boots bit into their backs, but they held fast.

There in the utter blackness and silence the trapped man strained for what seemed ages. His arms ached and throbbed till he feared he would collapse, his whole body trembled and the great vein on his sweat-bedewed forehead stood out alarmingly.

At last a thin ray of faint daylight filtered in from the tomb above. With renewed vigor he pushed until the crack had widened several inches. Then, summoning every ounce of strength, for an instant he held the great rock with one hand while with the other he reached for the far end. His fingers crept around the thick block, he made, one last tremendous effort and the slab swung into perpendicular, locking there as it had done before.

His strength spent, he staggered gasping against the wall while the natives scrambled up and out with an almost monkey-like agility. Beeba reached a hand down and helped Ashbrooke out. "Get the electric drill — we've got to get Phil out of there!" he shouted as soon as he had regained his breath.

In a few minutes they were dragging the heavy apparatus to the edge of the pit. At first the natives were loth to climb down into the gloomy place again, but when the professor fingered the butt of his revolver nervously, they obeyed with alacrity.

Under the blaze of two electric lanterns, Ashbrooke watched the powerful drill quickly cut through the soft stone wall beyond which Phil had disappeared. He called from time to time but received no answer. As soon as a large enough hole was made, he squeezed through into what appeared to be a large chamber. But he had no time to take note of his surroundings, for the first object the light fell upon was the huddled form of Phil lying on the floor. He quickly knelt beside him, and was feeling his pulse when to his relief the young man opened his eyes and looked about him dazedly. He saw Ashbrooke and tried to smile.

"Something lit on me," he said weakly, "bowled me over and I cracked my head on the floor." At that moment a bright illumination dazzled them as Beeba, the wall demolished, stepped through carrying an electric lantern. The professor helped Phil to his feet.

"How do you feel? Want to go outside and get some fresh air?" he inquired.

"No, I'm all right — just a sore lump on my head," Phil assured him.

Together they looked about them. The chamber in which they stood was fairly large and almost square. A few articles of furniture, a gold-encrusted chariot and several large urns of preserved fruit were grouped about in the tomb, but the scene that caught their attention and held it was in the center of the room.

From a hole in the ceiling, water dripped slowly into a small oval pool which was apparently quite deep. At either end of the pool an upright mast was sunk into the stone floor, and between the masts, above the water, was suspended a hammock-like swing in which reposed a mummy. On a low stand at the brink of the pool were an ornate little jar and a small carved box.

For the first time in his life Phil saw the professor really excited. "Just wait till I get my camera in here!" he exclaimed. "What will the British Museum say to the arrangement and position of *that* mummy! Why, Phil, we've found something new — absolutely new!"

But Phil was gazing toward the mouth of the tunnel by which they had entered. "That's what hit me," he said quietly, "look!"

Ashbrooke turned.

From an axle set high upon the wall above the opening extended a long wooden beam, parallel and close to the side of the chamber. On the end of the beam was affixed a wicked-looking metal blade set so that when the wooden arms swung down, it would sweep quite close to the floor, thus decapitating or seriously injuring a person who might be emerging through the ten-inch crack the electric drill had just enlarged. The beam was discharged by pressure against a small wooden trigger set on the floor.

"I kicked that trigger with my foot as I stood up," said Phil. "If I'd crawled one foot farther — zowie!" He made an unpleasant gesture. "As it was," he continued; "it was only the shaft that hit me and knocked me over. It's a good thing I stood up as soon as I found I could. Even so, I don't think that knife missed me very far."

"Why, say, Phil, that thing seems to be cocked ready to go off again. How could it reset itself. . . . There's something mighty queer here, I tell you! See if there is any way a person could get out of this chamber except through our tunnel. That heavy beam couldn't swing back up in place itself. . . . We'd better set it off, though, or one of the men might get hurt."

He advanced, kicked the trigger with his boot and leaped backward. The murderous weapon swept down with a creak, but instead of swinging back up again as a thing of pendulum construction might naturally be expected to do, it remained suspended in the air on the farthest extremity of its arc.

"There must be a catch of some sort up there," said the professor, indicating the hole where the axle disappeared in the wall, "but that's all the more reason why it couldn't swing back in place by itself. . . . *Someone was in here while you lay unconscious!*"

"If there was," said Phil uneasily, "he's in here yet. You can see for yourself there's nobody here but that mummy over there."

"And I hardly think he'd do it," supplemented Ashbrooke smilingly. Instinctively both men turned their gaze toward the grim brown profile that was visible over the edge of the ornamented hammock. Suddenly Phil gripped Ashbrooke's arm.

"Look! For God's sake, look! The thing's moving!"

The professor took a step forward and his jaw dropped. Then it snapped shut and he straightened up. He cleared his throat.

"Bunk! Your imagination's playing tricks, or else it's air currents swinging that hammock. Three-thousand-year-old mummies don't move!"

Phil shuddered. "I *hope* it was my imagination."

At that instant Beeba, who a few minutes before had gone back into the tunnel, burst in.

"Stone door closed again!" he gasped.

There was a stunned silence. Then the professor asked a question. "When did it close?"

"Just then."

"About thirty seconds ago?"

"Yes. Swung down shut — nothing touched it."

For several seconds Ashbrooke was lost in thought. Then he exclaimed: "Phil, run up underneath the trap-door and watch. I've got an idea."

The young man cast a last wide-eyed glance at the mummy, then trotted down the tunnel, leaping the pile of stones where the barrier had been removed. The professor called to him.

"All set," came back the reply.

Ashbrooke walked over beneath the long wooden arm that still hung motionless. He stood on tiptoe, grasped it just above the blade and pulled downward.

"Anything happening?" he shouted at the tunnel-mouth.

"No!"

He pulled harder. The beam moved downward a few inches.

"Say, this trap-door's beginning to open!" yelled Phil excitedly from the tunnel. The professor released his grip on the arm. It jerked back up into its original position.

"The door's dropped back shut again now!"

"All right, that's what I wanted to find out. Come back in here now."

As Phil re-entered the chamber, Ashbrooke smiled and pointed at the beam's axle.

"This is a really simple arrangement, and ingenious, too. See that axle? Well, that's the same axle that the stone slab is hung on. As we pulled open the trap-door, we automatically drew this swinging arm up into place and set it. When that was set, the trap-door was locked open, but when you touched the trigger and released the beam, the stone slab fell back down and bottled us up in here. We've got the drill down here now, so we'll cut the trap-door down. Then we can't get caught."

"Let's break up this unpleasant-looking business, too," suggested Phil, pointing to the knife and the beam.

After they shoveled the loose stone out of the tunnel, removed the heavy slab from its axle and took down the swinging beam, it was past time for their evening meal. Ashbrooke suggested that they reserve the examination of their discoveries till the next morning. Phil agreed with him.

III

"Better bring the folding table, too, Phil," called the professor from the door of the tomb; "I want to examine that mummy before we bring him out." He turned to Beeba, who stood beside him. "Are the batteries in the lanterns in good shape?" The native nodded and followed him down the ladder which they had placed in the pit to facilitate entrance and exit.

When Phil emerged from the tunnel into the chamber of the pool, Ashbrooke was preparing to take a flashlight picture. Phil unfolded the long, low portable table he had brought with him and set it up. Then he moved over and stood beside the professor.

"I expect that's Za, there," he remarked by way of conversation, pointing at the mummy. Ashbrooke was busy and did not answer, so Phil wandered over closer to the pool. He took from his pocket the translation of the inscription that had brought them there. He reread it . . . *"By the sting of the box and the juice of the jar."* . . . His glance fell on the stand that held the squat jar and the carved box. He looked back at the professor, completely engrossed in putting a slide in his camera. Acting on a sudden impulse, Phil quickly picked up both the box and the jar and walked out. Ashbrooke did not notice his departure.

When Phil returned from concealing the two objects beneath his cot, he smelled the odor of burnt magnesium powder and found the professor in a highly satisfied humor.

"Let's take him down now and have a close look at him. I may take some more pictures, too, for he seems to be clothed differently from any mummy I ever saw before; in fact, he's virtually naked."

They moved toward the hammock. "The ropes are slipped over hooks in each of the poles," observed Phil; "we can unhook them and swing hammock and all over onto the floor."

"Good idea," commented the professor.

The ropes easily unhooked, and for a moment the two men held the thing low above the water, standing across the pool from each other preparatory to swinging it ashore.

"Wow! This fellow weighs a ton!" groaned Phil, bracing his feet to keep from slipping into the water.

"It's those ornaments on the hammock," explained Ashbrooke. "He's fastened in, too. Whoever took care of him fixed a nice safe berth. All right now, heave ho!"

They swung together. At the same instant, the dry, crumbly old ropes parted and with a splash the hammock and mummy plunged beneath the dark waters of the pool.

The professor stepped back in disgust. Phil sat on the dusty floor regarding the piece of rope in his hand.

"Confound the luck!" expostulated Ashbrooke. "I wonder how deep that water is. Now he won't be worth a thing if we do get him out."

He tied a small rock to a six-foot piece of cord and sounded the pool. The stone sank the full length without touching.

"We could make a grappling iron," suggested Phil. He eyed the surface of the water. "Look at the bubbles coming up, would you?"

"Yes, that dried-up old mummy will soak up water like a sponge."

"I'd like to get him out," said Phil. "I'll see if I can rig up some sort to tackle right now."

"All right. And in the meantime I'll look over this stuff." Asbbrooke indicated the other contents of the tomb.

Phil met Beeba standing spell-bound in the tomb above, watching another great white spider crawl slowly up the wall. Phil, too, was struck with revulsion at the hideous sight the creature presented, but being somewhat of an entomologist, he was also intensely interested.

"Is it poisonous?" he asked.

Beeba shrugged his shoulders.

"Then why are you so afraid of it?"

The native turned horror-wide eyes upon him in an inarticulate reply.

"Did you ever hear of anyone's being bitten by one?"

Beeba admitted that he never had, but added that a horrible death would be sure to follow if one were. Phil smiled.

"Well, I never saw a spider like this before, so I think I'll add him to my collection. He seems to be a sleepy beggar — ought to be easy to capture." He stepped outside and returned a few minutes later with a glass jar and a stick. Holding the jar at arm's length beneath the creature, he dislodged it with the stick, quickly clapped the lid on and the huge spider was his captive. It lay sprawled helplessly on the bottom of the jar. Phil turned to Beeba.

"Simple, wasn't it?"

The native turned and walked away, shaking his head. "Bad business!" Phil heard him mutter as he left.

IV

A thorough search of the little camp revealed absolutely nothing with which even the crudest kind of grappling iron could be improvised. At noon the professor came up from the chamber in high glee, bearing a bundle of papyrus rolls which Phil knew would occupy him for some time.

After lunch the young man decided to go to the military post, some ten miles distant, to borrow a grappling iron and incidentally to pay a call of Major Knepper, the officer in charge of the post and a friend of his.

As he slipped into a clean white shirt, his eyes fell upon the glass jar and the spider within. He pondered a moment. His collection was stored back in Cairo, he told himself, and, too, he lacked the paraphernalia to properly preserve the creature, so why not make Major Knepper a present of it? He knew that the major was a well-known collector and would be able to inform him as to the name and habits of the thing.

After a fifteen minutes' whirlwind ride, he drew up by the officers' quarters at the post. He found the major at his desk, and when the necessary formalities and informalities of greeting an old friend were disposed of, broached the subject of a grappling iron. Knepper dispatched an orderly to search through the supply house.

"Say, Bill, I've got something out in the machine for you," exclaimed Phil, suddenly remembering the spider. He stepped out and got the jar. Major Knepper examined the motionless form through the glass.

"It's what is called a tomb-spider around here," he informed him. "We get hold of one every now and then. Although almost every large collection contains one or two, nobody knows very much about them. Somehow or other, no one seems to want to make a detailed and careful study of the things. I, personally, have investigated a little and found that they lack the nasty viciousness so marked in most of the other very large species of the spider family. It's queer, though, for these spiders have by far the largest venom sacs I have ever seen. Just a moment and I'll show you. . . . You don't mind if I spoil this one, do you?"

"No, go ahead," Phil replied.

Deftly Knepper removed the huge spider from the jar, killed it and impaled the body on a small dissecting board. A few minutes of skilful work with a sharp penknife, and he laid aside two soft, yellowish, oval sacs the size of ripe cherries.

"Once, prompted by a morbid curiosity," he continued, "I took some of this venom and analyzed it. I found it to be of an entirely different nature from the irritating poison of other spiders; in fact, as far as I could ascertain, it wasn't even poisonous. But then, I'm not much of a chemist and there are a great many things that scientists don't know yet. Rather a trivial matter all the way round, too, don't you think?"

"Yes, I suppose that the private life of a rare spider doesn't matter a great deal one way or another," agreed Phil with a smile.

"Have you noticed, though, that the mere sight of one will incapacitate for work any native in Egypt? They'll step over a deadly snake and never give it a second thought, but let one of these sluggish, helpless old spiders appear on the scene and they're paralyzed."

"Yes, it seems to be one of their pet superstitions," laughed Phil.

"There's no figuring out a native's way of thinking," sighed the major.

The orderly returned carrying a small grappling iron on a twenty-five foot chain. Phil thanked Knepper and said goodbye.

He drove slowly on the return trip to camp and did a great deal of thinking. Remembering the box and jar concealed beneath the cot in his tent, he determined to investigate as soon as he arrived. But mostly he thought about large, white spiders. . . .

Finding Professor Ashbrooke engrossed and oblivious among his papyrus rolls, Phil went to his tent, placed the box and the jar on his desk and started his investigation. He selected the jar. It opened easily.

He found it to be nearly filled with a thick, clear odorless liquid which covered several leafy twigs. Phil lifted one out by means of forceps. The leaves and stems were perfectly preserved, and after consulting a naturalist's handbook, he recognized it as a rather uncommon, though not rare, shrub which could be found in that locality. Rather disappointed by the commonplace nature of his find, nevertheless he resolved to obtain a growing specimen of that shrub on the morrow.

He turned his attention to the box. Finding no lock or clasp, he surmised from the elaborate carvings on the front that the lid must be operated by a hidden spring. Painstakingly he set about to find it.

As he worked about the box he noticed an unpleasant odor, but when his fingers suddenly stumbled upon the spring and the lid flew open, he sprang up and covered his nose with his handkerchief, for there, coated with a jellylike preservative, lay fully a dozen huge white tomb-spiders!

V

"May I have that mummy, professor?" asked Phil, pointing to the dripping form of Za, the scribe, which they had just recovered from the pool and removed from his hammock.

"You may have it as far as I'm concerned," replied Ashbrooke; "it's spoiled for exhibition purposes . . . But what on earth do you want it for, Phil?"

"Oh, I have a little theory I'd like to try out, that's all."

"It's all right with me," consented the professor; "I'm going to finish translating those papyrus rolls. They give some new facts on old Egyptian law that are mighty interesting." He hurried out through the tunnel to the ladder which led to the outside world, leaving Phil alone in the chamber of the pool.

Throwing several rough towels about the mummy, he quickly lifted it onto the examination table under the direct blaze of the electric lights. Unfolding the towels, he intently scrutinized the inert figure.

Za, the scribe, had been a well-formed man of medium stature. His skin was dark, his hair close-cropped and jetblack, hands small with exceptionally long fingers.

Phil could see at once that this man had not been subjected to the usual mummification processes. The body was intact and free from the long, closely-wound linen wrappings characteristic of all other mummies. He wore but a single light garment and sandals, with an armlet of hammered silver above his elbow — a costume such as any ancient Egyptian might have worn about his private estate, the young man thought.

He lifted an arm toward him. It moved stiffly in its socket. As he turned it over, palm up, the elbow cracked sharply. The limb was but slightly shrunken, the flesh firm and cold. He held the heavy upper arm in his hand and gripped it. With a little more elasticity and quite a bit more warmth, it could easily have been that of a sleeping man. Phil flexed the arm slowly. The biceps muscle rolled evenly under the smooth, brown skin.

Suddenly Phil began to wonder how this man had met his death. In an effort to discover some wound or sign or disease he removed the clothing and examined the body minutely. Numerous scars attested that Za had been a fearless warrior in his day, but they were all old and completely healed. Poison, perhaps, Phil decided. Poisons were in vogue then and the keeper of a treasure would be a likely victim.

The features of the mummy attracted the young man's attention — the closed eyes, the straight-bridged nose, the set lips and the slightly sunken cheeks. He stood close by and regarded them for some time. Then he narrowed his eyes, cupped his chin in his hand and leaned over, peering searchingly into the dark countenance as if trying to find the answer to the mummy's secret. Tentatively he reached out a forefinger and pushed back an eylid. He looked beneath and compressed his lips as if afraid to make an exclamation. Then again he stared fixedly at the face before him for quite a long time.

When he left the chamber of the pool, a strange light was burning in his eyes. . . .

VI

Phil arose early after a sleepless night. Bolting a hasty breakfast, he tramped around over the surrounding country till about noon. On his return he bore three small bushes which he had dug up by the roots. Two of these he carefully transplanted behind his tent, reserving the third for immediate employment.

Seated at his portable desk, he held a powerful magnifying glass over a limb of the shrub and painstakingly compared it with a portion of the preserved twig he had discovered in the jar from the chamber of the pool.

Convinced at last that they were one and the same plant, he went into Ashbrooke's tent, and, not finding the professor there, helped himself to one of a set of nature books. Settling himself on a camp stool, he thumbed through the section dealing with shrubs and bushes till he came to an account of the Mona bush. There was only a single, terse paragraph, but to Phil one sentence stood out sharply from among the rest:

"This herb was believed by the ancient Egyptians to have magical properties, and the juice of the leaves was much used by them in the preparation of their medicines."

Replacing the book on the shelf, he went down the ladder into the cool underground vault where lay Za, the scribe. The body was completely covered with a heavy canvas which Phil had purposely drenched with water. He removed the covering and wiped the trickling drops from the quiet brown face. The band of silver now fitted its owner's arm as snugly as it had done in life, Phil observed. He was satisfied that the body had absorbed enough water to counteract the drying effect of the preservative, if indeed a preservative had been used.

Phil grew feverishly excited. He flexed the arms several times, noticing that the joints were not so stiff as before and that the flesh was softer and more elastic. Then he studied the translation on the slip of paper. *"By the juice of the jar."* . . . The jar had contained sprigs of the Mona bush. . . . That must mean that the juice of the leaves was in some way connected with the riddle. The juice of the leaves of the Mona bush had been used by the ancient Egyptians in their medicines. . . .

Phil plucked one of the thick oval leaves from the twig he had brought with him and crushed it beneath his thumb on the table beside the mummy. Instantly a strong, pungent vegetable odor, utterly unlike anything he had ever smelled before, assailed his nostrils. It crept like the scent of incense through the damp, still air of the underground tomb, an odor both pleasant and unpleasant.

Puzzled, and fighting against the fantastic ideas and whisperings that flitted through his mind, Phil walked aimlessly about the tomb-chamber for a few minutes, pausing to study a crude sketch on the wall, or to gaze wide-eyed into the black depths of the pool from which the mummy had been retrieved. Still finding no solution to his problem. Phil turned back to the low table and Za, the scribe. Suddenly he gave an exclamation of disgust, for upon the table, apparently materialized out of the thin air, were two gigantic tomb-spiders. The young man took a quick step forward in an effort to prevent the hideous things from molesting the body, but checked himself when he saw that that did not seem to be their object. Rather, they seemed eagerly searching for something which they could not see.

Standing by the side of the table, Phil watched the two things scurry back and forth with more display of energy than he had believed them capable of. Interested, he leaned forward and noted their every move.

Almost frantically, the two great white spiders wove about, often brushing the side of the mummy in their erratic course. Suddenly the larger of the two ranged within an inch or so of the crushed leaf of the Mona bush. As if frozen in its tracks it stopped for an instant, then flexed its thick hairy legs and pounced upon the sticky green clot of juice and pulp. A moment later the other spider had done the same. Their bloated bodies relaxed and they lay quietly, seemingly finding satisfaction in the strong, peculiar odor.

His face a study in conflicting disgust, puzzlement and interest, Phil watched intently. But when he saw one of the unlovely pair endeavour to sink his fangs into the wooden table, and, failing to do so, exude an unbelievable quantity of his thick yellow venom, disgust came to the fore and with a shuddered oath the young man swept the two loathsome creatures to the floor and ground them into the dust under his heavy boot-heel.

Feeling somewhat better, he glanced again at the crushed leaf. Queer, he told himself, how a mere odor could excite those sluggish spiders into such a frenzy! Then, like the flash of a lightning bolt, the idea came to him.

The juice of the jar! In the same metaphor the sting of the box would be the bite of a tomb-spider, for had not the little carved box been packed with preserved spiders? And the age-old legends surrounding them, and what Major Knepper had told him . . . about their having the largest venom sacs . . . seemingly not poisonous . . . very little known. . . . Why, perhaps —!

Phil dashed out of the chamber, through the tunnel and up the ladder into the tomb above. He collided with Professor Ashbrooke in the doorway. Grasping him by the arm, the younger man led him back down into the chamber of the pool, talking rapidly all the while and with passionate earnestness. His eyes burned feverishly and his face quivered.

At first the professor's weatherbeaten countenance showed surprise and a mild annoyance at Phil's outburst. As he assimilated some of the rapid flow of talk, his expression changed to one of incredulous astonishment, then to anxiety for his companion's sanity, till finally he made the young man cease and began to question him. Phil repeated what he had said. Professor Ashbrooke's fingers worked nervously, he compressed his lips till they were almost bloodless, and a faint glimmer of the queer light that shone so brightly from Phil's eyes began to appear in his.

An hour later both men were standing beside the still form which lay on the table in the chamber of the pool. They conversed in low, vibrant tones, casting frequent glances at their silent companion, Za, the scribe.

The professor spoke excitedly of rare forms of catelepsy, of the lost art of Egyptian medicine — and also of the jewels of Ahma-Ka.

VII

The batteries in the electric lanterns were exhausted and there were no others in camp.

Thus it was that in the center of a ring of flickering yellow candle flames, a weird and unearthly scene took place in the dark dampness of a tomb beneath a tomb — in the chamber of the pool.

The strange, unforgettable odor of the crushed leaves of the Mona bush hung stiflingly heavy in the chill, motionless air. On the low table lay the body of Za, the scribe. Their faces tense, Phil and Professor Ashbrooke stood over him.

The older man was applying a thick green liquid to the mummy. It was the juice of a great many leaves of the Mona bush. Some he rubbed on the legs and thighs, then a circular spot on the stomach, a little over the heart, liberal applications on the arms and shoulders, while the remainder he used on the back of the neck. This done, both men donned heavy rubber gloves. Phil lifted a tin box from the floor, a box with airholes pierced through the lid. He opened it and spilled its contents full upon the bare chest of the mummy, then stepped back quickly and averted his face.

Tomb-spiders had not been hard to obtain by using the odor of crushed Mona bush leaves as a lure. . . .

The professor, too, was standing with his back to the weird and horrible scene. He spoke without turning.

"How many preserved spiders was it that you found in the little carved box?"

"Fourteen." Unconsciously both men spoke in subdued tones.

"And you're using fourteen now?"

"Yes."

"What if they're not enough?"

"I've got three more in this jar to use as a last resort."

"How long do you suppose it will take?"

"I haven't the slightest idea."

For some time there was absolute silence in the twilight of the tomb. In the tall corners the shadows quivered like great black beasts held on leash.

"Oh, but a thing like this *couldn't* be!" Ashbrooke burst out, "It's impossible! Horrible!"

"We've gone too far now — all that's left to do is to follow through the procedure and see whether our wild hopes and fancies are true."

Presently Phil steeled his nerves and turned slowly around. Squatting in clusters over the body were the spiders; motionless, their fangs sunk deep as they pumped their mysterious toxin into the dead veins of the mummy. It was with difficulty that he restrained himself from turning and fleeing at once from the blood-curdling and eery sight.

As rapidly as possible he plucked the tenacious things from the body and replaced them in the tin box, his hands protected by the rubber gloves. Ashbrooke applied a stethoscope to the bare brown chest. He listened breathlessly for a few seconds, then sighed and shook his head. Phil began to chafe one of the cold wrists.

"We'll allow an hour for the stuff to do its work. If nothing happens then, we'll use the other three spiders. After that we'll give up the whole wild business, bury this body and try to forget that we were so foolish — so heathenly superstitious, I might better say."

Three-quarters of the hour had elapsed before the death like hush was again broken. The towering, monstrous shadows in the far recesses of the tomb became more restless as the candles burned low and lower. The white, strained faces of the two men stood out sharply in the semi darkness, their bodies indistinct and shapeless.

The professor felt for a pulse in one of the thin, muscular wrists, then shook his head again.

"Get those other three spiders out, Phil," he said. "I think we're going to need them."

"Let's wait a few minutes more," replied the other. He, too, picked up a wrist and held it.

Standing very quietly, his fingertips resting lightly on the pulse, Phil strained every ounce of his powers of perception. Suddenly he gasped. Surely it couldn't be that — no, it must have been his imagination . . . but there it came again . . . Then he uttered an exclamation that caused Ashbrooke to start, for beyond the shadow of a doubt he had detected a faint pulse in the cold wrist of the three-thousand-year-old mummy!

In a few quick words Phil informed the professor, who immediately seized the stethoscope and pressed it to the chest once more. He passed the instrument to Phil. The young man listened for a moment before he could hear, coming as if from a great distance, the slow, faint, but unmistakable sound of heart-beats.

"What about the temperature?" he breathed in an awed whisper. Ashbrooke snatched a thermometer from the armpit of the reclining figure and looked at it dubiously.

"Only gone up two degrees," he announced. "Hadn't we better try a stimulant? It isn't called for, but it couldn't do any harm and it might hasten matters a great deal."

Phil nodded his acquiescence. The professor poured a liberal portion of brandy down the throat of the slowly reviving man before them.

Afterward neither Phil nor Professor Ashbrooke could hazard a guess as to how long they kept vigil over the body of Za, the scribe. Phil remembered lighting new candles twice. Neither slept.

Slowly, very slowly, the thermometer climbed and the heartbeats increased in strength and volume. At the end of the fifth hour respiration was noticeable. Once the lips twitched. Just as the exhausted watchers were about to give way to the growing weariness that excitement can not always dispel, the eyelids were slowly raised for a moment, then drooped. Soon the heavy breathing of the man was quite audible and the limbs rolled limply.

"He's asleep," whispered the professor.

Snatching short naps by relays, Phil and Ashbrooke passed the next twelve hours. At the end of that time both the pulse and the temperature were almost normal. Phil absented himself for some time and returned with a pot of steaming coffee. The professor had just finished his second cup when he glanced down at Za.

"Look!" he exclaimed.

Phil followed his pointing finger and saw with astonishment that Za was staring at the ceiling with wide-open eyes. Motionless as statues, they watched him slowly turn his gaze to one side till he seemed to be regarding a spot on Phil's shirt-front. The young man felt a disturbing little cold shiver scamper up his spine as the unwinking stare rose inch by inch. Before he knew it, he was looking straight into the deep black eyes of a man who had supposedly died three thousand years before!

The eyes were misty and unfocused, like those of a very young baby. Spellbound, Phil watched them shift and squint till they regarded him squarely. For a moment they gazed into each other's eyes, then a few faint lines wrinkled Za's forehead. In the same slow, deliberate manner he blinked his eyes a few times, then changed his position very slightly. The effort seemed to cause him pain, for he frowned quite noticeably.

Presently he began to open and close his mouth uneasily and to lick his dry lips with a still dryer tongue. Ashbrooke hastily supplied half a glass of cool water. Za swallowed several times and turned his head to stare with increased interest at his benefactor.

Gradually his animation increased till at the end of perhaps two hours he assayed to raise himself to a sitting position. He fell back weakly, but with the aid of the other two was soon swinging his legs slowly to and fro as he sat on the edge of the table. Phil and the professor hovered about him excitedly, hardly daring to believe their own eyes and half fearing that he might fall back any moment into a lifeless mummy once more.

By degrees his eyes brightened, his facial expression increased and his whole demeanor livened. He pointed at the pitcher of water and was able to hold the cup with which Phil supplied him and to drink from it copiously.

Soon he evinced a desire to walk. Phil and the professor supporting and assisting him, he hobbled stiffly a few paces, then halted and looked about. A queer, dull glow came into his black eyes as he recognized his surroundings. By turns he inspected the pool, the empty chests and the mouth of the tunnel. When he saw his empty, gold-weighted hammock lying on the floor he made several unsuccessful efforts to speak. Finally he uttered a few words in a guttural tongue.

The professor shook his head and made gestures to show that he did not understand.

"Try writing in hieroglyphics," suggested Phil. Ashbrooke took his pencil and painstakingly constructed on a leaf from his notebook a single sentence to the effect that they did not understand his language, and inquiring if he desired anything to eat. He handed the paper and pencil to Za.

The Egyptian scrutinized it a few moments examined the pencil curiously, then grasping it in his fist like a dagger with a few incredibly dexterous motions set down a reply in well-formed characters. The professor translated carefully to Phil.

"He says that it is difficult for him to speak and that he is not hungry."

Phil was seized by a sudden inspiration. "Ask him where the jewels of Ahma-Ka are. This resurrection may not last but a few hours."

Ashbrooke nodded rapidly and narrowed his eyes. "I'd better work up to it gradually," he whispered from the corner of his mouth.

He made several trifling inquiries about the architecture of the tomb, to which Za replied briefly. Impatience getting the best of him, the professor put the question direct.

"Where are the jewels of Ahma-Ka?"

The brown-skinned man looked at the paper fully a minute before he raised his head. Phil was startled at the uncanny red light which appeared to glow from his eyes. He regarded Ashbrooke till the latter grew uneasy. Then the disturbing glow was suddenly extinguished and to the amazement of the two white men, he pointed at the black glassy surface of the pool!

Za made his way unassisted to the edge, knelt, and extended his arm to the elbow in the water. After a few minutes of groping he brought up a loop of heavy, handwrought chain. Stretching it tight, he pulled. As Phil and the professor stepped quickly to his side, he made an upward gesture.

"He means for us to pull up on the chain," exclaimed Phil.

Under their combined efforts they lifted a heavy object a few inches and felt it grate to one side. The two white men, believing it to be an urn or chest containing the precious stones, endeavored to bring it to the surface. Za checked them and pointed again at the surface of the pool. The level of the water was rapidly lowering!

"We must have lifted a plug out of the bottom," cried Ashbrooke excitedly.

When grappling for the body of Za they had found the pool to be more than nine feet in depth, so it was some time later when they watched the last of the water gurgle out through a rectangular hole in one corner. By the side of the drain was a corresponding stone block, to the top of which the chain was attached leading to a heavy staple set in the stone a few inches below where the surface of the water had been.

But the object that attracted their wide-eyed attention was a small chest in the exact center of the pit, its priceless magnificence — gleaming softly through the silt and slime which partly covered it.

Heedless of the expression on Za's face, Phil seized a candle, lowered himself over the edge and dropped lightly down beside the chest. As Ashbrooke brushed by the motionless Egyptian he unconsciously noted that the odor of the Mona bush was still strong upon him.

A moment later Phil and the professor were bending over the open chest and tearing away the rotted leather case within. Suddenly a scintillating blaze of multi-colored light burst out from within as the candle-light fell upon a great mass of wondrous gems, glistening with water and reflecting a rainbow-like radiance into the faces of the two men who leaned close, drinking in the beauty.

A sound from above caused them to look up. Instantly their surprise and delight were replaced by sudden terror, for upon the edge of the pit, his eyes blazing a maniacal red, stood Za, the scribe. He held aloft a heavy carved stand and slowly gathered himself to send it crashing down upon them. Seeing that he was observed, he paused. His dry, blackened lips writhed back from his yellow teeth in a fiendish mockery of a smile and the low cackle of a madman grated from between his set jaws.

Looking above and beyond him, Phil was conscious of something else — a huge, white, hairy something that twinkled across the ceiling and halted above the maniac. As Za drew himself to his full height and tightened his grip on his brutal weapon, the white, handlike thing upon the ceiling dropped, alighting tenaciously as a burr on the back of the brown man's neck. Za shrieked and dropped the stand to one side. He fell to his knees, clutching at the horror on his back.

Phil hastily tucked the little casket of jewels under his arm and scrambled up out of the pit after the professor. There both men stopped aghast at the horrible sight on the tomb floor before them.

A mighty tomb-spider, a giant of its kind, was clamped in a deathlike grip to the spot on Za's neck that reeked of the odor of crushed leaves from the Mona bush. The huge thing's thick, hairy legs twisted and knotted themselves convulsively as its greedy fangs sank deep. The brown man writhed in agony, his glazing eyes rolling wildly in their sockets. One arm shot out and grasped Phil by the ankle dragging him toward the edge of the empty pool. The young man screamed in mortal terror and kicked himself free. His glance swept down into the pit, and as if touched by a high-voltage wire his whole body suddenly stiffened. The color drained swiftly from his face, leaving it a ghastly gray. The case of jewels slipped unheeded from his fear paralyzed arms and crashed to the floor, sending the glittering baubles rolling in the dust . . . *Trooping up out of the foul subterranean darkness of the great square drainage hole at the bottom of the pit, came countless thousands of great white spiders!* In an undulating tide of furry evilness they crept up from the lower chamber that had been their prison and from which the water had just driven them. The professor, too, saw the advancing horde of horror, and the two men's eyes met in unutterable terror.

A low moan from the dying Za broke the spell. Snatching up a huge handful of the wondrous stones, Phil led the dash for the doorway, where for a moment he paused and looked back.

As Za, his spinal cord severed, sank at last into the eternal rest which should have been his three thousand years before, he rolled limply over on his back, crushing under him the bloated form of the immense spider. With a noise like the bursting of a great oily bubble the creature's thin skin split, and it spattered out into a formless blot. The blood from the lacerated neck swelled into the sticky puddle that had been a tomb-spider, and trickled out to meet the oncoming wave of glittering eyes and writhing legs that was flowing soundlessly over the edge of the pit.

Body and Soul[*]

had had a strenuous day, for the mild epidemic of summer grippe had lasted over into September, and my round of calls had been double the usual number. "Thank heaven, I can relax for seven or eight hours," I murmured piously as I pulled the single blanket up around my chin and settled myself for the night. The hall clock had just struck twelve, and I had no appointments earlier than nine the following morning. "If only nobody is so inconsiderate as to break a leg or get the bellyache," I mumbled drowsily, "I'll not stir from this bed until —"

As if to demonstrate the futility of self-congratulation, there came a sudden thunderous clamor at the front door. Someone was beating the panels with both his fists, raining frenzied blows on the wood with his feet and shrieking at the top of his voice, "Let me in! Doctor — Dr. Trowbridge, let me in! For God's sake, let me in!"

"The devil!" I ejaculated, rising resentfully and feeling for my slippers and dressing-gown. "Couldn't he have had the decency to ring the bell?"

"Let me in, let me in, Dr. Trowbridge!" the frantic hail came again as I rounded the bend of the stairs. "Let me in — quick!"

"All right, all right!" I counseled testily, undoing the lock and chain-fastener. "Just a min —"

The caller ceased his battering-ram assault on the door as I swung it back and catapulted past me into the hall, almost carrying me off my feet as he did so. "Quick, shut it — shut the door!" he gasped, wheeling in his tracks to snatch the knob from my hand and force the door to. "It's out there — it's outside there, I tell you!"

"What the mischief —" I began, half puzzled, half angry, as I took quick stock of the intruder.

He was a young man, twenty-five or -six, I judged, dressed somewhat foppishly in a suit of mohair dinner clothes, his jacket and waistcoat badly rumpled, his once stiff evening shirt and collar reduced to a pulpy mass of sweat-soaked linen, and the foamy froth of drool disfiguring the corners of his flaccid mouth. As he turned on me to repeat his hysterical warning, I noticed that he caught his breath with considerable difficulty and that there was a strong hint of liquor in his speech.

"See here, young man, what do you mean?" I demanded sternly. "Haven't you any better sense than to knock a man out of bed at this ungodly hour to tell him that —"

"Ssssh!" he interrupted with the exaggerated caution of the half-tipsy. "Sssh, Dr. Trowbridge, I think I hear it coming up the steps.

* "Body and Soul" was written by Seabury Quinn, pseud. of Jerome Burk (1889 – 1969), and published in *Weird Tales*, Sep. 1928.

Is the door locked? Quick, in here!" Snatching me by the arm he dragged me unceremoniously into the surgery.

"Now see here, confound you!" I remonstrated. "This is going a bit too far. If you expect to get away with this sort of thing, I'll mighty soon show you —"

"Trowbridge, *mon vieux*, what is it? What does the alarm portend?" Jules de Grandin, a delicate mauve-silk dressing-gown drawn over his lilac pajamas, slippers of violet snake-skin on his womanishly small feet, tiptoed into the room, his little blue eyes round with wonder and curiosity. "I thought I heard someone in extremity calling," he continued, looking from the visitor to me, then back again with his quick, stock-taking glance. "Is it that someone dies and requires our assistance through the door to the better world, or —"

"It looks as if some drunken young fool is trying to play a practical joke on us," I returned grimly, bending a stern look on the boy who cowered in the chair beside my desk. "I've half a mind to prescribe four ounces of castor oil and stand by while he takes it!"

De Grandin regarded the young man with his steady, unwinking stare a moment, then: "What frightens you, *mon brave*?" he demanded, far too gently, I thought. "*Parbleu*, but, you look as though you had been playing tag with Satan himself!"

"I have — I have!" the youth replied quaveringly. "I tell you, it jumped at me just as I came past the park entrance, and I wasn't a hundred yards ahead when Dr. Trowbridge let me in!"

"U'm?" the Frenchman twisted the ends of his little blond mustache meditatively. "And this 'It' which pursued you, it is what?"

"I don't know," the other responded. "I was walking home from a dance at the Sigma Delta Tau house — been stagging it, you know — and stopped by the Victory Monument to light a cigarette when something — dam' if I know what — jumped out o' the bushes at me and made a grab at my throat. It missed my neck by a couple o' inches, but snatched my hat, and I didn't take any time to see what it would do next. I'd 'a' been going yet if my wind hadn't given out, and I happened to think that Dr. Trowbridge lives in this block and that he'd most likely be up, or within call, anyhow, so I rushed up the steps and hammered on the door till he let me in.

"Will you let me stay here overnight?" he concluded, turning to me appealingly. "I'm Dick Ratliff — Henry Ratliff's nephew, you know — and honest, Doctor, I'm scared stiff to go out in that street again till daylight."

"H'm," I murmured judicially, surveying the young fool reflectively. He was not a bad-looking boy — quite otherwise — and I could well imagine he presented a personable enough appearance when his clothing was in better array and his head less fuddled with bad liquor. "How much have you had to drink tonight, young man?"

"Two drinks, sir," he returned promptly, looking me squarely in the eye, and, though my better judgment told me he was lying like a witness at a Senate investigation, I believed him.

"I think you're a damn fool," I told him with more candor than courtesy. "You were probably so full of rotgut that your own shadow gave you a start back there by the park gate, and you've been trying to outrace it for the last four blocks. You'll be heartily ashamed of yourself in the morning, but I've a spare bed, and you may as well sleep off your debauch here as in some police station, I suppose."

"Thank you, sir," he answered humbly. "I don't blame you for thinking I've got the jim-jams — I know my story sounds crazy — but I'm telling you the truth. Something did jump out at me, and almost succeeded in grabbing me by the throat. It wasn't just imagination, and it wasn't booze, either, but — my God, look!"

The exclamation ended in a shrill crescendo, and the lad half leaped from his chair, pointing with a shaking forefinger at the little window over the examination table, then slumped back as though black-jacked, his hands falling limply to the floor, his head lolling drunkenly forward on his breast.

Both de Grandin and I wheeled about, facing the window. "Good lord!" I exclaimed as my gaze penetrated the shining, night-backed panes.

"*Grand Dieu — ç'est le diable en personne!*" the little Frenchman cried.

Staring into the dimly lighted room was such a visage as might bring shudders of horripilation to a bronze statue. It was a long, cadaverous face, black with the dusky hue of old and poorly cured rawhide, bony as a death's-head, yet covered with a multitude of tiny horizontal wrinkles. The fleshless, leathery lips were drawn back from a set of broken and discolored teeth which reminded me somehow of the cruel dentition of a shark, and the corded, rugous neck supporting the withered face was scarcely thicker than a man's wrist. From the bare, black scalp there hung a single lock of coarse, straggling hair. But terrible as the features were, terrifying as were the unfleshed lips and cheeks and brow, the tiny, deep-set eyes almost fallen backward from their sockets were even more horrible. Small as the eyes of a rodent, set, unwavering in their stare, they reminded me, as they gleamed with hellish malevolence in their settings of shrunken, wrinkled skin, of twin poisonous spiders awaiting the chance to pounce upon their prey. It might have been a trick of the lamplight, but to me it seemed that the organs shone with a diabolical luminance of their own as they regarded us with a sort of mirthless smile.

"Good heavens, what is it?" I choked, half turning to my companion, yet keeping most of my glance fixed on the baneful, hypnotic orbs glaring at me through the windowpane.

"God knows," returned de Grandin, "but by the belly of Jonah's whale, we shall see if he be proof against shot and powder!" Whipping a tiny Ortgies automatic from his dressing-gown pocket he brought its blunt muzzle in line with the window and pressed the trigger. Seven, eight shots rang out so quickly that the last seemed no more than the echo of the first; the plate glass pane was perforated like a sieve within an area of three square inches; and the sharp, acrid smell of smokeless powder bit the mucous membrane of my nostrils.

"After him, Friend Trowbridge!" de Grandin cried, flinging aside the empty pistol and bolting through the door, down the hallway and across the porch. "*Barbe d'une oie*, but we shall see how he liked the pills I dealt him!"

The September moon rode serenely in the dark-blue sky; a little vagrant breeze, coming from the bay, rustled the boughs of the curbside maple trees; and from the downtown section there came to us, faintly, the muted clangor of the all-night trolley cars and the occasional hoot of a cruising taxicab's horn. After the bedlam of the Frenchman's shots the early autumn night seemed possessed of a stillness which bore in on our eardrums like a tangible sound, and, like visitors in an empty church, we pursued our quest in silence, communicating only in low, breathless whispers. From house to hedge, over lawn and rosebed and tennis court we pushed our search, scanning every square inch of land, peering under rosebushes and rhododendron plants, even turning over the galvanized iron trash-can which stood by my kitchen stoop. No covert large enough to have shielded a rat did we leave unexplored, yet of the awful thing which had gazed through the surgery window we found no sign or trace, though we hunted till the eastern sky began to pale with streaks of rose and pearl and amethyst and the rattling milk carts broke the nighttime quiet with their early-morning clatter.

"Good mornin', Dr. de Grandin." Detective Sergeant Costello rose from his seat in the consulting-room as de Grandin and I entered. "'Tis sorry I am to be disturbin' ye so early in th' mornin', more especially as I know what store ye set by yer breakfast" — he grinned broadly at his sally — "but th' fact is, sor, there's been a tidy little murder committed up th' street, an' I'm wondering if ye'd be discommodin' yerself to th' extent o' comin' up to Professor Kolisko's house and takin' a look around before th' coroner's physician messes everything up an' carts th' remains off to the morgue for an autopsy."

"A murder?" de Grandin's little eyes snapped with sudden excitement. "Do you say a murder? My friend, you delight me!"

"Yes, sor, I knew y'd be pleased to hear about it," the Irishman answered soberly. "Will we be goin' up to th' house at once, sor?"

"But of course, by all means," de Grandin assented. "Trowbridge, my friend, you will have the charity to convey us thither, will you not? Come, let us hasten to this Monsieur Kolisko's house and observe what we can see. And" — his little eyes twinkled as he spoke — "I beseech you, implore the so excellent Nora to reserve sufficient breakfast against the time of our return. *Mordieu*, already I feel my appetite assuming giant proportions!"

Two minutes later the detective, de Grandin and I were speeding uptown toward the isolated cottage where Urban Kolisko, one-time professor of psychology at the University at Warsaw, had passed the declining years of his life as a political refugee.

"Tell me, Friend Costello," the Frenchman demanded; "this Monsieur Kolisko, how did he die?"

"H'm, that's just what's puzzlin' all of us," the detective admitted. "All we know about th' case is that Murphy, who has th' beat where th' old felly lived wuz passin' by there a little after midnight an' heard th' devil's own row goin' on inside. The lights, wuz all goin' in th' lower part o' th' house, which warn't natural, an' when Murphy stopped to hear what it wuz all about, he thought he heard someone shoutin' an' swearin', an' once or twice th' crack o' a whip, then nothin' at all.

"Murphy's a good lad, sor; I've knowed him, man an' boy, these last eighteen years, an' he did just what I'd expected o' him. Went up an' knocked on th' door, an' when he couldn't get no response, broke it in. There was hell broke loose for certain, sor."

"Ah?" returned de Grandin. "What did the excellent Murphy observe?"

"Plenty," Costello replied laconically. "Ye'll be seein' it for yerself in a minute."

Inside the Kolisko house was that peculiar hush which does reverence to the Grim Reaper's visits. Acting on telephoned instructions, Officer Murphy mounted guard before the door, permitting no one to enter the place, and the scene in the small, poorly lighted living-room was exactly as he had come upon it several hours earlier. Like most dyed-in-the-wool students, Kolisko had regarded his home merely as a place to sleep, eat and store books. The room was lined from floor to ceiling on all sides with rough deal shelving which groaned and sagged under the weight of ponderous volumes in every language known to print. Piles of other books, unable to find accommodation on the shelves, were littered about the floor. The rough, bench-like table and the littered, untidy desk which stood between the two small windows were also piled high with books.

Between the desk and table, flat on its back, staring endlessly at the rough whitewashed ceiling with bulging, sightless eyes, lay the relic of Professor Kolisko. Clothed in a tattered bathrobe and soiled pajamas the body lay, and it was not a pretty sight even to a medical man to whom death in its unloveliest phases is no stranger. Kolisko had been thin to the point of emaciation, and his scrawniness was accentuated in death. His white-thatched head was thrown back and bent grotesquely to one side, his straggling white beard thrust upward truculently, and his lower jaw had fallen downward with the flaccidity of death, half an inch or so of tongue protruding beyond the line of his lower teeth. Any doctor, soldier or undertaker — any man whose business has to do habitually with death — could not fail to recognize the signs. The man was dead, and had been so for upward of seven hours.

"Howly Mither!" Costello's brogue came strongly to the surface as he blessed himself involuntarily. "Will ye be lookin' at th' awfulness o' him, sors?"

"U'm," murmured Jules de Grandin, sinking to one knee beside the corpse, raising the lolling head and fingering the back of the neck with quick, practiced hands, then brushing back the bristling beard to examine the scrawny throat attentively, "he had cause to be dead, this one. See, Friend Trowbridge" — taking my hand he guided my fingers slowly down the dead man's neck, then pointed to the throat — "there is a clean fracture of the spine between the third and fourth dorsal vertebræ probably involving a rupture of the cord, as well. The autopsy will disclose that. And here" — he tapped the throat with a well-manicured forefinger — "are the marks of strangulation. *Mordieu*, whatever gripped this poor one's neck possessed a hold like Death himself, for he not only choked him, but broke his spine as well! If it were not for one thing, I should say such strength — such ferocity of grip — could only have been exerted by one of the great apes, but —"

He broke off, staring with preoccupied, unseeing eyes at the farther wall.

"But what, sor?" Costello prompted as the little man's silence continued.

"*Parbleu*, it could not be an ape and leave such a thumb-mark, my friends," de Grandin returned. "The gorilla, the orangutan, the chimpanzee, all have such strength of hand as to accomplish what we see here, but they are not human, no matter how much they parody mankind. Their thumbs are undeveloped; the thumb which closed on this one's neck was long and thin, more like a finger than a thumb. See for yourselves, it closed about the throat, meeting the fingers which clasped it on the other side. *Mordieu*, if we are to find this murderer we must look for one with twice the length and five times the strength of hand of the average man. Bethink you — this one's grip was great enough to snap Kolisko's spine like a clay-pipe stem by merely squeezing his neck! *Dieu de Dieu*, but he will be an uncomfortable one to meet in the dark!"

"Sergeant Costello," Murphy's hail came sharply from the cottage door, "they're comin'; Coroner Martin an' Dr. Schuester just drove up!"

"All right, Murphy, good lad!" Costello returned, then glanced sharply at de Grandin. "Leave him be, Doc," he ordered. "If the coroner an' Dr. Schuester catch us monkeyin' with their property there'll be hell poppin' at headquarters."

"Very good, my friend," de Grandin rejoined, rising and brushing the dust from his trousers knees, "we have seen as much of the body as we desire. Let them have it and perform their gruesome rites; we shall look elsewhere for what we seek."

Coroner Martin and his physician came bustling in almost as the little Frenchman ceased speaking, glanced casually at Costello and suspiciously at de Grandin and me, then went at their official duties with only a mumbled word of greeting.

"What do you make of it?" I inquired as we drove toward my house.

"*Eh bien*, as yet I make nothing," de Grandin returned. "The man was killed by paralysis resulting from a broken neck, although the pressure on his windpipe would have been sufficient to have slain him, had it but continued long enough. We know his murderer possessed hands of extraordinary strength and size, and is, therefore, in all probability, a man of more than usual height. Thus far we step with assurance. When the coroner has finished with the deceased gentleman's premises, we shall afford ourselves the pleasure of a protracted search; before that we shall request our good friend Costello to inquire into

Monsieur Kolisko's antecedents and discover if he possessed any enemies, especially any enemies capable of doing him to death in this manner. Meantime I famish for my breakfast. I am hungry as a cormorant."

The boasted appetite was no mere figure of speech. Three bowls of steaming cereal, two generous helpings of bacon and eggs, half a dozen cups of well-creamed coffee disappeared into his interior before he pushed back his chair and lighted a rank-smelling French cigarette with a sigh of utter content. "*Eh bien*, but it is difficult to think on an empty stomach," he assured me as he blew a column of smoke toward the ceiling. "Me, I am far from my best when there is nothing but flatulence beneath my belt. I require stimu — *Mon Dieu*, what a fool I am!"

Striking his forehead with the heel of his hand, he rose so abruptly that his chair almost capsized behind him. "What's the matter?" I asked, but he waved my question and me aside with an impatient hand.

"*Non, non*, do not stop me, do not hinder me, my friend!" he ordered. "Me, I have important duties to perform, if it be not too late to do them. Go upon your errands of mercy, Friend Trowbridge, and should you chance to return before I quit the surgery, I pray you leave me undisturbed. I have to do that which is needful, and I must do it uninterrupted, if you please."

Having thus served notice on me that I would be unwelcome in my own workshop, he turned and fled toward the front door like a luckless debtor pursued by collectors.

It was nearly four o'clock that afternoon when I returned from my round of calls and tiptoed past the surgery door, only to find my caution unnecessary, for de Grandin sat in the cool, darkened library, smoking a cigar and chuckling over some inane story in *L' Illustration*.

"Finish the important duties?" I asked, regarding him ironically.

"But certainly," he returned. "First, dear friend, I must apologize most humbly for my so abominable rudeness of this morning. It is ever my misfortune, I fear, to show only incivility to those who most deserve my courtesy, but I was all afire with the necessity of haste when I spoke. Great empty-head that I was, I had completely forgotten for the moment that one of the best places to seek clues of a murder is the person of the victim himself, and when I did remember I was almost beside myself until I ascertained to which *entrepreneur des pompes funèbres* — How do you say it? Undertaker? — my God, what a language! — Monsieur Kolisko's body had been entrusted by the coroner. Friend Costello informed me that Monsieur Mitchell was in charge, and to the excellent Mitchell I hurried post-haste, begging that he would permit me one little minute alone with the deceased before he commenced his ministrations."

"H'm, and did you find anything?" I asked.

"*Parbleu*, yes; I found almost too much. From the nails of Monsieur Kolisko's hands I rescued some fragments, and in your surgery I subjected them to microscopic examination. They proved to be — what do you say?"

"Tobacco?" I hazarded.

"Tobacco!" he scoffed. "Friend Trowbridge, sometimes I think you foolish; at others I fear you are merely stupid. Beneath the dead man's finger-nails I found some bits of human skin — and a fragment of human hair."

"Well," I returned unenthusiastically, "what of it? Kolisko was an exceedingly untidy sort of person — the kind who cared so little for social amenities that he was apt to scratch himself vigorously when he chose, and probably he was also addicted to the habit of scrabbling through his beard with his fingers. Most of those European scientists with birds' nests sprouting from their chins are that sort, you know. He was shockingly uncouth, and —"

"And you annoy me most thoroughly, Friend Trowbridge," the little Frenchman broke in. "Listen, attend me, regard that which I am about to tell you: The skin and hair which I did find were black, my friend, black as bitumen, and subjected to chemical reagents, showed themselves to be strongly impregnated with natron, oil of cedar and myrrh. What have you to say now?"

"Why —"

"And if these things suggest an Egyptian mummy to you, as they may if you think steadily for the next ten or more years, I make so bold as to ask what would a professor of psychology be doing in contact with a mummy. *Hein*? Answer me that, if you please. Had he been an Egyptologist, or even a student of comparative anatomy, there would be reason for it, but a psychologist — it does not make sense!"

"Well, then, why bother about it?" I retorted.

"Ah, but I think maybe, perhaps, there is an answer to the riddle, after all," he insisted. "Recall the events of last night, if you please. Remember how that young Monsieur Ratliff came bawling like a frightened calf to our door, begging to be taken in and protected from something which assaulted him in the public thoroughfares. Recollect how we suspected him of an overindulgence in alcohol, and how, as we were about to turn him out, there appeared at our window a most unpleasant-looking thing which made mock of Jules de Grandin's marksmanship. *Parbleu*, yes, you will recall all that, as well as that the ungrateful Ratliff child did sneak away from the house without so much as saying 'thank you' for our hospitality while we were out with Sergeant Costello viewing Monsieur Kolisko's remains."

"Then you'd suggest —" I began incredulously, but he rose with an impatient shrug.

"Ah bah, I think nothing, my friend," he assured me. "He who thinks without knowing is a fool. A connection there may be between that which we saw last night and that which we viewed this morning. We shall see, perhaps. I have an engagement to search Kolisko's house with Sergeant Costello this evening, and I suggest you accompany us. There may be that there which shall cause your eyes to pop from out your face with wonder. Meantime, I hear visitors in the reception-room. Go to your duties, my friend. Some neurotic old lady undoubtlessly desires you to sympathize with her latest symptoms."

"Well, sor," confided Sergeant Costello as he, de Grandin and I set out for the Kolisko cottage that evening, "this case beats th' Jews, an' th' Jews beat the devil."

"Indeed?" responded de Grandin politely.

"It sure does. We've been over Kolisko's antecedents, as ye might call 'em, an' th' devil a thing can we find that might lead us to a clue as to who killed him. 'Twas little enough they knew about him, at best, for he was a stand-offish old felly wid never a word for anybody, except when he wanted sumpin, which warn't often. He had a few Polack cronies, but they wuz few an' far between. Five months ago a felly broke into his house an' stole some stuff o' triflin' value, an' shot up a State trooper while tryin' to escape to th' next town. Kolisko appeared agin 'im at th' trial, as wuz his dooty, for he wuz subpoenaed, an' later visited 'im in jail, I understand, but this, felly — name o' Heschler, he wuz — didn't take anny too kindly to th' professor's visits, an' he cut 'em out."

"Ah," de Grandin nursed his narrow chin in the cradle of his hand, "perhaps it is that this Heschler harbored malice and wreaked vengeance on Monsieur Kolisko for the part he had in his conviction?"

"P'raps," agreed Costello shortly, "but 'tain't likely."

"And why not?" the Frenchman demanded shortly. Like most men who keep their own counsel, he was easily annoyed by others' reticence.

"Because they burned him at Camden last night, sor."

"Burned? How do you mean —"

"Sure, burned him. Bumped 'im off, rubbed 'im out, gave 'im th' chair — electrocuted 'im. He was a murderer, warn't he?" Costello elucidated.

"U'm," the Frenchman gulped over the information like one trying to clear his mouth of an unpalatable morsel, "you are doubtless right, Sergeant; we may regard this Heschler as eliminated — perhaps."

"P'raps?" echoed the amazed Irishman as I brought the car to a halt before the cottage door. "P'raps me neck! If you'll listen to me, I'll say he's been eliminated altogether entirely by th' State executioner!"

Our search was startlingly unproductive. A few letters in envelopes with foreign postmarks, receipts for small bills for groceries and kindred household items, one or two invitations to meetings of learned societies — this was the sum total produced by an hour's rummaging among the dead man's papers.

"*Tiens*, it would seem we have come on the chase of the wild goose," de Grandin admitted disconsolately, wiping the sweat from his forehead with a pale blue silk handkerchief. "*Zut*, it seems impossible that any man should have so much paper of so little importance. Me, I think that —"

"Here's sumpin that might help us, if it's papers ye're after," Costello interrupted, appearing at the kitchen door with a rough wooden box in his hand. "I found it behint th' stove, sor. Most of it seems of little enough account, but you might find sumpin that'd —"

"Aside, stand aside, my friend!" the Frenchman ordered, leaping on the box like a famished cat on a mouse and scattering its contents over the living-room table. "What have we here? *Mordieu*, another receipt from that twenty-times-damned Public Service Company! Name of a rooster, did the man do nothing but contract and pay bills for electric light? Another one — and another! *Grand Dieu*, if I find but one more of these receipts I shall require a strait-waistcoat to restrain myself. What, another — ah, *triomphe*! At last we find something else!" From the pile of scrambled papers he unearthed a small, black-leather book and began riffling through its pages.

Pausing to read an inscription at random, he regarded the page with upraised brows and pursed lips, seated himself beside the table and brought his eyes to within a few inches of the small, crabbed writing with which the book seemed filled.

Five minutes he sat thus studying the memoranda, his brows gradually rising till I feared they would impinge upon the line of his smoothly combed blond hair. Finally: "My friends, this is of the importance," he assured us, looking quickly from one to the other with his queer, direct glance. "Monsieur Kolisko made these entries in his diary in mingled Polish and French. I shall endeavor to render them into English tonight, and tomorrow morning we shall go over them together. Thus far I have read little, but that little may explain much, or I am much mistaken."

"Trowbridge, my friend," de Grandin requested the following morning when my round of calls was finished, "will you please read what I have written? All night I labored over this translation, and this morning my eyes are not sufficient to the task of reading my own script."

He thrust a sheaf of neatly written foolscap into my hands, then lighted a cigarette and leaned back in his chair, his small hands locked behind his head, his eyes half closed, as he surveyed Costello and me lazily.

Glancing from de Grandin to the waiting detective, I set my pince-nez firmly on my nose and began:

> April 5 — Michel was here again last night, nagging me with his silly talk of the soul and its immortality. To think that one so well educated should entertain such childish ideas! I would have ordered him from the house in anger, as I did once before, had he not been more than usually insulting. After taunting me with the old story about a body's being weighed a few minutes after death and found lighter than before, thereby proving that something of material weight had passed from it, he challenged me to prove the non-existence of any entity separate from the physical being. Fool! It is he who asserts the proposition, not I. Yet I must think of some way to confound him, or he will be everlastingly reminding me that I failed to meet his test.

> April 10 — Michel is a greater fool than I thought. I hold him and his faith in the hollow of my hand, and by his own act. Last night he proposed the wildest scheme ever broached by man. The burglar who

broke into my house last month has been sentenced to death for killing a policeman. Michel would have me see the fellow in prison, arrange for a transmigration of his soul to a body which he will secure, and await results of the experiment. It is childish folly; I insult my own intelligence by agreeing to it, but I must silence Michel and his everlasting patter of the soul's immortality. I shall undertake the task, if only to prove my cousin a fool.

May 16 —Yesterday I saw Heschler in prison. The poor fellow was almost beside himself with joy when I told him of Michel's wild plan. Not dying, but fear of punishment in the world to come seems to terrify the man. If I can provide a tenement for his soul which will enable it to remain away from the seat of judgment a little longer, he will be content, even though he has to live in the body of a child, a cripple or one already bowed with age. Living out the span of life in the second body we provide, he will so conduct himself as to win pardon for misdeeds committed in the frame he now wears, he vows. Poor, hoodwinked fool! Like all Christians, he is bound hand and foot by the old superstitions which have come down to us through the ages. That Heschler, the burglar, should adhere to the Christus myth, the God fairy-tale, is not surprising, for he is but an ignorant clod; but that my cousin Michel Kolisko, a learned man, should give credit to beliefs which were outworn and disproved in the nineteenth century is beyond my understanding.

May 30 — Today I had another talk with Heschler. He is pitiably anxious to begin the experiment. It was childishly simple. Ordering him to gaze steadfastly into my eyes through the bars of his cell, I soon had him completely hypnotized. "You will hereafter cease to dread your coming execution," I told him. "From this time forth you will think of nothing but the opportunity of living on in another body which is to be afforded you. At the moment of execution you will concentrate all your will upon entering the body which will be waiting at my home to receive your soul." He nodded as I gave each command, and I left him. It will not be necessary to repeat my orders. He was already half insane with the obsession of prolonging his life. My work was more than half done before I gave him the directions. I shall not see him again.

The next page bore a clipping from the Newark Call:

Adolph Heschler, confined in the penitentiary at Camden awaiting execution for the murder of State Trooper James Donovan on the night of March 20th last, seems resigned to his fate. When first taken to the state prison he seemed in deadly fear of death and spent most of his time in prayer. Prison officials say that he began to show signs of resignation following the memorial services on May 30th, and it is said he declares his conscience is cleared by the thought that he shall be allowed the opportunity of atoning for his misdeeds. Curiously enough, Heschler, who has heretofore shown the most devout appreciation of the ministrations of the prison's Catholic chaplain, will have nothing further to do with the spiritual advisor, declaring "atonement for his sins has been arranged." There is talk of having him examined by a lunacy commission before the date set for his execution.

Another translation of the diary followed:

> August 30 — Michel has come with the body. It is a mummy! When I expressed my astonishment, he told me it was the best possible corpse for the purpose. After hearing him, I realized he has the pseudo-logic of the mildly insane. The body of one who has died from natural causes or by violence would be unfitted for our purposes, he says, since some of its organs must inevitably be unable to function properly. This mummy is not a true mummy, but the body of an Egyptian guilty of sacrilege, who was sealed up alive in a tomb during the Hyksos dynasty. He died of asphyxia, in all probability, and his body is in perfect condition, except for the dehydration due to lying so many thousands of years in a perfectly dry atmosphere. Michel rescued the mummy during his last expedition to Egypt, and tells me there was evidence of the man's having made a terrific struggle before death put an end to his sufferings. Other bodies, properly mummified, were found in the same tomb, and the dying man had overturned many of the cases and spilled their contents about the place. His body was so thoroughly impregnated with the odor of the spices and preservatives, absorbed from the mummies lying in the tomb, that it was not for some time his discoverers realized he had not been eviscerated and embalmed. Michel assures me the dead man will be perfectly able to act as an envelope for Heschler's soul when the electrocution has been performed. Cousin Michel, if this body does but so much as wiggle its fingers or toes after the authorities have killed Heschler, I will believe — I will believe.

I laid down the final page of de Grandin's translation and looked wonderingly at him. "Where's the rest of it?" I demanded. "Couldn't you do any more last night?"

"The rest," he answered ironically, "is for us to find out, my friends. The journal stops with the entry you have just read. There was no more."

"Humph," Sergeant, Costello commented, "crazy as a pair o' fish out o' water, weren't they? Be gorry, gentlemen, I'm thinkin' it's a crazy man we'd best be lookin' for. I can see it all plain, now. This here Cousin Michael o' Professor Kolisko' was a religious fy-nat-ic, as th' felly says, an' th' pair o' 'em got to fightin' among themselves an' th' professor came out second best. That's th' answer, or my name ain't —"

The sudden shrilling of the office telephone interrupted him. "Sergeant Costello, please," a sharp voice demanded as I picked up the receiver.

"Yeah, this is Costello speakin'," the detective announced, taking the instrument from me. "Yep. All right, go ahead. What? Just like th' other one? My Gawd!"

"What is it?" de Grandin and I asked in chorus as he put down the receiver and turned a serious face to us.

"Miss Adkinson, an old lady livin' by herself out by th' cemetery, has been found murdered," he replied slowly, "*an' th' marks on her throat tally exactly wid those on Professor Kolisko's!*"

"*Cordieu*!" de Grandin shouted, leaping from his chair as if it had suddenly become white-hot. "We must hasten, we must rush, we must fly to that house, my friends! We must examine the body, we must assure ourselves before some bungling coroner's physician spoils everything!"

Two minutes later we were smashing the speed ordinances in an effort to reach the Adkinson house before Coroner Martin arrived.

Stark tragedy repeated itself in the Adkinson cottage. The old lady, gaunt with the leanness of age to which time has not been over-kind, lay in a crumpled heap on her kitchen floor, and a moment's examination disclosed the same livid marks on her throat and the same horrifying limberness of neck which we had observed when viewing Professor Kolisko's body.

"By Gawd, gentlemen, this is terrible!" Costello swore as he turned from the grisly relic. "Here's an old man kilt at night an' a harmless old woman murdered in broad daylight, an' no one to tell us anything certain about th' murderer!"

"Ha, do you say so?" de Grandin responded sharply, his little eyes flashing with excitement. "*Parbleu*, my friend, but you are greatly wrong, as wrong as can be. There is one who can tell us, and tell us he shall, if I must wring the truth from him with my bare hands!"

"What d'ye mean —?" Sergeant Costello began, but the little Frenchman had already turned toward the door, dragging frantically at my elbow.

"Clutch everything, *mes amis*," he commanded. "Retain all; me, I go to find him who can tell us what we need to know. *Mordieu*, I shall find him though he takes refuge in the nethermost subcellar of hell! Come, Trowbridge, my friend; I would that you drive me to the station where I can entrain for New York."

Shortly after seven o'clock that evening I answered the furious ringing of my telephone to hear de Grandin's excited voice come tumbling out of the receiver. "Come at once, my friend," he ordered, fairly stuttering in his elation. "Rush with all speed to the Carmelite Fathers' retreat in East Thirty-second Street. Bring the excellent Costello with you, too, for there is one here who can shed the light of intelligence on our ignorance."

"Who is it —?" I began, but the sharp click of a receiver smashed into its hook cut short my query, and I turned in disgust from the unresponsive instrument to transmit the Frenchman's message to Sergeant Costello.

Within sight of Bellevue's grim mortuary, enshrouded by the folds of drab East River fog as a body is wrapped in its winding-sheet, the little religious community seemed as incongruously out of place in the heart of New York's poverty-ridden East Side as a nun in a sweatshop. Striding up and down the polished floor of the bare, immaculately clean reception-room was Jules de Grandin, a glowing cigarette between his fingers, his tiny, waxed mustache standing straight out from the corners of his mouth like the whiskers of an excited tomcat. "At last!" he breathed as Costello and I followed the porter from the front door to the public room. "*Morbleu*, I thought you had perished on the way."

"Monsieur," he paused in his restless pacing and stopped before the figure sitting motionless in the hard, straight-backed chair at the farther side of the room, "you will please tell these gentlemen what you have told me and be of haste in doing so. We have small time to waste."

I glanced curiously at the seated man. His strong resemblance to the dead Kolisko was remarkable. He possessed a mop of untidy, iron-gray hair and a rather straggling gray beard; his forehead was high, narrow and startlingly white, almost transparent, and the skin of his face was puckered into hundreds of little, wrinkles as though his skull had shrunk, leaving the epidermis without support. His eyes, however, differed radically from Kolisko's, for even in death the professor's orbs had shown a hard, implacable nature, whereas this man's eyes, though shaded by beetling, overhanging brows, were soft and brown. Somehow, they reminded me of the eyes of an old and very gentle dog begging not to be beaten.

"I am Michel Kolisko," he began, clearing his throat with a soft, deprecating cough. "Urban Kolisko was my cousin, son of my father's brother. We grew up together in Poland, attended the same schools and colleges, and dreamed the same dreams of Polish independence. I was twenty, Urban was twenty-three when the Tsar's officers swooped down on our fathers, carried them off to rot in Siberia, and confiscated most of our family's fortune. Both of us were suspected of complicity in the revolutionary movement, and fled for our lives, Urban to Paris, I to Vienna. He matriculated at the Sorbonne and devoted himself to the study of psychology; I studied medicine in Vienna, then went to Rome, and finally took up Egyptology as my life's work.

"Twenty years passed before I saw my cousin again. The Russian proscription had been raised, and he had gone to Warsaw, where he taught in the university. When I went there to visit him, I was shocked to learn he had abandoned God and taken to the worship of the material world. Kant, Spencer, Richet, Wundt — these were his prophets and his priests; the God of our fathers he disowned and denied. I argued with him, pleaded with him to return to his childhood's belief, and he turned me out of his house.

"Once again he earned the displeasure of the Tsar and escaped arrest only by a matter of moments. Fleeing to this country, he took up residence in your city, and devoted himself to penning revolutionary propaganda and atheistic theses. Broken in health, but with sufficient money to insure me of a quiet old age, I followed him to America and made it the work of my declining years to convert him from his apostasy.

"This spring it seemed I was beginning to succeed, for he showed more patience with me than ever before; but he was a hardened sinner, his heart was steeled against the call of consciousness, even as was Pharaoh's of old. He challenged me to offer evidence of God's truth, and promised he would turn again to religion if I could."

For a moment the speaker paused in his monotonous, almost mumbled recitation, wrung his bloodless hands together in a gesture of despair, pressed his fingers to his forehead, as though to crowd back departing reason, then took up his story, never raising his voice, never stressing one word more than another, keeping his eyes fixed on vacancy. He reminded me of a child reciting a distasteful lesson by rote.

"I see we were both mad, now," he confided drearily. "Mad, mad with the sense of our own importance, for Urban defied divine providence, and I forgot that it is not man's right to attempt to prove God's truth as revealed to us by his ordained ministers. It is ours to believe, and to question not. But I was carried away by the fervor of my mission. 'If I can shake Urban's doubts, I shall surely win a crown of glory,' I told myself, 'for surely there is great joy in heaven over one sinner who repents.' And so I went about the sacrilegious business of the test.

"Among the curios I had brought from Egypt was the body of a man sealed alive in a tomb during the Hyksos rule. It was not really a mummy, for no embalming had been performed, but the superheated atmosphere of the tomb in which he had been incarcerated had shriveled his tissues until it was difficult to tell him from a body mummified by artificial methods. Only three or four such bodies are known; one is the celebrated Flinders mummy, and the others are in French and British museums. I had intended leaving mine to the Metropolitan when I died.

"I brought this body to Urban's house the night before Heschler, the condemned murderer, was to be executed, and we laid it on the library table. Urban viewed it with disgust and skepticism, but I prayed over it, begging God to work a miracle, to permit the body to move, if only very slightly, and so convince my poor, misguided cousin. You know, gentlemen" — he turned his sorrowful, lackluster eyes on us with a melancholy smile — "such things are not entirely unknown. Sudden changes in temperature or in the moisture content of the atmosphere often lead to a movement as the dehydrated tissues take up water from the air. The mummy of Rameses the Great, for instance, moved its arm when first exposed to the outdoor air.

"A few minutes after midnight was the time set for Heschler's electrocution, and as the town clocks began rounding the hour I felt as though the heavens must fall if no sign were manifested to us.

"Urban sat beside the mummy, smoking his pipe and sneering — part of the time reading an impious book by Freud. I bowed my head in silent prayer, asking for a miracle to save him despite his hardness of heart. The city hall clock struck the quarter hour, then the half, and still there was no sound. Urban laid his pipe and book aside and looked at me with his familiar sneer, then turned as though to thrust the body of the Egyptian from the table — then it sat up!

"Like a sleeper waking from a dream, like a patient coming forth from the ether it was — the corpse that had been dead four thousand years rose from the table and looked at us. For a moment it seemed to smile with its fleshless lips, then it looked down at itself, and gave a scream of surprise and fury.

"'So!' it shrieked; 'so this is the body you've given me to work out my salvation! This is the form in which I must walk the earth until my sins be wiped away, is it? You've tricked me, cheated me; but I'll have vengeance. No one living can harm me, and I'll take my toll of human kind before I finally go forth to stew and burn in Satan's fires!'

"It was stiff and brittle, but somehow it managed to crawl from the table and make at Urban. He seized a heavy whip which hung on the wall and struck the thing on the head with its loaded butt. The blow would have killed an ordinary man — indeed, I saw the mummy's dried-up skull cave in beneath the force of Urban's flailings, but it never faltered in its attack, never missed a step in its pursuit of vengeance.

"Then I went mad. I fled from that accursed house and buried myself in this retreat, where I have spent every moment since, denying myself both food and sleep, deeming every second left me all too short to beg divine forgiveness for the terrible sacrilege I have committed."

"So, my friends, you see?" de Grandin turned to Costello and me as the half-hysterical Pole concluded his preposterous narrative.

"Sure, I do," the detective returned. "Didn't th' felly say he's mad? Be dad, they say crazy folks tell th' truth, an' he ain't stretchin' it none when he says his steeple's full o' bats."

"Ah bah!" de Grandin shot back. "You weary me, my friend."

To Kolisko he said: "Your story supplies the information which we so sorely needed, sir. Whatever the result of your experiment, your motives were good, nor do I think the good God will be too hard upon you. If you do truly wish forgiveness, pray that we shall be successful in destroying the monster before more harm is done. *Cordieu*, but we shall need all your prayers, and a vast deal of luck as well, I think; for killing that which is already dead is no small task.

"Now what?" Demanded Costello with a sidelong glance at de Grandin as we emerged from the religious house. "Got some more loonies for us to listen to?"

"*Parbleu*, if you will but give ear to your own prattle, you shall have all that sort of conversation you wish, I think, *cher Sergent*," the little Frenchman jerked back with a smile which took half the acid from his words. Then:

"Friend Trowbridge, convoy our good, unbelieving friend to Harrisonville and await my return. I have one or two things to attend to before I join you; but when I come I think I can promise you a show the like of which you have not before seen. *Au revoir, mes enfants*."

Ten o'clock sounded on the city's clocks; eleven; half-past. Costello and I consumed innumerable cigars and more than one portion of some excellent cognac I had stored in my cellar since the days before prohibition; still no sign of my little friend. The sergeant was on the point of taking his departure when a light step sounded on the porch and de Grandin came bounding into the consulting-room, his face wreathed in smiles, a heavy-looking parcel gripped under his right arm.

"*Bien*, my friends, I find you in good time," he greeted, poured himself a monstrous stoup of amber liquor, then helped himself to one of my cigars. "I think it high time we were on our way. There is that to do which may take considerable doing this night, but I would not that we delay our expedition because of difficulties in the road."

"Be gorry, he's caught it from th' other nut!" Costello confided to the surrounding atmosphere with a serio-comic grimace. "Which crazy house are we goin' to now, sor?"

"Where but to the house of Monsieur Kolisko?" returned the Frenchman with a grin. "I think there will be another there before long, and it is highly expedient that we be there first."

"Humph, if it's Coroner Martin or his physician, you needn't be worryin' yourself anny," Costello assured him. "They'll be takin' no more interest in th' case till someone else gets kilt, I'm thinkin'."

"*Morbleu*, then their days of interest are ended, or Jules de Grandin is a colossal liar," was the response. "Come; *allons vite!*"

The lowest workings of a coal mine were not darker than the Kolisko house when we let ourselves in some fifteen minutes later. Switching on the electric light, de Grandin proceeded to unpack his parcel, taking from it a folded black object which resembled a deflated association football. Next he produced a shining nickel-plated apparatus consisting of a thick upright cylinder and a transverse flat piece which opened in two on hinges, disclosing an interior resembling a waffle-iron with small, close-set knobs. Into a screw-stopped opening in the hollow cylinder of the contrivance he poured several ounces of gray-black powder; then, taking the flat rubber bag, he hurried from the house to my car, attached the valve of the bag to my tire pump and proceeded to inflate the rubber bladder almost to the bursting point. This done, he attached the bag to a valve in the nickeled cylinder by a two-foot length of rubber hose, poured some liquid over the corrugated "waffle-iron" at the top of the cylinder, and, with the inflated bag hugged under his arm, as a Highland piper might hold the bag of his pipes, he strode across the room, snapped off the light, and took his station near the open window.

Several times Costello and I addressed him, but each time he cut us short with a sharp, irritable "Sssh!" continuing his crouching watch beside the window, staring intently into the shaded garden beyond.

It must have been some three-quarters of an hour later that we sensed, rather than heard, the scuffling of light footfalls on the grass outside, heard the door-knob cautiously tested, then the scuttering of more steps, scarcely louder than the sound of wind-blown leaves, as the visitor rounded the cottage wall and made for the window beside which de Grandin mounted guard.

A puff of autumn wind, scented with the last blooms of summer's rosebeds, sent the light clouds drifting from before the moon's pale lantern, and, illuminated in the pallid light of the night's goddess, we saw framed at the window-square the terrifying vision which had followed young Ratliff's story of his escape two nights before.

"My Gawd!" Costello's bass voice was shrill and treble with sudden terror as the thing gazed malevolently in at us. Next instant his heavy service revolver was out, and shot after shot poured straight into the hideous, grinning face at the window.

He might as well have fired boiled beans from a pea-shooter for all the effect his bullets had. Distinctly I saw a portion of the mummy's ear clipped off by a flying slug of lead, saw an indentation sink in the thing's head half an inch above the right eye as a soft-nosed bullet tore through skin and withered flesh and frontal bone; but the emaciated body never paused in its progress. One withered leg was lifted across the window sill; two long, unfleshed arms, terminating in hands of enormous length, were thrust out toward the Irishman; a grin of such hellish hatred and triumph as I had never conceived possible disfigured the object's visage as it pressed onward, its long, bony fingers opening and closing con vulsively, as though they already felt their victim's neck within their grasp.

"*Monsieur*, you do play truant from hell!" De Grandin's announcement was made in the most casual manner as he rose from his half-kneeling posture beside the window and placed himself directly in the mummy's path, but there was a quaver in his voice which betrayed the intensity of his emotion.

A noise — you could hardly call it a snarl nor yet a scream, but a sound midway between the two — emanated from the thing's desiccated throat as it turned on him, threw out one hand and snatched at his throat.

There was a tiny spark of light, as though a match had been struck, then a mighty, bursting blaze, as if time had turned backward in its flight for a second and the midday sun had thrown its beams through the midnight blackness of the room, a swishing, whistling sound, as of air suddenly released from tremendous pressure, and a shriek of mad, insupportable anguish. Then the fierce blazing of some inflammable substance suddenly set alight. My eyes started from my face as I seemed to see the mummy's scraggly limbs and emaciated torso writhe within a very inferno of fire. Then:

"*Cher Sergent*, it might be well to call the fire department; this place will surely burn about our ears unless *les pompiers* hurry with their hose, I fear," remarked Jules de Grandin as calmly as though advising us the night was fine.

"But — but — howly mither o' Moses!" Sergeant Costello demanded as we turned from watching the firemen salvaging the remnants of Kolisko's cottage. "How did ye manage it, Doctor de Grandin, sor? May I never eat another mess o' corned beef an' cabbage if I didn't shoot th' thing clean through th' head wid me gun, an' it never so much as batted an eye, yet ye burned it up as clean as —"

"Precisely, *mon vieux*," the Frenchman admitted with a chuckle. "Have you never heard the adage that one must fight the Devil with fire? It was something like that which I did.

"No later than night before last a young man came crying and whimpering at Friend Trowbridge's door, begging for shelter from some ghastly thing which pursued him through the streets. Both Trowbridge and I thought he suffered from an overdose of the execrable liquor with which Monsieur Volstead has flooded this unhappy land, but before we could boot him from the door, behold, the same thing which you so unsuccessfully shot tonight did stick its unlovely countenance against our window, and I, who always go armed lest some miscreant do me a mischief, did fire eight shots directly into his face. Believe me, my friend, when Jules de Grandin shoots, he does not miss, and that night I shot exceptionally well. Yet when Friend Trowbridge and I searched the garden, neither hide nor hair of the one who should have been eight times dead did we find. 'There is something here which will take much explaining,' I say to me after we could not find him.

"Next morning you did come and tell us of Professor Kolisko's murder, and when we had viewed his remains, I wondered much what sort of creature could have done this thing. The pressure exerted on his neck were superhuman, but the marks of the hand were not those of an ape, for no ape possesses such a long, thin thumb.

"Then we did find the dead professor's diary and I have the tiny shivers playing tag with each other up and down my back as I read and translate it. It sounds like the dream of one crazed with dope, I know, but there was the possibility of truth in it. Do you know the vampire, my friends?"

"The vampire?" I echoed.

"*Précisement*; the vampire you have said it. He is not always one who can not die because of sin or misfortune in life. No. Sometimes he is a dead body possessed by some demon — perhaps by some unhappy, earthbound spirit. Yes.

"Now, as I read the professor's journal, I see that every thing which had transpired were most favorable for the envampirement of that body which his cousin had brought from Egypt so long ago. Yet the idea seemed — how do you say? — ah, yes — to have the smell of the fish on it.

"But when you came and say Miss Adkinson have been erased in the same manner as Professor Kolisko, I begin to wonder if perhaps I have not less nuts in my belfry than I at first thought. In Professor Kolisko's journal there was reference to his cousin. 'How does it come that this cousin have not come forward and told us what, if anything, he knows?' I ask me as we view the poor dead woman's body, and the answer was, 'He has most doubtless seen that which will not be believed, and hides because he fears arrest on a false charge of murder.'

"Right away I rush to New York and inquire at the *Musée Metropolitain* for the address of Monsieur Michel Kolisko, the Egyptologist. I find his living-quarters in East Eighty-sixth Street. Then they tell me he have gone to the Carmelite retreat. *Morbleu*, had he hidden in lost Atlantis, I should have hunted him out, for I desired speech with him!

"At first he would not talk, dreading I intended to drag him to the jail, but after I had spoken with him for a time, he opened his heart, and told me what he later told you.

"Now, what to do? By Monsieur Kolisko's story, it were useless to battle with this enlivened mummy, for the body of him was but the engine moved by an alien spirit — he had no need of brains, hearts and such things as we must use. Also, I knew from experience, bullets were as useless against him as puffs of wind against a fortress wall. 'Very well,' I tell me, 'he may be invulnerable to bullets and blows, but living or dead, he is still a mummy — a dry, desiccated mummy — and we have had no rain lately. It are entirely unlikely that he have gotten greatly moistened in his trips through the streets, and all mummies are as tinder to fire. *Mordieu*, did they not once use them as fuel for locomotives in Egypt when railways were first built there? Yes.'

"And so I prepare the warm reception for him. At one time and another I have taken photographs at night, and to do so I have used magnesium flares — what you call flashlight powder. At a place where they sell such things in New York I procure a flashlight burner — a hollow cylinder for the powder magazine with a benzine wick at its top and a tube through which air can be blown to force the powder through the burning petrol and so give a continuous blaze. I get me also a rubber bag which I can inflate and attach to the windpipe of the apparatus, thus leaving my lips free for swearing and other important things, and also giving a greater force of air.

"I reason: 'Where will this living mummy go most naturally? Why not to the house where he received his new life, for the town in which he goes about committing murder is still new to him?' And so, when *Monsieur la Momie* returns to the place of his second nativity, I am all ready for him. Your shots, they are as ineffectual as were mine two nights ago, but I have my magnesium flare ready, and as he turns on me I blow the fierce flame from it all over him. He are dry like tinder, the fire seized on him like a hungry little boy on a jam-tart, and — *pouf* — he is burn up, incinerated; he is no more!"

"Do you actually mean Heschler's soul entered that dried-up body?" I demanded.

The Frenchman shook his head. "I do not know," he replied. "Perhaps it were Heschler; more likely not. The air is full of strange and terrible things, my friend. Not for nothing did the old divines call Satan the Prince of the Powers of the Air. How do we know some of those elementals who are ever on the watch to do mankind an injury did not hear the mad Kolisko's scheme and take advantage of the opportunity to enter into the mummy's body? Such things have been before; why may they not be again?"

"But —" I commenced.

"But —" expostulated Sergeant Costello.

"But, my friends," the little man cut in "did you behold how dry that so abominable mummy was before I applied the fire?"

"Yes," I answered wonderingly.

"*Cordieu*, he was wet as the broad Atlantic Ocean beside the dryness of Jules de Grandin at this moment! Friend Trowbridge, unless my memory plays me false, I beheld a bottle of cognac upon your office table. Come, I faint, I die, I perish; talk to me no more till I have consumed the remainder of that bottle, I do beseech you!"

A List of Books for Further Reading

Frost, Brian J. *The Essential Guide to Mummy Literature.* Maryland: Scarecrow Press, Inc., 2008.

Joshi, S. T. (Editor). *Icons of Horror and the Supernatural: An Encyclopedia of Our Worst Nightmares.* (Vol. 1). Connecticut: Greenwood Press, 2007.

Luckhurst, Roger. *The Mummy's Curse: The True History of a Dark Fantasy.* United Kingdom: Oxford University Press, 2012.

Alcott, Louisa May. *The Uncollected Works of Louisa May Alcott.* (Vol. 1). Arizona: Ironweed Press, 2001.

Blackwood, Algernon. *The Tales of Algernon Blackwood.* New York: E.P. Dutton & Co., Inc., 1939.

Bleiler, E. F. (Editor). *The Best Supernatural Tales of Arthur Conan Doyle.* New York: Dover Publications, 1978.

Christie, Agatha. *Poirot Investigates.* New York: Dodd Mead, 1925.

Clark, Barrett H. and Lieber, Maxim. (Editors). *Great Short Stories of the World.* London: William Heinemann LTD., 1926.

Connors, Scott and Hilger, Ron. (Editors). *Clark Ashton Smith: The End of the Story* (The Collected Fantasies, Vol. 1). New York: Night Shade Books, 2006.

Cory, Charles B. *Montezuma's Castle & Other Weird Tales.* Leonaur Press, 2009.

Costain, T. B. and Beechcroft, J. (Editors). *Stories to Remember.* New York: Doubleday, 1956.

Davies, David Stuart. (Editor). *Return from the Dead.* London: Wordsworth Editions, 2004.

Davies, David Stuart. (Editor). *Sir Arthur Conan Doyle: Tales of Unease.* London: Wordsworth Editions, 2008.

Derleth, August. (Editor). *The Sleeping and the Dead.* Chicago: Pellegrini and Cudahy, 1947.

Doyle, Arthur Conan. *The Conan Doyle Stories Omnibus.* London: John Murray, 1929.

Dziemianowicz, Stefan R. et al. (Editors). *100 Creepy Little Creatures.* New York: Barnes and Noble, 1994.

Elliott, M. J. (Editor). *H. P. Lovecraft: The Horror in the Museum & Other Stories.* London: Wordsworth Editions, 2010.

Elliott, M. J. (Editor). *H. P. Lovecraft: The Lurking Fear & Other Stories*. London: Wordsworth Editions, 2013.

Elliott, M. J. (Editor). *Robert E. Howard: The Haunter of the Ring & Other Tales*. London: Wordsworth Editions, 2008.

Frayling, Christopher. (Editor). *The Face of Tutankhamun*. Boston: Faber and Faber, 1992.

Gautier, Théophile. *Clarimonde and Other Stories*. England: Tartarus Press, 2011.

Gautier, Théophile. *One of Cleopatra's Nights and Other Fantastic Romances*. New York: B. Worthington, 1882.

Ghidalia, Vic. (Editor). *The Mummy Walks Among Us*. Connecticut: Xerox Corp. Publishing, 1971.

Greenberg, Martin H. (Editor). *Mummy Stories*. Boston: Severn House Publisher, 1990.

Griffith, George. *The Raid of 'Le Vengeur' and Other Stories*. London: Ferret Fantasy LTD, 1974.

Haining, Peter. (Editor). *The Best Short Stories of Rider Haggard*. London: Michael Joseph, 1981.

Haining, Peter. (Editor). *The Mummy: Stories of the Living Corpse*. New York: Seven House Publishing, 1989.

Hearn, Lafcadio. *Stray Leaves from Strange Literature*. Boston: Houghton, Mifflin, and Co.: 1884.

Howard, Robert E. *The Horror Stories of Robert E. Howard*. New York: Ballantine Books, 2008.

Hyne, C. J. Cutcliffe. *Atoms of Empire*. New York: Macmillan, 1904.

Irish, John P. (Editor). *Fitz-James O'Brien: Gothic Short Stories*. (3/e). Texas: A Bit O'Irish Press, 2017.

Iliowizi, Henry. *The Weird Orient*. Philadelphia, Henry T. Coates & Co.: 1900.

Johnson, John J. and Shurin, Jared. (Editors). *Unearthed*. London: Jurassic: 2013.

Jones, Stephen. (Editor). *The Emperor of Dreams: The Lost Worlds of Clark Ashton Smith*. London: Gollancz, 2002.

Leadbeater, C. W. *The Perfume of Egypt*. India, The Theosophist Office: 1912.

Lovecraft, H. P. *At the Mountains of Madness and Other Novels*. Wisconsin: Arkham House Publishers, Inc., 1946.

Lovecraft, H. P. *Dagon and Other Macabre Tales*. Wisconsin: Arkham House Publishers, Inc., 1965.

Lovecraft, H. P. *The Dunwich Horror and Others*. Wisconsin: Arkham House Publishers, Inc., 1963.

Lovecraft, H. P. *The Horror in the Museum and Other Revisions*. Wisconsin: Arkham House Publishers, Inc., 1989.

Menville, Douglas and Reginald, R. (Editors). *Dreamers of Dreams*. New York: Arno Press, 1978.

O'Donnell, Elliott. *Byways of Ghost-Land*. London: William Rider and Son, Ltd.: 1911.

Parry, Michael. (Editor). *The Rivals of Dracula*. London: Corgi Books, 1977.

Poe, Edgar Allan. *Poetry and Tales*. New York: The Library of America, 1984.

Pronzini, Bill. (Editor). *Mummy! A Chrestomathy of Cryptology*. New York: Arbor House, 1980.

Rohmer, Sax. *Tales of Secret Egypt*. New York: McKinlay, Stone & Mackenzie, 1920.

Rohmer, Sax. *The Dream Detective*. New York: A.L. Burt Company, 1925.

Singer, Kurt. (Editor). *Weird Tales of the Supernatural*. London: W.H. Allen, 1966.

Smith, Andrew. (Editor). *Lost in a Pyramid & Other Classic Mummy Stories*. London: The British Library, 2016.

Smith, Clark Ashton. *A Rendezvous in Averoigne*. Wisconsin: Arkham House Publishers, Inc., 1988.

Smith, Clark Ashton. *Out of Space and Time*. Lincoln: University of Nebraska Press, 2006.

Stephens, John Richard. (Editor). *Into the Mummy's Tomb*. New York: Berkley Books, 2001.

Suffling, Ernest Richard. *The Story Hunter or Tales of the Weird and Wild*. British Library, 1896.

Thomson, Christine Campbell. (Editor). *More Not At Night*. London: Selwyn & Blount, Ltd., 1926.

Vanderburgh, George A. (Editor). *Seabury Quinn: The Horror on the Links: The Complete Tales of Jules de Grandin*. (Vol. 1). New York: Night Shade Books, 2017.

Weinberg, Robert, et al. (Editors). *Between Time and Terror*. New York: Penguin Books, 1995.